VILLETTE

VILLETTE

◆

Charlotte Brontë

Introduction and Notes by
DR SALLY MINOGUE
Canterbury Christ Church University College

WORDSWORTH CLASSICS

For my husband
ANTHONY JOHN RANSON
with love from your wife, the publisher.
Eternally grateful for your unconditional love.

Readers who are interested in other titles from
Wordsworth Editions are invited to visit our website at
www.wordsworth-editions.com

This edition first published 1993 by
Wordsworth Editions Limited
8B East Street, Ware, Hertfordshire SG12 9HJ
Introduction and Notes added 1999

ISBN 978 1 85326 072 8

Text © Wordsworth Editions Limited 1993
Introduction and Notes © Sally Minogue 1993

Wordsworth® is a registered trade mark of
Wordsworth Editions Limited

Wordsworth Editions
is the company founded in 1987 by
MICHAEL TRAYLER

Typeset in Great Britain by Antony Gray
Printed and bound by Clays Ltd, Elcograf S.p.A.

CONTENTS

INTRODUCTION   ix

VOLUME ONE

1   *Bretton*   1
2   *Paulina*   8
3   *The Playmates*   14
4   *Miss Marchmont*   29
5   *Turning a New Leaf*   36
6   *London*   41
7   *Villette*   51
8   *Madame Beck*   60
9   *Isidore*   73
10 *Dr John*   83
11 *The Portress's Cabinet*   90
12 *The Casket*   96
13 *A Sneeze Out of Season*   105
14 *The Fête*   115
15 *The Long Vacation*   140

VOLUME TWO

16 *Auld Lang Syne*   153
17 *La Terrasse*   166

18 We Quarrel   175
19 The Cleopatra   182
20 The Concert   193
21 Reaction   212
22 The Letter   227
23 Vashti   236
24 M. de Bassompierre   248
25 The Little Countess   260
26 A Burial   273
27 The Hôtel Crécy   287

VOLUME THREE

28 The Watchguard   303
29 Monsieur's Fête   314
30 M. Paul   326
31 The Dryad   336
32 The First Letter   345
33 M. Paul Keeps His Promise   353
34 Malevola   361
35 Fraternity   372
36 The Apple of Discord   383
37 Sunshine   396
38 Cloud   410
39 Old and New Acquaintance   431
40 The Happy Pair   441
41 Faubourg Clotilde   447
42 Finis   460

    NOTES   463

GENERAL INTRODUCTION

Wordsworth Classics are inexpensive editions designed to appeal to the general reader and students. We commissioned teachers and specialists to write broad-ranging, jargon-free Introductions and to provide Notes that would assist the understanding of our readers, rather than interpret the stories for them. In the same spirit, because the pleasures of reading are inseparable from the surprises, secrets and revelations that all narratives contain, we strongly advise you to enjoy this book before turning to the Introduction.

KEITH CARABINE
General Advisor

INTRODUCTION

Villette is really two novels. One is encountered on first reading: a novel of false starts and ambiguous endings, of double names and double identities, setting the bourgeois English Protestant world typified by the Bretton (Briton) household against a different, Catholic bourgeoisie, that of Brussels/Villette, which holds the promise of change, thrill, love almost by virtue of its foreignness. This *Villette* offers Gothic excitements and Dickensian coincidences alongside its realism and caution of tone – a novel of some romance to offset its undoubted pain. If the reader wishes to experience this first *Villette* with innocence unalloyed, s/he should go straight to the first page of the novel, and save this Introduction for the end. Then s/he could go on to the second reading of the novel, the second *Villette*, a different novel entirely. For now, we *know* that the self-effacing narrator of the early chapters, whose name is not revealed until the start of Chapter II, and whose antecedents we never discover, is in fact the heroine of her own story; we know that Bretton and its charms – not least of them John Graham Bretton – will reappear in a foreign land and lure Lucy with their promise of happiness; we know that happiness will be hers, but not the sunny golden variety found by Dr John and Polly; and we know, perhaps most importantly for our understanding of what kind of novel this is, that the nun is no supernatural being, no Gothic horror, indeed no hallucination born of Lucy's mental strain, but a mere disguise for a silly fop and a sillier love affair. We start this second reading knowing that our narrator withholds, deceives, distorts, teases; she is not translucent, as her name suggests, but opaque. Indeed, even as she reveals so much of herself to us, much still remains hidden and in doubt, especially in the novel's final page; in certain ways Lucy remains as opaque as her story's ending.

The dual personality of the novel is what principally distinguishes it from its nineteenth-century counterparts, and it produces effects of peculiar resonance in the late twentieth century; the fictional world of the Nun, the Banshee and the shipwreck collides with elements subversive of any fictional world whatsoever – unreliable narrator, self-reflexive narrative, participant reader, lack of closure – and from the collision rises a cry of anguish such as might issue from Munch's silent image.[1] For this is a novel deeply marked by suffering. Harriet Martineau indeed felt it to be 'almost intolerably painful'[2] in a judgement echoing that of Samuel Johnson on Cordelia's death in *King Lear*. The comparison with *Lear*, disproportionate as it may seem, can stand, because through this largely realist fiction the tragic weight of lone suffering is brought into the heart of an ordinary, bright, social world, where we can recognise it in all its banal horror. No Goneril and Regan here, only prying Madame Beck and Jesuitical Père Silas, to both of whom Lucy extends a narrative sympathy in which the reader is inevitably involved; yet both do their best to prolong Lucy's pain and deny her personal contentment. No blind chance or blasted heath, but the glossy indifference of those who are happy to those who are unhappy. Dr John's wanton boy carelessly raises Lucy's hopes and calls up her love, then as carelessly abandons her to tame and

1 Edward Munch's 'The Scream' (also variously translated as 'The Cry' and 'The Shriek'), though produced in 1885, seems prescient of certain twentieth-century horrors, personal and public.
2 Review, *Daily News*, 3 February 1853, reprinted in McNees (1996), Vol.3, p. 589

constrain her own passions as she can, passions he doesn't even understand. He stays happily oblivious of the pain he has wrought, goes on to a contented, successful, fulfilled life, basking in his wife's doll-like devotion as he once bathed in his mother's indulgent adoration; and Lucy forgives him, perhaps even continues to love him, open-eyed. In recounting the 'blessed' (p. 408) future life of Dr John and Polly, she gently reminds the – perhaps less forgiving – reader of her creed: 'I *do* believe there are some human beings so born, so reared, so guided from a soft cradle to a calm and late grave, that no excessive suffering penetrates their lot and no tempestuous blackness overcasts their journey' (p. 408). And not only these 'natures elect, harmonious and benign' (p. 408) meet this happy fate, but also the less benevolent and downright malign, as we learn from the penultimate line of the novel: 'Madame Beck prospered all the days of her life; so did Père Silas; Madame Walravens fulfilled her ninetieth year before she died' (p. 463). Well, that's life, Brontë seems to intimate here, and we remember Lucy's picture of Human Justice (her nicely ironic public-examination topic), 'a red, random beldame' who beats the 'weak, wronged and sickly' with her poker, and treats the 'strong, lively and violent' to a token menace followed by a 'liberal shower of sugar-plums' (p. 377). The irony here, which would be comic if it were not so savage, promotes an imaginative relish, the language spilling over in what by this stage we recognise as a characteristic tripartite structure. This is a picture that the late-twentieth-century reader well recognises, but it was a markedly unconventional one to paint in 1853, not least for the linguistic vigour with which the picture is painted.

Central to the tragic aspect of the novel is the final chapter (xv) of Volume One (in the original triple-decker publication), 'The Long Vacation'. The writing here, again, sets *Villette* apart from the fiction of its time, even from Brontë's own ground-breaking *Jane Eyre*. (Perhaps the difference was too much for her readership; though critically acclaimed, *Villette* did not achieve the spectacular popular success of *Jane Eyre*, which ran to three editions within six months.) Personal and individual as the pain is, bourgeois and social as the setting is, none the less in this chapter Lucy might as well be out on the heath in the storm with madness threatening. Indeed there is a storm, as often in this novel, which both echoes and aggravates her despair. But the writing does not depend on externals for its power. Lucy's distress is internal, mental, spiritual; at times her mental vertigo verges on the ontological, questioning

the very nature of the self in relation to existence. In consequence
her universe can feel Godless, for, though she prays 'to Heaven for
consolation and support', none comes, except the conviction that
she must be among those for whom God ordains that they must
'deeply suffer while they live' (p. 144). Even as Lucy professes not
to 'arraign the mercy or justice of God for this' (p. 144), her painful
isolation argues against her, so that while she may accept, the
reader, especially today's reader, may not. Robert Martin contends
that in *Villette*, with its deep affiliation to Protestantism (amounting
to a possibly offensive anti-Catholicism), and its extensive Christian
reference and wider metaphor, 'there is a resurgence of Christian
faith', a faith notably questioned in her previous novels.[3] But the
spiritual void so brilliantly evoked in 'The Long Vacation' speaks of
a universe, blind and in chaos, in which nature itself is estranging
and estranged – 'I too felt those autumn suns and saw those harvest
moons, and I almost wished to be covered in with earth and turf . . .
for I could not live on their light, nor make them comrades, nor
yield them affection.' (p. 145) – in which the thought of other
human beings and their comfort mocks rather than sustains, and in
which God exists only by virtue of the suffering he inflicts. It is not
surprising that Lucy, alienated thus from all that gives her world
meaning, comes close to alienation from herself. Her 'peculiarly
agonising depression' (p. 145) turns to night terror when, in the
midst of sleeplessness, she has a dream which seems scarcely that: 'a
nameless experience that had the hue, the mien, the terror, the very
tone of a visitation from eternity' (p. 146). In this fearful state she
has no hope for the future and engages with the prospect of death
itself as a less dreadful alternative. Here again is the hallmark
triplicate phrasing found where Brontë is particularly concerned to
be exact to the full complexity and depth of an experience; while the
reader can find her adjectival accretions relentless, here they are in
perfect keeping with the remorseless nature of the agony she
describes. This chapter is the most heavily revised of Volume One
in manuscript, and Brontë continued to refine it at proof stage. A
sustained, almost pitiless, account of a passage of despair, it has no
equal in its own century, and few in our own – to which it speaks so
fully.

But, in the way of nineteenth-century novels, Volume Two
succeeds Volume One, and hope springs freshly from despair. We
have already had two new beginnings within the space of Volume

3 Martin (1966), p. 147

One, first with Miss Marchmont and second with the move to
Villette, but in the three-part publishing structure of the nineteenth-
century novel, a new volume provides a particularly significant new
beginning. So in Chapter xvi negation gives way to affirmation as
Lucy, willy-nilly, engages with existence again. Brontë distances
herself from this engagement in a strikingly modern way: 'the
faculties soon settled each in its place; the life-machine presently
resumed its wonted and regular working' (p. 153). Lucy will not, she
could not, plumb such horrors again; they have proved survivable.
But they remain deep in the reader's imagination, and of course in
her own, even as the friendly sunshine of Dr John's disposition plays
on its surface awhile, and aids her recovery. For recover she does,
and this is as central to the power of the novel as was her collapse. If
despair is the watchword of Volume One, benevolence is that of
Volume Two, the central structural plank of the novel. And Lucy's
return to health, to life, to her at-oneness with herself, is remarkably
expressed in fictional terms through her almost literal return to the
comfort and security briefly known in the past. Waking in a strange
room, she finds it none the less strangely familiar; the domesticity of
her recognitions (a blue armchair, a table, two footstools) is
completely in keeping with the solidity, the very ordinariness, which
is to be the key to her comfort and her restoration. If there is bathos
here, it is deliberate, and deeply true. For all it needs, it seems, to
save Lucy from the chill waters of despair is what as human beings
we all hope for, indeed expect: the society of some others who love
us and whom we love, the comfort and security of a home, the belief
that these will still be there even when we are absent from them.
These are symbolised on Lucy's reawakening by the transplantation
of her early Bretton home, where her visits, we recall, 'resembled the
sojourn of Christian and Hopeful beside a certain pleasant stream'
(p. 2), into the foreign climate of Villette. The innocent past *can*
return and Lucy can take up residence in it, can feel the reviving
warmth of bourgeois comforts which, for her, are as spiritual as they
are material. And this home is peopled: 'When I had said my
prayers, and when I was undressed and laid down, I felt that I still
had friends' (p. 165). However much she may temper this sense of
security with poignant reminders not to be importunate – ' "Do not
let me think of them too often, too much, too fondly" ' (p 165),
which recalls her earlier prophetic advice to the child Polly about
Graham: ' " . . . don't fret, and don't expect too much of him, or else
he will feel you to be troublesome, and then it is all over" ' (p. 27) '–
moderation is not her *forte*, while it is the very essence of the Bretton

household. In one of the multiple ironies of the novel, the domestic
beneficence which brings Lucy back to life is too mild and too bland
ever truly to suit her, though it contains what she most desires. But
once she desires, she desires excessively; the image of stoicism and
moderation she may be, but it is a forced moderation, bred out of
passion. All this she knows about herself (as, on our second reading,
do we), and so even as she begs herself not to want too much, she
knows both that she will, and that she will suffer for it.

At such points the knowledge acquired from a first reading
informs our understanding of the novel, and leads us to a harsher
judgement on those surrounding Lucy than she permits herself.
Perhaps too we look at Lucy a little harder; some readers find her
too self-pitying, her martyrdom a sort of inverted arrogance. In this
way Brontë also keeps a certain ironic distance from her narrator
and inserts her own judgements, though she always leaves room to
extend, adapt or overturn a position. Indeed the novel is about the
process of judging, and as first readers we have had an early warning
against misjudgement when we initially assume that the central
character will be Polly/Paulina. We take as little notice of the
nameless narrator in the first chapter as those around her, and Polly
is our focus. Only gradually is it borne in upon us that Lucy is to
carry the story forward, and that Polly is (as we think) to disappear
from it. As we were wrong about Lucy's effacement, so we will be
wrong about Polly's disappearance, and gradually we learn to tread
more warily and make fewer summary judgements. Thus the
flibbertigibbet Ginevra unexpectedly wins our respect because she
seems truly to care for Lucy, and perhaps more so because Lucy
truly cares for her, albeit in curmudgeonly fashion. Paulina never
quite grows up, petrified into childishness by the early parting from
her father; but Lucy likes her, and shows us why we might like her
too (p. 347). Mrs. Bretton seems the model of equanimity, incapable
of disturbance, yet she betrays in her letter to Lucy a frank
admiration for the charms of her son that is almost erotic (p. 254);
the point here is not so much that she feels it but that she avows it,
and to someone she knows will share it. Her letter is full of the
acknowledged desire of a lover to talk about the one loved –
foreshadowing the more acceptable desire of Paulina to talk of Dr
John to Lucy (pp. 397–8). Lucy is, however, a more reluctant
recipient of Paulina's 'confidences which left her lips, sweet honey,
and sometimes dropped in my ear – molten lead.' (p. 398). Indeed
she registers protest to both Paulina and Dr John as they seek her
complicity in their mutual admiration, but it is only to the reader

that she confesses the extent of her pain, and she maintains a constant fairness to her tormentors, recognising that both are in their way more innocent than she is. In these insights and extensions of understanding, and not only from Lucy's viewpoint, Brontë constantly surprises the reader into empathy. In this way she imperceptibly leads us to a readerly generosity, a refusal of prediction, which persists to the last page, where even the fate of M. Paul, and so of Lucy too, is left up to whether we have 'sunny imaginations' (p. 462) or no.

Finally, however, we do stand back from the novel as Lucy cannot, and here surely Brontë guides our view. Dr John perhaps comes in for the sternest scrutiny, and adjectives which elsewhere might be laudatory begin to carry a deprecatory tarnish. 'Golden', 'sunny', 'supple', 'cheerful', 'bland', 'benignant', 'blithe', 'blessed', 'suave' come to bespeak surface rather than depth, and in the end John Graham Bretton is seen to be shallow. One of the earliest epithets Brontë uses of him, 'faithless-looking' (p. 11), comes back to haunt him. She has Lucy retract its implication as soon as she has used it, emphasising that the perfidy is a matter of appearance rather than actuality. But Dr John does prove faithless to Lucy, and there is even at times a certain venom in the appraising eye the author casts on him. 'Cool young Briton!' (p. 242) realises Lucy at Vashti's turbulent theatrical performance, a remark which marks the start of her withdrawal from him, moments before the fatal event which will instigate his much fuller withdrawal from her – the fire, and the consequent remeeting with Paulina. But while that night marks 'a deep-red cross' (p. 243) on Lucy's book of life, the fire turns out to be no more than a brief flare: 'Next morning's papers explained that it was but some loose drapery on which a spark had fallen, and which had blazed up and been quenched in a moment' (p. 247). This dry chapter-ending is characteristic: an ordinary event, presented in full realist fashion, is invested with multiple significance; and while Brontë's metaphors can jar the modern reader, and occasionally obscure more than they reveal, at their best they carry their full symbolic freight without sacrificing anything of their realism. Bathos is again Brontë's technique in this example, evident in that mundane reference to newspapers. But the metaphorical work has already been done, in the inflamed and inflammatory language of the chapter. Lucy, Snowe in name only, burns in response to Vashti, while Dr John stays 'cool'; Vashti's emotional heat virtually sets the theatre alight whereupon John shows 'cordial calm' (p. 243). Similarly Lucy sits firm in the fire while Paulina is knocked down, almost crushed; her childlike weakness can allow John his strength. For him Lucy would have proved too strong, too hot; a small fire, soon put out, is Dr John's portion. It is, in its quiet, laconic way, a cruel judgement.

Is the cruelty and bitterness to be found in *Villette* Charlotte Brontë's own rather than that of her created narrator, Lucy? Certainly it is difficult in places to separate their positions, and the relationship between fiction and reality, never straightforward, is particularly vexed in the case of *Villette*. There is no doubt that the formative events of Brontë's life in the Pensionnat Heger in Brussels in 1842–3 (ten years prior to the writing of the novel) are the imaginative basis for *Villette*. Many episodes from that period are given exact fictional counterparts, most notably M. Heger's intellectual flirtation with his pupil, down to the evocative detail of his smoking his cigar into her desk, mimicked in the portrait of M. Paul; and Charlotte's dark night of the soul in her own long vacation, and her subsequent confession in a Catholic church. The Lucy/Paul relationship, being both successful and non-adulterous, is of course markedly different from Charlotte's with M. Heger – though both, probably, were unconsummated. The pain of her eventual rejection by Heger goes rather into the fictional relationship between Lucy and Dr John, most obviously in the treasured letters he sends her and their symbolic burial. For while George Smith, Brontë's publisher, was in part the model for Dr John, the affectionate and relaxed letters they exchanged have none of the air of desperation we find in Brontë's to Heger. These leave no doubt of the strength of her feeling for him, and strongly suggest that at some stage he encouraged that feeling. None of his letters to her survive but Rebecca Fraser in her biography of Brontë intriguingly provides two pieces of evidence of Heger's flirtatious tendencies with his pupils. One is a letter from Mme Heger to a former pupil reminiscing familiarly about his once having kissed this pupil and made an illicit declaration of feeling to her; Madame's tone is utterly secure and indeed indulgent. The second is a letter from M. Heger to another English pupil written in his eighties, well after Charlotte's death.[4] If his letters to Charlotte had the same playful, semi-erotic edge, they must have been hard to resist. But his continuing to flirt with others, even by letter, after wounding Charlotte as he knew he had, looks like selfish irresponsibility. 'Faithless' comes to mind. Reading Brontë's repeated and

4 Fraser (1988), pp. 189–90

unanswered letters pleading for just 'crumbs' of comfort from her 'master'[5] is more painful than any fiction – particularly when we learn that Heger used the margin of one of these sad missives to note down the address of his shoemaker. Feet of clay indeed. Mme Heger, by contrast, cared enough to retrieve the torn-up pieces and sew them together; only her jealous watchfulness preserved the evidence of Charlotte's consuming love.

Our intimate knowledge of Brontë here has, however, served her badly; many critics, including recent feminist ones, have seen *Villette* at least in part as the fictional fulfilment of the author's own desires.[6] Brontë had been rightly furious with Thackeray when he had introduced her as 'Jane Eyre' to his mother at a public lecture, and he it was again who first elided Lucy Snowe with her author: 'The poor little woman of genius! I can read a great deal of her life as I fancy in her book, and see that rather than have fame . . . she wants some Tomkins or another to love . . . '.[7] Such crude readings of *Villette* as autobiographical, even where they are given a psycho-analytic gloss, are reductive both of the life and of the art. Whatever her personal investment in the novel, Brontë's larger aim was to speak, not of her particular life, but of life in general, perhaps of aspects of life which she was peculiarly fitted through her experiences to understand, aspects not commonly dealt with in the fiction of her day. She defends her particular brand of realism against the rather more conventional expectations of her publisher, George Smith, and his colleague, William Smith Williams, both of whom voiced some criticisms of *Villette* as they received it volume by volume. Brontë seems always to have been tart about criticism, but in this case her defence rises above the personal. To Williams' objections that the first two volumes lacked excitement, she concurs that 'the regular novel-reader' (a haughty phrase which includes him) will not find 'the colours dashed on to the canvas with the proper amount of daring' but avers that they must take what they get: ' . . . my palette affords no brighter tints; were I to attempt to deepen the reds, or burnish the yellows, I should but botch'. To Smith's objections of inconsistency in the development of Dr John,

5 Wise and Symington (1980), Vol. 2, p. 23. The history of Brontë's relation-ship with M. Heger, and her surviving letters, can be found in Volumes One and Two of the *Letters*.
6 Moglen argues this position most thoroughly, and Gilbert and Gubar, Gordon, Jacobus and Keefe all commit themselves to it at some stage.
7 Letter to Lucy Baxter, 11 March 1853, reprinted in Orel (1997), p. 106

and in the change of tack in Volume Three, with the focus on M. Paul, she rebukes: 'The spirit of romance would have indicated another course, far more flowery and inviting . . . but this would have been unlike life, inconsistent with truth – at variance with probability.'[8] Both men are firmly smacked down, and we feel here Brontë's real authority as an artist. *Villette* undoubtedly draws on personal love and pain, but (unlike the rather leaden *The Professor*, written in 1846 in the immediate aftermath of the Brussels events) it transforms these into the imaginative representation of so much more: what it is to be; what it is to desire not to be; what the self is, and how its relation to other selves moderates and qualifies it; how chance externals, of appearance and economics, affect what we are. Thackeray's self-satisfied reduction of all this to a desire for 'some Tomkins', like later readings of the novel in terms of its author's neuroses, misses the greatness of *Villette*.

In the last three chapters of Volume Two these searching questions about existence are once more brought to the fore. Paulina artlessly, but also thoughtlessly and callously, expresses surprise at Lucy's occupation as schoolteacher; indeed she is surprised that she needs an occupation at all. Her 'Well, I never knew what you were, nor ever thought of asking: for me you were always Lucy Snowe' (p. 266) betrays a supreme incomprehension of the way in which identity can be shaped by accidents of birth. At the same time Paulina's indifference to materialist dimensions of identity answers to that proud sense of self for which Lucy has struggled through all the pain of the long vacation, a selfhood which may have emerged from the specifics of her social and economic isolation but which seems to her, and indeed to the reader, to go deeper than economics, history or culture. Paulina, and even her apparently wiser father, try to co-opt Lucy, offering her three times her current salary to be Paulina's companion and teacher. But Lucy knows, what Paulina in her attempt to help Lucy doesn't, that, thus paid, she would not remain 'always Lucy Snowe'; her identity depends precisely on her independence from those with whom she might have personal relationships, on the very poverty for which she is pitied. Ginevra, for all her shallowness, never makes the Bassompierres' mistake; she knows full well that any relationship she has with Lucy depends on Lucy's indulgence of her rather than vice versa, and she is intrigued by Lucy's impenetrability and unknowableness. In Chapter xxvII, the final

8 Wise and Symington (1980), Vol. 4, p. 17 and pp. 22–3 respectively

chapter of Volume Two, she asks, more directly than even Lucy herself, ' "Who *are* you, Miss Snowe?" ' (p. 287), goes on to ponder whether " ' . . . you really are the nobody I once thought you" ' (p. 288) and finally moves to the ostensibly metaphysical, " 'But *are* you anybody?" ' (p. 289). And though in one way her questions are, like Ginevra herself, stolidly physical (since they pertain to class and position, and so finally, in the resolutely bourgeois society of the novel, to money), they also reflect a curiosity about how Lucy can exist on the very margins of society, where she is, paradoxically, also a threat to it. Soon that question can turn into something more abstract, and more pressing, as Ginevra's italics suggest. The fear of invisibility which pervades the creation of Lucy, most acutely described when Lucy encounters 'a stilly pause, a wordless silence, a long blank of oblivion . . . seven weeks as bare as seven sheets of blank paper' (pp. 245), is a fear of non-existence itself, when existence seems to depend on the recognition of others. Lucy combats this by deliberately making herself *less* visible, and creating herself almost entirely within. Only we, as readers, are privy to that creation, and know its instability and frailty, but also its profound strength. When, in Chapter XXVI, Lucy faces her apparent demon, the nun, and demands, 'Who are you? and why do you come to me?' (p. 277), she shows that strength. Alone, unaided, her love buried and a cold moon shining, she faces down her visitant, just as she looks hard at her own reality. The time has come for her to move forward.

The final volume of *Villette* brings the happiness that Dr John advised her to cultivate. Certainly, as she trenchantly says, 'happiness is not a potato' (p. 233); but the good doctor is not so wrong. Lucy has cultivated herself, and M. Paul sees what she really is – not a 'nobody', not a 'somebody', but an independent self. His best gift to her is not his love, but his absence; she can have him, through the now-familiar device of his letters, but also have herself. Lucy's joyful three years in her own house – rooms of her own, both occupation and home, that home always missing before – may scarcely seem like having her cake and eating it. But *Villette* never gives us what we expect. Quite its most brilliant surprises are left to the last few pages, first with the revelation of the nun's identity, and then with the double ending. When Lucy shakes apart the 'nun' on her bed, Brontë dismantles for good the Gothic framework she had depended on in *Jane Eyre:* 'I tore her up – the incubus! I held her on high – the goblin! I shook her loose – the mystery!' (p. 439). Again we feel Bronte's linguistic pleasure in this act of destruction, the dramatic syntax and punctuation ironically echoing the very inflation she is stylistically puncturing. (This comic deflation is something the novel excels in, witness Lucy's forensic debunking of the portrait of Cleopatra.) The final indignity for the nun, and for the Gothic, is to be mundanely bundled up and stuffed under Lucy's pillow – upon which 'I deeply slept' (p. 440). The despatch of M. Paul to a fate determined by the reader's imagination is a further sign of Brontë's impatience with the conventions of her chosen form. Again she rounds on the happy ending of *Jane Eyre*, reminding us that only 'sunny imaginations' picture 'union and a happy succeeding life' (pp. 462–3). Since 'sunny' is Dr John's adjective, we feel the shadow of Brontë's disapproval on such an ending. Still, she leaves us the choice, with a lack of closure which looks forward to the modernism of the twentieth century.

Other modernist features abound in *Villette*: its daring 'double love'[9] which raised the eyebrows of contemporaries; its dwelling on male beauty and female desire; its blurring of male and female lines when Lucy, half-man, half-woman, makes love to Ginevra on the stage as she cannot – quite – off it; its placing of the woman, and a plain woman at that, at the centre of her own story, her satisfaction dependent on the absence of a man rather than his presence, and on the presence of work rather than its absence; its sense of the abyss yawning below the social inanities of existence. These qualities made many of Brontë's contemporaries uncomfortable – especially the men. Thackeray called the novel 'plaguey',[10] and Matthew Arnold felt that 'the writer's mind contains nothing but hunger, rebellion, and rage';[11] for him these were faults. It took twentieth-century feminist criticism to convert them into virtues. Kate Millett gives probably the earliest feminist account, and still one of the finest, of *Villette*, acutely characterising it as 'too subversive to be popular'.[12] *Villette* will continue to disturb and subvert, not only through its revolutionary examination of female identity, but in its representation of the shifting nature of *human* identity, its hiddenness, the final unknowableness of one human being to another. That it is able at the same time to make the reader feel the deepest sympathy both for those who float easily on life's surface and for those who struggle bravely with life's pain is Charlotte

9 Martineau, cited above
10 Letter to Mrs Procter, 28 March 1853, quoted in Gordon (1995), p. 283
11 Letter to Mrs Forster, 14 April 1853, quoted in Allott (1973), p. 93
12 Millett (1977), p. 140

Brontë's consummate achievement. Certainly, it was the novel I reached for to calm mind and body in an actual storm, the hurricane of 1987; by candle and gasfire light I reached back to Brontë's century – and she reached forward to mine.

DR SALLY MINOGUE
Canterbury Christ Church
University College

BIBLIOGRAPHY

Biography

Rebecca Fraser, *Charlotte Brontë*, Methuen, London 1988

Elizabeth Gaskell, *The Life of Charlotte Bronte* (Smith, Elder & Co., 1857), ed. Alan Shelston, Penguin, Harmondsworth 1975

Lyndall Gordon, *Charlotte Brontë: A Passionate Life*, Vintage, London 1995

Helene Moglen, *Charlotte Brontë: The Self Conceived*, W. W. Norton & Co., New York 1978; combines biography with extensive analysis of the novels in terms of the life

Harold Orel (ed.), *The Brontës: Interviews and Recollections*, Macmillan, London 1997

Thomas J. Wise and John A. Symington (eds), *The Brontës: Their Lives, Friendships and Correspondence* (first edition, 1933), reprinted in 2 vols, Basil Blackwell, Oxford 1980

Criticism

Miriam Allott (ed.), *Charlotte Brontë: Jane Eyre and Villette*, Casebook Series, Macmillan, London 1973; particularly useful for contemporary and later-nineteenth-century reception of *Villette*

Kathleen Blake, *Love and the Woman Question in Victorian Literature: The Art of Self-Postponement*, Barnes and Noble, New Jersey 1983

Charles Burkhart, 'The Nuns of *Villette*', *Victorian Newsletter*, 44, 1973, pp. 8–13

Janice Carlisle, 'The Face in the Mirror: *Villette* and the Conventions of Autobiography', *Journal of English Literary History*, 46, 1979, pp. 262–89

Rosemary Clark-Beattie, 'Fables of Rebellion: Anti-Catholicism and the Structure of *Villette*', *Journal of English Literary History*, 53, 1986, pp. 821–47

R. A. Colby, '*Villette* and the Life of the Mind', *Publications of the Modern Language Association of America*, 75, 1960, pp. 410–19

Enid L. Duthie, *The Foreign Vision of Charlotte Brontë*, Macmillan, London 1975; relates the Brussels experience to Brontë's fiction

Terry Eagleton, *Myths of Power* (first edition, 1975), reprinted with a new introduction, Macmillan, London 1988; an early Marxist account of the Brontës' work

Inga-Stina Ewbank, *Their Proper Sphere: A Study of the Brontë Sisters as Early Victorian Female Novelists*, Arnold, London 1966

Sandra M. Gilbert and Susan S. Gubar, *The Madwoman in the Attic: the Woman Writer and the Nineteenth-Century Literary Imagination*, Yale University Press, New Haven and London 1979; highly influential feminist account

Robert B. Heilman, 'Charlotte Brontë's "New" Gothic', in *From Jane Austen to Conrad*, R. C. Rathbone and M. Steinmann (eds), University of Minnesota Press, 1958; excellent account of Brontë's revolutionary use of Gothic techniques

Mary Jacobus, 'The Buried Letter: Feminism and Romanticism in *Villette*', in *Women Writing and Writing About Women*, Mary Jacobus (ed.), Croom Helm, London 1979

Robert Keefe, *Charlotte Brontë's World of Death*, University of Texas Press, Austin 1979

Karen Lawrence, 'The Cypher: Disclosure and Reticence in *Villette*', in *Tradition and the Talents of Women*, Florence Howe (ed.), University of Illinois Press, Urbana 1991

Robert B. Martin, *The Accents of Persuasion*, Faber and Faber, London 1966

John Maynard, *Charlotte Brontë and Sexuality*, Cambridge University Press, 1984; counters the 'neurotic' view of Brontë's work

Eleanor McNees (ed.), *The Brontë Sisters: Critical Assessments*, Helm Information, Robertsbridge, East Sussex 1996; Vol. 3 relates to *Villette*

Jane Miller, *Women Writing About Men*, Virago, London 1986

Kate Millett, *Sexual Politics* (first English edition, 1971), Virago, London 1977; see pp. 140–7; early, highly influential, feminist criticism – revolutionary without being reductive

Margot Peters, *Charlotte Brontë: Style in the Novel*, University of Wisconsin Press, 1973

F. B. Pinion, *A Brontë Companion: Literary Assessments, Background, and Reference*, Macmillan, London 1975

Carolyn Platt, 'How Feminist is *Villette*?', *Women and Literature*, 3, 1975, pp. 16–26

Robert M. Polhemus, *Erotic Faith: Being in Love from Jane Austen to D. H. Lawrence*, University of Chicago Press, Chicago and London 1990; see Chapter 6

Nancy S. Rabinowitz, ' "Faithful Narrator" or "Partial Eulogist" First-Person Narration in Brontë's *Villette*', *Journal of Narrative Technique*, 15, 1985, pp. 244–55

Fannie E. Ratchford, *The Brontës' Web of Childhood* (first edition, 1941), Russell and Russell, New York 1964; traces some aspects of *Villette* to Brontë's Angrian writings

Elaine Showalter, *A Literature of Their Own: British Women Novelists from Brontë to Lessing*, Princeton University Press, 1977; Virago, London 1978, revised 1982

Sally Shuttleworth, *Charlotte Brontë and Victorian Psychology*, Cambridge University Press, 1996

VOLUME ONE

CHAPTER I

Bretton

My godmother lived in a handsome house in the clean and ancient town of Bretton. Her husband's family had been residents there for generations, and bore, indeed, the name of their birthplace – Bretton of Bretton: whether by coincidence, or because some remote ancestor had been a personage of sufficient importance to leave his name to his neighbourhood, I know not.

When I was a girl I went to Bretton about twice a year, and well I liked the visit. The house and its inmates specially suited me. The large peaceful rooms, the well-arranged furniture, the clear wide windows, the balcony outside, looking down on a fine antique street, where Sundays and holidays seemed always to abide – so quiet was its atmosphere, so clean its pavement – these things pleased me well.

One child in a household of grown people is usually made very much of, and in a quiet way I was a good deal taken notice of by Mrs Bretton, who had been left a widow, with one son, before I knew her; her husband, a physician, having died while she was yet a young and handsome woman.

She was not young, as I remember her, but she was still handsome, tall, well-made, and though dark for an Englishwoman, yet wearing always the clearness of health in her brunette cheeks, and its vivacity in a pair of fine, cheerful black eyes. People esteemed it a grievous pity that she had not conferred her complexion on her son, whose eyes were blue – though, even in boyhood, very piercing – and the colour of his long hair such as friends did not venture to specify, except as the sun shone on it, when they called it golden. He inherited the lines of his mother's features, however; also her good teeth, her stature (or the promise of her stature, for he was not yet full-grown), and, what was better, her health without flaw, and her spirits of that tone and equality which are better than a fortune to the possessor.

In the autumn of the year – I was staying at Bretton; my godmother having come in person to claim me of the kinsfolk with whom was at that time fixed my permanent residence. I believe she then plainly saw events coming, whose very shadow I scarce guessed; yet of which the faint suspicion sufficed to impart unsettled sadness, and made me glad to change scene and society.

Time always flowed smoothly for me at my godmother's side; not with tumultuous swiftness, but blandly, like the gliding of a full river through a plain. My visits to her resembled the sojourn of Christian and Hopeful[1] beside a certain pleasant stream, with 'green trees on each bank, and meadows beautified with lilies all the year round.' The charm of variety there was not, nor the excitement of incident; but I liked peace so well, and sought stimulus so little, that when the latter came I almost felt it a disturbance, and wished rather it had still held aloof.

One day a letter was received of which the contents evidently caused Mrs Bretton surprise and some concern. I thought at first it was from home, and trembled, expecting I knew not what disastrous communication; to me, however, no reference was made, and the cloud seemed to pass.

The next day, on my return from a long walk, I found, as I entered my bed-room, an unexpected change. In addition to my own French bed in its shady recess, appeared in a corner a small crib, draped with white; and in addition to my mahogany chest of drawers, I saw a tiny rosewood chest. I stood still, gazed, and considered.

'Of what are these things the signs and tokens?' I asked. The answer was obvious. 'A second guest is coming: Mrs Bretton expects other visitors.'

On descending to dinner, explanations ensued. A little girl, I was told, would shortly be my companion: the daughter of a friend and distant relation of the late Dr Bretton's. This little girl, it was added, had recently lost her mother; though indeed, Mrs Bretton ere long subjoined, the loss was not so great as might at first appear. Mrs Home (Home it seems was the name) had been a very pretty, but a giddy, careless woman, who had neglected her child, and disappointed and disheartened her husband. So far from congenial had the union proved, that separation at last ensued – separation by mutual consent, not after any legal process. Soon after this event, the lady having over-exerted herself at a ball, caught cold, took a fever, and died after a very brief illness. Her husband, naturally a man of very sensitive feelings, and shocked inexpressibly by too sudden communication of the news, could hardly, it seems, now be persuaded but that some over-severity on his part – some deficiency in patience and indulgence – had contributed to hasten her end. He had brooded over this idea till his spirits were seriously affected; the medical men insisted on travelling being tried as a remedy, and meanwhile Mrs Bretton had offered to take charge of his little girl. 'And I hope,' added my godmother in conclusion, 'the child will not be like her mama; as silly and frivolous a little flirt as ever sensible man was weak enough to marry. For,' said she, 'Mr Home *is* a sensible man in his way, though not very practical: he is fond of science, and lives half his life in a laboratory trying experiments – a thing his butterfly wife could neither comprehend nor endure; and indeed,' confessed my godmother, 'I should not have liked it myself.'

In answer to a question of mine, she further informed me that her late husband used to say, Mr Home had derived this scientific turn from a maternal uncle, a French savant; for he came, it seems, of mixed French and Scottish origin, and had connections now living in France, of whom more than one wrote *de* before his name, and called himself noble.

That same evening at nine o'clock, a servant was despatched to meet the coach by which our little visitor was expected. Mrs Bretton and I sat alone in the drawing-room waiting her coming; John Graham Bretton being absent on a visit to one of his school-fellows who lived in the country. My godmother read the evening paper while she waited; I sewed. It was a wet night; the rain lashed the panes, and the wind sounded angry and restless.

'Poor child!' said Mrs Bretton from time to time. 'What weather for her journey! I wish she were safe here.'

A little before ten the door-bell announced Warren's return. No sooner was the door opened than I ran down into the hall: there lay a trunk and some band-boxes, beside them stood a person like a nurse-girl, and at the foot of the stair-case was Warren with a shawled bundle in his arms.

'Is that the child?' I asked.

'Yes, miss.'

I would have opened the shawl, and tried to get a peep at the face, but it was hastily turned from me to Warren's shoulder.

'Put me down, please,' said a small voice when Warren opened the drawing-room door, 'and take off this shawl,' continued the speaker, extracting with its minute hand the pin, and with a sort of fastidious haste doffing the clumsy wrapping. The creature which now appeared made a deft attempt to fold the shawl; but the drapery was much too heavy and large to be sustained or wielded by those hands and arms. 'Give it to Harriet, please,' was then the direction, 'and she can put it away.' This said, it turned and fixed its eyes on Mrs Bretton.

'Come here, little dear,' said that lady. 'Come and let me see if you are cold and damp: come and let me warm you at the fire.'

The child advanced promptly. Relieved of her wrapping, she appeared exceedingly tiny; but was a neat, completely-fashioned little figure, light, slight, and straight. Seated on my godmother's ample lap, she looked a mere doll; her neck, delicate as wax, her head of silky curls, increased, I thought, the resemblance.

Mrs Bretton talked in little fond phrases as she chafed the child's hands, arms, and feet; first she was considered with a wistful gaze, but soon a smile answered her. Mrs Bretton was not generally a caressing woman: even with her deeply-cherished son, her manner was rarely sentimental, often the reverse; but when this small stranger smiled at her, she kissed it, asking –

'What is my little one's name?'

'Missy.'

'But besides Missy?'

'Polly, papa calls her.'

'Will Polly be content to live with me?'

'Not *always*; but till papa comes home. Papa is gone away.' She shook her head expressively.

'He will return to Polly, or send for her.'

'Will he, ma'am? Do you know he will?'

'I think so.'

'But Harriet thinks not: at least not for a long while. He is ill.'

Her eyes filled. She drew her hand from Mrs Bretton's, and made a movement to leave her lap; it was at first resisted, but she said –

'Please, I wish to go: I can sit on a stool.'

She was allowed to slip down from the knee, and taking a foot-stool, she carried it to a corner where the shade was deep, and there seated herself. Mrs Bretton, though a commanding, and in grave matters even a peremptory woman, was often passive in trifles: she allowed the child her way. She said to me, 'Take no notice at present.' But I did take notice: I watched Polly rest her small elbow on her small knee, her head on her hand; I observed her draw a square-inch or two of pocket handkerchief from the doll-pocket of her doll-skirt, and then I heard her weep. Other children in grief or pain cry aloud, without shame or restraint; but this being wept: the tiniest occasional sniff testified to her emotion. Mrs Bretton did not hear it: which was quite as well. Ere long, a voice, issuing from the corner, demanded –

'May the bell be rung for Harriet?'

I rang; the nurse was summoned and came.

'Harriet, I must be put to bed,' said her little mistress. 'You must ask where my bed is.'

Harriet signified that she had already made that inquiry.

'Ask if you sleep with me, Harriet.'

'No, missy,' said the nurse: 'You are to share this young lady's room,' designating me.

Missy did not leave her seat, but I saw her eyes seek me. After some minutes' silent scrutiny, she emerged from her corner.

'I wish you, ma'am, good night,' said she to Mrs Bretton; but she passed me mute.

'Good night, Polly,' I said.

'No need to say good night, since we sleep in the same chamber;' was the reply with which she vanished from the drawing-room. We heard Harriet propose to carry her up-stairs. 'No need,' was again her answer – ' No need, no need:' and her small step toiled wearily up the staircase.

On going to bed an hour afterwards, I found her still wide awake. She had arranged her pillows so as to support her little person in a sitting posture; her hands, placed one within the other, rested quietly on the sheet, with an old-fashioned calm most unchildlike. I abstained from speaking to her for some time, but just before extinguishing the light, I recommended her to lie down.

'By and by,' was the answer.

'But you will take cold, missy.'

She took some tiny article of raiment from the chair at her crib side, and with it covered her shoulders. I suffered her to do as she pleased. Listening awhile in the darkness, I was aware that she still wept – wept under restraint, quietly and cautiously.

On awaking with daylight, a trickling of water caught my ear. Behold! there she was risen and mounted on a stool near the wash-stand, with pains and difficulty inclining the ewer (which she could not lift) so as to pour its contents into the basin. It was curious to watch her as she washed and dressed, so small, busy, and noiseless. Evidently she was little accustomed to perform her own toilet; and the buttons, strings, hooks and eyes, offered difficulties which she encountered with a perseverance good to witness. She folded her nightdress, she smoothed the drapery of her couch quite neatly; withdrawing into a corner, where the sweep of the white curtain

concealed her, she became still. I half rose, and advanced my head
to see how she was occupied. On her knees, with her forehead bent
on her hands, I perceived that she was praying.

Her nurse tapped at the door. She started up.

'I am dressed, Harriet,' said she: 'I have dressed myself, but I do
not feel neat. Make me neat!'

'Why did you dress yourself, missy?'

'Hush! speak low, Harriet, for fear of waking *the girl*' (meaning
me, who now lay with my eyes shut). 'I dressed myself to learn,
against the time you leave me.'

'Do you want me to go?'

'When you are cross, I have many a time wanted you to go, but
not now. Tie my sash straight; make my hair smooth, please.'

'Your sash is straight enough. What a particular little body you
are!'

'It must be tied again. Please to tie it.'

'There, then. When I am gone you must get that young lady to
dress you.'

'On no account.'

'Why? She is a very nice young lady. I hope you mean to behave
prettily to her, missy, and not show your airs.'

'She shall dress me on no account.'

'Comical little thing!'

'You are not passing the comb straight through my hair, Harriet:
the line will be crooked.'

'Ay, you are ill to please. Does that suit?'

'Pretty well. Where should I go now that I am dressed?'

'I will take you into the breakfast-room.'

'Come, then.'

They proceeded to the door. She stopped.

'Oh! Harriet, I wish this was papa's house! I don't know these
people.'

'Be a good child, missy.'

'I am good, but I ache here;' putting her hand to her heart, and
moaning while she reiterated 'Papa! papa!'

I roused myself and started up, to check this scene while it was yet
within bounds.

'Say good morning to the young lady,' dictated Harriet.

She said 'good morning,' and then followed her nurse from the
room. Harriet temporarily left that same day, to go to her own
friends, who lived in the neighbourhood.

On descending, I found Paulina (the child called herself Polly, but her full name was Paulina Mary) seated at the breakfast table, by Mrs Bretton's side; a mug of milk stood before her, a morsel of bread filled her hand, which lay passive on the table-cloth: she was not eating.

'How we shall conciliate this little creature,' said Mrs Bretton to me, 'I don't know: she tastes nothing, and, by her looks, she has not slept.'

I expressed my confidence in the effects of time and kindness.

'If she were to take a fancy to anybody in the house, she would soon settle; but not till then,' replied Mrs Bretton.

CHAPTER 2

Paulina

SOME DAYS ELAPSED, and it appeared she was not likely to take much of a fancy to anybody in the house. She was not exactly naughty or wilful: she was far from disobedient; but an object less conducive to comfort – to tranquillity even – than she presented, it was scarcely possible to have before one's eyes. She moped: no grown person could have performed that uncheering business better; no furrowed face of adult exile, longing for Europe at Europe's antipodes, ever bore more legibly the signs of home sickness than did her infant visage. She seemed growing old and unearthly. I, Lucy Snowe, plead guiltless of that curse, an overheated and discursive imagination; but whenever, opening a room-door, I found her seated in a corner alone, her head on her pigmy hand, that room seemed to me not inhabited, but haunted.

And again, when of moonlight nights, on waking, I beheld her figure, white and conspicuous in its night-dress, kneeling upright in bed, and praying like some Catholic or Methodist enthusiast – some precocious fanatic or untimely saint – I scarcely know what thoughts I had; but they ran risk of being hardly more rational and healthy than that child's mind must have been.

I seldom caught a word of her prayers, for they were whispered low: sometimes, indeed, they were not whispered at all, but put up unuttered; such rare sentences as reached my ear still bore the burden, 'Papa; my dear papa!' This, I perceived, was a one-idead nature; betraying that monomaniac tendency I have ever thought the most unfortunate with which man or woman can be cursed.

What might have been the end of this fretting, had it continued unchecked, can only be conjectured: it received, however, a sudden turn.

One afternoon Mrs Bretton, coaxing her from her usual station in a corner, had lifted her into the window-seat, and, by way of occupying her attention, told her to watch the passengers and count how many ladies should go down the street in a given time. She had sat listlessly, hardly looking, and not counting, when – my eye being fixed on hers – I witnessed in its irid and pupil a startling transfiguration. These sudden, dangerous natures – *sensitive* as they are called – offer many a curious spectacle to those whom a cooler temperament has secured from participation in their angular vagaries. The fixed and heavy gaze swum, trembled, then glittered in fire; the small overcast brow cleared; the trivial and dejected features lit up; the sad countenance vanished, and in its place appeared a sudden eagerness, an intense expectancy.

'It *is*!' were her words.

Like a bird or a shaft, or any other swift thing, she was gone from the room. How she got the house-door open I cannot tell; probably it might be ajar; perhaps Warren was in the way and obeyed her behest, which would be impetuous enough. I – watching calmly from the window – saw her, in her black frock and tiny braided apron (to pinafores she had an antipathy), dart half the length of the street; and, as I was on the point of turning, and quietly announcing to Mrs Bretton that the child was run out mad, and ought instantly to be pursued, I saw her caught up, and rapt at once from my cool observation, and from the wondering stare of the passengers. A gentleman had done this good turn, and now, covering her with his cloak, advanced to restore her to the house whence he had seen her issue.

I concluded he would leave her in a servant's charge and withdraw; but he entered: having tarried a little while below, he came upstairs.

His reception immediately explained that he was known to Mrs Bretton. She recognized him; she greeted him, and yet she was fluttered, surprised, taken unawares. Her look and manner were even expostulatory; and in reply to these, rather than her words, he said, –

'I could not help it, madam: I found it impossible to leave the country without seeing with my own eyes how she settled.'

'But you will unsettle her.'

'I hope not. And how is papa's little Polly?'

This question he addressed to Paulina, as he sat down and placed her gently on the ground before him.

'How is Polly's papa?' was the reply, as she leaned on his knee, and gazed up into his face.

It was not a noisy, not a wordy scene: for that I was thankful; but it was a scene of feeling too brimful, and which, because the cup did not foam up high or furiously overflow, only oppressed one the more. On all occasions of vehement, unrestrained expansion, a sense of disdain or ridicule comes to the weary spectator's relief; whereas I have ever felt most burdensome that sort of sensibility which bends of its own will, a giant slave under the sway of good sense.

Mr Home was a stern-featured – perhaps I should rather say, a hard-featured man: his forehead was knotty, and his cheek-bones were marked and prominent. The character of his face was quite Scotch; but there was feeling in his eye, and emotion in his now agitated countenance. His northern accent in speaking harmonized with his physiognomy. He was at once proud-looking and homely-looking.

He laid his hand on the child's uplifted head. She said –

'Kiss Polly.'

He kissed her. I wished she would utter some hysterical cry, so that I might get relief and be at ease. She made wonderfully little noise: she seemed to have got what she wanted – *all* she wanted, and to be in a trance of content. Neither in mien nor features was this creature like her sire, and yet she was of his strain: her mind had been filled from his, as the cup from the flagon.

Indisputably Mr Home owned manly self-control, however he might secretly feel on some matters. 'Polly,' he said, looking down on this little girl, 'go into the hall; you will see papa's greatcoat lying on a chair; put your hand into the pockets, you will find a pocket-handkerchief; bring it to me.'

She obeyed; went and returned deftly and nimbly. He was talking to Mrs Bretton when she came back, and she waited with the handkerchief in her hand. It was a picture, in its way, to see her, with her tiny stature and trim, neat shape, standing at his knee. Seeing that he continued to talk, apparently unconscious of her return, she took his hand, opened the unresisting fingers, insinuated into them the handkerchief, and closed them upon it one by one. He still seemed not to see or feel her; but by-and-by, he lifted her to his knee; she nestled against him, and though neither looked at or spoke to the other for an hour following, I suppose both were satisfied.

During tea, the minute thing's movements and behaviour gave, as usual, full occupation to the eye. First she directed Warren, as he placed the chairs.

'Put papa's chair here, and mine near it, between papa and Mrs Bretton: *I* must hand his tea.'

She took her own seat, and beckoned with her hand to her father.

'Be near me, as if we were at home, papa.'

And again, as she intercepted his cup in passing, and would stir the sugar and put in the cream herself, 'I always did it for you at home, papa: nobody could do it as well, not even your own self.'

Throughout the meal she continued her attentions: rather absurd they were. The sugar-tongs were too wide for one of her hands, and she had to use both in wielding them; the weight of the silver cream-ewer, the bread and butter plates, the very cup and saucer tasked her insufficient strength and dexterity; but she would lift this, hand that, and luckily contrived through it all to break nothing. Candidly speaking, I thought her a little busy-body; but her father, blind like other parents, seemed perfectly content to let her wait on him, and even wonderfully soothed by her offices.

'She is my comfort!' he could not help saying to Mrs Bretton. That lady had her own 'comfort' and nonpareil on a much larger scale, and for the moment, absent; so she sympathized with his foible.

This second 'comfort' came on the stage in the course of the evening. I knew this day had been fixed for his return, and was aware that Mrs Bretton had been expecting him through all its hours. We were seated round the fire, after tea, when Graham joined our circle: I should rather say, broke it up – for, of course, his arrival made a bustle; and then, as Mr Graham was fasting, there was refreshment to be provided. He and Mr Home met as old acquaintance; of the little girl he took no notice for a time.

His meal over, and numerous questions from his mother answered, he turned from the table to the hearth. Opposite where he had placed himself was seated Mr Home, and at his elbow, the child. When I say *child* I use an inappropriate and undescriptive term – a term suggesting any picture rather than that of the demure little person in a mourning frock and white chemisette,[2] that might just have fitted a good-sized doll – perched now on a high chair beside a stand, whereon was her toy work-box of white varnished wood, and holding in her hands a shred of a handkerchief, which she was professing to hem, and at which she bored perseveringly with a needle, that in her fingers seemed almost a skewer, pricking herself ever and anon, marking the cambric with a track of minute red dots; occasionally starting when the perverse weapon – swerving from her control – inflicted a deeper stab than usual; but still silent, diligent, absorbed, womanly.

Graham was at that time a handsome, faithless-looking youth of sixteen. I say faithless-looking, not because he was really of a very perfidious disposition, but because the epithet strikes me as proper to describe the fair, Celtic (not Saxon) character of his good looks; his waved light auburn hair, his supple symmetry, his smile frequent, and destitute neither of fascination nor of subtlety, (in no bad sense.) A spoiled, whimsical boy he was in those days.

'Mother,' he said, after eyeing the little figure before him in silence for some time, and when the temporary absence of Mr Home from the room relieved him from the half-laughing bashfulness, which was all he knew of timidity – 'Mother, I see a young lady in the present society to whom I have not been introduced.'

'Mr Home's little girl, I suppose you mean,' said his mother.

'Indeed, ma'am,' replied her son, 'I consider your expression of the least ceremonious: Miss Home *I* should certainly have said, in venturing to speak of the gentlewoman to whom I allude.'

'Now, Graham, I will not have that child teazed. Don't flatter yourself that I shall suffer you to make her your butt.'

'Miss Home,' pursued Graham, undeterred by his mother's remonstrance, 'might I have the honour to introduce myself, since no one else seems willing to render you and me that service? Your slave, John Graham Bretton.'

She looked at him; he rose and bowed quite gravely. She deliberately put down thimble, scissors, work; descended with precaution from her perch, and curtsying with unspeakable seriousness, said, 'How do you do?'

'I have the honour to be in fair health, only in some measure fatigued with a hurried journey. I hope, ma'am, I see you well.'

'Tor-rer-ably well,' was the ambitious reply of the little woman; and she now essayed to regain her former elevation, but finding this could not be done without some climbing and straining – a sacrifice of decorum not to be thought of – and being utterly disdainful of aid in the presence of a strange young gentleman, she relinquished the high chair for a low stool: towards that low stool Graham drew in his chair.

'I hope, ma'am, the present residence, my mother's house, appears to you a convenient place of abode?'

'Not par-tic-er-er-ly: I want to go home.'

'A natural and laudable desire, ma'am; but one which, notwithstanding, I shall do my best to oppose. I reckon on being able to get out of you a little of that precious commodity called amusement, which mama and Mistress Snowe there fail to yield me.'

'I shall have to go with papa soon: I shall not stay long at your mother's.'

'Yes, yes; you will stay with me I am sure. I have a pony on which you shall ride, and no end of books with pictures to show you.'

'Are *you* going to live here now?'

'I am. Does that please you? Do you like me?'

'No.'

'Why?'

'I think you queer.'

'My face, ma'am?'

'Your face and all about you. You have long red hair.'

'Auburn hair, if you please: mama calls it auburn, or golden, and so do all her friends. But even with my "long red hair," (and he waved his mane with a sort of triumph – tawny he himself well knew that it was, and he was proud of the leonine hue) 'I cannot possibly be queerer than is your ladyship.'

'You call me queer?'

'Certainly.'

(After a pause) 'I think I shall go to bed.'

'A little thing like you ought to have been in bed many hours since; but you probably sat up in the expectation of seeing me?'

'No, indeed.'

'You certainly wished to enjoy the pleasure of my society. You knew I was coming home, and would wait to have a look at me.'

'I sat up for papa, and not for you.'

'Very good, Miss Home. I am going to be a favourite: preferred before papa soon, I dare say.'

She wished Mrs Bretton and myself good night; she seemed hesitating whether Graham's deserts entitled him to the same attention, when he caught her up with one hand, and with that one hand held her poised aloft above his head. She saw herself thus lifted up on high, in the glass over the fireplace. The suddenness, the freedom, the disrespect of the action were too much.

'For shame, Mr Graham!' was her indignant cry, 'put me down!' – and when again on her feet, 'I wonder what you would think of me if I were to treat you in that way, lifting you with my hand' (raising that mighty member) 'as Warren lifts the little cat?'

So saying, she departed.

CHAPTER 3

The Playmates

MR HOME STAYED TWO DAYS. During his visit he could not be prevailed on to go out: he sat all day long by the fireside, sometimes silent, sometimes receiving and answering Mrs Bretton's chat, which was just of the proper sort for a man in his morbid mood – not over-sympathetic, yet not too uncongenial; sensible, and even with a touch of the motherly – she was sufficiently his senior to be permitted this touch.

As to Paulina, the child was at once happy and mute, busy and watchful. Her father frequently lifted her to his knee; she would sit there till she felt or fancied he grew restless; then it was –

'Papa, put me down; I shall tire you with my weight.'

And the mighty burden slid to the rug, and establishing itself on carpet or stool just at 'papa's' feet, the white work-box and the scarlet-speckled handkerchief came into play. This handkerchief it seems was intended as a keepsake for 'papa,' and must be finished before his departure; consequently the demand on the sempstress's industry (she accomplished about a score of stitches in half an hour) was stringent.

The evening, by restoring Graham to the maternal roof (his days were passed at school), brought us an accession of animation – a quality not diminished by the nature of the scenes pretty sure to be enacted between him and Miss Paulina.

A distant and haughty demeanour had been the result of the indignity put upon her the first evening of his arrival: her usual answer, when he addressed her, was –

'I can't attend to you; I have other things to think about.' Being implored to state *what* things: 'Business.'

Graham would endeavour to seduce her attention by opening his desk and displaying its multifarious contents: seals, bright sticks of wax, pen-knives, with a miscellany of engravings – some of them gaily coloured – which he had amassed from time to time. Nor was this powerful temptation wholly unavailing: her eyes, furtively raised from her work, cast many a peep towards the writing-table, rich in scattered pictures. An etching of a child playing with a

Blenheim spaniel happened to flutter to the floor.

'Pretty little dog!' said she, delighted.

Graham prudently took no notice. Ere long, stealing from her corner, she approached to examine the treasure more closely. The dog's great eyes and long ears, and the child's hat and feathers, were irresistible.

'Nice picture!' was her favourite criticism.

'Well – you may have it,' said Graham.

She seemed to hesitate. The wish to possess was strong, but to accept would be a compromise of dignity. No. She put it down and turned away.

'You won't have it then, Polly?'

'I would rather not, thank you.'

'Shall I tell you what I will do with the picture if you refuse it?'

She half turned to listen.

'Cut it into strips for lighting the taper.'

'No!'

'But I shall.'

'Please – don't.'

Graham waxed inexorable on hearing the pleading tone; he took the scissors from his mother's work-casket.

'Here goes!' said he, making a menacing flourish. 'Right through Fido's head, and splitting little Harry's nose.'

'No! *No!* NO!'

'Then come to me. Come quickly, or it is done.'

She hesitated, lingered, but complied.

'Now, will you have it?' he asked, as she stood before him.

'Please.'

'But I shall want payment.'

'How much?'

'A kiss.'

'Give the picture first into my hand.'

Polly, as she said this, looked rather faithless in her turn. Graham gave it. She absconded a debtor, darted to her father, and took refuge on his knee. Graham rose in mimic wrath and followed. She buried her face in Mr Home's waistcoat.

'Papa – papa – send him away!'

'I'll not be sent away,' said Graham.

With face still averted, she held out her hand to keep him off.

'Then, I shall kiss the hand,' said he; but that moment it became a miniature fist, and dealt him payment in a small coin that was not kisses.

Graham – not failing in his way to be as wily as his little playmate – retreated apparently quite discomfited; he flung himself on a sofa, and resting his head against the cushion, lay like one in pain. Polly, finding him silent, presently peeped at him. His eyes and face were covered with his hands. She turned on her father's knee, and gazed at her foe anxiously and long. Graham groaned.

'Papa, what is the matter?' she whispered.

'You had better ask him, Polly.'

'Is he hurt?' (groan second.)

'He makes a noise as if he were,' said Mr Home.

'Mother,' suggested Graham, feebly, 'I think you had better send for the doctor. Oh my eye!' (renewed silence broken only by sighs from Graham.)

'If I were to become blind – ?' suggested this last.

His chastiser could not bear the suggestion. She was beside him directly.

'Let me see your eye: I did not mean to touch it, only your mouth; and I did not think I hit so *very* hard.'

Silence answered her. Her features worked, – 'I am sorry; I am sorry!'

Then succeeded emotion, faltering, weeping.

'Have done trying that child, Graham,' said Mrs Bretton.

'It is all nonsense, my pet,' cried Mr Home.

And Graham once more snatched her aloft, and she again punished him; and while she pulled his lion's locks, termed him –

'The naughtiest, rudest, worst, untruest person that ever was.'

On the morning of Mr Home's departure, he and his daughter had some conversation in a window-recess by themselves; I heard part of it.

'Couldn't I pack my box and go with you, papa?' she whispered earnestly.

He shook his head.

'Should I be a trouble to you?'

'Yes, Polly.'

'Because I am little?'

'Because you are little and tender. It is only great, strong people that should travel. But don't look sad, my little girl; it breaks my heart. Papa will soon come back to his Polly.'

'Indeed, indeed, I am not sad, scarcely at all.'

'Polly would be sorry to give papa pain; would she not?'

'Sorrier than sorry.'

'Then Polly must be cheerful: not cry at parting; not fret afterwards. She must look forward to meeting again, and try to be happy meanwhile. Can she do this?'

'She will try.'

'I see she will. Farewell, then. It is time to go.'

'*Now?* – just *now?*'

'Just now.'

She held up quivering lips. Her father sobbed, but she, I remarked, did not. Having put her down, he shook hands with the rest present, and departed.

When the street-door closed, she dropped on her knees at a chair with a cry – 'Papa!'

It was low and long; a sort of 'Why hast thou forsaken me?'³ During an ensuing space of some minutes, I perceived she endured agony. She went through, in that brief interval of her infant life, emotions such as some never feel; it was in her constitution: she would have more of such instants if she lived. Nobody spoke. Mrs Bretton, being a mother, shed a tear or two. Graham, who was writing, lifted up his eyes and gazed at her. I, Lucy Snowe, was calm.

The little creature, thus left unharassed, did for herself what none other could do – contended with an intolerable feeling; and, ere long, in some degree, repressed it. That day she would accept solace from none; nor the next day: she grew more passive afterwards.

On the third evening, as she sat on the floor, worn and quiet, Graham, coming in, took her up gently, without a word. She did not resist: she rather nestled in his arms, as if weary. When he sat down, she laid her head against him; in a few minutes she slept; he carried her upstairs to bed. I was not surprised that, the next morning, the first thing she demanded was, 'Where is Mr Graham?'

It happened that Graham was not coming to the breakfast-table; he had some exercises to write for that morning's class, and had requested his mother to send a cup of tea into the study. Polly volunteered to carry it: she must be busy about something, look after somebody. The cup was entrusted to her: for, if restless, she was also careful. As the study was opposite the breakfast-room, the doors facing across the passage, my eye followed her.

'What are you doing?' she asked, pausing on the threshold.

'Writing,' said Graham.

'Why don't you come to take breakfast with your mama?'

'Too busy.'

'Do you want any breakfast?'

'Of course.'

'There then.'

And she deposited the cup on the carpet, like a jailer putting a prisoner's pitcher of water through his cell-door, and retreated. Presently she returned.

'What will you have besides tea – what to eat?'

'Anything good. Bring me something particularly nice; that's a kind little woman.'

She came back to Mrs Bretton.

'Please, ma'am, send your boy something good.'

'You shall choose for him, Polly; what shall my boy have?'

She selected a portion of whatever was best on the table, and, ere long, came back with a whispered request for some marmalade, which was not there. Having got it, however (for Mrs Bretton refused the pair nothing), Graham was shortly after heard lauding her to the skies; promising that, when he had a house of his own, she should be his housekeeper, and perhaps – if she showed any culinary genius – his cook; and, as she did not return, and I went to look after her, I found Graham and her breakfasting *tête-à-tête* – she standing at his elbow, and sharing his fare: excepting the marmalade, which she delicately refused to touch; lest, I suppose, it should appear that she had procured it as much on her own account as his. She constantly evinced these nice perceptions and delicate instincts.

The league of acquaintanceship thus struck up was not hastily dissolved; on the contrary, it appeared that time and circumstances served rather to cement than loosen it. Ill-assimilated as the two were in age, sex, pursuits, &c., they somehow found a great deal to say to each other. As to Paulina, I observed that her little character never properly came out, except with young Bretton. As she got settled, and accustomed to the house, she proved tractable enough with Mrs Bretton; but she would sit on a stool at that lady's feet all day long, learning her task, or sewing, or drawing figures with a pencil on a slate, and never kindling once to originality, or showing a single gleam of the peculiarities of her nature. I ceased to watch her under such circumstances: she was not interesting. But the moment Graham's knock sounded of an evening, a change occurred; she was instantly at the head of the staircase. Usually her welcome was a reprimand or a threat.

'You have not wiped your shoes properly on the mat. I shall tell your mama.'

'Little busybody! Are you there?'

'Yes – and you can't reach me: I am higher up than you' (peeping between the rails of the bannister; she could not look over them).

'Polly!'

'My dear boy!' (such was one of her terms for him, adopted in imitation of his mother.)

'I am fit to faint with fatigue,' declared Graham, leaning against the passage-wall in seeming exhaustion. 'Dr Digby' (the headmaster) 'has quite knocked me up with over-work. Just come down and help me to carry up my book.'

'Ah! you're cunning!'

'Not at all, Polly – it is positive fact. I'm as weak as a rush. Come down.'

'Your eyes are quiet like the cat's, but you'll spring.'

'Spring? Nothing of the kind: it isn't in me. Come down.'

'Perhaps I may – if you'll promise not to touch – not to snatch me up, and not to whirl me round.'

'I? I couldn't do it!' (sinking into a chair.)

'Then put the books down on the first step, and go three yards off.'

This being done, she descended warily, and not taking her eyes from the feeble Graham. Of course her approach always galvanized him to new and spasmodic life: the game of romps was sure to be exacted. Sometimes she would be angry; sometimes the matter was allowed to pass smoothly, and we could hear her say as she led him up-stairs:

'Now, my dear boy, come and take your tea – I am sure you must want something.'

It was sufficiently comical to observe her as she sat beside Graham, while he took that meal. In his absence she was a still personage, but with him the most officious, fidgetty little body possible. I often wished she would mind herself and be tranquil; but no – herself was forgotten in him: he could not be sufficiently well waited on, nor carefully enough looked after; he was more than the Grand Turk in her estimation. She would gradually assemble the various plates before him, and, when one would suppose all he could possibly desire was within his reach, she would find out something else:

'Ma'am,' she would whisper to Mrs Bretton, – 'perhaps your son would like a little cake – sweet cake, you know – there is some in there' (pointing to the side-board cupboard). Mrs Bretton, as a rule, disapproved of sweet cake at tea, but still the request was urged, – 'One little piece – only for him – as he goes to school: girls – such as me and Miss Snowe – don't need treats, but *he* would like it.'

Graham did like it very well, and almost always got it. To do him justice, he would have shared his prize with her to whom he owed it; but that was never allowed: to insist, was to ruffle her for the evening. To stand by his knee, and monopolize his talk and notice, was the reward she wanted – not a share of the cake.

With curious readiness did she adapt herself to such themes as interested him. One would have thought the child had no mind or life of her own, but must necessarily live, move, and have her being in another: now that her father was taken from her, she nestled to Graham, and seemed to feel by his feelings: to exist in his existence. She learned the names of all his school-fellows in a trice; she got by heart their characters as given from his lips: a single description of an individual seemed to suffice. She never forgot, or confused identities: she would talk with him the whole evening about people she had never seen, and appear completely to realize their aspect, manners, and dispositions. Some she learned to mimic: an under-master, who was an aversion of young Bretton's, had, it seems, some peculiarities, which she caught up in a moment from Graham's representation, and rehearsed for his amusement; this, however, Mrs Bretton disapproved and forbade.

The pair seldom quarrelled; yet once a rupture occurred, in which her feelings received a severe shock.

One day Graham, on the occasion of his birthday, had some friends – lads of his own age – to dine with him. Paulina took much interest in the coming of these friends; she had frequently heard of them; they were amongst those of whom Graham oftenest spoke. After dinner, the young gentlemen were left by themselves in the dining-room, where they soon became very merry and made a good deal of noise. Chancing to pass through the hall, I found Paulina sitting alone on the lowest step of the staircase, her eyes fixed on the glossy panels of the dining-room door, where the reflection of the hall-lamp was shining; her little brow knit in anxious meditation.

'What are you thinking about, Polly?'

'Nothing particular; only I wish that door was clear glass – that I might see through it. The boys seem very cheerful, and I want to go to them: I want to be with Graham, and watch his friends.'

'What hinders you from going?'

'I feel afraid: but may I try, do you think? May I knock at the door, and ask to be let in?'

I thought perhaps they might not object to have her as a playmate, and therefore encouraged the attempt.

She knocked – too faintly at first to be heard, but on a second essay the door unclosed; Graham's head appeared; he looked in high spirits but impatient.

'What do you want, you little monkey?'

'To come to you.'

'Do you indeed? As if I would be troubled with you! Away to mama and Mistress Snowe, and tell them to put you to bed.' The auburn head and bright flushed face vanished, – the door shut peremptorily. She was stunned.

'Why does he speak so? He never spoke so before,' she said in consternation. 'What have I done?'

'Nothing, Polly; but Graham is busy with his school friends.'

'And he likes them better than me! He turns me away now they are here!'

I had some thoughts of consoling her, and of improving the occasion by inculcating some of those maxims of philosophy whereof I had ever a tolerable stock ready for application. She stopped me, however, by putting her fingers in her ears at the first words I uttered, and then lying down on the mat with her face against the flags; nor could either Warren or the cook root her from that position: she was allowed to lie, therefore, till she chose to rise of her own accord.

Graham forgot his impatience the same evening, and would have accosted her as usual when his friends were gone, but she wrenched herself from his hand; her eye quite flashed; she would not bid him good-night; she would not look in his face. The next day he treated her with indifference, and she grew like a bit of marble. The day after, he teazed her to know what was the matter; her lips would not unclose. Of course he could not feel real anger on his side: the match was too unequal in every way; he tried soothing and coaxing. 'Why was she angry? What had he done?' By-and-by tears answered him; he petted her and they were friends. But she was one on whom such incidents were not lost: I remarked that never after this rebuff did she seek him, or follow him, or in any way solicit his notice. I told her once to carry a book or some other article to Graham when he was shut up in his study.

'I shall wait till he comes out,' said she, proudly; 'I don't choose to give him the trouble of rising to open the door.'

Young Bretton had a favourite pony on which he often rode out; from the window she always watched his departure and return. It was her ambition to be permitted to have a ride round the court-yard on this pony; but far be it from her to ask such a favour. One day she descended to the yard to watch him dismount; as she leaned against the gate, the longing wish for the indulgence of a ride glittered in her eye.

'Come, Polly, will you have a canter?' asked Graham, half carelessly. I suppose she thought he was *too* careless.

'No thank you,' said she, turning away with the utmost coolness.

'You'd better;' pursued he. 'You will like it, I am sure.'

'Don't think I should care a fig about it,' was the response.

'That is not true. You told Lucy Snowe you longed to have a ride.'

'Lucy Snowe is a tatter-box,' I heard her say: (her imperfect articulation was the least precocious thing she had about her), and with this, she walked into the house. Graham coming in soon after, observed to his mother, –

'Mama, I believe that creature is a changeling: she is a perfect cabinet of oddities; but I should be dull without her: she amuses me a great deal more than you or Lucy Snowe.'

'Miss Snowe,' said Paulina to me once (she had now got into the habit of occasionally chatting with me when we were alone in our room at night), 'do you know on what day in the week I like Graham best?'

'How can I possibly know anything so strange? Is there one day out of the seven when he is otherwise than on the other six?'

'To be sure! Can't you see? Don't you know? I find him the most excellent on a Sunday; then we have him the whole day, and he is quiet, and, in the evening, *so* kind.'

This observation was not altogether groundless: going to church, &c., kept Graham quiet on the Sunday, and the evening he generally dedicated to a serene, though rather indolent sort of enjoyment by the parlour fireside. He would take possession of the couch, and then he would call Polly.

Graham was a boy not quite as other boys are; all his delight did not lie in action: he was capable of some intervals of contemplation; he could take a pleasure too in reading, nor was his selection of books wholly indiscriminate: there were glimmerings of characteristic preference and even of instinctive taste in the choice. He rarely, it is true, remarked on what he read, but I have seen him sit and think of it.

Polly being near him, kneeling on a little cushion or the carpet, a conversation would begin in murmurs, not inaudible, though subdued. I caught a snatch of their tenor now and then; and, in truth, some influence better and finer than that of every day, seemed to soothe Graham at such times into no ungentle mood.

'Have you learned any hymns this week, Polly?'

'I have learned a very pretty one, four verses long. Shall I say it?'

'Speak nicely, then: don't be in a hurry.'

The hymn being rehearsed, or rather half-chanted, in a little singing voice, Graham would take exceptions at the manner, and proceed to give a lesson in recitation. She was quick in learning, apt in imitating; and, besides, her pleasure was to please Graham: she proved a ready scholar. To the hymn would succeed some reading – perhaps a chapter in the Bible; correction was seldom required here, for the child could read any simple narrative chapter very well; and, when the subject was such as she could understand and take an interest in, her expression and emphasis were something remarkable. Joseph cast into the pit; the calling of Samuel; Daniel[4] in the lion's den; – these were favourite passages: of the first especially she seemed perfectly to feel the pathos.

'Poor Jacob!' she would sometimes say, with quivering lips. 'How he loved his son Joseph! As much,' she once added – 'as much, Graham, as I love you: if you were to die' (and she re-opened the book, sought the verse, and read), 'I should "refuse to be comforted, and go down into the grave to your mourning."'

With these words she gathered Graham in her little arms, drawing his long-tressed head towards her. The action, I remember, struck me as strangely rash; exciting the feeling one might experience on seeing an animal dangerous by nature, and but half-tamed by art, too heedlessly fondled. Not that I feared Graham would hurt, or very roughly check her; but I thought she ran risk of incurring such a careless, impatient repulse, as would be worse almost to her than a blow. On the whole, however, these demonstrations were borne passively: sometimes even a sort of complacent wonder at her earnest partiality would smile not unkindly in his eyes. Once he said: –

'You like me almost as well as if you were my little sister, Polly.'

'Oh! I *do* like you,' said she; 'I *do* like you very much.'

I was not long allowed the amusement of this study of character. She had scarcely been at Brètton two months, when a letter came from Mr Home, signifying that he was now settled amongst his maternal kinsfolk on the Continent, that, as England was become wholly distasteful to him, he had no thoughts of returning thither, perhaps, for years; and that he wished his little girl to join him immediately.

'I wonder how she will take this news?' said Mrs Bretton, when she had read the letter. *I* wondered, too, and I took upon myself to communicate it.

Repairing to the drawing-room – in which calm and decorated apartment she was fond of being alone, and where she could be implicitly trusted, for she fingered nothing, or rather soiled nothing she fingered – I found her seated, like a little Odalisque,[5] on a couch, half shaded by the drooping draperies of the window near. She seemed happy; all her appliances for occupation were about her; the white wood work-box, a shred or two of muslin, an end or two of ribbon, collected for conversion into doll-millinery. The doll, duly night-capped and night-gowned, lay in its cradle; she was rocking it to sleep, with an air of the most perfect faith in its possession of sentient and somnolent faculties; her eyes, at the same time, being engaged with a picture-book, which lay open on her lap.

'Miss Snowe,' said she in a whisper, 'this is a wonderful book. Candace' (the doll, christened by Graham; for, indeed, its begrimed complexion gave it much of an Ethiopian aspect) – 'Candace is asleep now, and I may tell you about it; only we must both speak low, lest she should waken. This book was given me by Graham; it tells about distant countries, a long, long way from England, which no traveller can reach without sailing thousands of miles over the sea. Wild men live in these countries, Miss Snowe, who wear clothes different from ours: indeed, some of them wear scarcely any clothes, for the sake of being cool, you know; for they have very hot weather. Here is a picture of thousands gathered in a desolate place – a plain, spread with sand – round a man in black, – a good, *good* Englishman, – a missionary, who is preaching to them under a palm-tree.' (She showed a little coloured cut to that effect.) 'And here are pictures' (she went on) 'more stranger' (grammar was occasionally forgotten) 'than that. There is the wonderful Great Wall of China; here is a Chinese lady, with a foot littler than mine. There is a wild horse of Tartary; and here – most strange of all – is a land of ice and snow, without green fields, woods, or gardens. In this land, they found some mammoth bones: there are no mammoths now. You don't know what it was; but I can tell you, because Graham told me. A mighty, goblin creature, as high as this room, and as long as the hall; but not a fierce, flesh-eating thing, Graham thinks. He believes, if I met one in a forest, it would not kill me, unless I came quite in its way; when it would trample me down amongst the bushes, as I might tread on a grasshopper in a hay-field without knowing it.'

Thus she rambled on.

'Polly,' I interrupted, 'should you like to travel?'

'Not just yet,' was the prudent answer; 'but perhaps in twenty years, when I am grown a woman, as tall as Mrs Bretton, I may travel with Graham. We intend going to Switzerland, and climbing Mount Blanck; and some day we shall sail over to South America, and walk to the top of Kim – kim – borazo.'[6]

'But how would you like to travel now, if your papa was with you?'

Her reply – not given till after a pause – evinced one of those unexpected turns of temper peculiar to her: –

'Where is the good of talking in that silly way?' said she. 'Why do you mention papa? What is papa to you? I was just beginning to be happy, and not think about him so much; and there it will be all to do over again!'

Her lip trembled. I hastened to disclose the fact of a letter having been received, and to mention the directions given that she and Harriet should immediately rejoin this dear papa. 'Now, Polly, are you not glad?' I added.

She made no answer. She dropped her book, and ceased to rock her doll; she gazed at me with gravity and earnestness.

'Shall you not like to go to papa?'

'Of course,' she said at last in that trenchant manner she usually employed in speaking to me; and which was quite different from that she used with Mrs Bretton, and different again from the one dedicated to Graham. I wished to ascertain more of what she thought; but no: she would converse no more. Hastening to Mrs Bretton, she questioned her, and received the confirmation of my news. The weight and importance of these tidings kept her perfectly serious the whole day. In the evening, at the moment Graham's entrance was heard below, I found her at my side. She began to arrange a locket-ribbon about my neck, she displaced and replaced the comb in my hair; while thus busied, Graham entered.

'Tell him by-and-by,' she whispered; 'tell him I am going.'

In the course of tea-time I made the desired communication. Graham, it chanced, was at that time greatly preoccupied about some school-prize, for which he was competing. The news had to be told twice before it took proper hold of his attention; and even then he dwelt on it but momently.

'Polly going? What a pity! Dear little Mousie, I shall be sorry to lose her: she must come to us again, mama.'

And hastily swallowing his tea, he took a candle and a small table to himself and his books, and was soon buried in study.

'Little Mousie' crept to his side, and lay down on the carpet at his feet, her face to the floor; mute and motionless she kept that post and position till bed-time. Once I saw Graham – wholly unconscious of her proximity – push her with his restless foot. She receded an inch or two. A minute after one little hand stole out from beneath her face, to which it had been pressed, and softly caressed the heedless foot. When summoned by her nurse she rose and departed very obediently, having bid us all a subdued good-night.

I will not say that I dreaded going to bed, an hour later; yet I certainly went with an unquiet anticipation that I should find that child in no peaceful sleep. The forewarning of my instinct was but fulfilled, when I discovered her, all cold and vigilant, perched like a white bird on the outside of the bed. I scarcely knew how to accost her; she was not to be managed like another child. She, however, accosted me. As I closed the door, and put the light on the dressing-table, she turned to me with these words: –

'I cannot – *cannot* sleep; and in this way I cannot – *cannot* live!'

I asked what ailed her.

'Dedful miz-er-y!' said she, with her piteous lisp.

'Shall I call Mrs Bretton?'

'That is downright silly,' was her impatient reply; and, indeed, I well knew that if she had heard Mrs Bretton's foot approach, she would have nestled quiet as a mouse under the bedclothes. While lavishing her eccentricities regardlessly before me – for whom she professed scarcely the semblance of affection – she never showed my godmother one glimpse of her inner self: for her, she was nothing but a docile, somewhat quaint little maiden. I examined her; her cheek was crimson; her dilated eye was both troubled and glowing, and painfully restless: in this state it was obvious she must not be left till morning. I guessed how the case stood.

'Would you like to bid Graham good-night again?' I asked. 'He is not gone to his room yet.'

She at once stretched out her little arms to be lifted. Folding a shawl round her, I carried her back to the drawing-room. Graham was just coming out.

'She cannot sleep without seeing and speaking to you once more,' I said. 'She does not like the thought of leaving you.'

'I've spoilt her,' said he, taking her from me with good humour, and kissing her little hot face and burning lips. 'Polly, you care for me more than for papa, now – '

'I *do* care for you, but you care nothing for me,' was her whisper.

She was assured to the contrary, again kissed, restored to me, and I carried her away; but, alas! not soothed.

When I thought she could listen to me I said –

'Paulina, you should not grieve that Graham does not care for you so much as you care for him. It must be so.'

Her lifted and questioning eyes asked why.

'Because he is a boy and you are a girl; he is sixteen and you are only six; his nature is strong and gay, and yours is otherwise.'

'But I love him so much; he *should* love me a little.'

'He does. He is fond of you. You are his favourite.'

'Am I Graham's favourite?'

'Yes, more than any little child I know.'

The assurance soothed her; she smiled in her anguish.

'But,' I continued, 'don't fret, and don't expect too much of him, or else he will feel you to be troublesome, and then it is all over.'

'All over!' she echoed softly, 'then I'll be good. I'll try to be good, Lucy Snowe.'

I put her to bed.

'Will he forgive me this one time?' she asked, as I undressed myself. I assured her that he would; that as yet he was by no means alienated; that she had only to be careful for the future.

'There is no future,' said she: 'I am going. Shall I ever – ever – see him again, after I leave England?'

I returned an encouraging response. The candle being extinguished, a still half-hour elapsed. I thought her asleep, when the little white shape once more lifted itself in the crib, and the small voice asked, – ' Do you like Graham, Miss Snowe?'

'Like him! Yes, a little.'

'Only a little! Do you like him as I do?'

'I think not. No. Not as you do.'

'Do you like him much?'

'I told you I liked him a little. Where is the use of caring for him so very much? He is full of faults.'

'Is he?'

'All boys are.'

'More than girls?'

'Very likely. Wise people say it is folly to think anybody perfect; and as to likes and dislikes, we should be friendly to all, and worship none.'

'Are you a wise person?'

'I mean to try to be so. Go to sleep.'

'I *cannot* go to sleep. Have you no pain just here' (laying her elfish hand on her elfish breast), 'when you think *you* shall have to leave Graham; for *your* home is not here?'

'Surely, Polly,' said I, 'you should not feel so much pain when you are very soon going to rejoin your father. Have you forgotten him? Do you no longer wish to be his little companion?'

Dead silence succeeded this question.

'Child, lie down and sleep,' I urged.

'My bed is cold,' said she. 'I can't warm it.'

I saw the little thing shiver. 'Come to me,' I said, wishing, yet scarcely hoping, that she would comply: for she was a most strange, capricious, little creature, and especially whimsical with me. She came, however, instantly, like a small ghost gliding over the carpet. I took her in. She was chill; I warmed her in my arms. She trembled nervously; I soothed her. Thus tranquillized and cherished she at last slumbered.

'A very unique child,' thought I, as I viewed her sleeping countenance by the fitful moonlight, and cautiously and softly wiped her glittering eyelids and her wet cheeks with my handkerchief. 'How will she get through this world, or battle with this life? How will she bear the shocks and repulses, the humiliations and desolations, which books, and my own reason tell me are prepared for all flesh?'

She departed the next day; trembling like a leaf when she took leave, but exercising self-command.

CHAPTER 4

Miss Marchmont

ON QUITTING BRETTON, which I did a few weeks after Paulina's departure – little thinking then I was never again to visit it: never more to tread its calm old streets – I betook myself home, having been absent six months. It will be conjectured that I was of course glad to return to the bosom of my kindred. Well! the amiable conjecture does no harm, and may therefore be safely left uncontradicted. Far from saying nay, indeed, I will permit the reader to picture me, for the next eight years, as a bark slumbering through halcyon weather, in a harbour still as glass – the steersman stretched on the little deck, his face up to heaven, his eyes closed: buried, if you will, in a long prayer. A great many women and girls are supposed to pass their lives something in that fashion; why not I with the rest?

Picture me then idle, basking, plump, and happy, stretched on a cushioned deck, warmed with constant sunshine, rocked by breezes indolently soft. However, it cannot be concealed that, in that case, I must somehow have fallen over-board, or that there must have been wreck at last. I too well remember a time – a long time, of cold, of danger, of contention. To this hour, when I have the nightmare, it repeats the rush and saltness of briny waves in my throat, and their icy pressure on my lungs. I even know there was a storm, and that not of one hour nor one day. For many days and nights neither sun nor stars appeared; we cast with our own hands the tackling out of the ship; a heavy tempest lay on us; all hope that we should be saved was taken away. In fine, the ship was lost, the crew perished.

As far as I recollect, I complained to no one about these troubles. Indeed, to whom could I complain? Of Mrs Bretton I had long lost sight. Impediments, raised by others, had, years ago, come in the way of our intercourse, and cut it off. Besides, time had brought changes for her too: the handsome property of which she was left guardian for her son, and which had been chiefly invested in some joint-stock undertaking, had melted, it was said, to a fraction of its original amount. Graham, I learned from incidental rumours, had adopted a profession; both he and his mother were gone from Bretton, and were understood to be now in London. Thus, there remained no possibility of dependence on others; to myself alone could I look. I know not that I was of a self-reliant or active nature; but self-reliance and exertion were forced upon me by circumstances, as they are upon thousands besides; and when Miss Marchmont, a maiden lady of our neighbourhood, sent for me, I obeyed her behest, in the hope that she might assign me some task I could undertake.

Miss Marchmont was a woman of fortune, and lived in a handsome residence; but she was a rheumatic cripple, impotent, foot and hand, and had been so for twenty years. She always sat up-stairs: her drawing-room adjoined her bed-room. I had often heard of Miss Marchmont, and of her peculiarities (she had the character of being very eccentric), but till now had never seen her. I found her a furrowed, gray-haired woman, grave with solitude, stern with long affliction, irritable also, and perhaps exacting. It seemed that a maid, or rather companion, who had waited on her for some years, was about to be married; and she, hearing of my bereaved lot, had sent for me, with the idea that I might supply this person's place. She made the proposal to me after tea, as she and I sat alone by her fireside.

'It will not be an easy life,' said she candidly, 'for I require a good deal of attention, and you will be much confined; yet, perhaps, contrasted with the existence you have lately led, it may appear tolerable.'

I reflected. Of course it ought to appear tolerable, I argued inwardly; but somehow, by some strange fatality, it would not. To live here, in this close room, the watcher of suffering, sometimes, perhaps, the butt of temper, through all that was to come of my youth; while all that was gone had passed, to say the least, not blissfully – my heart sunk one moment, then it revived; for though I forced myself to *realize* evils, I think I was too prosaic to *idealize*, and consequently to exaggerate them.

'My doubt is whether I should have strength for the undertaking,' I observed.

'That is my own scruple,' said she; 'for you look a worn-out creature.'

So I did. I saw myself in the glass, in my mourning-dress, a faded, hollow-eyed vision. Yet I thought little of the wan spectacle. The blight, I believed, was chiefly external: I still felt life at life's sources.

'What else have you in view – anything?'

'Nothing clear as yet: but I may find something.'

'So you imagine: perhaps you are right. Try your own method, then; and if it does not succeed, test mine. The chance I have offered shall be left open to you for three months.'

This was kind. I told her so, and expressed my gratitude. While I was speaking, a paroxysm of pain came on. I ministered to her; made the necessary applications, according to her directions, and, by the time she was relieved, a sort of intimacy was already formed between us. I, for my part, had learned from the manner in which she bore this attack, that she was a firm, patient woman (patient under physical pain, though sometimes perhaps excitable under long mental canker); and she, from the good-will with which I succoured her, discovered that she could influence my sympathies (such as they were). She sent for me the next day; for five or six successive days she claimed my company. Closer acquaintance, while it developed both faults and eccentricities, opened, at the same time, a view of a character I could respect. Stern and even morose as she sometimes was, I could wait on her and sit beside her with that calm which always blesses us when we are sensible that our manners, presence, contact, please and soothe the persons we serve. Even when she scolded me – which she did, now and then, very tartly – it was in such a way as did not humiliate, and left no sting; it was rather like an irascible mother rating her daughter, than a harsh mistress lecturing a dependent: lecture, indeed, she could not, though she could occasionally storm. Moreover, a vein of reason ever ran through her passion: she was logical even when fierce. Ere long a growing sense of attachment began to present the thought of staying with her as companion in quite a new light; in another week I had agreed to remain.

Two hot, close rooms thus became my world; and a crippled old woman, my mistress, my friend, my all. Her service was my duty – her pain, my suffering – her relief, my hope – her anger, my punishment – her regard, my reward. I forgot that there were fields, woods, rivers, seas, an everchanging sky outside the steam-dimmed lattice of this sick-chamber; I was almost content to forget it. All within me became narrowed to my lot. Tame and still by habit, disciplined by destiny, I demanded no walks in the fresh air; my appetite needed no more than the tiny messes served for the invalid. In addition she gave me the originality of her character to study: the steadiness of her virtues, I will add, the power of her passions, to admire, the truth of her feelings to trust. All these things she had, and for these things I clung to her.

For these things I would have crawled on with her for twenty years, if for twenty years longer her life of endurance had been

protracted. But another decree was written. It seemed I must be
stimulated into action. I must be goaded, driven, stung, forced to
energy. My little morsel of human affection, which I prized as if it
were a solid pearl, must melt in my fingers and slip thence like a
dissolving hailstone. My small adopted duty must be snatched from
my easily contented conscience. I had wanted to compromise with
Fate: to escape occasional great agonies by submitting to a whole life
of privation and small pains. Fate would not so be pacified; nor would
Providence sanction this shrinking sloth and cowardly indolence.

One February night – I remember it well – there came a voice
near Miss Marchmont's house, heard by every inmate, but
translated, perhaps, only by one. After a calm winter, storms were
ushering in the spring. I had put Miss Marchmont to bed; I sat at
the fireside sewing. The wind was wailing at the windows: it had
wailed all day; but, as night deepened, it took a new tone – an accent
keen, piercing, almost articulate to the ear; a plaint, piteous and
disconsolate to the nerves, trilled in every gust.

'Oh, hush! hush!' I said in my disturbed mind, dropping my work,
and making a vain effort to stop my ears against that subtle, searching
cry. I had heard that very voice ere this, and compulsory observation
had forced on me a theory as to what it boded. Three times in the
course of my life, events had taught me that these strange accents in
the storm – this restless, hopeless cry – denote a coming state of the
atmosphere unpropitious to life. Epidemic diseases, I believed, were
often heralded by a gasping, sobbing, tormented, long-lamenting east
wind. Hence, I inferred, arose the legend of the Banshee.[7] I fancied,
too, I had noticed – but was not philosopher enough to know
whether there was any connection between the circumstances – that
we often at the same time hear of disturbed volcanic action in distant
parts of the world; of rivers suddenly rushing above their banks; and
of strange high tides flowing furiously in on low sea-coasts. 'Our
globe,' I had said to myself, 'seems at such periods torn and
disordered; the feeble amongst us wither in her distempered breath,
rushing hot from steaming volcanoes.'

I listened, and trembled; Miss Marchmont slept.

About midnight, the storm in one half hour fell to a dead calm.
The fire, which had been burning dead, glowed up vividly. I felt the
air change, and become keen. Raising blind and curtain, I looked
out, and saw in the stars the keen sparkle of a sharp frost.

Turning away, the object that met my eyes was Miss Marchmont
awake, lifting her head from the pillow, and regarding me with
unusual earnestness.

'Is it a fine night?' she asked.

I replied in the affirmative.

'I thought so,' she said; 'for I feel so strong, so well. Raise me. I feel young to-night,' she continued; 'young, light-hearted, and happy. What if my complaint be about to take a turn, and I am yet destined to enjoy health? It would be a miracle!'

'And these are not the days of miracles,' I thought to myself, and wondered to hear her talk so. She went on directing her conversation to the past, and seeming to recall its incidents, scenes, and personages with singular vividness.

'I love Memory to-night,' she said: 'I prize her as my best friend. She is just now giving me a deep delight; she is bringing back to my heart, in warm and beautiful life, realities – not mere empty ideas – but what were once realities, and that I long have thought decayed, dissolved, mixed in with grave-mould. I possess just now the hours, the thoughts, the hopes of my youth. I renew the love of my life – its only love – almost its only affection; for I am not a particularly good woman: I am not amiable. Yet I have had my feelings, strong and concentrated; and these feelings had their object; which, in its single self, was dear to me, as, to the majority of men and women, are all the unnumbered points on which they dissipate their regard. While I loved, and while I was loved, what an existence I enjoyed! What a glorious year I can recall – how bright it comes back to me! What a living spring – what a warm, glad summer – what soft moonlight, silvering the autumn evenings – what strength of hope under the ice-bound waters and frost-hoar fields of that year's winter! Through that year my heart lived with Frank's heart. O my noble Frank – my faithful Frank – my *good* Frank! so much better than myself – his standard in all things so much higher! This I can now see and say – if few women have suffered as I did in his loss, few have enjoyed what I did in his love. It was a far better kind of love than common; I had no doubts about it or him: it was such a love as honoured, protected, and elevated, no less than it gladdened her to whom it was given. Let me now ask, just at this moment, when my mind is so strangely clear, – let me reflect why it was taken from me? For what crime was I condemned, after twelve months of bliss, to undergo thirty years of sorrow?'

'I do not know,' she continued, after a pause: 'I cannot *cannot* see the reason; yet at this hour I can say with sincerity, what I never tried to say before – Inscrutable God, Thy will be done! And at this moment I can believe that death will restore me to Frank. I never believed it till now.'

'He is dead, then?' I inquired in a low voice.

'My dear girl,' she said, 'one happy Christmas Eve I dressed and decorated myself, expecting my lover, very soon to be my husband, would come that night to visit me. I sat down to wait. Once more I see that moment – I see the snow-twilight stealing through the window over which the curtain was not dropped, for I designed to watch him ride up the white walk; I see and feel the soft firelight warming me, playing on my silk dress, and fitfully showing me my own young figure in a glass. I see the moon of a calm winter night float full, clear and cold, over the inky mass of shrubbery, and the silvered turf of my grounds. I wait, with some impatience in my pulse, but no doubt in my breast. The flames had died in the fire, but it was a bright mass yet; the moon was mounting high, but she was still visible from the lattice; the clock neared ten; he rarely tarried later than this, but once or twice he had been delayed so long.

'Would he for once fail me? No – not even for once; and now he was coming – and coming fast – to atone for lost time. "Frank! you furious rider," I said inwardly, listening gladly, yet anxiously, to his approaching gallop, "you shall be rebuked for this: I will tell you it is *my* neck you are putting in peril; for whatever is yours is, in a dearer and tenderer sense, mine." There he was: I saw him; but I think tears were in my eyes; my sight was so confused. I saw the horse; I heard it stamp – I saw at least a mass; I heard a clamour. *Was* it a horse? or what heavy, dragging thing was it, crossing, strangely dark, the lawn? How could I name that thing in the moonlight before me? or how could I utter the feeling which rose in my soul?

'I could only run out. A great animal – truly, Frank's black horse – stood trembling, panting, snorting before the door; a man held it: Frank, as I thought.

' "What is the matter?" I demanded. Thomas, my own servant, answered by saying sharply, "Go into the house, madam." And then calling to another servant, who came hurrying from the kitchen as if summoned by some instinct, "Ruth, take missis into the house directly." But I was kneeling down in the snow, beside something that lay there – something that I had seen dragged along the ground – something that sighed, that groaned on my breast, as I lifted and drew it to me. He was not dead; he was not quite unconscious. I had him carried in; I refused to be ordered about and thrust from him. I was quite collected enough, not only to be my own mistress, but the mistress of others. They had begun by trying to treat me like a child, as they always do with people struck by God's hand; but I gave place to none except the surgeon; and when he had done what he could, I took my dying Frank to myself. He had strength to fold me in his arms; he had power to speak my name; he heard me as I prayed over him very softly; he felt me as I tenderly and fondly comforted him.

' "Maria," he said, "I am dying in Paradise." He spent his last breath in faithful words for me. When the dawn of Christmas morning broke, my Frank was with God.

'And that,' she went on, 'happened thirty years ago. I have suffered since. I doubt if I have made the best use of all my calamities. Soft, amiable natures they would have refined to saintliness; of strong, evil spirits they would have made demons; as for me, I have only been a woe-struck and selfish woman.'

'You have done much good,' I said; for she was noted for her liberal almsgiving.

'I have not withheld money, you mean, where it could assuage affliction. What of that? It cost me no effort or pang to give. But I think from this day I am about to enter a better frame of mind, to prepare myself for reunion with Frank. You see I still think of Frank more than of God; and unless it be counted that in thus loving the creature so much, so long, and so exclusively, I have not at least blasphemed the Creator, small is my chance of salvation. What do you think, Lucy, of these things? Be my chaplain and tell me.'

This question I could not answer: I had no words. It seemed as if she thought I *had* answered it.

'Very right, my child. We should acknowledge God merciful, but not always for us comprehensible. We should accept our own lot whatever it be, and try to render happy that of others. Should we not? Well, to-morrow I will begin by trying to make you happy. I will endeavour to do something for you, Lucy: something that will benefit you when I am dead. My head aches now with talking too much; still I am happy. Go to bed. The clock strikes two. How late you sit up; or rather how late I, in my selfishness, keep you up. But go now; have no more anxiety for me: I feel I shall rest well.'

She composed herself as if to slumber. I, too, retired to my crib in a closet within her room. The night passed in quietness; quietly her doom must at last have come: peacefully and painlessly: in the morning she was found without life, nearly cold, but all calm and undisturbed. Her previous excitement of spirits and change of mood had been the prelude of a fit; one stroke sufficed to sever the thread of an existence so long fretted by affliction.

CHAPTER 5

Turning a New Leaf

MY MISTRESS BEING DEAD, and I once more alone, I had to look out for a new place. About this time I might be a little – a very little, shaken in nerves. I grant I was not looking well, but on the contrary, thin, haggard, and hollow-eyed; like a sitter-up at night, like an over-wrought servant, or a placeless person in debt. In debt, however, I was not; nor quite poor; for though Miss Marchmont had not had time to benefit me, as, on that last night, she said she intended, yet after the funeral, my wages were duly paid by her second cousin, the heir, an avaricious-looking man, with pinched nose and narrow temples, who, indeed, I heard long afterwards, turned out a thorough miser: a direct contrast to his generous kinswoman, and a foil to her memory, blessed to this day by the poor and needy. The possessor, then, of fifteen pounds; of health though worn not broken, and of a spirit in similar condition; I might still, in comparison with many people, be regarded as occupying an enviable position. An embarrassing one it was, however, at the same time; as I felt with some acuteness on a certain day, of which the corresponding one in the next week was to see my departure from my present abode, while with another I was not provided.

In this dilemma I went, as a last and sole resource, to see and consult an old servant of our family; once my nurse, now housekeeper at a grand mansion not far from Miss Marchmont's. I spent some hours with her; she comforted, but knew not how to advise me. Still all inward darkness, I left her about twilight; a walk of two miles lay before me; it was a clear, frosty night. In spite of my solitude, my poverty, and my perplexity, my heart, nourished and nerved with the vigour of a youth that had not yet counted twenty-three summers, beat light and not feebly. Not feebly, I am sure, or I should have trembled in that lonely walk, which lay through still fields, and passed neither village nor farm-house, nor cottage; I should have quailed in the absence of moonlight, for it was by the leading of stars only I traced the dim path; I should have quailed still more in the unwonted presence of that which to-night shone in the north, a moving mystery – the Aurora Borealis. But this solemn stranger influenced me otherwise than through my fears. Some new power it seemed to bring. I drew in energy with the keen, low breeze that blew on its path. A bold thought was sent to my mind; my mind was made strong to receive it.

'Leave this wilderness,' it was said to me, 'and go out hence.'

'Where?' was the query.

I had not very far to look: gazing from this country parish in the flat, rich middle of England – I mentally saw within reach what I had never yet beheld with my bodily eyes; I saw London.

The next day I returned to the hall, and asking once more to see the housekeeper, I communicated to her my plan.

Mrs Barrett was a grave, judicious woman, though she knew little more of the world than myself; but grave and judicious as she was, she did not charge me with being out of my senses: and, indeed, I had a staid manner of my own which ere now had been as good to me as cloak and hood of hodden gray; since under its favour I had been enabled to achieve with impunity, and even approbation, deeds that if attempted with an excited and unsettled air, would in some minds have stamped me as a dreamer and zealot.

The housekeeper was slowly propounding some difficulties, while she prepared orange-rind for marmalade, when a child ran past the window and came bounding into the room. It was a pretty child, and as it danced, laughing, up to me – for we were not strangers (nor, indeed, was its mother – a young married daughter of the house – a stranger) – I took it on my knee. Different as were our social positions now, this child's mother and I had been schoolfellows, when I was a girl of ten and she a young lady of sixteen; and I remembered her – good-looking, but dull – in a lower class than mine.

I was admiring the boy's handsome dark eyes, when the mother, young Mrs Leigh, entered. What a beautiful and kind-looking woman was the good-natured and comely, but unintellectual girl become! Wifehood and maternity had changed her thus, as I have since seen them change others even less promising than she. Me she had forgotten. I was changed too; though not, I fear, for the better. I made no attempt to recall myself to her memory: why should I? She came for her son to accompany her in a walk, and behind her followed a nurse carrying an infant. I only mention the incident because, in addressing the nurse, Mrs Leigh spoke French (very bad French, by the way, and with an incorrigibly bad accent, again forcibly reminding me of our school-days); and I found the woman was a foreigner. The little boy chattered volubly in French too. When the whole party were withdrawn, Mrs Barrett remarked that her young lady had brought that foreign nurse home with her two years ago, on her return from a Continental excursion; that she was treated almost as well as a governess, and had nothing to do but walk out with the baby and chatter French with Master Charles; 'and,' added Mrs Barrett, 'she says there are many Englishwomen in foreign families as well placed as she.'

I stored up this piece of casual information, as careful housewives store seemingly worthless shreds and fragments for which their prescient minds anticipate a possible use some day. Before I left my old friend, she gave me the address of a respectable old-fashioned inn in the city, which, she said, my uncles used to frequent in former days.

In going to London, I ran less risk and evinced less enterprise than the reader may think. In fact, the distance was only fifty miles. My means would suffice both to take me there, to keep me a few days, and also to bring me back if I found no inducement to stay. I regarded it as a brief holiday, permitted for once to work-weary faculties, rather than as an adventure of life and death. There is nothing like taking all you do at a moderate estimate: it keeps mind and body tranquil; whereas grandiloquent notions are apt to hurry both into fever.

Fifty miles were then a day's journey, (for I speak of a time gone by: my hair which till a late period withstood the frosts of time, lies now at last, white under a white cap, like snow beneath snow.) About nine o'clock of a wet February night I reached London.

My reader, I know, is one who would not thank me for an elaborate reproduction of poetic first impressions; and it is well, inasmuch as I had neither time nor mood to cherish such; arriving as I did late, on a dark, raw, and rainy evening, in a Babylon and a wilderness of which the vastness and the strangeness tried to the utmost any powers of clear thought and steady self-possession with which, in the absence of more brilliant faculties, Nature might have gifted me.

When I left the coach, the strange speech of the cabmen and others waiting round, seemed to me odd as a foreign tongue. I had never before heard the English language chopped up in that way. However, I managed to understand and to be understood, so far as to get myself and trunk safely conveyed to the old inn whereof I had the address. How difficult, how oppressive, how puzzling seemed my flight! In London for the first time; at an inn for the first time; tired with travelling; confused with darkness; palsied with cold;

unfurnished with either experience or advice to tell me how to act, and yet – to act obliged.

Into the hands of Common-sense I confided the matter. Common-sense, however, was as chilled and bewildered as all my other faculties, and it was only under the spur of an inexorable necessity that she spasmodically executed her trust. Thus urged, she paid the porter: considering the crisis, I did not blame her too much that she was hugely cheated; she asked the waiter for a room; she timorously called for the chambermaid; what is far more, she bore, without being wholly overcome, a highly supercilious style of demeanour from that young lady, when she appeared.

I recollect this same chambermaid was a pattern of town prettiness and smartness. So trim her waist, her cap, her dress – I wondered how they had all been manufactured. Her speech had an accent which in its mincing glibness seemed to rebuke mine as by authority; her spruce attire flaunted an easy scorn at my plain country garb.

'Well, it can't be helped,' I thought, 'and then the scene is new, and the circumstances; I shall gain good.'

Maintaining a very quiet manner towards this arrogant little maid, and subsequently observing the same towards the parsonic-looking, black-coated, white-neckclothed waiter, I got civility from them ere long. I believe at first they thought I was a servant; but in a little while they changed their minds, and hovered in a doubtful state between patronage and politeness.

I kept up well till I had partaken of some refreshment, warmed myself by a fire, and was fairly shut into my room; but, as I sat down by the bed and rested my head and arms on the pillow, a terrible oppression overcame me. All at once my position rose on me like a ghost. Anomalous; desolate, almost blank of hope, it stood. What was I doing here alone in great London? What should I do on the morrow? What prospects had I in life? What friends had I on earth? Whence did I come? Whither should I go? What should I do?

I wet the pillow, my arms, and my hair, with rushing tears. A dark interval of most bitter thought followed this burst; but I did not regret the step taken, nor wish to retract it. A strong, vague persuasion, that it was better to go forward than backward, and that I *could go* forward – that a way, however narrow and difficult, would in time open – predominated over other feelings: its influence hushed them so far, that at last I became sufficiently tranquil to be able to say my prayers and seek my couch. I had just extinguished my candle and lain down, when a deep, low, mighty tone swung through the night. At first I knew it not; but it was uttered twelve times, and at the twelfth colossal hum and trembling knell, I said: 'I lie in the shadow of St. Paul's.'

CHAPTER 6

London

THE NEXT DAY was the first of March, and when I awoke, rose, and opened my curtain, I saw the risen sun struggling through fog. Above my head, above the house-tops, co-elevate almost with the clouds, I saw a solemn, orbed mass, dark-blue and dim – THE DOME. While I looked, my inner self moved; my spirit shook its always-fettering wings half loose; I had a sudden feeling as if I, who had never yet truly lived, were at last about to taste life: in that morning my soul grew as fast as Jonah's gourd.

'I did well to come,' I said, proceeding to dress with speed and care. 'I like the spirit of this great London which I feel around me. Who but a coward would pass his whole life in hamlets, and for ever abandon his faculties to the eating rust of obscurity?'

Being dressed, I went down, not travel-worn and exhausted, but tidy and refreshed. When the waiter came in with my breakfast, I managed to accost him sedately, yet cheerfully; we had ten minutes' discourse, in the course of which we became usefully known to each other.

He was a gray-haired, elderly man; and, it seemed, had lived in his present place twenty years. Having ascertained this, I was sure he must remember my two uncles, Charles and Wilmot, who, fifteen years ago, were frequent visitors here. I mentioned their names; he recalled them perfectly, and with respect. Having intimated my connection, my position in his eyes was henceforth clear, and on a right footing. He said I was like my uncle Charles: I suppose he spoke truth, because Mrs Barrett was accustomed to say the same thing. A ready and obliging courtesy now replaced his former uncomfortably doubtful manner: henceforth I need no longer be at a loss for a civil answer to a sensible question.

The street on which my little sitting-room window looked was narrow, perfectly quiet, and not dirty: the few passengers were just such as one sees in provincial towns: here was nothing formidable; I felt sure I might venture out alone.

Having breakfasted, out I went. Elation and pleasure were in my heart: to walk alone in London seemed of itself an adventure.

Presently I found myself in Paternoster-row – classic ground this. I entered a bookseller's shop, kept by one Jones; I bought a little book – a piece of extravagance I could ill afford; but I thought I would one day give or send it to Mrs Barrett. Mr Jones, a dried-in man of business, stood behind his desk; he seemed one of the greatest, and I one of the happiest, of beings.

Prodigious was the amount of life I lived that morning. Finding myself before St. Paul's, I went in; I mounted to the dome: I saw thence London, with its river, and its bridges, and its churches; I saw antique Westminster, and the green Temple Gardens, with sun upon them, and a glad, blue sky of early spring above; and, between them and it, not too dense a cloud of haze.

Descending, I went wandering whither chance might lead, in a still ecstacy of freedom and enjoyment; and I got – I knew not how – I got into the heart of city life. I saw and felt London at last: I got into the Strand; I went up Cornhill; I mixed with the life passing along; I dared the perils of crossings. To do this, and to do it utterly alone, gave me, perhaps an irrational, but a real pleasure. Since those days, I have seen the West-end, the parks, the fine squares; but I love the city far better. The city seems so much more in earnest: its business, its rush, its roar, are such serious things, sights, and sounds. The city is getting its living – the West-end but enjoying its pleasure. At the West-end you may be amused, but in the city you are deeply excited.

Faint, at last, and hungry (it was years since I had felt such healthy hunger), I returned, about two o'clock, to my dark, old, and quiet inn. I dined on two dishes – a plain joint, and vegetables; both seemed excellent (how much better than the small, dainty messes Miss Marchmont's cook used to send up to my kind, dead mistress and me, and to the discussion of which we could not bring half an appetite between us). Delightfully tired, I lay down on three chairs for an hour (the room did not boast a sofa). I slept, then I woke and thought for two hours.

My state of mind, and all accompanying circumstances, were just now such as most to favour the adoption of a new, resolute, and daring – perhaps desperate – line of action. I had nothing to lose. Unutterable loathing of a desolate existence past forbade return. If I failed in what I now designed to undertake, who, save myself, would suffer? If I died far away from – home, I was going to say, but I had no home – from England, then, who would weep?

I might suffer; I was inured to suffering: death itself had not, I thought, those terrors for me which it has for the softly reared. I had, ere this, looked on the thought of death with a quiet eye. Prepared, then, for any consequences, I formed a project.

That same evening I obtained from my friend, the waiter, information respecting the sailing of vessels for a certain continental port, Boue-Marine.[8] No time, I found, was to be lost: that very night I must take my berth. I might, indeed, have waited till the morning before going on board, but would not run the risk of being too late.

'Better take your berth at once ma'am,' counselled the waiter. I agreed with him, and having discharged my bill, and acknowledged my friend's services at a rate which I now know was princely, and which in his eyes must have seemed absurd – and indeed, while pocketing the cash, he smiled a faint smile which intimated his opinion of the donor's *savoir-faire* – he proceeded to call a coach. To the driver he also recommended me, giving at the same time an injunction about taking me, I think, to the wharf, and not leaving me to the watermen; which that functionary promised to observe, but failed in keeping his promise. On the contrary, he offered me up as an oblation, served me as a dripping roast, making me alight in the midst of a throng of watermen.

This was an uncomfortable crisis. It was a dark night. The coachman instantly drove off as soon as he had got his fare; the watermen commenced a struggle for me and my trunk. Their oaths I hear at this moment: they shook my philosophy more than did the night, or the isolation, or the strangeness of the scene. One laid hands on my trunk. I looked on and waited quietly; but when another laid hands on me, I spoke up, shook off his touch, stepped at once into a boat, desired austerely that the trunk should be placed beside me – 'Just there,' – which was instantly done; for the owner of the boat I had chosen became now an ally: I was rowed off.

Black was the river as a torrent of ink: lights glanced on it from the piles of building round, ships rocked on its bosom. They rowed me up to several vessels; I read by lantern-light their names painted in great white letters on a dark ground. 'The Ocean,' 'The Phoenix,' 'The Consort,' 'The Dolphin,' were passed in turns; but 'The Vivid' was my ship, and it seemed she lay further down.

Down the sable flood we glided; I thought of the Styx, and of Charon[9] rowing some solitary soul to the Land of Shades. Amidst the strange scene, with a chilly wind blowing in my face, and midnight-clouds dropping rain above my head; with two rude rowers for companions, whose insane oaths still tortured my ear, I asked myself if I was wretched or terrified. I was neither. Often in my life have I been far more so under comparatively safe circumstances. 'How is this?' said I. 'Methinks I am animated and alert, instead of being depressed and apprehensive?' I could not tell how it was.

'THE VIVID' started out, white and glaring, from the black night at last. 'Here you are!' said the waterman, and instantly demanded six shillings.

'You ask too much,' I said. He drew off from the vessel and swore he would not embark me till I paid it. A young man, the steward as I found afterwards, was looking over the ship's side; he grinned a smile in anticipation of the coming contest; to disappoint him, I paid the money. Three times that afternoon I had given crowns where I should have given shillings; but I consoled myself with the reflection, 'It is the price of experience.'

'They've cheated you!' said the steward exultantly when I got on board. I answered phlegmatically that 'I knew it,' and went below.

A stout, handsome, and showy woman was in the ladies' cabin; I asked to be shown my berth; she looked hard at me, muttered something about its being unusual for passengers to come on board at that hour, and seemed disposed to be less than civil. What a face she had – so comely – so insolent and so selfish!

'Now that I am on board, I shall certainly stay here,' was my answer. 'I will trouble you to show me my berth.'

She complied, but sullenly. I took off my bonnet, arranged my things, and lay down. Some difficulties had been passed through; a sort of victory was won: my homeless, anchorless, unsupported mind had again leisure for a brief repose: till the 'Vivid' arrived in harbour, no further action would be required of me, but then... Oh! I could not look forward. Harassed, exhausted, I lay in a half-trance.

The stewardess talked all night; not to me, but to the young steward, her son and her very picture. He passed in and out of the cabin continually: they disputed, they quarrelled, they made it up again twenty times in the course of the night. She professed to be writing a letter home, – she said – to her father; she read passages of it aloud, heeding me no more than a stock – perhaps she believed me asleep: several of these passages appeared to comprise family secrets, and bore special reference to one 'Charlotte,' a younger sister who, from the bearing of the epistle, seemed to be on the brink of perpetrating a romantic and imprudent match; loud was the protest of this elder lady against the distasteful union. The dutiful son laughed his mother's correspondence to scorn. She defended it, and raved at him. They were a strange pair. She might be thirty-nine or forty, and was buxom and blooming as a girl of twenty. Hard, loud, vain and vulgar, her mind and body alike seemed brazen and imperishable. I should think, from her childhood, she must have lived in public stations; and in her youth might very likely have been a bar-maid.

Towards morning her discourse ran on a new theme: 'the Watsons,' a certain expected family-party of passengers, known to her, it appeared, and by her much esteemed on account of the handsome profit realized in their fees. She said, 'it was as good as a little fortune to her whenever this family crossed.'

At dawn all were astir, and by sunrise the passengers came on board. Boisterous was the welcome given by the stewardess to the 'Watsons,' and great was the bustle made in their honour. They were four in number, two males and two females. Besides them, there was but one other passenger – a young lady, whom a gentlemanly, though languid-looking man escorted. The two groups offered a marked contrast. The Watsons were doubtless rich people, for they had the confidence of conscious wealth in their bearing; the women – youthful both of them, and one perfectly handsome, as far as physical beauty went – were dressed richly, gaily, and absurdly out of character for the circumstances. Their bonnets with bright flowers, their velvet cloaks and silk dresses seemed better suited for park or promenade than for a damp packet-deck. The men were of low stature, plain, fat, and vulgar; the oldest, plainest, greasiest, broadest, I soon found was the husband – the bridegroom I suppose, for she was very young – of the beautiful girl. Deep was my amazement at this discovery; and deeper still when I perceived that, instead of being desperately wretched in such a union, she was gay even to giddiness. 'Her laughter,' I reflected, 'must be the mere frenzy of despair.' And even while this thought was crossing my mind, as I stood leaning quiet and solitary against the ship's side, she came tripping up to me, an utter stranger, with a camp stool in her hand, and smiling a smile of which the levity puzzled and startled me, though it showed a perfect set of perfect teeth, she offered me the accommodation of this piece of furniture. I declined it, of course with all the courtesy I could put into my manner; she danced off heedless and lightsome. She must have been good-natured; but what had made her marry that individual, who was at least as much like an oil-barrel as a man?

The other lady-passenger, with the gentleman-companion, was quite a girl, pretty and fair; her simple print dress, untrimmed straw-bonnet, and large shawl, gracefully worn, formed a costume plain to quakerism: yet, for her, becoming enough. Before the gentleman quitted her, I observed him throwing a glance of scrutiny over all the passengers, as if to ascertain in what company his charge would be left. With a most dissatisfied air did his eye turn from the ladies with the gay flowers: he looked at me, and then he spoke to his daughter, niece, or whatever she was; she also glanced in my direction, and slightly curled her short, pretty lip. It might be myself, or it might be my homely mourning-habit that elicited this mark of contempt; more likely both. A bell rang; her father (I afterwards knew that it was her father) kissed her and returned to land. The packet[10] sailed.

Foreigners say that it is only English girls who can thus be trusted to travel alone, and deep is their wonder at the daring confidence of English parents and guardians. As for the 'jeunes Miss,' by some their intrepidity is pronounced masculine and 'inconvenant,'[11] others regard them as the passive victims of an educational and theological system which wantonly dispenses with proper 'surveillance.' Whether this particular young lady was of the sort that can the most safely be left unwatched, I do not know: or rather did not *then* know; but it soon appeared that the dignity of solitude was not to her taste. She paced the deck once or twice backwards and forwards; she looked with a little sour air of disdain at the flaunting silks and velvets, and the bears which thereon danced attendance, and eventually she approached me and spoke.

'Are you fond of a sea-voyage?' was her question.

I explained that my *fondness* for a sea-voyage had yet to undergo the test of experience: I had never made one.

'Oh how charming!' cried she. 'I quite envy you the novelty: first impressions, you know, are so pleasant. Now I have made so many, I quite forget the first: I am quite *blasée* about the sea and all that.'

I could not help smiling.

'Why do you laugh at me?' she inquired, with a frank testiness that pleased me better than her other talk.

'Because you are so young to be *blasée* about anything.'

'I am seventeen' (a little piqued).

'You hardly look sixteen. Do you like travelling alone?'

'Bah! I care nothing about it. I have crossed the Channel ten times, alone; but then I take care never to be long alone: I always make friends.'

'You will scarcely make many friends this voyage, I think' (glancing at the Watson-group, who were now laughing and making a great deal of noise on deck).

'Not of those odious men and women,' said she: 'such people should be steerage passengers. Are you going to school?'

'No.'

'Where are you going?'

'I have not the least idea – beyond, at least, the Port of Boue-marine.'

She stared, then carelessly ran on:

'I am going to school. Oh the number of foreign schools I have been at in my life! And yet I am quite an ignoramus. I know nothing – nothing in the world – I assure you; except that I play and dance beautifully, – and French and German of course I know, to speak; but I can't read or write them very well. Do you know they wanted me to translate a page of an easy German book into English the other day, and I couldn't do it. Papa was so mortified: he says it looks as if M. de Bassompierre – my god-papa, who pays all my school-bills – had thrown away all his money. And then, in matters of information – in history, geography, arithmetic, and so on, I am quite a baby; and I write English so badly – such spelling and grammar, they tell me. Into the bargain I have quite forgotten my religion; they call me a Protestant, you know, but really I am not sure whether I am one or not: I don't well know the difference between Romanism and Protestantism. However, I don't in the least care for that. I was a Lutheran once at Bonn – dear Bonn! – charming Bonn! – where there were so many handsome students. Every nice girl in our school had an admirer; they knew our hours for walking out, and almost always passed us on the promenade: "Schönes Mädchen,"[12] we used to hear them say. I was excessively happy at Bonn!'

'And where are you now?' I inquired.

'Oh! at – *chose*,'[13] said she.

Now Miss Ginevra Fanshawe (such was this young person's name) only substituted this word '*chose*' in temporary oblivion of the real name. It was a habit she had: '*chose*' came in at every turn in her conversation – the convenient substitute for any missing word in any language she might chance at the time to be speaking. French girls often do the like; from them she had caught the custom. '*Chose*,' however, I found, in this instance, stood for Villette – the great capital of the great kingdom of Labassecour.

'Do you like Villette?' I asked.

'Pretty well. The natives, you know, are intensely stupid and vulgar; but there are some nice English families.'

'Are you in a school?'

'Yes.'

'A good one?'

'Oh no! horrid: but I go out every Sunday, and care nothing about the *maîtresses* or the *professeurs*, or the *élèves*,[14] and send lessons *au diable*;[15] (one daren't say that in English, you know, but it sounds quite right in French,) and thus I get on charmingly . . .. You are laughing at me again?'

'No – I am only smiling at my own thoughts.'

'What are they?' (without waiting for an answer) – 'Now *do* tell me where you are going.'

'Where Fate may lead me. My business is to earn a living where I can find it.'

'To earn!' (in consternation) 'are you poor then?'

'As poor as Job.'

(After a pause) 'Bah! how unpleasant! But *I* know what it is to be poor: they are poor enough at home – papa and mama, and all of them. Papa is called Captain Fanshawe; he is an officer on half-pay, but well-descended, and some of our connections are great enough; but my uncle and god-papa de Bassompierre, who lives in France, is the only one that helps us: he educates us girls. I have five sisters and three brothers. By-and-by we are to marry – rather elderly gentlemen, I suppose, with cash: papa and mama manage that. My sister Augusta is married now to a man much older-looking than papa. Augusta is very beautiful – not in my style – but dark; her husband, Mr Davies, had the yellow fever in India, and he is still the colour of a guinea; but then he is rich, and Augusta has her carriage and establishment, and we all think she has done perfectly well. Now this is better than "earning a living," as you say. By the way, are you clever?'

'No – not at all.'

'You can play, sing, speak three or four languages?'

'By no means.'

'Still I think you are clever' (a pause and a yawn). 'Shall you be sea-sick?'

'Shall you?'

'Oh, immensely! as soon as ever we get in sight of the sea: I begin, indeed, to feel it already. I shall go below; and won't I order about that fat, odious stewardess? Heureusement je sais faire aller mon monde.'[16] Down she went.

It was not long before the other passengers followed her: throughout the afternoon I remained on deck alone. When I recall the tranquil, and even happy mood in which I passed those hours, and remember, at the same time, the position in which I was placed: its hazardous – some would have said its hopeless – character; I feel that, as –

> Stone walls do not a prison make,
> Nor iron bars – a cage.[17]

so peril, loneliness, an uncertain future, are not oppressive evils, so long as the frame is healthy and the faculties are employed; so long, especially, as Liberty lends us her wings, and Hope guides us by her star.

I was not sick till long after we passed Margate, and deep was the pleasure I drank in with the sea-breeze; divine the delight I drew from the heaving channel-waves, from the sea-birds on their ridges, from the white sails on their dark distance, from the quiet, yet beclouded sky, overhanging all. In my reverie, methought I saw the continent of Europe, like a wide dream-land, far away. Sunshine lay on it, making the long coast one line of gold; tiniest tracery of clustered town and snow-gleaming tower, of woods deep-massed, of heights serrated, of smooth pasturage and veiny stream, embossed the metal-bright prospect. For background, spread a sky, solemn and dark-blue, and – grand with imperial promise, soft with tints of enchantment – strode from north to south a God-bent bow, an arch of hope.

Cancel the whole of that, if you please, reader – or rather let it stand, and draw thence a moral – an alternative, text-hand copy –

Day-dreams are delusions of the demon.

Becoming excessively sick, I faltered down into the cabin.

Miss Fanshawe's berth chanced to be next mine; and, I am sorry to say, she tormented me with an unsparing selfishness during the whole time of our mutual distress. Nothing could exceed her impatience and fretfulness. The Watsons, who were very sick too, and on whom the stewardess attended with shameless partiality, were stoics compared with her. Many a time since have I noticed, in persons of Ginevra Fanshawe's light, careless temperament, and fair, fragile style of beauty, an entire incapacity to endure: they seem to sour in adversity, like small-beer in thunder: the man who takes such a woman for his wife, ought to be prepared to guarantee her an existence all sunshine. Indignant at last with her teazing peevishness, I curtly requested her 'to hold her tongue.' The rebuff did her good, and it was observable that she liked me no worse for it.

As dark night drew on, the sea roughened: larger waves swayed strong against the vessel's side. It was strange to reflect that blackness and water were round us, and to feel the ship ploughing straight on her pathless way, despite noise, billow, and rising gale. Articles of furniture began to fall about, and it became needful to lash them to their places; the passengers grew sicker than ever; Miss Fanshawe declared, with groans, that she must die.

'Not just yet, honey,' said the stewardess. 'We're just in port.' Accordingly, in another quarter of an hour, a calm fell upon us all; and about midnight the voyage ended.

I was sorry: yes, I was sorry. My resting-time was past; my difficulties – my stringent difficulties – recommenced. When I went on deck, the cold air and black scowl of the night seemed to rebuke me for my presumption in being where I was: the lights of the foreign sea-port town, glimmering round the foreign harbour, met me like unnumbered threatening eyes. Friends came on board to welcome the Watsons; a whole family of friends surrounded and bore away Miss Fanshawe; I – but I dared not for one moment dwell on a comparison of positions.

Yet where should I go? I must go somewhere. Necessity dare not be nice. As I gave the stewardess her fee – and she seemed surprised at receiving a coin of more value than, from such a quarter, her coarse calculations had probably reckoned on – I said:

'Be kind enough to direct me to some quiet, respectable inn, where I can go for the night.'

She not only gave me the required direction, but called a commissionaire, and bid him take charge of me, and – *not* my trunk, for that was gone to the custom-house.

I followed this man along a rudely-paved street, lit now by a fitful gleam of moonlight; he brought me to the inn. I offered him sixpence, which he refused to take; supposing it not enough, I changed it for a shilling; but this also he declined, speaking rather sharply, in a language to me unknown. A waiter, coming forward into the lamp-lit inn-passage, reminded me, in broken English, that my money was foreign money, not current here. I gave him a sovereign to change. This little matter settled, I asked for a bedroom; supper I could not take: I was still sea-sick and unnerved, and trembling all over. How deeply glad I was when the door of a very small chamber at length closed on me and my exhaustion. Again I might rest: though the cloud of doubt would be as thick tomorrow as ever; the necessity for exertion more urgent, the peril (or destitution) nearer, the conflict (for existence) more severe.

CHAPTER 7

Villette

I AWOKE NEXT MORNING with courage revived and spirits refreshed: physical debility no longer enervated my judgment; my mind felt prompt and clear.

Just as I finished dressing, a tap came to the door; I said, 'Come in,' expecting the chambermaid, whereas a rough man walked in and said, –

'Gif me your keys, Meess.'

'Why?' I asked.

'Gif!' said he impatiently; and as he half-snatched them from my hand, he added, 'All right! haf your tronc soon.'

Fortunately it did turn out all right: he was from the custom-house. Where to go to get some breakfast I could not tell; but I proceeded, not without hesitation, to descend.

I now observed what I had not noticed in my extreme weariness last night, viz., that this inn was, in fact, a large hotel; and as I slowly descended the broad staircase, halting on each step (for I was in wonderfully little haste to get down), I gazed at the high ceiling above me, at the painted walls around, at the wide windows which filled the house with light, at the veined marble I trode (for the steps were all of marble, though uncarpeted and not very clean), and contrasting all this with the dimensions of the closet assigned to me as a chamber, with the extreme modesty of its appointments, I fell into a philosophizing mood.

Much I marvelled at the sagacity evinced by waiters and chambermaids in proportioning the accommodation to the guest. How could inn-servants and ship-stewardesses everywhere tell at a glance that I, for instance, was an individual of no social significance and little burdened by cash? They *did* know it, evidently: I saw quite well that they all, in a moment's calculation, estimated me at about the same fractional value. The fact seemed to me curious and pregnant: I would not disguise from myself what it indicated, yet managed to keep up my spirits pretty well under its pressure.

Having at last landed in a great hall, full of skylight glare, I made my way somehow to what proved to be the coffee-room. It cannot be denied that on entering this room I trembled somewhat; felt uncertain, solitary, wretched; wished to Heaven I knew whether I was doing right or wrong; felt convinced it was the last, but could not help myself. Acting in the spirit and with the calm of a fatalist, I sat down at a small table, to which a waiter presently brought me some breakfast; and I partook of that meal in a frame of mind not greatly calculated to favour digestion. There were many other people breakfasting at other tables in the room; I should have felt rather more happy if amongst them all I could have seen any women; however, there was not one – all present were men. But nobody seemed to think I was doing anything strange; one or two gentlemen glanced at me occasionally, but none stared obtrusively: I suppose if there was anything eccentric in the business, they accounted for it by this word 'Anglaise!'[18]

Breakfast over, I must again move – in what direction? 'Go to Villette,' said an inward voice; prompted doubtless by the recollection of this slight sentence uttered carelessly and at random by Miss Fanshawe, as she bid me good-bye:

'I wish you would come to Madame Beck's; she has some marmots whom you might look after: she wants an English gouvernante, or was wanting one two months ago.'

Who Madame Beck was, where she lived, I knew not; I had asked, but the question passed unheard: Miss Fanshawe, hurried away by her friends, left it unanswered. I presumed Villette to be her residence – to Villette I would go. The distance was forty miles. I knew I was catching at straws; but in the wide and weltering deep where I found myself, I would have caught at cobwebs. Having inquired about the means of travelling to Villette, and secured a seat in the Diligence,[19] I departed on the strength of this outline – this shadow of a project. Before you pronounce on the rashness of the proceeding, reader, look back to the point whence I started; consider the desert I had left, note how little I perilled: mine was the game where the player cannot lose and may win.

Of an artistic temperament, I deny that I am; yet I must possess something of the artist's faculty of making the most of present pleasure: that is to say, when it is of the kind to my taste; I enjoyed that day, though we travelled slowly, though it was cold, though it rained. Somewhat bare, flat, and treeless was the route along which our journey lay; and slimy canals crept, like half-torpid green snakes, beside the road; and formal pollard willows edged level fields, tilled like kitchen-garden beds. The sky too was monotonously gray; the atmosphere was stagnant and humid; yet amidst all these deadening influences, my fancy budded fresh and my heart basked in sunshine. These feelings, however, were well kept in check by the secret but ceaseless consciousness of anxiety lying in wait on enjoyment, like a tiger crouched in a jungle. The breathing of that beast of prey was in my ear always; his fierce heart panted close against mine; he never stirred in his lair but I felt him: I knew he waited only for sun-down to bound ravenous from his ambush.

I had hoped we might reach Villette ere night set in, and that thus I might escape the deeper embarrassment which obscurity seems to throw round a first arrival at an unknown bourne; but, what with our slow progress and long stoppages – what with a thick fog and small, dense rain – darkness that might almost be felt, had settled on the city by the time we gained its suburbs.

I know we passed through a gate where soldiers were stationed – so much I could see by lamplight; then, having left behind us the miry Chaussée,[20] we rattled over a pavement of strangely rough and flinty surface. At a bureau, the diligence stopped, and the passengers alighted. My first business was to get my trunk: a small matter enough, but important to me. Understanding that it was best not to be importunate or over-eager about luggage, but to wait and watch quietly the delivery of other boxes till I saw my own, and then promptly claim and secure it, I stood apart; my eye fixed on that part of the vehicle in which I had seen my little portmanteau safely stowed, and upon which, piles of additional bags and boxes were now heaped. One by one, I saw these removed, lowered, and seized on. I was sure mine ought to be by this time visible: it was not. I had tied on the direction card with a piece of green ribbon, that I might know it at a glance: not a fringe or fragment of green was perceptible. Every package was removed; every tin-case and brown paper parcel; the oil-cloth cover was lifted; I saw with distinct vision that not an umbrella, cloak, cane, hat-box or band-box remained.

And my portmanteau, with my few clothes and the little pocket-book enclasping the remnant of my fifteen pounds, where were they?

I ask this question now, but I could not ask it then. I could say nothing whatever; not possessing a phrase of *speaking* French: and it was French, and French only, the whole world seemed now gabbling round me. *What* should I do? Approaching the conductor, I just laid my hand on his arm, pointed to a trunk, then to the diligence-roof, and tried to express a question with my eyes. He misunderstood me, seized the trunk indicated, and was about to hoist it on the vehicle.

'Let that alone – will you?' said a voice in good English; then, in correction, 'Qu'est ce que vous faîtes donc? Cette malle est à moi.'[21]

But I had heard the Fatherland accents; they rejoiced my heart; I turned:

'Sir,' said I, appealing to the stranger, without in my distress noticing what he was like, 'I cannot speak French. May I entreat you to ask this man what he has done with my trunk?'

Without discriminating, for the moment, what sort of face it was to which my eyes were raised and on which they were fixed, I felt in its expression half-surprise at my appeal and half-doubt of the wisdom of interference.

'*Do* ask him; I would do as much for you,' said I.

I don't know whether he smiled, but he said in a gentlemanly tone; that is to say, a tone not hard nor terrifying, –

'What sort of trunk was yours?'

I described it, including in my description the green ribbon. And forthwith he took the conductor under hand, and I felt, through all the storm of French which followed, that he raked him fore and aft. Presently he returned to me.

'The fellow avers he was overloaded, and confesses that he removed your trunk after you saw it put on, and has left it behind at Boue-Marine with other parcels; he has promised, however, to forward it to-morrow; the day after, therefore, you will find it safe at this bureau.'

'Thank you,' said I: but my heart sank.

Meantime what should I do? Perhaps this English gentleman saw the failure of courage in my face; he inquired kindly,

'Have you any friends in this city?'

'No, and I don't know where to go.'

There was a little pause, in the course of which, as he turned more fully to the light of a lamp above him, I saw that he was a young, distinguished, and handsome man; he might be a lord, for anything I knew: nature had made him good enough for a prince, I thought. His face was very pleasant; he looked high but not arrogant, manly but not overbearing. I was turning away, in the deep consciousness of all absence of claim to look for further help from such a one as he.

'Was all your money in your trunk?' he asked, stopping me.

How thankful was I to be able to answer with truth, –

'No. I have enough in my purse' (for I had near twenty francs) 'to keep me at a quiet inn till the day after to-morrow; but I am quite a stranger in Villette, and don't know the streets and the inns.'

'I can give you the address of such an inn as you want,' said he; 'and it is not far off: with my direction you will easily find it.'

He tore a leaf from his pocket-book, wrote a few words and gave it to me. I *did* think him kind; and as to distrusting him, or his advice, or his address, I should almost as soon have thought of distrusting the Bible. There was goodness in his countenance, and honour in his bright eyes.

'Your shortest way will be to follow the boulevard, and cross the park,' he continued; 'but it is too late and too dark for a woman to go through the park alone; I will step with you thus far.'

He moved on, and I followed him, through the darkness and the small soaking rain. The Boulevard was all deserted, its path miry, the water dripping from its trees; the park was black as midnight. In the double gloom of trees and fog, I could not see my guide; I could only follow his tread. Not the least fear had I: I believe I would have followed that frank tread, through continual night, to the world's end.

'Now,' said he, when the park was traversed, 'you will go along this broad street till you come to steps; two lamps will show you where they are: these steps you will descend: a narrower street lies below; following that, at the bottom you will find your inn. They speak English there, so your difficulties are now pretty well over. Good-night.'

'Good-night, sir,' said I: 'accept my sincerest thanks.' And we parted.

The remembrance of his countenance, which I am sure wore a light not unbenignant to the friendless – the sound in my ear of his voice, which spoke a nature chivalric to the needy and feeble, as well as the youthful and fair – were a sort of cordial to me long after. He was a true young English gentleman.

On I went, hurrying fast through a magnificent street and square, with the grandest houses round, and amidst them the huge outline of more than one overbearing pile; which might be palace, or church – I could not tell. Just as I passed a portico, two moustachioed men came suddenly from behind the pillars; they were smoking cigars, their dress implied pretensions to the rank of gentlemen, but, poor things! they were very plebeian in soul. They spoke with insolence, and, fast as I walked, they kept pace with me a long way. At last I met a sort of patrol, and my dreaded hunters were turned from the pursuit; but they had driven me beyond my reckoning: when I could collect my faculties, I no longer knew where I was; the staircase I must long since have passed; puzzled, out of breath, all my pulses throbbing in inevitable agitation, I knew not where to turn. It was terrible to think of again encountering those bearded, sneering simpletons; yet the ground must be retraced, and the steps sought out.

I came at last to an old and worn flight, and, taking it for granted that this must be the one indicated, I descended them. The street into which they led was indeed narrow, but it contained no inn. On I wandered. In a very quiet and comparatively clean and well-paved street, I saw a light burning over the door of a rather large house, loftier by a storey than those round it. *This* might be the inn at last. I hastened on: my knees now trembled under me: I was getting quite exhausted.

No inn was this. A brass-plate embellished the great Porte-cochère:[22] 'Pensionnat de Demoiselles'[23] was the inscription; and beneath, a name, 'Madame Beck.'

I started. About a hundred thoughts volleyed through my mind in a moment. Yet I planned nothing, and considered nothing: I had not time. Providence said, 'Stop here; this is *your* inn.' Fate took me in her strong hand; mastered my will; directed my actions: I rung the door-bell.

While I waited, I would not reflect. I fixedly looked at the street-stones, where the door-lamp shone, and counted them, and noted their shapes, and the glitter of wet on their angles. I rang again. They opened at last. A bonne in a smart cap stood before me.

'May I see Madame Beck?' I inquired.

I believe if I had spoken French she would not have admitted me; but, as I spoke English, she concluded I was a foreign teacher come on business connected with the Pensionnat, and, even at that late hour, she let me in, without a word of reluctance or a moment of hesitation.

The next moment I sat in a cold, glittering salon, with porcelain stove unlit, and gilded ornaments, and polished floor. A pendule on the mantel-piece struck nine o'clock.

A quarter of an hour passed. How fast beat every pulse in my frame! How I turned cold and hot by turns! I sat with my eyes fixed on the door – a great white folding-door, with gilt mouldings: I watched to see a leaf move and open. All had been quiet: not a mouse had stirred; the white doors were closed and motionless.

'You ayre Engliss?' said a voice at my elbow. I almost bounded, so unexpected was the sound; so certain had I been of solitude.

No ghost stood beside me, nor anything of spectral aspect; merely a motherly, dumpy little woman, in a large shawl, a wrapping-gown, and a clean, trim night-cap.

I said I was English, and immediately, without further prelude, we fell to a most remarkable conversation. Madame Beck (for Madame Beck it was – she had entered by a little door behind me, and, being shod with the shoes of silence, I had heard neither her entrance nor approach) – Madame Beck had exhausted her command of insular speech when she said 'You ayre Engliss,' and she now proceeded to work away volubly in her own tongue. I answered in mine. She partly understood me, but as I did not at all understand her – though we made together an awful clamour (anything like madame's gift of utterance I had not hitherto heard or imagined) – we achieved little progress. She rang, ere long, for aid; which arrived in the shape of a 'maîtresse,' who had been partly educated in an Irish convent, and was esteemed a perfect adept in the English language. A bluff little personage this maîtresse was – Labassecourienne from top to toe: and how she did slaughter the speech of Albion![24] However, I told her a plain tale, which she translated. I told her how I had left my own country, intent on extending my knowledge, and gaining my bread; how I was ready to turn my hand to any useful thing, provided it was not wrong or degrading: how I would be a child's-nurse or a lady's-maid, and would not refuse even housework adapted to my strength. Madame heard this; and, questioning her countenance, I almost thought the tale won her ear:

'Il n'y a que les Anglaises pour ces sortes d'entreprises,' said she: 'sont-elles donc intrépides ces femmes là!'[25]

She asked my name, my age; she sat and looked at me – not pityingly, not with interest: never a gleam of sympathy, or a shade of compassion, crossed her countenance during the interview. I felt she was not one to be led an inch by her feelings: grave and considerate, she gazed, consulting her judgment and studying my narrative. A bell rang.

'Voilà pour la prière du soir!'[26] said she, and rose. Through her interpreter, she desired me to depart now, and come back on the morrow; but this did not suit me: I could not bear to return to the perils of darkness and the street. With energy, yet with a collected and controlled manner, I said, addressing herself personally, and not the maîtresse:

'Be assured, madame, that by instantly securing my services, your interests will be served and not injured: you will find me one who will wish to give, in her labour, a full equivalent for her wages; and if you hire me, it will be better that I should stay here this night: having no acquaintance in Villette, and not possessing the language of the country, how can I secure a lodging?'

'It is true;' said she, 'but at least you can give a reference?'

'None.'

She inquired after my luggage: I told her when it would arrive. She mused. At that moment a man's step was heard in the vestibule, hastily proceeding to the outer door. (I shall go on with this part of my tale as if I had understood all that passed; for though it was then scarce intelligible to me, I heard it translated afterwards).

'Who goes out now?' demanded Madame Beck, listening to the tread.

'M. Paul,' replied the teacher. 'He came this evening to give a reading to the first class.'

'The very man I should at this moment most wish to see. Call him.'

The teacher ran to the salon door. M. Paul was summoned. He entered: a small, dark and spare man, in spectacles.

'Mon cousin,' began madame, 'I want your opinion. We know your skill in physiognomy; use it now. Read that countenance.'

The little man fixed on me his spectacles. A resolute compression of the lips, and gathering of the brow, seemed to say that he meant to see through me, and that a veil would be no veil for him.

'I read it,' he pronounced.

'Et qu'en dites-vous?'

'Mais – bien des choses,' was the oracular answer.

'Bad or good?'

'Of each kind, without doubt,' pursued the diviner.

'May one trust her word?'

'Are you negotiating a matter of importance?'

'She wishes me to engage her as bonne or gouvernante; tells a tale full of integrity, but gives no reference.'

'She is a stranger?'

'An Englishwoman, as one may see.'

'She speaks French?'

'Not a word.'

'She understands it?'

'No.'

'One may then speak plainly in her presence?'

'Doubtless.'

He gazed steadily. 'Do you need her services?'

'I could do with them. You know I am disgusted with Madame Svini.'

Still he scrutinized. The judgment, when it at last came, was as indefinite as what had gone before it.

'Engage her. If good predominates in that nature, the action will bring its own reward; if evil – eh bien! ma cousine, ce sera toujours une bonne oeuvre.' And with a bow and a 'bon soir,' this vague arbiter of my destiny vanished. And madame did engage me that very night – by God's blessing I was spared the necessity of passing forth again into the lonesome, dreary, hostile street.

CHAPTER 8

Madame Beck

BEING DELIVERED into the charge of the maîtresse, I was led through a long, narrow passage into a foreign kitchen, very clean but very strange. It seemed to contain no means of cooking – neither fireplace nor oven; I did not understand that the great black furnace which filled one corner, was an efficient substitute for these. Surely pride was not already beginning its whispers in my heart; yet I felt a sense of relief when, instead of being left in the kitchen, as I half-anticipated, I was led forward to a small inner room termed a 'cabinet.' A cook in a jacket, a short petticoat and sabots, brought my supper: to wit, – some meat, nature unknown, served in an odd and acid, but pleasant sauce; some chopped potatoes, made savoury with, I know not what: vinegar and sugar, I think; a tartine, or slice of bread and butter, and a baked pear. Being hungry, I ate and was grateful.

After the 'Prière du Soir,' madame herself came to have another look at me. She desired me to follow her up-stairs. Through a series of the queerest little dormitories – which, I heard afterwards, had once been nuns' cells: for the premises were in part of ancient date – and through the oratory – a long, low, gloomy room, where a crucifix hung, pale, against the wall, and two tapers kept dim vigils – she conducted me to an apartment where three children were asleep in three tiny beds. A heated stove made the air of this room oppressive; and, to mend matters, it was scented with an odour rather strong than delicate: a perfume, indeed, altogether surprising and unexpected under the circumstances, being like the combination of smoke with some spirituous essence – a smell, in short, of whiskey.

Beside a table, on which flared the remnant of a candle guttering to waste in the socket, a coarse woman, heterogeneously clad in a broad-striped showy silk dress and a stuff apron, sat in a chair fast asleep. To complete the picture, and leave no doubt as to the state of matters, a bottle and an empty glass stood at the sleeping beauty's elbow.

Madame contemplated this remarkable tableau with great calm;

she neither smiled nor scowled: no impress of anger, disgust, or surprise, ruffled the equality of her grave aspect; she did not even wake the woman. Serenely pointing to a fourth bed, she intimated that it was to be mine; then, having extinguished the candle and substituted for it a night-lamp, she glided through an inner door, which she left ajar: the entrance to her own chamber, a large, well-furnished apartment; as was discernible through the aperture.

My devotions that night were all thanksgiving: strangely had I been led since morning – unexpectedly had I been provided for. Scarcely could I believe that not forty-eight hours had elapsed since I left London, under no other guardianship than that which protects the passenger-bird – with no prospect but the dubious cloud-tracery of hope.

I was a light sleeper; in the dead of night I suddenly awoke. All was hushed, but a white figure stood in the room – Madame in her night-dress. Moving without perceptible sound, she visited the three children in the three beds; she approached me: I feigned sleep, and she studied me long. A small pantomime ensued, curious enough. I dare say she sat a quarter of an hour on the edge of my bed, gazing at my face. She then drew nearer, bent close over me; slightly raised my cap, and turned back the border so as to expose my hair; she looked at my hand lying on the bed-clothes. This done, she turned to the chair where my clothes lay: it was at the foot of the bed. Hearing her touch and lift them, I opened my eyes with precaution, for I own I felt curious to see how far her taste for research would lead her. It led her a good way: every article did she inspect. I divined her motive for this proceeding, viz., the wish to form from the garments a judgment respecting the wearer, her station, means, neatness, &c. The end was not bad, but the means were hardly fair or justifiable. In my dress was a pocket; she fairly turned it inside out: she counted the money in my purse; she opened a little memorandum-book, coolly perused its contents, and took from between the leaves a small plaited lock of Miss Marchmont's grey hair. To a bunch of three keys, being those of my trunk, desk, and work-box, she accorded special attention: with these, indeed, she withdrew a moment to her own room. I softly rose in my bed and followed her with my eye: these keys, reader, were not brought back till they had left on the toilet of the adjoining room the impress of their wards in wax. All being thus done decently and in order, my property was returned to its place, my clothes were carefully refolded. Of what nature were the conclusions deduced from this scrutiny? Were they favourable or otherwise? Vain question. Madame's face of stone (for of stone in its present night-aspect it looked: it had been human and, as I said before, motherly, in the salon) betrayed no response.

Her duty done – I felt that in her eyes this business was a duty – she rose, noiseless as a shadow: she moved towards her own chamber; at the door she turned, fixing her eye on the heroine of the bottle, who still slept and loudly snored. Mrs Svini (I presumed this was Mrs Svini, Anglicé or Hibernice,[27] Sweeny) – Mrs Sweeny's doom was in Madame Beck's eye – an immutable purpose that eye spoke: madame's visitations for shortcomings might be slow, but they were sure. All this was very un-English: truly I was in a foreign land.

The morrow made me further acquainted with Mrs Sweeny. It seems she had introduced herself to her present employer as an English lady in reduced circumstances: a native, indeed, of Middlesex, professing to speak the English tongue with the purest metropolitan accent. Madame – reliant on her own infallible expedients for finding out the truth in time – had a singular intrepidity in hiring service off-hand (as indeed seemed abundantly proved in my own case). She received Mrs Sweeny as nursery-governess to her three children. I need hardly explain to the reader that this lady was in effect a native of Ireland; her station I do not pretend to fix: she boldly declared that she had 'had the bringing-up of the son and daughter of a marquis.' I think, myself, she might possibly have been hanger-on – nurse, fosterer, or washer-woman, in some Irish family: she spoke a smothered brogue, curiously overlaid with mincing cockney inflections. By some means or other she had acquired, and now held in possession, a wardrobe of rather suspicious splendour – gowns of stiff and costly silk, fitting her indifferently and apparently made for other proportions than those they now adorned; caps with real lace borders, and – the chief item in the inventory, the spell by which she struck a certain awe through the household, quelling the otherwise scornfully disposed teachers and servants, and, so long as her broad shoulders *wore* the folds of that majestic drapery, even influencing madame herself – a *real Indian shawl* – 'un véritable Cachmire,' as Madame Beck said, with mixed reverence and amaze. I feel quite sure that without this 'Cachmire' she would not have kept her footing in the pensionnat for two days: by virtue of it, and it only, she maintained the same a month.

But when Mrs Sweeny knew that I was come to fill her shoes, then it was that she declared herself – then did she rise on Madame Beck in her full power – then come down on me with her

concentrated weight. Madame bore this revelation and visitation so
well, so stoically, that I for very shame could not support it
otherwise than with composure. For one little moment Madame
Beck absented herself from the room; ten minutes after, an agent of
the police stood in the midst of us. Mrs Sweeny and her effects were
removed. Madame's brow had not been ruffled during the scene –
her lips had not dropped one sharply accented word.

This brisk little affair of the dismissal was all settled before
breakfast: order to march given, policeman called, mutineer expelled,
'chambre d'enfants' fumigated and cleansed, windows thrown open,
and every trace of the accomplished Mrs Sweeny – even to the fine
essence and spiritual fragrance which gave token so subtle and so
fatal of the head and front of her offending – was annihilated from
the Rue Fossette: all this, I say, was done between the moment of
Madame Beck's issuing like Aurora[28] from her chamber, and that in
which she coolly sat down to pour out her first cup of coffee.

About noon, I was summoned to dress madame. (It appeared my
place was to be a hybrid between gouvernante[29] and lady's-maid.)
Till noon, she haunted the house in her wrapping-gown, shawl, and
soundless slippers. How would the lady-chief of an English school
approve this custom?

The dressing of her hair puzzled me; she had plenty of it; auburn,
unmixed with grey: though she was forty years old. Seeing my
embarrassment, she said, 'You have not been a femme de chambre
in your own country?' And taking the brush from my hand and
setting me aside, not ungently or disrespectfully, she arranged it
herself. In performing other offices of the toilet, she half-directed,
half-aided me, without the least display of temper or impatience.
N.B. that was the first and last time I was required to dress her.
Henceforth, on Rosine, the portress, devolved that duty.

When attired, Madame Beck appeared a personage of a figure
rather short and stout, yet still graceful in its own peculiar way: that
is, with the grace resulting from proportion of parts. Her
complexion was fresh and sanguine, not too rubicund; her eye, blue
and serene; her dark silk dress fitted her as a French sempstress
alone can make a dress fit; she looked well, though a little
bourgeoise: as bourgeoise, indeed, she was. I know not what of
harmony pervaded her whole person; and yet her face offered
contrast, too; its features were by no means such as are usually seen
in conjunction with a complexion of such blended freshness and
repose: their outline was stern; her forehead was high but narrow; it
expressed capacity and some benevolence, but no expanse; nor did

her peaceful yet watchful eye ever know the fire which is kindled in the heart or the softness which flows thence. Her mouth was hard: it could be a little grim; her lips were thin. For sensibility and genius, with all their tenderness and temerity, I felt somehow that madame would be the right sort of Minos[30] in petticoats.

In the long run, I found that she was something else in petticoats too. Her name was Modeste Maria Beck, née Kint: it ought to have been Ignacia.[31] She was a charitable woman, and did a great deal of good. There never was a mistress whose rule was milder. I was told that she never once remonstrated with the intolerable Mrs Sweeny, despite her tipsiness, disorder, and general neglect; yet Mrs Sweeny had to go, the moment her departure became convenient. I was told, too, that neither masters nor teachers were found fault with in that establishment; yet both masters and teachers were often changed: they vanished and others filled their places, none could well explain how.

The establishment was both a pensionnat and an externat: the externes or day-pupils exceeded one hundred in number; the boarders were about a score. Madame must have possessed high administrative powers: she ruled all these, together with four teachers, eight masters, six servants, and three children, managing at the same time to perfection the pupils' parents and friends; and that without apparent effort; without bustle, fatigue, fever, or any symptom of undue excitement: occupied she always was – busy, rarely. It is true that madame had her own system for managing and regulating this mass of machinery; and a very pretty system it was: the reader has seen a specimen of it, in that small affair of turning my pocket inside out, and reading my private memoranda. 'Surveillance,' 'espionage,' – these were her watch-words.

Still, madame knew what honesty was, and liked it – that is, when it did not obtrude its clumsy scruples in the way of her will and interest. She had a respect for 'Angleterre'; and as to 'les Anglaises,' she would have the women of no other country about her own children, if she could help it.

Often in the evening, after she had been plotting and counter-plotting, spying and receiving the reports of spies all day, she would come up to my room – a trace of real weariness on her brow – and she would sit down and listen while the children said their little prayers to me in English: the Lord's Prayer, and the hymn beginning 'Gentle Jesus,' these little Catholics were permitted to repeat at my knee; and, when I had put them to bed, she would talk to me (I soon gained enough French to be able to understand, and even answer her) about England and Englishwomen, and the reasons for what she was pleased to term their superior intelligence, and more real and reliable probity. Very good sense she often showed; very sound opinions she often broached: she seemed to know that keeping girls in distrustful restraint, in blind ignorance, and under a surveillance that left them no moment and no corner for retirement, was not the best way to make them grow up honest and modest women; but she averred that ruinous consequences would ensue if any other method were tried with continental children – they were so accustomed to constraint, that relaxation, however guarded, would be misunderstood and fatally presumed on: she was sick, she would declare, of the means she had to use, but use them she must; and after discoursing, often with dignity and delicacy, to me, she would move away on her 'souliers de silence,'[32] and glide ghost-like through the house, watching and spying everywhere, peering through every key-hole, listening behind every door.

After all, madame's system was not bad – let me do her justice. Nothing could be better than all her arrangements for the physical well-being of her scholars. No minds were overtasked; the lessons were well distributed and made incomparably easy to the learner; there was a liberty of amusement, and a provision for exercise which kept the girls healthy; the food was abundant and good: neither pale nor puny faces were anywhere to be seen in the Rue Fossette. She never grudged a holiday; she allowed plenty of time for sleeping, dressing, washing, eating; her method in all these matters was easy, liberal, salutary, and rational: many an austere English school-mistress would do vastly well to imitate it – and I believe many would be glad to do so, if exacting English parents would let them.

As Madame Beck ruled by espionage, she of course had her staff of spies: she perfectly knew the quality of the tools she used, and while she would not scruple to handle the dirtiest for a dirty occasion – flinging this sort from her like refuse rind, after the orange has been duly squeezed – I have known her fastidious in seeking pure metal for clean uses; and when once a bloodless and rustless instrument was found, she was careful of the prize, keeping it in silk and cotton-wool. Yet, woe be to that man or woman who relied on her one inch beyond the point where it was her interest to be trustworthy: interest was the master-key of madame's nature – the mainspring of her motives – the alpha and omega of her life. I have seen her *feelings* appealed to, and I have smiled in half-pity, half-scorn at the appellants. None ever gained her ear through that channel, or swayed her purpose by that means. On the contrary, to attempt to touch her heart was the surest way to rouse her antipathy, and to make of her a secret foe. It proved to her that she had no heart to be touched: it reminded her where she was impotent and dead. Never was the distinction between charity and mercy better exemplified than in her. While devoid of sympathy, she had a sufficiency of rational benevolence: she would give in the readiest manner to people she had never seen – rather, however, to classes than to individuals. 'Pour les pauvres,'[33] she opened her purse freely – against *the poor man*, as a rule, she kept it closed. In philanthropic schemes, for the benefit of society at large, she took a cheerful part; no private sorrow touched her: no force or mass of suffering concentrated in one heart had power to pierce hers. Not the agony in Gethsemane, not the death on Calvary, could have wrung from her eyes one tear.

I say again, madame was a very great and a very capable woman. That school offered for her powers too limited a sphere; she ought to have swayed a nation: she should have been the leader of a turbulent legislative assembly. Nobody could have brow-beaten her, none irritated her nerves, exhausted her patience, or over-reached her astuteness. In her own single person, she could have comprised the duties of a first minister and a superintendent of police. Wise, firm, faithless; secret, crafty, passionless; watchful and inscrutable; acute and insensate – withal perfectly decorous – what more could be desired?

The sensible reader will not suppose that I gained all the knowledge here condensed for his benefit in one month, or in one half-year. No! what I saw at first was the thriving outside of a large and flourishing educational establishment. Here was a great houseful of healthy, lively girls, all well-dressed and many of them handsome, gaining knowledge by a marvellously easy method, without painful exertion or useless waste of spirits; not, perhaps, making very rapid progress in anything; taking it easy, but still always employed, and never oppressed. Here was a corps of teachers and masters more stringently tasked, as all the real head-labour was to be done by them, in order to save the pupils, yet having their duties so arranged that they relieved each other in quick succession whenever the work was severe; here, in short, was a foreign school; of which the life, movement, and variety made it a complete and most charming contrast to many English institutions of the same kind.

Behind the house was a large garden, and, in summer, the pupils almost lived out of doors amongst the rose-bushes and the fruit-trees. Under the vast and vine-draped berceau,[34] madame would take her seat on summer afternoons, and send for the classes, in turns, to sit round her and sew and read. Meantime, masters came and went, delivering short and lively lectures, rather than lessons, and the pupils made notes of their instructions, or did *not* make them – just as inclination prompted; secure that, in case of neglect, they could copy the notes of their companions. Besides the regular monthly *jours de sortie*, the Catholic fête-days brought a succession of holidays all the year round; and sometimes on a bright summer morning, or soft summer evening, the boarders were taken out for a long walk into the country, regaled with *gaufres*[35] and *vin blanc*,[36] or new milk and *pain bis*,[37] or *pistolets au beurre* (rolls) and coffee. All this seemed very pleasant, and madame appeared goodness itself; and the teachers not so bad, but they might be worse; and the pupils, perhaps, a little noisy and rough, but types of health and glee.

Thus did the view appear, seen through the enchantment of distance; but there came a time when distance was to melt for me, when I was to be called down from my watch-tower of the nursery, whence I had hitherto made my observations, and was to be compelled into closer intercourse with this little world of the Rue Fossette.

I was one day sitting up-stairs, as usual, hearing the children their English lessons, and at the same time turning a silk dress for madame, when she came sauntering into the room with that absorbed air, and brow of hard thought she sometimes wore, and which made her look so little genial. Dropping into a seat opposite mine, she remained some minutes silent. Désirée, the eldest girl, was reading to me some little essay of Mrs Barbauld's, and I was making her translate currently from English to French as she proceeded, by way of ascertaining that she comprehended what she read: madame listened.

Presently, without preface or prelude, she said, almost in the tone of one making an accusation, 'Meess, in England you were a governess.'

'No, madame,' said I smiling, 'you are mistaken.'

'Is this your first essay at teaching – this attempt with my children?'

I assured her it was. Again she became silent; but looking up, as I took a pin from the cushion, I found myself an object of study: she held me under her eye; she seemed turning me round in her thoughts – measuring my fitness for a purpose, weighing my value in a plan. Madame had, ere this, scrutinized all I had, and I believe she esteemed herself cognizant of much that I was; but from that day, for the space of about a fortnight, she tried me by new tests.

She listened at the nursery door when I was shut in with the children; she followed me at a cautious distance when I walked out with them, stealing within ear-shot whenever the trees of park or boulevard afforded a sufficient screen: a strict preliminary process having thus been observed, she made a move forward.

One morning, coming on me abruptly, and with the semblance of hurry, she said she found herself placed in a little dilemma. Mr Wilson, the English master, had failed to come at his hour, she feared he was ill; the pupils were waiting in classe; there was no one to give a lesson; should I, for once, object to giving a short dictation exercise, just that the pupils might not have it to say they had missed their English lesson?

'In classe, madame?' I asked.

'Yes, in classe: in the second division.'

'Where there are sixty pupils,' said I; for I knew the number, and with my usual base habit of cowardice, I shrunk into my sloth, like a snail into its shell, and alleged incapacity and impracticability as a pretext to escape action. If let to myself, I should infallibly have let this chance slip. Inadventurous, unstirred by impulses of practical ambition, I was capable of sitting twenty years teaching infants the hornbook, turning silk dresses, and making children's frocks. Not that true contentment dignified this infatuated resignation: my work had neither charm for my taste, nor hold on my interest; but it seemed to me a great thing to be without heavy anxiety, and relieved from intimate trial; the negation of severe suffering was the nearest approach to happiness I expected to know. Besides, I seemed to hold two lives – the life of thought, and that of reality; and, provided the former was nourished with a sufficiency of the strange necromantic joys of fancy, the privileges of the latter might remain limited to daily bread, hourly work, and a roof of shelter.

'Come,' said madame, as I stooped more busily than ever over the cutting out of a child's pinafore, 'leave that work.'

'But Fifine wants it, madame.'

'Fifine must want it, then, for *I* want *you.*'

And as Madame Beck did really want and was resolved to have me – as she had long been dissatisfied with the English master, with his short-comings in punctuality, and his careless method of tuition – as, too, *she* did not lack resolution and practical activity, whether *I* lacked them or not – she, without more ado, made me relinquish thimble and needle; my hand was taken into hers, and I was conducted down stairs. When we reached the carré, a large square hall between the dwelling-house and the pensionnat, she paused, dropped my hand, faced, and scrutinized me. I was flushed, and tremulous from head to foot; tell it not in Gath,[38] I believe I was crying. In fact, the difficulties before me were far from being wholly imaginary; some of them were real enough; and not the least substantial lay in my want of mastery over the medium through which I should be obliged to teach. I had, indeed, studied French closely since my arrival in Villette; learning its practice by day, and its theory in every leisure moment at night, to as late an hour as the rule of the house would allow candle-light, but I was far from yet being able to trust my powers of correct oral expression.

'Dîtes donc,' said madame sternly, 'vous sentez-vous réellement trop faible?'[39]

I might have said 'Yes,' and gone back to nursery obscurity, and there, perhaps, mouldered for the rest of my life; but, looking up at madame, I saw in her countenance a something that made me think twice ere I decided. At that instant, she did not wear a woman's aspect, but rather a man's. Power of a particular kind strongly limned itself in all her traits, and that power was not *my* kind of power: neither sympathy, nor congeniality, nor submission, were the emotions it awakened. I stood – not soothed, nor won, nor overwhelmed. It seemed as if a challenge of strength between opposing gifts was given, and I suddenly felt all the dishonour of my diffidence – all the pusillanimity of my slackness to aspire.

'Will you,' said she, 'go backward or forward?' indicating with her hand, first, the small door of communication with the dwelling-house, and then the great double portals of the classes or school-rooms.

'En avant,'[40] I said.

'But,' pursued she, cooling as I warmed, and continuing the hard look, from very antipathy to which I drew strength and determination, 'can you face the classes, or are you over-excited?'

She sneered slightly in saying this – nervous excitability was not much to madame's taste.

'I am no more excited than this stone,' I said, tapping the flag with my toe: 'or than you,' I added, returning her look.

'Bon! But let me tell you these are not quiet, decorous English girls you are going to encounter. Ce sont des Labassecouriennes, rondes, franches, brusques, et tant soit peu rebelles.'[41]

I said: 'I know; and I know, too, that though I have studied French hard since I came here, yet I still speak it with far too much hesitation – too little accuracy to be able to command their respect: I shall make blunders that will lay me open to the scorn of the most ignorant. Still I mean to give the lesson.'

'They always throw over timid teachers,' said she.

'I know that, too, madame; I have heard how they rebelled against and persecuted Miss Turner' – a poor, friendless English teacher, whom madame had employed, and lightly discarded; and to whose piteous history I was no stranger.

'C'est vrai,'[42] said she, coolly. 'Miss Turner had no more command over them than a servant from the kitchen would have had. She was weak and wavering; she had neither tact nor intelligence, decision nor dignity. Miss Turner would not do for these girls at all.'

I made no reply, but advanced to the closed school-room door.

'You will not expect aid from me, or from any one,' said madame. 'That would at once set you down as incompetent for your office.'

I opened the door, let her pass with courtesy, and followed her. There were three school-rooms, all large. That dedicated to the second division, where I was to figure, was considerably the largest, and accommodated an assemblage more numerous, more turbulent, and infinitely more unmanageable than the other two. In after days, when I knew the ground better, I used to think sometimes (if such a comparison may be permitted), that the quiet, polished, tame first division, was to the robust, riotous, demonstrative second division, what the English House of Lords is to the House of Commons.

The first glance informed me that many of the pupils were more than girls – quite young women; I knew that some of them were of noble family (as nobility goes in Labassecour), and I was well convinced that not one amongst them was ignorant of my position in madame's household. As I mounted the estrade (a low platform, raised a step above the flooring), where stood the teacher's chair and desk, I beheld opposite to me a row of eyes and brows that threatened stormy weather – eyes full of an insolent light, and brows hard and unblushing as marble. The continental 'female' is quite a different being to the insular 'female' of the same age and class: I never saw such eyes and brows in England. Madame Beck introduced me in one cool phrase, sailed from the room, and left me alone in my glory.

I shall never forget that first lesson, nor all the undercurrent of life and character it opened up to me. Then first did I begin rightly to see the wide difference that lies between the novelist's and poet's ideal 'jeune fille,'[43] and the said 'jeune fille' as she really is.

It seemed that three titled belles in the first row had sat down predetermined that a *bonne d'enfants*[44] should not give them lessons in English. They knew they had succeeded in expelling obnoxious teachers before now; they knew that madame would at any time throw overboard a professeur or maîtresse who became unpopular with the school – that she never assisted a weak official to retain his place – that if he had not strength to fight, or tact to win his way – down he went: looking at 'Miss Snowe' they promised themselves an easy victory.

Mesdemoiselles Blanche, Virginie, and Angélique opened the campaign by a series of titterings and whisperings; these soon swelled into murmurs and short laughs, which the remoter benches caught up and echoed more loudly. This growing revolt of sixty against one, soon became oppressive enough; my command of French being so limited, and exercised under such cruel constraint.

Could I but have spoken in my own tongue, I felt as if I might have gained a hearing; for, in the first place, though I knew I looked a poor creature, and in many respects actually was so, yet nature had given me a voice that could make itself heard, if lifted in excitement or deepened by emotion. In the second place, while I had no flow, only a hesitating trickle of language, in ordinary circumstances, yet – under stimulus such as was now rife through the mutinous mass – I could, in English, have rolled out readily phrases stigmatizing their proceedings as such proceedings deserved to be stigmatized; and then with some sarcasm, flavoured with contemptuous bitterness, for the ringleaders, and relieved with easy banter for the weaker, but less knavish followers, it seemed to me that one might possibly get command over this wild herd and bring them into training, at least. All I could now do was to walk up to Blanche – Mademoiselle de Melcy, a young baronne – the eldest, tallest, handsomest, and most vicious – stand before her desk, take from under her hand her exercise-book, remount the estrade, deliberately read the composition, which I found very stupid, and as deliberately, and in the face of the whole school, tear the blotted page in two.

This action availed to draw attention and check noise. One girl alone, quite in the background, persevered in the riot with undiminished energy. I looked at her attentively. She had a pale face, hair like night, broad strong eyebrows, decided features, and a dark, mutinous, sinister eye: I noted that she sat close by a little door, which door, I was well aware, opened into a small closet where books were kept. She was standing up for the purpose of conducting her clamour with freer energies. I measured her stature and calculated her strength. She seemed both tall and wiry; but, so the conflict were brief and the attack unexpected, I thought I might manage her.

Advancing up the room, looking as cool and careless as I possibly could, in short, *ayant l'air de rien*;[45] I slightly pushed the door and found it was ajar. In an instant, and with sharpness, I had turned on her. In another instant she occupied the closet, the door was shut, and the key in my pocket.

It so happened that this girl, Dolores by name and a Catalonian by race, was the sort of character at once dreaded and hated by all her associates; the act of summary justice above noted, proved popular: there was not one present but, in her heart, liked to see it done. They were stilled for a moment; then a smile – not a laugh – passed from desk to desk: then – when I had gravely and tranquilly returned to the estrade, courteously requested silence, and commenced a dictation as if nothing at all had happened – the pens travelled peacefully over the pages, and the remainder of the lesson passed in order and industry.

'C'est bien,' said Madame Beck, when I came out of class, hot and a little exhausted. 'Ça ira.'[46]

She had been listening and peeping through a spy-hole the whole time.

From that day I ceased to be nursery-governess, and became English teacher. Madame raised my salary; but she got thrice the work out of me she had extracted from Mr Wilson, at half the expense.

CHAPTER 9

Isidore

MY TIME was now well and profitably filled up. What with teaching others and studying closely myself, I had hardly a spare moment. It was pleasant. I felt I was getting on; not lying the stagnant prey of mould and rust, but polishing my faculties and whetting them to a keen edge with constant use. Experience of a certain kind lay before me, on no narrow scale. Villette is a cosmopolitan city, and in this school were girls of almost every European nation, and likewise of very varied rank in life. Equality is much practised in Labassecour; though not republican in form, it is nearly so in substance, and at the desks of Madame Beck's establishment the young countess and the young bourgeoise sat side by side: nor could you always by outward indications decide which was noble and which plebeian; except that, indeed, the latter had often franker and more courteous manners, while the former bore away the bell for a delicately balanced combination of insolence and deceit. In the former there was often quick French blood mixed with their marsh-phlegm: I regret to say that the effect of this vivacious fluid chiefly appeared in the oilier glibness with which flattery and fiction ran from the tongue, and in a manner lighter and livelier, but quite heartless and insincere.

To do all parties justice, the honest aboriginal Labassecouriennes had an hypocrisy of their own too; but it was of a coarse order, such as could deceive few. Whenever a lie was necessary for their occasions, they brought it out with a careless ease and breadth altogether untroubled by the rebuke of conscience. Not a soul in Madame Beck's house, from the scullion to the directress herself, but was above being ashamed of a lie; they thought nothing of it: to invent might not be precisely a virtue, but it was the most venial of faults. 'J'ai menti plusieurs fois'[47] formed an item of every girl's and woman's monthly confession: the priest heard unshocked, and absolved unreluctant. If they had missed going to mass, or read a chapter of a novel, that was another thing: these were crimes whereof rebuke and penance were the unfailing meed.

While yet but half-conscious of this state of things, and

unlearned in its results, I got on in my new sphere very well. After
the first few difficult lessons, given amidst peril and on the edge of
a moral volcano, that rumbled under my feet and sent sparks and
hot fumes into my eyes, the eruptive spirit seemed to subside, as far
as I was concerned. My mind was a good deal bent on success: I
could not bear the thought of being baffled by mere undisciplined
disaffection and wanton indocility, in the first attempt to get on in
life. Many hours of the night I used to lie awake thinking what plan
I had best adopt to get a reliable hold on these mutineers, to bring
this stiff-necked tribe under permanent influence. In the first place,
I saw plainly that aid in no shape was to be expected from Madame:
her righteous plan was to maintain an unbroken popularity with
the pupils, at any and every cost of justice or comfort to the
teachers. For a teacher to seek her alliance in any crisis of
insubordination was equivalent to securing her own expulsion. In
intercourse with her pupils, Madame only took to herself what was
pleasant, amiable, and recommendatory; rigidly requiring of her
lieutenants sufficiency for every annoying crisis, where to act with
adequate promptitude was to be unpopular. Thus, I must look only
to myself.

Imprimis – it was clear as the day that this swinish multitude were
not to be driven by force. They were to be humoured, borne with
very patiently: a courteous though sedate manner impressed them; a
very rare flash of raillery did good. Severe or continuous mental
application they could not, or would not, bear: heavy demand on
the memory, the reason, the attention, they rejected point-blank.
Where an English girl of not more than average capacity and
docility, would quietly take a theme and bind herself to the task of
comprehension and mastery, a Labassecourienne would laugh in
your face, and throw it back to you with the phrase, – 'Dieu que
c'est difficile! Je n'en veux pas. Cela m'ennuie trop.'[48]

A teacher who understood her business would take it back at
once, without hesitation, contest, or expostulation – proceed with
even exaggerated care to smoothe every difficulty, to reduce it to
the level of their understandings, return it to them thus modified,
and lay on the lash of sarcasm with unsparing hand. They would
feel the sting, perhaps wince a little under it, but they bore no
malice against this sort of attack, provided the sneer was not *sour*
but *hearty*, and that it held well up to them, in a clear light and bold
type, so that she who ran might read, their incapacity, ignorance,
and sloth. They would riot for three additional lines to a lesson; but
I never knew them rebel against a wound given to their self-respect:

the little they had of that quality was trained to be crushed, and it rather liked the pressure of a firm heel, than otherwise.

By degrees, as I acquired fluency and freedom in their language, and could make such application of its more nervous idioms as suited their case, the elder and more intelligent girls began rather to like me, in their way: I noticed that whenever a pupil had been roused to feel in her soul the stirring of worthy emulation, or the quickening of honest shame, from that date she was won. If I could but once make their (usually large) ears burn under their thick, glossy hair, all was comparatively well. By-and-by bouquets began to be laid on my desk in the morning: by way of acknowledgment for this little foreign attention, I used sometimes to walk with a select few during recreation. In the course of conversation it befel once or twice that I made an unpremeditated attempt to rectify some of their singularly distorted notions of principle, especially I expressed my ideas of the evil and baseness of a lie. In an unguarded moment, I chanced to say that, of the two errors, I considered falsehood worse than an occasional lapse in church-attendance. The poor girls were tutored to report in Catholic ears whatever the Protestant teacher said. An edifying consequence ensued. Something – an unseen, an indefinite, a nameless something – stole between myself and these my best pupils: the bouquets continued to be offered, but conversation thenceforth became impracticable. As I paced the alleys or sat in the berceau, a girl never came to my right hand but a teacher, as if by magic, appeared at my left. Also, wonderful to relate, Madame's shoes of silence brought her continually to my back, as quick, noiseless, and unexpected, as some wandering zephyr.

The opinion of my Catholic acquaintance concerning my spiritual prospects was somewhat naively expressed to me on one occasion. A pensionnaire, to whom I had rendered some little service, exclaimed one day as she sat beside me:

'Mademoiselle, what a pity you are a Protestant!'

'Why, Isabelle?'

'Parceque, quand vous serez morte – vous brûlerez tout de suite dans l'Enfer.'

'Croyez-vous?'

'Certainement que j'y crois: tout le monde le sait; et d'ailleurs le prêtre me l'a dit.'

Isabelle was an odd, blunt little creature. She added, *sotto voce:*

'Pour assurer votre salut là-haut, on ferait bien de vous brûler toute vive ici-bas.'[49]

I laughed, as, indeed, it was impossible to do otherwise.

Has the reader forgotten Miss Ginevra Fanshawe? If so, I must be allowed to re-introduce that young lady as a thriving pupil of Madame Beck's, for such she was. On her arrival in the Rue Fossette, two or three days after my sudden settlement there, she encountered me with very little surprise. She must have had good blood in her veins, for never was any duchess more perfectly, radically, unaffectedly *nonchalante* than she: a weak, transient amaze was all she knew of the sensation of wonder. Most of her other faculties seemed to be in the same flimsy condition: her liking and disliking, her love and hate, were mere cobweb and gossamer; but she had one thing about her that seemed strong and durable enough, and that was – her selfishness.

She was not proud; and – *bonne d'enfants* as I was – she would forthwith have made of me a sort of friend and confidant. She teased me with a thousand vapid complaints about school-quarrels and household economy: the cookery was not to her taste – the people about her, teachers and pupils, she held to be despicable, because they were foreigners. I bore with her abuse of the Friday's salt-fish and hard eggs – with her invective against the soup, the bread, the coffee – with some patience for a time; but at last, wearied by iteration, I turned crusty and put her to rights – a thing I ought to have done in the very beginning, for a salutary setting down always agreed with her.

Much longer had I to endure her demands on me in the way of work. Her wardrobe, so far as concerned articles of external wear, was well and elegantly supplied; but there were other habiliments not so carefully provided: what she had, needed frequent repair. She hated needle-drudgery herself, and she would bring her hose, &c., to me in heaps, to be mended. A compliance of some weeks threatening to result in the establishment of an intolerable bore – I at last distinctly told her she must make up her mind to mend her own garments. She cried on receiving this information, and accused me of having ceased to be her friend; but I held by my decision, and let the hysterics pass as they could.

Notwithstanding these foibles, and various others needless to mention – but by no means of a refined or elevating character – how pretty she was! How charming she looked, when she came down on a sunny Sunday morning, well-dressed and well-humoured, robed in pale lilac silk, and with her fair long curls reposing on her white shoulders. Sunday was a holiday which she always passed with friends resident in town; and amongst these friends she speedily gave me to understand was one who would fain become something more. By glimpses and hints it was shown me, and by the general buoyancy of her look and manner it was ere long proved that ardent admiration – perhaps genuine love – was at her command. She called her suitor 'Isidore': this, however, she intimated was not his real name, but one by which it pleased her to baptize him – his own, she hinted, not being 'very pretty.' Once, when she had been bragging about the vehemence of 'Isidore's' attachment, I asked if she loved him in return.

'Comme cela,' said she: 'he is handsome, and he loves me to distraction, so that I am well amused. Ça suffit.'[50]

Finding that she carried the thing on longer than, from her very fickle tastes, I had anticipated, I one day took it upon me to make serious inquiries as to whether the gentleman was such as her parents, and especially her uncle – on whom, it appeared, she was dependent – would be likely to approve. She allowed that this was very doubtful, as she did not believe 'Isidore' had much money.

'Do you encourage him?' I asked.

'Furieusement, sometimes,' said she.

'Without being certain that you will be permitted to marry him?'

'Oh how dowdyish you are! I don't want to be married. I am too young.'

'But if he loves you as much as you say, and yet it comes to nothing in the end, he will be made miserable.'

'Of course he will break his heart. I should be shocked and disappointed if he didn't.'

'I wonder whether this M. Isidore is a fool?' said I.

'He is, about me; but he is wise in other things, à ce qu'on dit.[51] Mrs Cholmondeley considers him extremely clever: she says he will push his way by his talents; all I know is, that he does little more than sigh in my presence, and that I can wind him round my little finger.'

Wishing to get a more definite idea of this love-stricken M. Isidore, whose position seemed to me of the least secure, I requested her to favour me with a personal description; but she could not describe: she had neither words, nor the power of putting them together so as to make graphic phrases. She even seemed not properly to have noticed him: nothing of his looks, of the changes in his countenance, had touched her heart or dwelt in her memory – that he was 'beau, mais plutôt bel homme, que joli garçon,'[52] was all she could assert. My patience would often have failed, and my interest flagged, in listening to her, but for one thing. All the hints she dropped, all the details she gave, went unconsciously to prove, to my thinking, that M. Isidore's homage was offered with great delicacy and respect. I informed her very plainly that I believed him much too good for her, and intimated with equal plainness my impression that she was but a vain coquette. She laughed, shook her curls from her eyes, and danced away as if I had paid her a compliment.

Miss Ginevra's school-studies were little better than nominal; there were but three things she practised in earnest, viz., music, singing, and dancing; also embroidering the fine cambric handkerchiefs which she could not afford to buy ready-worked: such mere trifles as lessons in history, geography, grammar, and arithmetic, she left undone, or got others to do for her. Very much of her time was spent in visiting. Madame, aware that her stay at school was now limited to a certain period which would not be extended whether she made progress or not, allowed her great license in this particular. Mrs Cholmondeley – her *chaperon* – a gay fashionable lady, invited her whenever she had company at her own house, and sometimes took her to evening parties at the houses of her acquaintance. Ginevra perfectly approved this mode of procedure – it had but one inconvenience; she was obliged to be well dressed, and she had not money to buy variety of dresses. All her thoughts turned on this difficulty; her whole soul was occupied with expedients for effecting its solution. It was wonderful to witness the activity of her otherwise indolent mind on this point, and to see the much-daring intrepidity to which she was spurred by a sense of necessity, and the wish to shine.

She begged boldly of Mrs Cholmondeley – boldly, I say: not with an air of reluctant shame, but in this strain: –

'My darling Mrs C., I have nothing in the world fit to wear for your party next week; you *must* give me a book-muslin dress, and then a *ceinture bleu celeste*:[53] *do* – there's an angel! will you?'

The 'darling Mrs C.' yielded at first; but finding that applications increased as they were complied with, she was soon obliged, like all Miss Fanshawe's friends, to oppose resistance to encroachment. After a while I heard no more of Mrs Cholmondeley's presents; but still, visiting went on, and the absolutely necessary dresses continued to be supplied: also many little expensive *etceterae* – gloves, bouquets, even trinkets. These things, contrary to her custom, and even nature – for she was not secretive – were most sedulously kept out of sight for a time; but one evening when she was going to a large party, for which particular care and elegance of costume were demanded, she could not resist coming to my chamber to show herself in all her splendour.

Beautiful she looked: so young, so fresh, and with a delicacy of skin and flexibility of shape altogether English, and not found in the list of continental female charms. Her dress was new, costly, and perfect. I saw at a glance that it lacked none of those finishing details which cost so much, and give to the general effect such an air of tasteful completeness.

I viewed her from top to toe. She turned airily round that I might survey her on all sides. Conscious of her charms, she was in her best humour: her rather small blue eyes sparkled gleefully; she was going to bestow on me a kiss, in her school girl fashion of showing her delight: but I said, 'Steady! Let us be steady, and know what we are about, and find the meaning of our magnificence' – and so put her off at arm's length, to undergo cooler inspection.

'Shall I do?' was her question.

'Do?' said I. 'There are different ways of doing; and, by my word, I don't understand yours.'

'But how do I look?'

'You look well dressed.'

She thought the praise not warm enough, and proceeded to direct attention to the various decorative points of her attire. 'Look at this *parure*,'[34] said she. 'The brooch, the ear-rings, the bracelets: no one in the school has such a set – not madame herself.'

'I see them all.' (Pause.) 'Did M. de Bassompierre give you those jewels?'

'My uncle knows nothing about them.'

'Were they presents from Mrs Cholmondeley?'

'Not they, indeed. Mrs Cholmondeley is a mean, stingy creature; she never gives me anything now.'

I did not choose to ask any further questions, but turned abruptly away.

'Now, old Crusty – old Diogenes'[55] (these were her familiar terms for me when we disagreed), 'what is the matter now?'

'Take yourself away. I have no pleasure in looking at you or your *parure*.'

For an instant, she seemed taken by surprise.

'What now, Mother Wisdom? I have not got into debt for it – that is, not for the jewels, nor the gloves, nor the bouquet. My dress is certainly not paid for, but uncle de Bassompierre will pay it in the bill: he never notices items, but just looks at the total; and he is so rich, one need not care about a few guineas more or less.'

'Will you go? I want to shut the door . . . Ginevra, people may tell you you are very handsome in that ball-attire; but, in *my* eyes, you will never look so pretty as you did in the gingham gown and plain straw bonnet you wore when I first saw you.'

'Other people have not your puritanical tastes:' was her angry reply. 'And, besides, I see no right you have to sermonize me.'

'Certainly! I have little right; and you, perhaps, have still less to come flourishing and fluttering into my chamber – a mere jay in borrowed plumes. I have not the least respect for your feathers, Miss Fanshawe; and especially the peacock's eyes, you call a *parure*: very pretty things, if you had bought them with money which was your own, and which you could well spare, but not at all pretty under present circumstances.'

'On est là pour Mademoiselle Fanshawe!'[56] was announced by the portress, and away she tripped.

This semi-mystery of the *parure* was not solved till two or three days afterwards, when she came to make a voluntary confession.

'You need not be sulky with me,' she began, 'in the idea that I am running somebody, papa or M. de Bassompierre, deeply into debt. I assure you nothing remains unpaid for, but the few dresses I have lately had: all the rest is settled.'

'There,' I thought, 'lies the mystery, considering that they were not given you by Mrs Cholmondeley, and that your own means are limited to a few shillings, of which I know you to be excessively careful.'

'Ecoutez!' she went on, drawing near and speaking in her most confidential and coaxing tone; for my 'sulkiness' was inconvenient to her: she liked me to be in a talking and listening mood, even if I only talked to chide, and listened to rail. 'Ecoutez, chère grogneuse![57] I will tell you all how and about it; and you will then see, not only how right the whole thing is, but how cleverly managed. In the first place, *I must* go out. Papa himself said that he wished me to see something of the world: he particularly remarked to Mrs Cholmondeley, that, though I was a sweet creature enough, I had rather a bread-and-butter-eating, school-girl air; of which it was his special desire that I should get rid, by an introduction to society here, before I make my regular *début* in England. Well, then, if I go out, I *must* dress. Mrs Cholmondeley is turned shabby, and will give nothing more; it would be too hard upon uncle to make him pay for *all* the things I need: *that* you can't deny – *that* agrees with your own preachments. Well, but SOMEBODY who heard me (quite by chance, I assure you) complaining to Mrs

Cholmondeley of my distressed circumstances, and what straits I was put to for an ornament or two: *somebody*, far from grudging one a present, was quite delighted at the idea of being permitted to offer some trifle. You should have seen what a *blanc-bec*[58] he looked when he first spoke of it: how he hesitated and blushed, and positively trembled from fear of a repulse.'

'That will do, Miss Fanshawe. I suppose I am to understand that M. Isidore is the benefactor: that it is from him you have accepted that costly *parure*; that he supplies your bouquets and your gloves?'

'You express yourself so disagreeably,' said she, 'one hardly knows how to answer; what I mean to say is, that I occasionally allow Isidore the pleasure and honour of expressing his homage, by the offer of a trifle.'

'It comes to the same thing . . . Now, Ginevra, to speak the plain truth, I don't very well understand these matters; but I believe you are doing very wrong – seriously wrong. Perhaps, however, you now feel certain that you will be able to marry M. Isidore – your parents and uncle have given their consent – and, for your part, you love him entirely?'

'Mais pas du tout!' (she always had recourse to French, when about to say something specially heartless and perverse). 'Je suis sa reine, mais il n'est pas mon roi.'[59]

'Excuse me, I must believe this language is mere nonsense and coquetry. There is nothing great about you, yet you are above profiting by the good nature and the purse of a man to whom you feel absolute indifference. You love M. Isidore far more than you think, or will avow.'

'No. I danced with a young officer the other night, whom I love a thousand times more than he. I often wonder why I feel so very cold to Isidore, for everybody says he is handsome, and other ladies admire him; but, somehow, he bores me: let me see now how it is . . . '

And she seemed to make an effort to reflect. In this I encouraged her. 'Yes!' I said, 'try to get a clear idea of the state of your mind. To me, it seems in a great mess – chaotic as a rag-bag.'

'It is something in this fashion,' she cried out ere long: 'the man is too romantic and devoted, and he expects something more of me than I find it convenient to be. He thinks I am perfect: furnished with all sorts of sterling qualities and solid virtues, such as I never had, nor intend to have. Now, one can't help, in his presence, rather trying to justify his good opinion; and it does so tire one to be goody, and to talk sense, – for he really thinks I am sensible. I am far more at my ease with you, old lady – you, you dear crosspatch – who take me at my lowest, and know me to be coquettish, and ignorant, and flirting, and fickle, and silly, and selfish, and all the other sweet things you and I have agreed to be a part of my character.'

'This is all very well,' I said, making a strenuous effort to preserve that gravity and severity which ran risk of being shaken by this whimsical candour, 'but it does not alter that wretched business of the presents. Pack them up, Ginevra, like a good, honest girl, and send them back.'

'Indeed, I won't,' said she stoutly.

'Then you are deceiving M. Isidore. It stands to reason that by accepting his presents you give him to understand he will one day receive an equivalent, in your regard . . .'

'But he won't,' she interrupted: 'he has his equivalent now, in the pleasure of seeing me wear them – quite enough for him: he is only bourgeois.'

This phrase, in its senseless arrogance, quite cured me of the temporary weakness which had made me relax my tone and aspect. She rattled on:

'My present business is to enjoy youth, and not to think of fettering myself, by promise or vow, to this man or that. When first I saw Isidore, I believed he would help me to enjoy it. I believed he would be content with my being a pretty girl; and that we should meet and part and flutter about like two butterflies, and be happy. Lo, and behold! I find him at times as grave as a judge, and deep-feeling and thoughtful. Bah! Les penseurs, les hommes profonds et passionés, ne sont pas à mon gout. Le Colonel Alfred de Hamal suits me far better. Va pour les beaux fats et les jolis fripons! Vive les joies et les plaisirs! A bas les grandes passions et les sévères vertus!'

She looked for an answer to this tirade. I gave none.

'J'aime mon beau colonel,' she went on: 'Je n'aimerai jamais son rival. Je ne serai jamais femme de bourgeois, moi!'[60]

I now signified that it was imperatively necessary my apartment should be relieved of the honour of her presence: she went away laughing.

CHAPTER 10

Dr John

MADAME BECK was a most consistent character; forbearing with all the world, and tender to no part of it. Her own children drew her into no deviation from the even tenor of her stoic calm. She was solicitous about her family, vigilant for their interests, and physical well-being; but she never seemed to know the wish to take her little children upon her lap, to press their rosy lips with her own, to gather them in a genial embrace, to shower on them softly the benignant caress, the loving word.

I have watched her sometimes sitting in the garden, viewing the little ones afar off, as they walked in a distant alley with Trinette, their *bonne*; in her mien spoke care and prudence: I knew she often pondered anxiously what she called 'leur avenir;'[61] but if the youngest, a puny and delicate, but engaging child, chancing to spy her, broke from its nurse, and toddling down the walk, came all eager and laughing and panting to clasp her knee, madame would just calmly put out one hand, so as to prevent inconvenient concussion from the child's sudden onset: 'Prends garde, mon enfant!'[62] she would say unmoved, patiently permit it to stand near her a few moments, and then, without smile or kiss, or endearing syllable, rise and lead it back to Trinette.

Her demeanour to the eldest girl was equally characteristic in another way. This was a vicious child. 'Quelle peste que cette Désirée! Quel poison que cet enfant là!'[63] were the expressions dedicated to her, alike in kitchen and in school-room. Amongst her other endowments she boasted an exquisite skill in the art of provocation, sometimes driving her *bonne* and the servants almost wild. She would steal to their attics, open their drawers and boxes, wantonly tear their best caps and soil their best shawls; she would watch her opportunity to get at the beaufet of the salle à manger, where she would smash articles of porcelain or glass – or to the cupboard of the store-room, where she would plunder the preserves, drink the sweet wine, break jars and bottles, and so contrive as to throw the onus of suspicion on the cook and the kitchen-maid. All

this when madame saw, and of which when she received report, her
sole observation, uttered with matchless serenity, was:

'Désirée a besoin d'une surveillance toute particulière.'[64]
Accordingly she kept this promising olive-branch a good deal at her
side. Never once, I believe, did she tell her faithfully of her faults,
explain the evil of such habits, and show the results which must
thence ensue. Surveillance must work the whole cure. It failed of
course. Désirée was kept in some measure from the servants, but
she teased and pillaged her mama instead. Whatever, belonging to
madame's work-table or toilet, she could lay her hands on, she stole
and hid. Madame saw all this, but she still pretended not to see: she
had not rectitude of soul to confront the child with her vices. When
an article disappeared whose value rendered restitution necessary,
she would profess to think that Désirée had taken it away in play,
and beg her to restore it. Désirée was not to be so cheated: she had
learned to bring falsehood to the aid of theft, and would deny
having touched the brooch, ring, or scissors. Carrying on the
hollow system, the mother would calmly assume an air of belief, and
afterwards ceaselessly watch and dog the child till she tracked her to
her hiding-places – some hole in the garden-wall – some chink or
cranny in garret or out-house. This done, madame would send
Désirée out for a walk with her *bonne*, and profit by her absence to
rob the robber. Désirée proved herself the true daughter of her
astute parent, by never suffering either her countenance or manner
to betray the least sign of mortification on discovering the loss.

The second child Fifine, was said to be like its dead father.
Certainly, though the mother had given it her healthy frame, her
blue eye and ruddy cheek, not from her was derived its moral being.
It was an honest, gleeful little soul: a passionate, warm-tempered,
bustling creature it was too, and of the sort likely to blunder often
into perils and difficulties. One day it bethought itself to fall from
top to bottom of a steep flight of stone steps; and when madame,
hearing the noise (she always heard every noise), issued from the
salle à manger and picked it up, she said quietly, –

'Cet enfant a un os de cassé.'[65]

At first we hoped this was not the case. It was, however, but too
true: one little plump arm hung powerless.

'Let meess' (meaning me) 'take her,' said madame; 'et qu'on aille
tout de suite chercher un fiacre.'[66]

In a *fiacre* she promptly, but with admirable coolness and self-
possession, departed to fetch a surgeon.

It appeared she did not find the family-surgeon at home; but that mattered not: she sought until she laid her hand on a substitute to her mind, and brought him back with her. Meantime I had cut the child's sleeve from its arm, undressed and put it to bed.

We none of us, I suppose (by *we* I mean the bonne, the cook, the portress, and myself, all which personages were now gathered in the small and heated chamber), looked very scrutinizingly at the new doctor when he came into the room. I, at least, was taken up with endeavouring to soothe Fifine; whose cries (for she had good lungs) were appalling to hear. These cries redoubled in intensity as the stranger approached her bed; when he took her up, 'Let alone!' she cried passionately, in her broken English (for she spoke English as did the other children). 'I will not you: I will Dr Pillule!'

'And Dr Pillule is my very good friend,' was the answer, in perfect English; 'but he is busy at a place three leagues off, and I am come in his stead. So now, when we get a little calmer, we must commence business; and we will soon have that unlucky little arm bandaged and in right order.'

Hereupon he called for a glass of *eau sucrée*,[67] fed her with some teaspoonsful of the sweet liquid (Fifine was a frank gourmande; anybody could win her heart through her palate), promised her more when the operation should be over, and promptly went to work. Some assistance being needed, he demanded it of the cook, a robust, strong-armed woman, but she, the portress, and the nurse instantly fled. I did not like to touch that small, tortured limb, but, thinking there was no alternative, my hand was already extended to do what was requisite. I was anticipated: Madame Beck had put out her own hand – hers was steady while mine trembled.

'Ça vaudra mieux,'[68] said the doctor, turning from me to her.

He showed wisdom in his choice. Mine would have been feigned stoicism, forced fortitude. Hers was neither forced nor feigned.

'Merci Madame: très bien, fort bien!' said the operator when he had finished. 'Voilà un sang-froid bien opportun, et qui vaut mille élans de sensibilité déplacée.'[69]

He was pleased with her firmness, she with his compliment. It is likely too that his whole general appearance, his voice, mien, and manner wrought impressions in his favour. Indeed, when you looked well at him, and when a lamp was brought in – for it was evening and now waxing dusk – you saw that, unless Madame Beck had been less than woman, it could not well be otherwise. This young doctor (he *was* young) had no common aspect. His stature looked imposingly tall in that little chamber, and amidst that group of Dutch-made women; his profile was clear, fine, and expressive:

perhaps his eye glanced from face to face rather too vividly, too quickly, and too often, but it had a most pleasant character, and so had his mouth; his chin was full, cleft, Grecian, and perfect. As to his smile, one could not in a hurry make up one's mind as to the descriptive epithet it merited; there was something in it that pleased, but something too that brought surging up into the mind all one's foibles and weak points: all that could lay one open to a laugh; yet Fifine liked this doubtful smile, and thought the owner genial: much as he had hurt her, she held out her hand to bid him a friendly good-night. He patted the little hand kindly, and then he and madame went down stairs together; she talking in her highest tide of spirits and volubility; he listening with an air of good-natured amenity, dashed with that unconscious roguish archness I find it difficult to describe.

I noticed that though he spoke French well, he spoke English better; he had, too, an English complexion, eyes, and form. I noticed more. As he passed me in leaving the room, turning his face in my direction one moment – not to address me, but to speak to madame, yet so standing, that I almost necessarily looked up at him – a recollection which had been struggling to form in my memory, since the first moment I heard his voice, started up perfected. This was the very gentleman to whom I had spoken at the bureau; who had helped me in the matter of the trunk; who had been my guide through the dark, wet park. Listening, as he passed down the long vestibule out into the street, I recognized his very tread: it was the same firm and equal stride I had followed under the dripping trees.

It was to be concluded that this young surgeon-physician's first visit to the Rue Fossette would be his last. The respectable Dr Pillule being expected home the next day, there appeared no reason why his temporary substitute should again represent him; but the Fates had written their decree to the contrary.

Dr Pillule had been summoned to see a rich old hypochondriac at the antique university town of Bouquin-Moisi, and upon his prescribing change of air and travel as remedies, he was retained to accompany the timid patient on a tour of some weeks; it but remained, therefore, for the new doctor to continue his attendance at the Rue Fossette.

I often saw him when he came, for madame would not trust the little invalid to Trinette, but required me to spend much of my time in the nursery. I think he was skilful. Fifine recovered rapidly under his care, yet even her convalescence did not hasten his dismissal.

Destiny and Madame Beck seemed in league, and both had ruled that he should make deliberate acquaintance with the vestibule, the private staircase, and upper chambers of the Rue Fossette.

No sooner did Fifine emerge from his hands than Désirée declared herself ill. That possessed child had a genius for simulation, and captivated by the attentions and indulgences of a sick-room, she came to the conclusion that an illness would perfectly accommodate her tastes, and took her bed accordingly. She acted well, and her mother still better; for while the whole case was transparent to Madame Beck as the day, she treated it with an astonishingly well-assured air of gravity and good faith.

What surprised me was that Dr John (so the young Englishman had taught Fifine to call him, and we all took from her the habit of addressing him by this name, till it became an established custom, and he was known by no other in the Rue Fossette) – that Dr John consented tacitly to adopt madame's tactics, and to fall in with her manoeuvres. He betrayed, indeed, a period of comic doubt, cast one or two rapid glances from the child to the mother, indulged in an interval of self-consultation, but finally resigned himself with a good grace to play his part in the farce. Désirée ate like a raven, gambolled day and night in her bed, pitched tents with the sheets and blankets, lounged like a Turk amidst pillows and bolsters, diverted herself with throwing her shoes at her bonne and grimacing at her sisters – overflowed, in short, with unmerited health and evil spirits – only languishing when her mama and the physician paid their diurnal visit. Madame Beck, I knew, was glad, at any price, to have her daughter in bed out of the way of mischief; but I wondered that Dr John did not tire of the business.

Every day, on this mere pretext of a motive, he gave punctual attendance; madame always received him with the same empressement, the same sunshine for himself, the same admirably counterfeited air of concern for her child. Dr John wrote harmless prescriptions for the patient, and viewed her mother with a shrewdly sparkling eye. Madame caught his rallying looks without resenting them – she had too much good sense for that. Supple as the young doctor seemed, one could not despise him – this pliant part was evidently not adopted in the design to curry favour with his employer: while he liked his office at the Pensionnat, and lingered strangely about the Rue Fossette, he was independent, almost careless in his carriage there; and yet, too, he was often thoughtful and preoccupied.

It was not perhaps my business to observe the mystery of his bearing, or search out its origin or aim; but, placed as I was, I could hardly help it. He laid himself open to my observation, according to my presence in the room just that degree of notice and consequence a person of my exterior habitually expects: that is to say, about what is given to unobtrusive articles of furniture, chairs of ordinary joiner's work, and carpets of no striking pattern. Often, while waiting for madame, he would muse, smile, watch, or listen like a man who thinks himself alone. I, meantime, was free to puzzle over his countenance and movements, and wonder what could be the meaning of that peculiar interest and attachment – all mixed up with doubt and strangeness, and inexplicably ruled by some presiding spell – which wedded him to this demi-convent, secluded in the built-up core of a capital. He, I believe, never remembered that I had eyes in my head; much less a brain behind them.

Nor would he ever have found this out, but that one day, while he sat in the sunshine, and I was observing the colouring of his hair, whiskers, and complexion – the whole being of such a tone as a strong light brings out with somewhat perilous force (indeed I recollect I was driven to compare his beamy head in my thoughts to that of the 'golden image' which Nebuchadnezzar[70] the king had set up), an idea new, sudden, and startling, riveted my attention with an overmastering strength and power of attraction. I know not to this day how I looked at him – the force of surprise, and also of conviction, made me forget myself – and I only recovered wonted consciousness when I saw that his notice was arrested, and that it had caught my movement in a clear little oval mirror fixed in the side of the window recess – by the aid of which reflector madame often secretly spied persons walking in the garden below. Though of so gay and sanguine a temperament, he was not without a certain nervous sensitiveness which made him ill at ease under a direct, inquiring gaze. On surprising me thus, he turned and said in a tone which, though courteous, had just so much dryness in it as to mark a shade of annoyance, as well as to give to what was said the character of rebuke: –

'Mademoiselle does not spare me: I am not vain enough to fancy that it is my merits which attract her attention; it must then be some defect. Dare I ask – what?'

I was confounded, as the reader may suppose, yet not with an irrecoverable confusion, being conscious that it was from no emotion of incautious admiration, nor yet in a spirit of unjustifiable inquisitiveness, that I had incurred this reproof. I might have cleared myself on the spot, but would not. I did not speak. I was not in the habit of speaking to him. Suffering him, then, to think what he chose, and accuse me of what he would, I resumed some work I had dropped, and kept my head bent over it during the remainder of his stay. There is a perverse mood of the mind which is rather soothed than irritated by misconstruction; and in quarters where we can never be rightly known, we take pleasure, I think, in being consummately ignored. What honest man on being casually taken for a housebreaker, does not feel rather tickled than vexed at the mistake?

CHAPTER 11

The Portresse's Cabinet

IT WAS SUMMER and very hot. Georgette, the youngest of Madame Beck's children, took a fever. Désirée, suddenly cured of her ailments, was, together with Fifine, packed off to Bonne-Maman in the country, by way of precaution against infection. Medical aid was now really needed, and Madame, choosing to ignore the return of Dr Pillule, who had been at home a week, conjured his English rival to continue his visits. One or two of the *pensionnaires* complained of headache, and in other respects seemed slightly to participate Georgette's ailment. 'Now, at last,' I thought, 'Dr Pillule must be recalled: the prudent directress will never venture to permit the attendance of so young a man on the pupils.'

The directress was very prudent, but she could also be intrepidly venturous. She actually introduced Dr John to the school-division of the premises, and established him in attendance on the proud and handsome Blanche de Melcy, and the vain, flirting Angélique, her friend. Dr John, I thought, testified a certain gratification at this mark of confidence; and if discretion of bearing could have justified the step, it would by him have been amply justified. Here, however, in this land of convents and confessionals, such a presence as his was not to be suffered with impunity in a 'Pensionnat de demoiselles.' The school gossiped, the kitchen whispered, the town caught the rumour, parents wrote letters and paid visits of remonstrance. Madame, had she been weak, would now have been lost: a dozen rival educational houses were ready to improve this false step – if false step it were – to her ruin; but Madame was not weak, and little Jesuit though she might be, yet I clapped the hands of my heart, and with its voice cried 'brava!' as I watched her able bearing, her skilled management, her temper and her firmness on this occasion.

She met the alarmed parents with a good-humoured, easy grace: for nobody matched her in, I know not whether to say the possession or the assumption of a certain 'rondeur et franchise de bonne femme,'[71] which on various occasions gained the point aimed at with instant and complete success, where severe gravity and serious reasoning would probably have failed.

'Ce pauvre Docteur Jean!' she would say, chuckling and rubbing joyously her fat, little, white hands; 'ce cher jeune homme! le meilleur créature du monde!'[72] and go on to explain how she happened to be employing him for her own children, who were so fond of him they would scream themselves into fits at the thought of another doctor; how where she had confidence for her own, she thought it natural to repose trust for others, and au reste it was only the most temporary expedient in the world: Blanche and Angélique had the migraine; Dr John had written a prescription; voilà tout!

The parents' mouths were closed. Blanche and Angelique saved her all remaining trouble by chanting loud duets in their physician's praise; the other pupils echoed them, unanimously declaring that when they were ill they would have Dr John and nobody else; and madame laughed, and the parents laughed too. The Labassecouriens must have a large organ of philoprogenitiveness: at least the indulgence of offspring is carried by them to excessive lengths; the law of most households being the children's will. Madame now got credit for having acted on this occasion in a spirit of motherly partiality: she came off with flying colours; people liked her as a directress better than ever.

To this day I never fully understood why she thus risked her interest for the sake of Dr John. What people said, of course I know well: the whole house – pupils, teachers, servants included – affirmed that she was going to marry him. So they had settled it: difference of age seemed to make no obstacle in their eyes; it was to be so.

It must be admitted that appearances did not wholly discountenance this idea; madame seemed so bent on retaining his services, so oblivious of her former protégé, Pillule. She made, too, such a point of personally receiving his visits, and was so unfailingly cheerful, blithe, and benignant in her manner to him. Moreover, she paid, about this time, marked attention to dress: the morning deshabille, the night-cap and shawl, were discarded; Dr John's early visits always found her with auburn braids all nicely arranged, silk dress trimly fitted on, neat laced brodequins[73] in lieu of slippers: in short the whole toilette complete as a model, and fresh as a flower. I scarcely think, however, that her intention in this went further than just to show a very handsome man that she was not quite a plain woman: and plain she was not. Without beauty of feature or elegance of form, she pleased. Without youth and its gay graces, she cheered. One never tired of seeing her: she was never monotonous, or insipid, or colourless, or flat. Her unfaded hair, her eye with its temperate blue light, her cheek with its wholesome fruit-like bloom – these things pleased in moderation, but with constancy.

Had she, indeed, floating visions of adopting Dr John as a husband, taking him to her well-furnished home, endowing him with her savings, which were said to amount to a moderate competency, and making him comfortable for the rest of his life? Did Dr John suspect her of such visions? I have met him coming out of her presence with a mischievous half-smile about his lips, and in his eyes a look as of masculine vanity elate and tickled. With all his good looks and good-nature, he was not perfect; he must have been very imperfect if he roguishly encouraged aims he never intended to be successful. But did he not intend them to be successful? People said he had no money, that he was wholly dependent upon his profession. Madame – though perhaps some fourteen years his senior – was yet the sort of woman never to grow old, never to wither, never to break down. They certainly were on good terms. *He* perhaps was not in love; but how many people ever *do* love, or at least marry for love in this world? We waited the end.

For what *he* waited I do not know, nor for what he watched; but the peculiarity of his manner, his expectant, vigilant, absorbed, eager look, never wore off: it rather intensified. He had never been quite within the compass of my penetration, and I think he ranged farther and farther beyond it.

One morning little Georgette had been more feverish and consequently more peevish; she was crying and would not be pacified. I thought a particular draught ordered, disagreed with her, and I doubted whether it ought to be continued; I waited impatiently for the doctor's coming in order to consult him.

The door-bell rung, he was admitted; I felt sure of this, for I heard his voice addressing the portresse. It was his custom to mount straight to the nursery, taking about three degrees of the staircase at once, and coming upon us like a cheerful surprise. Five minutes elapsed – ten – and I saw and heard nothing of him. What could he be doing? Possibly waiting in the corridor below. Little Georgette still piped her plaintive wail, appealing to me by her familiar term, 'Minnie, Minnie, me very poorly!' till my heart ached. I descended to ascertain why he did not come. The corridor was empty. Whither was he vanished? Was he with madame in the salle à manger? Impossible: I had left her but a short time since, dressing in her own chamber. I listened. Three pupils were just then hard at work practising in three proximate rooms – the dining room and the greater and lesser drawing-rooms, between which and the corridor there was but the portresse's cabinet communicating with the salons, and intended originally for a boudoir. Farther off, at a fourth instrument in the oratory, a whole class of a dozen or more were taking a singing lesson, and just then joining in a 'barcarole'[74] (I think they called it), whereof I yet remember these words 'fraîchë brisë' and 'Venisë.' Under these circumstances what could I hear? A great deal, certainly; had it only been to the purpose.

Yes; I heard a giddy treble laugh in the above-mentioned little cabinet, close by the door of which I stood – that door half-unclosed; a man's voice in a soft, deep, pleading tone, uttered some words, whereof I only caught the adjuration, 'For God's sake!' Then, after a second's pause, forth issued Dr John, his eye full-shining, but not with either joy or triumph; his fair English cheek high-coloured; a baffled, tortured, anxious, and yet a tender meaning on his brow.

The open door served me as a screen; but had I been full in his way I believe he would have passed without seeing me. Some mortification, some strong vexation had hold of his soul: or rather, to write my impressions now as I received them at the time, I should say some sorrow, some sense of injustice. I did not so much think his pride was hurt, as that his affections had been wounded – cruelly wounded it seemed to me. But who was the torturer? What being in that house had him so much in her power? Madame I believed to be in her chamber; the room whence he had stepped was dedicated to the portresse's sole use; and she, Rosine Matou, an unprincipled though pretty little French grisette,[75] airy, fickle, dressy, vain, and mercenary – it was not, surely, to *her* hand he owed the ordeal through which he seemed to have passed?

But while I pondered, her voice, clear though somewhat sharp, broke out in a lightsome French song, trilling through the door still ajar: I glanced in, doubting my senses. There at the table she sat in a smart dress of 'jaconas rose,' trimming a tiny blond cap: not a living thing save herself was in the room, except indeed some gold-fish in a glass globe, some flowers in pots, and a broad July sunbeam.

Here was a problem: but I must go upstairs to ask about the medicine.

Dr John sat in a chair at Georgette's bedside; madame stood before him; the little patient had been examined and soothed, and now lay composed in her crib. Madame Beck, as I entered, was discussing the physician's own health, remarking on some real or fancied change in his looks, charging him with over-work, and recommending rest and change of air. He listened good-naturedly, but with laughing indifference, telling her that she was 'trop bonne,' and that he felt perfectly well. Madame appealed to me – Dr John following her movement with a slow glance which seemed to express languid surprise at reference being made to a quarter so insignificant.

'What do you think, Mees Lucie?' asked madame. 'Is he not paler and thinner?'

It was very seldom that I uttered more than monosyllables in Dr John's presence; he was the kind of person with whom I was likely ever to remain the neutral, passive thing he thought me. Now, however, I took license to answer in a phrase: and a phrase I purposely made quite significant.

'He looks ill at this moment; but perhaps it is owing to some temporary cause: Dr John may have been vexed or harassed.' I cannot tell how he took this speech, as I never sought his face for information. Georgette here began to ask me in her broken English if she might have a glass of *eau sucrée*. I answered her in English. For the first time, I fancy, he noticed that I spoke his language; hitherto he had always taken me for a foreigner, addressing me as 'mademoiselle,' and giving in French the requisite directions about the children's treatment. He seemed on the point of making a remark, but thinking better of it, held his tongue.

Madame recommenced advising him; he shook his head laughing, rose and bid her good morning, with courtesy, but still with the regardless air of one whom too much unsolicited attention was surfeiting and spoiling.

When he was gone, madame dropped into the chair he had just left; she rested her chin in her hand; all that was animated and amiable vanished from her face: she looked stony and stern, almost mortified and morose. She sighed; a single, but a deep sigh. A loud bell rang for morning school. She got up; as she passed a dressing-table with a glass upon it, she looked at her reflected image. One single white hair streaked her nut-brown tresses; she plucked it out with a shudder. In the full summer daylight, her face, though it still had the colour, could plainly be seen to have lost the texture of youth; and then, where were youth's contours? Ah, madame! wise as you were, even *you* knew weakness. Never had I pitied madame before, but my heart softened towards her, when she turned darkly from the glass. A calamity had come upon her. That hag Disappointment was greeting her with a grisly 'all-hail!' and her soul rejected the intimacy.

But Rosine! My bewilderment there surpasses description. I embraced five opportunities of passing her cabinet that day, with a view to contemplating her charms, and finding out the secret of their influence. She was pretty, young, and wore a well-made dress. All very good points, and, I suppose, amply sufficient to account, in any philosophic mind, for any amount of agony and distraction in a young man like Dr John. Still, I could not help forming half a wish that the said doctor were my brother; or at least that he had a sister or a mother who would kindly sermonize him. I say *half* a wish; I broke it and flung it away before it became a whole one, discovering in good time its exquisite folly. 'Somebody,' I argued, 'might as well sermonize madame about her young physician: and what good would that do?'

I believe madame sermonized herself. She did not behave weakly, or make herself in any shape ridiculous. It is true she had neither strong feelings to overcome, nor tender feelings by which to be miserably pained. It is true likewise that she had an important avocation, a real business to fill her time, divert her thoughts, and divide her interest. It is especially true that she possessed a genuine good sense which is not given to all women or to all men; and by dint of these combined advantages she behaved wisely, she behaved well. Brava! once more, Madame Beck. I saw you matched against an Apollyon[76] of a predilection; you fought a good fight, and you overcame!

CHAPTER 12

The Casket

BEHIND THE HOUSE at the Rue Fossette there was a garden – large, considering that it lay in the heart of a city, and to my recollection at this day it seems pleasant: but time, like distance, lends to certain scenes an influence so softening; and where all is stone around, blank wall and hot pavement, how precious seems one shrub, how lovely an enclosed and planted spot of ground!

There went a tradition that Madame Beck's house had in old days been a convent. That in years gone by – how long gone by I cannot tell, but I think some centuries – before the city had overspread this quarter, and when it was tilled ground and avenue, and such deep and leafy seclusion as ought to embosom a religious house – that something had happened on this site which, rousing fear and inflicting horror, had left to the place the inheritance of a ghost story. A vague tale went of a black and white nun, sometimes, on some night or nights of the year, seen in some part of this vicinage. The ghost must have been built out ages ago, for there were houses all round now; but certain convent-relics, in the shape of old and huge fruit-trees, yet consecrated the spot; and, at the foot of one – a Methuselah of a pear-tree, dead, all but a few boughs which still faithfully renewed their perfumed snow in spring, and their honey-sweet pendants in autumn – you saw, in scraping away the mossy earth between the half-bared roots, a glimpse of slab, smooth, hard, and black. The legend went, unconfirmed and unaccredited, but still propagated, that this was the portal of a vault, emprisoning deep beneath that ground, on whose surface grass grew and flowers bloomed, the bones of a girl whom a monkish conclave of the drear middle ages had here buried alive, for some sin against her vow. Her shadow it was that tremblers had feared, through long generations after her poor frame was dust; her black robe and white veil that, for timid eyes, moonlight and shade had mocked, as they fluctuated in the night-wind through the garden-thicket.

Independently of romantic rubbish, however, that old garden had its charms. On summer mornings I used to rise early, to enjoy them

alone; on summer evenings, to linger solitary, to keep tryste with
the rising moon, or taste one kiss of the evening breeze, or fancy
rather than feel the freshness of dew descending. The turf was
verdant, the gravelled walks were white; sun-bright nasturtiums
clustered beautiful about the roots of the doddered orchard giants.
There was a large berceau, above which spread the shade of an
acacia; there was a smaller, more sequestered bower, nestled in the
vines which ran all along a high and gray wall, and gathered their
tendrils in a knot of beauty, and hung their clusters in loving
profusion about the favoured spot where jasmine and ivy met and
married them.

Doubtless at high noon, in the broad, vulgar middle of the day,
when Madame Beck's large school turned out rampant, and externes
and pensionnaires were spread abroad, vying with the denizens of
the boys' college close at hand, in the brazen exercise of their lungs
and limbs – doubtless *then* the garden was a trite, trodden-down
place enough. But at sunset or the hour of *salut*, when the externes
were gone home, and the boarders quiet at their studies; pleasant
was it then to stray down the peaceful alleys, and hear the bells of St.
Jean Baptiste peal out with their sweet, soft, exalted sound.

I was walking thus one evening, and had been detained, farther
within the verge of twilight than usual, by the still deepening calm,
the mellow coolness, the fragrant breathing with which flowers no
sunshine could win now answered the persuasion of the dew. I saw
by a light in the oratory window that the Catholic household were
then gathered to evening prayer – a rite, from attendance on which,
I now and then, as a Protestant, exempted myself.

'One moment longer,' whispered solitude and the summer moon,
'stay with us: all is truly quiet now; for another quarter of an hour
your presence will not be missed: the day's heat and bustle have
tired you; enjoy these precious minutes.'

The windowless backs of houses built in this garden, and in
particular the whole of one side was skirted by the rear of a long line
of premises – being the boarding-houses of the neighbouring
college. This rear, however, was all blank stone, with the exception
of certain attic loop-holes high up, opening from the sleeping-
rooms of the women-servants, and also one casement in a lower
story said to mark the chamber or study of a master. But, though
thus secure, an alley, which ran parallel with the very high wall on
that side of the garden, was forbidden to be entered by the pupils. It
was called indeed 'l'allée défendue,' and any girl setting foot there
would have rendered herself liable to as severe a penalty as the mild

rules of Madame Beck's establishment permitted. Teachers might indeed go there with impunity; but as the walk was narrow, and the neglected shrubs were grown very thick and close on each side, weaving overhead a roof of branch and leaf which the sun's rays penetrated but in rare chequers, this alley was seldom entered even during day, and after dusk was carefully shunned.

From the first I was tempted to make an exception to this rule of avoidance: the seclusion, the very gloom of the walk attracted me. For a long time the fear of seeming singular scared me away; but by degrees, as people became accustomed to me and my habits, and to such shades of peculiarity as were engrained in my nature – shades, certainly not striking enough to interest, and perhaps not prominent enough to offend, but born in and with me, and no more to be parted with than my identity – by slow degrees I became a frequenter of this strait and narrow path. I made myself gardener of some tintless flowers that grew between its closely-ranked shrubs; I cleared away the relics of past autumns, choking up a rustic seat at the far end. Borrowing of Goton, the cuisinière, a pail of water and a scrubbing-brush, I made this seat clean. Madame saw me at work and smiled approbation: whether sincerely or not I don't know; but she *seemed* sincere.

'Voyez-vous,' cried she, 'comme elle est propre cette demoiselle Lucie? Vous aimez donc cette allée,[77] meess?'

'Yes,' I said, 'it is quiet and shady.'

'C'est juste,' cried she with her air of bonté; and she kindly recommended me to confine myself to it as much as I chose, saying, that as I was not charged with the surveillance, I need not trouble myself to walk with the pupils: only I might permit her children to come there, to talk English with me.

On the night in question, I was sitting on the hidden seat reclaimed from fungi and mould, listening to what seemed the far-off sounds of the city. Far-off, in truth, they were not: this school was in the city's centre; hence, it was but five minutes' walk to the park, scarce ten – to buildings of palatial splendour. Quite near were wide streets brightly lit, teeming at this moment with life: carriages were rolling through them, to balls or to the opera. The same hour which tolled curfew for our convent, which extinguished each lamp, and dropped the curtain round each couch, rung for the gay city about us the summons to festal enjoyment. Of this contrast I thought not, however: gay instincts my nature had few; ball or opera I had never seen; and though often I had heard them described, and even wished to see them, it was not the wish of one who hopes to partake a pleasure if she could only reach it – who feels fitted to shine in some bright distant sphere, could she but thither win her way; it was no yearning to attain, no hunger to taste; only the calm desire to look on a new thing.

A moon was in the sky, not a full moon but a young crescent. I saw her through a space in the boughs over-head. She and the stars, visible beside her, were no strangers where all else was strange: my childhood knew them. I had seen that golden sign with the dark globe in its curve leaning back on azure, beside an old thorn at the top of an old field, in Old England, in long past days, just as it now leaned back beside a stately spire in this continental capital.

Oh, my childhood! I had feelings: passive as I lived, little as I spoke, cold as I looked, when I thought of past days, I *could* feel. About the present, it was better to be stoical; about the future – such a future as mine – to be dead. And in catalepsy and a dead trance, I studiously held the quick of my nature.

At that time, I well remember whatever could excite – certain accidents of the weather, for instance, were almost dreaded by me, because they woke the being I was always lulling, and stirred up a craving cry I could not satisfy. One night a thunderstorm broke; a sort of hurricane shook us in our beds: the Catholics rose in panic and prayed to their saints. As for me, the tempest took hold of me with tyranny: I was roughly roused and obliged to live. I got up and dressed myself, and creeping outside the casement close by my bed, sat on its ledge, with my feet on the roof of a lower adjoining building. It was wet, it was wild, it was pitch-dark. Within the dormitory they gathered round the night-lamp in consternation, praying loud. I could not go in: too resistless was the delight of staying with the wild hour, black and full of thunder, pealing out such an ode as language never delivered to man – too terribly glorious, the spectacle of clouds, split and pierced by white and blinding bolts.

I did long, achingly, then and for four-and-twenty hours afterwards, for something to fetch me out of my present existence, and lead me upwards and onwards. This longing, and all of a similar kind, it was necessary to knock on the head; which I did, figuratively, after the manner of Jael to Sisera,[78] driving a nail through their temples. Unlike Sisera, they did not die: they were but transiently stunned, and at intervals would turn on the nail with a rebellious wrench; then did the temples bleed, and the brain thrill to its core.

To-night, I was not so mutinous, nor so miserable. My Sisera lay quiet in the tent, slumbering; and if his pain ached through his slumbers, something like an angel – the Ideal – knelt near, dropping balm on the soothed temples, holding before the sealed eyes a magic glass, of which the sweet, solemn visions were repeated in dreams, and shedding a reflex from her moonlight wings and robe over the transfixed sleeper, over the tent threshold, over all the landscape lying without. Jael, the stern woman, sat apart, relenting somewhat over her captive; but more prone to dwell on the faithful expectation of Heber coming home. By which words I mean that the cool peace and dewy sweetness of the night filled me with a mood of hope: not hope on any definite point, but a general sense of encouragement and heart-ease.

Should not such a mood, so sweet, so tranquil, so unwonted, have been the harbinger of good? Alas, no good came of it! Presently the rude Real burst coarsely in – all evil, grovelling, and repellent as she too often is.

Amid the intense stillness of that pile of stone overlooking the walk, the trees, the high wall, I heard a sound; a casement [all the windows here are casements, opening on hinges] creaked. Ere I had time to look up and mark where, in which story, or by whom unclosed, a tree overhead shook, as if struck by a missile; some object dropped prone at my feet.

Nine was striking by St. Jean Baptiste's clock; day was fading, but it was not dark: the crescent-moon aided little, but the deep gilding of that point in heaven where the sun burned last, and the crystalline clearness of a wide space above, sustained the summer twilight; even in my dark walk I could, by approaching an opening, have managed to read print of a small type. Easy was it to see then that the missile was a box, a small box of white and coloured ivory: its loose lid opened in my hand; violets lay within, violets smothering a closely-folded bit of pink paper, a note, superscribed, 'Pour la robe grise.' I wore indeed a dress of French gray.

Good. Was this a billet-doux? A thing I had heard of, but hitherto had not had the honour of seeing or handling. Was it this sort of commodity I held between my finger and thumb at this moment?

Scarcely: I did not dream it for a moment. Suitor or admirer my very thoughts had not conceived. All the teachers had dreams of some lover; one (but she was naturally of a credulous turn) believed in a future husband. All the pupils above fourteen knew of some prospective bridegroom; two or three were already affianced by their parents, and had been so from childhood: but into the realm of feelings and hopes which such prospects open, my speculations, far less my presumptions, had never once had warrant to intrude. If the other teachers went into town, or took a walk on the boulevards, or only attended mass, they were very certain (according to the accounts brought back) to meet with some individual of the 'opposite sex,' whose rapt, earnest gaze assured them of their power to strike and to attract. I can't say that my experience tallied with theirs, in this respect. I went to church and I took walks, and am very well convinced that nobody minded me. There was not a girl or woman in the Rue Fossette who could not, and did not testify to having received an admiring beam from our young doctor's blue eyes, at one time or other. I am obliged, however humbling it may sound, to except myself: as far as I was concerned, those blue eyes were guiltless and calm as the sky, to whose tint theirs seemed akin. So it came to pass that I heard the others talk, wondered often at their gaiety, security and self-satisfaction, but did not trouble myself to look up and gaze along the path they seemed so certain of treading. This then was no billet-doux; and it was in settled conviction to the contrary that I quietly opened it. Thus it ran – I translate: –

'Angel of my dreams! A thousand, thousand thanks for the promise kept: scarcely did I venture to hope its fulfilment. I believed you, indeed, to be half in jest; and then you seemed to think the enterprise beset with such danger – the hour so untimely, the alley so strictly secluded – often, you said, haunted by that dragon, the English teacher – une véritable bégueule Britannique à ce que vous dites – espèce de monstre, brusque et rude comme un vieux caporal de grenadiers, et revêche comme une religieuse'[79] (the reader will excuse my modesty in allowing this flattering sketch of my amiable self to retain the slight veil of the original tongue.) 'You are aware,' went on this precious effusion, 'that little Gustave, on account of his illness, has been removed to a master's chamber – that favoured chamber, whose lattice overlooks your prison-ground. There, I, the best uncle in the world, am admitted to visit him. How tremblingly I approached the window and glanced into your Eden – an Eden for me, though a desert for you! – how I feared to behold vacancy, or the dragon aforesaid! How my heart palpitated with delight when, through apertures in the envious boughs, I at once caught the gleam of your graceful straw-hat, and the waving of your gray dress – dress that I should recognize amongst a thousand. But why, my angel, will you not look up? Cruel, to deny me one ray of those adorable eyes! – how a single glance would have revived me! I write this in fiery haste; while the physician examines Gustave, I snatch an opportunity to enclose it in a small casket, together with a bouquet of flowers, the sweetest that blow – yet less sweet than thee, my Peri – my all-charming! Ever thine – thou well knowest whom!'

'I wish I did know whom,' was my comment; and the wish bore even closer reference to the person addressed in this choice document, than to the writer thereof. Perhaps it was from the fiancé of one of the engaged pupils; and, in that case, there was no great harm done or intended – only a small irregularity. Several of the girls, the majority indeed, had brothers or cousins at the neighbouring college. But, 'la robe grise, le chapeau de paille,' here surely was a clue – a very confusing one. The straw-hat was an ordinary garden head-screen, common to a score besides myself. The gray dress hardly gave more definite indication. Madame Beck herself ordinarily wore a gray dress just now; another teacher, and three of the pensionnaires, had had gray dresses purchased of the same shade and fabric as mine: it was a sort of every-day wear which happened at that time to be in vogue.

Meanwhile, as I pondered, I knew I must go in. Lights, moving in the dormitory, announced that prayers were over, and the pupils going to bed. Another half hour and all doors would be locked – all lights extinguished. The front door yet stood open, to admit into the heated house the coolness of the summer night; from the portresse's cabinet close by shone a lamp, showing the long vestibule with the two-leaved drawing-room doors on one side, the great street-door closing the vista.

All at once, quick rang the bell – quick, but not loud – a cautious tinkle – a sort of warning, metal whisper. Rosine darted from her cabinet and ran to open. The person she admitted stood with her two minutes in parley: there seemed a demur, a delay. Rosine came to the garden door, lamp in hand; she stood on the steps, lifting her lamp, looking round vaguely.

'Quel conte!' she cried with a coquettish laugh. 'Personne n'y a été.'[80]

'Let me pass,' pleaded a voice I knew: 'I ask but five minutes;' and a familiar shape, tall and grand (as we of the Rue Fossette all thought it), issued from the house, and strode down amongst the beds and walks. It was sacrilege – the intrusion of a man into that spot, at that hour; but he knew himself privileged, and perhaps he trusted to the friendly night. He wandered down the alleys, looking on this side and on that – he was lost in the shrubs, trampling flowers and breaking branches in his search – he penetrated at last the 'forbidden walk.' There I met him, like some ghost, I suppose.

'Dr John! it is found.'

He did not ask by whom, for with his quick eye he perceived that I held it in my hand.

'Do not betray her,' he said, looking at me as if I were indeed a dragon.

'Were I ever so disposed to treachery, I cannot betray what I do not know,' was my answer. 'Read the note, and you will see how little it reveals.'

'Perhaps you have read it,' I thought to myself; and yet I could not believe he wrote it: that could hardly be his style: besides, I was fool enough to think there would be a degree of hardship in his calling me such names. His own look vindicated him; he grew hot, and coloured as he read.

'This is indeed too much: this is cruel, this is humiliating,' were the words that fell from him. I thought it *was* cruel, when I saw his countenance so moved. No matter whether he was to blame or not; somebody, it seemed to me, must be more to blame.

'What shall you do about it?' he inquired of me. 'Shall you tell Madame Beck what you have found, and cause a stir – an esclandre?'

I thought I ought to tell, and said so; adding that I did not believe there would be either stir or esclandre: madame was much too prudent to make a noise about an affair of that sort connected with her establishment.

He stood looking down and meditating. He was both too proud and too honourable to entreat my secrecy on a point which duty evidently commanded me to communicate. I wished to do right, yet loathed to grieve or injure him. Just then Rosine glanced out through the open door; she could not see us, though between the trees I could plainly see her: her dress was gray, like mine. This circumstance, taken in connection with prior transactions, suggested to me that perhaps the case, however deplorable, was one in which I was under no obligation whatever to concern myself. Accordingly, I said, –

'If you can assure me that none of Madame Beck's pupils are implicated in this business, I shall be very happy to stand aloof from all interference. Take the casket, the bouquet, and the billet; for my part, I gladly forget the whole affair.'

'Look there!' he whispered suddenly, as his hand closed on what I offered, and at the same time he pointed through the boughs.

I looked. Behold madame, in shawl, wrapping-gown, and slippers, softly descending the steps, and stealing like a cat round the garden: in two minutes she would have been upon Dr John. If *she* were like a cat, however, *he*, quite as much, resembled a leopard: nothing could be lighter than his tread when he chose. He watched, and as she turned a corner, he took the garden at two noiseless bounds.

She reappeared, and he was gone. Rosine helped him, instantly interposing the door between him and his huntress. I too might have got away, but I preferred to meet madame openly.

Though it was my frequent and well-known custom to spend twilight in the garden, yet, never till now, had I remained so late. Full sure was I that madame had missed – was come in search of me, and designed now to pounce on the defaulter unawares. I expected a reprimand. No. Madame was all goodness. She tendered not even a remonstrance; she testified no shade of surprise. With that consummate tact of hers, in which I believe she was never surpassed by living thing, she even professed merely to have issued forth to taste 'la brise du soir.'

'Quelle belle nuit!' cried she, looking up at the stars – the moon was now gone down behind the broad tower of Jean Baptiste. 'Qu'il fait bon! que l'air est frais!'

And, instead of sending me in, she detained me to take a few turns with her down the principal alley. When at last we both re-entered, she leaned affably on my shoulder by way of support in mounting the front-door steps; at parting, her cheek was presented to my lips, and 'Bon soir, ma bonne amie; dormez bien!'[81] was her kindly adieu for the night.

I caught myself smiling as I lay awake and thoughtful on my couch – smiling at madame. The unction, the suavity of her behaviour offered, for one who knew her, a sure token that suspicion of some kind was busy in her brain. From some aperture or summit of observation, through parted bough or open window, she had doubtless caught a glimpse, remote or near, deceptive or instructive, of that night's transactions. Finely accomplished as she was in the art of surveillance, it was next to impossible that a casket could be thrown into her garden, or an interloper could cross her walks to seek it, without that she, in shaken branch, passing shade, unwonted footfall, or stilly murmur (and though Dr John had spoken very low in the few words he dropped to me, yet the hum of his man's voice pervaded, I thought, the whole conventual ground) without, I say, that she should have caught intimation of things extraordinary transpiring on her premises. *What* things, she might by no means see, or at that time be able to discover; but a delicious little ravelled plot lay tempting her to disentanglement; and in the midst, folded round and round in cobwebs, had she not secured 'Meess Lucie,' clumsily involved, like the foolish fly she was?

CHAPTER 13

A Sneeze out of Season

I HAD OCCASION TO SMILE – nay, to laugh, at madame again, within the space of four and twenty hours after the little scene treated of in the last chapter.

Villette owns a climate as variable, though not so humid, as that of any English town. A night of high wind followed upon that soft sunset, and all the next day was one of dry storm – dark, beclouded, yet rainless, – the streets were dim with sand and dust, whirled from the boulevards. I know not that even lovely weather would have tempted me to spend the evening-time of study and recreation, where I had spent it yesterday. My alley, and, indeed, all the walks and shrubs in the garden, had acquired a new, but not a pleasant interest; their seclusion was now become precarious; their calm – insecure. That casement which rained billets, had vulgarized the once dear nook it overlooked; and elsewhere, the eyes of the flowers had gained vision, and the knots in the tree-boles listened like secret ears. Some plants there were, indeed, trodden down by Dr John in his search, and his hasty and heedless progress, which I wished to prop up, water, and revive; some foot-marks, too, he had left on the beds: but these, in spite of the strong wind, I found a moment's leisure to efface very early in the morning, ere common eyes had discovered them. With a pensive sort of content, I sat down to my desk and my German, while the pupils settled to their evening lessons, and the other teachers took up their needlework.

The scene of the 'Etude du soir' was always the refectory, a much smaller apartment than any of the three classes or schoolrooms; for here none, save the boarders, were ever admitted, and these numbered only a score. Two lamps hung from the ceiling over the two tables; these were lit at dusk, and their kindling was the signal for school-books being set aside, a grave demeanour assumed, general silence enforced, and then commenced 'la lecture pieuse.' This said 'lecture pieuse' was, I soon found, mainly designed as a wholesome mortification of the Intellect, a useful humiliation of the

Reason; and such a dose for Common Sense as she might digest at her leisure, and thrive on as she best could.

The book brought out (it was never changed, but when finished, recommenced) was a venerable volume, old as the hills – gray as the Hôtel de Ville.

I would have given two francs for the chance of getting that book once into my hands, turning over the sacred yellow leaves, ascertaining the title, and perusing with my own eyes the enormous figments which, as an unworthy heretic, it was only permitted me to drink in with my bewildered ears. This book contained legends of the saints. Good God! (I speak the words reverently) what legends they were. What gasconading rascals those saints must have been, if they first boasted these exploits or invented these miracles! These legends, however, were no more than monkish extravagances, over which one laughed inwardly; there were, besides, priestly matters, and the priestcraft of the book was far worse than its monkery. The ears burned on each side of my head as I listened, perforce, to tales of moral martyrdom inflicted by Rome; the dread boasts of confessors, who had wickedly abused their office, trampling to deep degradation high-born ladies, making of countesses and princesses the most tormented slaves under the sun. Stories like that of Conrad and Elizabeth of Hungary,[82] recurred again and again, with all its dreadful viciousness, sickening tyranny and black impiety: tales that were nightmares of oppression, privation, and agony.

I sat out this 'lecture pieuse' for some nights as well as I could, and as quietly too; only once breaking off the points of my scissors by involuntarily sticking them somewhat deep in the worm-eaten board of the table before me. But, at last, it made me so burning hot, and my temples and my heart and my wrist throbbed so fast, and my sleep afterwards was so broken with excitement, that I could sit no longer. Prudence recommended henceforward a swift clearance of my person from the place, the moment that guilty old book was brought out. No Mause Headrigg ever felt a stronger call to take up her testimony against Sergeant Bothwell,[83] than I – to speak my mind in this matter of the popish 'lecture pieuse.' However, I did manage somehow to curb and rein in; and though always, as soon as Rosine came to light the lamps, I shot from the room quickly, yet also I did it quietly; seizing that vantage moment given by the little bustle before the dead silence, and vanishing whilst the boarders put their books away.

When I vanished – it was into darkness; candles were not allowed to be carried about, and the teacher who forsook the refectory, had only the unlit hall, school-room, or bed-room, as a refuge. In winter I sought the long classes, and paced them fast to keep myself warm – fortunate if the moon shone, and if there were only stars, soon reconciled to their dim gleam, or even to the total eclipse of their absence. In summer it was never quite dark, and then I went upstairs to my own quarter of the long dormitory, opened my own casement (that chamber was lit by five casements large as great doors), and leaning out, looked forth upon the city beyond the garden, and listened to band-music from the park or the palace-square, thinking meantime my own thoughts, living my own life in my own still, shadow-world.

This evening, fugitive as usual before the Pope and his works, I mounted the staircase, approached the dormitory, and quietly opened the door which was always kept carefully shut, and which, like every other door in this house, revolved noiselessly on well-oiled hinges. Before I *saw*, I *felt* that life was in the great room, usually void: not that there was either stir or breath, or rustle of sound, but Vacuum lacked, Solitude was not at home. All the white beds – the 'lits d'ange,' as they were poetically termed – lay visible at a glance; all were empty: no sleeper reposed therein. The sound of a drawer cautiously slid out struck my ear; stepping a little to one side, my vision took a free range, unimpeded by falling curtains. I now commanded my own bed and my own toilet, with a locked work-box upon it, and locked drawers underneath.

Very good. A dumpy, motherly, little body, in decent shawl and the cleanest of possible night-caps, stood before this toilet, hard at work, apparently doing me the kindness of 'tidying out' the 'meuble.' Open stood the lid of the work-box, open the top drawer; duly and impartially was each succeeding drawer opened in turn: not an article of their contents but was lifted and unfolded, not a paper but was glanced over, not a little box but was unlidded; and beautiful was the adroitness, exemplary the care with which the search was accomplished. Madame wrought at it like a true star, 'unhasting yet unresting.' I will not deny that it was with a secret glee I watched her. Had I been a gentleman, I believe madame would have found favour in my eyes, she was so handy, neat, thorough in all she did: some people's movements provoke the soul by their loose awkwardness, hers – satisfied by their trim compactness. I stood, in short, fascinated; but it was necessary to make an effort to break this spell: a retreat must be beaten. The searcher might have turned and caught me; there would have been nothing for it then but a scene, and she and I would have had to come all at once, with a sudden clash, to a thorough knowledge of each other: down would have gone conventionalities, away swept disguises, and *I* should have looked into her eyes, and *she* into mine – we should have known that we could work together no more, and parted in this life for ever.

Where was the use of tempting such a catastrophe? I was not angry, and had no wish in the world to leave her. I could hardly get another employer whose yoke would be so light and so easy of carriage; and truly, I liked madame for her capital sense, whatever I might think of her principles: as to her system, it did me no harm; she might work me with it to her heart's content: nothing would come of the operation. Loverless and inexpectant of love, I was as safe from spies in my heart-poverty, as the beggar from thieves in his destitution of purse. I turned, then, and fled; descending the stairs with progress as swift and soundless as that of the spider, which at the same instant ran down the bannister.

How I laughed when I reached the school-room. I knew now she had certainly seen Dr John in the garden; I knew what her thoughts were. The spectacle of a suspicious nature so far misled by its own inventions, tickled me much. Yet as the laugh died, a kind of wrath smote me, and then bitterness followed: it was the rock struck, and Meribah's waters gushing out. I never had felt so strange and contradictory an inward tumult as I felt for an hour that evening: soreness and laughter, and fire, and grief, shared my heart between them. I cried hot tears; not because madame mistrusted me – I did not care twopence for her mistrust – but for other reasons. Complicated, disquieting thoughts broke up the whole repose of my nature. However, that turmoil subsided: next day I was again Lucy Snowe.

On revisiting my drawers, I found them all securely locked; the closest subsequent examination could not discover change or apparent disturbance in the position of one object. My few dresses were folded as I had left them; a certain little bunch of white violets that had once been silently presented to me by a stranger (a stranger to me, for we had never exchanged words), and which I had dried and kept for its sweet perfume between the folds of my best dress, lay there unstirred; my black silk scarf, my lace chemisettes and collars were unrumpled. Had she creased one solitary article, I own I should have felt much greater difficulty in forgiving her; but finding all straight and orderly, I said, 'Let bygones be bygones. I am unharmed: why should I bear malice?'

A thing there was which puzzled myself, and I sought in my brain a key to that riddle almost as sedulously as madame had sought a guide to useful knowledge in my toilet drawers. How was it that Dr John, if he had not been accessory to the dropping of that casket into the garden, should have known that it *was* dropped, and appeared so promptly on the spot to seek it? So strong was the wish to clear up this point that I began to entertain this daring suggestion:

'Why may I not, in case I should ever have the opportunity, ask Dr John himself to explain this coincidence?'

And so long as Dr John was absent, I really believed I had courage to test him with such a question.

Little Georgette was now convalescent; and her physician accordingly made his visits very rare: indeed, he would have ceased them altogether, had not madame insisted on his giving an occasional call till the child should be quite well.

She came into the nursery one evening just after I had listened to Georgette's lisped and broken prayer, and had put her to bed. Taking the little one's hand, she said:

'Cette enfant a toujours un peu de fièvre.' And presently afterwards, looking at me with a quicker glance than was habitual to her quiet eye, 'Le Docteur John l'a-t-il vue dernièrement? Non, n'est-ce pas?'

Of course, she knew this better than any other person in the house. 'Well,' she continued, 'I am going out, pour faire quelques courses en fiacre. I shall call on Dr John, and send him to the child. I will that he sees her this very evening; her cheeks are flushed, her pulse is quick: *you* will receive him – for my part, I shall be from home.'

Now the child was well enough, only warm with the warmth of July; it was scarcely less needful to send for a priest to administer extreme unction, than for a doctor to prescribe a dose; also madame rarely made 'courses' as she called them, in the evening: moreover, this was the first time she had chosen to absent herself on the occasion of a visit from Dr John. The whole arrangement indicated some plan; this I saw, but without the least anxiety. 'Ha! ha! madame,' laughed Light-heart the Beggar, 'your crafty wits are on the wrong tack.'

She departed, attired very smartly in a shawl of price, and a certain *chapeau vert tendre*[84] – hazardous, as to its tint, for any complexion less fresh than her own, but, to her, not unbecoming. I wondered what she intended: whether she really would send Dr John or not; or whether indeed he would come: he might be engaged.

Madame had charged me not to let Georgette sleep till the doctor came; I had therefore sufficient occupation in telling her nursery tales and palavering the little language for her benefit. I affected Georgette; she was a sensitive and a loving child: to hold her in my lap, or carry her in my arms was to me a treat. To-night she would have me lay my head on the pillow of her crib; she even put her little arms round my neck. Her clasp and the nestling action with which she pressed her cheek to mine, made me almost cry with a tender pain. Feeling of no kind abounded in that house; this pure little drop from a pure little source was too sweet: it penetrated deep, and subdued the heart, and sent a gush to the eyes.

Half an hour or an hour passed; Georgette murmured in her soft lisp that she was growing sleepy. 'And you *shall* sleep,' thought I, 'malgré maman and médecin, if they are not here in ten minutes.'

Hark! There was the ring, and there the tread, astonishing the staircase by the fleetness with which it left the steps behind. Rosine introduced Dr John, and, with a freedom of manner not altogether peculiar to herself, but characteristic of the domestics of Villette generally, she stayed to hear what he had to say. Madame's presence would have awed her back to her own realm of the vestibule and the cabinet – for mine, or that of any other teacher or pupil, she cared not a jot. Smart, trim and pert, she stood, a hand in each pocket of her gay grisette apron, eyeing Dr John with no more fear or shyness than if he had been a picture instead of a living gentleman.

'Le marmot n'a rien n'est ce pas?' said she, indicating Georgette with a jerk of her chin.

'Pas beaucoup,'[85] was the answer, as the doctor hastily scribbled with his pencil some harmless prescription.

'Eh bien!' pursued Rosine, approaching him quite near, while he put up his pencil. 'And the box – did you get it? Monsieur went off like a coup de vent the other night; I had not time to ask him.'

'I found it: yes.'

'And who threw it then?' continued Rosine, speaking quite freely the very words I should so much have wished to say, but had no address or courage to bring out: how short some people make the road to a point which, for others, seems unattainable!

'That may be my secret,' rejoined Dr John briefly, but with no sort of hauteur: he seemed quite to understand the Rosine or grisette character.

'Mais enfin,' continued she, nothing abashed, 'monsieur knew it was thrown, since he came to seek it – how did he know?'

'I was attending a little patient in the college near,' said he, 'and saw it dropped out of his chamber window, and so came to pick it up.'

How simple the whole explanation! The note had alluded to a physician as then examining 'Gustave.'

'Ah ça!' pursued Rosine, 'Il n'y a donc rien là-dessous: pas de mystère, pas d'amourette, par exemple?'

'Pas plus que sur ma main,' responded the doctor, showing his palm.

'Quel dommage!' responded the grisette: 'et moi – à qui tout cela commencait à donner des idées.'

'Vraiment! vous en êtes pour vos frais,'[86] was the doctor's cool rejoinder.

She pouted. The doctor could not help laughing at the sort of 'moue' she made: when he laughed, he had something peculiarly good-natured and genial in his look. I saw his hand incline to his pocket.

'How many times have you opened the door for me within this last month?' he asked.

'Monsieur ought to have kept count of that,' said Rosine, quite readily.

'As if I had not something better to do!' rejoined he; but I saw him give her a piece of gold, which she took unscrupulously, and then danced off to answer the door-bell, ringing just now every five minutes, as the various servants came to fetch the half-boarders.

The reader must not think too hardly of Rosine; on the whole, she was not a bad sort of person, and had no idea there could be any disgrace in grasping at whatever she could get, or any effrontery in chattering like a pie to the best gentleman in Christendom.

I had learnt something from the above scene besides what concerned the ivory box: viz., that not on the robe de jaconas, pink or gray, nor yet on the frilled and pocketted apron, lay the blame of breaking Dr John's heart: these items of array were obviously guiltless as Georgette's little blue tunic. So much the better. But who then was the culprit? What was the ground – what the origin – what the perfect explanation of the whole business? Some points had been cleared, but how many yet remained obscure as night?

'However,' I said to myself, 'it is no affair of yours;' and turning from the face on which I had been unconsciously dwelling with a questioning gaze, I looked through the window which commanded the garden below. Dr John, meantime, standing by the bed-side, was slowly drawing on his gloves and watching his little patient, as her eyes closed and her rosy lips parted in coming sleep. I waited till he should depart as usual, with a quick bow and scarce articulate 'good night.' Just as he took his hat, my eyes, fixed on the tall houses bounding the garden, saw the one lattice, already commemorated, cautiously open; forth from the aperture projected a hand and a white handkerchief; both waved. I know not whether the signal was answered from some viewless quarter of our own dwelling; but immediately after there fluttered from the lattice a falling object, white and light – billet the second, of course.

'There!' I ejaculated involuntarily.

'Where?' asked Dr John with energy, making direct for the window. 'What is it?'

'They have gone and done it again,' was my reply. 'A handkerchief waved and something fell:' and I pointed to the lattice, now closed and looking hypocritically blank.

'Go at once; pick it up and bring it here,' was his prompt direction; adding, 'nobody will take notice of *you*: *I* should be seen.'

Straight I went. After some little search, I found a folded paper, lodged on the lower branch of a shrub; I seized and brought it direct to Dr John. This time, I believe not even Rosine saw me.

He instantly tore the billet into small pieces, without reading it.

'It is not in the least *her* fault, you must remember,' he said, looking at me.

'*Whose* fault?' I asked. '*Who is* it?'

'You don't yet know, then?'

'Not in the least.'

'Have you no guess?'

'None.'

'If I knew you better, I might be tempted to risk some confidence, and thus secure you as guardian over a most innocent and excellent, but somewhat inexperienced being.'

'As a duenna?' I asked.

'Yes,' said he abstractedly. 'What snares are round her!' he added musingly: and now, certainly for the first time, he examined my face, anxious, doubtless, to see if any kindly expression there, would warrant him in recommending to my care and indulgence some ethereal creature, against whom powers of darkness were plotting. I felt no particular vocation to undertake the surveillance of ethereal creatures; but recalling the scene at the bureau, it seemed to me that I owed *him* a good turn: if I *could* help him then I would, and it lay not with me to decide how. With as little reluctance as might be, I intimated that 'I was willing to do what I could towards taking care of any person in whom he might be interested.'

'I am no farther interested than as a spectator,' said he, with a modesty, admirable, as I thought, to witness. 'I happen to be acquainted with the rather worthless character of the person who, from the house opposite, has now twice invaded the sanctity of this place; I have also met in society the object at whom these vulgar attempts are aimed. Her exquisite superiority and innate refinement ought, one would think, to scare impertinence from her very idea. It is not so, however; and innocent, unsuspicious as she is, I would guard her from evil if I could. In person, however, I can do nothing: I cannot come near her' – he paused.

'Well, I am willing to help you,' said I, 'only tell me how.' And busily, in my own mind, I ran over the list of our inmates, seeking this paragon, this pearl of great price, this gem without flaw. 'It must be madame,' I concluded. '*She* only, amongst us all, has the art even to *seem* superior: but as to being unsuspicious, inexperienced, &c., Dr John need not distract himself about that. However, this is just his whim, and I will not contradict him; he shall be humoured: his angel shall be an angel.'

'Just notify the quarter to which my care is to be directed,' I continued gravely: chuckling, however, to myself over the thought of being set to chaperon Madame Beck or any of her pupils.

Now Dr John had a fine set of nerves, and he at once felt by instinct, what no more coarsely constituted mind would have detected; namely, that I was a little amused at him. The colour rose to his cheek; with half a smile he turned and took his hat – he was going. My heart smote me.

'I will – I will help you,' said I eagerly. 'I will do what you wish. I will watch over your angel; I will take care of her, only tell me who she is.'

'But you *must* know,' said he, then with earnestness, yet speaking very low, 'So spotless, so good, so unspeakably beautiful! impossible that one house should contain two like her. I allude, of course – '

Here the latch of Madame Beck's chamber-door (opening into the nursery) gave a sudden click, as if the hand holding it had been slightly convulsed; there was the suppressed explosion of an irrepressible sneeze. These little accidents will happen to the best of us. Madame – excellent woman! – was there on duty. She had come home quietly, stolen up-stairs on tip-toe; she was in her chamber. If she had not sneezed, she would have heard all, and so should I; but that unlucky sternutation routed Dr John. While he stood aghast, she came forward alert, composed, in the best yet most tranquil spirits: no novice to her habits but would have thought she was just come in, and scouted the idea of her ear having been glued to the key-hole for at least ten minutes. She affected to sneeze again, declared she was 'enrhumée,' and then proceeded volubly to recount her 'courses en fiacre.' The prayer-bell rang, and I left her with the doctor.

CHAPTER 14

The Fête

As soon as Georgette was well, madame sent her away into the country. I was sorry; I loved the child, and her loss made me poorer than before. But I must not complain. I lived in a house full of robust life; I might have had companions, and I chose solitude. Each of the teachers in turn made me overtures of special intimacy; I tried them all. One I found to be an honest woman, but a narrow thinker, a coarse feeler, and an egotist. The second was a Parisienne, externally refined – at heart, corrupt – without a creed, without a principle, without an affection: having penetrated the outward crust of decorum in this character, you found a slough beneath. She had a wonderful passion for presents; and, in this point, the third teacher – a person otherwise characterless and insignificant – closely resembled her. This last-named had also one other distinctive property – that of avarice. In her reigned the love of money for its own sake. The sight of a piece of gold would bring into her eyes a green glisten, singular to witness. She once, as a mark of high favour, took me upstairs, and, opening a secret drawer, showed me a hoard – a mass of coarse, large coin – about fifteen guineas, in five-franc pieces. She loved this hoard as a bird loves its eggs. These were her savings. She would come and talk to me about them with an infatuated and persevering dotage, strange to behold in a person not yet twenty-five.

The Parisienne, on the other hand, was prodigal and profligate (in disposition, that is: as to action, I do not know). That latter quality showed its snake-head to me but once, peering out very cautiously. A curious kind of reptile it seemed, judging from the glimpse I got; its novelty whetted my curiosity: if it would have come out boldly, perhaps I might philosophically have stood my ground, and coolly surveyed the long thing from forked tongue to scaly tail-tip; but it merely rustled in the leaves of a bad novel; and, on encountering a hasty and ill-advised demonstration of wrath, recoiled and vanished, hissing. She hated me from that day.

This Parisienne was always in debt; her salary being anticipated, not only in dress, but in perfumes, cosmetics, confectionery, and condiments. What a cold, callous epicure she was in all things! I see her now. Thin in face and figure, sallow in complexion, regular in features, with perfect teeth, lips like a thread, a large, prominent chin, a well-opened, but frozen eye, of light at once craving and ingrate. She mortally hated work, and loved what she called pleasure; being an insipid, heartless, brainless dissipation of time.

Madame Beck knew this woman's character perfectly well. She once talked to me about her, with an odd mixture of discrimination, indifference, and antipathy. I asked why she kept her in the establishment. She answered plainly, 'because it suited her interest to do so;' and pointed out a fact I had already noticed, namely, that Mademoiselle St. Pierre possessed, in an almost unique degree, the power of keeping order amongst her undisciplined ranks of scholars. A certain petrifying influence accompanied and surrounded her: without passion, noise, or violence, she held them in check as a breezeless frost-air might still a brawling stream. She was of little use as far as communication of knowledge went, but for strict surveillance and maintenance of rules she was invaluable. 'Je sais bien qu'elle n'a pas de principes, ni, peut-être, de moeurs,' admitted madame frankly; but added, with philosophy, 'son maintien en classe est toujours convenable et rempli même d'une certaine dignité: c'est tout ce qu'il faut. Ni les élèves, ni les parents ne regardent plus loin; ni, par conséquent, moi non plus.'[87]

A strange, frolicsome, noisy little world was this school: great pains were taken to hide chains with flowers: a subtle essence of Romanism pervaded every arrangement: large sensual indulgence (so to speak) was permitted by way of counterpoise to jealous spiritual restraint. Each mind was being reared in slavery; but, to prevent reflection from dwelling on this fact, every pretext for physical recreation was seized and made the most of. There, as elsewhere, the CHURCH strove to bring up her children robust in body, feeble in soul, fat, ruddy, hale, joyous, ignorant, unthinking, unquestioning. 'Eat, drink, and live!' she says. 'Look after your bodies; leave your souls to me. I hold their cure – guide their course: I guarantee their final fate.' A bargain, in which every true Catholic deems himself a gainer. Lucifer just offers the same terms: 'All this power will I give thee, and the glory of it; for that is delivered unto me, and to whomsoever I will I give it. If thou, therefore, wilt worship me, all shall be thine!'

About this time – in the ripest glow of summer – Madame Beck's house became as merry a place as a school could well be. All day long the broad folding-doors and the two-leaved casements stood wide open: settled sunshine seemed naturalized in the atmosphere; clouds were far off, sailing away beyond sea, resting, no doubt, round islands such as England – that dear land of mists – but withdrawn wholly from the drier continent. We lived far more in the garden than under a roof: classes were held, and meals partaken of, in the 'grand berceau.' Moreover, there was a note of holiday preparation, which almost turned freedom into license. The autumnal long vacation was but two months distant; but before that, a great day – an important ceremony – none other than the fête of madame – awaited celebration.

The conduct of this fête devolved chiefly on Mademoiselle St. Pierre; madame herself being supposed to stand aloof, disinterestedly unconscious of what might be going forward in her honour. Especially, she never knew, never in the least suspected that a subscription was annually levied on the whole school for the purchase of a handsome present. The polite tact of the reader will please to leave out of the account a brief, secret consultation on this point in madame's own chamber.

'What will you have this year?' was asked by her Parisian lieutenant.

'Oh, no matter! Let it alone. Let the poor children keep their francs.' And madame looked benign and modest.

The St. Pierre would here protrude her chin; she knew madame by heart; she always called her airs of 'bonté' – 'des grimaces.' She never even professed to respect them one instant.

'Vite!' she would say coldly. 'Name the article. Shall it be jewellery or porcelain, haberdashery or silver?'

'Eh bien! Deux ou trois cuillers et autant de fourchettes en argent.'[88]

And the result was a handsome case, containing 300 francs worth of plate.

The programme of the fête-day's proceedings comprised: Presentation of plate, collation in the garden, dramatic performance (with pupils and teachers for actors), a dance and supper. Very gorgeous seemed the effect of the whole to me, as I well remember. Zélie St. Pierre understood these things and managed them ably.

The Play was the main point; a month's previous drilling being there required. The choice too of the actors required knowledge and care; then came lessons in elocution, in attitude, and then the fatigue of countless rehearsals. For all this, as may well be supposed,

St. Pierre did not suffice: other management, other accomplishments than hers were requisite here. They were supplied in the person of a master – M. Paul Emanuel, professor of literature. It was never my lot to be present at the histrionic lessons of M. Paul, but I often saw him as he crossed the *carré* (a square hall between the dwelling-house and school-house). I heard him too in the warm evenings, lecturing with open doors, and his name, with anecdotes of him, resounded in one's ears from all sides. Especially our former acquaintance, Miss Ginevra Fanshawe, who had been selected to take a prominent part in the play – used, in bestowing upon me a large portion of her leisure, to lard her discourse with frequent allusions to his sayings and doings. She esteemed him hideously plain, and used to profess herself frightened almost into hysterics at the sound of his step or voice. A dark little man he certainly was; pungent and austere. Even to me he seemed a harsh apparition, with his close-shorn, black head, his broad, sallow brow, his thin cheek, his wide and quivering nostril, his thorough glance and hurried bearing. Irritable he was; one heard that, as he apostrophised with vehemence the awkward squad under his orders. Sometimes he would break out on these raw amateur actresses with a passion of impatience at their falseness of conception, their coldness of emotion, their feebleness of delivery. 'Ecoutez!' he would cry; and then his voice rang through the premises like a trumpet; and when, mimicking it, came the small pipe of a Ginevra, a Mathilde, or a Blanche, one understood why a hollow groan of scorn, or a fierce hiss of rage rewarded the tame echo.

'Vous n'êtes donc que des poupées?' I heard him thunder. 'Vous n'avez pas de passions – vous autres? Vous ne sentez donc rien? Votre chair est de neige, votre sang de glace? Moi, je veux que tout cela s'allume, qu'il ait une vie, une âme!'[89]

Vain resolve! And when he at last found it *was* vain, he suddenly broke the whole business down. Hitherto he had been teaching them a grand tragedy; he tore the tragedy in morsels, and came next day with a compact little comic trifle. To this they took more kindly; he presently knocked it all into their smooth round pates.

Mademoiselle St. Pierre always presided at M. Emanuel's lessons, and I was told that the polish of her manner, her seeming attention, her tact and grace, impressed that gentleman very favourably. She had, indeed, the art of pleasing, for a given time, whom she would; but the feeling would not last: in an hour it was dried like dew, vanished like gossamer.

The day preceding madame's fête was as much a holiday as the fête itself. It was devoted to clearing out, cleaning, arranging and decorating the three schoolrooms. All within doors was the gayest bustle; neither upstairs nor down could a quiet isolated person find rest for the sole of her foot; accordingly, for my part, I took refuge in the garden. The whole day did I wander or sit there alone, finding warmth in the sun, shelter among the trees, and a sort of companionship in my own thoughts. I well remember that I exchanged but two sentences that day with any living being: not that I felt solitary; I was glad to be quiet. For a looker-on, it sufficed to pass through the rooms once or twice, observe what changes were being wrought, how a green-room and a dressing-room were being contrived, a little stage with scenery erected, how M. Paul Emanuel, in conjunction with Mademoiselle St. Pierre, was directing all, and how an eager band of pupils, amongst them Ginevra Fanshawe, were working gaily under his control.

The great day arrived. The sun rose hot and unclouded, and hot and unclouded it burned on till evening. All the doors and all the windows were set open, which gave a pleasant sense of summer freedom – and freedom the most complete seemed indeed the order of the day. Teachers and pupils descended to breakfast in dressing-gowns and curl-papers: anticipating 'avec délices' the toilette of the evening, they seemed to take a pleasure in indulging that forenoon a luxury of slovenliness; like aldermen, fasting in preparation for a feast. About nine o'clock, A.M., an important functionary, the 'coiffeur,' arrived. Sacrilegious to state, he fixed his head-quarters in the oratory, and there, in presence of *bénitier*, candle, and crucifix, solemnized the mysteries of his art. Each girl was summoned in turn to pass through his hands; emerging from them with head as smooth as a shell, intersected by faultless white lines, and wreathed about with Grecian plaits that shone as if lacquered. I took my turn with the rest, and could hardly believe what the glass said when I applied to it for information afterwards; the lavish garlandry of woven brown hair amazed me – feared it was not all my own, and it required several convincing pulls to give assurance to the contrary. I then acknowledged in the coiffeur a first-rate artist – one who certainly made the most of indifferent materials.

The oratory closed, the dormitory became the scene of ablutions, arrayings and bedizenings curiously elaborate. To me it was, and ever must be an enigma, how they contrived to spend so much time in doing so little. The operation seemed close, intricate, prolonged: the result simple. A clear white muslin dress, a blue sash (the Virgin's colours), a pair of white, or straw-colour kid gloves – such was the gala uniform, to the assumption whereof that houseful of teachers and pupils devoted three mortal hours. But though simple, it must be allowed the array was perfect – perfect in fashion, fit, and freshness; every head being also dressed with exquisite nicety, and a certain compact taste – suiting the full, firm comeliness of Labassecourien contours, though too stiff for any more flowing and flexile style of beauty – the general effect was, on the whole, commendable.

In beholding this diaphanous and snowy mass, I well remember feeling myself to be a mere shadowy spot on a field of light; the courage was not in me to put on a transparent white dress: something thin I must wear – the weather and rooms being too hot to give substantial fabrics sufferance, so I had sought through a dozen shops till I lit upon a crape-like material of purple-gray – the colour, in short, of dun mist, lying on a moor in bloom. My *tailleuse* had kindly made it as well as she could: because, as she judiciously observed, it was 'si triste – si peu voyant,' care in the fashion was the more imperative: it was well she took this view of the matter, for I had no flower, no jewel to relieve it; and, what was more, I had no natural rose of complexion.

We become oblivious of these deficiencies in the uniform routine of daily drudgery, but they *will* force upon us their unwelcome blank on those bright occasions when beauty should shine.

However, in this same gown of shadow, I felt at home and at ease; an advantage I should not have enjoyed in anything more brilliant or striking. Madame Beck, too, kept me in countenance; her dress was almost as quiet as mine, except that she wore a bracelet, and a large brooch bright with gold and fine stones. We chanced to meet on the stairs, and she gave me a nod and smile of approbation. Not that she thought I was looking well – a point unlikely to engage her interest – but she considered me dressed 'convenablement,' 'décemment,' and la Convenance et la Décence were the two calm deities of madame's worship. She even paused, laid on my shoulder her gloved hand, holding an embroidered and perfumed handkerchief, and confided to my ear a sarcasm on the other teachers (whom she had just been complimenting to their faces). 'Nothing so absurd,' she said, 'as for des femmes mûres "to dress themselves like girls of fifteen" – quant à la St. Pierre, elle a l'air d'une vieille coquette qui fait l'ingénue.'[90]

Being dressed at least a couple of hours before anybody else, I felt a pleasure in betaking myself – not to the garden, where servants were busy propping up long tables, placing seats, and spreading cloths in readiness for the collation – but to the school-rooms, now empty, quiet, cool, and clean; their walls fresh stained, their planked floors fresh scoured and scarce dry; flowers fresh gathered adorning the recesses in pots, and draperies, fresh hung, beautifying the great windows.

Withdrawing to the first classe, a smaller and neater room than the others, and taking from the glazed book-case, of which I kept the key, a volume whose title promised some interest, I sat down to read. The glass-door of this 'classe,' or school-room, opened into the large berceau; acacia-boughs caressed its panes, as they stretched across to meet a rose-bush blooming by the opposite lintel: in this rose-bush, bees murmured busy and happy. I commenced reading. Just as the stilly hum, the embowering shade, the warm, lonely calm of my retreat were beginning to steal meaning from the page, vision from my eyes, and to lure me along the track of reverie, down into some deep dell of dream-land – just then, the sharpest ring of the street-door bell to which that much-tried instrument had ever thrilled, snatched me back to consciousness.

Now, the bell had been ringing all the morning, as workmen, or servants, or *coiffeurs*, or *tailleuses*, went and came on their several errands. Moreover, there was good reason to expect it would ring all the afternoon, since about one hundred externes were yet to arrive in carriages or fiacres: nor could it be expected to rest during the evening, when parents and friends would gather thronging to the play. Under these circumstances, a ring – even a sharp ring – was a matter of course: yet this particular peal had an accent of its own, which chased my dream, and startled my book from my knee.

I was stooping to pick up this last, when – firm, fast, straight – right on through vestibule, along corridor, across carré, through first division, second division, grande salle – strode a step, quick, regular, intent. The closed door of the first classe – my sanctuary – offered no obstacle; it burst open, and a paletôt and a bonnet grec filled the void; also two eyes first vaguely struck upon, and then hungrily dived into me.

'C'est cela!' said a voice. 'Je la connais: c'est l'Anglaise. Tant pis. Toute Anglaise, et par conséquent, toute bégueule qu'elle soit – elle fera mon affaire, ou je saurai pourquoi.'[91]

Then, with a certain stern politeness (I suppose he thought I had not caught the drift of his previous uncivil mutterings), and in a jargon the most execrable that ever was heard, 'Meess – play you must: I am planted there.'

'What can I do for you, M. Paul Emanuel?' I inquired: for M. Paul Emanuel it was, and in a state of no little excitement.

'Play you must. I will not have you shrink, or frown, or make the prude. I read your skull, that night you came; I see your moyens: play you can; play you must.'

'But how, M. Paul? What do you mean?'

'There is no time to be lost,' he went on now speaking in French; 'and let us thrust to the wall all reluctance, all excuses, all minauderies. You must take a part.'

'In the vaudeville?'

'In the vaudeville. You have said it.'

I gasped, horror-struck. *What* did the little man mean?

'Listen!' he said. 'The case shall be stated, and you shall then answer me Yes, or No; and according to your answer shall I ever after estimate you.'

The scarce-suppressed impetus of a most irritable nature glowed in his cheek, fed with sharp shafts his glances, a nature – the injudicious, the mawkish, the hesitating, the sullen, the affected, above all, the unyielding, might quickly render violent and implacable. Silence and attention was the best balm to apply: I listened.

'The whole matter is going to fail,' he began. 'Louise Vanderkelkov has fallen ill – at least so her ridiculous mother asserts; for my part, I feel sure she might play if she would: it is only good-will that lacks. She was charged with a *rôle*, as you know, or do *not* know – it is equal: without that *rôle* the play is stopped. There are now but a few hours in which to learn it: not a girl in this school would hear reason, and accept the task. Forsooth, it is not an interesting, not an amiable, part; their vile *amour-propre* – that base quality of which women have so much – would revolt from it. Englishwomen are either the best or the worst of their sex. Dieu sait que je les déteste comme la peste, ordinairement' (this between his recreant teeth). 'I apply to an Englishwoman to rescue me. What is her answer – Yes, or No?'

A thousand objections rushed into my mind. The foreign language, the limited time, the public display. Inclination recoiled, Ability faltered, Self-respect (that 'vile quality') trembled. 'Non, non, non!' said all these; but looking up at M. Paul, and seeing in his vexed, fiery, and searching eye, a sort of appeal behind all its menace – my lips dropped the word 'oui.' For a moment, his rigid countenance relaxed with a quiver of content: quickly bent up again, however, he went on, –

'Vite a l'ouvrage! Here is the book; here is your *rôle*: read.' And I read. He did not commend; at some passages he scowled and stamped. He gave me a lesson: I diligently imitated. It was a disagreeable part, – a man's – an empty-headed fop's. One could put

into it neither heart nor soul: I hated it. The play – a mere trifle –
ran chiefly on the efforts of a brace of rivals to gain the hand of a
fair coquette. One lover was called the 'Ours,' a good and gallant
but unpolished man, a sort of diamond in the rough; the other was a
butterfly, a talker, and a traitor: and I was to be the butterfly, talker,
and traitor.

I did my best – which was bad, I know: it provoked M. Paul; he
fumed. Putting both hands to the work, I endeavoured to do better
than my best; I presume he gave me credit for good intentions; he
professed to be partially content. 'Ça ira!' he cried; and as voices
began sounding from the garden, and white dresses fluttering
among the trees, he added: 'You must withdraw: you must be alone
to learn this. Come with me.'

Without being allowed time or power to deliberate, I found myself
in the same breath convoyed along as in a species of whirlwind, up
stairs, up two pair of stairs, nay, actually up three (for this fiery little
man seemed as by instinct to know his way everywhere); to the
solitary and lofty attic was I borne, put in and locked in, the key
being on the door, and that key he took with him, and vanished.

The attic was no pleasant place: I believe he did not know how
unpleasant it was, or he never would have locked me in with so little
ceremony. In this summer weather, it was hot as Africa; as in winter,
it was always cold as Greenland. Boxes and lumber filled it; old
dresses draped its unstained wall – cobwebs its unswept ceiling.
Well was it known to be tenanted by rats, by black beetles, and by
cockroaches – nay, rumour affirmed that the ghostly Nun of the
garden had once been seen here. A partial darkness obscured one
end, across which, as for deeper mystery, an old russet curtain was
drawn, by way of screen to a sombre band of winter cloaks, pendant
each from its pin like a malefactor from his gibbet. From amongst
these cloaks, and behind that curtain, the Nun was said to issue. I
did not believe this, nor was I troubled by apprehension thereof; but
I saw a very dark and large rat, with a long tail, come gliding out
from that squalid alcove; and, moreover, my eye fell on many a
black beetle, dotting the floor. These objects discomposed me
more, perhaps, than it would be wise to say, as also did the dust,
lumber, and stifling heat of the place. The last inconvenience would
soon have become intolerable, had I not found means to open and
prop up the sky-light, thus admitting some freshness. Underneath
this aperture I pushed a large empty chest, and having mounted
upon it a smaller box, and wiped from both the dust, I gathered my
dress (my best, the reader must remember, and therefore a

legitimate object of care) fastidiously round me, ascended this species of extempore throne, and being seated, commenced the acquisition of my task; while I learned, not forgetting to keep a sharp look-out on the black beetles and cockroaches, of which, more even, I believe, than of the rats, I sat in mortal dread.

My impression at first was that I had undertaken what it really was impossible to perform, and I simply resolved to do my best and be resigned to fail. I soon found, however, that one part in so short a piece was not more than memory could master at a few hours' notice. I learned and learned on, first in a whisper, and then aloud. Perfectly secure from human audience, I acted my part before the garret-vermin. Entering into its emptiness, frivolity, and falsehood, with a spirit inspired by scorn and impatience, I took my revenge on this 'fat,' by making him as fatuitous as I possibly could.

In this exercise the afternoon passed: day began to glide into evening; and I, who had eaten nothing since breakfast, grew excessively hungry. Now I thought of the collation, which doubtless they were just then devouring in the garden far below. (I had seen in the vestibule a basketful of small *pâtés à la crême*, than which nothing in the whole range of cookery seemed to me better). A *pâté*, or a square of cake, it seemed to me would come very *apropos*; and as my relish for these dainties increased, it began to appear somewhat hard that I should pass my holiday, fasting and in prison. Remote as was the attic from the street-door and vestibule, yet the ever-tinkling bell was faintly audible here; and also the ceaseless roll of wheels on the tormented pavement. I knew that the house and garden were thronged, and that all was gay and glad below; here it began to grow dusk: the beetles were fading from my sight; I trembled lest they should steal on me a march, mount my throne unseen, and, unsuspected, invade my skirts. Impatient and apprehensive, I recommenced the rehearsal of my part merely to kill time. Just as I was concluding, the long-delayed rattle of the key in the lock came to my ear – no unwelcome sound. M. Paul (I could just see through the dusk that it *was* M. Paul, for light enough still lingered to show the velvet blackness of his close-shorn head, and the sallow ivory of his brow) looked in.

'Brava!' cried he, holding the door open, and remaining at the threshold. 'J'ai tout entendu. C'est assez bien. Encore!'

A moment I hesitated.

'Encore!' said he sternly. 'Et point de grimaces! A bas la timidité!'[92]

Again I went through the part, but not half so well as I had spoken it alone.

'Enfin, elle le sait,' said he, half dissatisfied, 'and one cannot be fastidious or exacting under the circumstances.' Then he added, 'You may yet have twenty minutes for preparation: au revoir!' And he was going.

'Monsieur,' I called out, taking courage.

'Eh bien. Qu'est ce que c'est, mademoiselle?'

'J'ai bien faim.'

'Comment, vous avez faim! Et la collation?'

'I know nothing about it. I have not seen it, shut up here.'

'Ah! C'est vrai,'[93] cried he.

In a moment my throne was abdicated, the attic evacuated; an inverse repetition of the impetus which had brought me up into the attic, instantly took me down – down – down to the very kitchen. I thought I should have gone to the cellar. The cook was imperatively ordered to produce food, and I, as imperatively, was commanded to eat. To my great joy this food was limited to coffee and cake: I had feared wine and sweets, which I did not like. How he guessed that I should like a *petit pâté à la crême* I cannot tell; but he went out and procured me one from some quarter. With considerable willingness I ate and drank, keeping the *petit pâté* till the last, as a *bonne bouche*. M. Paul superintended my repast, and almost forced upon me more than I could swallow.

'A la bonne heure,' he cried, when I signified that I really could take no more, and, with uplifted hands, implored to be spared the additional roll on which he had just spread butter. 'You will set me down as a species of tyrant and Blue-beard, starving women in a garret; whereas, after all, I am no such thing. Now, mademoiselle, do you feel courage and strength to appear?'

I said, I thought I did; though, in truth, I was perfectly confused, and could hardly tell how I felt: but this little man was of the order of beings who must not be opposed, unless you possessed an all-dominant force sufficient to crush him at once.

'Come then,' said he, offering his hand.

I gave him mine, and he set off with a rapid walk, which obliged me to run at his side in order to keep pace. In the carré he stopped a moment; it was lit with large lamps; the wide doors of the classes were open, and so were the equally wide garden-doors; orange-trees in tubs, and tall flowers in pots, ornamented these portals on each side; groups of ladies and gentlemen in evening-dress stood and walked amongst the flowers. Within, the long vista of the school-rooms presented a thronging, undulating, murmuring, waving, streaming multitude, all rose, and blue, and half translucent white.

There were lustres burning overhead; far off there was a stage, a solemn green curtain, a row of foot-lights.

'N'est-ce pas que c'est beau?' demanded my companion.

I should have said it was, but my heart got up into my throat. M. Paul discovered this, and gave me a side-scowl and a little shake for my pains.

'I will do my best, but I wish it was over,' said I; then I asked: 'Are we to walk through that crowd?'

'By no means: I manage matters better: we pass through the garden – here.'

In an instant we were out of doors; the cool, calm night revived me somewhat. It was moonless, but the reflex from the many glowing windows lit the court brightly, and even the alleys – dimly. Heaven was cloudless, and grand with the quiver of its living fires. How soft are the nights of the continent! How bland, balmy, safe! No sea-fog; no chilling damp: mistless as noon, and fresh as morning.

Having crossed court and garden, we reached the glass door of the first classe. It stood open, like all other doors that night; we passed, and then I was ushered into a small cabinet, dividing the first classe from the grande salle. This cabinet dazzled me, it was so full of light: it deafened me, it was so clamorous with voices: it stifled me, it was so hot, choking, thronged.

'De l'ordre! Du silence!' cried M. Paul. 'Is this chaos?' he demanded; and there was a hush. With a dozen words, and as many gestures, he turned out half the persons present, and obliged the remnant to fall into rank. Those left were all in costume: they were the performers, and this was the green-room. M. Paul introduced me. All stared and some tittered. It was a surprise: they had not expected the Englishwoman would play in a *vaudeville*. Ginevra Fanshawe, beautifully dressed for her part, and looking fascinatingly pretty, turned on me a pair of eyes as round as beads. In the highest spirit, unperturbed by fear or bashfulness, delighted indeed at the thought of shining off before hundreds – my entrance seemed to transfix her with amazement in the midst of her joy. She would have exclaimed, but M. Paul held her and all the rest in check.

Having surveyed and criticised the whole troop, he turned to me.

'You, too, must be dressed for your part.'

'Dressed – dressed like a man!' exclaimed Zélie St. Pierre, darting forwards; adding with officiousness, 'I will dress her myself.'

To be dressed like a man did not please, and would not suit me. I had consented to take a man's name and part; as to his dress – *halte là*! No. I would keep my own dress; come what might. M. Paul might storm, might rage: I would keep my own dress. I said so, with a voice as resolute in intent, as it was low, and perhaps unsteady, in utterance.

He did not immediately storm or rage, as I fully thought he would: he stood silent. But Zélie again interposed.

'She will make a capital *petit-maître*. Here are the garments, all – all complete: somewhat too large, but I will arrange all that. Come chère amie – belle Anglaise!'

And she sneered, for I was not 'belle.' She seized my hand, she was drawing me away. M. Paul stood impassible – neutral.

'You must not resist,' pursued St. Pierre – for resist I did. 'You will spoil all, destroy the mirth of the piece, the enjoyment of the company, sacrifice everything to your *amour-propre*. This would be too bad – monsieur will never permit this?'

She sought his eye. I watched, likewise, for a glance. He gave her one, and then he gave me one. 'Stop!' he said slowly, arresting St. Pierre, who continued her efforts to drag me after her. Everybody awaited the decision. He was not angry, not irritated; I perceived that and took heart.

'You do not like these clothes?' he asked, pointing to the masculine vestments.

'I don't object to some of them, but I won't have them all.'

'How must it be, then? How, accept a man's part, and go on the stage dressed as a woman? This is an amateur affair, it is true – a *vaudeville de pensionnat*; certain modifications I might sanction, yet something you must have to announce you as of the nobler sex.'

'And I will, monsieur; but it must be arranged in my own way: nobody must meddle; the things must not be forced upon me. Just let me dress myself.'

Monsieur, without another word, took the costume from St. Pierre, gave it to me, and permitted me to pass into the dressing-room. Once alone, I grew calm, and collectedly went to work. Retaining my woman's garb without the slightest retrenchment, I merely assumed in addition, a little vest, a collar, and cravat, and a paletôt of small dimensions; the whole being the costume of a brother of one of the pupils. Having loosened my hair out of its braids, made up the long back hair close, and brushed the front hair to one side, I took my hat and gloves in my hand and came out. M. Paul was waiting and so were the others. He looked at me. 'That may pass in a Pensionnat,' he pronounced. Then added, not unkindly, 'Courage, mon ami! Un peu de sang froid – un peu d'aplomb, M. Lucien, et tout ira bien.'[94]

St. Pierre sneered again, in her cold, snaky manner.

I was irritable, because excited, and I could not help turning upon her and saying, that if she were not a lady and I a gentleman, I should feel disposed to call her out.

'After the play, after the play,' said M. Paul. 'I will then divide my pair of pistols between you, and we will settle the dispute according to form: it will only be the old quarrel of France and England.'

But now the moment approached for the performance to commence. M. Paul setting us before him, harangued us briefly, like a general addressing soldiers about to charge. I don't know what he said, except that he recommended each to penetrate herself well with a sense of her personal significance. God knows, I thought this advice superfluous for some of us. A bell tinkled. I and two more were ushered on to the stage. The bell tinkled again. I had to speak the very first words.

'Do not look at the crowd, nor think of it,' whispered M. Paul in my ear. 'Imagine yourself in the garret, acting to the rats.'

He vanished. The curtain drew up – shrivelled to the ceiling; the bright lights, the long room, the gay throng burst upon us. I thought of the black beetles, the old boxes, the worm-eaten bureaus. I said my say badly; but I said it. That first speech was the difficulty; it revealed to me this fact, that it was not the crowd I feared, so much as my own voice. Foreigners and strangers, the crowd were nothing to me. Nor did I think of them. When my tongue once got free, and my voice took its true pitch, and found its natural tone, I thought of nothing but the personage I represented – and of M. Paul, who was listening, watching, prompting in the side-scenes.

By-and-by, feeling the right power come – the spring demanded gush and rise inwardly – I became sufficiently composed to notice my fellow-actors. Some of them played very well; especially Ginevra Fanshawe, who had to coquette between two suitors, and managed admirably: in fact she was in her element. I observed that she once or twice threw a certain marked fondness, and pointed partiality into her manner towards me – the fop. With such emphasis and animation did she favour me, such glances did she dart out into the listening and applauding crowd, that to me – who knew her – it presently became evident she was acting *at* some one; and I followed her eye, her smile, her gesture, and ere long discovered that she had at least singled out a handsome and distinguished aim for her shafts; full in the path of those arrows – taller than other spectators, and therefore more sure to receive them – stood, in attitude quiet but intent, a well-known form – that of Dr John.

The spectacle seemed somehow suggestive. There was language in Dr John's look, though I cannot tell what he said; it animated me: I drew out of it a history; I put my idea into the part I performed; I threw it into my wooing of Ginevra. In the 'Ours,' or sincere lover, I saw Dr John. Did I pity him, as erst? No, I hardened my heart, rivalled and out-rivalled him. I knew myself but a fop, but where *he* was outcast *I* could please. Now I know I acted as if wishful and resolute to win and conquer. Ginevra seconded me; between us we half-changed the nature of the *rôle*, gilding it from top to toe. Between the acts M. Paul told us he knew not what possessed us, and half expostulated, 'C'est peut-être plus beau que votre modèle,' said he, 'mais ce n'est pas juste.'[95] I know not what possessed me either; but somehow, my longing was to eclipse the 'Ours:' *i.e.*, Dr John. Ginevra was tender; how could I be otherwise than chivalric? Retaining the letter, I recklessly altered the spirit of the *rôle*. Without heart, without interest, I could not play it at all. It must be played – in went the yearned-for seasoning – thus flavoured, I played it with relish.

What I felt that night, and what I did, I no more expected to feel and do, than to be lifted in a trance to the seventh heaven. Cold, reluctant, apprehensive, I had accepted a part to please another: ere long, warming, becoming interested, taking courage, I acted to please myself. Yet the next day, when I thought it over, I quite disapproved of these amateur performances; and though glad that I had obliged M. Paul, and tried my own strength for once, I took a firm resolution never to be drawn into a similar affair. A keen relish for dramatic expression had revealed itself as part of my nature; to cherish and exercise this new-found faculty might gift me with a world of delight, but it would not do for a mere looker-on at life: the strength and longing must be put by; and I put them by, and fastened them in with the lock of a resolution which neither Time nor Temptation has since picked.

No sooner was the play over and *well* over, than the choleric and arbitrary M. Paul underwent a metamorphosis. His hour of managerial responsibility past, he at once laid aside his magisterial austerity; in a moment he stood amongst us, vivacious, kind, and social, shook hands with us all round, thanked us separately, and announced his determination that each of us should in turn be his partner in the coming ball. On his claiming my promise, I told him I did not dance. 'For once I must,' was the answer; and if I had not slipped aside and kept out of his way, he would have compelled me to this second performance. But I had acted enough for one evening; it was time I retired into myself and my ordinary life. My dun-coloured dress did well enough under a paletôt on the stage, but would not suit a waltz or a quadrille. Withdrawing to a quiet nook, whence unobserved I could observe – the ball, its splendours and its pleasures passed before me as a spectacle.

Again Ginevra Fanshawe was the belle, the fairest and the gayest present; she was selected to open the ball: very lovely she looked, very gracefully she danced, very joyously she smiled. Such scenes were her triumphs – she was the child of pleasure. Work or suffering found her listless and dejected, powerless and repining; but gaiety expanded her butterfly's wings, lit up their gold-dust and bright spots, made her flash like a gem, and flush like a flower. At all ordinary diet and plain beverage she would pout; but she fed on creams and ices like a humming-bird on honeypaste: sweet wine was her element and sweet cake her daily bread. Ginevra lived her full life in a ball-room; elsewhere she drooped dispirited.

Think not, reader, that she thus bloomed and sparkled for the mere sake of M. Paul her partner, or that she lavished her best graces that night for the edification of her companions only, or for that of the parents and grand-parents, who filled the carré and lined the ball-room; under circumstances so insipid and limited, with motives so chilly and vapid, Ginevra would scarce have deigned to walk one quadrille, and weariness and fretfulness would have replaced animation and good-humour, but she knew of a leaven in the otherwise heavy festal mass which lightened the whole; she tasted a condiment which gave it zest; she perceived reasons justifying the display of her choicest attractions.

In the ball-room, indeed, not a single male spectator was to be seen who was not married and a father – M. Paul excepted – that gentleman, too, being the sole creature of his sex permitted to lead out a pupil to the dance; and this exceptional part was allowed him, partly as a matter of old-established custom (for he was a kinsman of Madame Beck's, and high in her confidence), partly because he would always have his own way and do as he pleased, and partly because – wilful, passionate, partial, as he might be – he was the soul of honour, and might be trusted with a regiment of the fairest and purest, in perfect security that under his leadership they would come to no harm. Many of the girls – it may be noted in parenthesis – were not pure-minded at all, very much otherwise; but they no more dare betray their natural coarseness in M. Paul's presence, than they dare tread purposely on his corns, laugh in his face during a stormy apostrophe, or speak above their breath while some crisis of irritability was covering his human visage with the mask of an intelligent tiger. M. Paul, then, might dance with whom he would – and woe be to the interference which put him out of step.

Others there were admitted as spectators – with (seeming) reluctance, through prayers, by influence, under restriction, by special and difficult exercise of Madame Beck's gracious good-nature, and whom she all the evening – with her own personal surveillance – kept far aloof at the remotest, drearest, coldest, darkest side of the carré – a small, forlorn, band of 'jeunes gens;' these being all of the best families, grown-up sons of mothers present, and whose sisters were pupils in the school. That whole evening was madame on duty beside these 'jeunes gens' – attentive to them as a mother, but strict with them as a dragon. There was a sort of cordon sketched before them, which they wearied her with prayers to be permitted to pass, and just to revive themselves by one dance with that 'belle blonde,' or that 'jolie brune,' or 'cette jeune fille magnifique aux cheveux noirs comme le jais.'

'Taisez-vous!' madame would reply, heroically and inexorably. 'Vous ne passerez pas à moins que ce ne soit sur mon cadavre, et vous ne danserez qu'avec la nonnette du jardin'[96] (alluding to the legend). And she majestically walked to and fro along their disconsolate and impatient line, like a little Bonaparte in a mouse-coloured silk gown.

Madame knew something of the world; madame knew much of human nature. I don't think that another directress in Villette would have dared to admit a 'jeune homme' within her walls; but madame knew that by granting such admission, on an occasion like the present, a bold stroke might be struck, and a great point gained.

In the first place, the parents were made accomplices to the deed, for it was only through their mediation it was brought about. Secondly: the admission of these rattlesnakes, so fascinating and so dangerous, served to draw out madame precisely in her strongest character – that of a first-rate *surveillante*. Thirdly: their presence furnished a most piquant ingredient to the entertainment: the pupils knew it, and saw it, and the view of such golden apples shining afar off, animated them with a spirit no other circumstance could have kindled. The children's pleasure spread to the parents; life and mirth circulated quickly round the ball-room; the 'jeunes gens' themselves, though restrained, were amused: for madame never permitted them to feel dull – and thus Madame Beck's fête annually ensured a success unknown to the fête of any other directress in the land.

I observed that Dr John was at first permitted to walk at large through the classes: there was about him a manly, responsible look, that redeemed his youth, and half-expiated his beauty; but as soon as the ball began, madame ran up to him.

'Come, Wolf; come,' said she, laughing: 'You wear sheep's clothing, but you must quit the fold notwithstanding. Come; I have a fine menagerie of twenty here in the carré: let me place you amongst my collection.'

'But first suffer me to have one dance with one pupil of my choice.'

'Have you the face to ask such a thing? It is madness: it is impiety. Sortez, sortez, et au plus vite.'

She drove him before her, and soon had him enclosed within the cordon.

Ginevra being, I suppose, tired with dancing, sought me out in my retreat. She threw herself on the bench beside me, and (a demonstration I could very well have dispensed with) cast her arms round my neck.

'Lucy Snowe! Lucy Snowe!' she cried in a somewhat sobbing voice, half hysterical.

'What in the world is the matter?' I drily said.

'How do I look – how do I look to-night?' she demanded.

'As usual,' said I; 'preposterously vain.'

'Caustic creature! You never have a kind word for me; but in spite of you, and all other envious detractors, I know I am beautiful: I feel it, I see it – for there is a great looking-glass in the dressing-room, where I can view my shape from head to foot. Will you go with me now, and let us two stand before it?'

'I will, Miss Fanshawe: you shall be humoured even to the top of your bent.'

The dressing-room was very near, and we stepped in. Putting her arm through mine, she drew me to the mirror. Without resistance, remonstrance, or remark, I stood and let her self-love have its feast and triumph: curious to see how much it could swallow – whether it was possible it could feed to satiety – whether any whisper of consideration for others could penetrate her heart, and moderate its vain-glorious exultation.

Not at all. She turned me and herself round; she viewed us both on all sides; she smiled, she waved her curls, she retouched her sash, she spread her dress, and finally, letting go my arm, and curtseying with mock respect, she said:

'I would not be you for a kingdom.'

The remark was too *naïve* to rouse anger; I merely said:

'Very good.'

'And what would *you* give to be ME?' she inquired.

'Not a bad sixpence – strange as it may sound,' I replied. 'You are but a poor creature.'

'You don't think so in your heart.'

'No; for in my heart you have not the outline of a place: I only occasionally turn you over in my brain.'

'Well, but,' said she, in an expostulatory tone, 'just listen to the difference of our positions, and then see how happy am I, and how miserable are you.'

'Go on; I listen.'

'In the first place: I am the daughter of a gentleman of family, and though my father is not rich, I have expectations from an uncle. Then, I am just eighteen, the finest age possible. I have had a continental education, and though I can't spell, I have abundant accomplishments. I *am* pretty; *you* can't deny that; I may have as many admirers as I choose. This very night I have been breaking the hearts of two gentlemen, and it is the dying look I had from one of them just now, which puts me in such spirits. I do so like to watch them turn red and pale, and scowl and dart fiery glances at each other, and languishing ones at me. There is *me* – happy ME; now for *you*, poor soul!

'I suppose you are nobody's daughter, since you took care of little children when you first came to Villette: you have no relations; you can't call yourself young at twenty-three; you have no attractive accomplishments – no beauty. As to admirers, you hardly know what they are; you can't even talk on the subject: you sit dumb when the other teachers quote their conquests. I believe you never were in love, and never will be; you don't know the feeling: and so much the better, for though you might have your own heart broken, no living heart will you ever break. Isn't it all true?'

'A good deal of it is true as gospel, and shrewd besides. There must be good in you, Ginevra, to speak so honestly; that snake, Zélie St. Pierre, could not utter what you have uttered. Still, Miss Fanshawe, hapless as I am, according to your showing, sixpence I would not give to purchase you, body and soul.'

'Just because I am not clever, and that is all *you* think of. Nobody in the world but you cares for cleverness.'

'On the contrary, I consider you *are* clever, in your way – very smart indeed. But you were talking of breaking hearts – that edifying amusement into the merits of which I don't quite enter;

pray on whom does your vanity lead you to think you have done execution to-night?'

She approached her lips to my ear – 'Isidore and Alfred de Hamal are both here,' she whispered.

'Oh! they are? I should like to see them.'

'There's a dear creature! your curiosity is roused at last. Follow me, I will point them out.'

She proudly led the way – 'But you cannot see them well from the classes,' said she, turning, 'Madame keeps them too far off. Let us cross the garden, enter by the corridor, and get close to them behind: we shall be scolded if we are seen, but never mind.'

For once, I did not mind. Through the garden we went – penetrated into the corridor by a quiet private entrance, and approaching the carré, yet keeping in the corridor shade, commanded a near view of the band of 'jeunes gens.'

I believe I could have picked out the conquering de Hamal even undirected. He was a straight-nosed, very correct-featured, little dandy. I say *little* dandy, though he was not beneath the middle standard in stature; but his lineaments were small, and so were his hands and feet; and he was pretty and smooth, and as trim as a doll: so nicely dressed, so nicely curled, so booted and gloved and cravated – he was charming indeed. I said so: 'What a dear personage!' cried I, and commended Ginevra's taste warmly; and asked her what she thought de Hamal might have done with the precious fragments of that heart she had broken – whether he kept them in a scent-vial, and conserved them in otto of roses? I observed, too, with a deep rapture of approbation, that the colonel's hands were scarce larger than Miss Fanshawe's own, and suggested that this circumstance might be convenient, as he could wear her gloves at a pinch. On his dear curls, I told her I doated; and as to his low, Grecian brow, and exquisite classic head-piece, I confessed I had no language to do such perfections justice.

'And if he were your lover?' suggested the cruelly exultant Ginevra.

'Oh! heavens, what bliss!' said I; 'but do not be inhuman, Miss Fanshawe: to put such thoughts into my head is like showing poor outcast Cain a far glimpse of Paradise.'

'You like him then?'

'As I like sweets, and jams, and comfits, and conservatory flowers.'

Ginevra admired my taste, for all these things were her adoration; she could then readily credit that they were mine too.

'Now for Isidore,' I went on. I own I felt still more curious to see him than his rival; but Ginevra was absorbed in the latter.

'Alfred was admitted here to-night,' said she, 'through the influence of his aunt, Madame la Baronne de Dorlodot; and now, having seen him, can you not understand why I have been in such spirits all the evening, and acted so well and danced with such life, and why I am now happy as a queen? Dieu! Dieu! It was such good fun to glance first at him and then at the other, and madden them both.'

'But that other – where is he? Show me Isidore.'

'I don't like.'

'Why not?'

'I am ashamed of him.'

'For what reason?'

'Because – because' (in a whisper) 'he has such – such whiskers, orange – red – there now!'

'The murder is out,' I subjoined. 'Never mind, show him, all the same; I engage not to faint.'

She looked round. Just then an English voice spoke behind her and me.

'You are both standing in a draught; you must leave this corridor.'

'There is no draught, Dr John,' said I turning.

'She takes cold so easily,' he pursued, looking at Ginevra with extreme kindness. 'She is delicate; she must be cared for: fetch her a shawl.'

'Permit me to judge for myself,' said Miss Fanshawe, with hauteur. 'I want no shawl.'

'Your dress is thin, you have been dancing, you are heated.'

'Always preaching,' retorted she; 'always coddling and admonishing.'

The answer Dr John would have given, did not come; that his heart was hurt became evident in his eye; darkened, and saddened, and pained, he turned a little aside, but was patient. I knew where there were plenty of shawls near at hand; I ran and fetched one.

'She shall wear this if I have strength to make her,' said I, folding it well round her muslin dress, covering carefully her neck and her arms. 'Is that Isidore?' I asked, in a somewhat fierce whisper.

She pushed up her lip, smiled, and nodded.

'*Is that* Isidore?' I repeated, giving her a shake: I could have given her a dozen.

'C'est lui-même,' said she. 'How coarse he is, compared with the Colonel-Count! And then – oh, ciel! – the whiskers!'

Dr John now passed on.

'The Colonel-Count!' I echoed. 'The doll – the puppet – the manikin – the poor inferior creature! A mere lackey for Dr John: his valet, his foot-boy! Is it possible that fine generous gentleman – handsome as a vision – offers you his honourable hand and gallant heart, and promises to protect your flimsy person and wretchless mind through the storms and struggles of life – and you hang back – you scorn, you sting, you torture him! Have you power to do this? Who gave you that power? Where is it? Does it lie all in your beauty – your pink and white complexion and your yellow hair? Does this bind his soul at your feet, and bend his neck under your yoke? Does this purchase for you his affection, his tenderness, his thoughts, his hopes, his interest, his noble, cordial love – and will you not have it? Do you scorn it? You are only dissembling: you are not in earnest; you love him; you long for him; but you trifle with his heart to make him more surely yours?'

'Bah! How you run on! I don't understand half you have said.'

I had got her out into the garden ere this. I now set her down on a seat and told her she should not stir till she had avowed which she meant in the end to accept – the man or the monkey.

'Him you call the man,' said she, 'is bourgeois, sandy-haired, and answers to the name of John! – cela suffit: je n'en veux pas. Colonel de Hamal is a gentleman of excellent connections, perfect manners, sweet appearance, with pale interesting face, and hair and eyes like an Italian. Then too he is the most delightful company possible – a man quite in my way; not sensible and serious like the other, but one with whom I can talk on equal terms – who does not plague, and bore, and harass me with depths, and heights, and passions, and talents for which I have no taste. There now. Don't hold me so fast.'

I slackened my grasp, and she darted off. I did not care to pursue her.

Somehow I could not avoid returning once more in the direction of the corridor to get another glimpse of Dr John; but I met him on the garden-steps, standing where the light from a window fell broad. His well-proportioned figure was not to be mistaken, for I doubt whether there was another in that assemblage his equal. He carried his hat in his hand; his uncovered head, his face and fine brow were most handsome and manly. *His* features were not delicate, not slight like those of a woman, nor were they cold, frivolous, and feeble; though well cut, they were not so chiselled, so frittered away, as to lose in power and significance what they gained in unmeaning symmetry. Much feeling spoke in them at times, and more sat silent in his eye. Such at least were my thoughts of him: to me he seemed all this. An inexpressible sense of wonder occupied me as I looked at this man, and reflected that *he* could be slighted.

It was not my intention to approach or address him in the garden, our terms of acquaintance not warranting such a step; I had only meant to view him in the crowd – myself unseen: coming upon him thus alone, I withdrew. But he was looking out for me, or rather for her who had been with me; therefore he descended the steps, and followed me down the alley.

'You know Miss Fanshawe? I have often wished to ask whether you knew her,' said he.

'Yes: I know her.'

'Intimately?'

'Quite as intimately as I wish.'

'What have you done with her now?'

'Am I her keeper?' I felt inclined to ask; but I simply answered, 'I have shaken her well, and would have shaken her better, but she escaped out of my hands and ran away.'

'Would you favour me,' he asked, 'by watching over her this one evening, and observing that she does nothing imprudent – does not, for instance, run out into the night-air immediately after dancing?'

'I may, perhaps, look after her a little, since you wish it; but she likes her own way too well to submit readily to control.'

'She is so young, so thoroughly artless,' said he.

'To me she is an enigma,' I responded.

'Is she?' he asked – much interested. 'How?'

'It would be difficult to say how – difficult, at least, to tell *you* how.'

'And why me?'

'I wonder she is not better pleased that you are so much her friend.'

'But she has not the slightest idea how much I *am* her friend. That is precisely the point I cannot teach her. May I inquire did she ever speak of me to you?'

'Under the name of "Isidore" she has talked about you often; but I must add that it is only within the last ten minutes I have discovered that you and "Isidore" are identical. It is only, Dr John, within that brief space of time I have learned that Ginevra Fanshawe is the person, under this roof, in whom you have long been interested – that she is the magnet which attracts you to the Rue Fossette, that for her sake you venture into this garden, and seek out caskets dropped by rivals.'

'You know all?'

'I know so much.'

'For more than a year I have been accustomed to meet her in society. Mrs Cholmondeley, her friend, is an acquaintance of mine; thus I see her every Sunday. But you observed that under the name of "Isidore" she often spoke of me: may I – without inviting you to a breach of confidence – inquire what was the tone, what the feeling of her remarks? I feel somewhat anxious to know, being a little tormented with uncertainty as to how I stand with her.'

'Oh, she varies: she shifts and changes like the wind.'

'Still, you can gather some general idea – ?'

'I can,' thought I, 'but it would not do to communicate that general idea to you. Besides, if I said she did not love you, I know you would not believe me.'

'You are silent,' he pursued. 'I suppose you have no good news to impart. No matter. If she feels for me positive coldness and aversion, it is a sign I do not deserve her.'

'Do you doubt yourself? Do you consider yourself the inferior of Colonel de Hamal?'

'I love Miss Fanshawe far more than de Hamal loves any human being, and would care for and guard her better than he. Respecting de Hamal, I fear she is under an illusion; the man's character is known to me, all his antecedents, all his scrapes. He is not worthy of your beautiful young friend.'

'My "beautiful young friend" ought to know that, and to know or feel who is worthy of her,' said I. 'If her beauty or her brains will not serve her so far, she merits the sharp lesson of experience.'

'Are you not a little severe?'

'I am excessively severe – more severe than I choose to show you. You should hear the strictures with which I favour my "beautiful young friend," only that you would be unutterably shocked at my want of tender considerateness for her delicate nature.'

'She is so lovely, one cannot but be loving towards her. You – every woman older than herself, must feel for such a simple, innocent, girlish fairy, a sort of motherly or elder sisterly fondness. Graceful angel! Does not your heart yearn towards her when she pours into your ear her pure, child-like confidences? How you are privileged!' And he sighed.

'I cut short these confidences somewhat abruptly now and then,' said I. 'But excuse me, Dr John, may I change the theme for one instant? What a god-like person is that de Hamal! What a nose on his face – perfect! Model one in putty or clay, you could not make a

better, or straighter, or neater; and then, such classic lips and chin –
and his bearing – sublime!'

'De Hamal is an unutterable puppy, besides being a very white-
livered hero.'

'You, Dr John, and every man of a less refined mould than he,
must feel for him a sort of admiring affection, such as Mars and the
coarser deities may be supposed to have borne the young, graceful
Apollo.'

'An unprincipled, gambling, little jackanapes!' said Dr John
curtly, 'whom, with one hand, I could lift up by the waistband any
day, and lay low in the kennel, if I liked.'

'The sweet seraph!' said I. 'What a cruel idea! Are you not a little
severe, Dr John?'

And now I paused. For the second time that night I was going
beyond myself – venturing out of what I looked on as my natural
habits – speaking in an unpremeditated, impulsive strain, which
startled me strangely when I halted to reflect. On rising that
morning, had I anticipated that before night I should have acted the
part of a gay lover in a vaudeville; and an hour after, frankly
discussed with Dr John the question of his hapless suit, and rallied
him on his illusions? I had no more presaged such feats than I had
looked forward to an ascent in a balloon, or a voyage to Cape Horn.

The Doctor and I, having paced down the walk, were now
returning; the reflex from the window again lit his face: he smiled,
but his eye was melancholy. How I wished that he could feel
heart's-ease! How I grieved that he brooded over pain, and pain
from such a cause! He, with his great advantages, *he* to love in vain!
I did not then know that the pensiveness of reverse is the best phase
for some minds; nor did I reflect that some herbs, 'though scentless
when entire, yield fragrance when they're bruised.'

'Do not be sorrowful, do not grieve,' I broke out. 'If there is in
Ginevra one spark of worthiness of your affection, she will – she
must feel devotion in return. Be cheerful, be hopeful, Dr John. Who
should hope, if not you?'

In return for this speech I got – what, it must be supposed, I
deserved – a look of some surprise: I thought also of some
disapprobation. We parted, and I went into the house very chill.
The clocks struck and the bells tolled midnight; people were leaving
fast: the fête was over; the lamps were fading. In another hour all
the dwelling-house, and all the Pensionnat, were dark and hushed. I
too was in bed, but not asleep. To me it was not easy to sleep after a
day of such excitement.

CHAPTER 15

The Long Vacation

FOLLOWING MADAME BECK's fête, with its three preceding weeks of relaxation, its brief twelve hours' burst of hilarity and dissipation, and its one subsequent day of utter languor, came a period of reaction; two months of real application, of close, hard study. These two months, being the last of the 'année scolaire,' were indeed the only genuine working months in the year. To them was procrastinated – into them concentrated, alike by professors, mistresses, and pupils – the main burden of preparation for the examinations preceding the distribution of prizes. Candidates for rewards had then to work in good earnest; masters and teachers had to set their shoulders to the wheel, to urge on the backward, and diligently aid and train the more promising. A showy demonstration – a telling exhibition – must be got up for public view, and all means were fair to this end.

I scarcely noted how the other teachers went to work; I had my own business to mind: and my task was not the least onerous, being to imbue some ninety sets of brains with a due tincture of what they considered a most complicated and difficult science, that of the English language; and to drill ninety tongues in what, for them, was an almost impossible pronunciation – the lisping and hissing dentals of the Isles.

The examination-day arrived. Awful day! Prepared for with anxious care, dressed for with silent despatch – nothing vaporous or fluttering now – no white gauze or azure streamers; the grave, close, compact was the order of the toilette. It seemed to me that I was this day especially doomed – the main burden and trial falling on me alone of all the female teachers. The others were not expected to examine in the studies they taught; the professor of literature, M. Paul, taking upon himself this duty. He, this school-autocrat, gathered all and sundry reins into the hollow of his one hand; he irefully rejected any colleague; he would not have help. Madame herself, who evidently rather wished to undertake the examination in geography – her favourite study, which she taught well – was forced to succumb, and be subordinate to her despotic kinsman's direction. The whole staff of instructors, male and female, he set aside, and stood on the examiner's estrade alone. It irked him that he was forced to make one exception to this rule. He could not manage English: he was obliged to leave that branch of education in the English teacher's hands; which he did, not without a flash of naïve jealousy.

A constant crusade against the 'amour-propre' of every human-being, but himself, was the crotchet of this able, but fiery and grasping little man. He had a strong relish for public representation in his own person, but an extreme abhorrence of the like display in any other. He quelled, he kept down where he could; and where he could not, he fumed like a bottled storm.

On the evening preceding the examination-day, I was walking in the garden, as were the other teachers and all the boarders. M. Emanuel joined me in the 'allée défendue'; his cigar was at his lips; his paletôt – a most characteristic garment of no particular shape – hung dark and menacing; the tassel of his bonnet grec sternly shadowed his left temple; his black whiskers curled like those of a wrathful cat; his blue eye had a cloud in its glitter.

'Ainsi,' he began, abruptly fronting and arresting me, 'vous allez trôner comme une reine; demain – trôner à mes côtés? Sans doute vous savourez d'avance les délices de l'autorité. Je crois voir en vous je ne sais quoi de rayonnante, petite ambitieuse!'[97]

Now the fact was, he happened to be entirely mistaken. I did not – could not – estimate the admiration or the good opinion of to-morrow's audience at the same rate he did. Had that audience numbered as many personal friends and acquaintance for me, as for him, I know not how it might have been: I speak of the case as it stood. On me school-triumphs shed but a cold lustre. I had wondered – and I wondered now – how it was that for him they seemed to shine as with hearth-warmth and hearth-glow. *He* cared for them perhaps too much; *I*, probably, too little. However, I had my own fancies as well as he. I liked, for instance, to see M. Emanuel jealous; it lit up his nature, and woke his spirit; it threw all sorts of queer lights and shadows over his dun face, and into his violet-azure eyes (he used to say that his black hair and blue eyes were 'une de ses beautés'). There was a relish in his anger; it was artless, earnest, quite unreasonable, but never hypocritical. I uttered no disclaimer then of the complacency he attributed to me; I merely asked where the English examination was to come in – whether at the commencement or close of the day?

'I hesitate,' said he, 'whether at the very beginning, before many

persons are come, and when your aspiring nature will not be gratified
by a large audience, or quite at the close, when everybody is tired, and
only a jaded and worn-out attention will be at your service.'

'Que vous êtes dur, monsieur!' I said, affecting dejection.

'One ought to be "dur" with you. You are one of those beings
who must be *kept down*. I know you! I know you! Other people in
this house see you pass, and think that a colourless shadow has gone
by. As for me, I scrutinized your face once, and it sufficed.'

'You are satisfied that you understand me?'

Without answering directly, he went on, 'Were you not gratified
when you succeeded in that *vaudeville*? *I* watched you, and saw a
passionate ardour for triumph in your physiognomy. What fire shot
into the glance! Not mere light, but flame: je me tins pour averti.'[98]

'What feeling I had on that occasion, monsieur – and pardon me,
if I say, you immensely exaggerate both its quality and quantity –
was quite abstract. I did not care for the vaudeville. I hated the part
you assigned me. I had not the slightest sympathy with the audience
below the stage. They are good people, doubtless, but do I know
them? Are they anything to me? Can I care for being brought
before their view again to-morrow? Will the examination be
anything but a task to me – a task I wish well over?'

'Shall I take it out of your hands?'

'With all my heart; if you do not fear failure.'

'But I should fail. I only know three phrases of English, and a few
words: par exemple, de sonn, de mone, de stare – est-ce bien dit?
My opinion is that it would be better to give up the thing
altogether: to have no English examination, eh?'

'If madame consents; I consent.'

'Heartily?'

'Very heartily.'

He smoked his cigar in silence. He turned suddenly.

'Donnez-moi la main,' said he, and the spite and jealousy melted
out of his face, and a generous kindliness shone there instead.

'Come, we will not be rivals, we will be friends;' he pursued. 'The
examination shall take place, and I will choose a good moment; and
instead of vexing and hindering, as I felt half inclined ten minutes
ago – for I have my malevolent moods: I always had, from childhood
– I will aid you sincerely. After all, you are solitary and a stranger,
and have your way to make and your bread to earn; it may be well
that you should become known. We will be friends: do you agree?'

'Out of my heart, monsieur. I am glad of a friend. I like that
better than a triumph.'

'Pauvrette!'[99] said he, and turned away and left the alley.

The examination passed over well; M. Paul was as good as his word, and did his best to make my part easy. The next day came the distribution of prizes; that also passed; the school broke up; the pupils went home, and now began the long vacation.

That vacation! Shall I ever forget it? I think not. Madame Beck went, the first day of the holidays, to join her children at the sea-side; all the three teachers had parents or friends with whom they took refuge; every professor quitted the city; some went to Paris, some to Boue-Marine; M. Paul set forth on a pilgrimage to Rome; the house was left quite empty, but for me, a servant, and a poor deformed and imbecile pupil, a sort of crétin whom her stepmother in a distant province would not allow to return home.

My heart almost died within me; miserable longings strained its chords. How long were the September days! How silent, how lifeless! How vast and void seemed the desolate premises! How gloomy the forsaken garden – gray now with the dust of a town-summer departed. Looking forward at the commencement of those eight weeks, I hardly knew how I was to live to the end. My spirits had long been gradually sinking; now that the prop of employment was withdrawn, they went down fast. Even to look forward was not to hope: the dumb future spoke no comfort, offered no promise, gave no inducement to bear present evil in reliance on future good. A sorrowful indifference to existence often pressed on me – a despairing resignation to reach betimes the end of all things earthly. Alas! When I had full leisure to look on life as life must be looked on by such as me, I found it but a hopeless desert: tawny sands, with no green field, no palm-tree, no well in view. The hopes which are dear to youth, which bear it up and lead it on, I knew not and dared not know. If they knocked at my heart sometimes, an inhospitable bar to admission must be inwardly drawn. When they turned away thus rejected, tears sad enough sometimes flowed; but it could not be helped: I dared not give such guests lodging. So mortally did I fear the sin and weakness of presumption.

Religious reader, you will preach to me a long sermon about what I have just written, and so will you, moralist; and you, stern sage: you, stoic, will frown; you, cynic, sneer; you, epicure, laugh. Well, each and all, take it your own way. I accept the sermon, frown, sneer and laugh; perhaps you are all right: and perhaps, circumstanced like me, you would have been, like me, wrong. The first month was, indeed, a long, black, heavy month to me.

The crétin did not seem unhappy. I did my best to feed her well and keep her warm, and she only asked food and sunshine, or when that lacked, fire. Her weak faculties approved of inertion: her brain, her eyes, her ears, her heart slept content; they could not wake to work, so lethargy was their Paradise.

Three weeks of that vacation were hot, fair, and dry, but the fourth and fifth were tempestuous and wet. I do not know why that change in the atmosphere made a cruel impression on me, why the raging storm and beating rain crushed me with a deadlier paralysis than I had experienced while the air remained serene: but so it was, and my nervous system could hardly support what it had for many days and nights to undergo in that huge, empty house. How I used to pray to Heaven for consolation and support! With what dread force the conviction would grasp me that Fate was my permanent foe, never to be conciliated. I did not, in my heart, arraign the mercy or justice of God for this; I concluded it to be a part of his great plan that some must deeply suffer while they live, and I thrilled in the certainty that of this number, I was one.

It was some relief when an aunt of the crétin, a kind old woman, came one day, and took away my strange, deformed companion. The hapless creature had been at times a heavy charge; I could not take her out beyond the garden, and I could not leave her a minute alone; for her poor mind, like her body, was warped: its propensity was to evil. A vague bent to mischief, an aimless malevolence made constant vigilance indispensable. As she very rarely spoke, and would sit for hours together moping and mowing and distorting her features with indescribable grimaces, it was more like being prisoned with some strange tameless animal, than associating with a human being. Then there were personal attentions to be rendered which required the nerve of a hospital nurse; my resolution was so tried, it sometimes fell dead-sick. These duties should not have fallen on me; a servant, now absent, had rendered them hitherto, and in the hurry of holiday departure, no substitute to fill this office had been provided. This tax and trial were by no means the least I have known in life. Still, menial and distasteful as they were, my mental pain was far more wasting and wearing. Attendance on the crétin deprived me often of the power and inclination to swallow a meal, and sent me faint to the fresh air, and the well or fountain in the court; but this duty never wrung my heart, or brimmed my eyes, or scalded my cheek with tears hot as molten metal.

The cretin being gone, I was free to walk out. At first I lacked courage to venture very far from the Rue Fossette, but by degrees I sought the city-gates, and passed them, and then went wandering

away far along chaussées, through fields, beyond cemeteries,
Catholic and Protestant, beyond farmsteads, to lanes and little
woods, and I know not where. A goad thrust me on, a fever forbade
me to rest; a want of companionship maintained in my soul the
cravings of a most deadly famine. I often walked all day, through the
burning noon and the arid afternoon, and the dusk evening, and
came back with moonrise.

While wandering in solitude, I would sometimes picture the
present probable position of others, my acquaintance. There was
Madame Beck at a cheerful watering-place with her children, her
mother, and a whole troop of friends who had sought the same
scene of relaxation. Zélie St. Pierre was at Paris, with her relatives;
the other teachers were at their homes. There was Ginevra
Fanshawe whom certain of her connections had carried on a
pleasant tour southward. Ginevra seemed to me the happiest. She
was on the route of beautiful scenery; these September suns shone
for her on fertile plains, where harvest and vintage matured under
their mellow beam. These gold and crystal moons rose on her
vision over blue horizons waved in mountain lines.

But all this was nothing; I too felt those autumn suns and saw those
harvest moons, and I almost wished to be covered in with earth and
turf, deep out of their influence; for I could not live on their light,
nor make them comrades, nor yield them affection. But Ginevra had
a kind of spirit with her, empowered to give constant strength and
comfort, to gladden daylight and embalm darkness; the best of the
good genii that guard humanity curtained her with his wings, and
canopied her head with his bending form. By True Love was Ginevra
followed: never could she be alone. Was she insensible to this
presence? It seemed to me impossible: I could not realize such
deadness. I imagined her grateful in secret, loving now with reserve;
but purposing one day to show how much she loved: pictured her
faithful hero half conscious of her coy fondness, and comforted by
that consciousness: I conceived an electric chord of sympathy
between them, a fine chain of mutual understanding, sustaining
union through a separation of a hundred leagues – carrying, across
mound and hollow, communication by prayer and wish. Ginevra
gradually became with me a sort of heroine. One day, perceiving this
growing illusion, I said, 'I really believe my nerves are getting
overstretched: my mind has suffered somewhat too much; a malady is
growing upon it – what shall I do? How shall I keep well?'

Indeed there was no way to keep well under the circumstances.
At last a day and night of peculiarly agonizing depression were

succeeded by physical illness; I took perforce to my bed. About this time the Indian summer closed and the equinoctial storms began; and for nine dark and wet days, of which the Hours rushed on all turbulent, deaf, dishevelled – bewildered with sounding hurricane – I lay in a strange fever of the nerves and blood. Sleep went quite away. I used to rise in the night, look round for her, beseech her earnestly to return. A rattle of the window, a cry of the blast only replied – Sleep never came!

I err. She came once, but in anger. Impatient of my importunity she brought with her an avenging dream. By the clock of St. Jean Baptiste, that dream remained scarce fifteen minutes – a brief space, but sufficing to wring my whole frame with unknown anguish; to confer a nameless experience that had the hue, the mien, the terror, the very tone of a visitation from eternity. Between twelve and one that night a cup was forced to my lips, black, strong, strange, drawn from no well, but filled up seething from a bottomless and boundless sea. Suffering, brewed in temporal or calculable measure, and mixed for mortal lips, tastes not as this suffering tasted. Having drank and woke, I thought all was over: the end come and past by. Trembling fearfully – as consciousness returned – ready to cry out on some fellow-creature to help me, only that I knew no fellow-creature was near enough to catch the wild summons – Goton in her far distant attic could not hear – I rose on my knees in bed. Some fearful hours went over me: indescribably was I torn, racked and oppressed in mind. Amidst the horrors of that dream I think the worst lay here. Methought the well-loved dead, who had loved *me* well in life, met me elsewhere, alienated: galled was my inmost spirit with an unutterable sense of despair about the future. Motive there was none why I should try to recover or wish to live; and yet quite unendurable was the pitiless and haughty voice in which Death challenged me to engage his unknown terrors. When I tried to pray I could only utter these words: –

'From my youth up Thy terrors have I suffered with a troubled mind.'[100]

Most true was it.

On bringing me my tea next morning Goton urged me to call in a doctor. I would not: I thought no doctor could cure me.

One evening – and I was not delirious: I was in my sane mind, I got up – I dressed myself, weak and shaking. The solitude and the stillness of the long dormitory could not be borne any longer; the ghastly white beds were turning into spectres – the coronal of each became a death's head, huge and sun-bleached – dead dreams of an

THE LONG VACATION   147

elder world and mightier race lay frozen in their wide gaping eye-
holes. That evening more firmly than ever fastened into my soul the
conviction that Fate was of stone, and Hope a false idol – blind,
bloodless, and of granite core. I felt, too, that the trial God had
appointed me was gaining its climax, and must now be turned by my
own hands, hot, feeble, trembling as they were. It rained still, and
blew; but with more clemency, I thought, than it had poured and
raged all day. Twilight was falling, and I deemed its influence
pitiful; from the lattice I saw coming night-clouds trailing low like
banners drooping. It seemed to me that at this hour there was
affection and sorrow in Heaven above for all pain suffered on earth
beneath; the weight of my dreadful dream became alleviated – that
insufferable thought of being no more loved, no more owned, half-
yielded to hope of the contrary – I was sure this hope would shine
clearer if I got out from under this house-roof, which was crushing
as the slab of a tomb, and went outside the city to a certain quiet
hill, a long way distant in the fields. Covered with a cloak (I could
not be delirious, for I had sense and recollection to put on warm
clothing), forth I set. The bells of a church arrested me in passing;
they seemed to call me in to the *salut*, and I went in. Any solemn
rite, any spectacle of sincere worship, any opening for appeal to
God was as welcome to me then as bread to one in extremity of
want. I knelt down with others on the stone pavement. It was an old
solemn church, its pervading gloom not gilded but purpled by light
shed through stained glass.

Few worshippers were assembled, and, the *salut* over, half of them
departed. I discovered soon that those left, remained to confess. I
did not stir. Carefully every door of the church was shut; a holy
quiet sank upon, and a solemn shade gathered about us. After a
space, breathless and spent in prayer, a penitent approached the
confessional. I watched. She whispered her avowal; her shrift was
whispered back; she returned consoled. Another went, and another.
A pale lady, kneeling near me, said in a low, kind voice: –

'Go you, now; I am not quite prepared.'

Mechanically obedient, I rose and went. I knew what I was about;
my mind had run over the intent with lightning-speed. To take this
step could not make me more wretched than I was; it might soothe
me.

The priest within the confessional never turned his eyes to regard
me; he only quietly inclined his ear to my lips. He might be a good
man, but this duty had become to him a sort of form: he went
through it with the phlegm of custom. I hesitated; of the formula of

confession, I was ignorant: instead of commencing with the prelude usual, I said: –

'Mon père, je suis Protestante.'[101]

He directly turned. He was not a native priest; of that class, the cast of physiognomy is, almost invariably, grovelling: I saw by his profile and brow he was a Frenchman; though gray and advanced in years, he did not, I think, lack either feeling or intelligence. He inquired, not unkindly, why, being a Protestant, I came to him?

I said, I was perishing for a word of advice or an accent of comfort. I had been living for some weeks quite alone; I had been ill; I had a pressure of affliction on my mind of which it would hardly any longer endure the weight.

'Was it a sin, a crime?' he inquired, somewhat startled.

I reassured him on this point, and, as well as I could, I showed him the mere outline of my experience.

He looked thoughtful, surprised, puzzled. 'You take me unawares,' said he. 'I have not had such a case as yours before: ordinarily we know our routine and are prepared, but this makes a great break in the common course of confession. I am hardly furnished with counsel fitting the circumstances.'

Of course, I had not expected he would be; but the mere relief of communication in an ear which was human and sentient, yet consecrated – the mere pouring out of some portion of long accumulating, long pent-up pain into a vessel whence it could not be again diffused – had done me good. I was already solaced.

'Must I go, father?' I asked of him, as he sat silent.

'My daughter,' he said kindly – and I am sure he was a kind man: he had a compassionate eye – 'for the present you had better go; but I assure you your words have struck me. Confession, like other things, is apt to become formal and trivial with habit. You have come and poured your heart out; a thing seldom done. I would fain think your case over, and take it with me to my oratory. Were you of our faith I should know what to say – a mind so tossed can find repose but in the bosom of retreat, and the punctual practice of piety. The world, it is well known, has no satisfaction for that class of natures. Holy men have bidden penitents like you to hasten their path upward by penance, self-denial, and difficult good works. Tears are given them here for meat and drink – bread of affliction and waters of affliction – their recompense comes hereafter. It is my own conviction that these impressions under which you are smarting are messengers from God to bring you back to the true church. You were made for our faith: depend upon it our faith alone could heal and help you – Protestantism is altogether too dry, cold, prosaic for you. The further I look into this matter, the more plainly I see it is entirely out of the common order of things. On no account would I lose sight of you. Go, my daughter, for the present; but return to me again.'

I rose and thanked him. I was withdrawing when he signed me to return.

'You must not come to this church,' said he: 'I see you are ill, and this church is too cold; you must come to my house: I live – ' (and he gave me his address). 'Be there to-morrow morning at ten.'

In reply to this appointment, I only bowed; and pulling down my veil, and gathering round me my cloak, I glided away.

Did I, do you suppose, reader, contemplate venturing again within that worthy priest's reach? As soon should I have thought of walking into a Babylonish furnace. That priest had arms which could influence me; he was naturally kind, with a sentimental French kindness, to whose softness I knew myself not wholly impervious. Without respecting some sorts of affection, there was hardly any sort, having a fibre of root in reality, which I could rely on my force wholly to withstand. Had I gone to him, he would have shown me all that was tender, and comforting, and gentle, in the honest popish superstition. Then he would have tried to kindle, blow and stir up in me the zeal of good works. I know not how it would all have ended. We all think ourselves strong in some points; we all know ourselves weak in many; the probabilities are that had I visited Numéro 10, Rue des Mages, at the hour and day appointed, I might just now, instead of writing this heretic narrative, be counting my beads in the cell of a certain Carmelite convent on the Boulevard of Crécy in Villette. There was something of Fénelon[102] about that benign old priest; and whatever most of his brethren may be, and whatever I may think of his Church and creed (and I like neither), of himself I must ever retain a grateful recollection. He was kind when I needed kindness; he did me good. May Heaven bless him!

Twilight had passed into night, and the lamps were lit in the streets, ere I issued from that sombre church. To turn back was now become possible to me; the wild longing to breathe this October wind on the little hill far without the city-walls had ceased to be an imperative impulse, and was softened into a wish with which Reason could cope: she put it down, and I turned, as I thought, to the Rue Fossette. But I had become involved in a part of the city with which I was not familiar; it was the old part, and full of narrow streets of picturesque, ancient, and mouldering houses. I was much too weak to be very collected, and I was still too careless of my own welfare and safety, to be cautious. I grew embarrassed; I got immeshed in a net-work of turns unknown. I was lost, and had no resolution to ask guidance of any passenger.

If the storm had lulled a little at sunset, it made up now for lost time. Strong and horizontal thundered the current of the wind from north-west to south-east; it brought rain like spray, and sometimes, a sharp hail like shot; it was cold and pierced me to the vitals. I bent my head to meet it, but it beat me back. My heart did not fail at all in this conflict; I only wished that I had wings and could ascend the gale, spread and repose my pinions on its strength, career in its course, sweep where it swept. While wishing this, I suddenly felt colder where before I was cold, and more powerless where before I was weak. I tried to reach the porch of a great building near, but the mass of frontage and the giant-spire turned black and vanished from my eyes. Instead of sinking on the steps as I intended, I seemed to pitch headlong down an abyss. I remember no more.

END OF VOLUME ONE

CHAPTER 16

Auld Lang Syne

WHERE MY SOUL went during that swoon I cannot tell. Whatever she saw, or wherever she travelled in her trance on that strange night, she kept her own secret; never whispering a word to Memory, and baffling Imagination by an indissoluble silence. She may have gone upward, and come in sight of her eternal home, hoping for leave to rest now, and deeming that her painful union with matter was at last dissolved. While she so deemed, an angel may have warned her away from heaven's threshold, and, guiding her weeping down, have bound her, once more, all shuddering and unwilling, to that poor frame, cold and wasted, of whose companionship she was grown more than weary.

I know she re-entered her prison with pain, with reluctance, with a moan and a long shiver. The divorced mates, Spirit and Substance, were hard to re-unite: they greeted each other, not in an embrace, but a racking sort of struggle. The returning sense of sight came upon me, red, as if it swam in blood; suspended hearing rushed back loud, like thunder; consciousness revived in fear: I sat up appalled, wondering into what region, amongst what strange beings I was waking. At first I knew nothing I looked on: a wall was not a wall – a lamp not a lamp. I should have understood what we call a ghost, as well as I did the commonest object; which is another way of intimating that all my eye rested on struck it as spectral. But the faculties soon settled each in its place; the life-machine presently resumed its wonted and regular working.

Still, I knew not where I was; only in time I saw I had been removed from the spot where I fell: I lay on no portico-step; night and tempest were excluded by walls, windows, and ceiling. Into some house I had been carried, – but what house?

I could only think of the pensionnat in the Rue Fossette. Still half-dreaming, I tried hard to discover in what room they had put me; whether the great dormitory, or one of the little dormitories. I was puzzled, because I could not make the glimpses of furniture I saw, accord with my knowledge of any of these apartments. The empty white beds were wanting, and the long line of large windows. 'Surely,' thought I, 'it is not to Madame Beck's own chamber they have carried me!' And here my eye fell on an easy chair covered with blue damask. Other seats, cushioned to match, dawned on me by degrees; and at last I took in the complete fact of a pleasant parlour, with a wood-fire on a clear-shining hearth, a carpet where arabesques of bright blue relieved a ground of shaded fawn; pale walls over which a slight but endless garland of azure forget-me-nots ran mazed and bewildered amongst myriad gold leaves and tendrils. A gilded mirror filled up the space between two windows, curtained amply with blue damask. In this mirror I saw myself laid, not in bed, but on a sofa. I looked spectral; my eyes larger and more hollow, my hair darker than was natural, by contrast with my thin and ashen face. It was obvious, not only from the furniture, but from the position of windows, doors, and fire-place, that this was an unknown room in an unknown house.

Hardly less plain was it that my brain was not yet settled; for, as I gazed at the blue arm-chair, it appeared to grow familiar; so did a certain scroll-couch, and not less so the round centre-table, with a blue covering, bordered with autumn-tinted foliage; and, above all, two little footstools with worked covers, and a small ebony-framed chair, of which the seat and back were also worked with groups of brilliant flowers on a dark ground.

Struck with these things, I explored further. Strange to say, old acquaintance were all about me, and 'auld lang syne' smiled out of every nook. There were two oval miniatures over the mantelpiece, of which I knew by heart the pearls about the high and powdered 'heads;' the velvets circling the white throats; the swell of the full muslin kerchiefs; the pattern of the lace sleeve-ruffles. Upon the mantel-shelf there were two china vases, some relics of a diminutive tea-service, as smooth as enamel and as thin as egg-shell, and a white centre-ornament, a classic group in alabaster, preserved under glass. Of all these things I could have told the peculiarities, numbered the flaws or cracks, like any *clairvoyante*. Above all, there was a pair of handscreens, with elaborate pencil-drawings finished like line-engravings; these, my very eyes ached at beholding again, recalling hours when they had followed, stroke by stroke and touch by touch, a tedious, feeble, finical, school-girl pencil held in these fingers, now so skeleton-like.

Where was I? Not only in what spot of the world, but in what year of our Lord? For all these objects were of past days, and of a distant country. Ten years ago I bade them good-bye; since my fourteenth year they and I had never met. I gasped audibly, 'Where am I?'

A shape hitherto unnoticed, stirred, rose, came forward; a shape inharmonious with the environment, serving only to complicate the riddle further. This was no more than a sort of native bonne, in a common-place bonne's cap and print-dress. She spoke neither French nor English, and I could get no intelligence from her, not understanding her phrases of dialect. But she bathed my temples and forehead with some cool and perfumed water, and then she heightened the cushion on which I reclined, made signs that I was not to speak, and resumed her post at the foot of the sofa.

She was busy knitting; her eyes thus drawn from me, I could gaze on her without interruption. I did mightily wonder how she came there, or what she could have to do among the scenes, or with the days of my girlhood. Still more I marvelled what those scenes and days could now have to do with me.

Too weak to scrutinize thoroughly the mystery, I tried to settle it by saying it was a mistake, a dream, a fever-fit; and yet I knew there could be no mistake, and that I was not sleeping, and I believed I was sane. I wished the room had not been so well lighted, that I might not so clearly have seen the little pictures, the ornaments, the screens, the worked chair. All these objects, as well as the blue-damask furniture, were, in fact, precisely the same, in every minutest detail, with those I so well remembered, and with which I had been so thoroughly intimate, in the drawing-room of my godmother's house at Bretton. Methought the apartment only was changed, being of different proportions and dimensions.

I thought of Bedreddin Hassan,[103] transported in his sleep from Cairo to the gates of Damascus. Had a Genius stooped his dark wing down the storm to whose stress I had succumbed, and gathering me from the church-steps, and 'rising high into the air,' as the eastern tale said, had he borne me over land and ocean, and laid me quietly down beside a hearth of Old England? But no; I knew the fire of that hearth burned before its Lares[104] no more – it went out long ago, and the household gods had been carried elsewhere.

The bonne turned again to survey me, and seeing my eyes wide open, and, I suppose, deeming their expression perturbed and excited, she put down her knitting. I saw her busied for a moment at a little stand; she poured out water, and measured drops from a phial: glass in hand, she approached me. What dark-tinged draught might she now be offering? what Genii-elixir or Magi-distillation?

It was too late to inquire – I had swallowed it passively, and at once. A tide of quiet thought now came gently caressing my brain; softer and softer rose the flow, with tepid undulations smoother than balm. The pain of weakness left my limbs, my muscles slept. I lost power to move; but, losing at the same time wish, it was no privation. That kind bonne placed a screen between me and the lamp; I saw her rise to do this, but do not remember seeing her resume her place: in the interval between the two acts, I 'fell on sleep.'

At waking, lo! all was again changed. The light of high day surrounded me; not, indeed, a warm, summer light, but the leaden gloom of raw and blustering autumn. I felt sure now that I was in the pensionnat – sure by the beating rain on the casement; sure by the 'wuther' of wind amongst trees, denoting a garden outside; sure by the chill, the whiteness, the solitude, amidst which I lay. I say *whiteness* – for the dimity curtains, dropped before a French bed, bounded my view.

I lifted them; I looked out. My eye, prepared to take in the range of a long, large, and white-washed chamber, blinked baffled, on encountering the limited area of a small cabinet – a cabinet with sea-green walls; also, instead of five wide and naked windows, there was one high lattice, shaded with muslin festoons: instead of two dozen little stands of painted wood, each holding a basin and an ewer, there was a toilette table dressed, like a lady for a ball, in a white robe over a pink skirt; a polished and large glass crowned, and a pretty pincushion frilled with lace adorned it. This toilette, together with a small, low, green and white chintz arm-chair, a wash-stand topped with a marble slab, and supplied with utensils of pale-green ware, sufficiently furnished the tiny chamber.

Reader, I felt alarmed! Why? you will ask. What was there in this simple and somewhat pretty sleeping-closet to startle the most timid? Merely this – These articles of furniture could not be real, solid arm-chairs, looking-glasses, and wash-stands – they must be the ghosts of such articles; or, if this were denied as too wild an hypothesis – and, confounded as I was, I *did* deny it – there remained but to conclude that I had myself passed into an abnormal state of mind; in short, that I was very ill and delirious: and even then, mine was the strangest figment with which delirium had ever harassed a victim.

I knew – I was obliged to know – the green chintz of that little chair; the little snug chair itself, the carved, shining-black, foliated frame of that glass; the smooth, milky-green of the china vessels on the stand; the very stand too, with its top of gray marble, splintered at one corner; – all these I was compelled to recognize and to hail, as last night I had, perforce, recognized and hailed the rosewood, the drapery, the porcelain, of the drawing-room.

Bretton! Bretton! and ten years ago shone reflected in that mirror. And why did Bretton and my fourteenth year haunt me thus? Why, if they came at all, did they not return complete? Why hovered before my distempered vision the mere furniture, while the rooms and the locality were gone? As to that pin-cushion made of crimson satin, ornamented with gold beads and frilled with thread-lace, I had the same right to know it as to know the screens – I had made it myself. Rising with a start from the bed, I took the cushion in my hand and examined it. There was the cipher 'L. L. B.' formed in gold beads, and surrounded with an oval wreath embroidered in white silk. These were the initials of my godmother's name – Louisa Lucy Bretton.

Am I in England? Am I at Bretton? I muttered; and hastily pulling up the blind with which the lattice was shrouded, I looked out to try and discover *where* I was; half-prepared to meet the calm, old, handsome buildings and clean gray pavement of St. Ann's Street, and to see at the end, the towers of the minster: or, if otherwise, fully expectant of a town view somewhere, a rue in Villette, if not a street in a pleasant and ancient English city.

I looked, on the contrary, through a frame of leafage, clustering round the high lattice, and forth thence to a grassy mead-like level, a lawn-terrace with trees rising from the lower ground beyond – high forest-trees, such as I had not seen for many a day. They were now groaning under the gale of October, and between their trunks I traced the line of an avenue, where yellow leaves lay in heaps and drifts, or were whirled singly before the sweeping west wind. Whatever landscape might lie further must have been flat, and these tall beeches shut it out. The place seemed secluded, and was to me quite strange: I did not know it at all.

Once more I lay down. My bed stood in a little alcove; on turning my face to the wall, the room with its bewildering accompaniments became excluded. Excluded? No! For as I arranged my position in this hope, behold, on the green space between the divided and looped-up curtains, hung a broad, gilded picture-frame enclosing a portrait. It was drawn – well drawn, though but a sketch – in water-colours; a head, a boy's head, fresh, life-like, speaking, and animated. It seemed a youth of sixteen, fair-complexioned, with sanguine health in his cheek; hair long, not dark, and with a sunny sheen; penetrating eyes, an arch mouth, and a gay smile. On the whole a most pleasant face to look at, especially for those claiming a right to that youth's affection – parents, for instance, or sisters. Any romantic little school-girl might almost have loved it in its frame. Those eyes looked as if when somewhat older, they would flash a lightning response to love: I cannot tell whether they kept in store the steady-beaming shine of faith. For whatever sentiment met him in form too facile, his lips menaced, beautifully but surely, caprice and light esteem.

Striving to take each new discovery as quietly as I could, I whispered to myself –

'Ah! that portrait used to hang in the breakfast-room, over the mantel-place: somewhat too high, as I thought. I well remember how I used to mount a music-stool for the purpose of unhooking it, holding it in my hand, and searching into those bonny wells of eyes, whose glance under their hazel lashes seemed like a pencilled laugh; and well I liked to note the colouring of the cheek, and the expression of the mouth.' I hardly believed fancy could improve on the curve of that mouth, or of the chin; even my ignorance knew that both were beautiful, and pondered, perplexed over this doubt: 'How it was that what charmed so much, could at the same time so keenly pain?' Once, by way of test, I took little Missy Home, and, lifting her in my arms, told her to look at the picture.

'Do you like it, Polly?' I asked. She never answered, but gazed long, and at last a darkness went trembling through her sensitive eye, as she said, 'Put me down.' So I put her down, saying to myself: 'The child feels it too.'

All these things did I now think over, adding, 'He had his faults, yet scarce ever was a finer nature; liberal, suave, impressible.' My reflections closed in an audibly pronounced word, 'Graham!'

'Graham!' echoed a sudden voice at the bedside. 'Do you want Graham?'

I looked. The plot was but thickening; the wonder but culminating. If it was strange to see that well-remembered pictured form on the wall, still stranger was it to turn and behold the equally well-remembered living form opposite – a woman, a lady, most real and substantial, tall, well-attired, wearing widow's silk, and such a cap as best became her matron and motherly braids of hair. Hers, too, was a good face; too marked, perhaps, now for beauty, but not for sense or character. She was little changed; something sterner, something more robust – but she was my godmother still: the distinct vision of Mrs Bretton.

I kept quiet, yet internally I was much agitated: my pulse fluttered, and the blood left my cheek, which turned cold.

'Madam, where am I?' I inquired.

'In a very safe asylum; well protected for the present: make your mind quite easy till you get a little better; you look ill this morning.'

'I am so entirely bewildered, I do not know whether I can trust my senses at all, or whether they are misleading me in every particular: but you speak English, do you not, madam?'

'I should think you might hear that: it would puzzle me to hold a long discourse in French.'

'You do not come from England?'

'I am lately arrived thence. Have you been long in this country? You seem to know my son?'

'Do I, madam? Perhaps I do. Your son – the picture there?'

'That is his portrait as a youth. While looking at it, you pronounced his name.'

'Graham Bretton?'

She nodded.

'I speak to Mrs Bretton, formerly of Bretton, – shire?'

'Quite right; and you, I am told, are an English teacher in a foreign school here: my son recognized you as such.'

'How was I found, madam, and by whom?'

'My son shall tell you that by-and-by,' said she; 'but at present you are too confused and weak for conversation: try to eat some breakfast, and then sleep.'

Notwithstanding all I had undergone – the bodily fatigue, the perturbation of spirits, the exposure to weather – it seemed that I was better: the fever, the real malady which had oppressed my frame, was abating; for, whereas during the last nine days I had taken no solid food, and suffered from continual thirst, this morning, on breakfast being offered, I experienced a craving for nourishment: an inward faintness which caused me eagerly to taste the tea this lady offered, and to eat the morsel of dry toast she allowed in accompaniment. It was only a morsel, but it sufficed; keeping up my strength till some two or three hours afterwards, when the bonne brought me a little cup of broth and a biscuit.

As evening began to darken, and the ceaseless blast still blew wild and cold, and the rain streamed on, deluge-like, I grew weary – very weary of my bed. The room, though pretty, was small: I felt it confining; I longed for a change. The increasing chill and gathering gloom, too, depressed me; I wanted to see – to feel firelight. Besides, I kept thinking of the son of that tall matron: when should I see him? Certainly not till I left my room.

At last the bonne came to make my bed for the night. She

prepared to wrap me in a blanket and place me in the little chintz
chair; but, declining these attentions, I proceeded to dress myself.
The business was just achieved, and I was sitting down to take
breath, when Mrs Bretton once more appeared.

'Dressed!' she exclaimed, smiling with that smile I so well knew –
a pleasant smile, though not soft; – 'You are quite better then?
Quite strong – eh?'

She spoke to me so much as of old she used to speak that I almost
fancied she was beginning to know me. There was the same sort of
patronage in her voice and manner that, as a girl, I had always
experienced from her – a patronage I yielded to and even liked; it
was not founded on conventional grounds of superior wealth or
station (in the last particular there had never been any inequality;
her degree was mine) but on natural reasons of physical advantage:
it was the shelter the tree gives the herb. I put a request without
further ceremony.

'Do let me go down stairs, madam; I am so cold and dull here.'

'I desire nothing better, if you are strong enough to bear the
change,' was her reply. 'Come then; here is an arm.' And she offered
me hers: I took it, and we descended one flight of carpeted steps to
a landing where a tall door, standing open, gave admission into the
blue damask room. How pleasant it was in its air of perfect domestic
comfort! How warm in its amber lamp-light and vermilion fire-
flush! To render the picture perfect, tea stood ready on the table –
an English tea, whereof the whole shining service glanced at me
familiarly; from the solid silver urn, of antique pattern, and the
massive pot of the same metal, to the thin porcelain cups, dark with
purple and gilding. I knew the very seed-cake of peculiar form,
baked in a peculiar mould, which always had a place on the tea-table
at Bretton. Graham liked it, and there it was as of yore – set before
Graham's plate with the silver knife and fork beside it. Graham was
then expected to tea: Graham was now, perhaps, in the house; ere
many minutes I might see him.

'Sit down – sit down,' said my conductress, as my step faltered a
little in passing to the hearth. She seated me on the sofa, but I soon
passed behind it, saying the fire was too hot; in its shade I found
another seat which suited me better. Mrs Bretton was never wont to
make a fuss about any person or anything; without remonstrance
she suffered me to have my own way. She made the tea, and she
took up the newspaper. I liked to watch every action of my
godmother; all her movements were so young: she must have been
now above fifty, yet neither her sinews nor her spirit seemed yet

touched by the rust of age. Though portly, she was alert, and though serene, she was at times impetuous – good health and an excellent temperament kept her green as in her spring.

While she read, I perceived she listened – listened for her son. She was not the woman ever to confess herself uneasy, but there was yet no lull in the weather, and if Graham were out in that hoarse wind – roaring still unsatisfied – I well knew his mother's heart would be out with him.

'Ten minutes behind his time,' said she, looking at her watch; then, in another minute, a lifting of her eyes from the page, and a slight inclination of her head towards the door, denoted that she heard some sound. Presently her brow cleared; and then even my ear, less practised, caught the iron clash of a gate swung to, steps on gravel, lastly the door-bell. He was come. His mother filled the tea-pot from the urn, she drew nearer the hearth the stuffed and cushioned blue chair – her own chair by right, but I saw there was one who might with impunity usurp it. And when that *one* came up the stairs – which he soon did, after, I suppose, some such attention to the toilet as the wild and wet night rendered necessary, and strode straight in –

'Is it you, Graham?' said his mother, hiding a glad smile and speaking curtly.

'Who else should it be, mama?' demanded the Unpunctual, possessing himself irreverently of the abdicated throne.

'Don't you deserve cold tea, for being late?'

'I shall not get my deserts, for the urn sings cheerily.'

'Wheel yourself to table, lazy boy: no seat will serve you but mine; if you had one spark of a sense of propriety, you would always leave that chair for the Old Lady.'

'So I should; only the dear Old Lady persists in leaving it for me. How is your patient, mama?'

'Will she come forward and speak for herself?' said Mrs Bretton, turning to my corner; and at this invitation, forward I came. Graham courteously rose up to greet me. He stood tall on the hearth, a figure justifying his mother's unconcealed pride.

'So you are come down,' said he; 'you must be better then – much better. I scarcely expected we should meet thus, or here. I was alarmed last night, and if I had not been forced to hurry away to a dying patient, I certainly would not have left you; but my mother herself is something of a doctoress, and Martha an excellent nurse. I saw the case was a fainting-fit, not necessarily dangerous. What brought it on, I have yet to learn, and all particulars; meantime, I trust you really do feel better.'

'Much better,' I said calmly. 'Much better, I thank you, Dr John.'

For, reader, this tall young man – this darling son – this host of mine – this Graham Bretton, *was* Dr John: he, and no other; and, what is more, I ascertained this identity scarcely with surprise. What is more, when I heard Graham's step on the stairs, I knew what manner of figure would enter, and for whose aspect to prepare my eyes. The discovery was not of to-day, its dawn had penetrated my perceptions long since. Of course I remembered young Bretton well; and though ten years (from sixteen to twenty-six) may greatly change the boy as they mature him to the man, yet they could bring no such utter difference as would suffice wholly to blind my eyes, or baffle my memory. Dr John Graham Bretton retained still an affinity to the youth of sixteen: he had his eyes; he had some of his features; to wit, all the excellently-moulded lower half of the face; I found him out soon. I first recognized him on that occasion, noted several chapters back, when my unguardedly-fixed attention had drawn on me the mortification of an implied rebuke. Subsequent observation confirmed, in every point, that early surmise. I traced in the gesture, the port, and the habits of his manhood, all his boy's promise. I heard in his now deep tones the accent of former days. Certain turns of phrase, peculiar to him of old, were peculiar to him still; and so was many a trick of eye and lip, many a smile, many a sudden ray levelled from the irid under his well-charactered brow.

To *say* anything on the subject, to *hint* at my discovery, had not suited my habits of thought, or assimilated with my system of feeling. On the contrary, I had preferred to keep the matter to myself. I liked entering his presence covered with a cloud he had not seen through, while he stood before me under a ray of special illumination, which shone all partial over his head, trembled about his feet, and cast light no farther.

Well I knew that to him it could make little difference, were I to come forward and announce 'This is Lucy Snowe!' So I kept back in my teacher's place; and as he never asked my name, so I never gave it. He heard me called 'Miss,' and 'Miss Lucy;' he never heard the surname, 'Snowe.' As to spontaneous recognition – though I, perhaps, was still less changed than he – the idea never approached his mind, and why should I suggest it?

During tea, Dr John was kind, as it was his nature to be; that meal over, and the tray carried out, he made a cosy arrangement of the cushions in a corner of the sofa, and obliged me to settle amongst them. He and his mother also drew to the fire, and ere we had sat ten minutes, I caught the eye of the latter fastened steadily upon me. Women are certainly quicker in some things than men.

'Well,' she exclaimed, presently; 'I have seldom seen a stronger likeness! Graham, have you observed it?'

'Observed what? What ails the Old Lady now? How you stare, mama! One would think you had an attack of second-sight.'

'Tell me, Graham, of whom does that young lady remind you?' pointing to me.

'Mama, you put her out of countenance. I often tell you abruptness is your fault; remember, too, that to you she is a stranger, and does not know your ways.'

'Now, when she looks down; now, when she turns sideways, who is she like, Graham?'

'Indeed, mama, since you propound the riddle, I think you ought to solve it!'

'And you have known her some time, you say – ever since you first began to attend the school in the Rue Fossette; – yet you never mentioned to me that singular resemblance!'

'I could not mention a thing of which I never thought, and which I do not now acknowledge. What *can* you mean?'

'Stupid boy! look at her.'

Graham did look: but this was not to be endured; I saw how it must end, so I thought it best to anticipate.

'Dr John,' I said, 'has had so much to do and think of, since he and I shook hands at our last parting in St. Ann's Street, that, while I readily found out Mr Graham Bretton, some months ago, it never occurred to me as possible that he should recognize Lucy Snowe.'

'Lucy Snowe! I thought so! I knew it!' cried Mrs Bretton. And she at once stepped across the hearth and kissed me. Some ladies would, perhaps, have made a great bustle upon such a discovery without being particularly glad of it; but it was not my godmother's habit to make a bustle, and she preferred all sentimental demonstration in bas-relief. So she and I got over the surprise with few words and a single salute; yet I daresay she was pleased, and I know I was. While we renewed old acquaintance, Graham, sitting opposite, silently disposed of his paroxysm of astonishment.

'Mama calls me a stupid boy, and I think I am so;' at length he said, 'for, upon my honour, often as I have seen you, I never once suspected this fact: and yet I perceive it all now. Lucy Snowe! To be sure! I recollect her perfectly, and there she sits; not a doubt of it. But,' he added, 'you surely have not known me as an old acquaintance all this time, and never mentioned it?'

'That I have,' was my answer.

Dr John commented not. I suppose he regarded my silence as eccentric, but he was indulgent in refraining from censure. I dare say, too, he would have deemed it impertinent to have interrogated me very closely, to have asked me the why and wherefore of my reserve; and, though he might feel a little curious, the importance of the case was by no means such as to tempt curiosity to infringe on discretion.

For my part, I just ventured to inquire whether he remembered the circumstance of my once looking at him very fixedly; for the slight annoyance he had betrayed on that occasion, still lingered sore in my mind.

'I think I do!' said he: 'I think I was even cross with you.'

'You considered me a little bold, perhaps?' I inquired.

'Not at all. Only, shy and retiring as your general manner was, I wondered what personal or facial enormity in me proved so magnetic to your usually averted eyes.'

'You see how it was, now?'

'Perfectly.'

And here Mrs Bretton broke in with many, many questions about past times; and for her satisfaction I had to recur to gone-by troubles, to explain causes of seeming estrangement, to touch on single-handed conflict with Life, with Death, with Grief, with Fate. Dr John listened, saying little. He and she then told me of changes they had known: even with them, all had not gone smoothly, and fortune had retrenched her once abundant gifts. But so courageous a mother, with such a champion in her son, was well fitted to fight a good fight with the world, and to prevail ultimately. Dr John himself was one of those on whose birth benign planets have certainly smiled. Adversity might set against him her most sullen front: he was the man to beat her down with smiles. Strong and cheerful, and firm and courteous; not rash, yet valiant; he was the aspirant to woo Destiny herself, and to win from her stone eye-balls a beam almost loving.

In the profession he had adopted, his success was now quite decided. Within the last three months, he had taken this house (a small chateau, they told me, about half a league without the Porte de Crécy); this country site being chosen for the sake of his mother's health, with which town air did not now agree. Hither he had invited Mrs Bretton, and she, on leaving England, had brought with her such residue furniture of the former St. Ann's Street mansion, as she had thought fit to keep unsold. Hence my bewilderment at the phantoms of chairs, and the wraiths of looking glasses, tea urns, and tea cups.

As the clock struck eleven, Dr John stopped his mother.

'Miss Snowe must retire now,' he said; 'she is beginning to look very pale. To-morrow I will venture to put some questions respecting the cause of her loss of health. She is much changed indeed, since last July, when I saw her enact with no little spirit, the part of a very killing fine gentleman. As to last night's catastrophe, I am sure thereby hangs a tale, but we will inquire no further this evening. Good-night, Miss Lucy.'

And so, he kindly led me to the door, and holding a wax candle, lighted me up the one flight of steps.

When I had said my prayers, and when I was undressed and laid down, I felt that I still had friends. Friends, not professing vehement attachment, not offering the tender solace of well-matched and congenial relationship; on whom, therefore, but moderate demand of affection was to be made, of whom but moderate expectation formed; but towards whom, my heart softened instinctively and yearned with an importunate gratitude, which I entreated Reason betimes to check.

'Do not let me think of them too often, too much, too fondly,' I implored; 'let me be content with a temperate draught of this living stream: let me not run athirst, and apply passionately to its welcome waters: let me not imagine in them a sweeter taste than earth's fountains know. Oh! would to God! I may be enabled to feel enough sustained by an occasional, amicable intercourse, rare, brief, unengrossing and tranquil: quite tranquil!'

Still repeating this word, I turned to my pillow; and, *still* repeating it, I steeped that pillow with tears.

CHAPTER 17

La Terrasse

THESE STRUGGLES with the natural character, the strong native bent of the heart, may seem futile and fruitless, but in the end they do good. They tend, however slightly, to give the actions, the conduct, that turn which Reason approves, and which Feeling, perhaps, too often opposes: they certainly make a difference in the general tenor of a life, and enable it to be better regulated, more equable, quieter on the surface; and it is on the surface only the common gaze will fall. As to what lies below, leave that with God. Man, your equal, weak as you, and not fit to be your judge, may be shut out thence: take it to your Maker – show Him the secrets of the spirit He gave – ask Him how you are to bear the pains He has appointed – kneel in His presence, and pray with faith for light in darkness, for strength in piteous weakness, for patience in extreme need. Certainly, at some hour, though perhaps not *your* hour, the waiting waters will stir; in *some* shape, though perhaps not the shape you dreamed, which your heart loved, and for which it bled, the healing herald will descend. The cripple and the blind, and the dumb, and the possessed, will be led to bathe. Herald, come quickly! Thousands lie round the pool, weeping and despairing, to see it, through slow years, stagnant. Long are the 'times' of Heaven: the orbits of angel messengers seem wide to mortal vision; they may en-ring ages: the cycle of one departure and return may clasp unnumbered generations; and dust, kindling to brief suffering life, and, through pain, passing back to dust, may meanwhile perish out of memory again, and yet again. To how many maimed and mourning millions is the first and sole angel visitant, him easterns call Azrael.

I tried to get up next morning, but while I was dressing, and at intervals drinking cold water from the *carafe* on my washstand, with design to brace up that trembling weakness which made dressing so difficult, in came Mrs Bretton.

'Here is an absurdity!' was her morning accost. 'Not so,' she added, and dealing with me at once in her own brusque, energetic fashion – that fashion which I used formerly to enjoy seeing applied to her son, and by him vigorously resisted – in two minutes she consigned me captive to the French bed.

'There you lie till afternoon,' said she. 'My boy left orders before he went out that such should be the case, and I can assure you my son is master and must be obeyed. Presently you shall have breakfast.'

Presently she brought that meal – brought it with her own active hands – not leaving me to servants. She seated herself on the bed while I ate. Now it is not everybody, even amongst our respected friends and esteemed acquaintance, whom we like to have near us, whom we like to watch us, to wait on us, to approach us with the proximity of a nurse to a patient. It is not every friend whose eye is a light in a sick room, whose presence is there a solace: but all this was Mrs Bretton to me; all this she had ever been. Food or drink never pleased me so well as when it came through her hands. I do not remember the occasion when her entrance into a room had not made that room cheerier. Our natures own predilections and antipathies alike strange. There are people from whom we secretly shrink, whom we would personally avoid, though reason confesses that they are good people: there are others with faults of temper, &c., evident enough, beside whom we live content, as if the air about them did us good. My godmother's lively black eye and clear brunette cheek, her warm, prompt hand, her self-reliant mood, her decided bearing, were all beneficial to me as the atmosphere of some salubrious climate. Her son used to call her 'the old lady;' it filled me with pleasant wonder to note how the alacrity and power of five-and-twenty still breathed from her and around her.

'I would bring my work here,' she said, as she took from me the emptied tea-cup, 'and sit with you the whole day, if that overbearing John Graham had not put his veto upon such a proceeding. "Now, mama," said he, when he went out, "take notice, you are not to knock up your god-daughter with gossip," and he particularly desired me to keep close to my own quarters, and spare you my fine company. He says, Lucy, he thinks you have had a nervous fever, judging from your look, – is that so?'

I replied that I did not quite know what my ailment had been, but that I had certainly suffered a good deal, especially in mind. Further, on this subject, I did not consider it advisable to dwell, for the details of what I had undergone belonged to a portion of my existence in which I never expected my godmother to take a share. Into what a new region would such a confidence have led that hale, serene nature! The difference between her and me might be figured by that between the stately ship, cruising safe on smooth seas, with its full complement of crew, a captain gay and brave, and venturous and provident; and the life-boat, which most days of the year lies dry and solitary in an old, dark boat-house, only putting to sea when the billows run high in rough weather, when cloud encounters water, when danger and death divide between them the rule of the great deep. No, the 'Louisa Bretton' never was out of harbour on such a night, and in such a scene: her crew could not conceive it; so the half-drowned life-boat man keeps his own counsel, and spins no yarns.

She left me, and I lay in bed content: it was good of Graham to remember me before he went out.

My day was lonely, but the prospect of coming evening abridged and cheered it. Then, too, I felt weak, and rest seemed welcome; and after the morning hours were gone by – those hours which always bring, even to the necessarily unoccupied, a sense of business to be done, of tasks waiting fulfilment, a vague impression of obligation to be employed – when this stirring time was past, and the silent descent of afternoon hushed housemaid steps on the stairs and in the chambers, I then passed into a dreamy mood, not unpleasant.

My calm little room seemed somehow like a cave in the sea. There was no colour about it, except that white and pale green, suggestive of foam and deep water; the blanched cornice was adorned with shell-shaped ornaments, and there were white mouldings like dolphins in the ceiling-angles. Even that one touch of colour visible in the red satin pincushion bore affinity to coral; even that dark, shining glass might have mirrored a mermaid. When I closed my eyes, I heard a gale, subsiding at last, bearing upon the house-front like a settling swell upon a rock-base. I heard it drawn and withdrawn far, far off, like a tide retiring from a shore of the upper world – a world so high above, that the rush of its largest waves, the dash of its fiercest breakers could sound down in this submarine home, only like murmurs and a lullaby.

Amidst these dreams came evening, and then Martha brought a light; with her aid I was quickly dressed, and, stronger now than in the morning, I made my way down to the blue saloon unassisted.

Dr John, it appears, had concluded his round of professional calls earlier than usual; his form was the first object that met my eyes as I entered the parlour; he stood in that window-recess opposite the door, reading the close type of a newspaper by such dull light as closing day yet gave. The fire shone clear, but the lamp stood on the table unlit, and tea was not yet brought up.

As to Mrs Bretton, my active godmother – who, I afterwards found, had been out in the open air all day – lay half-reclined in her deep-cushioned chair, actually lost in a nap. Her son seeing me, came forward. I noticed that he trod carefully, not to wake the sleeper; he also spoke low: his mellow voice never had any sharpness in it; modulated as at present, it was calculated rather to soothe than startle slumber.

'This is a quiet little chateau,' he observed, after inviting me to sit near the casement, 'I don't know whether you may have noticed it in your walks: though, indeed, from the chaussée it is not visible; just a mile beyond the Porte de Crécy, you turn down a lane which soon becomes an avenue, and that leads you on, through meadow and shade, to the very door of this house. It is not a modern place, but built somewhat in the old style of the Basse-Ville. It is rather a manoir than a chateau; they call it "La Terrasse," because its front rises from a broad turfed walk, whence steps lead down a grassy slope to the avenue. See yonder! The moon rises: she looks well through the tree boles.'

Where, indeed, does the moon not look well? What is the scene, confined or expansive, which her orb does not hallow? Rosy or fiery, she mounted now above a not distant bank; even while we watched her flushed ascent, she cleared to gold, and in very brief space, floated up stainless into a now calm sky. Did moonlight soften or sadden Dr Bretton? Did it touch him with romance? I think it did. Albeit of no sighing mood, he sighed in watching it: sighed to himself quietly. No need to ponder the cause or the course of that sigh; I knew it was wakened by beauty: I knew it pursued Ginevra. Knowing this, the idea pressed upon me that it was in some sort my duty to speak the name he meditated. Of course he was ready for the subject: I saw in his countenance a teeming plenitude of comment, question and interest; a pressure of language and sentiment, only checked, I thought, by sense of embarrassment how to begin. To spare him this embarrassment was my best, indeed my sole use. I had but to utter the idol's name, and love's tender litany would flow out. I had just found a fitting phrase: 'You know that Miss Fanshawe is gone on a tour with the Cholmondeleys,' and was opening my lips to speak it, when he scattered my plans by introducing another theme.

'The first thing this morning,' said he, putting his sentiment in his pocket, turning from the moon, and sitting down, 'I went to the Rue Fossette, and told the cuisinière that you were safe and in good hands. Do you know I actually found that she had not yet discovered your absence from the house: she thought you safe in the great dormitory. With what care must you have been waited on!'

'Oh! all that is very conceivable,' said I. 'Goton could do nothing for me but bring me a little tisane and a crust of bread, and I had rejected both so often during the past week, that the good woman got tired of useless journeys from the dwelling-house kitchen to the school-dormitory, and only came once a day at noon, to make my bed. Believe, however, that she is a good-natured creature, and would have been delighted to cook me cotelettes de mouton, if I could have eaten them.'

'What did Madame Beck mean by leaving you alone?'

'Madame Beck could not foresee that I should fall ill.'

'Your nervous system bore a good share of the suffering?'

'I am not quite sure what my nervous system is, but I was dreadfully low-spirited.'

'Which disables me from helping you by pill or potion. Medicine can give nobody good spirits. My art halts at the threshold of Hypochondria: she just looks in and sees a chamber of torture, but can neither say nor do much. Cheerful society would be of use; you should be as little alone as possible; you should take plenty of exercise.'

Acquiescence and a pause followed these remarks. They sounded all right, I thought, and bore the safe sanction of custom, and the well-worn stamp of use.

'Miss Snowe,' recommenced Dr John – my health, nervous system included, being now somewhat to my relief, discussed and done with – 'is it permitted me to ask what your religion now is? Are you a Catholic?'

I looked up in some surprise – 'A Catholic? No! Why suggest such an idea?'

'The manner in which you were consigned to me last night, made me doubt.'

'I consigned to you? But, indeed, I forget. It remains yet for me to learn how I fell into your hands.'

'Why, under circumstances that puzzled me. I had been in attendance all day yesterday on a case of singularly interesting and critical character; the disease being rare, and its treatment doubtful: I saw a similar and still finer case in a hospital at Paris; but that will not interest you. At last a mitigation of the patient's most urgent symptoms (acute pain is one of its accompaniments) liberated me, and I set out homeward. My shortest way lay through the Basse Ville, and as the night was excessively dark, wild and wet, I took it.

In riding past an old church belonging to a community of Béguines, I saw by a lamp burning over the porch or deep arch of the entrance, a priest lifting some object in his arms. The lamp was bright enough to reveal the priest's features clearly, and I recognized him; he was a man I have often met by the sick beds of both rich and poor: and, chiefly, the latter. He is, I think, a good old man, far better than most of his class in this country; superior, indeed, in every way: better informed, as well as more devoted to duty. Our eyes met, he called on me to stop; what he supported was a woman, fainting or dying. I alighted.

' "This person is one of your countrywomen," he said: "save her, if she is not dead.'

'My countrywoman, on examination, turned out to be the English teacher at Madame Beck's pensionnat. She was perfectly unconscious, perfectly bloodless, and nearly cold.

' "What does it all mean?" was my inquiry.

'He communicated a curious account: that you had been to him that evening at confessional; that your exhausted and suffering appearance, coupled with some things you had said – '

'Things I had said? I wonder what things!'

'Awful crimes, no doubt; but he did not tell me what: there, you know, the seal of the confessional checked his garrulity and my curiosity. Your confidences, however, had not made an enemy of the good father; it seems he was so struck, and felt so sorry that you should be out on such a night alone, he had esteemed it a Christian duty to watch when you quitted the church, and so to manage as not to lose sight of you, till you should have reached home. Perhaps the worthy man might, half unconsciously, have blent in this proceeding, some little of the subtilty of his class: it might have been his resolve to learn the locality of your home – did you impart that in your confession?'

'I did not: on the contrary, I carefully avoided the shadow of an indication; and as to my confession, Dr John, I suppose you will think me mad for taking such a step, but I could not help it: I suppose it was all the fault of what you call my "nervous system." I cannot put the case into words, but, my days and nights were grown intolerable; a cruel sense of desolation pained my mind: a feeling that would make its way, rush out, or kill me – like (and this you will understand, Dr John) the current which passes through the heart, and which, if aneurism or any other morbid cause obstructs its natural channels, seeks abnormal outlet. I wanted companionship, I wanted friendship, I wanted counsel. I could find none of these in closet, or chamber, so I went and sought them in church and confessional. As to what I said, it was no confidence, no narrative. I have done nothing wrong: my life has not been active enough for any dark deed, either of romance or reality: all I poured out was a dreary, desperate complaint.'

'Lucy, you ought to travel for about six months: why, your calm nature is growing quite excitable! Confound Madame Beck! Has the little buxom widow no bowels, to condemn her best teacher to solitary confinement?'

'It was not Madame Beck's fault,' said I; 'it is no living being's fault, and I won't hear any one blamed.'

'Who is in the wrong then, Lucy?'

'Me – Dr John – me; and a great abstraction on whose wide shoulders I like to lay the mountains of blame they were sculptured to bear: me and Fate.'

' "Me" must take better care in future,' said Dr John – smiling, I suppose, at my bad grammar.

'Change of air – change of scene; those are my prescriptions,' pursued the practical young doctor. 'But to return to our muttons, Lucy. As yet, Père Silas, with all his tact (they say he is a Jesuit), is no wiser than you choose him to be; for, instead of returning to the Rue Fossette, your fevered wanderings – there must have been high fever – '

'No, Dr John: the fever took its turn that night – now, don't make out that I was delirious, for I know differently.'

'Good! you were as collected as myself at this moment, no doubt! Your wanderings had taken an opposite direction to the Pensionnat. Near the Béguinage, amidst the stress of flood and gust, and in the perplexity of darkness, you had swooned and fallen. The priest came to your succour, and the physician, as we have seen, supervened. Between us we procured a fiacre and brought you here. Père Silas, old as he is, would carry you up stairs, and lay you on that couch himself. He would certainly have remained with you till suspended animation had been restored; and so should I, but, at that juncture, a hurried messenger arrived from the dying patient I had scarcely left – the last duties were called for – the physician's last visit and the priest's last rite; extreme unction could not be deferred. Père Silas and myself departed together, my mother was spending the evening abroad; we gave you in charge to Martha, leaving directions, which it seems she followed successfully. Now, are you a Catholic?'

'Not yet,' said I, with a smile. 'And never let Père Silas know where I live, or he will try to convert me; but give him my best and truest thanks when you see him, and if ever I get rich I will send him money for his charities. See, Dr John, your mother wakes; you ought to ring for tea.'

Which he did; and, as Mrs Bretton sat up – astonished and indignant at herself for the indulgence to which she had succumbed, and fully prepared to deny that she had slept at all – her son came gaily to the attack:

'Hushaby, mama! Sleep again. You look the picture of innocence in your slumbers.'

'My slumbers, John Graham! What are you talking about? You know I never *do* sleep by day: it was the slightest doze possible.'

'Exactly! a seraph's gentle lapse – a fairy's dream. Mama, under such circumstances, you always remind me of Titania.'

'That is because you, yourself, are so like Bottom.'[105]

'Miss Snowe – did you ever hear anything like mama's wit? She is a most sprightly woman of her size and age.'

'Keep your compliments to yourself, sir, and do not neglect your own size: which seems to me a good deal on the increase. Lucy, has he not rather the air of an incipient John Bull? He used to be slender as an eel, and now I fancy in him a sort of heavy-dragoon bent – a beef-eater tendency. Graham, take notice! If you grow fat I disown you.'

'As if you could not sooner disown your own personality! I am indispensable to the old lady's happiness, Lucy. She would pine away in green and yellow melancholy if she had not my six feet of iniquity to scold. It keeps her lively – it maintains the wholesome ferment of her spirits.'

The two were now standing opposite to each other, one on each side the fire-place; their words were not very fond, but their mutual looks atoned for verbal deficiencies. At least, the best treasure of Mrs Bretton's life was certainly casketed in her son's bosom; her dearest pulse throbbed in his heart. As to him, of course another love shared his feelings with filial love; and, no doubt, as the new passion was the latest born, so he assigned it in his emotions Benjamin's portion. Ginevra! Ginevra! Did Mrs Bretton yet know at whose feet her own young idol had laid his homage? Would she approve that choice? I could not tell; but I could well guess that if she knew Miss Fanshawe's conduct towards Graham: her alternations between coldness and coaxing, and repulse and allurement; if she could at all suspect the pain with which she had tried him; if she could have seen, as I had seen, his fine spirits subdued and harassed, his inferior preferred before him, his subordinate made the instrument of his humiliation – *then* Mrs Bretton would have pronounced Ginevra imbecile, or perverted, or both. Well – I thought so too.

That second evening passed as sweetly as the first – *more* sweetly indeed: we enjoyed a smoother interchange of thought; old troubles were not reverted to, acquaintance was better cemented; I felt happier, easier, more at home. That night – instead of crying myself asleep – I went down to dreamland by a pathway bordered with pleasant thoughts.

CHAPTER 18

We Quarrel

DURING THE FIRST DAYS of my stay at the Terrace, Graham never took a seat near me, or in his frequent pacing of the room approached the quarter where I sat, or looked preoccupied, or more grave than usual, but I thought of Miss Fanshawe and expected her name to leap from his lips. I kept my ear and mind in perpetual readiness for the tender theme; my patience was ordered to be permanently under arms, and my sympathy desired to keep its cornucopia replenished and ready for outpouring. At last, and after a little inward struggle which I saw and respected, he one day launched into the topic. It was introduced delicately; anonymously as it were.

'Your friend is spending her vacation in travelling, I hear?' 'Friend, forsooth!' thought I to myself: but it would not do to contradict; he must have his own way; I must own the soft impeachment: friend let it be. Still, by way of experiment, I could not help asking whom he meant?

He had taken a seat at my work-table; he now laid hands on a reel of thread which he proceeded recklessly to unwind.

'Ginevra – Miss Fanshawe, has accompanied the Cholmondeleys on a tour through the south of France?'

'She has.'

'Do you and she correspond?'

'It will astonish you to hear that I never once thought of making application for that privilege.'

'You have seen letters of her writing?'

'Yes; several to her uncle.'

'They will not be deficient in wit and naïveté; there is so much sparkle, and so little art in her soul?'

'She writes comprehensibly enough when she writes to M. de Bassompierre: he who runs may read.' (In fact, Ginevra's epistles to her wealthy kinsman were commonly business documents, unequivocal applications for cash.)

'And her handwriting? It must be pretty, light, ladylike, I should think?'

It was, and I said so.

'I verily believe that all she does is well done,' said Dr John; and as I seemed in no hurry to chime in with this remark, he added: 'You, who know her, could you name a point in which she is deficient?'

'She does several things very well.' ('Flirtation amongst the rest,' subjoined I, in thought.)

'When do you suppose she will return to town?' he soon inquired.

'Pardon me, Dr John, I must explain. You honour me too much in ascribing to me a degree of intimacy with Miss Fanshawe I have not the felicity to enjoy. I have never been the depositary of her plans and secrets. You will find her particular friends in another sphere than mine: amongst the Cholmondeleys, for instance.'

He actually thought I was stung with a kind of jealous pain similar to his own! 'Excuse her;' he said, 'judge her indulgently; the glitter of fashion misleads her, but she will soon find out that these people are hollow, and will return to you with augmented attachment and confirmed trust. I know something of the Cholmondeleys; superficial, showy, selfish people: depend on it, at heart Ginevra values you beyond a score of such.'

'You are very kind,' I said briefly. A disclaimer of the sentiments attributed to me burned on my lips, but I extinguished the flame. I submitted to be looked upon as the humiliated, cast-off, and now pining confidante of the distinguished Miss Fanshawe: but, reader, it was a hard submission.

'Yet, you see,' continued Graham, 'while I comfort *you*, I cannot take the same consolation to myself; I cannot hope she will do me justice. De Hamal is most worthless, yet I fear he pleases her: wretched delusion!'

My patience really gave way, and without notice: all at once. I suppose illness and weakness had worn it and made it brittle.

'Dr Bretton,' I broke out, 'there is no delusion like your own. On all points but one you are a man, frank, healthful, right-thinking, clear-sighted: on this exceptional point you are but a slave. I declare, where Miss Fanshawe is concerned, you merit no respect; nor have you mine.'

I got up, and left the room very much excited.

This little scene took place in the morning; I had to meet him again in the evening, and then I saw I had done mischief. He was not made of common clay, not put together out of vulgar materials; while the outlines of his nature had been shaped with breadth and vigour, the details embraced workmanship of almost feminine delicacy: finer, much finer, than you could be prepared to meet with; than you could believe inherent in him, even after years of acquaintance. Indeed, till some over-sharp contact with his nerves had betrayed, by its effects, their acute sensibility, this elaborate construction must be ignored; and the more especially because the sympathetic faculty was not prominent in him: to feel, and to seize quickly another's feelings, are separate properties; a few constructions possess both, some neither. Dr John had the one gift in exquisite perfection; and because I have admitted that he was not endowed with the other in equal degree, the reader will considerately refrain from passing to an extreme, and pronouncing him *un*sympathizing, unfeeling: on the contrary, he was a kind, generous man. Make your need known, his hand was open. Put your grief into words, he turned no deaf ear. Expect refinements of perception, miracles of intuition, and realize disappointment. This night, when Dr John entered the room, and met the evening lamp, I saw well and at one glance his whole mechanism.

To one who had named him 'slave,' and, on any point, banned him from respect, he must now have peculiar feelings. That the epithet was well applied, and the ban just, might be; he put forth no denial that it was so: his mind even candidly revolved that unmanning possibility. He sought in this accusation the cause of that ill-success which had got so galling a hold of his mental peace. Amid the worry of a self-condemnatory soliloquy, his demeanour seemed grave, perhaps cold, both to me and his mother. And yet there was no bad feeling, no malice, no rancour, no littleness in his countenance, beautiful with a man's best beauty, even in its depression. When I placed his chair at the table, which I hastened to do, anticipating the servant, and when I handed him his tea, which I did with trembling care, he said –

'Thank you, Lucy,' in as kindly a tone of his full pleasant voice as ever my ear welcomed.

For my part, there was only one plan to be pursued; I must expiate my culpable vehemence, or I must not sleep that night. This would not do at all; I could not stand it: I made no pretence of capacity to wage war on this footing. School solitude, conventual silence and stagnation, anything seemed preferable to living embroiled with Dr John. As to Ginevra, she might take the silver wings of a dove, or any other fowl that flies, and mount straight up to the highest place, among the highest stars, where her lover's highest flight of fancy chose to fix the constellation of her charms:

never more be it mine to dispute the arrangement. Long I tried to catch his eye. Again and again that eye just met mine; but, having nothing to say, it withdrew, and I was baffled. After tea, he sat, sad and quiet, reading a book. I wished I could have dared to go and sit near him, but it seemed that if I ventured to take that step, he would infallibly evince hostility and indignation. I longed to speak out, and I dared not whisper. His mother left the room; then, moved by insupportable regret, I just murmured the words 'Dr Bretton.'

He looked up from his book; his eyes were not cold or malevolent, his mouth was not cynical; he was ready and willing to hear what I might have to say: his spirit was of vintage too mellow and generous to sour in one thunder-clap.

'Dr Bretton, forgive my hasty words: *do, do* forgive them.'

He smiled that moment I spoke. 'Perhaps I deserved them, Lucy. If you don't respect me, I am sure it is because I am not respectable. I fear I am an awkward fool: I must manage badly in some way, for where I wish to please, it seems I don't please.'

'Of that you cannot be sure; and even if such be the case, is it the fault of your character, or of another's perceptions? But now, let me unsay what I said in anger. In one thing, and in all things, I deeply respect you. If you think scarcely enough of yourself, and too much of others, what is that but an excellence?'

'Can I think too much of Ginevra?'

'*I* believe you may; *you* believe you can't. Let us agree to differ. Let me be pardoned; that is what I ask.'

'Do you think I cherish ill-will for one warm word?'

'I see you do not and cannot; but just say, "Lucy, I forgive you!" Say that, to ease me of the heart-ache.'

'Put away your heart-ache, as I will put away mine: for you wounded me a little, Lucy. Now, when the pain is gone, I more than forgive: I feel grateful, as to a sincere well-wisher.'

'I *am* your sincere well-wisher: you are right.'

Thus our quarrel ended.

Reader, if in the course of this work, you find that my opinion of Dr John undergoes modification, excuse the seeming inconsistency. I give the feeling as at the time I felt it; I describe the view of character as it appeared when discovered.

He showed the fineness of his nature by being kinder to me after that misunderstanding than before. Nay, the very incident which, by my theory, must in some degree estrange me and him, changed, indeed, somewhat our relations; but not in the sense I painfully anticipated. An invisible, but a cold something, very slight, very transparent, but very chill: a sort of screen of ice had hitherto, all through our two lives, glazed the medium through which we exchanged intercourse. Those few warm words, though only warm with anger, breathed on that frail frost-work of reserve; about this time, it gave note of dissolution. I think from that day, so long as we continued friends, he never in discourse stood on topics of ceremony with me. He seemed to know that if he would but talk about himself, and about that in which he was most interested, my expectation would always be answered, my wish always satisfied. It follows, as a matter of course, that I continued to hear much of 'Ginevra.'

'Ginevra!' He thought her so fair, so good; he spoke so lovingly of her charms, her sweetness, her innocence, that, in spite of my plain prose knowledge of the reality, a kind of reflected glow began to settle on her idea, even for me. Still, reader, I am free to confess, that he often talked nonsense; but I strove to be unfailingly patient with him. I had had my lesson: I had learned how severe for me was the pain of crossing, or grieving, or disappointing him. In a strange and new sense, I grew most selfish, and quite powerless to deny myself the delight of indulging his mood, and being pliant to his will. He still seemed to me most absurd when he obstinately doubted, and desponded about his power to win in the end Miss Fanshawe's preference. The fancy became rooted in my own mind more stubbornly than ever, that she was only coquetting to goad him, and that, at heart, she coveted every one of his words and looks. Sometimes he harassed me, in spite of my resolution to bear and hear; in the midst of the indescribable gall-honey pleasure of thus bearing and hearing, he struck so on the flint of what firmness I owned, that it emitted fire once and again. I chanced to assert one day, with a view to stilling his impatience, that in my own mind, I felt positive Miss Fanshawe *must* intend eventually to accept him.

'Positive! It was easy to say so, but had I any grounds for such assurance?'

'The best grounds.'

'Now, Lucy, *do* tell me what!'

'You know them as well as I; and, knowing them, Dr John, it really amazes me that you should not repose the frankest confidence in her fidelity. To doubt, under the circumstances, is almost to insult.'

'Now you are beginning to speak fast and to breathe short; but speak a little faster and breathe a little shorter, till you have given an explanation – a full explanation: I must have it.'

'You shall, Dr John. In some cases, you are a lavish, generous man: you are a worshipper ever ready with the votive offering; should Père Silas ever convert *you*, you will give him abundance of alms for his poor, you will supply his altar with tapers, and the shrine of your favourite saint you will do your best to enrich: Ginevra, Dr John – '

'Hush!' said he, 'don't go on.'

'Hush, I will *not*: and go on I *will*: Ginevra has had her hands filled from your hands more times than I can count. You have sought for her the costliest flowers; you have busied your brain in devising gifts, the most delicate: such, one would have thought, as only a woman could have imagined; and in addition, Miss Fanshawe owns a set of ornaments, to purchase which your generosity must have verged on extravagance.'

The modesty Ginevra herself had never evinced in this matter, now flushed all over the face of her admirer.

'Nonsense!' he said, destructively snipping a skein of silk with my scissors. 'I offered them to please myself: I felt she did me a favour in accepting them.'

'She did more than a favour, Dr John: she pledged her very honour that she would make you some return; and if she cannot pay you in affection, she ought to hand out a business-like equivalent, in the shape of some rouleaux of gold pieces.'

'But you don't understand her; she is far too disinterested to care for my gifts, and too simple-minded to know their value.'

I laughed out: I had heard her adjudge to every jewel its price; and well I knew money-embarrassment, money-schemes, money's worth, and endeavours to realize supplies, had, young as she was, furnished the most frequent, and the favourite stimulus of her thoughts for years.

He pursued. 'You should have seen her whenever I have laid on her lap some trifle; so cool, so unmoved: no eagerness to take, not even pleasure in contemplating. Just from amiable reluctance to grieve me, she would permit the bouquet to lie beside her, and perhaps consent to bear it away. Or, if I achieved the fastening of a bracelet on her ivory arm, however pretty the trinket might be (and I always carefully chose what seemed to *me* pretty, and what of course was not valueless), the glitter never dazzled her bright eyes: she would hardly cast one look on my gift.'

'Then, of course, not valuing it, she would unloose, and return it to you?'

'No; for such a repulse she was too good-natured. She would

consent to seem to forget what I had done, and retain the offering with lady-like quiet and easy oblivion. Under such circumstances, how can a man build on acceptance of his presents as a favourable symptom? For my part, were I to offer her all I have, and she to take it, such is her incapacity to be swayed by sordid considerations, I should not venture to believe the transaction advanced me one step.'

'Dr John,' I began, 'Love is blind;' but just then a blue, subtle ray sped sideways from Dr John's eye: it reminded me of old days, it reminded me of his picture: it half led me to think that part, at least, of his professed persuasion of Miss Fanshawe's *naïveté* was assumed; it led me dubiously to conjecture that perhaps, in spite of his passion for her beauty, his appreciation of her foibles might possibly be less mistaken, more clear-sighted, than from his general language was presumable. After all it might be only a chance look, or at best, the token of a merely momentary impression. Chance or intentional, real or imaginary, it closed the conversation.

CHAPTER 19

The Cleopatra

MY STAY AT LA TERRASSE was prolonged a fortnight beyond the close of the vacation. Mrs Bretton's kind management procured me this respite. Her son having one day delivered the dictum that 'Lucy was not yet strong enough to go back to that den of a Pensionnat,' she at once drove over to the Rue Fossette, had an interview with the directress, and procured the indulgence, on the plea of prolonged rest and change being necessary to perfect recovery. Hereupon, however, followed an attention I could very well have dispensed with, viz. – a polite call from Madame Beck.

That lady – one fine day – actually came out in a fiacre as far as the chateau. I suppose she had resolved within herself to see what manner of place Dr John inhabited. Apparently, the pleasant site and neat interior surpassed her expectations; she eulogized all she saw, pronounced the blue salon 'une pièce magnifique,'[106] profusely congratulated me on the acquisition of friends, 'tellement dignes, aimables, et respectables,'[107] turned also a neat compliment in my favour, and, upon Dr John coming in, ran up to him with the utmost buoyancy, opening at the same time such a fire of rapid language, all sparkling with felicitations and protestations about his 'chateau,' – 'madame sa mère, la digne châtelaine:'[108] also his looks; which indeed were very flourishing, and at the moment additionally embellished by the good-natured but amused smile with which he always listened to madame's fluent and florid French. In short, Madame shone in her very best phase that day, and came in and went out quite a living catherine-wheel of compliments, delight, and affability. Half-purposely, and half to ask some question about school-business, I followed her to the carriage, and looked in after she was seated and the door closed. In that brief fraction of time what a change had been wrought! An instant ago, all sparkles and jests, she now sat sterner than a judge and graver than a sage. Strange little woman!

I went back and teased Dr John about Madame's devotion to him. How he laughed! What fun shone in his eyes as he recalled some of her fine speeches, and repeated them, imitating her voluble delivery! He had an acute sense of humour, and was the finest company in the world – when he could forget Miss Fanshawe.

To 'sit in sunshine calm and sweet' is said to be excellent for weak people; it gives them vital force. When little Georgette Beck was recovering from her illness, I used to take her in my arms and walk with her in the garden by the hour together, beneath a certain wall hung with grapes which the Southern sun was ripening: that sun cherished her little pale frame quite as effectually as it mellowed and swelled the clustering fruit.

There are human tempers, bland, glowing, and genial, within whose influence it is as good for the poor in spirit to live, as it is for the feeble in frame to bask in the glow of noon. Of the number of these choice natures were certainly both Dr Bretton's and his mother's. They liked to communicate happiness, as some like to occasion misery: they did it instinctively; without fuss, and apparently, with little consciousness: the means to give pleasure rose spontaneously in their minds. Every day while I stayed with them, some little plan was proposed which resulted in beneficial enjoyment. Fully occupied as was Dr John's time, he still made it in his way to accompany us in each brief excursion. I can hardly tell how he managed his engagements; they were numerous, yet by dint of system, he classed them in an order which left him a daily period of liberty. I often saw him hard-worked, yet seldom over-driven; and never irritated, confused, or oppressed. What he did was accomplished with the ease and grace of all-sufficing strength; with the bountiful cheerfulness of high and unbroken energies. Under his guidance I saw, in that one happy fortnight, more of Villette, its environs, and its inhabitants, than I had seen in the whole eight months of my previous residence. He took me to places of interest in the town, of whose names I had not before so much as heard; with willingness and spirit he communicated much note-worthy information. He never seemed to think it a trouble to talk to me, and, I am sure, it was never a task to me to listen. It was not his way to treat subjects coldly and vaguely; he rarely generalized, never prosed. He seemed to like nice details almost as much as I liked them myself; he seemed observant of character: and not superficially observant, either. These points gave the quality of interest to his discourse; and the fact of his speaking direct from his own resources, and not borrowing or stealing from books – here a dry fact, and there a trite phrase, and elsewhere a hackneyed opinion – ensured a freshness, as welcome as it was rare. Before my eyes, too, his disposition seemed to unfold another phase; to pass to a fresh day: to rise in new and nobler dawn.

His mother possessed a good development of benevolence, but he owned a better and larger. I found, on accompanying him to the Basse-Ville – the poor and crowded quarter of the city – that his errands there were as much those of the philanthropist as the physician. I understood presently that – cheerfully, habitually, and in single-minded unconsciousness of any special merit distinguishing his deeds – he was achieving, amongst a very wretched population, a world of active good. The lower orders liked him well; his poor patients in the hospitals welcomed him with a sort of enthusiasm.

But stop – I must not, from the faithful narrator, degenerate into the partial eulogist. Well, full well, do I know that Dr John was not perfect, any more than I am perfect. Human fallibility leavened him throughout: there was no hour, and scarcely a moment of the times I spent with him, that in act, or speech, or look, he did not betray something that was not a god. A god could not have the cruel vanity of Dr John, nor his sometime levity. No immortal could have resembled him in his occasional temporary oblivion of all but the present – in his passing passion for that present; shown not coarsely, by devoting it to material indulgence, but selfishly, by extracting from it whatever it could yield of nutriment to his masculine self-love: his delight was to feed that ravenous sentiment, without thought of the price of provender, or care for the cost of keeping it sleek and high-pampered.

The reader is requested to note a seeming contradiction in the two views which have been given of Graham Bretton – the public and private – the out-door and the in-door view. In the first, the public, he is shown oblivious of self; as modest in the display of his energies, as earnest in their exercise. In the second, the fireside picture, there is expressed consciousness of what he has and what he is; pleasure in homage, some recklessness in exciting, some vanity in receiving the same. Both portraits are correct.

It was hardly possible to oblige Dr John quietly and in secret. When you thought that the fabrication of some trifle dedicated to his use had been achieved unnoticed, and that, like other men, he would use it when placed ready for his use, and never ask whence it came, he amazed you by a smilingly-uttered observation or two proving that his eye had been on the work from commencement to close: that he had noted the design, traced its progress, and marked its completion. It pleased him to be thus served, and he let his pleasure beam in his eye and play about his mouth.

This would have been all very well, if he had not added to such kindly and unobtrusive evidence a certain wilfulness in discharging what he called debts. When his mother worked for him, he paid her by showering about her his bright animal spirits, with even more affluence than his gay, taunting, teasing, loving wont. If Lucy Snowe were discovered to have put her hand to such work, he planned, in recompense, some pleasant recreation.

I often felt amazed at his perfect knowledge of Villette; a knowledge not merely confined to its open streets, but penetrating to all its galleries, salles, and cabinets: of every door which shut in an object worth seeing, of every museum, of every hall, sacred to art or science, he seemed to possess the 'Open! Sesame.' I never had a head for science, but an ignorant, blind, fond instinct inclined me to art. I liked to visit the picture-galleries, and I dearly liked to be left there alone. In company, a wretched idiosyncracy forbade me to see much or to feel anything. In unfamiliar company, where it was necessary to maintain a flow of talk on the subjects in presence, half an hour would knock me up, with a combined pressure of physical lassitude and entire mental incapacity. I never yet saw the well-reared child, much less the educated adult, who could not put me to shame, by the sustained intelligence of its demeanour under the ordeal of a conversable sociable visitation of pictures, historical sites or buildings, or any lions of public interest. Dr Bretton was a cicerone after my own heart; he would take me betimes, ere the galleries were filled, leave me there for two or three hours, and call for me when his own engagements were discharged. Meantime, I was happy; happy, not always in admiring, but in examining, questioning, and forming conclusions. In the commencement of these visits, there was some misunderstanding and consequent struggle between Will and Power. The former faculty exacted approbation of that which it was considered orthodox to admire; the latter groaned forth its utter inability to pay the tax; it was then self-sneered at, spurred up, goaded on to refine its taste, and whet its zest. The more it was chidden, however, the more it wouldn't praise. Discovering gradually that a wonderful sense of fatigue resulted from these conscientious efforts, I began to reflect whether I might not dispense with that great labour, and concluded eventually that I might, and so sank supine into a luxury of calm before ninety-nine out of a hundred of the exhibited frames.

It seemed to me that an original and good picture was just as scarce as an original and good book; nor did I, in the end, tremble to say to myself, standing before certain *chef d'oeuvres* bearing great names, 'These are not a whit like nature. Nature's daylight never had that colour; never was made so turbid, either by storm or cloud, as it is laid out there, under a sky of indigo: and that indigo is not ether; and those dark weeds plastered upon it are not trees.' Several very well executed and complacent-looking fat women struck me as by no means the goddesses they appeared to consider themselves. Many scores of marvellously-finished little Flemish pictures, and also of sketches, excellent for fashion-books, displaying varied costumes in the handsomest materials, gave evidence of laudable industry whimsically applied. And yet there were fragments of truth here and there which satisfied the conscience, and gleams of light that cheered the vision. Nature's power here broke through in a mountain snow-storm; and there her glory in a sunny southern day. An expression in this portrait proved clear insight into character; a face in this historical painting, by its vivid filial likeness, startlingly reminded you that genius gave it birth. These exceptions I loved: they grew dear as friends.

One day, at a quiet early hour, I found myself nearly alone in a certain gallery, wherein one particular picture of pretentious size, set up in the best light, having a cordon of protection stretched before it, and a cushioned bench duly set in front for the accommodation of worshipping connoisseurs, who, having gazed themselves off their feet, might be fain to complete the business sitting: this picture, I say, seemed to consider itself the queen of the collection.

It represented a woman, considerably larger, I thought, than the life. I calculated that this lady, put into a scale of magnitude suitable for the reception of a commodity of bulk, would infallibly turn from fourteen to sixteen stone. She was, indeed, extremely well fed: very much butcher's meat – to say nothing of bread, vegetables, and liquids – must she have consumed to attain that breadth and height, that wealth of muscle, that affluence of flesh. She lay half-reclined on a couch: why, it would be difficult to say; broad daylight blazed round her; she appeared in hearty health, strong enough to do the work of two plain cooks; she could not plead a weak spine; she ought to have been standing, or at least sitting bolt upright. She had no business to lounge away the noon on a sofa. She ought likewise to have worn decent garments; a gown covering her properly, which was not the case: out of abundance of material – seven-and-twenty yards, I should say, of drapery – she managed to make inefficient raiment. Then, for the wretched untidiness surrounding her, there could be no excuse. Pots and pans – perhaps I ought to say vases and goblets – were rolled here and there on the foreground; a perfect rubbish of flowers was mixed amongst them, and an absurd and disorderly mass of curtain upholstery smothered the couch and cumbered the floor. On referring to the catalogue, I found that this notable production bore name 'Cleopatra.'

Well, I was sitting wondering at it (as the bench was there, I thought I might as well take advantage of its accommodation), and thinking that while some of the details – as roses, gold cups, jewels, &c. – were very prettily painted, it was on the whole an enormous piece of claptrap; the room, almost vacant when I entered, began to fill. Scarcely noticing this circumstance (as, indeed, it did not matter to me) I retained my seat; rather to rest myself than with a view to studying this huge, dark-complexioned gipsy-queen; of whom, indeed, I soon tired, and betook myself for refreshment to the contemplation of some exquisite little pictures of still life: wild-flowers, wild-fruit, mossy wood-nests, casketing eggs that looked like pearls seen through clear green sea-water; all hung modestly beneath that coarse and preposterous canvas.

Suddenly a light tap visited my shoulder. Starting, turning, I met a face bent to encounter mine; a frowning, almost a shocked face it was.

'Que faites-vous ici?' said a voice.

'Mais, monsieur, je m'amuse.'

'Vous vous amusez! et à quoi, s'il vous plaît? Mais d'abord, faites-moi le plaisir de vous lever: prenez mon bras, et allons de l'autre côté.'[109]

I did precisely as I was bid. M. Paul Emanuel (it was he) returned from Rome, and now a travelled man, was not likely to be less tolerant of insubordination now, than before this added distinction laurelled his temples.

'Permit me to conduct you to your party,' said he, as we crossed the room.

'I have no party.'

'You are not alone?'

'Yes, monsieur.'

'Did you come here unaccompanied?'

'No, monsieur. Dr Bretton brought me here.'

'Dr Bretton and Madame his mother, of course?'

'No; only Dr Bretton.'

'And he told you to look at *that* picture?'

'By no means: I found it out for myself.'

M. Paul's hair was shorn close as raven down, or I think it would have bristled on his head. Beginning now to perceive his drift, I had a certain pleasure in keeping cool, and working him up.

'Astounding insular audacity!' cried the Professor. 'Singulières femmes que ces Anglaises!'

'What is the matter, monsieur?'

'Matter! How dare you, a young person, sit coolly down, with the self-possession of a garçon, and look at *that* picture?'

'It is a very ugly picture, but I cannot at all see why I should not look at it.'

'Bon! bon! Speak no more of it. But you ought not to be here alone.'

'If, however, I have no society – no *party*, as you say? And then, what does it signify whether I am alone, or accompanied? nobody meddles with me.'

'Taisez-vous, et asseyez-vous là – là!' Setting down a chair with emphasis in a particularly dull corner, before a series of most specially dreary 'cadres.'

'Mais, monsieur.'

'Mais, mademoiselle, asseyez-vous, et ne bougez pas – entendez-vous? jusqu'à ce qu'on vienne vous chercher, ou que je vous donne la permission.'

'Quel triste coin!' cried I, 'et quels laids tableaux!'[110]

And 'laids,' indeed, they were; being a set of four, denominated in the catalogue 'La vie d'une femme.'[111] They were painted rather in a remarkable style – flat, dead, pale and formal. The first represented a 'Jeune Fille,' coming out of a church-door, a missal in her hand, her dress very prim, her eyes cast down, her mouth pursed up – the image of a most villainous little precocious she-hypocrite. The second, a 'Mariée' with a long white veil, kneeling at a prie-dieu in her chamber, holding her hands plastered together, finger to finger, and showing the whites of her eyes in a most exasperating manner. The third, a 'Jeune Mère,' hanging disconsolate over a clayey and puffy baby with a face like an unwholesome full moon. The fourth, a 'Veuve,' being a black woman, holding by the hand a black little girl, and the twain studiously surveying an elegant French monument, set up in a corner of some Père la Chaise. All these four 'Anges' were grim and gray as burglars, and cold and vapid as ghosts. What women to live with! insincere, ill-humoured, bloodless, brainless nonentities! As bad in their way as the indolent gipsy-giantess, the Cleopatra, in hers.

It was impossible to keep one's attention long confined to these masterpieces, and so, by degrees, I veered round, and surveyed the gallery.

A perfect crowd of spectators was by this time gathered round the Lioness, from whose vicinage I had been banished; nearly half this crowd were ladies, but M. Paul afterwards told me, these were 'des dames,' and it was quite proper for them to contemplate what no 'demoiselle' ought to glance at. I assured him plainly I could not agree in this doctrine, and did not see the sense of it; whereupon, with his usual absolutism, he merely requested my silence, and also, in the same breath, denounced my mingled rashness and ignorance. A more despotic little man than M. Paul never filled a professor's chair. I noticed, by the way, that he looked at the picture himself quite at his ease, and for a very long while: he did not, however, neglect to glance from time to time my way, in order, I suppose, to make sure that I was obeying orders, and not breaking bounds. By and by, he again accosted me.

'Had I not been ill?' he wished to know: 'he understood I had.'

'Yes, but I was now quite well.'

'Where had I spent the vacation?'

'Chiefly in the Rue Fossette; partly with Madame Bretton.'

'He had heard that I was left alone in the Rue Fossette; was that so?'

'Not quite alone: Marie Broc' (the crétin) 'was with me.'

He shrugged his shoulders; varied and contradictory expressions played rapidly over his countenance. Marie Broc was well known to M. Paul; he never gave a lesson in the third division (containing the least advanced pupils), that she did not occasion in him a sharp conflict between antagonistic impressions. Her personal appearance, her repulsive manners, her often unmanageable disposition, irritated his temper, and inspired him with strong antipathy; a feeling he was too apt to conceive where his taste was offended or his will thwarted. On the other hand, her misfortunes constituted a strong claim on his forbearance and compassion – such a claim as it was not in his nature to deny; hence resulted almost daily drawn battles between impatience and disgust on the one hand, pity and a sense of justice on the other; in which, to his credit be it said, it was very seldom that the former feelings prevailed: when they did, however, M. Paul showed a phase of character which had its terrors. His passions were strong, his aversions and attachments alike vivid; the force he exerted in holding both in check, by no means mitigated an observer's sense of their vehemence. With such tendencies, it may well be supposed he often excited in ordinary minds fear and dislike;

yet it was an error to fear him: nothing drove him so nearly frantic as the tremor of an apprehensive and distrustful spirit; nothing soothed him like confidence tempered with gentleness. To evince these sentiments, however, required a thorough comprehension of his nature; and his nature was of an order rarely comprehended.

'How did you get on with Marie Broc?' he asked, after some minutes' silence.

'Monsieur, I did my best; but it was terrible to be alone with her!'

'You have, then, a weak heart! You lack courage; and, perhaps, charity. Yours are not the qualities which might constitute a Sister of Mercy.'

[He was a religious little man, in his way: the self-denying and self-sacrificing part of the Catholic religion commanded the homage of his soul.]

'I don't know, indeed: I took as good care of her as I could; but when her aunt came to fetch her away, it was a great relief.'

'Ah! you are an egotist. There are women who have nursed hospitals-full of similar unfortunates. You could not do that?'

'Could Monsieur do it himself?'

'Women who are worthy the name ought infinitely to surpass our coarse, fallible, self-indulgent sex, in the power to perform such duties.'

'I washed her, I kept her clean, I fed her, I tried to amuse her; but she made mouths at me instead of speaking.'

'You think you did great things?'

'No; but as great as I *could* do.'

'Then limited are your powers, for in tending one idiot, you fell sick.'

'Not with that, monsieur; I had a nervous fever: my mind was ill.'

'Vraiment! Vous valez peu de chose.[112] You are not cast in an heroic mould; your courage will not avail to sustain you in solitude; it merely gives you the temerity to gaze with sang-froid at pictures of Cleopatra.'

It would have been easy to show anger at the teasing, hostile tone of the little man. I had never been angry with him yet, however, and had no present disposition to begin.

'Cleopatra!' I repeated, quietly. 'Monsieur, too, has been looking at Cleopatra; what does he think of her?'

'Cela ne vaut rien,' he responded. 'Une femme superbe – une taille d'imperatrice, des formes de Junon, mais une personne dont je ne voudrais ni pour femme, ni pour fille, ni pour soeur. Aussi vous ne jeterez plus un seul coup d'oeil de sa côté.'[113]

'But I have looked at her a great many times while Monsieur has been talking: I can see her quite well from this corner.'

'Turn to the wall and study your four pictures of a woman's life.'

'Excuse me, M. Paul; they are too hideous: but if you admire them, allow me to vacate my seat and leave you to their contemplation.'

'Mademoiselle,' he said, grimacing a half-smile, or what he intended for a smile, though it was but a grim and hurried manifestation. 'You nurslings of Protestantism astonish me. You unguarded Englishwomen walk calmly amidst red-hot ploughshares and escape burning. I believe, if some of you were thrown into Nebuchadnezzar's hottest furnace, you would issue forth untraversed by the smell of fire.'

'Will Monsieur have the goodness to move an inch to one side?'

'How! At what are you gazing now? You are not recognizing an acquaintance amongst that group of jeunes gens?'

'I think so. Yes, I see there a person I know.'

In fact, I had caught a glimpse of a head too pretty to belong to any other than the redoubted Colonel de Hamal. What a very finished, highly-polished little pate it was! What a figure, so trim and natty! What womanish feet and hands! How daintily he held a glass to one of his optics! with what admiration he gazed upon the Cleopatra! and then, how engagingly he tittered and whispered a friend at his elbow! Oh, the man of sense! Oh, the refined gentleman of superior taste and tact! I observed him for about ten minutes, and perceived that he was exceedingly taken with this dusk and portly Venus of the Nile. So much was I interested in his bearing, so absorbed in divining his character by his looks and movements, I temporarily forgot M. Paul; in the interim a group came between that gentleman and me; or possibly his scruples might have received another and worse shock from my present abstraction, causing him to withdraw voluntarily: at any rate, when I again looked round, he was gone.

My eye, pursuant of the search, met not him, but another and dissimilar figure, well seen amidst the crowd, for the height as well as the port lent each its distinction. This way came Dr John, in visage, in shape, in hue, as unlike the dark, acerb, and caustic little professor, as the fruit of the Hesperides[114] might be unlike the sloe in the wild thicket; as the high-couraged but tractable Arabian is unlike the rude and stubborn 'sheltie.'[115] He was looking for me, but had not yet explored the corner where the schoolmaster had just put me. I remained quiet; yet another minute I would watch.

He approached de Hamal; he paused near him; I thought he had a pleasure in looking over his head; Dr Bretton, too, gazed on the Cleopatra. I doubt if it were to his taste: he did not simper like the little Count; his mouth looked fastidious, his eye cool; without demonstration he stepped aside, leaving room for others to approach. I saw now that he was waiting, and, rising, I joined him.

We took one turn round the gallery; with Graham it was very pleasant to take such a turn. I always liked dearly to hear what he had to say about either pictures or books; because, without pretending to be a connoisseur, he always spoke his thought, and that was sure to be fresh: very often it was also just and pithy. It was pleasant also to tell him some things he did not know – he listened so kindly, so teachably; unformalized by scruples lest so to bend his bright handsome head, to gather a woman's rather obscure and stammering explanation, should emperil the dignity of his manhood. And when he communicated information in return, it was with a lucid intelligence that left all his words clear graven on the memory: no explanation of his giving, no fact of his narrating, did I ever forget.

As we left the gallery, I asked him what he thought of the Cleopatra (after making him laugh by telling him how Professor Emanuel had sent me to the right-about, and taking him to see the sweet series of pictures recommended to my attention.)

'Pooh!' said he, 'My mother is a better-looking woman. I heard some French fops, yonder, designating her as "le type du voluptueux;" if so, I can only say, "le voluptueux" is little to my liking. Compare that mulatto with Ginevra!'

CHAPTER 20

The Concert

ONE MORNING, Mrs Bretton, coming promptly into my room, desired me to open my drawers and show her my dresses; which I did, without a word.

'That will do,' said she, when she had turned them over. 'You must have a new one.'

She went out. She returned presently with a dress-maker. She had me measured. 'I mean,' said she, 'to follow my own taste, and to have my own way in this little matter.'

Two days after came home—a pink dress!

'That is not for me,' I said, hurriedly, feeling that I would almost as soon clothe myself in the costume of a Chinese lady of rank.

'We shall see whether it is for you or not,' rejoined my godmother, adding with her resistless decision: 'Mark my words. You will wear it this very evening.'

I thought I should not: I thought no human force should avail to put me into it. A pink dress! I knew it not. It knew not me. I had not proved it.

My godmother went on to decree that I was to go with her and Graham to a concert that same night: which concert, she explained, was a grand affair to be held in the large salle, or hall of the principal musical society. The most advanced of the pupils of the Conservatoire were to perform: it was to be followed by a lottery 'au bénéfice des pauvres;' and to crown all, the King, Queen, and Prince of Labassecour were to be present. Graham, in sending tickets, had enjoined attention to costume as a compliment due to royalty: he also recommended punctual readiness by seven o'clock.

About six, I was ushered up-stairs. Without any force at all, I found myself led and influenced by another's will, unconsulted, unpersuaded, quietly over-ruled. In short the pink dress went on, softened by some drapery of black lace. I was pronounced to be en grande tenue, and requested to look in the glass. I did so with some fear and trembling; with more fear and trembling, I turned away. Seven o'clock struck; Dr Bretton was come; my godmother and I went down. *She* was clad in brown velvet; as I walked in her shadow, how I envied her those folds of grave, dark majesty! Graham stood in the drawing-room doorway.

'*I do* hope he will not think I have been decking myself out to draw attention,' was my uneasy aspiration.

'Here, Lucy, are some flowers,' said he, giving me a bouquet. He took no further notice of my dress than was conveyed in a kind smile and satisfied nod, which calmed at once my sense of shame and fear of ridicule. For the rest, the dress was made with extreme simplicity, guiltless of flounce or furbelow; it was but the light fabric and bright tint which scared me, and since Graham found in it nothing absurd, my own eye consented soon to become reconciled.

I suppose people who go every night to places of public amusement, can hardly enter into the fresh gala feeling with which an opera or a concert is enjoyed by those for whom it is a rarity. I am not sure that I expected great pleasure from the concert, having but a very vague notion of its nature, but I liked the drive there well. The snug comfort of the close carriage on a cold though fine night, the pleasure of setting out with companions so cheerful and friendly, the sight of the stars glinting fitfully through the trees as we rolled along the avenue; then the freer burst of the night-sky when we issued forth to the open chaussée, the passage through the city gates, the lights there burning, the guards there posted, the pretence of inspection to which we there submitted, and which amused us so much – all these small matters had for me, in their novelty, a peculiar exhilarating charm. How much of it lay in the atmosphere of friendship diffused about me, I know not: Dr John and his mother were both in their finest mood, contending animatedly with each other the whole way, and as frankly kind to me as if I had been of their kin.

Our way lay through some of the best streets of Villette, streets brightly lit, and far more lively now than at high noon. How brilliant seemed the shops! How glad, gay, and abundant flowed the tide of life along the broad pavement! While I looked, the thought of the Rue Fossette came across me – of the walled-in garden and school-house, and of the dark, vast 'classes,' where, as at this very hour, it was my wont to wander all solitary, gazing at the stars through the high, blindless windows, and listening to the distant voice of the reader in the refectory, monotonously exercised upon the 'lecture pieuse.' Thus must I soon again listen and wander; and this shadow of the future stole with timely sobriety across the radiant present.

By this time we had got into a current of carriages all tending in one direction, and soon the front of a great illuminated building blazed before us. Of what I should see within this building, I had, as before intimated, but an imperfect idea; for no place of public entertainment had it ever been my lot to enter yet.

We alighted under a portico where there was a great bustle and a great crowd, but I do not distinctly remember further details, until I found myself mounting a majestic staircase wide and easy of ascent, deeply and softly carpeted with crimson, leading up to great doors closed solemnly, and whose panels were also crimson-clothed.

I hardly noticed by what magic these doors were made to roll back – Dr John managed these points; roll back they did, however, and within was disclosed a hall – grand, wide, and high, whose sweeping circular walls, and domed hollow ceiling, seemed to me all dead gold (thus with nice art was it stained), relieved by cornicing, fluting and garlandry, either bright, like gold burnished, or snow-white, like alabaster, or white and gold mingled in wreaths of gilded leaves and spotless lilies: wherever drapery hung, wherever carpets were spread, or cushions placed, the sole colour employed was deep crimson. Pendant from the dome, flamed a mass that dazzled me – a mass, I thought, of rock-crystal, sparkling with facets, streaming with drops, ablaze with stars, and gorgeously tinged with dews of gems dissolved, or fragments of rainbows shivered. It was only the chandelier, reader, but for me it seemed the work of eastern genii: I almost looked to see if a huge, dark cloudy hand – that of the Slave of the Lamp – were not hovering in the lustrous and perfumed atmosphere of the cupola, guarding its wondrous treasure.

We moved on – I was not at all conscious whither – but at some turn we suddenly encountered another party approaching from the opposite direction. I just now see that group, as it flashed upon me for one moment. A handsome middle-aged lady in dark velvet; a gentleman who might be her son – the best face, the finest figure, I thought, I had ever seen; a third person in a pink dress and black lace mantle.

I noted them all – the third person as well as the other two – and for the fraction of a moment, believed them all strangers, thus receiving an impartial impression of their appearance. But the impression was hardly felt and not fixed, before the consciousness that I faced a great mirror, filling a compartment between two pillars, dispelled it: the party was our own party. Thus for the first, and perhaps only time in my life, I enjoyed the 'giftie' of seeing myself as others see me. No need to dwell on the result. It brought a jar of discord, a pang of regret; it was not flattering, yet, after all, I ought to be thankful: it might have been worse.

At last, we were seated in places commanding a good general view of that vast and dazzling, but warm and cheerful hall. Already it was filled, and filled with a splendid assemblage. I do not know that the women were very beautiful, but their dresses were so perfect; and foreigners, even such as are ungraceful in domestic privacy, seem to possess the art of appearing graceful in public: however blunt and boisterous those every-day and home movements connected with peignoir and papillotes, there is a slide, a bend, a carriage of the head and arms, a mien of the mouth and eyes, kept nicely in reserve for gala use – always brought out with the grande toilette, and duly put on with the 'parure.'

Some fine forms there were here and there, models of a peculiar style of beauty; a style, I think, never seen in England: a solid, firm-set, sculptural style. These shapes have no angles: a caryatid in marble is almost as flexible; a Phidian goddess[116] is not more perfect in a certain still and stately sort. They have such features as the Dutch painters give to their madonnas: low-country classic features, regular but round, straight but stolid; and for their depth of expressionless calm, of passionless peace, a polar snow-field could alone offer a type. Women of this order need no ornament, and they seldom wear any; the smooth hair, closely braided, supplies a sufficient contrast to the smoother cheek and brow; the dress cannot be too simple; the rounded arm and perfect neck require neither bracelet nor chain.

With one of these beauties I once had the honour and rapture to be perfectly acquainted: the inert force of the deep, settled love she bore herself, was wonderful; it could only be surpassed by her proud impotency to care for any other living thing. Of blood, her cool veins conducted no flow; placid lymph filled and almost obstructed her arteries.

Such a Juno[117] as I have described, sat full in our view – a sort of mark for all eyes, and quite conscious that so she was, but proof to the magnetic influence of gaze or glance: cold, rounded, blonde, and beauteous, as the white column, capitalled with gilding, which rose at her side.

Observing that Dr John's attention was much drawn towards her, I entreated him in a low voice 'for the love of heaven to shield well his heart. You need not fall in love with *that* lady,' I said, 'because, I tell you before-hand, you might die at her feet, and she would not love you again.'

'Very well,' said he, 'and how do you know that the spectacle of her grand insensibility might not with me be the strongest stimulus to homage? The sting of desperation is, I think, a wonderful irritant to my emotions: but' (shrugging his shoulders) 'you know nothing about these things; I'll address myself to my mother. Mama, I'm in a dangerous way. '

'As if that interested me!' said Mrs Bretton.

'Alas! the cruelty of my lot!' responded her son. 'Never man had a more unsentimental mother than mine: she never seems to think that such a calamity can befall her as a daughter-in-law.'

'If I don't, it is not for want of having that same calamity held over my head: you have threatened me with it for the last ten years. "Mama, I am going to be married soon!" was the cry before you were well out of jackets.'

'But, mother, one of these days it will be realized. All of a sudden, when you think you are most secure, I shall go forth like Jacob or Esau, or any other patriarch, and take me a wife: perhaps of these which are of the daughters of the land.'

'At your peril, John Graham! that is all.'

'This mother of mine means me to be an old bachelor. What a jealous old lady it is! But now just look at that splendid creature in the pale blue satin dress, and hair of paler brown, with "reflets satinés" as those of her robe. Would you not feel proud, mama, if I were to bring that goddess home some day, and introduce her to you as Mrs Bretton, junior?'

'You will bring no goddess to La Terrasse: that little chateau will not contain two mistresses; especially if the second be of the height, bulk, and circumference of that mighty doll in wood and wax, and kid and satin.'

'Mama, she would fill your blue chair so admirably!'

'Fill my chair? I defy the foreign usurper! a rueful chair should it be for her: but hush, John Graham! Hold your tongue, and use your eyes.'

During the above skirmish, the hall which, I had thought, seemed full at our entrance, continued to admit party after party, until the semicircle before the stage presented one dense mass of heads, sloping from floor to ceiling. The stage, too, or rather the wide temporary platform, larger than any stage, desert half an hour since, was now overflowing with life; round two grand pianos, placed about the centre, a white flock of young girls, the pupils of the Conservatoire, had noiselessly poured. I had noticed their gathering, while Graham and his mother were engaged in discussing the belle in blue satin, and had watched with interest the process of arraying and marshalling them. Two gentlemen, in each of whom I recognized an acquaintance, officered this virgin troop. One, an artistic looking man, bearded, and with long hair, was a noted pianiste, and also the first music teacher in Villette; he attended twice a week at Madame Beck's pensionnat, to give lessons to the few pupils whose parents were rich enough to allow their daughters the privilege of his instructions; his name was M. Josef Emanuel, and he was half-brother to M. Paul: which potent personage was now visible in the person of the second gentleman.

M. Paul amused me; I smiled to myself as I watched him, he seemed so thoroughly in his element – standing conspicuous in presence of a wide and grand assemblage, arranging, restraining, over-aweing about one hundred young ladies. He was, too, so perfectly in earnest – so energetic, so intent, and, above all, so absolute: and yet what business had he there? What had he to do with music or the Conservatoire – he who could hardly distinguish one note from another? I knew that it was his love of display and authority which had brought him there – a love not offensive, only because so naïve. It presently became obvious that his brother, M. Josef, was as much under his control as were the girls themselves. Never was such a little hawk of a man as that M. Paul! Ere long, some noted singers and musicians dawned upon the platform: as these stars rose, the comet-like professor set. Insufferable to him were all notorieties and celebrities: where he could not outshine, he fled.

And now all was prepared: but one compartment of the hall waited to be filled – a compartment covered with crimson, like the grand staircase and doors, furnished with stuffed and cushioned benches, ranged on each side of two red regal chairs, placed solemnly under a canopy.

A signal was given, the doors rolled back, the assembly stood up, the orchestra burst out, and, to the welcome of a choral burst, enter the King, the Queen, the Court of Labassecour.

Till then, I had never set eyes on living king or queen; it may consequently be conjectured how I strained my powers of vision to take in these specimens of European royalty. By whomsoever majesty is beheld for the first time, there will always be experienced a vague surprise bordering on disappointment, that the same does not appear seated, en permanence, on a throne, bonneted with a crown, and furnished, as to the hand, with a sceptre. Looking out for a king and queen, and seeing only a middle-aged soldier and a rather young lady, I felt half cheated, half pleased.

Well do I recall that King – a man of fifty, a little bowed, a little gray: there was no face in all that assembly which resembled his. I had never read, never been told anything of his nature or his habits; and at first the strong hieroglyphics graven as with iron stylet on his brow, round his eyes, beside his mouth, puzzled and baffled instinct. Ere long, however, if I did not *know*, at least *I felt*, the meaning of those characters written without hand. There sat a silent sufferer – a nervous, melancholy man. Those eyes had looked on the visits of a certain ghost – had long waited the comings and goings of that strangest spectre, Hypochondria. Perhaps he saw her now on that stage, over against him, amidst all that brilliant throng. Hypochondria has that wont, to rise in the midst of thousands – dark as Doom, pale as Malady, and well nigh strong as Death. Her comrade and victim thinks to be happy one moment – 'Not so,' says she; 'I come.' And she freezes the blood in his heart, and beclouds the light in his eye.

Some might say it was the foreign crown pressing the King's brows which bent them to that peculiar and painful fold; some might quote the effects of early bereavement. Something there might be of both these; but these as embittered by that darkest foe of humanity – constitutional melancholy. The Queen, his wife, knew this: it seemed to me, the reflection of her husband's grief lay, a subduing shadow, on her own benignant face. A mild, thoughtful, graceful woman that princess seemed; not beautiful, not at all like the women of solid charms and marble feelings described a page or two since. Hers was a somewhat slender shape; her features, though distinguished enough, were too suggestive of reigning dynasties and royal lines to give unqualified pleasure. The expression clothing that profile was agreeable in the present instance; but you could not avoid connecting it with remembered effigies, where similar lines appeared, under phase ignoble; feeble, or sensual, or cunning, as the case might be. The Queen's eye, however, was her own; and pity, goodness, sweet sympathy, blessed it with divinest light. She moved no sovereign, but a lady – kind, loving, elegant. Her little son, the Prince of Labassecour, and young Duc de Dindonneau, accompanied her: he leaned on his mother's knee; and, ever and anon, in the course of that evening, I saw her observant of the monarch at her side, conscious of his beclouded abstraction, and desirous to rouse him from it by drawing his attention to their son. She often bent her head to listen to the boy's remarks, and would then smilingly repeat them to his sire. The moody King started, listened, smiled, but invariably relapsed as soon as his good angel ceased speaking. Full mournful and significant was that spectacle! Not the less so because, both for the aristocracy and the honest bourgeoisie of Labassecour, its peculiarity seemed to be wholly invisible: I could not discover that one soul present was either struck or touched.

With the King and Queen had entered their court, comprising two or three foreign ambassadors; and with them came the élite of the foreigners then resident in Villette. These took possession of the crimson benches; the ladies were seated; most of the men remained standing: their sable rank, lining the background, looked like a dark foil to the splendour displayed in front. Nor was this splendour without varying light and shade and gradation: the middle distance was filled with matrons in velvets and satins, in plumes and gems; the benches in the foreground, to the Queen's right hand, seemed devoted exclusively to young girls, the flower – perhaps, I should rather say, the bud – of Villette aristocracy. Here were no jewels, no head-dresses, no velvet pile or silken sheen: purity, simplicity, and aërial grace reigned in that virgin band. Young heads simply braided, and fair forms (I was going to write *sylph* forms, but that would have been quite untrue: several of these 'jeunes filles,' who had not numbered more than sixteen or seventeen years, boasted contours as robust and solid as those of a stout Englishwoman of five-and-twenty) – fair forms robed in white, or pale rose, or placid blue, suggested thoughts of heaven and angels. I knew a couple, at least, of these 'rose et blanches' specimens of humanity. Here was a pair of Madame Beck's late pupils – Mesdemoiselles Mathilde and Angélique: pupils, who, during their last year at school, ought to have been in the first class, but whose brains had never got them beyond the second division. In English, they had been under my own charge, and hard work it was to get them to translate rationally a page of 'The Vicar of Wakefield.'[118] Also during three months I had one of them for my vis-à-vis at table, and the quantity of household bread, butter, and stewed fruit, she would habitually consume at 'second déjeuner' was a real world's wonder – to be exceeded only by the fact of her actually pocketing slices she could not eat. Here be truths – wholesome truths, too.

I knew another of these seraphs – the prettiest, or, at any rate, the least demure and hypocritical-looking of the lot: she was seated by the daughter of an English peer, also an honest, though haughty-looking girl; both had entered in the suite of the British embassy. She (*i.e.* my acquaintance) had a slight pliant figure, not at all like the forms of the foreign damsels; her hair, too, was not close-braided, like a shell or a skull-cap of satin; it looked *like* hair, and waved from her head, long, curled, and flowing. She chatted away volubly, and seemed full of a light-headed sort of satisfaction with herself and her position. I did not look at Dr Bretton; but I knew that he, too, saw Ginevra Fanshawe: he had become so quiet, he answered so briefly his mother's remarks, he so often suppressed a sigh. Why should he sigh? He had confessed a taste for the pursuit of love under difficulties; here was full gratification for that taste. His lady-love beamed upon him from a sphere above his own: he could not come near her; he was not certain that he could win from her a look. I watched to see if she would so far favour him. Our seat was not far from the crimson benches; we must inevitably be seen thence, by eyes so quick and roving as Miss Fanshawe's, and very soon those optics of hers were upon us: at least, upon Dr and Mrs Bretton. I kept rather in the shade and out of sight, not wishing to be immediately recognized: she looked quite steadily at Dr John, and then she raised a glass to examine his mother; a minute or two afterwards she laughingly whispered her neighbour; upon the performance commencing, her rambling attention was attracted to the platform.

On the concert I need not dwell; the reader would not care to have my impressions thereanent: and, indeed, it would not be worth while to record them, as they were the impressions of an ignorance crasse. The young ladies of the Conservatoire, being very much frightened, made rather a tremulous exhibition on the two grand pianos. M. Josef Emanuel stood by them while they played; but he had not the tact or influence of his kinsman, who, under similar circumstances, would certainly have *compelled* pupils of his to demean themselves with heroism and self-possession. M. Paul would have placed the hysteric debutantes between two fires – terror of the audience, and terror of himself – and would have inspired them with the courage of desperation, by making the latter terror incomparably the greater: M. Josef could not do this.

Following the white muslin pianistes came a fine, full-grown, sulky lady in white satin. She sang. Her singing just affected me like the tricks of a conjuror: I wondered how she did it – how she made her voice run up and down, and cut such marvellous capers; but a simple Scotch melody, played by a rude street minstrel, has often moved me more deeply.

Afterwards stepped forth a gentleman, who, bending his body a good deal in the direction of the King and Queen, and frequently approaching his white-gloved hand to the region of his heart, vented a bitter outcry against a certain 'fausse Isabelle.' I thought he seemed especially to solicit the Queen's sympathy; but, unless I am egregiously mistaken, her Majesty lent her attention rather with the calm of courtesy than the earnestness of interest. This gentleman's state of mind was very harrowing, and I was glad when he wound up his musical exposition of the same.

Some rousing choruses struck me as the best part of the evening's entertainment. There were present deputies from all the best provincial choral societies; genuine, barrel-shaped, native Labassecouriens. These worthies gave voice without mincing the matter: their hearty exertions had at least this good result – the ear drank thence a satisfying sense of power.

Through the whole performance – timid instrumental duets, conceited vocal solos, sonorous, brass-lunged choruses – my attention gave but one eye and one ear to the stage, the other being permanently retained in the service of Dr Bretton: I could not forget him, nor cease to question how he was feeling, what he was thinking, whether he was amused or the contrary. At last he spoke.

'And how do you like it all, Lucy? You are very quiet,' he said, in his own cheerful tone.

'I am quiet,' I said, 'because I am so very, *very* much interested: not merely with the music, but with everything about me.'

He then proceeded to make some further remarks, with so much equanimity and composure that I began to think he had really not seen what I had seen, and I whispered –

'Miss Fanshawe is here: have you noticed her?'

'Oh, yes! and I observed that you noticed her too.'

'Is she come with Mrs Cholmondeley, do you think?'

'Mrs Cholmondeley is there with a very grand party. Yes: Ginevra was in *her* train; and Mrs Cholmondeley was in Lady —'s train, who was in the Queen's train. If this were not one of the compact little minor European courts, whose very formalities are little more imposing than familiarities, and whose gala grandeur is but homeliness in Sunday array, it would sound all very fine.'

'Ginevra saw you, I think?'

'So do I think so. I have had my eye on her several times since you withdrew yours; and I have had the honour of witnessing a little spectacle which you were spared.'

I did not ask what: I waited voluntary information; which was presently given.

'Miss Fanshawe,' he said, 'has a companion with her – a lady of rank. I happen to know Lady Sara by sight; her noble mother has called me in professionally. She is a proud girl, but not in the least insolent, and I doubt whether Ginevra will have gained ground in her estimation by making a butt of her neighbours.'

'What neighbours?'

'Merely myself and my mother. As to me it is all very natural: nothing, I suppose, can be fairer game than the young bourgeois doctor; but my mother? I never saw her ridiculed before. Do you know, the curling lip, and sarcastically levelled glass thus directed, gave me a most curious sensation?'

'Think nothing of it, Dr John: it is not worth while. If Ginevra were in a giddy mood, as she is eminently to-night, she would make no scruple of laughing at that mild, pensive Queen, or that melancholy King. She is not actuated by malevolence, but sheer, heedless folly. To a feather-brained school-girl nothing is sacred.'

'But you forget: I have not been accustomed to look on Miss Fanshawe in the light of a feather-brained school-girl. Was she not my divinity—the angel of my career?'

'Hem! There was your mistake.'

'To speak the honest truth, without any false rant or assumed romance, there actually was a moment, six months ago, when I thought her divine. Do you remember our conversation about the presents? I was not quite open with you in discussing that subject: the warmth with which you took it up amused me. By way of having the full benefit of your lights, I allowed you to think me more in the dark than I really was. It was that test of the presents which first proved Ginevra mortal. Still her beauty retained its fascination: three days – three hours ago, I was very much her slave. As she passed me to-night, triumphant in beauty, my emotions did her homage; but for one luckless sneer, I should yet be the humblest of her servants. She might have scoffed at me, and, while wounding, she would not soon have alienated me: through myself, she could not in ten years have done what, in a moment, she has done through my mother.'

He held his peace awhile. Never before had I seen so much fire and so little sunshine in Dr John's blue eye, as just now.

'Lucy,' he recommenced, 'look well at my mother, and say, without fear or favour, in what light she now appears to you.'

'As she always does – an English middle-class gentlewoman; well, though gravely dressed, habitually independent of pretence, constitutionally composed and cheerful.'

'So she seems to me – bless her! The merry may laugh *with* mama, but the weak only will laugh *at* her. She shall not be ridiculed, with my consent at least; nor without my – my scorn – my antipathy – my – '

He stopped: and it was time – for he was getting excited – more it seemed than the occasion warranted. I did not then know that he had witnessed double cause for dissatisfaction with Miss Fanshawe. The glow of his complexion, the expansion of his nostril, the bold curve which disdain gave his well-cut under lip, showed him in a new and striking phase. Yet the rare passion of the constitutionally suave and serene is not a pleasant spectacle; nor did I like the sort of vindictive thrill which passed through his strong young frame.

'Do I frighten you, Lucy?' he asked.

'I cannot tell why you are so very angry.'

'For this reason,' he muttered in my ear: 'Ginevra is neither a pure angel nor a pure-minded woman.'

'Nonsense! you exaggerate: she has no great harm in her.'

'Too much for me. *I* can see where *you* are blind. Now, dismiss the subject. Let me amuse myself by teasing mama: I will assert that she is flagging. Mama, pray rouse yourself.'

'John, I will certainly rouse you, if you are not better conducted. Will you and Lucy be silent, that I may hear the singing?'

They were then thundering in a chorus, under cover of which all the previous dialogue had taken place.

'*You* hear the singing, mama! Now, I will wager my studs – which are genuine – against your paste brooch – '

'My paste brooch, Graham? Profane boy! you know that it is a stone of value.'

'Oh! that is one of your superstitions: you were cheated in the business.'

'I am cheated in fewer things than you imagine. How do you happen to be acquainted with young ladies of the court, John? I have observed two of them pay you no small attention during the last half hour.'

'I wish you would not observe them.'

'Why not? Because one of them satirically levels her eye-glass at me? She is a pretty, silly girl: but are you apprehensive that her titter will discomfit the old lady?'

'The sensible, admirable old lady! Mother, you are better to me than ten wives yet.'

'Don't be demonstrative, John, or I shall faint, and you will have to carry me out; and if that burden were laid upon you, you would reverse your last speech, and exclaim, "Mother, ten wives could hardly be worse to me than you are!" '

The concert over, the Lottery 'au bénéfice des Pauvres' came next: the interval between was one of general relaxation, and the pleasantest imaginable stir and commotion. The white flock was cleared from the platform; a busy throng of gentlemen crowded it instead, making arrangements for the drawing; and amongst these – the busiest of all – re-appeared that certain well-known form, not tall but active, alive with the energy and movement of three tall men. How M. Paul did work! How he issued directions, and at the same time, set his own shoulder to the wheel! Half-a-dozen assistants were at his beck to remove the pianos, &c.; no matter, he must add to their strength his own. The redundancy of his alertness was half-vexing, half-ludicrous: in my mind I both disapproved and derided most of this fuss. Yet, in the midst of prejudice and annoyance, I could not, while watching, avoid perceiving a certain not disagreeable naïveté in all he did and said; nor could I be blind to certain vigorous characteristics of his physiognomy, rendered conspicuous now by the contrast with a throng of tamer faces: the deep, intent keenness of his eye, the power of his forehead – pale, broad, and full – the mobility of his most flexible mouth. He lacked the calm of force, but its movement and its fire he signally possessed.

Meantime the whole hall was astir; most people rose and remained standing, for a change; some walked about, all talked and laughed. The crimson compartment presented a peculiarly animated scene. The long cloud of gentlemen, breaking into fragments, mixed with the rainbow line of ladies; two or three officer-like men approached the King and conversed with him. The Queen, leaving her chair, glided along the rank of young ladies, who all stood up as she passed; and to each in turn I saw her vouchsafe some token of kindness – a gracious word, look or smile. To the two pretty English girls, Lady Sara and Ginevra Fanshawe, she addressed several sentences; as she left them, both, and especially the latter, seemed to glow all over with gratification. They were afterwards accosted by several ladies, and a little circle of gentlemen gathered round them; amongst these – the nearest to Ginevra – stood the Count de Hamal.

'This room is stiflingly hot;' said Dr Bretton, rising with sudden impatience. 'Lucy – mother – will you come a moment to the fresh air?'

'Go with him Lucy;' said Mrs Bretton. 'I would rather keep my seat.'

Willingly would I have kept mine also, but Graham's desire must take precedence of my own; I accompanied him.

We found the night-air keen; or at least, I did: he did not seem to feel it; but it was very still, and the star-sown sky spread cloudless. I was wrapped in a fur shawl. We took some turns on the pavement; in passing under a lamp, Graham encountered my eye.

'You look pensive, Lucy: is it on my account?'

'I was only fearing that you were grieved.'

'Not at all: so be of good cheer – as I am. Whenever I die, Lucy, my persuasion is that it will not be of heart complaint. I may be stung, I may seem to droop for a time, but no pain or malady of sentiment has yet gone through my whole system. You have always seen me cheerful at home?'

'Generally.'

'I am glad she laughed at my mother. I would not give the old lady for a dozen beauties. That sneer did me all the good in the world. Thank you, Miss Fanshawe!' And he lifted his hat from his waved locks, and made a mock reverence.

'Yes,' he said, 'I thank her. She has made me feel that nine parts in ten of my heart have always been sound as a bell, and the tenth bled from a mere puncture: a lancet-prick that will heal in a trice.'

'You are angry just now, heated and indignant; you will think and feel differently to-morrow.'

'*I* heated and indignant! You don't know me. On the contrary, the heat is gone: I am cool as the night – which, by the way, may be too cool for you. We will go back.'

'Dr John – this is a sudden change.'

'Not it: or if it be, there are good reasons for it – two good reasons: I have told you one. But now let us re-enter.'

We did not easily regain our seats; the lottery was begun, and all was excited confusion; crowds blocked the sort of corridor along which we had to pass: it was necessary to pause for a time. Happening to glance round – indeed I half fancied I heard my name pronounced – I saw quite near, the ubiquitous, the inevitable M. Paul. He was looking at me gravely and intently: at me, or rather, at my pink dress – sardonic comment on which gleamed in his eye. Now it was his habit to indulge in strictures on the dress, both of the teachers and pupils, at Madame Beck's – a habit which the former, at least, held to be an offensive impertinence: as yet I had not suffered from it – my sombre daily attire not being calculated to attract notice. I was in no mood to permit any new encroachment to-night: rather than accept his banter, I would ignore his presence, and accordingly steadily turned my face to the sleeve of Dr John's coat: finding in that same black sleeve a prospect more redolent of pleasure and comfort, more genial, more friendly, I thought, than was offered by the dark little Professor's unlovely visage. Dr John seemed unconsciously to sanction the preference by looking down and saying in his kind voice,

'Ay, keep close to my side, Lucy: these crowding burghers are no respecters of persons.'

I could not, however, be true to myself. Yielding to some influence, mesmeric or otherwise – an influence unwelcome, displeasing, but effective – I again glanced round to see if M. Paul was gone. No, there he stood on the same spot, looking still, but with a changed eye; he had penetrated my thought and read my wish to shun him. The mocking but not ill-humoured gaze was turned to a swarthy frown, and when I bowed, with a view to conciliation, I got only the stiffest and sternest of nods in return.

'Whom have you made angry, Lucy?' whispered Dr Bretton, smiling. 'Who is that savage-looking friend of yours?'

'One of the professors at Madame Beck's: a very cross little man.'

'He looks mighty cross just now: what have you done to him? What is it all about? Ah, Lucy, Lucy! tell me the meaning of this.'

'No mystery, I assure you. M. Emanuel is very exigeant, and because I looked at your coat sleeve, instead of curtseying and dipping to him, he thinks I have failed in respect.'

'The little – ' began Dr John: I know not what more he would have added, for at that moment I was nearly thrown down amongst the feet of the crowd. M. Paul had rudely pushed past, and was elbowing his way with such utter disregard to the convenience and security of all round him, that a very uncomfortable pressure was the consequence.

'I think he is what he himself would call "méchant," said Dr Bretton. I thought so, too.

Slowly and with difficulty we made our way along the passage, and at last regained our seats. The drawing of the lottery lasted nearly an hour; it was an animating and amusing scene; and as we each held tickets, we shared in the alternations of hope and fear raised by each turn of the wheel. Two little girls, of five and six years old, drew the numbers; and the prizes were duly proclaimed from the platform. These prizes were numerous, though of small value. It so fell out, that Dr John and I each gained one: mine was a cigar-case, his a lady's head-dress – a most airy sort of blue and silver turban, with a streamer of plumage on one side, like a light snowy cloud. He was excessively anxious to make an exchange; but I could not be brought to hear reason, and to this day I keep my cigar-case: it serves, when I look at it, to remind me of old times, and one happy evening.

Dr John, for his part, held his turban at arm's length between his finger and thumb, and looked at it with a mixture of reverence and embarrassment highly provocative of laughter. The contemplation over, he was about coolly to deposit the delicate fabric on the ground between his feet; he seemed to have no shadow of an idea of the treatment or stowage it ought to receive: if his mother had not come to the rescue, I think he would finally have crushed it under his arm like an opera-hat; she restored it to the band-box whence it had issued.

Graham was quite cheerful all the evening, and his cheerfulness seemed natural and unforced. His demeanour, his look, is not easily described; there was something in it peculiar, and, in its way, original. I read in it no common mastery of the passions, and a fund of deep and healthy strength which, without any exhausting effort, bore down Disappointment and extracted her fang. His manner now, reminded me of qualities I had noticed in him when professionally engaged amongst the poor, the guilty, and the suffering, in the Basse-Ville: he looked at once determined, enduring, and sweet-tempered. Who could help liking him? *He* betrayed no weakness which harassed all your feelings with considerations as to how its faltering must be propped; from him broke no irritability which startled calm and quenched mirth; *his* lips let fall no caustic that burned to the bone; *his* eye shot no morose shafts that went cold and rusty and venomed through your heart: beside him was rest and refuge – around him, fostering sunshine.

And yet he had neither forgiven nor forgotten Miss Fanshawe. Once angered, I doubt if Dr Bretton were to be soon propitiated – once alienated, whether he were ever to be reclaimed. He looked at her more than once; not stealthily or humbly, but with a movement of hardy, open observation. De Hamal was now a fixture beside her; Mrs Cholmondeley sat near, and they and she were wholly absorbed in the discourse, mirth, and excitement, with which the crimson seats were as much astir as any plebeian part of the hall. In the course of some apparently animated discussion, Ginevra once or twice lifted her hand and arm; a handsome bracelet gleamed upon the latter. I saw that its gleam flickered in Dr John's eye – quickening therein a derisive, ireful sparkle; he laughed:

'I think,' he said, 'I will lay my turban on my wonted altar of offerings; there, at any rate, it would be certain to find favour: no grisette has a more facile faculty of acceptance. Strange! for after all, I know she is a girl of family.'

'But you don't know her education, Dr John,' said I. 'Tossed about all her life from one foreign school to another, she may justly proffer the plea of ignorance in extenuation of most of her faults. And then, from what she says, I believe her father and mother were brought up much as she has been brought up.'

'I always understood she had no fortune; and once I had pleasure in the thought,' said he.

'She tells me,' I answered, 'that they are poor at home; she always speaks quite candidly on such points: you never find her lying, as these foreigners will often lie. Her parents have a large family: they occupy such a station and possess such connections as, in their opinion, demand display; stringent necessity of circumstances and inherent thoughtlessness of disposition combined, have engendered reckless unscrupulousness as to how they obtain the means of sustaining a good appearance. This is the state of things, and the only state of things she has seen from childhood upwards.'

'I believe it – and I thought to mould her to something better: but, Lucy, to speak the plain truth, I have felt a new thing to-night, in looking at her and de Hamal. I felt it before noticing the impertinence directed at my mother. I saw a look interchanged between them immediately after their entrance, which threw a most unwelcome light on my mind.'

'How do you mean? You have long been aware of the flirtation they keep up?'

'Ay, flirtation! That might be an innocent girlish wile to lure on the true lover; but what I refer to was not flirtation: it was a look marking mutual and secret understanding – it was neither girlish nor innocent. No woman, were she as beautiful as Aphrodite, who could give or receive such a glance, shall ever be sought in marriage by me: I would rather wed a paysanne in a short petticoat and high cap – and be sure that she was honest.'

I could not help smiling. I felt sure he now exaggerated the case: Ginevra, I was certain, was honest enough, with all her giddiness. I told him so. He shook his head, and said he would not be the man to trust her with his honour.

'The only thing,' said I, 'with which you may safely trust her. She would unscrupulously damage a husband's purse and property, recklessly try his patience and temper: I don't think she would breathe, or let another breathe, on his honour.'

'You are becoming her advocate,' said he. 'Do you wish me to resume my old chains?'

'No: I am glad to see you free, and trust that free you will long remain. Yet be, at the same time, just.'

'I am so: just as Rhadamanthus,[118] Lucy. When once I am thoroughly estranged, I cannot help being severe. But look! the King and Queen are rising. I like that Queen: she has a sweet countenance. Mama, too, is excessively tired; we shall never get the old lady home if we stay longer.'

'I tired, John?' cried Mrs Bretton, looking at least as animated and as wide-awake as her son, 'I would undertake to sit you out yet: leave us both here till morning, and we should see which would look the most jaded by sunrise.'

'I should not like to try the experiment; for, in truth, mama, you are the most unfading of evergreens, and the freshest of matrons. It must then be on the plea of your son's delicate nerves and fragile constitution that I found a petition for our speedy adjournment.'

'Indolent young man! You wish you were in bed, no doubt; and I suppose you must be humoured. There is Lucy, too, looking quite done up. For shame, Lucy! At your age, a week of evenings-out would not have made me a shade paler. Come away, both of you; and you may laugh at the old lady as much as you please, but, for my part, I shall take charge of the band-box and turban.'

Which she did accordingly. I offered to relieve her, but was shaken off with kindly contempt: my godmother opined that I had enough to do to take care of myself. Not standing on ceremony now, in the midst of the gay 'confusion worse confounded' succeeding to the King and Queen's departure, Mrs Bretton preceded us, and promptly made us a lane through the crowd. Graham followed, apostrophizing his mother as the most flourishing grisette it had ever been his good fortune to see charged with carriage of a band-box; he also desired me to mark her affection for the sky-blue turban, and announced his conviction that she intended one day to wear it.

The night was now very cold and very dark, but with little delay we found the carriage. Soon we were packed in it, as warm and as snug as at a fire-side; and the drive home was, I think, still pleasanter than the drive to the concert. Pleasant it was, even though the coachman – having spent in the shop of a 'marchand de vin' a portion of the time we passed at the concert – drove us along the dark and solitary chaussée far past the turn leading down to La Terrasse; we, who were occupied in talking and laughing, not noticing the aberration – till at last, Mrs Bretton intimated that though she had always thought the chateau a retired spot, she did not know it was situated at the world's end, as she declared seemed now to be the case, for she believed we had been an hour and a half en route, and had not yet taken the turn down the avenue.

Then Graham looked out, and perceiving only dim-spread fields, with unfamiliar rows of pollards and limes ranged along their else invisible sunk-fences, began to conjecture how matters were, and calling a halt and descending, he mounted the box and took the reins himself. Thanks to him, we arrived safe at home about an hour and a half beyond our time.

Martha had not forgotten us; a cheerful fire was burning, and a neat supper spread in the dining-room: we were glad of both. The winter dawn was actually breaking before we gained our chambers. I took off my pink dress and lace mantle with happier feelings than I had experienced in putting them on. Not all, perhaps, who had shone brightly arrayed at that concert could say the same; for not all had been satisfied with friendship – with its calm comfort and modest hope.

CHAPTER 21

Reaction

YET THREE DAYS, and then I must go back to the Pensionnat. I almost numbered the moments of these days upon the clock; fain would I have retarded their flight; but they glided by while I watched them: they were already gone while I yet feared their departure.

'Lucy will not leave us to-day,' said Mrs Bretton, coaxingly, at breakfast; 'she knows we can procure a second respite.'

'I would not ask for one if I might have it for a word,' said I. 'I long to get the good-bye over, and to be settled in the Rue Fossette again. I must go this morning: I must go directly; my trunk is packed and corded.'

It appeared, however, that my going depended upon Graham; he had said he would accompany me, and it so fell out that he was engaged all day, and only returned home at dusk. Then ensued a little combat of words. Mrs Bretton and her son pressed me to remain one night more. I could have cried, so irritated and eager was I to be gone. I longed to leave them as the criminal on the scaffold longs for the axe to descend: that is, I wished the pang over. How much I wished it, they could not tell. On these points, mine was a state of mind out of their experience.

It was dark when Dr John handed me from the carriage at Madame Beck's door. The lamp above was lit; it rained a November drizzle, as it had rained all day: the lamplight gleamed on the wet pavement. Just such a night was it as that on which, not a year ago, I had first stopped at this very threshold; just similar was the scene. I remembered the very shapes of the paving-stones which I had noted with idle eye, while, with a thick-beating heart, I waited the un-closing of that door at which I stood – a solitary and a suppliant. On that night, too, I had briefly met him who now stood with me. Had I ever reminded him of that rencontre, or explained it? I had not, nor ever felt the inclination to do so: it was a pleasant thought, laid by in my own mind, and best kept there.

Graham rung the bell. The door was instantly opened, for it was just that period of the evening when the half-boarders took their departure – consequently, Rosine was on the alert.

'Don't come in,' said I to him; but he stepped a moment into the well-lighted vestibule. I had not wished him to see that 'the water stood in my eyes,' for his was too kind a nature ever to be needlessly shown such signs of sorrow. He always wished to heal – to relieve – when, physician as he was, neither cure nor alleviation were, perhaps, in his power.

'Keep up your courage, Lucy. Think of my mother and myself as true friends. We will not forget you.'

'Nor will I forget you, Dr John.'

My trunk was now brought in. We had shaken hands; he had turned to go, but he was not satisfied: he had not done or said enough to content his generous impulses.

'Lucy,' – stepping after me – 'shall you feel very solitary here?'

'At first I shall.'

'Well, my mother will soon call to see you; and, meantime, I'll tell you what I'll do. I'll write – just any cheerful nonsense that comes into my head – shall I?'

'Good, gallant heart!' thought I to myself; but I shook my head, smiling, and said, 'Never think of it: impose on yourself no such task. *You* write to *me*! – you'll not have time.'

'Oh! I will find or make time. Good-bye!'

He was gone. The heavy door crashed to: the axe had fallen – the pang was experienced.

Allowing myself no time to think or feel – swallowing tears as if they had been wine – I passed to madame's sitting-room to pay the necessary visit of ceremony and respect. She received me with perfectly well-acted cordiality – was even demonstrative, though brief, in her welcome. In ten minutes I was dismissed. From the salle à manger I proceeded to the refectory, where pupils and teachers were now assembled for evening study: again I had a welcome, and one not, I think, quite hollow. That over, I was free to repair to the dormitory.

'And will Graham really write?' I questioned, as I sank tired on the edge of the bed.

Reason, coming stealthily up to me through the twilight of that long, dim chamber, whispered sedately, –

'He may write once. So kind is his nature, it may stimulate him for once to make the effort. But it *cannot* be continued – it *may* not be repeated. Great were that folly which should build on such a promise—insane that credulity which should mistake the transitory rain-pool, holding in its hollow one draught, for the perennial spring yielding the supply of seasons.'

I bent my head: I sat thinking an hour longer. Reason still whispered me, laying on my shoulder a withered hand, and frostily touching my ear with the chill blue lips of eld.

'If,' muttered she, 'if he *should* write, what then? Do you meditate pleasure in replying? Ah, fool! I warn you! Brief be your answer. Hope no delight of heart – no indulgence to intellect: grant no expansion to feeling – give holiday *to* no single faculty: dally with no friendly exchange: foster no genial intercommunion . . . '

'But I have talked to Graham and you did not chide,' I pleaded.

'No,' said she, 'I needed not. Talk for you is good discipline. You converse imperfectly. While you speak, there can be no oblivion of inferiority – no encouragement to delusion: pain, privation, penury stamp your language . . .'

'But,' I again broke in, 'where the bodily presence is weak and the speech contemptible, surely there cannot be error in making written language the medium of better utterance than faltering lips can achieve?'

Reason only answered, 'At your peril you cherish that idea, or suffer its influence to animate any writing of yours!'

'But if I feel, may I *never* express?'

'*Never*!' declared Reason.

I groaned under her bitter sternness. Never – never – oh, hard word! This hag, this Reason, would not let me look up, or smile, or hope: she could not rest unless I were altogether crushed, cowed, broken-in, and broken-down. According to her, I was born only to work for a piece of bread, to await the pains of death, and steadily through all life to despond. Reason might be right; yet no wonder we are glad at times to defy her, to rush from under her rod and give a truant hour to Imagination – *her* soft, bright foe, *our* sweet Help, our divine Hope. We shall and must break bounds at intervals, despite the terrible revenge that awaits our return. Reason is vindictive as a devil: for me, she was always envenomed as a stepmother. If I have obeyed her it has chiefly been with the obedience of fear, not of love. Long ago I should have died of her ill-usage: her stint, her chill, her barren board, her icy bed, her savage, ceaseless blows; but for that kinder Power who holds my secret and sworn allegiance. Often has Reason turned me out by night, in midwinter, on cold snow, flinging for sustenance the gnawed bone dogs had forsaken: sternly has she vowed her stores held nothing more for me – harshly denied my right to ask better things . . . Then, looking up, have I seen in the sky a head amidst circling stars, of which the midmost and the brightest lent a ray sympathetic and attent. A spirit, softer and better than Human Reason, has descended with quiet flight to the waste – bringing all round her a sphere of air borrowed of eternal summer; bringing perfume of flowers which cannot fade – fragrance of trees whose fruit is life; bringing breezes pure from a world whose day needs no sun to lighten it. My hunger has this good angel appeased with food, sweet and strange, gathered amongst gleaning angels, garnering their dew-white harvest in the first fresh hour of a heavenly day; tenderly has she assuaged the insufferable tears which weep away life itself – kindly given rest to deadly weariness – generously lent hope and impulse to paralyzed despair. Divine, compassionate, succourable influence! When I bend the knee to other than God, it shall be at thy white and winged feet, beautiful on mountain or on plain. Temples have been reared to the Sun – altars dedicated to the Moon. Oh, greater glory! To thee neither hands build, nor lips consecrate; but hearts, through ages, are faithful to thy worship. A dwelling thou hast, too wide for walls, too high for dome – a temple whose floors are space – rites whose mysteries transpire in presence, to the kindling, the harmony of worlds!

Sovereign complete! thou hadst, for endurance, thy great army of martyrs; for achievement, thy chosen band of worthies. Deity unquestioned, thine essence foils decay!

This daughter of Heaven remembered me to-night; she saw me weep and she came with comfort: 'Sleep,' she said. 'Sleep, sweetly – I gild thy dreams!'

She kept her word, and watched me through a night's rest; but at dawn Reason relieved the guard. I awoke with a sort of start; the rain was dashing against the panes, and the wind uttering a peevish cry at intervals; the night-lamp was dying on the black circular stand in the middle of the dormitory: day had already broken. How I pity those whom mental pain stuns instead of rousing! This morning the pang of waking snatched me out of bed like a hand with a giant's gripe. How quickly I dressed in the cold of the raw dawn! How deeply I drank of the ice-cold water in my carafe! This was always my cordial, to which, like other dramdrinkers, I had eager recourse when unsettled by chagrin.

Ere long the bell rang its *réveillée* to the whole school. Being dressed, I descended alone to the refectory, where the stove was lit and the air was warm; through the rest of the house it was cold, with the nipping severity of a continental winter: though now but the beginning of November, a north wind had thus early brought a wintry blight over Europe. I remember the black stoves pleased me little when I first came; but now I began to associate with them a sense of comfort, and liked them, as in England, we like a fireside.

Sitting down before this dark comforter, I presently fell into a deep argument with myself on life and its chances, on destiny and her decrees. My mind, calmer and stronger now than last night, made for itself some imperious rules, prohibiting under deadly penalties all weak retrospect of happiness past; commanding a patient journeying through the wilderness of the present, enjoining a reliance on faith – a watching of the cloud and pillar which subdue while they guide, and awe while they illumine – hushing the impulse of fond idolatry, checking the longing out-look for a far-off promised land whose rivers are, perhaps, never to be reached save in dying dreams, whose sweet pastures are to be viewed but from the desolate and sepulchral summit of a Nebo.[120]

By degrees, a composite feeling of blended strength and pain wound itself wirily round my heart, sustained, or at least restrained, its throbbings, and made me fit for the day's work. I lifted my head.

As I said before, I was sitting near the stove, let into the wall beneath the refectory and the carré, and thus sufficing to heat both apartments. Piercing the same wall, and close beside the stove, was a window, looking also into the carré; as I looked up a cap-tassel, a brow, two eyes filled a pane of that window; the fixed gaze of those two eyes hit right against my own glance: they were watching me. I had not till that moment known that tears were on my cheek, but I felt them now.

This was a strange house, where no corner was sacred from intrusion, where not a tear could be shed, nor a thought pondered, but a spy was at hand to note and to divine. And this new, this out-door, this male spy, what business had brought him to the premises at this unwonted hour? What possible right had he to intrude on me thus? No other professor would have dared to cross the carré before the class-bell rang. M. Emanuel took no account of hours nor of claims: there was some book of reference in the first-classe library which he had occasion to consult; he had come to seek it: on his way he passed the refectory. It was very much his habit to wear eyes before, behind, and on each side of him: he had seen me through the little window – he now opened the refectory door, and there he stood.

'Mademoiselle, vous êtes triste.'

'Monsieur, j'en ai bien le droit.'

'Vous êtes malade de coeur et d'humeur,'[121] he pursued. 'You are at once mournful and mutinous. I see on your cheek two tears which I know are hot as two sparks, and salt as two crystals of the sea. While I speak you eye me strangely. Shall I tell you of what I am reminded while watching you?'

'Monsieur, I shall be called away to prayers shortly; my time for conversation is very scant and brief at this hour – excuse – '

'I excuse everything,' he interrupted; 'my mood is so meek, neither rebuff nor, perhaps insult could ruffle it. You remind me, then, of a young she wild creature, new caught, untamed, viewing with a mixture of fire and fear the first entrance of the breaker-in.'

Unwarrantable accost! – rash and rude if addressed to a pupil; to a teacher inadmissible. He thought to provoke a warm reply; I had seen him vex the passionate to explosion before now. In me his malice should find no gratification; I sat silent.

'You look,' said he, 'like one who would snatch at a draught of sweet poison, and spurn wholesome bitters with disgust.'

'Indeed, I never liked bitters; nor do I believe them wholesome. And to whatever is sweet, be it poison or food, you cannot, at least, deny its own delicious quality – sweetness. Better, perhaps, to die quickly a pleasant death, than drag on long a charmless life.'

'Yet,' said he, 'you should take your bitter dose duly and daily, if I had the power to administer it; and, as to the well-beloved poison, I would, perhaps, break the very cup which held it.'

I sharply turned my head away, partly because his presence utterly displeased me, and partly because I wished to shun questions: lest, in my present mood, the effort of answering should overmaster self-command.

'Come,' said he, more softly, 'tell me the truth – you grieve at being parted from friends – is it not so?'

The insinuating softness was not more acceptable than the inquisitorial curiosity. I was silent. He came into the room, sat down on the bench about two yards from me, and persevered long, and, for him, patiently, in attempts to draw me into conversation – attempts necessarily unavailing, because I *could* not talk. At last I entreated to be let alone. In uttering the request, my voice faltered, my head sank on my arms and the table. I wept bitterly, though quietly. He sat a while longer. I did not look up nor speak, till the closing door and his retreating steps told me that he was gone. These tears proved a relief.

I had time to bathe my eyes before breakfast, and I suppose I appeared at that meal as serene as any other person: not, however, quite as jocund-looking as the young lady who placed herself in the seat opposite mine, fixed on me a pair of somewhat small eyes twinkling gleefully, and frankly stretched across the table a white hand to be shaken. Miss Fanshawe's travels, gaieties, and flirtations agreed with her mightily; she had become quite plump, her cheeks looked as round as apples. I had seen her last in elegant evening attire. I don't know that she looked much less charming now in her school-dress, a kind of careless peignoir of a dark-blue material, dimly and dingily plaided with black. I even think this dusky wrapper gave her charms a triumph; enhancing by contrast the fairness of her skin, the freshness of her bloom, the golden beauty of her tresses.

'I am glad you are come back, Timon,'[122] said she. Timon was one of her dozen names for me. 'You don't know how often I have wanted you in this dismal hole.'

'Oh! have you? Then, of course, if you wanted me, you have something for me to do: stockings to mend, perhaps?' I never gave Ginevra a minute's or a farthing's credit for disinterestedness.

'Crabbed and crusty as ever!' said she. 'I expected as much: it would not be you if you did not snub one. But now, come, grandmother, I hope you like coffee as much, and pistolets as little as ever: are you disposed to barter?'

'Take your own way.'

This way consisted in a habit she had of making me convenient. She did not like the morning cup of coffee; its school brewage not being strong or sweet enough to suit her palate; and she had an excellent appetite, like any other healthy school-girl, for the morning pistolets or rolls, which were new-baked and very good, and of which a certain allowance was served to each. This allowance being more than I needed, I gave half to Ginevra; never varying in my preference, though many others used to covet the superfluity; and she in return would sometimes give me a portion of her coffee. This morning I was glad of the draught; hunger I had none, and with thirst I was parched. I don't know why I chose to give my bread rather to Ginevra than to another; nor why, if two had to share the convenience of one drinking-vessel, as sometimes happened – for instance, when we took a long walk into the country, and halted for refreshment at a farm I always contrived that she should be my convive, and rather liked to let her take the lion's share, whether of the white beer, the sweet wine, or the new milk: so it was, however, and she knew it; and, therefore, while we wrangled daily, we were never alienated.

After breakfast my custom was to withdraw to the first classe, and sit and read, or think (oftenest the latter) there alone, till the nine o'clock bell threw open all doors, admitted the gathered rush of externes and demi-pensionnaires, and gave the signal for entrance on that bustle and business to which, till five P.M., there was no relax.

I was just seated this morning, when a tap came to the door.

'Pardon, mademoiselle,' said a pensionnaire, entering gently; and having taken from her desk some necessary book or paper, she withdrew on tip-toe, murmuring, as she passed me, 'Que mademoiselle est appliquée!'

Appliquée, indeed! The means of application were spread before me, but I was doing nothing; and had done nothing, and meant to do nothing. Thus does the world give us credit for merits we have not. Madame Beck herself deemed me a regular bas-bleu, and often and solemnly used to warn me not to study too much, lest 'the blood should all go to my head.' Indeed, everybody in the Rue Fossette held a superstition that 'Meess Lucie' was learned; with the notable exception of M. Emanuel: who, by means peculiar to himself, and quite inscrutable to me, had obtained a not inaccurate inkling of my real qualifications, and used to take quiet opportunities of chuckling in my ear his malign glee over their scant measure. For my part, I never troubled myself about this penury. I dearly liked to think my own thoughts; I had great pleasure in reading a few books, but not many: preferring always those in whose style or sentiment the writer's individual nature was plainly stamped; flagging inevitably over characterless books, however clever and meritorious; perceiving well that, as far as my own mind was concerned, God had limited its powers and its action – thankful, I trust, for the gift bestowed, but unambitious of higher endowments, not restlessly eager after higher culture.

The polite pupil was scarcely gone, when, unceremoniously, without tap, in burst a second intruder. Had I been blind I should have known who this was. A constitutional reserve of manner had by this time told with wholesome and, for me, commodious effect, on the manners of my co-inmates; rarely did I now suffer from rude or intrusive treatment. When I first came, it would happen once and again that a blunt German would clap me on the shoulder, and ask me to run a race; or a riotous Labassecourienne seize me by the arm and drag me towards the play-ground: urgent proposals to take a swing at the 'Pas de Géant,' or to join in a certain romping hide-and-seek game called 'Un, deux, trois,' were formerly also of hourly occurrence; but all these little attentions had ceased some time ago – ceased, too, without my finding it necessary to be at the trouble of point-blank cutting them short. I had now no familiar

demonstration to dread or endure, save from one quarter; and as
that was English I could bear it. Ginevra Fanshawe made no scruple
of – at times – catching me as I was crossing the carré, whirling me
round in a compulsory waltz, and heartily enjoying the mental and
physical discomfiture her proceeding induced. Ginevra Fanshawe it
was who now broke in upon my 'learned leisure.' She carried a huge
music-book under her arm.

'Go to your practising,' said I to her at once: 'away with you to
the little salon!'

'Not till I have had a talk with you, chère amie. I know where you
have been spending your vacation, and how you have commenced
sacrificing to the graces, and enjoying life like any other belle. I saw
you at the concert the other night, dressed, actually, like anybody
else. Who is your tailleuse?'

'Tittle-tattle: how prettily it begins! My tailleuse! – a fiddlestick!
Come, sheer off, Ginevra. I really don't want your company.'

'But when I want yours so much, ange farouche,[123] what does a
little reluctance on your part signify? Dieu merci! we know how to
manoeuvre with our gifted compatriote – the learned "ourse
Britannique."[124] And so, Ourson, you know Isidore?'

'I know John Bretton.'

'Oh, hush!' (putting her fingers in her ears) 'you crack my
tympanums with your rude Anglicisms. But, how is our well-beloved
John? Do tell me about him. The poor man must be in a sad way.
What did he say to my behaviour the other night? Wasn't I cruel?'

'Do you think I noticed you?'

'It was a delightful evening. Oh, that divine de Hamal! And then
to watch the other sulking and dying in the distance; and the old
lady – my future mama-in-law! But I am afraid I and Lady Sara
were a little rude in quizzing her.'

'Lady Sara never quizzed her at all; and for what *you* did, don't
make yourself in the least uneasy: Mrs Bretton will survive *your*
sneer.'

'She may: old ladies are tough; but that poor son of hers! Do tell
me what he said: I saw he was terribly cut up.'

'He said you looked as if, at heart, you were already Madame de
Hamal.'

'Did he?' she cried, with delight. 'He noticed that? How
charming! I thought he would be mad with jealousy.'

'Ginevra, have you seriously done with Dr Bretton? Do you want
him to give you up?'

'Oh! you know he *can't* do that: but wasn't he mad?'

'Quite mad,' I assented; 'as mad as a March hare.'

'Well, and how *ever* did you get him home?'

'How *ever*, indeed! Have you no pity on his poor mother and me? Fancy us holding him tight down in the carriage, and he raving between us, fit to drive everybody delirious. The very coachman went wrong, somehow, and we lost our way.'

'You don't say so? You are laughing at me. Now, Lucy Snowe –'

'I assure you it is fact – and fact, also, that Dr Bretton would *not* stay in the carriage: he broke from us, and *would* ride outside.'

'And afterwards?'

'Afterwards – when we *did* reach home – the scene transcends description.'

'Oh, but describe it – you know it is such fun!'

'Fun for you, Miss Fanshawe; but' (with stern gravity) 'you know the proverb – "What is sport to one may be death to another." '

'Go on, there's a darling Timon.'

'Conscientiously, I cannot, unless you assure me you have some heart.'

'I have – such an immensity, you don't know!'

'Good! In that case, you will be able to conceive Dr Graham Bretton rejecting his supper in the first instance – the chicken, the sweet-bread prepared for his refreshment, left on the table untouched. Then but it is of no use dwelling at length on harrowing details. Suffice it to say, that never, in the most stormy fits and moments of his infancy, had his mother such work to tuck the sheets about him as she had that night.'

'He wouldn't lie still?'

'He wouldn't lie still: there it was. The sheets might be tucked in, but the thing was to keep them tucked in.'

'And what did he say?'

'Say! Can't you imagine him demanding his divine Ginevra, anathematizing that demon, de Hamal – raving about golden locks, blue eyes, white arms, glittering bracelets?'

'No, did he? He saw the bracelet?'

'Saw the bracelet? Yes, as plain as I saw it: and, perhaps, for the first time, he saw also the brand-mark with which its pressure has circled your arm. Ginevra,' (rising, and changing my tone) 'come, we will have an end of this. Go away to your practising.' And I opened the door.

'But you've not told me all.'

'You had better not wait until I *do* tell you all. Such extra communicativeness could give you no pleasure. March!'

'Cross thing!' said she; but she obeyed: and, indeed, the first classe was my territory, and she could not there legally resist a notice of quittance from me.

Yet, to speak the truth, never had I been less dissatisfied with her than I was then. There was pleasure in thinking of the contrast between the reality and my description – to remember Dr John enjoying the drive home, eating his supper with relish, and retiring to rest with Christian composure. It was only when I saw him really unhappy that I felt really vexed with the fair, frail cause of his suffering.

A fortnight passed; I was getting once more inured to the harness of school, and lapsing from the passionate pain of change to the palsy of custom. One afternoon in crossing the carré, on my way to the first classe, where I was expected to assist at a lesson of 'style and literature,' I saw, standing by one of the long and large windows, Rosine, the portress. Her attitude, as usual, was quite nonchalante. She always 'stood at ease;' one of her hands rested in her apron-pocket, the other, at this moment, held to her eyes a letter, whereof Mademoiselle coolly perused the address, and deliberately studied the seal.

A letter! The shape of a letter similar to that had haunted my brain in its very core for seven days past. I had dreamed of a letter last night. Strong magnetism drew me to that letter now; yet, whether I should have ventured to demand of Rosine so much as a glance at that white envelope, with the spot of red wax in the middle, I know not. No; I think I should have sneaked past in terror of a rebuff from Disappointment: my heart throbbed now as if I already heard the tramp of her approach. Nervous mistake! It was the rapid step of the Professor of Literature measuring the corridor. I fled before him. Could I but be seated quietly at my desk before his arrival, with the class under my orders all in disciplined readiness, he would, perhaps, exempt me from notice; but, if caught lingering in the carré, I should be sure to come in for a special harangue. I had time to get seated, to enforce perfect silence, to take out my work, and to commence it amidst the profoundest and best trained hush, ere M. Emanuel entered with his vehement burst of latch and panel, and his deep, redundant bow, prophetic of choler.

As usual he broke upon us like a clap of thunder; but instead of flashing lightning-wise from the door to the estrade, his career halted midway at my desk. Setting his face towards me and the

window, his back to the pupils and the room, he gave me a look –
such a look as might have licensed me to stand straight up and
demand what he meant – a look of scowling distrust.

'Voilà! pour vous,' said he, drawing his hand from his waistcoat,
and placing on my desk a letter – the very letter I had seen in
Rosine's hand – the letter whose face of enamelled white and single
Cyclops-eye[125] of vermilion-red had printed themselves so clear and
perfect on the retina of an inward vision. I knew it, I felt it to be the
letter of my hope, the fruition of my wish, the release from my
doubt, the ransom from my terror. This letter M. Paul, with his
unwarrantably interfering habits, had taken from the portress, and
now delivered it himself.

I might have been angry, but had not a second for the sensation.
Yes: I held in my hand not a slight note, but an envelope, which
must, at least, contain a sheet: it felt, not flimsy, but firm, substantial,
satisfying. And here was the direction, 'Miss Lucy Snowe,' in a clean,
clear, equal, decided hand; and there was the seal, round, full, deftly
dropped by untremulous fingers, stamped with the well-cut impress
of initials, 'J. G. B.' I experienced a happy feeling – a glad emotion
which went warm to my heart, and ran lively through all my veins.
For once a hope was realized. I held in my hand a morsel of real
solid joy: not a dream, not an image of the brain, not one of those
shadowy chances imagination pictures, and on which humanity
starves but cannot live; not a mess of that manna I drearily eulogized
awhile ago – which, indeed, at first melts on the lips with an
unspeakable and preternatural sweetness, but which, in the end, our
souls full surely loathe; longing deliriously for natural and earth-
grown food, wildly praying Heaven's Spirits to reclaim their own
spirit-dew and essence – an aliment divine, but for mortals deadly. It
was neither sweet hail, nor small coriander-seed – neither slight
wafer, nor luscious honey, I had lighted on; it was the wild savoury
mess of the hunter, nourishing and salubrious meat, forest-fed or
desert-reared, fresh, healthful, and life-sustaining. It was what the
old dying patriarch[126] demanded of his son Esau, promising him in
requital the blessing of his last breath. It was a godsend; and I
inwardly thanked the God who had vouchsafed it. Outwardly I only
thanked man, crying, 'Thank you, thank you, Monsieur!'

Monsieur curled his lip, gave me a vicious glance of the eye, and
strode to his estrade. M. Paul was not at all a good little man,
though he had good points.

Did I read my letter there and then? Did I consume the venison
at once and with haste, as if Esau's shaft flew every day?

I knew better. The cover with its address; the seal, with its three clear letters, was bounty and abundance for the present. I stole from the room, I procured the key of the great dormitory which was kept locked by day. I went to my bureau; with a sort of haste and trembling lest Madame should creep up-stairs and spy me, I opened a drawer, unlocked a box, and took out a case, and – having feasted my eyes with one more look, and approached the seal, with a mixture of awe and shame and delight, to my lips – I folded the untasted treasure, yet all fair and inviolate, in silver paper, committed it to the case, shut up box and drawer, reclosed, relocked the dormitory, and returned to class, feeling as if fairy tales were true and fairy gifts no dream. Strange, sweet insanity! And this letter, the source of my joy, I had not yet read: did not yet know the number of its lines.

When I re-entered the school-room, behold M. Paul raging like a pestilence! Some pupil had not spoken audibly or distinctly enough to suit his ear and taste, and now she and others were weeping, and he was raving from his estrade almost livid. Curious to mention, as I appeared, he fell on me.

'Was I the mistress of these girls? Did I profess to teach them the conduct befitting ladies? – and did I permit and, he doubted not, encourage them to strangle their mother-tongue in their throats, to mince and mash it between their teeth, as if they had some base cause to be ashamed of the words they uttered? Was this modesty? He knew better. It was a vile pseudo sentiment – the offspring or the forerunner of evil. Rather than submit to this mopping and mowing, this mincing and grimacing, this grinding of a noble tongue, this general affectation and sickening stubbornness of the pupils of the first class, he would throw them up for a set of insupportable petites-maîtresses, and confine himself to teaching the A B C to the babies of the third division.'

What could I say to all this? Really nothing; and I hoped he would allow me to be silent. The storm recommenced.

'Every answer to his queries was then refused? It seemed to be considered in *that* place – that conceited boudoir of a first classe, with its pretentious book-cases, its green-baized desks, its rubbish of flower-stands, its trash of framed pictures and maps, and its foreign surveillante, forsooth!—it seemed to be the fashion to think *there* that the Professor of Literature was not worthy of a reply! These were new ideas; imported, he did not doubt, straight from "la Grande Bretagne': they savoured of island insolence and arrogance.'

Lull the second – the girls, not one of whom was ever known to weep a tear for the rebukes of any other master, now all melting like snow-statues before the intemperate heat of M. Emanuel: I, not yet much shaken, sitting down, and venturing to resume my work.

Something – either in my continued silence or in the movement of my hand, stitching – transported M. Emanuel beyond the last boundary of patience; he actually sprung from his estrade. The stove stood near my desk, and he attacked it; the little iron door was nearly dashed from its hinges, the fuel was made to fly.

'Est-ce que vous avez l'intention de m'insulter?' said he to me, in a low, furious voice, as he thus outraged, under pretence of arranging, the fire.

It was time to soothe him a little if possible.

'Mais, monsieur,' said I, 'I would not insult you for the world. I remember too well that you once said we should be friends.'

I did not intend my voice to falter, but it did: more, I think, through the agitation of late delight than in any spasm of present fear. Still there certainly was something in M. Paul's anger – a kind of passion of emotion – that specially tended to draw tears. I was not unhappy, nor much afraid, yet I wept.

'Allons, allons!' said he presently, looking round and seeing the deluge universal. 'Decidedly I am a monster and a ruffian. I have only one pocket-handkerchief,' he added, 'but if I had twenty, I would offer you each one. Your teacher shall be your representative. Here, Miss Lucy.'

And he took forth and held out to me a clean silk handkerchief. Now a person who did not know M. Paul, who was unused to him and his impulses, would naturally have bungled at this offer – declined accepting the same – etcetera. But I too plainly felt this would never do: the slightest hesitation would have been fatal to the incipient treaty of peace. I rose and met the handkerchief half-way, received it with decorum, wiped therewith my eyes, and, resuming my seat, and retaining the flag of truce in my hand and on my lap, took especial care during the remainder of the lesson to touch neither needle nor thimble, scissors nor muslin. Many a jealous glance did M. Paul cast at these implements; he hated them mortally, considering sewing a source of distraction from the attention due to himself. A very eloquent lesson he gave, and very kind and friendly was he to the close. Ere he had done, the clouds were dispersed and the sun shining out – tears were exchanged for smiles.

In quitting the room he paused once more at my desk.

'And your letter?' said he, this time not quite fiercely.

'I have not yet read it, monsieur.'

'Ah! it is too good to read at once: you save it, as, when I was a boy, I used to save a peach whose bloom was very ripe?'

The guess came so near the truth, I could not prevent a suddenly-rising warmth in my face from revealing as much.

'You promise yourself a pleasant moment,' said he, 'in reading that letter; you will open it when alone – n'est-ce pas? Ah! a smile answers. Well, well! one should not be too harsh; "la jeunesse n'a qu'un temps." '[127]

'Monsieur, monsieur!' I cried or rather whispered after him, as he turned to go, 'do not leave me under a mistake. This is merely a friend's letter. Without reading it, I can vouch for that.'

'Je conçois, je conçois: on sait ce que c'est qu'un ami.[128] Bonjour, mademoiselle!'

'But, monsieur, here is your handkerchief.'

'Keep it, keep it, till the letter is read, then bring it me; I shall read the billet's tenor in your eyes.'

When he was gone, the pupils having already poured out of the school-room into the berceau, and thence into the garden and court to take their customary recreation before the five o'clock dinner, I stood a moment thinking, and absently twisting the handkerchief round my arm. For some reason – gladdened, I think, by a sudden return of the golden glimmer of childhood, roused by an unwonted renewal of its buoyancy, made merry by the liberty of the closing hour, and, above all, solaced at heart by the joyous consciousness of that treasure in the case, box, drawer up-stairs, I fell to playing with the handkerchief as if it were a ball, casting it into the air and catching it as it fell. The game was stopped by another hand than mine – a hand emerging from a paletôt-sleeve and stretched over my shoulder; it caught the extemporized plaything and bore it away with these sullen words:

'Je vois bien que vous vous moquez de moi et de mes effets.'[129]

Really that little man was dreadful: a mere sprite of caprice and ubiquity: one never knew either his whim or his whereabout.

CHAPTER 22

The Letter

WHEN ALL WAS STILL IN THE HOUSE; when dinner was over and the noisy recreation-hour past; when darkness had set in, and the quiet lamp of study was lit in the refectory; when the externes were gone home, the clashing door and clamorous bell hushed for the evening; when Madame was safely settled in the salle à manger in company with her mother and some friends; I then glided to the kitchen, begged a bougie for one half hour for a particular occasion, found acceptance of my petition at the hands of my friend Goton, who answered 'Mais certainement, chou-chou, vous en aurez deux, si vous voulez.'[130] And, light in hand, I mounted noiseless to the dormitory.

Great was my chagrin to find in that apartment a pupil gone to bed indisposed, – greater when I recognized amid the muslin night-cap borders, the 'figure chiffonnée' of Mistress Ginevra Fanshawe; supine at this moment, it is true – but certain to wake and overwhelm me with chatter when the interruption would be least acceptable: indeed, as I watched her, a slight twinkling of the eyelids warned me that the present appearance of repose might be but a ruse, assumed to cover sly vigilance over 'Timon's' movements: she was not to be trusted. And I had so wished to be alone, just to read my precious letter in peace.

Well, I must go to the classes. Having sought and found my prize in its casket, I descended. Ill-luck pursued me. The classes were undergoing sweeping and purification by candle-light, according to hebdomadal custom: benches were piled on desks, the air was dim with dust, damp coffee-grounds (used by Labassecourien housemaids instead of tea-leaves) darkened the floor; all was hopeless confusion. Baffled, but not beaten, I withdrew, bent as resolutely as ever on finding solitude *somewhere*.

Taking a key whereof I knew the repository, I mounted three staircases in succession, reached a dark, narrow, silent landing, opened a worm-eaten door, and dived into the deep, black, cold garret. Here none would follow me – none interrupt – not Madame herself. I shut the garret-door; I placed my light on a doddered and mouldy chest of drawers; I put on a shawl, for the air was ice-cold; I took my letter, trembling with sweet impatience; I broke its seal.

'Will it be long – will it be short?' thought I, passing my hand across my eyes to dissipate the silvery dimness of a suave, south wind shower.

It was long.

'Will it be cool? – will it be kind?'

It was kind.

To my checked, bridled, disciplined expectation, it seemed very kind; to my longing and famished thought it seemed, perhaps, kinder than it was.

So little had I hoped, so much had I feared; there was a fullness of delight in this taste of fruition – such, perhaps, as many a human being passes through life without ever knowing. The poor English teacher in the frosty garret, reading by a dim candle guttering in the wintry air, a letter simply good-natured – nothing more: though that good-nature then seemed to me god-like – was happier than most queens in palaces.

Of course, happiness of such shallow origin could but be brief; yet, while it lasted, it was genuine and exquisite: a bubble – but a sweet bubble – of real honey-dew. Dr John had written to me at length; he had written to me with pleasure; he had written in benignant mood, dwelling with sunny satisfaction on scenes that had passed before his eyes and mine – on places we had visited together – on conversations we had held – on all the little subject-matter, in short, of the last few halcyon weeks. But the cordial core of the delight was, a conviction the blithe, genial language generously imparted, that it had been poured out – not merely to content *me* – but to gratify *himself*. A gratification he might never more desire, never more seek – an hypothesis in every point of view approaching the certain; but *that* concerned the future. This present moment had no pain, no blot, no want; full, pure, perfect, it deeply blessed me. A passing seraph seemed to have rested beside me, leaned towards my heart, and reposed on its throb a softening, cooling, healing, hallowing wing. Dr John, you pained me afterwards: forgiven be every ill – freely forgiven – for the sake of that one dear remembered good!

Are there wicked things, not human, which envy human bliss? Are there evil influences haunting the air, and poisoning it for man? What was near me? . . .

Something in that vast solitary garret sounded strangely. Most surely and certainly I heard, as it seemed, a stealthy foot on that floor: a sort of gliding out from the direction of the black recess haunted by the malefactor cloaks. I turned: my light was dim; the room was long – but, as I live! I saw in the middle of that ghostly chamber a figure all black or white; the skirts straight, narrow, black; the head bandaged, veiled, white.

Say what you will, reader – tell me I was nervous, or mad; affirm that I was unsettled by the excitement of that letter; declare that I dreamed: this I vow – I saw there – in that room – on that night – an image like – a NUN.

I cried out; I sickened. Had the shape approached me I might have swooned. It receded: I made for the door. How I descended all the stairs I know not. By instinct I shunned the refectory, and shaped my course to Madame's sitting-room: I burst in. I said –

'There is something in the grenier: I have been there: I saw something. Go and look at it, all of you!'

I said, 'All of you;' for the room seemed to me full of people, though, in truth, there were but four present: Madame Beck; her mother, Madame Kint, who was out of health, and now staying with her on a visit; her brother M. Victor Kint, and another gentleman: who, when I entered the room, was conversing with the old lady, and had his back towards the door.

My mortal fear and faintness must have made me deadly pale. I felt cold and shaking. They all rose in consternation; they surrounded me. I urged them to go to the grenier; the sight of the gentlemen did me good and gave me courage: it seemed as if there was some help and hope, with men at hand. I turned to the door, beckoning them to follow. They wanted to stop me; but I said they must come this way: they must see what I had seen – something strange, standing in the middle of the garret. And, now, I remembered my letter, left on the drawers with the light. This precious letter! Flesh or spirit must be defied for its sake. I flew up-stairs, hastening the faster as I knew I was followed: they were obliged to come.

Lo! When I reached the garret-door, all within was dark as a pit: the light was out. Happily, some one – Madame, I think, with her usual calm sense – had brought a lamp from the room; speedily, therefore, as they came up, a ray pierced the opaque blackness. There stood the bougie quenched on the drawers; but where was the letter? And I looked for *that* now, and not for the nun.

'My letter! my letter!' I panted and plained, almost beside myself. I groped on the floor, wringing my hands wildly. Cruel, cruel doom! To have my bit of comfort preternaturally snatched from me, ere I had well tasted its virtue!

I don't know what the others were doing; I could not watch them:

they asked me questions I did not answer; they ransacked all corners; they prattled about this and that, disarrangement of cloaks, a breach or crack in the sky-light – I know not what. 'Something or somebody has been here,' was sagely averred.

'Oh! they have taken my letter!' cried the grovelling, groping, monomaniac.

'What letter, Lucy? My dear girl, what letter?' asked a known voice in my ear. Could I believe that ear? No: and I looked up. Could I trust my eyes? Had I recognized the tone? Did I now look on the face of the writer of that very letter? Was this gentleman near me in this dim garret, John Graham – Dr Bretton himself?

Yes: it was. He had been called in that very evening to prescribe for some access of illness in old Madame Kint; he was the second gentleman present in the salle à manger when I entered.

'Was it *my* letter, Lucy?'

'Your own: yours – the letter you wrote to me. I had come here to read it quietly. I could not find another spot where it was possible to have it to myself. I had saved it all day – never opened it till this evening: it was scarcely glanced over: I *cannot bear* to lose it. Oh, my letter!'

'Hush! don't cry and distress yourself so cruelly. What is it worth? Hush! Come out of this cold room; they are going to send for the police now to examine further: we need not stay here – come, we will go down.'

A warm hand, taking my cold fingers, led me down to a room where there was a fire. Dr John and I sat before the stove. He talked to me and soothed me with unutterable goodness, promising me twenty letters for the one lost. If there are words and wrongs like knives, whose deep-inflicted lacerations never heal – cutting injuries and insults of serrated and poison-dripping edge – so, too, there are consolations of tone too fine for the ear not fondly and for ever to retain their echo: caressing kindnesses – loved, lingered over through a whole life, recalled with unfaded tenderness, and answering the call with undimmed shine, out of that raven cloud foreshadowing Death himself. I have been told since, that Dr Bretton was not so nearly perfect as I thought him: that his actual character lacked the depth, height, compass, and endurance it possessed in my creed. I don't know: he was as good to me as the well is to the parched wayfarer – as the sun to the shivering jail-bird. I remember him heroic. Heroic at this moment will I hold him to be.

He asked me, smiling, why I cared for his letter so very much. I thought, but did not say, that I prized it like the blood in my veins. I only answered that I had so few letters to care for.

'I am sure you did not read it,' said he; 'or you would think nothing of it!'

'I read it, but only once. I want to read it again. I am sorry it is lost.' And I could not help weeping afresh.

'Lucy, Lucy, my poor little god-sister (if there be such a relationship), here – *here* is your letter. Why is it not better worth such tears, and such tenderly exaggerating faith?'

Curious, characteristic manœuvre! His quick eye had seen the letter on the floor where I sought it; his hand, as quick, had snatched it up. He had hidden it in his waistcoat pocket. If my trouble had wrought with a whit less stress and reality, I doubt whether he would ever have acknowledged or restored it. Tears of temperature one degree cooler than those I shed would only have amused Dr John.

Pleasure at regaining made me forget merited reproach for the teasing torment; my joy was great; it could not be concealed: yet I think it broke out more in countenance than language. I said little.

'Are you satisfied now?' asked Dr John

I replied that I was – satisfied and happy.

'Well then,' he proceeded, 'how do you feel physically? Are you growing calmer? Not much; for you tremble like a leaf still.'

It seemed to me, however, that I was sufficiently calm: at least I felt no longer terrified. I expressed myself composed.

'You are able, consequently, to tell me what you saw? Your account was quite vague, do you know? You looked white as the wall; but you only spoke of "something," not defining *what*. Was it a man? Was it an animal? *What* was it?'

'I never will tell exactly what I saw,' said I, 'unless some one else sees it too, and then I will give corroborative testimony; but otherwise, I shall be discredited and accused of dreaming.'

'Tell me,' said Dr Bretton; 'I will hear it in my professional character: I look on you now from a professional point of view, and I read, perhaps, all you would conceal – in your eye, which is curiously vivid and restless; in your cheek, which the blood has forsaken; in your hand, which you cannot steady. Come, Lucy, speak and tell me.'

'You would laugh – ?'

'If you don't tell me you shall have no more letters.'

'You are laughing now.'

'I will again take away that single epistle: being mine, I think I have a right to reclaim it.'

I felt raillery in his words: it made me grave and quiet; but I folded up the letter and covered it from sight.

'You may hide it, but I can possess it any moment I choose. You don't know my skill in sleight of hand: I might practise as a conjuror if I liked. Mama says sometimes, too, that I have a harmonizing property of tongue and eye; but you never saw that in me – did you Lucy?'

'Indeed – indeed – when you were a mere boy I used to see both: far more then than now – for now you are strong, and strength dispenses with subtlety. But still, Dr John, you have what they call in this country "un air fin," that nobody can mistake. Madame Beck saw it, and – '

'And liked it,' said he, laughing, 'because she has it herself. But, Lucy, give me that letter – you don't really care for it.'

To this provocative speech I made no answer. Graham in mirthful mood must not be humoured too far. Just now there was a new sort of smile playing about his lips – very sweet, but it grieved me somehow – a new sort of light sparkling in his eyes: not hostile, but not reassuring. I rose to go – I bid him good- night a little sadly.

His sensitiveness – that peculiar, apprehensive, detective faculty of his – felt in a moment the unspoken complaint – the scarce-thought reproach. He asked quietly if I was offended. I shook my head as implying a negative.

'Permit me, then, to speak a little seriously to you before you go. You are in a highly nervous state. I feel sure from what is apparent in your look and manner, however well-controlled, that whilst alone this evening in that dismal, perishing sepulchral garret – that dungeon under the leads, smelling of damp and mould, rank with phthisis and catarrh: a place you never ought to enter – that you saw, or *thought* you saw, some appearance peculiarly calculated to impress the imagination. I know you *are* not, nor ever were, subject to material terrors, fears of robbers, &c. – I am not so sure that a visitation bearing a spectral character would not shake your very mind. Be calm now. This is all a matter of the nerves, I see: but just specify the vision.'

'You will tell nobody?'

'Nobody – most certainly. You may trust me as implicitly as you did Père Silas. Indeed, the doctor is perhaps the safer confessor of the two, though he has not gray hair.'

'You will not laugh?'

'Perhaps I may, to do you good; but not in scorn. Lucy, I feel as a friend towards you, though your timid nature is slow to trust.'

He now looked like a friend: that indescribable smile and sparkle were gone; those formidable arched curves of lip, nostril, eyebrow, were depressed; repose marked his attitude – attention sobered his aspect. Won to confidence, I told him exactly what I had seen: ere now I had narrated to him the legend of the house – whiling away with that narrative an hour of a certain mild October afternoon, when he and I rode through Bois l'Etang.

He sat and thought, and while he thought, we heard them all coming down stairs.

'Are they going to interrupt?' said he, glancing at the door with an annoyed expression.

'They will not come here,' I answered; for we were in the little salon where Madame never sat in the evening, and where it was by mere chance that heat was still lingering in the stove. They passed the door and went on to the salle-à-manger.

'Now,' he pursued, 'they will talk about thieves, burglars, and so on: let them do so – mind you say nothing, and keep your resolution of describing your nun to nobody. She may appear to you again: don't start.'

'You think then,' I said, with secret horror, 'she came out of my brain, and is now gone in there, and may glide out again at an hour and a day when I look not for her?'

'I think it a case of spectral illusion: I fear, following on and resulting from long-continued mental conflict.'

'Oh, Doctor John – I shudder at the thought of being liable to such an illusion! It seemed so real. Is there no cure? – no preventive?'

'Happiness is the cure – a cheerful mind the preventive: cultivate both.'

No mockery in this world ever sounds to me so hollow as that of being told to *cultivate* happiness. What does such advice mean? Happiness is not a potato, to be planted in mould, and tilled with manure. Happiness is a glory shining far down upon us out of Heaven. She is a divine dew which the soul, on certain of its summer mornings, feels dropping upon it from the amaranth[131] bloom and golden fruitage of Paradise.

'Cultivate happiness!' I said briefly to the doctor: 'do *you* cultivate happiness? How do you manage?'

'I am a cheerful fellow by nature: and then ill-luck has never dogged me. Adversity gave me and my mother one passing scowl and brush, but we defied her, or rather laughed at her, and she went by.'

'There is no cultivation in all this.'

'I do not give way to melancholy.'

'Yes: I have seen you subdued by that feeling.'

'About Ginevra Fanshawe – eh?'

'Did she not sometimes make you miserable?'

'Pooh! stuff! nonsense! You see I am better now.'

If a laughing eye with a lively light, and a face bright with beaming and healthy energy, could attest that he was better, better he certainly was.

'You do not look much amiss, or greatly out of condition,' I allowed.

'And why, Lucy, can't you look and feel as I do – buoyant, courageous, and fit to defy all the nuns and flirts in Christendom? I would give gold on the spot just to see you snap your fingers. Try the manœuvre.'

'If I were to bring Miss Fanshawe into your presence just now?'

'I vow, Lucy, she should not move me: or, she should move me but by one thing – true, yes, and passionate love. I would accord forgiveness at no less a price.'

'Indeed! a smile of hers would have been a fortune to you a while since.'

'Transformed, Lucy: transformed! Remember, you once called me a slave! but I am a free man now!'

He stood up: in the port of his head, the carriage of his figure, in his beaming eye and mien, there revealed itself a liberty which was more than ease – a mood which was disdain of his past bondage.

'Miss Fanshawe,' he pursued, 'has led me through a phase of feeling which is over: I have entered another condition, and am now much disposed to exact love for love – passion for passion – and good measure of it too.'

'Ah, Doctor! Doctor! you said it was your nature to pursue Love under difficulties – to be charmed by a proud insensibility!'

He laughed, and answered, 'My nature varies: the mood of one hour is sometimes the mockery of the next. Well, Lucy' (drawing on his gloves), 'will the Nun come again to-night, think you?'

'I don't think she will.'

'Give her my compliments, if she does – Dr John's compliments – and entreat her to have the goodness to wait a visit from him. Lucy, was she a pretty nun? Had she a pretty face? You have not told me that yet; and *that is* the really important point.'

'She had a white cloth over her face,' said I, 'but her eyes glittered.'

'Confusion to her goblin trappings!' cried he, irreverently: 'but at least she had handsome eyes – bright and soft.'

'Cold and fixed,' was my reply.

'No, no, we'll none of her: she shall not haunt you, Lucy. Give her that shake of the hand, if she comes again. Will she stand *that*, do you think?'

I thought it too kind and cordial for a ghost to stand; and so was the smile which matched it, and accompanied his 'Good-night.'

And had there been anything in the garret? What did they discover? I believe, on the closest examination, their discoveries amounted to very little. They talked, at first, of the cloaks being disturbed; but Madame Beck told me afterwards she thought they hung much as usual: and as for the broken pane in the skylight, she affirmed that aperture was rarely without one or more panes broken or cracked: and besides, a heavy hail-storm had fallen a few days ago. Madame questioned me very closely as to what I had seen, but I only described an obscure figure clothed in black: I took care not to breathe the word 'nun,' certain that this word would at once suggest to her mind an idea of romance and unreality. She charged me to say nothing on the subject to any servant, pupil, or teacher, and highly commended my discretion in coming to her private salle-à-manger, instead of carrying the tale of horror to the school refectory. Thus the subject dropped. I was left secretly and sadly to wonder, in my own mind, whether that strange thing was of this world, or of a realm beyond the grave; or whether indeed it was only the child of malady, and I of that malady the prey.

CHAPTER 23

Vashti

To wonder sadly, did I say? No: a new influence began to act upon my life, and sadness, for a certain space, was held at bay. Conceive a dell, deep-hollowed in forest secrecy; it lies in dimness and mist: its turf is dank, its herbage pale and humid. A storm or an axe makes a wide gap amongst the oak-trees; the breeze sweeps in; the sun looks down; the sad, cold dell becomes a deep cup of lustre; high summer pours her blue glory and her golden light out of that beauteous sky, which till now the starved hollow never saw.

A new creed became mine – a belief in happiness.

It was three weeks since the adventure of the garret, and I possessed in that case, box, drawer up-stairs, casketed with that first letter, four companions like to it, traced by the same firm pen, sealed with the same clear seal, full of the same vital comfort. Vital comfort it seemed to me then: I read them in after years; they were kind letters enough – pleasing letters, because composed by one well-pleased; in the two last there were three or four closing lines half-gay, half-tender, 'by *feeling* touched, but not subdued.' Time, dear reader, mellowed them to a beverage of this mild quality; but when I first tasted their elixir, fresh from the fount so honoured, it seemed juice of a divine vintage: a draught which Hebe might fill, and the very gods approve.

Does the reader, remembering what was said some pages back, care to ask how I answered these letters: whether under the dry, stinting check of Reason, or according to the full, liberal impulse of Feeling?

To speak truth, I compromised matters; I served two masters: I bowed down in the house of Rimmon,[132] and lifted the heart at another shrine. I wrote to these letters two answers – one for my own relief, the other for Graham's perusal .

To begin with: Feeling and I turned Reason out of doors, drew against her bar and bolt, then we sat down, spread our paper, dipped in the ink an eager pen, and, with deep enjoyment, poured out our sincere heart. When we had done – when two sheets were covered with the language of a strongly-adherent affection, a rooted and active gratitude – (once, for all, in this parenthesis, I disclaim, with the utmost scorn, every sneaking suspicion of what are called 'warmer feelings:' women do not entertain these 'warmer feelings' where, from the commencement, through the whole progress of an acquaintance, they have never once been cheated of the conviction that to do so would be to commit a mortal absurdity: nobody ever launches into Love unless he has seen or dreamed the rising of Hope's star over Love's troubled waters) – when, then, I had given expression to a closely-clinging and deeply-honouring attachment – an attachment that wanted to attract to itself and take into its own lot all that was painful in the destiny of its object; that would, if it could, have absorbed and conducted away all storms and lightnings from an existence viewed with a passion of solicitude – then, just at that moment, the doors of my heart would shake, bolt and bar would yield, Reason would leap in, vigorous and revengeful, snatch the full sheets, read, sneer, erase, tear up, re-write, fold, seal, direct, and send a terse, curt missive of a page. She did right.

I did not live on letters only: I was visited, I was looked after; once a week I was taken out to La Terrasse; always I was made much of. Dr Bretton failed not to tell me *why* he was so kind: 'To keep away the nun,' he said; 'he was determined to dispute with her her prey. He had taken,' he declared, 'a thorough dislike to her, chiefly on account of that white face-cloth, and those cold gray eyes: the moment he heard of those odious particulars,' he affirmed, 'consummate disgust had incited him to oppose her; he was determined to try whether he or she was the cleverest, and he only wished she would once more look in upon me when he was present:' but *that* she never did. In short, he regarded me scientifically in the light of a patient, and at once exercised his professional skill, and gratified his natural benevolence, by a course of cordial and attentive treatment.

One evening, the first in December, I was walking by myself in the carré; it was six o'clock; the classe-doors were closed; but within, the pupils, rampant in the license of evening recreation, were counterfeiting a miniature chaos. The carré was quite dark, except a red light shining under and about the stove; the wide glass-doors and the long windows were frosted over; a crystal sparkle of starlight, here and there spangling this blanched winter veil, and breaking with scattered brilliants the paleness of its embroidery, proved it a clear night, though moonless. That I should dare to remain thus alone in darkness, showed that my nerves were regaining a healthy tone: I thought of the nun, but hardly feared her; though the staircase was behind me, leading up, through blind, black night, from landing to landing, to the haunted grenier. Yet I own my heart quaked, my pulse leaped, when I suddenly heard breathing and rustling, and turning, saw in the deep shadow of the steps a deeper shadow still—a shape that moved and descended. It paused a while at the classe door, and then it glided before me. Simultaneously came a clangor of the distant door-bell. Life-like sounds bring life-like feelings: this shape was too round and low for my gaunt nun: it was only Madame Beck on duty.

'Mademoiselle Lucy!' cried Rosine, bursting in, lamp in hand, from the corridor, 'On est là pour vous au salon.'

Madame saw me, I saw Madame, Rosine saw us both: there was no mutual recognition. I made straight for the salon. There I found what I own I anticipated I should find – Dr Bretton; but he was in evening-dress.

'The carriage is at the door,' said he; 'my mother has sent it to take you to the theatre; she was going herself but an arrival has prevented her: she immediately said, "Take Lucy in my place." Will you go?'

'Just now? I am not dressed,' cried I, glancing despairingly at my dark merino.

'You have half an hour to dress. I should have given you notice, but I only determined on going since five o'clock, when I heard there was to be a genuine regale in the presence of a great actress.'

And he mentioned a name that thrilled me – a name that, in those days, could thrill Europe. It is hushed now: its once restless echoes are all still; she who bore it went years ago to her rest: night and oblivion long since closed above her; but *then* her day – a day of Sirius[133] – stood at its full height, light and fervour.

'I'll go; I will be ready in ten minutes,' I vowed. And away I flew, never once checked, reader, by the thought which perhaps at this moment checks you: namely that to go anywhere with Graham and without Mrs Bretton could be objectionable. I could not have conceived, much less have expressed, to Graham such thought – such scruple – without risk of exciting a tyrannous self-contempt; of kindling an inward fire of shame so quenchless, and so devouring, that I think it would soon have licked up the very life in my veins. Besides, my godmother, knowing her son, and knowing me, would as soon have thought of chaperoning a sister with a brother, as of keeping anxious guard over our incomings and outgoings.

The present was no occasion for showy array; my dunmist crape would suffice, and I sought the same in the great oak-wardrobe in the dormitory, where hung no less than forty dresses. But there had been changes and reforms, and some innovating hand had pruned this same crowded wardrobe, and carried divers garments to the grenier – my crape amongst the rest. I must fetch it. I got the key, and went aloft fearless, almost thoughtless. I unlocked the door, I plunged in. The reader may believe it or not, but when I thus suddenly entered, that garret was not wholly dark as it should have been: from one point there shone a solemn light, like a star, but broader. So plainly it shone, that it revealed the deep alcove with a portion of the tarnished scarlet curtain drawn over it. Instantly, silently, before my eyes, it vanished; so did the curtain and alcove: all that end of the garret became black as night. I ventured no research; I had not time nor will; snatching my dress, which hung on the wall, happily near the door, I rushed out, relocked the door with convulsed haste, and darted downwards to the dormitory.

But I trembled too much to dress myself: impossible to arrange hair or fasten hooks-and-eyes with such fingers, so I called Rosine and bribed her to help me. Rosine liked a bribe, so she did her best, smoothed and plaited my hair as well as a coiffeur would have done, placed the lace collar mathematically straight, tied the neck-ribbon accurately – in short, did her work like the neat-handed Phillis she could be when she chose. Having given me my handkerchief and gloves, she took the candle and lighted me down stairs. After all, I had forgotten my shawl; she ran back to fetch it; and I stood with Dr John in the vestibule, waiting.

'What is this, Lucy?' said he, looking down at me narrowly. 'Here is the old excitement. Ho! the nun again?'

But I utterly denied the charge: I was vexed to be suspected of a second illusion. He was sceptical.

'She has been, as sure as I live,' said he; 'her figure crossing your eyes leaves on them a peculiar gleam and expression not to be mistaken.'

'She has *not* been,' I persisted: for, indeed, I could deny her apparition with truth.

'The old symptoms are there,' he affirmed; 'a particular pale, and what the Scotch call a "raised" look.'

He was so obstinate, I thought it better to tell him what I really *had* seen. Of course with him, it was held to be another effect of the same cause: it was all optical illusion – nervous malady, and so on. Not one bit did I believe him; but I dared not contradict: doctors are so self-opinionated, so immovable in their dry, materialist views.

Rosine brought the shawl, and I was bundled into the carriage.

The theatre was full – crammed to its roof: royal and noble were there; palace and hotel had emptied their inmates into those tiers so thronged and so hushed. Deeply did I feel myself privileged in having a place before that stage; I longed to see a being of whose powers I had heard reports which made me conceive peculiar anticipations. I wondered if she would justify her renown: with strange curiosity, with feelings severe and austere, yet of riveted interest, I waited. She was a study of such nature as had not encountered my eyes yet: a great and new planet she was: but in what state? I waited her rising.

She rose at nine that December night: above the horizon I saw her come. She could shine yet with pale grandeur and steady might; but that star verged already on its judgment day. Seen near, it was a chaos – hollow, half-consumed: an orb perished or perishing – half lava, half glow.

I had heard this woman termed 'plain,' and I expected bony harshness and grimness – something large, angular, sallow. What I saw was the shadow of a royal Vashti:[134] a queen, fair as the day once, turned pale now like twilight, and wasted like wax in flame.

For awhile – a long while – I thought it was only a woman, though an unique woman, who moved in might and grace before this multitude. By-and-by I recognized my mistake. Behold! I found upon her something neither of woman nor of man: in each of her eyes sat a devil. These evil forces bore her through the tragedy, kept up her feeble strength – for she was but a frail creature; and as the action rose and the stir deepened, how wildly they shook her with their passions of the pit! They wrote HELL on her straight, haughty brow. They tuned her voice to the note of torment. They writhed her regal face to a demoniac mask. Hate and Murder and Madness incarnate, she stood.

It was a marvellous sight: a mighty revelation.

It was a spectacle low, horrible, immoral.

Swordsmen thrust through, and dying in their blood on the arena sand; bulls goring horses disembowelled, make a meeker vision for the public eye – a milder condiment for a people's palate – than Vashti torn by seven devils: devils which cried sore and rent the tenement they haunted, but still refused to be exorcised.

Suffering had struck that stage empress; and she stood before her audience neither yielding to, nor enduring, nor in finite measure, resenting it: she stood locked in struggle, rigid in resistance. She stood, not dressed, but draped in pale antique folds, long and regular like sculpture. A background and entourage and flooring of deepest crimson threw her out, white like alabaster – like silver: rather be it said, like Death.

Where was the artist of the Cleopatra? Let him come and sit down and study this different vision. Let him seek here the mighty brawn, the muscle, the abounding blood, the full-fed flesh he worshipped: let all materialists draw nigh and look on.

I have said that she does not *resent* her grief. No; the weakness of that word would make it a lie. To her, what hurts becomes immediately embodied: she looks on it as a thing that can be attacked, worried down, torn in shreds. Scarcely a substance herself, she grapples to conflict with abstractions. Before calamity she is a tigress; she rends her woes, shivers them in convulsed abhorrence. Pain, for her, has no result in good; tears water no harvest of wisdom: on sickness, on death itself, she looks with the eye of a rebel. Wicked, perhaps, she is, but also she is strong; and her strength has conquered Beauty, has overcome Grace, and bound both at her side, captives peerlessly fair, and docile as fair. Even in the uttermost frenzy of energy is each maenad movement royally, imperially, incedingly upborne. Her hair, flying loose in revel or war, is still an angel's hair, and glorious under a halo. Fallen, insurgent, banished, she remembers the heaven where she rebelled. Heaven's light, following her exile, pierces its confines, and discloses their forlorn remoteness.

Place now the Cleopatra, or any other slug, before her as an obstacle, and see her cut through the pulpy mass as the scimitar of Saladin[135] clove the down cushion. Let Paul Peter Rubens[136] wake from the dead, let him rise out of his cerements, and bring into this presence all the army of his fat women; the magian power or prophet-virtue gifting that slight rod of Moses, could, at one waft, release and re-mingle a sea spell-parted, whelming the heavy host with the down-rush of overthrown sea-ramparts.

Vashti was not good, I was told; and I have said she did not look good: though a spirit, she was a spirit out of Tophet.[137] Well, if so much of unholy force can arise from below, may not an equal efflux of sacred essence descend one day from above?

What thought Dr Graham of this being?

For long intervals I forgot to look how he demeaned himself, or to question what he thought. The strong magnetism of genius drew my heart out of its wonted orbit; the sunflower turned from the south to a fierce light, not solar – a rushing, red, cometary light –

hot on vision and to sensation. I had seen acting before, but never anything like this: never anything which astonished Hope and hushed Desire; which outstripped Impulse and paled Conception; which, instead of merely irritating imagination with the thought of what *might* be done, at the same time fevering the nerves because it was *not* done, disclosed power like a deep, swollen, winter river, thundering in cataract, and bearing the soul, like a leaf, on the steep and steely sweep of its descent.

Miss Fanshawe, with her usual ripeness of judgment, pronounced Dr Bretton a serious, impassioned man, too grave and too impressible. Not in such light did I ever see him: no such faults could I lay to his charge. His natural attitude was not the meditative, nor his natural mood the sentimental; *impressionable* he was as dimpling water, but, almost as water, *unimpressible:* the breeze, the sun, moved him – metal could not grave, nor fire brand.

Dr John *could* think, and think well, but he was rather a man of action than of thought; he *could* feel, and feel vividly in his way, but his heart had no chord for enthusiasm: to bright, soft, sweet influences his eyes and lips gave bright, soft, sweet welcome, beautiful to see as dyes of rose and silver, pearl and purple, embuing summer clouds; for what belonged to storm, what was wild and intense, dangerous, sudden, and flaming, he had no sympathy, and held with it no communion. When I took time and regained inclination to glance at him, it amused and enlightened me to discover that he was watching that sinister and sovereign Vashti, not with wonder, nor worship, nor yet dismay, but simply with intense curiosity. Her agony did not pain him, her wild moan – worse than a shriek – did not much move him; her fury revolted him somewhat, but not to the point of horror. Cool young Briton! The pale cliffs of his own England do not look down on the tides of the channel more calmly than he watched the Pythian[138] inspiration of that night.

Looking at his face, I longed to know his exact opinions, and at last I put a question tending to elicit them. At the sound of my voice he awoke as if out of a dream; for he had been thinking, and very intently thinking, his own thoughts, after his own manner. 'How did he like Vashti?' I wished to know.

'Hm-m-m,' was the first scarce articulate but expressive answer; and then such a strange smile went wandering round his lips, a smile so critical, so almost callous! I suppose that for natures of that order his sympathies *were* callous. In a few terse phrases he told me his opinion of, and feeling towards, the actress: he judged her as a woman, not an artist: it was a branding judgment.

That night was already marked in my book of life, not with white, but with a deep-red cross. But I had not done with it yet; and other memoranda were destined to be set down in characters of tint indelible.

Towards midnight, when the deepening tragedy blackened to the death scene, and all held their breath, and even Graham bit in his under lip, and knit his brow, and sat still and struck – when the whole theatre was hushed, when the vision of all eyes centred in one point, when all ears listened towards one quarter – nothing being seen but the white form sunk on a seat, quivering in conflict with her last, her worst-hated, her visibly-conquering foe – nothing heard but her throes, her graspings, breathing yet of mutiny, panting still defiance: when, as it seemed, an inordinate will, convulsing a perishing mortal frame, bent it to battle with doom and death, fought every inch of ground, sold dear every drop of blood, resisted to the latest the rape of every faculty, *would* see, *would* hear, *would* breathe, *would* live, up to, within, well nigh *beyond* the moment when death says to all sense and all being –

'Thus far and no farther!'

Just then a stir, pregnant with omen, rustled behind the scenes – feet ran, voices spoke. What was it? demanded the whole house. A flame, a smell of smoke replied.

'Fire!' rang through the gallery. 'Fire!' was repeated, re-echoed, yelled forth: and then, and faster than pen can set it down, came panic, rushing, crushing – a blind, selfish, cruel chaos.

And Dr John? Reader, I see him yet, with his look of comely courage and cordial calm.

'Lucy will sit still, I know,' said he, glancing down at me with the same serene goodness, the same repose of firmness that I have seen in him when sitting at his side amid the secure peace of his mother's hearth. Yes, thus adjured, I think I would have sat still under a rocking crag: but, indeed, to sit still in actual circumstances was my instinct; and at the price of my very life, I would not have moved to give him trouble, thwart his will, or make demands on his attention. We were in the stalls, and for a few minutes there was a most terrible, ruthless pressure about us.

'How terrified are the women!' said he; 'but if the men were not almost equally so, order might be maintained. This is a sorry scene: I see fifty selfish brutes at this moment, each of whom, if I were near, I could conscientiously knock down. I see some women braver than some men. There is one yonder – Good God!'

While Graham was speaking, a young girl who had been very quietly and steadily clinging to a gentleman standing before us, was suddenly struck from her protector's arms by a big, butcherly intruder, and hurled under the feet of the crowd. Scarce two seconds lasted her disappearance. Graham rushed forwards; he and the gentleman, a powerful man though gray-haired, united their strength to thrust back the throng; her head and long hair fell back over his shoulder: she seemed unconscious.

'Trust her with me; I am a medical man,' said Dr John.

'If you have no lady with you, be it so,' was the answer. 'Hold her, and I will force a passage: we must get her to the air.'

'I have a lady,' said Graham, 'but she will be neither hindrance nor incumbrance.'

He summoned me with his eye: we were separated. Resolute, however, to rejoin him, I penetrated the living barrier, creeping under, where I could not get between or over.

'Fasten on me, and don't leave go,' he said; and I obeyed him.

Our pioneer proved strong and adroit; he opened the dense mass like a wedge; with patience and toil he at last bored through the flesh-and-blood rock – so solid, hot, and suffocating – and brought us to the fresh, freezing night.

'You are an Englishman?' said he, turning shortly on Dr Bretton, when we got into the street.

'An Englishman. And I speak to a countryman?' was the reply.

'Right. Be good enough to stand here two minutes, whilst I find my carriage.'

'Papa, I am not hurt,' said a girlish voice; 'am I with papa?'

'You are with a friend, and your father is close at hand.'

'Tell him I am not hurt, except just in my shoulder. Oh, my shoulder! They trode just here.'

'Dislocation, perhaps!' muttered the Doctor: 'let us hope there is no worse injury done. Lucy, lend a hand one instant.'

And I assisted while he made some arrangement of drapery and position for the ease of his suffering burden. She suppressed a moan, and lay in his arms quietly and patiently.

'She is very light,' said Graham, 'like a child!' and he asked in my ear, 'Is she a child, Lucy? Did you notice her age?'

'I am not a child – I am a person of seventeen,' responded the patient demurely and with dignity. Then, directly after:

'Tell papa to come; I get anxious.'

The carriage drove up; her father relieved Graham; but in the exchange from one bearer to another she was hurt, and moaned again.

'My darling!' said the father tenderly; then turning to Graham, 'You said, sir, you are a medical man?'

'I am: Dr Bretton, of La Terrasse.'

'Good. Will you step into my carriage?'

'My own carriage is here: I will seek it, and accompany you.'

'Be pleased, then, to follow us.' And he named his address: 'The Hôtel Crécy, in the Rue Crécy.'

We followed; the carriage drove fast; myself and Graham were silent. This seemed like an adventure.

Some little time being lost in seeking our own equipage, we reached the hotel, perhaps, about ten minutes after these strangers. It was an hotel in the foreign sense: a collection of dwelling-houses, not an inn – a vast, lofty pile, with a huge arch to its street-door, leading through a vaulted covered way, into a square all built round.

We alighted, passed up a wide, handsome public staircase, and stopped at Numéro 2 on the second landing; the first floor comprising the abode of I know not what 'prince Russe,' as Graham informed me. On ringing the bell at a second great door, we were admitted to a suite of very handsome apartments. Announced by a servant in livery, we entered a drawing-room whose hearth glowed with an English fire, and whose walls gleamed with foreign mirrors. Near the hearth appeared a little group; a slight form sunk in a deep arm-chair, one or two women busy about it, the iron-gray gentleman anxiously looking on.

'Where is Harriet? I wish Harriet would come to me,' said the girlish voice, faintly.

'Where is Mrs Hurst?' demanded the gentleman impatiently and somewhat sternly of the man-servant who had admitted us.

'I am sorry to say she is gone out of town, sir; my young lady gave her leave till to-morrow.'

'Yes – I did – I did. She is gone to see her sister; I said she might go: I remember now,' interposed the young lady; 'but I am so sorry, for Manon and Louison cannot understand a word I say, and they hurt me without meaning to do so.'

Dr John and the gentleman now interchanged greetings; and while they passed a few minutes in consultation, I approached the easy-chair, and seeing what the faint and sinking girl wished to have done, I did it for her.

I was still occupied in the arrangement, when Graham drew near; he was no less skilled in surgery than medicine, and, on examination, found that no further advice than his own was necessary to the treatment of the present case. He ordered her to be carried to her chamber, and whispered to me: –

'Go with the women, Lucy; they seem but dull; you can at least direct their movements, and thus spare her some pain. She must be touched very tenderly.'

The chamber was a room shadowy with pale-blue hangings, vaporous with curtainings and veilings of muslin; the bed seemed to me like snow-drift and mist – spotless, soft, and gauzy. Making the women stand apart, I undressed their mistress, without their well-meaning but clumsy aid. I was not in a sufficiently collected mood to note with separate distinctness every detail of the attire I removed, but I received a general impression of refinement, delicacy, and perfect personal cultivation; which, in a period of after-thought, offered in my reflections a singular contrast to notes retained of Miss Ginevra Fanshawe's appointments.

This girl was herself a small, delicate creature, but made like a model. As I folded back her plentiful yet fine hair, so shining and soft, and so exquisitely tended, I had under my observation a young, pale, weary, but high-bred face. The brow was smooth and clear; the eyebrows were distinct, but soft, and melting to a mere trace at the temples; the eyes were a rich gift of nature – fine and full, large, deep, seeming to hold dominion over the slighter subordinate features – capable, probably, of much significance at another hour and under other circumstances than the present, but now languid and suffering. Her skin was perfectly fair, the neck and hands veined finely like the petals of a flower; a thin glazing of the ice of pride, polished this delicate exterior, and her lip wore a curl – I doubt not inherent and unconscious, but which, if I had seen it first with the accompaniments of health and state, would have struck me as unwarranted, and proving in the little lady a quite mistaken view of life and her own consequence.

Her demeanour under the Doctor's hands at first excited a smile: it was not puerile – rather, on the whole, patient and firm – but yet, once or twice she addressed him with suddenness and sharpness, saying that he hurt her, and must contrive to give her less pain; I saw her large eyes, too, settle on his face like the solemn eyes of some pretty, wondering child. I know not whether Graham felt this examination: if he did, he was cautious not to check or discomfit it by any retaliatory look. I think he performed his work with extreme care and gentleness, sparing her what pain he could; and she acknowledged as much, when he had done, by the words: –

'Thank you, Doctor, and good-night,' very gratefully pronounced: as she uttered them, however, it was with a repetition of the serious, direct gaze, I thought, peculiar in its gravity and intentness.

Her injuries, it seemed, were not dangerous: an assurance which her father received with a smile that almost made one his friend – it was so glad and gratified. He now expressed his obligations to Graham with as much earnestness as was befitting an Englishman addressing one who has served him, but is yet a stranger; he also begged him to call the next day.

'Papa,' said a voice from the veiled couch, 'thank the lady, too: is she there?'

I opened the curtain with a smile, and looked in at her. She lay now at comparative ease; she looked pretty, though pale; her face was delicately designed, and if at first sight it appeared proud, I believe custom might prove it to be soft.

'I thank the lady very sincerely,' said her father: 'I fancy she has been very good to my child. I think we scarcely dare tell Mrs Hurst who has been her substitute and done her work; she will feel at once ashamed and jealous.'

And thus, in the most friendly spirit, parting greetings were interchanged; and refreshment having been hospitably offered, but by us, as it was late, refused, we withdrew from the Hôtel Crécy.

On our way back we repassed the theatre. All was silence and darkness: the roaring, rushing crowd all vanished and gone – the lamps, as well as the incipient fire, extinct and forgotten. Next morning's papers explained that it was but some loose drapery on which a spark had fallen, and which had blazed up and been quenched in a moment.

CHAPTER 24

M. de Bassompierre

THOSE WHO LIVE IN RETIREMENT, whose lives have fallen amid the seclusion of schools or of other walled-in and guarded dwellings, are liable to be suddenly and for a long while dropped out of the memory of their friends, the denizens of a freer world. Unaccountably, perhaps, and close upon some space of unusually frequent intercourse – some congeries of rather exciting little circumstances, whose natural sequel would rather seem to be the quickening than the suspension of communication – there falls a stilly pause, a wordless silence, a long blank of oblivion. Unbroken always is this blank; alike entire and unexplained. The letter, the message once frequent, are cut off; the visit, formerly periodical, ceases to occur; the book, paper, or other token that indicated remembrance, comes no more.

Always there are excellent reasons for these lapses, if the hermit but knew them. Though he is stagnant in his cell, his connections without are whirling in the very vortex of life. That void interval which passes for him so slowly that the very clocks seem at a stand, and the wingless hours plod by in the likeness of tired tramps prone to rest at milestones – that same interval, perhaps, teems with events, and pants with hurry for his friends.

The hermit – if he be a sensible hermit – will swallow his own thoughts, and lock up his own emotions during these weeks of inward winter. He will know that Destiny designed him to imitate, on occasion, the dormouse, and he will be conformable: make a tidy ball of himself, creep into a hole of life's wall, and submit decently to the drift which blows in and soon blocks him up, preserving him in ice for the season.

Let him say, 'It is quite right: it ought to be so, since so it is.' And, perhaps, one day his snow-sepulchre will open, spring's softness will return, the sun and south-wind will reach him; the budding of hedges, and carolling of birds and singing of liberated streams will call him to kindly resurrection. *Perhaps* this may be the case, perhaps not: the frost may get into his heart and never thaw more; when spring comes, a crow or a pie may pick out of the wall only his dormouse-bones. Well, even in that case, all will be right: it is to be supposed he knew from the first he was mortal, and must one day go the way of all flesh, 'As well soon as syne.'

Following that eventful evening at the theatre, came for me seven weeks as bare as seven sheets of blank paper: no word was written on one of them; not a visit, not a token.

About the middle of that time I entertained fancies that something had happened to my friends at La Terrasse. The mid-blank is always a beclouded point for the solitary: his nerves ache with the strain of long expectancy; the doubts hitherto repelled gather now to a mass and – strong in accumulation – roll back upon him with a force which savours of vindictiveness. Night, too, becomes an unkindly time, and sleep and his nature cannot agree: strange starts and struggles harass his couch; the sinister band of bad dreams, with horror of calamity, and sick dread of entire desertion at their head, join the league against him. Poor wretch! He does his best to bear up, but he is a poor, pallid, wasting wretch, despite that best.

Towards the last of those long seven weeks I admitted, what through the other six I had jealously excluded – the conviction that these blanks were inevitable: the result of circumstances, the fiat of fate, a part of my life's lot, and – above all – a matter about whose origin no question must ever be asked, for whose painful sequence no murmur ever uttered. Of course I did not blame myself for suffering: I thank God I had a truer sense of justice than to fall into any imbecile extravagances of self-accusation; and as to blaming others for silence, in my reason I well knew them blameless, and in my heart acknowledged them so: but it was a rough and heavy road to travel, and I longed for better days.

I tried different expedients to sustain and fill existence: I commenced an elaborate piece of lace-work, I studied German pretty hard, I undertook a course of regular reading of the driest and thickest books in the library; in all my efforts I was as orthodox as I knew how to be. Was there error somewhere? Very likely. I only know the result was as if I had gnawed a file to satisfy hunger, or drunk brine to quench thirst.

My hour of torment was the post-hour. Unfortunately I knew it too well, and tried as vainly as assiduously to cheat myself of that knowledge; dreading the rack of expectation, and the sick collapse of disappointment which daily preceded and followed upon that well-recognized ring.

I suppose animals kept in cages, and so scantily fed as to be always upon the verge of famine, await their food as I awaited a letter. Oh!

– to speak truth, and drop that tone of a false calm which long to sustain, outwears nature's endurance – I underwent in those seven weeks bitter fears and pains, strange inward trials, miserable defections of hope, intolerable encroachments of despair. This last came so near me sometimes that her breath went right through me. I used to feel it, like a baleful air or sigh, penetrate deep, and make motion pause at my heart, or proceed only under unspeakable oppression. The letter – the well-beloved letter – would not come; and it was all of sweetness in life I had to look for.

In the very extremity of want, I had recourse again, and yet again, to the little packet in the case – the five letters. How splendid that month seemed whose skies had beheld the rising of these five stars! It was always at night I visited them, and not daring to ask every evening for a candle in the kitchen, I bought a wax-taper and matches to light it, and at the study-hour stole up to the dormitory, and feasted on my crust from the Barmecide's loaf.[139] It did not nourish me: I pined on it, and got as thin as a shadow: otherwise I was not ill.

Reading there somewhat late one evening, and feeling that the power to read was leaving me – for the letters from incessant perusal were losing all sap and significance: my gold was withering to leaves before my eyes, and I was sorrowing over the disillusion – suddenly a quick tripping foot ran up the stairs. I knew Ginevra Fanshawe's step: she had dined in town that afternoon; she was now returned, and would come here to replace her shawl, &c., in the wardrobe.

Yes: in she came, dressed in bright silk, with her shawl falling from her shoulders, and her curls, half-uncurled in the damp of night, drooping careless and heavy upon her neck. I had hardly time to recasket my treasures and lock them up when she was at my side: her humour seemed none of the best.

'It has been a stupid evening: they are stupid people,' she began.

'Who? Mrs Cholmondeley? I thought you always found her house charming.'

'I have not been to Mrs Cholmondeley's.'

'Indeed! Have you made new acquaintance?'

'My uncle de Bassompierre is come.'

'Your uncle de Bassompierre! Are you not glad? – I thought he was a favourite.'

'You thought wrong: the man is odious; I hate him.'

'Because he is a foreigner? or for what other reason of equal weight?'

'He is not a foreigner. The man is English enough, goodness

knows; and had an English name till three or four years ago; but his mother was a foreigner, a de Bassompierre, and some of her family are dead and have left him estates, a title, and this name: he is quite a great man now.'

'Do you hate him for that reason?'

'Don't I know what mama says about him? He is not my own uncle, but married mama's sister. Mama detests him; she says he killed Aunt Ginevra with unkindness: he looks like a bear. Such a dismal evening!' she went on. 'I'll go no more to his big hotel. Fancy me walking into a room alone, and a great man fifty years old coming forwards, and after a few minutes' conversation actually turning his back upon me, and then abruptly going out of the room. Such odd ways! I daresay his conscience smote him, for they all say at home I am the picture of Aunt Ginevra. Mama often declares the likeness is quite ridiculous.'

'Were you the only visitor?'

'The only visitor? Yes: then there was missy, my cousin: little spoiled, pampered thing.'

'M. de Bassompierre has a daughter?'

'Yes, yes: don't tease one with questions. Oh dear! I am so tired.'

She yawned. Throwing herself without ceremony on my bed, she added, 'It seems Mademoiselle was nearly crushed to a jelly in a hubbub at the theatre some weeks ago.'

'Ah! indeed. And they live at a large hotel in the Rue Crécy?'

'Justement. How do *you* know?'

'I have been there.'

'Oh you have? Really! You go everywhere in these days. I suppose Mother Bretton took you? She and Esculapius[140] have the *entrée* of the de Bassompierre apartments: it seems "my son John" attended missy on the occasion of her accident – accident? Bah! All affectation! I don't think she was squeezed more than she richly deserves for her airs. And now there is quite an intimacy struck up: I heard something about "Auld lang syne," and what not? Oh, how stupid they all were!'

'*All*! You said you were the only visitor?'

'Did I? You see one forgets to particularize an old woman and her boy.'

'Dr and Mrs Bretton were at M. de Bassompierre's this evening?'

'Ay, ay! as large as life; and missy played the hostess. What a conceited doll it is!'

Soured and listless, Miss Fanshawe was beginning to disclose the causes of her prostrate condition. There had been a retrenchment of incense, a diversion or a total witholding of homage and attention: coquetry had failed of effect, vanity had undergone mortification. She lay fuming in the vapours.

'Is Miss de Bassompierre quite well now?' I asked.

'As well as you or I, no doubt; but she is an affected little thing, and gave herself invalid airs to attract medical notice. And to see the old dowager making her recline on a couch, and "my son John" prohibiting excitement, etcetera – faugh! the scene was quite sickening.'

'It would not have been so if the object of attention had been changed: if you had taken Miss de Bassompierre's place.'

'Indeed! I hate "my son John!" '

' "My son John!" – whom do you indicate by that name? Dr Bretton's mother never calls him so.'

'Then she ought. A clownish, bearish John he is.'

'You violate the truth in saying so; and as the whole of my patience is now spun off the distaff, I peremptorily desire you to rise from that bed, and vacate this room.'

'Passionate thing! Your face is the colour of a coquelicot. I wonder what always makes you so mighty testy à l'endroit du gros Jean? "John Anderson, my joe, John!" Oh! the distinguished name!'

Thrilling with exasperation, to which it would have been sheer folly to have given vent – for there was no contending with that unsubstantial feather, that mealy-winged moth – I extinguished my taper, locked my bureau, and left her, since she would not leave me. Small-beer as she was, she had turned insufferably acid.

The morrow was Thursday and a half-holiday. Breakfast was over; I had withdrawn to the first classe. The dreaded hour, the post-hour, was nearing, and I sat waiting it, much as a ghost-seer might wait his spectre. Less than ever was a letter probable; still, strive as I would, I could not forget that it was possible. As the moments lessened, a restlessness and fear almost beyond the average assailed me. It was a day of winter east wind, and I had now for some time entered into that dreary fellowship with the winds and their changes, so little known, so incomprehensible to the healthy. The north and east owned a terrible influence, making all pain more poignant, all sorrow sadder. The south could calm, the west sometimes cheer: unless, indeed, they brought on their wings the burden of thunder-clouds, under the weight and warmth of which all energy died.

Bitter and dark as was this January day, I remember leaving the classe, and running down without bonnet to the bottom of the long garden, and there lingering amongst the stripped shrubs; in the forlorn hope that the postman's ring might occur while I was out of hearing, and I might thus be spared the thrill which some particular nerve or nerves, almost gnawed through with the unremitting tooth of a fixed idea, were becoming wholly unfit to support. I lingered as long as I dared without fear of attracting attention by my absence. I muffled my head in my apron, and stopped my ears in terror of the torturing clang, sure to be followed by such blank silence, such barren vacuum for me. At last I ventured to re-enter the first-classe, where, as it was not yet nine o'clock, no pupils had been admitted. The first thing seen was a white object on my black desk, a white, flat object. The post had, indeed, arrived; by me unheard. Rosine had visited my cell, and, like some angel, had left behind her a bright token of her presence. That shining thing on the desk was indeed a letter, a real letter; I saw so much at the distance of three yards, and as I had but one correspondent on earth, from that one it must come. He remembered me yet. How deep a pulse of gratitude sent new life through my heart.

Drawing near, bending and looking on the letter, in trembling but almost certain hope of seeing a known hand, it was my lot to find, on the contrary, an autograph for the moment deemed unknown – a pale female scrawl, instead of a firm masculine character. I then thought fate was *too* hard upon me, and I said, audibly, 'This is cruel.'

But I got over that pain also. Life is still life, whatever its pangs: our eyes and ears and their use remain with us, though the prospect of what pleases be wholly withdrawn, and the sound of what consoles be quite silenced.

I opened the billet: by this time I had recognized its handwriting as perfectly familiar. It was dated 'La Terrasse,' and it ran thus: –

'DEAR LUCY, – It occurs to me to inquire what you have been doing with yourself for the last month or two? Not that I suspect you would have the least difficulty in giving an account of your proceedings. I daresay you have been just as busy and happy as ourselves at La Terrasse. As to Graham, his professional connection extends daily: he is so much sought after, so much engaged, that I tell him he will grow quite conceited. Like a right good mother, as I am, I do my best to keep him down: no flattery does he get from me, as you know. And yet, Lucy, he is a fine fellow; his mother's heart dances at the sight of him. After being hurried here and there the whole day, and passing the ordeal of fifty sorts of tempers, and combating a hundred caprices, and sometimes witnessing cruel sufferings – perhaps, occasionally, as I tell him, inflicting them – at night he still comes home to me in such kindly, pleasant mood, that, really, I seem to live in a sort of moral antipodes, and on these January evenings my day rises when other people's night sets in.

'Still he needs keeping in order, and correcting, and repressing, and I do him that good service; but the boy is so elastic there is no such thing as vexing him thoroughly. When I think I have at last driven him to the sullens, he turns on me with jokes for retaliation: but you know him and all his iniquities, and I am but an elderly simpleton to make him the subject of this epistle.

'As for me, I have had my old Bretton agent here on a visit, and have been plunged over head and ears in business matters. I do so wish to regain for Graham at least some part of what his father left him. He laughs to scorn my anxiety on this point, bidding me look and see how he can provide for himself and me too, and asking what the old lady can possibly want that she has not; hinting about sky-blue turbans; accusing me of an ambition to wear diamonds, keep livery servants, have an hotel, and lead the fashion amongst the English clan in Villette.

'Talking of sky-blue turbans, I wished you had been with us the other evening. He had come in really tired; and after I had given him his tea, he threw himself into my chair with his customary presumption. To my great delight, he dropped asleep. (You know how he teazes me about being drowsy; I, who never, by any chance, close an eye by daylight). While he slept, I thought he looked very bonny, Lucy: fool as I am to be so proud of him: but who can help it? Show me his peer. Look where I will I see nothing like him in Villette. Well, I took it into my head to play him a trick: so I brought out the sky-blue turban, and handling it and him with gingerly precaution, I managed to invest his brows with this grand adornment. I assure you it did not at all misbecome him; he looked quite Eastern, except that he is so fair. Nobody, however, can accuse him of having red hair *now* – it is genuine chestnut – a dark, glossy chestnut; and when I put my large Cashmere about him, there was as fine a young bey, dey, or pacha[141] improvised as you would wish to see.

'It was good entertainment; but only half-enjoyed, since I was alone: *you* should have been there.

'In due time my lord awoke: the looking-glass above the fireplace soon intimated to him his plight: as you may imagine, I now live under threat and dread of vengeance.

'But to come to the gist of my letter. I know Thursday is a half-holiday in the Rue Fossette: be ready, then, by five in the afternoon, at which hour I will send the carriage to take you out to La Terrasse. Be sure to come: you may meet some old acquaintance. Good-bye, my wise, dear, grave little god-daughter.

—Very truly yours,
'LOUISA BRETTON.'

Now, a letter like that sets one to rights! I might still be sad after reading that letter, but I was more composed; not exactly cheered, perhaps, but relieved. My friends, at least, were well and happy: no accident had occurred to Graham; no illness had seized his mother – calamities that had so long been my dream and thought. Their feelings for me too were – as they had been. Yet, how strange it was to look on Mrs Bretton's seven weeks and contrast them with my seven weeks! Also, how very wise it is in people placed in an exceptional position to hold their tongues and not rashly declare how such position galls them! The world can understand well enough the process of perishing for want of food: perhaps few persons can enter into or follow out that of going mad from solitary confinement. They see the long-buried prisoner disinterred, a maniac or an idiot! – how his senses left him – how his nerves first inflamed, underwent nameless agony, and then sunk to palsy – is a subject too intricate for examination, too abstract for popular comprehension. Speak of it! you might almost as well stand up in an European market-place, and propound dark sayings in that language and mood wherein Nebuchadnezzar, the imperial hypochondriac, communed with his baffled Chaldeans.[142] And long, long may the minds to whom such themes are no mystery – by whom their bearings are sympathetically seized – be few in number, and rare of rencounter. Long may it be generally thought that physical privations alone merit compassion, and that the rest is a figment. When the world was younger and haler than now, moral trials were a deeper mystery still: perhaps in all the land of Israel there was but one Saul – certainly but one David to soothe or comprehend him.

The keen, still cold of the morning was succeeded, later in the day, by a sharp breathing from Russian wastes: the cold zone sighed over the temperate zone, and froze it fast. A heavy firmament, dull, and thick with snow, sailed up from the north, and settled over expectant Europe. Towards afternoon began the descent. I feared no carriage would come – the white tempest raged so dense and wild. But trust my godmother! Once having asked, she would have her guest. About six o'clock I was lifted from the carriage over the already blocked-up front steps of the chateau, and put in at the door of La Terrasse.

Running through the vestibule, and up-stairs to the drawing-room, there I found Mrs Bretton – a summer-day in her own person. Had I been twice as cold as I was, her kind kiss and cordial clasp would have warmed me. Inured now for so long a time to rooms with bare boards, black benches, desks, and stoves, the blue saloon seemed to me gorgeous. In its Christmas-like fire alone there was a clear and crimson splendour which quite dazzled me.

When my godmother had held my hand for a little while, and chatted with me, and scolded me for having become thinner than when she last saw me, she professed to discover that the snow-wind had disordered my hair, and sent me up-stairs to make it neat, and remove my shawl.

Repairing to my own little sea-green room, there also I found a bright fire, and candles too were lit: a tall waxlight stood on each side the great looking-glass; but between the candles, and before the glass, appeared something dressing itself – an airy, fairy thing – small, slight, white – a winter spirit.

I declare, for one moment I thought of Graham and his spectral illusions. With distrustful eye I noted the details of this new vision. It wore white, sprinkled slightly with drops of scarlet; its girdle was red; it had something in its hair leafy, yet shining—a little wreath with an evergreen gloss. Spectral or not, here truly was nothing frightful, and I advanced.

Turning quick upon me, a large eye, under long lashes, flashed over me, the intruder: the lashes were as dark as long, and they softened with their pencilling the orb they guarded.

'Ah! you are come!' she breathed out, in a soft, quiet voice, and she smiled slowly, and gazed intently.

I knew her now. Having only once seen that sort of face, with that cast of fine and delicate featuring, I could not but know her.

'Miss de Bassompierre,' I pronounced.

'No,' was the reply, 'not Miss de Bassompierre for *you*.' I did not inquire who then she might be, but waited voluntary information.

'You are changed, but still you are yourself,' she said, approaching nearer. 'I remember you well – your countenance, the colour of your hair, the outline of your face. . .'

I had moved to the fire, and she stood opposite, and gazed into me; and as she gazed, her face became gradually more and more expressive of thought and feeling, till at last a dimness quenched her clear vision.

'It makes me almost cry to look so far back,' said she; 'but as to being sorry, or sentimental, don't think it: on the contrary, I am quite pleased and glad.'

Interested, yet altogether at fault, I knew not what to say. At last I stammered, 'I think I never met you till that night, some weeks ago, when you were hurt . . .?'

She smiled. 'You have forgotten then that I have sat on your knee, been lifted in your arms, even shared your pillow? You no longer remember the night when I came crying, like a naughty little child as I was, to your bedside, and you took me in? You have no memory for the comfort and protection by which you soothed an acute distress? Go back to Bretton. Remember Mr Home.'

At last I saw it all. 'And you are little Polly?'

'I am Paulina Mary Home de Bassompierre.'

How time can change! Little Polly wore in her pale, small features, her fairy symmetry, her varying expression, a certain promise of interest and grace; but Paulina Mary was become beautiful – not with the beauty that strikes the eye like a rose – orbed, ruddy, and replete; not with the plump, and pink, and flaxen attributes of her blond cousin Ginevra; but her seventeen years had brought her a refined and tender charm which did not lie in complexion, though hers was fair and clear; nor in outline, though her features were sweet, and her limbs perfectly turned; but, I think, rather in a subdued glow from the soul outward. This was not an opaque vase, of material however costly, but a lamp chastely lucent, guarding from extinction, yet not hiding from worship, a flame vital and vestal. In speaking of her attractions, I would not exaggerate language; but, indeed, they seemed to me very real and engaging. What though all was on a small scale? It was the perfume which gave this white violet distinction, and made it superior to the broadest camellia – the fullest dahlia that ever bloomed.

'Ah! and you remember the old time at Bretton?'

'Better,' said she, 'better, perhaps, than you. I remember it with minute distinctness: not only the time, but the days of the time, and the hours of the days.'

'You must have forgotten some things?'

'Very little, I imagine.'

'You were then a little creature of quick feelings: you must, long ere this, have outgrown the impressions with which joy and grief, affection and bereavement, stamped your mind ten years ago?'

'You think I have forgotten whom I liked, and in what degree I liked them when a child?'

'The sharpness must be gone – the point, the poignancy – the deep imprint must be softened away and effaced?'

'I have a good memory for those days.'

She looked as if she had. Her eyes were the eyes of one who can remember; one whose childhood does not fade like a dream, nor whose youth vanish like a sunbeam. She would not take life, loosely and incoherently, in parts, and let one season slip as she entered on another: she would retain and add; often review from the commencement, and so grow in harmony and consistency as she grew in years. Still I could not quite admit the conviction that *all* the pictures which now crowded upon me were vivid and visible to her. Her fond attachments, her sports and contests with a well-loved playmate, the patient, true devotion of her child's heart, her fears, her delicate reserves, her little trials, the last piercing pain of separation, . . . I retraced these things, and shook my head incredulous. She persisted. 'The child of seven years lives yet in the girl of seventeen,' said she.

'You used to be excessively fond of Mrs Bretton,' I remarked, intending to test her. She set me right at once.

'Not *excessively* fond,' said she; 'I liked her: I respected her, as I should now: she seems to me very little altered.'

'She is not much changed,' I assented.

We were silent a few minutes. Glancing round the room, she said –

'There are several things here that used to be at Bretton. I remember that pincushion and that looking-glass.'

Evidently she was not deceived in her estimate of her own memory; not, at least, so far.

'You think, then, you would have known Mrs Bretton?' I went on.

'I perfectly remembered her; the turn of her features, her olive complexion, and black hair, her height, her walk, her voice.'

'Dr Bretton, of course,' I pursued, 'would be out of the question: and, indeed, as I saw your first interview with him, I am aware that he appeared to you as a stranger.'

'That first night I was puzzled,' she answered.

'How did the recognition between him and your father come about?'

'They exchanged cards. The names Graham Bretton and Home de Bassompierre gave rise to questions and explanations. That was on the second day; but before then I was beginning to know something.'

'How – know something?'

'Why,' she said, 'how strange it is that most people seem so slow to feel the truth – not to see, but *feel*! When Dr Bretton had visited me a few times, and sat near and talked to me; when I had observed the look in his eyes, the expression about his mouth, the form of his chin, the carriage of his head, and all that we *do* observe in persons who approach us – how could I avoid being led by association to think of Graham Bretton? Graham was slighter than he, and not grown so tall, and had a smoother face, and longer and lighter hair, and spoke – not so deeply – more like a girl; but yet he *is* Graham, just as *I* am little Polly, or you are Lucy Snowe.'

I thought the same, but I wondered to find my thoughts hers: there are certain things in which we so rarely meet with our double that it seems a miracle when that chance befalls.

'You and Graham were once playmates.'

'And do you remember that?' she questioned in her turn.

'No doubt he will remember it also,' said I.

'I have not asked him: few things would surprise me so much as to find that he did. I suppose his disposition is still gay and careless?'

'Was it so formerly? Did it so strike you? Do you thus remember him?'

'I scarcely remember him in any other light. Sometimes he was studious; sometimes he was merry: but whether busy with his books or disposed for play, it was chiefly the books or game he thought of; not much heeding those with whom he read or amused himself.'

'Yet to you he was partial.'

'Partial to me? Oh, no! he had other playmates – his school-fellows; I was of little consequence to him, except on Sundays: yes, he was kind on Sundays. I remember walking with him hand in hand to St. Mary's, and his finding the places in my prayer-book; and how good and still he was on Sunday evenings! So mild for such a proud, lively boy; so patient with all my blunders in reading; and so wonderfully to be depended on, for he never spent those evenings from home: I had a constant fear that he would accept some invitation and forsake us; but he never did, nor seemed ever to wish to do it. Thus, of course, it can be no more. I suppose Sunday will now be Dr Bretton's dining-out day. . .'

'Children, come down!' here called Mrs Bretton from below. Paulina would still have lingered, but I inclined to descend: we went down.

CHAPTER 25

The Little Countess

CHEERFUL AS MY GODMOTHER NATURALLY WAS, and entertaining as, for our sakes, she made a point of being, there was no true enjoyment that evening at La Terrasse, till, through the wild howl of the winter-night, were heard the signal sounds of arrival. How often, while women and girls sit warm at snug fire-sides, their hearts and imaginations are doomed to divorce from the comfort surrounding their persons, forced out by night to wander through dark ways, to dare stress of weather, to contend with the snow-blast, to wait at lonely gates and stiles in wildest storms, watching and listening to see and hear the father, the son, the husband coming home.

Father and son came at last to the chateau: for the Count de Bassompierre that night accompanied Dr Bretton. I know not which of our trio heard the horses first; the asperity, the violence of the weather warranted our running down into the hall to meet and greet the two riders as they came in; but they warned us to keep our distance: both were white – two mountains of snow; and indeed Mrs Bretton, seeing their condition, ordered them instantly to the kitchen; prohibiting them, at their peril, from setting foot on her carpeted staircase till they had severally put off that mask of Old Christmas they now affected. Into the kitchen, however, we could not help following them: it was a large old Dutch kitchen, picturesque and pleasant. The little white Countess danced in a circle about her equally white sire, clapping her hands and crying, –

'Papa, papa, you look like an enormous Polar bear.'

The bear shook himself, and the little sprite fled far from the frozen shower. Back she came, however, laughing, and eager to aid in removing the arctic disguise. The Count, at last issuing from his dreadnought, threatened to overwhelm her with it as with an avalanche.

'Come, then,' said she, bending to invite the fall, and when it was playfully advanced above her head, bounding out of reach like some little chamois.

Her movements had the supple softness, the velvet grace of a kitten; her laugh was clearer than the ring of silver and crystal: as she took her sire's cold hands and rubbed them, and stood on tiptoe to reach his lips for a kiss, there seemed to shine round her a halo of loving delight. The grave and reverend signior looked down on her as men *do* look on what is the apple of their eye.

'Mrs Bretton,' said he; 'what am I to do with this daughter or daughterling of mine? She neither grows in wisdom nor in stature. Don't you find her pretty nearly as much the child as she was ten years ago?'

'She cannot be more the child than this great boy of mine,' said Mrs Bretton, who was in conflict with her son about some change of dress she deemed advisable, and which he resisted. He stood leaning against the Dutch dresser, laughing and keeping her at arm's length.

'Come, mama,' said he, 'by way of compromise, and to secure for us inward as well as outward warmth, let us have a Christmas wassail-cup, and toast Old England here, on the hearth.'

So, while the Count stood by the fire, and Paulina Mary still danced to and fro – happy in the liberty of the wide hall-like kitchen – Mrs Bretton herself instructed Martha to spice and heat the wassail-bowl, and, pouring the draught into a Bretton flagon, it was served round, reaming hot, by means of a small silver vessel, which I recognized as Graham's christening-cup.

'Here's to Auld Lang Syne!'[143] said the Count; holding the glancing cup on high. Then, looking at Mrs Bretton: –

'We twa ha" paidlet i" the burn
Fra morning-sun till dine,
But seas between us braid ha" roared
Sin" auld lang syne.
And surely ye'll be your pint-stoup,
As surely I'll be mine;
And we'll taste a cup o" kindness yet
For auld lang syne.'

'Scotch! Scotch!' cried Paulina; 'papa is talking Scotch: and Scotch he is, partly. We are Home and De Bassompierre, Caledonian and Gallic.'

'And is that a Scotch reel you are dancing, you Highland fairy?' asked her father. 'Mrs Bretton, there will be a green ring growing up in the middle of your kitchen shortly. I would not answer for her being quite cannie: she is a strange little mortal.'

'Tell Lucy to dance with me, papa: there is Lucy Snowe.'

Mr Home (there was still quite as much about him of plain Mr Home as of proud Count de Bassompierre) held his hand out to me, saying kindly, 'he remembered me well; and, even had his own memory been less trustworthy, my name was so often on his daughter's lips, and he had listened to so many long tales about me, I should seem like an old acquaintance.'

Every one now had tasted the wassail-cup except Paulina, whose pas de fée, ou de fantaisie, nobody thought of interrupting to offer so profanatory a draught; but she was not to be overlooked, nor baulked of her mortal privileges.

'Let me taste,' said she to Graham, as he was putting the cup on the shelf of the dresser out of her reach.

Mrs Bretton and Mr Home were now engaged in conversation. Dr John had not been unobservant of the fairy's dance; he had watched it, and he had liked it. To say nothing of the softness and beauty of the movements, eminently grateful to his grace-loving eye, that ease in his mother's house charmed him, for it set *him* at ease: again she seemed a child for him – again, almost his playmate. I wondered how he would speak to her; I had not yet seen him address her; his first words proved that the old days of 'little Polly' had been recalled to his mind by this evening's child-like light-heartedness.

'Your ladyship wishes for the tankard?'

'I think I said so. I think I intimated as much.'

'Couldn't consent to a step of the kind on any account. Sorry for it, but couldn't do it.'

'Why? I am quite well now: it can't break my collar-bone again, or dislocate my shoulder. Is it wine?'

'No; nor dew.'

'I don't want dew; I don't like dew: but what is it?'

'Ale – strong ale – old October; brewed, perhaps, when I was born.'

'It must be curious: is it good?'

'Excessively good.'

And he took it down, administered to himself a second dose of this mighty elixir, expressed in his mischievous eyes extreme contentment with the same, and solemnly replaced the cup on the shelf.

'I should like a little,' said Paulina, looking up; 'I never had any "old October:" is it sweet?'

'Perilously sweet,' said Graham.

She continued to look up exactly with the countenance of a child that longs for some prohibited dainty. At last the Doctor relented, took it down, and indulged himself in the gratification of letting her taste from his hand; his eyes, always expressive in the revelation of pleasurable feelings, luminously and smilingly avowed that it *was* a gratification; and he prolonged it by so regulating the position of the cup that only a drop at a time could reach the rosy, sipping lips by which its brim was courted.

'A little more – a little more,' said she, petulantly touching his hand with her forefinger, to make him incline the cup more generously and yieldingly. 'It smells of spice and sugar, but I can't taste it; your wrist is so stiff, and you are so stingy.'

He indulged her, whispering, however, with gravity: 'Don't tell my mother or Lucy; they wouldn't approve.'

'Nor do I,' said she, passing into another tone and manner as soon as she had fairly assayed the beverage, just as if it had acted upon her like some disenchanting draught, undoing the work of a wizard: 'I find it anything but sweet; it is bitter and hot, and takes away my breath. Your old October was only desirable while forbidden. Thank you, no more.'

And, with a slight bend – careless, but as graceful as her dance – she glided from him and rejoined her father.

I think she had spoken truth: the child of seven was in the girl of seventeen.

Graham looked after her a little baffled, a little puzzled; his eye was on her a good deal during the rest of the evening, but she did not seem to notice him.

As we ascended to the drawing-room for tea, she took her father's arm: her natural place seemed to be at his side; her eyes and her ears were dedicated to him. He and Mrs Bretton were the chief talkers of our little party, and Paulina was their best listener, attending closely to all that was said, prompting the repetition of this or that trait or adventure.

'And where were you at such a time, papa? And what did you say then? And tell Mrs Bretton what happened on that occasion.' Thus she drew him out.

She did not again yield to any effervescence of glee; the infantine sparkle was exhaled for the night: she was soft, thoughtful, and docile. It was pretty to see her bid good-night; her manner to Graham was touched with dignity: in her very slight smile and quiet bow spoke the Countess, and Graham could not but look grave, and bend responsive. I saw he hardly knew how to blend together in his ideas the dancing fairy and delicate dame.

Next day, when we were all assembled round the breakfast table, shivering and fresh from the morning's chill ablutions, Mrs Bretton pronounced a decree that nobody, who was not forced by dire necessity, should quit her house that day.

Indeed, egress seemed next to impossible; the drift darkened the lower panes of the casement, and, on looking out, one saw the sky and air vexed and dim, the wind and snow in angry conflict. There was no fall now, but what had already descended was torn up from the earth, whirled round by brief shrieking gusts, and cast into a hundred fantastic forms.

The Countess seconded Mrs Bretton.

'Papa shall not go out,' said she, placing a seat for herself beside her father's arm-chair. 'I will look after him. You won't go into town, will you, papa?'

'Aye, and No,' was the answer. 'If you and Mrs Bretton are *very* good to me, Polly – kind, you know, and attentive; if you pet me in a very nice manner, and make much of me, I may possibly be induced to wait an hour after breakfast and see whether this razor-edged wind settles. But, you see, you give me no breakfast; you offer me nothing: you let me starve.'

'Quick! please, Mrs Bretton, and pour out the coffee,' entreated Paulina, 'whilst I take care of the Count de Bassompierre in other respects: since he grew into a Count, he has needed *so* much attention.'

She separated and prepared a roll.

'There, papa, are your "pistolets" charged,' said she. 'And there is some marmalade, just the same sort of marmalade we used to have at Bretton, and which you said was as good as if it had been conserved in Scotland – '

'And which your little ladyship used to beg for my boy – do you remember that?' interposed Mrs Bretton. 'Have you forgotten how you would come to my elbow and touch my sleeve with the whisper, "please, ma'am, something good for Graham – a little marmalade, or honey, or jam?" '

'No, mama,' broke in Dr John, laughing, yet reddening; 'it surely was not so: I could not have cared for these things.'

'Did he or did he not, Paulina?'

'He liked them,' asserted Paulina.

'Never blush for it, John,' said Mr Home, encouragingly. 'I like them myself yet, and always did. And Polly showed her sense in catering for a friend's material comforts: it was I who put her into the way of such good manners – nor do I let her forget them. Polly, offer me a small slice of that tongue.'

'There, papa: but remember you are only waited upon with this assiduity, on condition of being persuadable, and reconciling yourself to La Terrasse for the day.'

'Mrs Bretton,' said the Count, 'I want to get rid of my daughter, to send her to school. Do you know of any good school?'

'There is Lucy's place – Madame Beck's.'

'Miss Snowe is in a school?'

'I am a teacher,' I said, and was rather glad of the opportunity of saying this. For a little while I had been feeling as if placed in a false position. Mrs Bretton and her son knew my circumstances; but the Count and his daughter did not. They might choose to vary by some shades their hitherto cordial manner towards me, when aware of my grade in society. I spoke then readily: but a swarm of thoughts I had not anticipated nor invoked, rose dim at the words, making me sigh involuntarily. Mr Home did not lift his eyes from his breakfast-plate for about two minutes, nor did he speak; perhaps he had not caught the words – perhaps he thought that on a confession of that nature, politeness would interdict comment: the Scotch are proverbially proud; and homely as was Mr Home in look, simple in habits and tastes, I have all along intimated that he was not without his share of the national quality. Was his a pseudo pride? was it real dignity? I leave the question undecided in its wide sense. Where it concerned me individually I can only answer: then, and always, he showed himself a true-hearted gentleman.

By nature he was a feeler and a thinker; over his emotions and his reflections spread a mellowing of melancholy; more than a mellowing: in trouble and bereavement it became a cloud. He did not know much about Lucy Snowe; what he knew, he did not very accurately comprehend: indeed his misconceptions of my character often made me smile; but he saw my walk in life lay rather on the shady side of the hill; he gave me credit for doing my endeavour to keep the course honestly straight; he would have helped me if he could: having no opportunity of helping, he still wished me well. When he did look at me, his eye was kind; when he did speak, his voice was benevolent.

'Yours,' said he, 'is an arduous calling. I wish you health and strength to win in it – success.'

His fair little daughter did not take the information quite so composedly: she fixed on me a pair of eyes wide with wonder – almost with dismay.

'Are you a teacher?' cried she. Then, having paused on the unpalatable idea, 'Well, I never knew what you were, nor ever thought of asking: for me, you were always Lucy Snowe.'

'And what am I now?' I could not forbear inquiring.

'Yourself, of course. But do you really teach here, in Villette?'

'I really do.'

'And do you like it?'

'Not always.'

'And why do you go on with it?'

Her father looked at, and, I feared, was going to check her; but he only said, 'Proceed, Polly, proceed with that catechism – prove yourself the little wiseacre you are. If Miss Snowe were to blush and look confused, I should have to bid you hold your tongue; and you and I would sit out the present meal in some disgrace; but she only smiles, so push her hard, multiply the cross-questions. Well, Miss Snowe, why do you go on with it?'

'Chiefly, I fear, for the sake of the money I get.'

'Not then from motives of pure philanthropy? Polly and I were clinging to that hypothesis, as the most lenient way of accounting for your eccentricity.'

'No – no, sir. Rather for the roof of shelter I am thus enabled to keep over my head; and for the comfort of mind it gives me to think that while I can work for myself, I am spared the pain of being a burden to anybody.'

'Papa, say what you will, I pity Lucy.'

'Take up that pity, Miss de Bassompierre: take it up in both hands, as you might a little callow gosling squattering out of bounds without leave; put it back in the warm nest of a heart whence it issued, and receive in your ear this whisper. If my Polly ever came to know by experience the uncertain nature of this world's goods, I should like her to act as Lucy acts: to work for herself, that she might burden neither kith nor kin.'

'Yes, papa,' said she, pensively and tractably. 'But poor Lucy! I thought she was a rich lady, and had rich friends.'

'You thought like a little simpleton: *I* never thought so. When I had time to consider Lucy's manner and aspect, which was not often, I saw she was one who had to guard and not be guarded; to act and not be served: and this lot has, I imagine, helped her to an experience for which, if she live long enough to realize its full benefit, she may yet bless Providence. But this school,' he pursued, changing his tone from grave to gay: 'Would Madame Beck admit my Polly, do you think, Miss Lucy?'

I said, there needed but to try madame; it would soon be seen: she was fond of English pupils. 'If you, sir,' I added, 'will but take Miss de Bassompierre in your carriage this very afternoon, I think I can answer for it that Rosine, the portress, will not be very slow in answering your ring; and madame, I am sure, will put on her best pair of gloves to come into the salon to receive you.'

'In that case,' responded Mr Home, 'I see no sort of necessity there is for delay. Mrs Hurst can send, what she calls, her young lady's "things" after her; Polly can settle down to her horn-book before night; and you, Miss Lucy, I trust, will not disdain to cast an occasional eye upon her, and let me know, from time to time, how she gets on. I hope you approve of the arrangement, Countess de Bassompierre?'

The Countess hemmed and hesitated. 'I thought,' said she, 'I thought I had finished my education – '

'That only proves how much we may be mistaken in our thoughts: I hold a far different opinion, as most of those will who have been auditors of your profound knowledge of life this morning. Ah, my little girl, thou hast much to learn; and papa ought to have taught thee more than he has done! Come, there is nothing for it but to try Madame Beck; and the weather seems settling, and I have finished my breakfast.'

'But, papa!'

'Well?'

'I see an obstacle.'

'I don't at all.'

'It is enormous, papa, it can never be got over; it is as large as you in your great coat, and the snowdrift on the top.'

'And, like that snowdrift, capable of melting?'

'No! it is of too – too solid flesh:[144] it is just your own self. Miss Lucy, warn Madame Beck not to listen to any overtures about taking me, because, in the end, it would turn out that she would have to take papa too: as he is so teasing, I will just tell tales about him. Mrs Bretton and all of you listen! About five years ago, when I was twelve years old, he took it into his head that he was spoiling me; that I was growing unfitted for the world, and I don't know what, and nothing would serve or satisfy him, but I must go to school. I cried, and so on; but M. de Bassompierre proved hard-hearted, quite firm and flinty, and to school I went. What was the result? In the most admirable manner, papa came to school likewise:

every other day he called to see me. Madame Aigredoux grumbled, but it was of no use; and so, at last, papa and I were both, in a manner, expelled. Lucy can just tell Madame Beck this little trait: it is only fair to let her know what she has to expect.'

Mrs Bretton asked Mr Home what he had to say in answer to this statement. As he made no defence, judgment was given against him, and Paulina triumphed.

But she had other moods besides the arch and naïve. After breakfast, when the two elders withdrew – I suppose to talk over certain of Mrs Bretton's business matters – and the Countess, Dr Bretton, and I were, for a short time, alone together – all the child left her; with us, more nearly her companions in age, she rose at once to the little lady: her very face seemed to alter; that play of feature, and candour of look, which, when she spoke to her father, made it quite dimpled and round, yielded to an aspect more thoughtful, and lines distincter and less *mobile*.

No doubt, Graham noted the change as well as I. He stood for some minutes near the window, looking out at the snow; presently he approached the hearth, and entered into conversation, but not quite with his usual ease: fit topics did not seem to rise to his lips; he chose them fastidiously, hesitatingly, and consequently infelicitously: he spoke vaguely of Villette – its inhabitants, its notable sights and buildings. He was answered by Miss de Bassompierre in quite womanly sort; with intelligence, with a manner not indeed wholly disindividualized: a tone, a glance, a gesture, here and there, rather animated and quick than measured and stately, still recalled little Polly; but yet there was so fine and even a polish, so calm and courteous a grace, gilding and sustaining these peculiarities, that a less sensitive man than Graham would not have ventured to seize upon them as vantage points, leading to franker intimacy.

Yet while Dr Bretton continued subdued, and, for him, sedate, he was still observant. Not one of those pretty impulses and natural breaks escaped him. He did not miss one characteristic movement, one hesitation in language, or one lisp in utterance. At times, in speaking fast, she still lisped; but coloured whenever such lapse occurred, and in a painstaking, conscientious manner, quite as amusing as the slight error, repeated the word more distinctly.

Whenever she did this, Dr Bretton smiled. Gradually, as they conversed, the restraint on each side slackened: might the conference have but been prolonged, I believe it would soon have become genial: already to Paulina's lip and cheek returned the wreathing, dimpling smile; she lisped once, and forgot to correct herself. And Dr John, I know not how *he* changed, but change he did. He did not grow gayer – no raillery, no levity sparkled across his aspect – but his position seemed to become one of more pleasure to himself, and he spoke his augmented comfort in readier language, in tones more suave. Ten years ago, this pair had always found abundance to say to each other; the intervening decade had not narrowed the experience or impoverished the intelligence of either: besides, there are certain natures of which the mutual influence is such, that the more they say, the more they have to say. For these, out of association grows adhesion, and out of adhesion, amalgamation.

Graham, however, must go: his was a profession, whose claims are neither to be ignored, nor deferred. He left the room; but before he could leave the house there was a return. I am sure he came back – not for the paper, or card in his desk, which formed his ostensible errand – but to assure himself, by one more glance, that Paulina's aspect was really such as memory was bearing away: that he had not been viewing her somehow by a partial, artificial light, and making a fond mistake. No! he found the impression true – rather, indeed, he gained, than lost, by this return: he took away with him a parting look – shy, but very soft – as beautiful, as innocent, as any little fawn could lift out of its cover of fern, or any lamb from its meadow-bed.

Being left alone, Paulina and I kept silence for some time; we both took out some work, and plied a mute and diligent task. The white-wood work-box of old days, was now replaced by one inlaid with precious mosaic, and furnished with implements of gold; the tiny and trembling fingers that could scarce guide the needle, though tiny still, were now swift and skilful: but there was the same busy knitting of the brow, the same little dainty mannerisms, the same quick turns and movements – now to replace a stray tress; and anon to shake from the silken skirt some imaginary atom of dust – some clinging fibre of thread.

That morning I was disposed for silence: the austere fury of the winter-day had on me an awing, hushing influence. That passion of January, so white and so bloodless, was not yet spent: the storm had raved itself hoarse, but seemed no nearer exhaustion. Had Ginevra Fanshawe been my companion in that morning-room, she would not have suffered me to muse and listen undisturbed. The presence just gone from us would have been her theme; and how she would have rung the changes on one topic! how she would have pursued and pestered me with questions and surmises – worried and oppressed me with comments and confidences I did not want, and longed to avoid.

Paulina Mary cast once or twice towards me a quiet, but penetrating glance of her dark, full eye; her lips half opened, as if to the impulse of coming utterance: but she saw and delicately respected my inclination for silence.

'This will not hold long,' I thought to myself; for I was not accustomed to find in women or girls any power of self-control, or strength of self-denial. As far as I knew them, the chance of a gossip about their usually trivial secrets, their often very washy and paltry feelings, was a treat not to be readily foregone.

The little Countess promised an exception: she sewed, till she was tired of sewing, and then she took a book.

As chance would have it, she had sought it in Dr Bretton's own compartment of the book-case; and it proved to be an old Bretton book – some illustrated work of natural history. Often had I seen her standing at Graham's side, resting that volume on his knee, and reading to his tuition; and, when the lesson was over, begging, as a treat, that he would tell her all about the pictures. I watched her keenly: here was a true test of that memory she had boasted: would her recollections now be faithful?

Faithful? It could not be doubted. As she turned the leaves, over her face passed gleam after gleam of expression, the least intelligent of which was a full greeting to the Past. And then she turned to the title-page, and looked at the name written in the schoolboy hand. She looked at it long; nor was she satisfied with merely looking: she gently passed over the characters the tips of her fingers, accompanying the action with an unconscious but tender smile, which converted the touch into a caress. Paulina loved the Past; but the peculiarity of this little scene was, that she *said* nothing: she could feel, without pouring out her feelings in a flux of words.

She now occupied herself at the bookcase for nearly an hour; taking down volume after volume, and renewing her acquaintance with each. This done, she seated herself on a low stool, rested her cheek on her hand, and thought, and still was mute.

The sound of the front door opened below, a rush of cold wind, and her father's voice speaking to Mrs Bretton in the hall, startled her at last. She sprang up: she was down-stairs in one second.

'Papa! papa! you are not going out?'

'My pet; I must go into town.'

'But it is too – *too* cold, papa.'

And then I heard M. de Bassompierre showing to her how he was well provided against the weather; and how he was going to have the carriage, and to be quite snugly sheltered; and, in short, proving that she need not fear for his comfort.

'But you will promise to come back here this evening, before it is quite dark; – you and Dr Bretton, both, in the carriage? It is not fit to ride.'

'Well, if I see the Doctor, I will tell him a lady has laid on him her commands to take care of his precious health, and come home early under my escort.'

'Yes, you must say "a lady;" and he will think it is his mother, and be obedient. And, papa, mind to come soon, for I *shall* watch and listen.'

The door closed, and the carriage rolled softly through the snow; and back returned the Countess, pensive and anxious.

She *did* listen, and watch, when evening closed; but it was in stillest sort: walking the drawing-room with quite noiseless step. She checked at intervals her velvet march; inclined her ear, and consulted the night sounds: I should rather say, the night silence; for now, at last, the wind was fallen. The sky, relieved of its avalanche, lay naked and pale: through the barren boughs of the avenue we could see it well, and note also the polar splendour of the new-year moon – an orb, white as a world of ice. Nor was it late when we saw also the return of the carriage.

Paulina had no dance of welcome for this evening. It was with a sort of gravity that she took immediate possession of her father, as he entered the room; but she at once made him her entire property, led him to the seat of her choice, and, while softly showering round him honeyed words of commendation for being so good and coming home so soon, you would have thought it was entirely by the power of her little hands he was put into his chair, and settled and arranged; for the strong man seemed to take pleasure in wholly yielding himself to this dominion – potent only by love.

Graham did not appear till some minutes after the Count. Paulina half turned when his step was heard: they spoke, but only a word or two; their fingers met a moment, but obviously with slight contact. Paulina remained beside her father; Graham threw himself into a seat on the other side of the room.

It was well that Mrs Bretton and Mr Home had a great deal to say to each other – almost an inexhaustible fund of discourse in old recollections; otherwise, I think, our party would have been but a still one that evening.

After tea, Paulina's quick needle and pretty golden thimble were busily plied by the lamp-light, but her tongue rested, and her eyes seemed reluctant to raise often their lids so smooth and so full-fringed. Graham too must have been tired with his day's work: he listened dutifully to his elders and betters, said very little himself, and followed with his eye the gilded glance of Paulina's thimble, as if it had been some bright moth on the wing, or the golden head of some darting little yellow serpent.

CHAPTER 26

A Burial

FROM THIS DATE my life did not want variety; I went out a good deal, with the entire consent of Madame Beck, who perfectly approved the grade of my acquaintance. That worthy directress had never from the first treated me otherwise than with respect; and when she found that I was liable to frequent invitations from a chateau and a great hotel, respect improved into distinction.

Not that she was fulsome about it: madame, in all things worldly, was in nothing weak; there was measure and sense in her hottest pursuit of self-interest, calm and considerateness in her closest clutch of gain; without, then, laying herself open to my contempt as a time-server and a toadie, she marked with tact that she was pleased people connected with her establishment should frequent such associates as must cultivate and elevate, rather than those who might deteriorate and depress. She never praised either me or my friends; only once when she was sitting in the sun in the garden, a cup of coffee at her elbow and the Gazette in her hand, looking very comfortable, and I came up and asked leave of absence for the evening, she delivered herself in this gracious sort: –

'Oui, oui, ma bonne amie: je vous donne la permission de coeur et de gré. Votre travail dans ma maison a toujours été admirable, rempli de zèle et de discrétion: vous avez bien le droit de vous amuser. Sortez donc tant que vous voudrez. Quant à votre choix de connaissances, j'en suis contente; c'est sage, digne, louable.'[145]

She closed her lips and resumed the Gazette.

The reader will not too gravely regard the little circumstance that about this time the triply-enclosed packet of five letters temporarily disappeared from my bureau. Blank dismay was naturally my first sensation on making the discovery; but in a moment I took heart of grace.

'Patience!' whispered I to myself. 'Let me say nothing, but wait peaceably; they will come back again.'

And they did come back: they had only been on a short visit to madame's chamber; having passed their examination, they came back duly and truly: I found them all right the next day.

I wonder what she thought of my correspondence. What estimate did she form of Dr John Bretton's epistolary powers? In what light did the often very pithy thoughts, the generally sound, and sometimes original opinions, set, without pretension, in an easily-flowing, spirited style, appear to her? How did she like that genial, half-humorous vein, which to me gave such delight? What did she think of the few kind words scattered here and there – not thickly, as the diamonds were scattered in the valley of Sinbad, but sparely, as those gems lie in unfabled beds? Oh, Madame Beck! how seemed these things to you?

I think in Madame Beck's eyes the five letters found a certain favour. One day after she had *borrowed* them (in speaking of so suave a little woman, one ought to use suave terms), I caught her examining me with a steady contemplative gaze, a little puzzled, but not at all malevolent. It was during that brief space between lessons, when the pupils turned out into the court for a quarter of an hour's recreation; she and I remained in the first classe alone: when I met her eye, her thoughts forced themselves partially through her lips.

'Il y a,' said she, 'quelquechose de bien remarquable dans le caractère Anglais.'

'How, Madame?'

She gave a little laugh, repeating the word 'how' in English.

'Je ne saurais vous dire "how;" mais, enfin, les Anglais ont des idées à eux, en amitie, en amour, en tout. Mais au moins il n'est pas besoin de les surveiller,'[146] she added, getting up and trotting away like the compact little pony she was.

'Then I hope,' murmured I to myself, 'you will graciously let alone my letters for the future.'

Alas! something came rushing into my eyes, dimming utterly their vision, blotting from sight the schoolroom, the garden, the bright winter sun, as I remembered that never more would letters, such as she had read, come to me. I had seen the last of them. That goodly river on whose banks I had sojourned, of whose waves a few reviving drops had trickled to my lips, was bending to another course: it was leaving my little hut and field forlorn and sand-dry, pouring its wealth of waters far away. The change was right, just, natural; not a word could be said: but I loved my Rhine, my Nile; I had almost worshipped my Ganges, and I grieved that the grand tide should roll estranged, should vanish like a false mirage. Though stoical, I was not quite a stoic; drops streamed fast on my hands, on my desk: I wept one sultry shower, heavy and brief.

But soon I said to myself, 'The Hope I am bemoaning suffered and made me suffer much: it did not die till it was full time: following an agony so lingering, death ought to be welcome.'

Welcome I endeavoured to make it. Indeed, long pain had made patience a habit. In the end I closed the eyes of my dead, covered its face, and composed its limbs with great calm.

The letters, however, must be put away, out of sight: people who have undergone bereavement always jealously gather together and lock away mementos: it is not supportable to be stabbed to the heart each moment by sharp revival of regret.

One vacant holiday afternoon (the Thursday) going to my treasure, with intent to consider its final disposal, I perceived – and this time with a strong impulse of displeasure – that it had been again tampered with: the packet was there, indeed, but the ribbon which secured it had been untied and retied; and by other symptoms I knew that my drawer had been visited.

This was a little too much. Madame Beck herself was the soul of discretion, besides having as strong a brain and sound a judgment as ever furnished a human head; that she should know the contents of my casket, was not pleasant, but might be borne. Little Jesuit inquisitress as she was, she could see things in a true light, and understand them in an unperverted sense; but the idea that she had ventured to communicate information, thus gained, to others; that she had, perhaps, amused herself with a companion over documents, in my eyes most sacred, shocked me cruelly. Yet, that such was the case I now saw reason to fear: I even guessed her confidant. Her kinsman, M. Paul Emanuel, had spent yesterday evening with her: she was much in the habit of consulting him, and of discussing with him matters she broached to no one else. This very morning, in class, that gentleman had favoured me with a glance which he seemed to have borrowed from Vashti, the actress; I had not at the moment comprehended that blue, yet lurid flash out of his angry eye, but I read its meaning now. *He*, I believed, was not apt to regard what concerned me from a fair point of view, nor to judge me with tolerance and candour: I had always found him severe and suspicious: the thought that these letters, mere friendly letters as they were, had fallen once, and might fall again, into his hands, jarred my very soul.

What should I do to prevent this? In what corner of this strange house was it possible to find security or secrecy? Where could a key be a safe-guard, or a padlock a barrier?

In the grenier? No, I did not like the grenier. Besides, most of the boxes and drawers there were mouldering, and did not lock. Rats, too, gnawed their way through the decayed wood; and mice made nests amongst the litter of their contents: my dear letters (most dear still, though Ichabod[147] was written on their covers) might be consumed by vermin; certainly the writing would soon become obliterated by damp. No; the grenier would not do – but where then?

While pondering this problem, I sat in the dormitory window-seat. It was a fine frosty afternoon; the winter sun, already setting, gleamed pale on the tops of the garden-shrubs: in the 'allée défendue' one great old pear-tree – the nun's pear-tree – stood up a tall dryad skeleton, gray, gaunt, and stripped. A thought struck me – one of those queer fantastic thoughts that will sometimes strike solitary people. I put on my bonnet, cloak and furs, and went out into the city.

Bending my steps to the old historical quarter of the town, whose hoar and overshadowed precincts I always sought by instinct in melancholy moods, I wandered on from street to street, till, having crossed a half-deserted 'place' or square, I found myself before a sort of broker's shop; an ancient place, full of ancient things.

What I wanted was a metal box which might be soldered, or a thick glass jar or bottle which might be stoppered and sealed hermetically. Amongst miscellaneous heaps, I found and purchased the latter article.

I then made a little roll of my letters, wrapped them in oiled silk, bound them with twine, and, having put them in the bottle, got the old Jew broker to stopper, seal, and make it air-tight. While obeying my directions, he glanced at me now and then, suspiciously, from under his frost-white eye-lashes. I believe he thought there was some evil deed on hand. In all this I had a dreary something – not pleasure – but a sad, lonely satisfaction. The impulse under which I acted, the mood controlling me, were similar to the impulse and the mood which had induced me to visit the confessional. With quick walking I regained the pensionnat just at dark, and in time for dinner.

At seven o'clock the moon rose. At half-past seven, when the pupils and teachers were at study, and Madame Beck was with her mother and children in the salle à manger, when the half-boarders were all gone home, and Rosine had left the vestibule, and all was still – I shawled myself, and, taking the sealed jar, stole out through the first-classe door, into the berceau and thence into the 'allée défendue.'

Methusaleh, the pear-tree, stood at the further end of this walk, near my seat: he rose up, dim and gray, above the lower shrubs round him. Now Methusaleh, though so very old, was of sound timber still; only there was a hole, or rather a deep hollow, near his root. I knew there was such a hollow, hidden partly by ivy and creepers growing thick round; and there I meditated hiding my treasure. But I was not only going to hide a treasure – I meant also to bury a grief. That grief over which I had lately been weeping as I wrapped it in its winding-sheet, must be interred.

Well, I cleared away the ivy, and found the hole; it was large enough to receive the jar, and I thrust it deep in. In a tool-shed at the bottom of the garden, lay the relics of building-materials, left by masons lately employed to repair a part of the premises. I fetched thence a slate and some mortar, put the slate on the hollow, secured it with cement, covered the whole with black mould, and, finally, replaced the ivy. This done, I rested, leaning against the tree; lingering, like any other mourner, beside a newly-sodded grave.

The air of the night was very still, but dim with a peculiar mist, which changed the moonlight into a luminous haze. In this air, or this mist, there was some quality – electrical, perhaps – which acted in strange sort upon me. I felt then as I had felt a year ago in England – on a night when the aurora borealis was streaming and sweeping round heaven, when, belated in lonely fields, I had paused to watch that mustering of an army with banners – that quivering of serried lances – that swift ascent of messengers from below the north star to the dark, high keystone of heaven's arch. I felt, not happy, far otherwise, but strong with reinforced strength.

If life be a war, it seemed my destiny to conduct it single-handed. I pondered now how to break up my winter-quarters – to leave an encampment where food and forage failed. Perhaps, to effect this change, another pitched battle must be fought with fortune; if so, I had a mind to the encounter: too poor to lose, God might destine me to gain. But what road was open? – what plan available?

On this question I was still pausing, when the moon, so dim hitherto, seemed to shine out somewhat brighter: a ray even gleamed white before me, and a shadow became distinct and marked. I looked more narrowly, to make out the cause of this well-defined contrast appearing a little suddenly in the obscure alley: whiter and blacker it grew on my eye: it took shape with instantaneous transformation. I stood about three yards from a tall, sable-robed, snowy-veiled woman.

Five minutes passed. I neither fled nor shrieked. She was there still. I spoke.

'Who are you? and why do you come to me?'

She stood mute. She had no face – no features: all below her brow was masked with a white cloth; but she had eyes, and they viewed me.

I felt, if not brave, yet a little desperate; and desperation will often suffice to fill the post and do the work of courage. I advanced one step. I stretched out my hand, for I meant to touch her. She seemed to recede. I drew nearer: her recession, still silent, became swift. A mass of shrubs, full-leaved evergreens – laurel and dense yew – intervened between me and what I followed. Having passed that obstacle, I looked and saw nothing. I waited. I said, – 'If you have any errand to me, come back and deliver it.' Nothing spoke or reappeared.

This time there was no Dr John to whom to have recourse: there was no one to whom I dared whisper the words, 'I have again seen the nun.'

Paulina Mary sought my frequent presence in the Rue Crécy. In the old Bretton days, though she had never professed herself fond of me, my society had soon become to her a sort of unconscious necessary. I used to notice that if I withdrew to my room, she would speedily come trotting after me, and opening the door and peeping in, say, with her little peremptory accent, –

'Come down. Why do you sit here by yourself? You must come into the parlour.'

In the same spirit she urged me now –

'Leave the Rue Fossette,' she said, 'and come and live with us. Papa would give you far more than Madame Beck gives you.'

Mr Home himself offered me a handsome sum – thrice my present salary – if I would accept the office of companion to his daughter. I declined. I think I should have declined had I been poorer than I was, and with scantier fund of resource, more stinted narrowness of future prospect. I had not that vocation. I could teach; I could give lessons; but to be either a private governess or a companion was unnatural to me. Rather than fill the former post in any great house, I would deliberately have taken a housemaid's place, bought a strong pair of gloves, swept bedrooms and staircases, and cleaned stoves and locks, in peace and independence. Rather than be a companion, I would have made shirts, and starved.

I was no bright lady's shadow – not Miss de Bassompierre's. Overcast enough it was my nature often to be; of a subdued habit I was: but the dimness and depression must both be voluntary – such as kept me docile at my desk, in the midst of my now well-accustomed pupils in Madame Beck's first classe; or alone, at my own bedside, in her dormitory, or in the alley and seat which were called mine, in her garden: my qualifications were not convertible, not adaptable; they could not be made the foil of any gem, the adjunct of any beauty, the appendage of any greatness in Christendom. Madame Beck and I, without assimilating, understood each other well. I was not *her* companion, nor her children's governess; she left me free: she tied me to nothing – not to herself – not even to her interests: once, when she had for a fortnight been called from home by a near relation's illness, and on her return, all anxious and full of care about her establishment, lest something in her absence should have gone wrong – finding that matters had proceeded much as usual, and that there was no evidence of glaring neglect – she made each of the teachers a present, in acknowledgement of steadiness. To my bedside she came at twelve o'clock at night, and told me she had no present for me. 'I must make fidelity advantageous to the St. Pierre,' said she; 'if I attempt to make it advantageous to you, there will arise misunderstanding between us – perhaps separation. One thing, however, I *can* do to please you – leave you alone with your liberty: c'est ce que je ferai.'

She kept her word. Every slight shackle she had ever laid on me, she, from that time, with quiet hand removed. Thus I had pleasure in voluntarily respecting her rules; gratification in devoting double time, in taking double pains with the pupils she committed to my charge.

As to Mary de Bassompierre, I visited her with pleasure, though I would not live with her. My visits soon taught me that it was unlikely even my occasional and voluntary society would long be indispensable to her. M. de Bassompierre, for his part, seemed impervious to this conjecture, blind to this possibility; unconscious as any child to the signs, the likelihoods, the fitful beginnings of what, when it drew to an end, he might not approve.

Whether or not he would cordially approve, I used to speculate. Difficult to say. He was much taken up with scientific interests; keen, intent, and somewhat oppugnant in what concerned his favourite pursuits, but unsuspicious and trustful in the ordinary affairs of life. From all I could gather, he seemed to regard his 'daughterling' as still but a child, and probably had not yet admitted the notion that others might look on her in a different light: he would speak of what should be done when 'Polly' was a woman, when she should be grown up; and 'Polly,' standing beside his chair, would sometimes smile and take his honoured head between her little hands, and kiss his iron-gray locks; and, at other times, she would pout and toss her curls: but she never said, 'Papa, I *am* grown up.'

She had different moods for different people. With her father she really was still a child, or child-like, affectionate, merry, and playful. With me she was serious, and as womanly as thought and feeling could make her. With Mrs Bretton she was docile and reliant, but not expansive. With Graham she was shy, at present very shy; at moments she tried to be cold; on occasion she endeavoured to shun him. His step made her start; his entrance hushed her; when he spoke, her answers failed of fluency; when he took leave, she remained self-vexed and disconcerted. Even her father noticed this demeanour in her.

'My little Polly,' he said once, 'you live too retired a life; if you grow to be a woman with these shy manners, you will hardly be fitted for society. You really make quite a stranger of Dr Bretton: how is this? Don't you remember that, as a little girl, you used to be rather partial to him?'

'*Rather*, papa,' echoed she, with her slightly dry, yet gentle and simple tone.

'And you don't like him now? What has he done?'

'Nothing. Y-e-s, I like him a little; but we are grown strange to each other.'

'Then rub it off, Polly: rub the rust and the strangeness off. Talk away when he is here, and have no fear of him!'

'*He* does not talk much. Is he afraid of me, do you think, papa?'

'Oh, to be sure! What man would not be afraid of such a little silent lady?'

'Then tell him some day not to mind my being silent. Say that it is my way, and that I have no unfriendly intention.'

'Your way, you little chatter-box? So far from being your way, it is only your whim!'

'Well, I'll improve, papa.'

And very pretty was the grace with which, the next day, she tried to keep her word. I saw her make the effort to converse affably with Dr John on general topics. The attention called into her guest's face a pleasurable glow; he met her with caution, and replied to her in his softest tones, as if there was a kind of gossamer happiness hanging in the air which he feared to disturb by drawing too deep a breath. Certainly, in her timid yet earnest advance to friendship, it could not be denied that there was a most exquisite and fairy charm.

When the Doctor was gone, she approached her father's chair.

'Did I keep my word, papa? Did I behave better?'

'My Polly behaved like a queen. I shall become quite proud of her if this improvement continues. By and by we shall see her receiving my guests with quite a calm, grand manner. Miss Lucy and I will have to look about us, and polish up all our best airs and graces lest we should be thrown into the shade. Still, Polly, there is a little flutter, a little tendency to stammer now and then, and even to lisp as you lisped when you were six years old.'

'No, papa,' interrupted she, indignantly, 'that can't be true.'

'I appeal to Miss Lucy. Did she not, in answering Dr Bretton's question as to whether she had ever seen the palace of the Prince of Bois l'Etang, say "yeth," she had been there "theveral" times?'

'Papa, you are satirical, you are méchant! I can pronounce all the letters of the alphabet as clearly as you can. But tell me this: you are very particular in making me be civil to Dr Bretton, do you like him yourself?'

'To be sure: for old acquaintance sake I like him: then he is a very good son to his mother; besides being a kind-hearted fellow and clever in his profession: yes, the callant[148] is well enough.'

'*Callant*! Ah, Scotchman! Papa, is it the Edinburgh or the Aberdeen accent you have?'

'Both, my pet, both; and doubtless the Glaswegian into the bargain: it is that which enables me to speak French so well: a gude Scots tongue always succeeds well at the French.'

'*The* French! Scotch again: incorrigible papa! You, too, need schooling.'

'Well, Polly, you must persuade Miss Snowe to undertake both you and me; to make you steady and womanly, and me refined and classical.'

The light in which M. de Bassompierre evidently regarded 'Miss Snowe,' used to occasion me much inward edification. What contradictory attributes of character we sometimes find ascribed to us, according to the eye with which we are viewed! Madame Beck esteemed me learned and blue; Miss Fanshawe, caustic, ironic, and cynical; Mr Home, a model teacher, the essence of the sedate and discreet: somewhat conventional perhaps, too strict, limited and scrupulous, but still the pink and pattern of governess-correctness; whilst another person, Professor Paul Emanuel, to wit, never lost an opportunity of intimating his opinion that mine was rather a fiery and rash nature – adventurous, indocile, and audacious. I smiled at them all. If any one knew me it was little Paulina Mary.

As I would not be Paulina's nominal and paid companion, genial and harmonious as I began to find her intercourse, she persuaded me to join her in some study, as a regular and settled means of sustaining communication: she proposed the German language, which, like myself, she found difficult of mastery. We agreed to take our lessons in the Rue Crécy of the same mistress; this arrangement threw us together for some hours of every week. M. de Bassompierre seemed quite pleased: it perfectly met his approbation that Madame Minerva Gravity should associate a portion of her leisure with that of his fair and dear child.

That other self-elected judge of mine, the professor in the Rue Fossette, discovering by some surreptitious, spying means, that I was no longer so stationary as hitherto, but went out regularly at certain hours of certain days, took it upon himself to place me under surveillance. People said M. Emanuel had been brought up amongst Jesuits. I should more readily have accredited this report had his manœuvres been better masked. As it was I doubted it. Never was a more undisguised schemer, a franker, looser intriguer. He would analyze his own machinations: elaborately contrive plots, and forthwith indulge in explanatory boasts of their skill. I know not whether I was more amused or provoked, by his stepping up to me one morning and whispering solemnly that he 'had his eye on me: *he* at least would discharge the duty of a friend and not leave me entirely to my own devices. My proceedings seemed at present very unsettled: he did not know what to make of them: he thought his cousin Beck very much to blame in suffering this sort of fluttering inconsistency in a teacher attached to her house. What had a person devoted to a serious calling, that of education, to do with Counts and Countesses, hotels and chateaux? To him, I seemed altogether "en l'air." On his faith, he believed I went out six days in the seven.'

I said, 'Monsieur exaggerated. I certainly had enjoyed the advantage of a little change lately, but not before it had become necessary; and the privilege was by no means exercised in excess.'

'Necessary! How was it necessary? I was well enough, he supposed? Change necessary! He would recommend me to look at the Catholic 'religieuses,' and study *their* lives. *They* asked no change.'

I am no judge of what expression crossed my face when he thus spoke, but it was one which provoked him: he accused me of being reckless, worldly, and epicurean; ambitious of greatness and feverishly athirst for the pomps and vanities of life. It seems I had no 'dévouement,' no 'recueillement'[149] in my character; no spirit of grace, faith, sacrifice, or self-abasement. Feeling the inutility of answering these charges, I mutely continued the correction of a pile of English exercises.

'He could see in me nothing Christian: like many other Protestants, I revelled in the pride and self-will of paganism.'

I slightly turned from him, nestling still closer under the wing of silence.

A vague sound grumbled between his teeth; it could not surely be a 'juron:' he was too religious for that; but I am certain I heard the word *sacré*.[150] Grievous to relate, the same word was repeated, with the unequivocal addition of *mille* something, when I passed him about two hours afterwards in the corridor, prepared to go and take my German lesson in the Rue Crécy. Never was a better little man, in some points, than M. Paul: never, in others, a more waspish little despot.

Our German mistress, Fräulein Anna Braun, was a worthy, hearty woman, of about forty-five; she ought, perhaps, to have lived in the days of Queen Elizabeth, as she habitually consumed, for her first and second breakfast, beer and beef: also, her direct and downright Deutsch nature seemed to suffer a sensation of cruel restraint from what she called our English reserve; though we thought we were very cordial with her: but we did not slap her on the shoulder, and if we consented to kiss her cheek, it was done quietly, and without any explosive smack. These omissions oppressed and depressed her considerably; still, on the whole, we got on very well. Accustomed to instruct foreign girls, who hardly ever will think and study for themselves – who have no idea of grappling with a difficulty, and overcoming it by dint of reflection or application – our progress, which, in truth, was very leisurely, seemed to astound her. In her eyes, we were a pair of glacial prodigies, cold, proud, and preternatural.

The young Countess *was* a little proud, a little fastidious: and perhaps, with her native delicacy and beauty, she had a right to these feelings; but I think it was a total mistake to ascribe them to me. I never evaded the morning salute, which Paulina would slip when she could; nor was a certain little manner of still disdain a weapon known in my armoury of defence; whereas, Paulina always kept it clear, fine and bright, and any rough German sally called forth at once its steely glisten.

Honest Anna Braun, in some measure, felt this difference; and while she half-feared, half-worshipped Paulina, as a sort of dainty nymph – an Undine – she took refuge with me, as a being all mortal, and of easier mood.

A book we liked well to read and translate was Schiller's Ballads;
Paulina soon learned to read them beautifully: the Fräulein would
listen to her with a broad smile of pleasure, and say her voice
sounded like music. She translated them too with a facile flow of
language, and in a strain of kindred and poetic fervour: her cheek
would flush, her lips tremblingly smile, her beauteous eyes kindle or
melt as she went on. She learnt the best by heart, and would often
recite them when we were alone together. One she liked well was
'Des Mädchens Klage:'[151] that is, she liked well to repeat the words,
she found plaintive melody in the sound; the sense she would
criticise. She murmured, as we sat over the fire one evening: –

> 'Du Heilige, rufe dein Kind zurück,
> Ich habe genossen das irdische Glück,
> Ich habe gelebt und geliebet!'

'Lived and loved!' said she, 'is that the summit of earthly happiness,
the end of life – to love? I don't think it is. It may be the extreme of
mortal misery, it may be sheer waste of time, and fruitless torture of
feeling. If Schiller had said to *be* loved – he might have come nearer
the truth. Is not that another thing, Lucy, to be loved?'

'I suppose it may be: but why consider the subject? What is love
to you? What do you know about it?'

She crimsoned, half in irritation, half in shame.

'Now, Lucy,' she said, 'I won't take that from you. It may be well
for papa to look on me as a baby: I rather prefer that he should thus
view me; but *you* know and shall learn to acknowledge that I am
verging on my nineteenth year.'

'No matter if it were your twenty-ninth; we will anticipate no
feelings by discussion and conversation: we will not talk about love.'

'Indeed, indeed!' said she – all in hurry and heat – 'you may think
to check and hold me in, as much as you please; but I *have* talked
about it, and heard about it too; and a great deal and lately, and
disagreeably and detrimentally: and in a way you wouldn't approve.'

And the vexed, triumphant, pretty, naughty being laughed. I
could not discern what she meant, and I would not ask her: I was
nonplussed. Seeing, however, the utmost innocence in her
countenance – combined with some transient perverseness and
petulance – I said at last, –

'Who talks to you disagreeably and detrimentally on such
matters? Who that has near access to you would dare to do it?'

'Lucy,' replied she more softly, 'it is a person who makes me miserable sometimes; and I wish she would keep away – I don't want her.'

'But who, Paulina, can it be? You puzzle me much.'

'It is – it is my cousin Ginevra. Every time she has leave to visit Mrs Cholmondeley she calls here, and whenever she finds me alone she begins to talk about her admirers. Love, indeed! You should hear all she has to say about love.'

'Oh, I have heard it,' said I, quite coolly; 'and on the whole, perhaps, it is as well you should have heard it too: it is not to be regretted, it is all right. Yet surely, Ginevra's mind cannot influence yours? You can look over both her head and her heart.'

'She does influence me very much. She has the art of disturbing my happiness and unsettling my opinions. She hurts me through the feelings and people dearest to me.'

'What does she say, Paulina? Give me some idea. There may be counteraction of the damage done.'

'The people I have longest and most esteemed are degraded by her. She does not spare Mrs Bretton – she does not spare. . . Graham – '

'No, I dare say: and how does she mix up these with her sentiment and her. . . *love*? She does mix them, I suppose?'

'Lucy, she is insolent; and I believe, false. You know Dr Bretton. We both know him. He may be careless and proud; but when was he ever mean or slavish? Day after day she shows him to me kneeling at her feet, pursuing her like her shadow. She – repulsing him with insult, and he imploring her with infatuation. Lucy, is it true? Is any of it true?'

'It may be true that he once thought her handsome: does she give him out as still her suitor?'

'She says she might marry him any day: he only waits her consent.'

'It is these tales which have caused that reserve in your manner towards Graham which your father noticed.'

'They have certainly made me all doubtful about his character. As Ginevra speaks, they do not carry with them the sound of unmixed truth: I believe she exaggerates – perhaps invents – but I want to know how far.'

'Suppose we bring Miss Fanshawe to some proof. Give her an opportunity of displaying the power she boasts.'

'I could do that to-morrow. Papa has asked some gentlemen to dinner, all savants. Graham who, papa is beginning to discover, is a savant, too – skilled, they say, in more than one branch of science –

is among the number. Now I should be miserable to sit at table unsupported, amidst such a party. I could not talk to Messieurs A – and Z –, the Parisian academicians: all my new credit for manner would be put in peril. You and Mrs Bretton must come for my sake; Ginevra, at a word, will join you.'

'Yes; then I will carry a message of invitation, and she shall have the chance of justifying her character for veracity.'

CHAPTER 27

The Hôtel Crécy

THE MORROW TURNED OUT a more lively and busy day than we – or than I, at least – had anticipated. It seems it was the birthday of one of the young princes of Labassecour – the eldest, I think, the Duc de Dindonneau – and a general holiday was given in his honour at the schools, and especially at the principal 'Athénée,' or college. The youth of that institution had also concocted, and were to present a loyal address; for which purpose they were to be assembled in the public building where the yearly examinations were conducted, and the prizes distributed. After the ceremony of presentation, an oration, or 'discours' was to follow from one of the professors.

Several of M. de Bassompierre's friends – the savants – being more or less connected with the Athénée, were expected to attend on this occasion; together with the worshipful municipality of Villette, M. le Chevalier Staas, the burgomaster, and the parents and kinsfolk of the Athenians in general. M. de Bassompierre was engaged by his friends to accompany them; his fair daughter would, of course, be of the party, and she wrote a little note to Ginevra and myself, bidding us come early that we might join her.

As Miss Fanshawe and I were dressing in the dormitory of the Rue Fossette, she (Miss F.) suddenly burst into a laugh.

'What now?' I asked; for she had suspended the operation of arranging her attire, and was gazing at me.

'It seems so odd,' she replied, with her usual half-honest, half-insolent unreserve, 'that you and I should now be so much on a level, visiting in the same sphere; having the same connections.'

'Why yes,' said I; 'I had not much respect for the connections you chiefly frequented awhile ago: Mrs Cholmondeley and Co. would never have suited me at all.'

'Who *are* you, Miss Snowe?' she inquired, in a tone of such undisguised and unsophisticated curiosity, as made me laugh in my turn.

'You used to call yourself a nursery-governess; when you first came here you really had the care of the children in this house: I have seen you carry little Georgette in your arms, like a bonne – few

governesses would have condescended so far – and now Madame
Beck treats you with more courtesy than she treats the Parisienne,
St. Pierre; and that proud chit, my cousin, makes you her bosom
friend!'

'Wonderful!' I agreed, much amused at her mystification. 'Who
am I indeed? Perhaps a personage in disguise. Pity I don't look the
character.'

'I wonder you are not more flattered by all this,' she went on:
'you take it with strange composure. If you really are the nobody I
once thought you, you must be a cool hand.'

'The nobody you once thought me!' I repeated, and my face grew
a little hot; but I would not be angry: of what importance was a
school-girl's crude use of the terms nobody and somebody? I
confined myself, therefore, to the remark that I had merely met
with civility; and asked 'what she saw in civility to throw the
recipient into a fever of confusion?'

'One can't help wondering at some things,' she persisted.

'Wondering at marvels of your own manufacture. Are you ready
at last?'

'Yes; let me take your arm.'

'I would rather not: we will walk side by side.'

When she took my arm, she always leaned upon me her whole
weight; and, as I was not a gentleman, or her lover, I did not like it.

'There, again!' she cried. 'I thought, by offering to take your arm,
to intimate approbation of your dress and general appearance: I
meant it as a compliment.'

'You did? You meant, in short, to express that you are not
ashamed to be seen in the street with me? That if Mrs
Cholmondeley should be fondling her lap-dog at some window, or
Colonel de Hamal picking his teeth in a balcony, and should catch a
glimpse of us, you would not quite blush for your companion?'

'Yes,' said she, with that directness which was her best point –
which gave an honest plainness to her very fibs when she told them
– which was, in short, the salt, the sole preservative ingredient of a
character otherwise not formed to keep.

I delegated the trouble of commenting on this 'yes' to my
countenance; or rather, my under-lip voluntarily anticipated my
tongue: of course, reverence and solemnity were not the feelings
expressed in the look I gave her.

'Scornful, sneering creature!' she went on, as we crossed a great
square, and entered the quiet, pleasant park, our nearest way to the Rue
Crécy. 'Nobody in this world was ever such a Turk to me as you are!'

'You bring it on yourself: let me alone: have the sense to be quiet: I will let you alone.'

'As if one *could* let you alone, when you are so peculiar and so mysterious!'

'The mystery and peculiarity being entirely the conception of your own brain – maggots – neither more nor less, be so good as to keep them out of my sight.'

'But *are* you anybody?' persevered she, pushing her hand, in spite of me, under my arm; and that arm pressed itself with inhospitable closeness against my side, by way of keeping out the intruder.

'Yes,' I said, 'I am a rising character: once an old lady's companion, then a nursery-governess, now a schoolteacher.'

'Do – *do* tell me who you are? I'll not repeat it,' she urged, adhering with ludicrous tenacity to the wise notion of an incognito she had got hold of; and she squeezed the arm of which she had now obtained full possession, and coaxed and conjured till I was obliged to pause in the park to laugh. Throughout our walk she rang the most fanciful changes on this theme; proving, by her obstinate credulity, or incredulity, her incapacity to conceive how any person not bolstered up by birth or wealth, not supported by some consciousness of name or connection, could maintain an attitude of reasonable integrity. As for me, it quite sufficed to my mental tranquillity that I was known where it imported that known I should be; the rest sat on me easily: pedigree, social position, and recondite intellectual acquisition, occupied about the same space and place in my interests and thoughts; they were my third-class lodgers – to whom could be assigned only the small sitting-room and the little back bed-room: even if the dining and drawing-rooms stood empty, I never confessed it to them, as thinking minor accommodations better suited to their circumstances. The world, I soon learned, held a different estimate: and I make no doubt, the world is very right in its view, yet believe also that I am not quite wrong in mine.

There are people whom a lowered position degrades morally, to whom loss of connection costs loss of self-respect: are not these justified in placing the highest value on that station and association which is their safeguard from debasement? If a man feels that he would become contemptible in his own eyes were it generally known that his ancestry were simple and not gentle, poor and not rich, workers and not capitalists, would it be right severely to blame him for keeping these fatal facts out of sight – for starting, trembling, quailing at the chance which threatens exposure? The longer we live, the more our experience widens; the less prone are we to judge our neighbour's conduct, to question the world's wisdom: wherever an accumulation of small defences is found, whether surrounding the prude's virtue or the man of the world's respectability, there, be sure, it is needed.

We reached the Hôtel Crécy; Paulina was ready; Mrs Bretton was with her; and, under her escort and that of M. de Bassompierre, we were soon conducted to the place of assembly, and seated in good seats, at a convenient distance from the Tribune.[152] The youth of the Athénée were marshalled before us, the municipality and their bourgmestre were in places of honour, the young princes, with their tutors, occupied a conspicuous position, and the body of the building was crowded with the aristocracy and first burghers of the town.

Concerning the identity of the professor by whom the 'discours' was to be delivered, I had as yet entertained neither care nor question. Some vague expectation I had that a savant would stand up and deliver a formal speech, half dogmatism to the Athenians, half flattery to the princes.

The Tribune was yet empty when we entered, but in ten minutes after it was filled; suddenly, in a second of time, a head, chest and arms, grew above the crimson desk. This head I knew: its colour, shape, port, expression, were familiar both to me and Miss Fanshawe; the blackness and closeness of cranium, the amplitude and paleness of brow, the blueness and fire of glance, were details so domesticated in the memory, and so knit with many a whimsical association, as almost by this their sudden apparition, to tickle fancy to a laugh. Indeed, I confess, for my part, I did laugh till I was warm; but then I bent my head, and made my handkerchief and a lowered veil the sole confidants of my mirth.

I think I was glad to see M. Paul; I think it was rather pleasant than otherwise, to behold him set up there, fierce and frank, dark and candid, testy and fearless, as when regnant on his estrade in class. His presence was such a surprise: I had not once thought of expecting him, though I knew he filled the chair of Belles Lettres in the college. With *him* in that Tribune, I felt sure that neither formalism nor flattery would be our doom; but for what was vouchsafed us, for what was poured suddenly, rapidly, continuously, on our heads – I own I was not prepared.

He spoke to the princes, the nobles, the magistrates and the burghers, with just the same ease, with almost the same pointed, choleric earnestness, with which he was wont to harangue the three divisions of the Rue Fossette. The collegians he addressed, not as school-boys, but as future citizens and embryo patriots. The times which have since come on Europe had not been foretold yet, and M. Emanuel's spirit seemed new to me. Who would have thought the flat and fat soil of Labassecour could yield political convictions and national feelings, such as were now strongly expressed? Of the bearing of his opinions I need here give no special indication; yet it may be permitted me to say that I believed the little man not more earnest than right in what he said: with all his fire he was severe and sensible, – he trampled Utopian theories under his heel; he rejected wild dreams with scorn; – but, when he looked in the face of tyranny – oh, then there opened a light in his eye worth seeing; and when he spoke of injustice, his voice gave no uncertain sound, but reminded me rather of the band-trumpet, ringing at twilight from the park.

I do not think his audience were generally susceptible of sharing his flame in its purity; but some of the college youth caught fire as he eloquently told them what should be their path and endeavour in their country's and in Europe's future. They gave him a long, loud, ringing cheer, as he concluded: with all his fierceness, he was their favourite professor.

As our party left the Hall, he stood at the entrance; he saw and knew me, and lifted his hat; he offered his hand in passing, and uttered the words 'Qu'en dîtes-vous?'[153] – question eminently characteristic, and reminding me, even in this his moment of triumph, of that inquisitive restlessness, that absence of what I considered desirable self-control, which were amongst his faults. He should not have cared just then to ask what I thought, or what anybody thought; but he *did* care, and he was too natural to conceal, too impulsive to repress his wish. Well! if I blamed his over-eagerness, I liked his *näiveté*. I would have praised him: I had plenty of praise in my heart; but, alas! no words on my lips. Who *has* words at the right moment? I stammered some lame expressions; but was truly glad when other people, coming up with profuse congratulations, covered my deficiency by their redundancy.

A gentleman introduced him to M. de Bassompierre; and the Count, who had likewise been highly gratified, asked him to join his friends (for the most part M. Emanuel's likewise), and to dine with them at the Hôtel Crécy. He declined dinner, for he was a man always somewhat shy in meeting the advances of the wealthy: there was a strength of sturdy independence in the stringing of his sinews – not obtrusive, but pleasant enough to discover as one advanced in knowledge of his character; he promised, however, to step in with his friend, M. A –, a French Academician, in the course of the evening.

At dinner that day, Ginevra and Paulina each looked, in her own way, very beautiful; the former, perhaps, boasted the advantage in material charms, but the latter shone pre-eminent for attractions more subtle and spiritual: for light and eloquence of eye, for grace of mien, for winning variety of expression. Ginevra's dress of deep crimson relieved well her light curls, and harmonized with her rose-like bloom. Paulina's attire – in fashion close, though faultlessly neat, but in texture clear and white – made the eye grateful for the delicate life of her complexion, for the soft animation of her countenance, for the tender depth of her eyes, for the brown shadow and bounteous flow of her hair – darker than that of her Saxon cousin, as were also her eyebrows, her eye-lashes, her full irids, and large mobile pupils – Nature having traced all these details slightly, and with a careless hand, in Miss Fanshawe's case; and in Miss de Bassompierre's, wrought them to a high and delicate finish.

Paulina was awed by the savants, but not quite to mutism: she conversed modestly, diffidently; not without effort, but with so true a sweetness, so fine and penetrating a sense, that her father more than once suspended his own discourse to listen, and fixed on her an eye of proud delight. It was a polite Frenchman, M. Z – , a very learned, but quite a courtly man, who had drawn her into discourse. I was charmed with her French; it was faultless – the structure correct, the idiom true, the accent pure; Ginevra, who had lived half her life on the Continent, could do nothing like it: not that words ever failed Miss Fanshawe, but real accuracy and purity she neither possessed, nor in any number of years would acquire. Here, too, M. de Bassompierre was gratified; for, on the point of language, he was critical.

Another listener and observer there was; one who, detained by some exigency of his profession, had come in late to dinner. Both ladies were quietly scanned by Dr Bretton, at the moment of taking his seat at the table; and that guarded survey was more than once renewed. His arrival roused Miss Fanshawe, who had hitherto appeared listless: she now became smiling and complacent, talked – though what she said was rarely to the purpose – or rather, was of a purpose somewhat mortifyingly below the standard of the occasion. Her light, disconnected prattle might have gratified Graham once; perhaps it pleased him still: perhaps it was only fancy which suggested the thought that, while his eye was filled and his ear fed, his taste, his keen zest, his lively intelligence, were not equally consulted and regaled. It is certain that, restless and exacting as seemed the demand on his attention, he yielded courteously all that was required: his manner showed neither pique nor coolness: Ginevra was his neighbour, and to her, during dinner, he almost exclusively confined his notice. She appeared satisfied, and passed to the drawing-room in very good spirits.

Yet, no sooner had we reached that place of refuge, than she again became flat and listless: throwing herself on a couch, she denounced both the 'discours' and the dinner as stupid affairs, and inquired of her cousin how she could hear such a set of prosaic 'gros-bonnets' as her father gathered about him. The moment the gentlemen were heard to move, her railings ceased: she started up, flew to the piano, and dashed at it with spirit. Dr Bretton entering, one of the first, took up his station beside her. I thought he would not long maintain that post: there was a position near the hearth to which I expected to see him attracted: this position he only scanned with his eye; while *he* looked, others drew in. The grace and mind of Paulina charmed these thoughtful Frenchmen: the fineness of her beauty, the soft courtesy of her manner, her immature, but real and inbred tact, pleased their national taste; they clustered about her, not indeed to talk science, which would have rendered her dumb, but to touch on many subjects in letters, in arts, in actual life, on which it soon appeared that she had both read and reflected. I listened. I am sure that though Graham stood aloof, he listened too: his hearing as well as his vision was very fine, quick, discriminating. I knew he gathered the conversation; I felt that the mode in which it was sustained suited him exquisitely – pleased him almost to pain.

In Paulina there was more force, both of feeling and character, than most people thought – than Graham himself imagined – than she would ever show to those who did not wish to see it. To speak truth, reader, there is no excellent beauty, no accomplished grace, no reliable refinement, without strength as excellent, as complete, as trustworthy. As well might you look for good fruit and blossom on a rootless and sapless tree, as for charms that will endure in a feeble and relaxed nature. For a little while, the blooming semblance of beauty may flourish round weakness; but it cannot bear a blast: it soon fades, even in serenest sunshine. Graham would have started had any suggestive spirit whispered of the sinew and the stamina sustaining that delicate nature; but I, who had known her as a child, knew, or guessed, by what a good and strong root her graces held to the firm soil of reality.

While Dr Bretton listened, and waited an opening in the magic circle, his glance, restlessly sweeping the room at intervals, lighted by chance on me; where I sat in a quiet nook not far from my godmother and M. de Bassompierre, who, as usual, were engaged in what Mr Home called 'a two-handed crack:' what the Count would have interpreted as a tête-à-tête. Graham smiled recognition, crossed the room, asked me how I was, told me I looked pale. I also had my own smile at my own thought: it was now about three months since Dr John had spoken to me – a lapse of which he was not even conscious. He sat down, and became silent. His wish was rather to look than converse. Ginevra and Paulina were now opposite to him: he could gaze his fill: he surveyed both forms – studied both faces.

Several new guests, ladies as well as gentlemen, had entered the room since dinner, dropping in for the evening conversation; and amongst the gentlemen, I may incidentally observe, I had already noticed by glimpses, a severe, dark professoral outline, hovering aloof in an inner saloon, seen only in vista. M. Emanuel knew many of the gentlemen present, but I think was a stranger to most of the ladies, excepting myself; in looking towards the hearth, he could not but see me, and naturally made a movement to approach; seeing, however, Dr Bretton also, he changed his mind and held back. If that had been all, there would have been no cause for quarrel; but not satisfied with holding back, he puckered his eye-brows, protruded his lip, and looked so ugly that I averted my eyes from the displeasing spectacle. M. Josef Emanuel had arrived, as well as his austere brother, and at this very moment was relieving Ginevra at the piano. What a master-touch succeeded her school-girl jingle! In what grand, grateful tones the instrument acknowledged the hand of the true artist!

'Lucy,' began Dr Bretton, breaking silence and smiling, as Ginevra glided before him, casting a glance as she passed by, 'Miss Fanshawe is certainly a fine girl.'

Of course I assented.

'Is there,' he pursued, 'another in the room as lovely?'

'I think there is not another as handsome.'

'I agree with you, Lucy: you and I do often agree in opinion, in taste, I think; or at least in judgment.'

'Do we?' I said, somewhat doubtfully.

'I believe if you had been a boy, Lucy, instead of a girl – my mother's god-son instead of her god-daughter – we should have been good friends: our opinions would have melted into each other.'

He had assumed a bantering air: a light, half-caressing, half-ironic, shone aslant in his eye. Ah, Graham! I have given more than one solitary moment to thoughts and calculations of your estimate of Lucy Snowe: was it always kind or just? Had Lucy been intrinsically the same, but possessing the additional advantages of wealth and station, would your manner to her, your value for her have been quite what they actually were? And yet by these questions

I would not seriously infer blame. No; you might sadden and trouble me sometimes; but then mine was a soon-depressed, an easily-deranged temperament – it fell if a cloud crossed the sun. Perhaps before the eye of severe equity, I should stand more at fault than you.

Trying then to keep down the unreasonable pain which thrilled my heart, on thus being made to feel that while Graham could devote to others the most grave and earnest, the manliest interest, he had no more than light raillery for Lucy, the friend of lang syne, I inquired calmly, –

'On what points are we so closely in accordance?'

'We each have an observant faculty. You, perhaps, don't give me credit for the possession; yet I have it.'

'But you were speaking of tastes: we may see the same objects, yet estimate them differently?'

'Let us bring it to the test. Of course, you cannot but render homage to the merits of Miss Fanshawe: now, what do you think of others in the room? – my mother, for instance; or the lions, yonder, Messieurs A – and Z – ; or, let us say, that pale little lady, Miss de Bassompierre?'

'You know what I think of your mother. I have not thought of Messieurs A – and Z –.'

'And the other?'

'I think she is, as you say, a pale little lady – pale, certainly, just now, when she is fatigued with over-excitement.'

'You don't remember her as a child?'

'I wonder, sometimes, whether you do?'

'I had forgotten her; but it is noticeable, that circumstances, persons, even words and looks, that had slipped your memory, may, under certain conditions, certain aspects of your own or another's mind, revive.'

'That is possible enough.'

'Yet,' he continued, 'the revival is imperfect – needs confirmation, partakes so much of the dim character of a dream, or of the airy one of a fancy, that the testimony of a witness becomes necessary for corroboration. Were you not a guest at Bretton ten years ago, when Mr Home brought his little girl, whom we then called "little Polly," to stay with mama?'

'I was there the night she came, and also the morning she went away.'

'Rather a peculiar child; was she not? I wonder how I treated her. Was I fond of children in those days? Was there anything gracious or kindly about me – great, reckless, school-boy as I was? But you don't recollect me, of course?'

'You have seen your own picture at La Terrasse. It is like you personally. In manner, you were almost the same yesterday as to-day.'

'But, Lucy, how is that? Such an oracle really whets my curiosity. What am I to-day? What was I the yesterday of ten years back?'

'Gracious to whatever pleased you – unkindly or cruel to nothing.'

'There you are wrong; I think I was almost a brute to you, for instance.'

'A brute! No, Graham: I should never have patiently endured brutality.'

'*This*, however, I *do* remember: quiet Lucy Snowe tasted nothing of my grace.'

'As little of your cruelty.'

'Why, had I been Nero himself, I could not have tormented a being inoffensive as a shadow.'

I smiled; but I also hushed a groan. Oh! – I wished he would just let me alone – cease allusion to me. These epithets – these attributes I put from me. His 'quiet Lucy Snowe,' his 'inoffensive shadow,' I gave him back; not with scorn, but with extreme weariness: theirs was the coldness and the pressure of lead; let him whelm me with no such weight. Happily, he was soon on another theme.

'On what terms were "little Polly" and I? Unless my recollections deceive me, we were not foes – '

'You speak very vaguely. Do you think little Polly's memory not more definite?'

'Oh! we don't talk of "little Polly" *now*. Pray say, Miss de Bassompierre; and, of course, such a stately personage remembers nothing of Bretton. Look at her large eyes, Lucy; can they read a word in the page of memory? Are they the same which I used to direct to a horn-book? She does not know that I partly taught her to read.'

'In the Bible on Sunday nights?'

'She has a calm, delicate, rather fine profile now: once what a little restless, anxious countenance was hers! What a thing is a child's preference – what a bubble! Would you believe it? that lady was fond of me!'

'I think she was in some measure fond of you,' said I, moderately.

'You don't remember then? I had forgotten; but I remember *now*. She liked me the best of whatever there was at Bretton.'

'You thought so.'

'I quite well recall it. I wish I could tell her all I recall; or rather, I wish some one, *you* for instance, would go behind and whisper it all in her ear, and I could have the delight – here, as I sit – of watching her look under the intelligence. Could you manage that, think you, Lucy, and make me ever grateful?'

'Could I manage to make you ever grateful?' said I. 'No, *I could not.*' And I felt my fingers work and my hands interlock: I felt, too, an inward courage, warm and resistant. In this matter I was not disposed to gratify Dr John: not at all. With a now welcome force, I realized his entire misapprehension of my character and nature. He wanted always to give me a rôle not mine. Nature and I opposed him. He did not at all guess what I felt: he did not read my eyes, or face, or gestures; though, I doubt not, all spoke. Leaning towards me coaxingly, he said, softly, '*Do* content me, Lucy.'

And I would have contented, or, at least, I would clearly have enlightened him, and taught him well never again to expect of me the part of officious soubrette in a love drama; when, following his soft, eager murmur, meeting almost his pleading, mellow – '*Do* content me, Lucy!' – a sharp hiss pierced my ear on the other side.

'Petite chatte, doucerette, coquette!' sibillated the sudden boa-constrictor; 'vous avez l'air bien triste, soumise, rêveuse, mais vous ne l'êtes pas; c'est moi qui vous le dis: Sauvage! la flamme à l'âme, l'éclair aux yeux!'[154]

'Oui; j'ai la flamme à l'âme, et je dois l'avoir!'[155] retorted I, turning in just wrath; but Professor Emanuel had hissed his insult and was gone.

The worst of the matter was, that Dr Bretton, whose ears, as I have said, were quick and fine, caught every word of this apostrophe; he put his handkerchief to his face and laughed till he shook.

'Well done, Lucy,' cried he; 'capital! petite chatte, petite coquette! Oh, I must tell my mother! Is it true, Lucy, or half-true? I believe it is: you redden to the colour of Miss Fanshawe's gown. And really, by my word, now I examine him, that is the same little man who was so savage with you at the concert: the very same, and in his soul he is frantic at this moment because he sees me laughing. Oh! I must tease him.'

And Graham, yielding to his bent for mischief, laughed, jested, and whispered on till I could bear no more, and my eyes filled.

Suddenly he was sobered: a vacant space appeared near Miss de Bassompierre; the circle surrounding her seemed about to dissolve. This movement was instantly caught by Graham's eye – ever-vigilant, even while laughing; he rose, took his courage in both hands, crossed the room, and made the advantage his own. Dr John, throughout his whole life, was a man of luck – a man of success. And why? Because he had the eye to see his opportunity, the heart to prompt to well-timed action, the nerve to consummate a perfect work. And no tyrant-passion dragged him back; no enthusiasms, no foibles encumbered his way. How well he looked at this very moment! When Paulina looked up as he reached her side, her glance mingled at once with an encountering glance, animated, yet modest; his colour, as he spoke to her, became half a blush, half a glow. He stood in her presence brave and bashful: subdued and unobtrusive, yet decided in his purpose and devoted in his ardour. I gathered all this by one view. I did not prolong my observation – time failed me, had inclination served: the night wore late; Ginevra and I ought already to have been in the Rue Fossette. I rose, and bade good-night to my godmother and M. de Bassompierre.

I know not whether Professor Emanuel had noticed my reluctant acceptance of Dr Bretton's badinage, or whether he perceived that I was pained, and that, on the whole, the evening had not been one flow of exultant enjoyment for the volatile, pleasure-loving, Mademoiselle Lucie; but, as I was leaving the room, he stepped up and inquired whether I had any one to attend me to the Rue Fossette. The professor *now* spoke politely, and even deferentially, and he looked apologetic and repentant; but I could not recognise his civility at a word, nor meet his contrition with crude, premature oblivion. Never hitherto had I felt seriously disposed to resent his brusqueries, or freeze before his fierceness; what he had said to-night, however, I considered unwarranted: my extreme disapprobation of the proceeding must be marked, however slightly. I merely said: –

'I am provided with attendance.'

Which was true, as Ginevra and I were to be sent home in the carriage; and I passed him with the sliding obeisance with which he was wont to be saluted in classe by pupils crossing his estrade.

Having sought my shawl I returned to the vestibule. M. Emanuel stood there as if waiting. He observed that the night was fine.

'Is it?' I said, with a tone and manner whose consummate chariness and frostiness I could not but applaud. It was so seldom I could properly act out my own resolution to be reserved and cool where I had been grieved or hurt, that I felt almost proud of this one successful effort. That 'Is it?' sounded just like the manner of other people. I had heard hundreds of such little minced, docked, dry phrases, from the pursed-up coral lips of a score of self-possessed, self-sufficing misses and mesdemoiselles. That M. Paul would not stand any prolonged experience of this sort of dialogue I knew; but he certainly merited a sample of the curt and arid. I believe he thought so himself, for he took the dose quietly. He

looked at my shawl and objected to its lightness. I decidedly told
him it was as heavy as I wished. Receding aloof, and standing apart,
I leaned on the banister of the stairs, folded my shawl about me, and
fixed my eyes on a dreary religious painting darkening the wall.

Ginevra was long in coming: tedious seemed her loitering. M.
Paul was still there, my ear expected from his lips an angry tone. He
came nearer. 'Now for another hiss!' thought I: had not the action
been too uncivil I could have stopped my ears with my fingers in
terror of the thrill. Nothing happens as we expect: listen for a coo
or a murmur; it is then you will hear a cry of prey or pain. Await a
piercing shriek, an angry threat, and welcome an amicable greeting,
a low kind whisper. M. Paul spoke gently: –

'Friends,' said he, 'do not quarrel for a word. Tell me, was it I or
ce grand fat d'Anglais'[156] (so he profanely denominated Dr Bretton),
'who made your eyes so humid, and your cheeks so hot as they are
even now?'

'I am not conscious of you, monsieur, or of any other having
excited such emotion as you indicate,' was my answer; and in giving
it, I again surpassed my usual self, and achieved a neat, frosty
falsehood.

'But what did I say?' he pursued, 'tell me: I was angry: I have
forgotten my words; what were they?'

'Such as it is best to forget!' said I, still quite calm and chill.

'Then it was *my* words which wounded you? Consider them
unsaid: permit my retractation; accord my pardon.'

'I am not angry, monsieur.'

'Then you are worse than angry – grieved. Forgive me, Miss
Lucy.'

'M. Emanuel, I *do* forgive you.'

'Let me hear you say, in the voice natural to you, and not in that
alien tone, "Mon ami, je vous pardonne." '[157]

He made me smile. Who could help smiling at his wistfulness, his
simplicity, his earnestness?

'Bon!' he cried; 'Voilà que le jour va poindre! Dîtes donc, mon ami.'

'Monsieur Paul, je vous pardonne.'

'I will have no monsieur: speak the other word, or I shall not
believe you sincere: another effort – *mon ami*, or else in English, –
my friend!'

Now, 'my friend' had rather another sound and significancy than
'*mon ami*,' it did not breathe the same sense of domestic and
intimate affection: '*mon ami*' I could *not* say to M. Paul; 'my friend,'
I could, and did say without difficulty. This distinction existed not

for him, however, and he was quite satisfied with the English phrase. He smiled. You should have seen him smile, reader; and you should have marked the difference between his countenance now, and that he wore half an hour ago. I cannot affirm that I had ever witnessed the smile of pleasure, or content, or kindness round M. Paul's lips, or in his eyes before. The ironic, the sarcastic, the disdainful, the passionately exultant, I had hundreds of times seen him express by what he called a smile, but any illuminated sign of milder or warmer feeling struck me as wholly new in his visage. It changed it as from a mask to a face: the deep lines left his features; the very complexion seemed clearer and fresher; that swart, sallow, southern darkness which spoke his Spanish blood, became displaced by a lighter hue. I know not that I have ever seen in any other human face an equal metamorphosis from a similar cause. He now took me to the carriage; at the same moment M. de Bassompierre came out with his niece.

In a pretty humour was Mistress Fanshawe; she had found the evening a grand failure: completely upset as to temper, she gave way to the most uncontrolled moroseness as soon as we were seated, and the carriage-door closed. Her invectives against Dr Bretton had something venomous in them. Having found herself impotent either to charm or sting him, hatred was her only resource; and this hatred she expressed in terms so unmeasured and proportion so monstrous, that, after listening for a while with assumed stoicism, my outraged sense of justice at last and suddenly caught fire. An explosion ensued: for I could be passionate, too; especially with my present fair but faulty associate, who never failed to stir the worst dregs of me. It was well that the carriage-wheels made a tremendous rattle over the flinty Choseville pavement, for I can assure the reader there was neither dead silence nor calm discussion within the vehicle. Half in earnest, half in seeming, I made it my business to storm down Ginevra. She had set out rampant from the Rue Crécy; it was necessary to tame her before we reached the Rue Fossette: to this end it was indispensable to show up her sterling value and high deserts; and this must be done in language of which the fidelity and homeliness might challenge comparison with the compliments of a John Knox to a Mary Stuart.[158] This was the right discipline for Ginevra; it suited her. I am quite sure she went to bed that night all the better and more settled in mind and mood, and slept all the more sweetly for having undergone a sound moral drubbing.

END OF VOLUME TWO

VOLUME THREE

CHAPTER 28

The Watchguard

M. PAUL EMANUEL owned an acute sensitiveness to the annoyance of interruption, from whatsoever cause, occurring during his lessons: to pass through the classe under such circumstances was considered by the teachers and pupils of the school, individually and collectively, to be as much as a woman's or girl's life was worth.

Madame Beck herself, if forced to the enterprise, would 'skurry' through, retrenching her skirts, and carefully coasting the formidable estrade, like a ship dreading breakers. As to Rosine, the portress – on whom, every half-hour, devolved the fearful duty of fetching pupils out of the very heart of one or other of the divisions, to take their music-lessons in the oratory, the great or little salon, the salle à manger, or some other piano-station – she would, upon her second or third attempt, frequently become almost tongue-tied from excess of consternation – a sentiment inspired by the unspeakable looks levelled at her through a pair of dart-dealing spectacles.

One morning I was sitting in the carré, at work upon a piece of embroidery which one of the pupils had commenced but delayed to finish, and while my fingers wrought at the frame, my ears regaled themselves with listening to the crescendos and cadences of a voice haranguing in the neighbouring classe, in tones that waxed momently more unquiet, more ominously varied. There was a good strong partition-wall between me and the gathering storm, as well as a facile means of flight through the glass-door to the court, in case it swept this way; so I am afraid I derived more amusement than alarm from these thickening symptoms. Poor Rosine was not so safe: four times that blessed morning had she made the passage of peril; and now, for the fifth time it became her dangerous duty to snatch, as it were, a brand from the burning – a pupil from under M. Paul's nose.

'Mon Dieu! mon Dieu!' cried she. 'Que vais-je devenir? Monsieur va me tuer, je suis sûre; car il est d'une colère!'[159]

Nerved by the courage of desperation, she opened the door.

'Mademoiselle La Malle au piano!' was her cry. Ere she could make good her retreat, or quite close the door, this voice uttered itself: –

'Dès ce moment! – la classe est défendue. La première qui ouvrira cette porte, ou passera par cette division, sera pendue – fut-ce Madame Beck elle-même!'[160]

Ten minutes had not succeeded the promulgation of this decree, when Rosine's French pantoufles were again heard shuffling along the corridor.

'Mademoiselle,' said she, 'I would not for a five franc piece go into that classe again just now: Monsieur's lunettes are really terrible; and here is a commissionaire come with a message from the Athénée. I have told Madame Beck I dare not deliver it, and she says I am to charge you with it.'

'Me? No, that is rather too bad! It is not in my line of duty. Come, come, Rosine! bear your own burden. Be brave – charge once more!'

'I, Mademoiselle? – impossible! Five times I have crossed him this day. Madame must really hire a gendarme for this service. Ouf! Je n'en puis plus!'

'Bah! you are only a coward. What is the message?'

'Precisely of the kind with which Monsieur least likes to be pestered: an urgent summons to go directly to the Athénée, as there is an official visitor – inspector – I know not what – arrived, and Monsieur *must* meet him: you know how he hates a *must*.'

Yes, I knew well enough. The restive little man detested spur or curb: against whatever was urgent or obligatory, he was sure to revolt. However, I accepted the responsibility – not, certainly, without fear, but fear blent with other sentiments, curiosity amongst them. I opened the door, I entered, I closed it behind me as quickly and quietly as a rather unsteady hand would permit; for to be slow or bustling, to rattle a latch, or leave a door gaping wide, were aggravations of crime, often more disastrous in result than the main crime itself. There I stood then, and there he sat; his humour was visibly bad – almost at its worst; he had been giving a lesson in arithmetic – for he gave lessons on any and every subject that struck his fancy – and arithmetic being a dry subject, invariably disagreed with him: not a pupil but trembled when he spoke of figures. He sat, bent above his desk: to look up at the sound of an entrance, at the occurrence of a direct breach of his will and law, was an effort he could not for the moment bring himself to make. It was quite as well: I thus gained time to walk up the long classe; and it suited my idiosyncracy far better to encounter the near burst of anger like his, than to bear its menace at a distance.

At his estrade I paused, just in front; of course I was not worthy of immediate attention: he proceeded with his lesson. Disdain would not do: he must hear and he must answer my message.

Not being quite tall enough to lift my head over his desk, elevated upon the estrade, and thus suffering eclipse in my present position, I ventured to peep round, with the design, at first, of merely getting a better view of his face, which had struck me when I entered as bearing a close and picturesque resemblance to that of a black and sallow tiger. Twice did I enjoy this side-view with impunity, advancing and receding unseen; the third time my eye had scarce dawned beyond the obscuration of the desk, when it was caught and transfixed through its very pupil – transfixed by the 'lunettes.' Rosine was right; these utensils had in them a blank and immutable terror, beyond the mobile wrath of the wearer's own unglazed eyes.

I now found the advantage of proximity: these shortsighted 'lunettes' were useless for the inspection of a criminal under Monsieur's nose; accordingly, he doffed them, and he and I stood on more equal terms.

I was glad I was not really much afraid of him – that, indeed, close in his presence, I felt no terror at all; for upon his demanding cord and gibbet to execute the sentence recently pronounced, I was able to furnish him with a needleful of embroidering thread with such accommodating civility as could not but allay some portion at least of his surplus irritation. Of course I did not parade this courtesy before public view: I merely handed the thread round the angle of the desk, and attached it, ready noosed, to the barred back of the Professor's chair.

'Que me voulez-vous?' said he, in a growl of which the music was wholly confined to his chest and throat, for he kept his teeth clenched, and seemed registering to himself an inward vow, that nothing earthly should wring from him a smile. My answer commenced uncompromisingly: –

'Monsieur,' I said, 'je veux l'impossible, des choses inouïes;'[161] and thinking it best not to mince matters, but to administer the 'douche' with decision, in a low but quick voice, I delivered the Athenian message, floridly exaggerating its urgency.

Of course, he would not hear a word of it. 'He would not go; he would not leave his present class, let all the officials in Villette send for him. He would not put himself an inch out of his way at the bidding of king, cabinet, and chambers together.'

I knew, however, that he *must* go; that, talk as he would, both his duty and interest commanded an immediate and literal compliance with the summons: I stood, therefore, waiting in silence, as if he had not yet spoken. He asked what more I wanted.

'Only Monsieur's answer to deliver to the commissionaire.'

He waved an impatient negative.

I ventured to stretch my hand to the bonnet-grec which lay in grim repose on the window-sill. He followed this daring movement with his eye, no doubt in mixed pity and amazement at its presumption.

'Ah!' he muttered, 'if it came to that – if Miss Lucy meddled with his bonnet-grec – she might just put it on herself, turn garçon for the occasion, and benevolently go to the Athénée in his stead.'

With great respect, I laid the bonnet on the desk, where its tassel seemed to give me an awful nod.

'I'll write a note of apology – that will do?' said he, still bent on evasion.

Knowing well it would *not* do, I gently pushed the bonnet towards his hand. Thus impelled, it slid down the polished slope of the varnished and unbaized desk, carried before it the light steel-framed 'lunettes,'[162] and, fearful to relate, they fell to the estrade. A score of times ere now had I seen them fall and receive no damage – this time, as Lucy Snowe's hapless luck would have it, they so fell that each clear pebble became a shivered and shapeless star.

Now, indeed, dismay seized me – dismay and regret. I knew the value of those 'lunettes:' M. Paul's sight was peculiar, not easily fitted, and these glasses suited him. I had heard him call them his treasures: as I picked them up, cracked and worthless, my hand trembled. Frightened through all my nerves I was to see the mischief I had done, but I think I was even more sorry than afraid. For some seconds I dared not look the bereaved Professor in the face; he was the first to speak.

'Là!' said he; 'me voilà veuf de mes lunettes! I think Mademoiselle Lucy will now confess that the cord and gallows are amply earned; she trembles in anticipation of her doom. Ah, traitress! traitress! You are resolved to have me quite blind and helpless in your hands!'

I lifted my eyes: his face, instead of being irate, lowering, and furrowed, was overflowing with the smile, coloured with the bloom I had seen brightening it that evening at the Hôtel Crécy. He was not angry – not even grieved. For the real injury he showed himself full of clemency; under the real provocation, patient as a saint. This event, which seemed so untoward – which I thought had ruined at once my chance of successful persuasion – proved my best help. Difficult of management so long as I had done him no harm, he became graciously pliant as soon as I stood in his presence, a conscious and contrite offender.

Still gently railing at me as 'une forte femme – une Anglaise terrible – une petite casse-tout'[163] – he declared that he dared not but obey one who had given such an instance of her dangerous prowess; it was absolutely like the 'grand Empereur,[164] smashing the vase to inspire dismay.' So, at last, crowning himself with his bonnet-grec, and taking his ruined 'lunettes' from my hand with a clasp of kind pardon and encouragement, he made his bow, and went off to the Athénée in first-rate humour and spirits.

After all this amiability, the reader will be sorry for my sake to hear that I was quarrelling with M. Paul again before night; yet so it was, and I could not help it.

It was his occasional custom – and a very laudable, acceptable custom, too – to arrive of an evening, always à l'improviste, unannounced, burst in on the silent hour of study, establish a sudden despotism over us and our occupations, cause books to be put away, work-bags to be brought out, and, drawing forth a single thick volume, or a handful of pamphlets, substitute for the besotted 'lecture pieuse,' drawled by a sleepy pupil, some tragedy made grand by grand reading, ardent by fiery action – some drama, whereof, for my part, I rarely studied the intrinsic merit; for M. Emanuel made it a vessel for an outpouring, and filled it with his native verve and passion like a cup with a vital brewage. Or else he would flash through our conventual darkness a reflex of a brighter world, show us a glimpse of the current literature of the day, read us passages from some enchanting tale, or the last witty feuilleton which had awakened laughter in the saloons of Paris; taking care always to expunge, with the severest hand, whether from tragedy, melo-drama, tale, or essay, whatever passage, phrase, or word, could be deemed unsuited to an audience of 'jeunes filles.' I noticed more than once, that where retrenchment without substitute would have left unmeaning vacancy, or introduced weakness, he could, and did, improvise whole paragraphs, no less vigorous than irreproachable: the dialogue – the description – he engrafted was often far better than that he pruned away.

Well, on the evening in question, we were sitting silent as nuns in a 'retreat,' the pupils studying, the teachers working. I remember my work; it was a slight matter of fancy, and it rather interested me;

it had a purpose; I was not doing it merely to kill time; I meant it when finished as a gift; and the occasion of presentation being near, haste was requisite, and my fingers were busy.

We heard the sharp bell-peal which we all knew; then the rapid step familiar to each ear: the words 'Voilà Monsieur!' had scarcely broken simultaneously from every lip, when the two-leaved door split (as split it always did for his admission – such a slow word as 'open' is inefficient to describe his movements), and he stood in the midst of us.

There were two study-tables, both long and flanked with benches; over the centre of each hung a lamp; beneath this lamp, on either side the table, sat a teacher; the girls were arranged to the right hand and the left; the eldest and most studious nearest the lamps or tropics; the idlers and little ones towards the north and south poles. Monsieur's habit was politely to hand a chair to some teacher, generally Zélie St. Pierre, the senior mistress; then to take her vacated seat; and thus avail himself of the full beam of Cancer or Capricorn, which, owing to his near sight, he needed.

As usual, Zélie rose with alacrity, smiling to the whole extent of her mouth, and the full display of her upper and under rows of teeth – that strange smile which passes from ear to ear, and is marked only by a sharp thin curve, which fails to spread over the countenance, and neither dimples the cheek nor lights the eye. I suppose Monsieur did not see her, or he had taken a whim that he would not notice her, for he was as capricious as women are said to be; then his 'lunettes' (he had got another pair) served him as an excuse for all sorts of little oversights and short-comings. Whatever might be his reason, he passed by Zélie, came to the other side of the table, and before I could start up to clear the way, whispered, 'Ne bougez pas,' and established himself between me and Miss Fanshawe, who always would be my neighbour, and have her elbow in my side, however often I declared to her, –

'Ginevra, I wish you were at Jericho.'

It was easy to say, 'Ne bougez pas;' but how could I help it? I must make him room, and I must request the pupils to recede that *I* might recede. It was very well for Ginevra to be gummed to me, 'keeping herself warm,' as she said, on the winter evenings, and harassing my very heart with her fidgetings and pokings, obliging me, indeed, sometimes to put an artful pin in my girdle by way of protection against her elbow; but I suppose M. Emanuel was not to be subjected to the same kind of treatment, so I swept away my working materials, to clear space for his book, and withdrew myself, to make room for his person; not, however, leaving more than a yard of interval, just what any reasonable man would have regarded as a convenient, respectful allowance of bench. But M. Emanuel never *was* reasonable; flint and tinder that he was! he struck and took fire directly.

'Vous ne voulez pas de moi pour voisin,' he growled: 'vous vous donnez des airs de caste; vous me traitez en paria;' he scowled. 'Soit! je vais arranger la chose!' And he set to work.

'Levez vous toutes, mesdemoiselles!'[165] cried he.

The girls rose. He made them all file off to the other table. He then placed me at one extremity of the long bench, and having duly and carefully brought me my work-basket, silk, scissors, all my implements, he fixed himself quite at the other end.

At this arrangement, highly absurd as it was, not a soul in the room dared to laugh; luckless for the giggler would have been the giggle. As for me, I took it with entire coolness. There I sat, isolated and cut off from human intercourse; I sat and minded my work, and was quiet, and not at all unhappy.

'Est-ce assez de distance?' he demanded.

'Monsieur en est l'arbitre,' said I.

'Vous savez bien que non. C'est vous qui avez créé ce vide immense: moi je n'y ai pas mis la main.'[166]

And with this assertion he commenced the reading.

For his misfortune he had chosen a French translation of what he called 'un drame de Williams Shackspire; le faux dieu,' he further announced, 'de ces sots païens, les Anglais.'[167] How far otherwise he would have characterized him had his temper not been upset, I scarcely need intimate.

Of course, the translation being French, was very inefficient; nor did I make any particular effort to conceal the contempt which some of its forlorn lapses were calculated to excite. Not that it behoved or beseemed me to *say* anything; but one can occasionally *look* the opinion it is forbidden to embody in words. Monsieur's lunettes being on the alert, he gleamed up every stray look; I don't think he lost one: the consequence was, his eyes soon discarded a screen, that their blaze might sparkle free, and he waxed hotter at the north pole to which he had voluntarily exiled himself, than, considering the general temperature of the room, it would have been reasonable to become under the vertical ray of Cancer itself.

The reading over, it appeared problematic whether he would depart with his anger unexpressed, or whether he would give it vent. Suppression was not much in his habits; but still, was what had been done to him definite enough to afford matter for overt reproof? I had not uttered a sound, and could not justly be deemed amenable to reprimand or penalty for having permitted a slightly freer action than usual to the muscles about my eyes and mouth.

The supper, consisting of bread, and milk diluted with tepid water, was brought in. In respectful consideration of the professor's presence, the rolls and glasses were allowed to stand instead of being immediately handed round.

'Take your supper, ladies,' said he, seeming to be occupied in making marginal notes to his 'Williams Shackspire.' They took it. I also accepted a roll and glass, but being now more than ever interested in my work, I kept my seat of punishment, and wrought while I munched my bread and sipped my beverage, the whole with easy *sang froid*; with a certain snugness of composure, indeed, scarcely in my habits, and pleasantly novel to my feelings. It seemed as if the presence of a nature so restless, chafing, thorny as that of M. Paul, absorbed all feverish and unsettling influences like a magnet, and left me none but such as were placid and harmonious.

He rose. 'Will he go away without saying another word?' Yes; he turned to the door.

No: he re-turned on his steps; but only, perhaps, to take his pencil-case, which had been left on the table.

He took it – shut the pencil in and out, broke its point against the wood, re-cut and pocketed it, and . . . walked promptly up to me.

The girls and teachers, gathered round the other table, were talking pretty freely: they always talked at meals; and, from the constant habit of speaking fast and loud at such times, did not now subdue their voices much.

M. Paul came and stood behind me. He asked at what I was working; and I said I was making a watchguard.

He asked, 'For whom?' And I answered, 'For a gentleman – one of my friends.'

M. Paul stooped down and proceeded – as novel-writers say, and as was literally true in his case – to 'hiss' into my ear some poignant words.

He said that, of all the women he knew, I was the one who could make herself the most consummately unpleasant: I was she with whom it was least possible to live on friendly terms. I had a 'caractère intraitable'[168] and perverse to a miracle. How I managed it, or what possessed me, he, for his part, did not know; but with whatever pacific and amicable intentions a person accosted me – crac! I turned concord to discord, good-will to enmity. He was sure, he – M. Paul – wished me well enough; he had never done me any harm that he knew of; he might, at least, he supposed, claim a right to be regarded as a neutral acquaintance, guiltless of hostile sentiments: yet, how I behaved to him! With what pungent vivacities – what an impetus of mutiny – what a 'fougue'[169] of injustice!

Here I could not avoid opening my eyes somewhat wide, and even slipping in a slight interjectional observation:

'Vivacities? Impetus? Fougue? I didn't know . . .'

'Chut! à l'instant! There! there I went – vive comme la poudre!'[170] He was sorry – he was very sorry: for my sake he grieved over the hapless peculiarity. This 'emportement,' this 'chaleur'[171] – generous, perhaps, but excessive – would yet, he feared, do me a mischief. It was a pity: I was not – he believed, in his soul – wholly without good qualities; and would I but hear reason, and be more sedate, more sober, less 'en l'air,' less 'coquette,' less taken by show, less prone to set an undue value on outside excellence – to make much of the attentions of people remarkable chiefly for so many feet of stature, 'des couleurs de poupée,' 'un nez plus ou moins bien fait,'[172] and an enormous amount of fatuity – I might yet prove an useful, perhaps an exemplary, character. But, as it was – And here, the little man's voice was for a minute choked.

I would have looked up at him, or held out my hand, or said a soothing word; but I was afraid, if I stirred, I should either laugh or cry; so odd, in all this, was the mixture of the touching and the absurd.

I thought he had nearly done: but no; he sat down that he might go on at his ease.

'While he, M. Paul, was on these painful topics, he would dare my anger for the sake of my good, and would venture to refer to a change he had noticed in my dress. He was free to confess that when he first knew me – or, rather, was in the habit of catching a passing glimpse of me from time to time – I satisfied him on this point: the gravity, the austere simplicity, obvious in this particular, were such as to inspire the highest hopes for my best interests. What fatal influence had impelled me lately to introduce flowers under the brim of my bonnet, to wear "des cols brodés,"[173] and even to appear on one occasion in a *scarlet gown* – he might indeed conjecture, but, for the present, would not openly declare.'

Again I interrupted, and this time not without an accent at once indignant and horror-struck.

'Scarlet, Monsieur Paul? It was not scarlet! It was pink, and pale pink, too; and further subdued by black lace.'

'Pink or scarlet, yellow or crimson, pea-green or sky-blue; it was all one: these were all flaunting, giddy colours; and as to the lace I talked of, *that* was but a "colifichet de plus."'[174] And he sighed over my degeneracy. 'He could not, he was sorry to say, be so particular on this theme as he could wish: not possessing the exact names of these "babioles,"[175] he might run into small verbal errors which would not fail to lay him open to my sarcasm, and excite my unhappily sudden and passionate disposition. He would merely say, in general terms – and in these general terms he knew he was correct – that my costume had of late assumed "des façons mondaines,"[176] which it wounded him to see.'

What 'façons mondaines' he discovered in my present winter merino and plain white collar, I own it puzzled me to guess: and when I asked him, he said it was all made with too much attention to effect – and besides, 'had I not a bow or ribbon at my neck?'

'And if you condemn a bow of ribbon for a lady, monsieur, you would necessarily disapprove of a thing like this for a gentleman?' – holding up my bright little chainlet of silk and gold. His sole reply was a groan – I suppose over my levity.

After sitting some minutes in silence, and watching the progress of the chain, at which I now wrought more assiduously than ever, he inquired:

'Whether what he had just said would have the effect of making me entirely detest him?'

I hardly remember what answer I made, or how it came about; I don't think I spoke at all, but I know we managed to bid good-night on friendly terms: and, even after M. Paul had reached the door, he turned back just to explain, 'that he would not be understood to speak in entire condemnation of the scarlet dress' ('Pink! pink!' I threw in) 'that he had no intention to deny it the merit of *looking* rather well' (the fact was, M. Emanuel's taste in colours decidedly leaned to the brilliant); 'only he wished to counsel me, whenever I wore it, to do so in the same spirit as if its material were "bure," and its hue "gris de poussière."'[177] 'And the flowers under my bonnet, monsieur?' I asked. 'They are very little ones – ?'

'Keep them little, then,' said he. 'Permit them not to become full-blown.'

'And the bow, monsieur – the bit of ribbon?'

'Va pour le ruban!'[178] was the propitious answer. And so we settled it.

'Well done, Lucy Snowe!' cried I to myself; 'you have come in for a pretty lecture – brought on yourself a "rude savon," and all through your wicked fondness for worldly vanities! Who would have thought it? You deemed yourself a melancholy sober-sides enough! Miss Fanshawe there regards you as a second Diogenes. M. de Bassompierre, the other day, politely turned the conversation when it ran on the wild gifts of the actress Vashti, because, as he kindly said, "Miss Snowe looked uncomfortable." Dr John Bretton knows you only as "quiet Lucy" – "a creature inoffensive as a shadow;" he has said, and you have heard him say it: "Lucy's disadvantages spring from over-gravity in tastes and manner – want of colour in character and costume." Such are your own and your friends' impressions; and behold! there starts up a little man, differing diametrically from all these, roundly charging you with being too airy and cheery – too volatile and versatile – too flowery and coloury. This harsh little man – this pitiless censor – gathers up all your poor scattered sins of vanity, your luckless chiffon of rose-colour, your small fringe of a wreath, your scrap of ribbon, your silly bit of lace, and calls you to account for the lot, and for each item. You are well habituated to be passed by as a shadow in Life's sunshine: it is a new thing to see one testily lifting his hand to screen his eyes, because you tease him with an obtrusive ray.'

CHAPTER 29

Monsieur's Fête

I WAS UP THE NEXT MORNING an hour before daybreak, and
finished my guard, kneeling on the dormitory floor beside the
centre stand, for the benefit of such expiring glimmer as the night-
lamp afforded in its last watch.

All my materials – my whole stock of beads and silk – were used
up before the chain assumed the length and richness I wished; I had
wrought it double, as I knew, by the rule of contraries, that to suit
the particular taste whose gratification was in view, an effective
appearance was quite indispensable. As a finish to the ornament, a
little gold clasp was needed; fortunately I possessed it in the
fastening of my sole necklace; I duly detached and re-attached it,
then coiled compactly the completed guard, and enclosed it in a
small box I had bought for its brilliancy, made of some tropic shell
of the colour called 'nacarat,'[179] and decked with a little coronal of
sparkling blue stones. Within the lid of the box, I carefully graved
with my scissors' point certain initials.

The reader will, perhaps, remember the description of Madame
Beck's fête; nor will he have forgotten that at each anniversary, a
handsome present was subscribed for and offered by the school.
The observance of this day was a distinction accorded to none but
Madame, and, in a modified form, to her kinsman and counsellor,
M. Emanuel. In the latter case it was an honour spontaneously
awarded, not plotted and contrived beforehand, and offered an
additional proof, amongst many others, of the estimation in which
– despite his partialities, prejudices, and irritabilities – the
professor of literature was held by his pupils. No article of value
was offered to him: he distinctly gave it to be understood, that he
would accept neither plate nor jewellery. Yet he liked a slight
tribute; the cost, the money-value, did not touch him: a diamond
ring, a gold snuff-box, presented with pomp, would have pleased
him less than a flower, or a drawing, offered simply and with
sincere feelings. Such was his nature. He was a man, not wise in

his generation, yet could he claim a filial sympathy with 'the
dayspring on high.'

M. Paul's fête fell on the first of March and a Thursday. It proved
a fine sunny day, and being likewise the morning on which it was
customary to attend mass; being also otherwise distinguished by the
half holiday which permitted the privilege of walking out, shopping,
or paying visits in the afternoon: these combined considerations
induced a general smartness and freshness of dress. Clean collars
were in vogue; the ordinary dingy woollen classe-dress was
exchanged for something lighter and clearer. Mademoiselle Zélie St.
Pierre, on this particular Thursday, even assumed a 'robe de soie,'
deemed in economical Labassecour an article of hazardous splendour
and luxury; nay, it was remarked that she sent for a 'coiffeur' to dress
her hair that morning; there were pupils acute enough to discover
that she had bedewed her handkerchief and her hands with a new and
fashionable perfume. Poor Zélie! It was much her wont to declare
about this time, that she was tired to death of a life of seclusion and
labour; that she longed to have the means and leisure for relaxation;
to have some one to work for her – a husband who would pay her
debts (she was wofully encumbered with debt), supply her wardrobe,
and leave her at liberty, as she said, to 'goûter un peu les plaisirs.' It
had long been rumoured, that her eye was upon M. Emanuel.
Monsieur Emanuel's eye was certainly often upon her. He would sit
and watch her perseveringly for minutes together. I have seen him
give her a quarter of an hour's gaze, while the class was silently
composing, and he sat throned on his estrade, unoccupied. Conscious
always of this basilisk attention, she would writhe under it, half-
flattered, half-puzzled, and Monsieur would follow her sensations,
sometimes looking appallingly acute; for in some cases, he had the
terrible unerring penetration of instinct, and pierced in its hiding-
place the last lurking thought of the heart, and discerned under florid
veilings the bare, barren places of the spirit: yes, and its perverted
tendencies, and its hidden false curves – all that men and women
would not have known – the twisted spine, the mal-formed limb that
was born with them, and far worse, the stain or disfigurement they
have perhaps brought on themselves. No calamity so accursed but M.
Emanuel could pity and forgive, if it were acknowledged candidly;
but where his questioning eyes met dishonest denial – where his
ruthless researches found deceitful concealment – oh, then, he could
be cruel, and I thought wicked! he could exultantly snatch the screen
from poor shrinking wretches, passionately hurry them to the
summit of the mount of exposure, and there show them all naked, all

false – poor living lies – the spawn of that horrid Truth which cannot be looked on unveiled. He thought he did justice; for my part I doubt whether man has a right to do such justice on man: more than once in these his visitations, I have felt compelled to give tears to his victims, and not spared ire and keen reproach on himself. He deserved it; but it was difficult to shake him in his firm conviction that the work was righteous and needed.

Breakfast being over and mass attended, the school-bell rung and the rooms filled: a very pretty spectacle was presented in classe. Pupils and teachers sat neatly-arrayed, orderly, and expectant, each bearing in her hand the bouquet of felicitation – the prettiest spring-flowers – all fresh, and filling the air with their fragrance: I only had no bouquet. I like to see flowers growing, but when they are gathered, they cease to please. I look on them as things rootless and perishable; their likeness to life makes me sad. I never offer flowers to those I love; I never wish to receive them from hands dear to me. Mademoiselle St. Pierre marked my empty hands – she could not believe I had been so remiss; with avidity her eye roved over and round me: surely I must have some solitary symbolic flower somewhere: some small knot of violets, something to win to myself praise for taste, commendation for ingenuity. The unimaginative 'Anglaise' proved better than the Parisienne's fears: she sat literally unprovided, as bare of bloom or leaf as the winter tree. This ascertained, Zélie smiled well pleased.

'How wisely you have acted to keep your money, Meess Lucie,' she said: 'silly I have gone and thrown away two francs on a bouquet of hot-house flowers!'

And she showed with pride her splendid nosegay.

But hush! a step: *the* step. It came prompt, as usual, but with a promptitude, we felt disposed to flatter ourselves, inspired by other feelings than mere excitability of nerve, and vehemence of intent. We thought our professor's 'foot-fall' (to speak romantically) had in it a friendly promise this morning; and so it had.

He entered in a mood which made him as good as a new sunbeam to the already well-lit first-classe. The morning light, playing amongst our plants and laughing on our walls, caught an added lustre from M. Paul's all-benignant salute. Like a true Frenchman (though I don't know why I should say so, for he was of strain neither French nor Labassecourien), he had dressed for the 'situation' and the occasion. Not by the vague folds, sinister and conspirator-like, of his soot-dark paletôt were the outlines of his person obscured; on the contrary, his figure (such as it was, I don't boast of it) was well set off by a civilized coat and a silken vest quite pretty to behold. The defiant and pagan bonnet-grec had vanished: bare-headed he came upon us, carrying a Christian hat in his gloved hand. The little man looked well, very well; there was a clearness of amity in his blue eye, and a glow of good feeling on his dark complexion, which passed perfectly in the place of beauty: one really did not care to observe that his nose, though far from small, was of no particular shape, his cheek thin, his brow marked and square, his mouth no rosebud: one accepted him as he was, and felt his presence the reverse of damping or insignificant.

He passed to his desk; he placed on the same his hat and gloves. 'Bon jour, mes amies,' said he, in a tone that somehow made amends to some amongst us for many a sharp snap and savage snarl: not a jocund, good-fellow tone, still less an unctuous priestly accent, but a voice he had belonging to himself – a voice used when his heart passed the word to his lips. That same heart *did* speak sometimes; though an irritable, it was not an ossified organ: in its core was a place, tender beyond a man's tenderness; a place that humbled him to little children, that bound him to girls and women: to whom, rebel as he would, he could not disown his affinity, nor quite deny that, on the whole, he was better with them than with his own sex.

'We all wish Monsieur a good-day, and present to him our congratulations on the anniversary of his fête,' said Mademoiselle Zélie, constituting herself spokeswoman of the assembly; and advancing, with no more twists of affectation than with her were indispensable to the achievement of motion, she laid her costly bouquet before him. He bowed over it.

The long train of offerings followed: all the pupils, sweeping past with the gliding step foreigners practise, left their tributes as they went by. Each girl so dexterously adjusted her separate gift that, when the last bouquet was laid on the desk, it formed the apex to a blooming pyramid – a pyramid blooming, spreading, and towering with such exuberance as, in the end, to eclipse the hero behind it. This ceremony over, seats were resumed, and we sat in dead silence, expectant of a speech.

I suppose five minutes might have elapsed, and the hush remained unbroken; ten – and there was no sound.

Many present began, doubtless, to wonder for what Monsieur waited: as well they might. Voiceless and viewless, stirless and wordless, he kept his station behind the pile of flowers.

At last there issued forth a voice, rather deep, as if it spoke out of a hollow:

'Est-ce là tout?'[180]

Mademoiselle Zélie looked round.

'You have all presented your bouquets?' inquired she of the pupils.

Yes; they had all given their nosegays from the eldest to the youngest, from the tallest to the most diminutive. The senior mistress signified as much.

'Est-ce là tout?' was reiterated in an intonation which, deep before, had now descended some notes lower.

'Monsieur,' said Mademoiselle St. Pierre, rising, and this time speaking with her own sweet smile, 'I have the honour to tell you that, with a single exception, every person in classe has offered her bouquet. For Meess Lucie, Monsieur will kindly make allowance; as a foreigner, she probably did not know our customs, or did not appreciate their significance. Meess Lucie has regarded this ceremony as too frivolous to be honoured by her observance.'

'Famous!' I muttered between my teeth; 'you are no bad speaker, Zélie, when you begin.'

The answer vouchsafed to Mademoiselle St. Pierre from the estrade, was given in the gesticulation of a hand from behind the pyramid. This manual action seemed to deprecate words, to enjoin silence.

A form, ere long, followed the hand. Monsieur emerged from his eclipse; and producing himself upon the front of his estrade, and gazing straight and fixedly before him at a vast 'mappe-monde' covering the wall opposite, he demanded a third time, and now in really tragic tones –

'Est-ce là tout?'

I might yet have made all right, by stepping forwards and slipping into his hand the ruddy little shell-box I, at that moment, held tight in my own. It was what I had fully purposed to do; but, first, the comic side of Monsieur's behaviour had tempted me to delay, and now, Mademoiselle St. Pierre's affected interference provoked contumacity. The reader not having hitherto had any cause to ascribe to Miss Snowe's character the most distant pretension to perfection, will be scarcely surprised to learn that she felt too perverse to defend herself from any imputation the Parisienne might choose to insinuate: and besides, M. Paul was so tragic, and took my defection so seriously, he deserved to be vexed. I kept, then, both my box and my countenance, and sat insensate as any stone.

'It is well!' dropped at length from the lips of M. Paul; and having uttered this phrase, the shadow of some great paroxysm – the swell of wrath, scorn, resolve – passed over his brow, rippled his lips, and lined his cheeks. Gulping down all further comment, he launched into his customary 'discours.'

I can't at all remember what this 'discours' was; I did not listen to it: the gulping-down process, the abrupt dismissal of his mortification or vexation, had given me a sensation which half-counteracted the ludicrous effect of the reiterated 'Est-ce là tout?'

Towards the close of the speech there came a pleasing diversion; my attention was again amusingly arrested.

Owing to some little accidental movement – I think I dropped my thimble on the floor, and in stooping to regain it, hit the crown of my head against the sharp corner of my desk; which casualties (exasperating to me, by rights, if to anybody) naturally made a slight bustle – M. Paul became irritated, and dismissing his forced equanimity, and casting to the winds that dignity and self-control with which he never cared long to encumber himself, he broke forth into the strain best calculated to give him ease.

I don't know how, in the progress of his 'discours,' he had contrived to cross the channel, and land on British ground but there I found him when I began to listen.

Casting a quick, cynical glance round the room – a glance which scathed, or was intended to scathe, as it crossed me – he fell with fury upon 'les Anglaises.'

Never have I heard English women handled as M. Paul that morning handled them: he spared nothing – neither their minds, morals, manners, nor personal appearance. I specially remember his abuse of their tall stature, their long necks, their thin arms, their slovenly dress, their pedantic education, their impious scepticism (!), their insufferable pride, their pretentious virtue: over which he ground his teeth malignantly, and looked as if, had he dared, he would have said singular things. Oh! he was spiteful, acrid, savage; and, as a natural consequence, detestably ugly.

'Little wicked venomous man!' thought I; 'am I going to harass myself with fears of displeasing *you*, or hurting *your* feelings? No, indeed; you shall be indifferent to me, as the shabbiest bouquet in your pyramid.'

I grieve to say I could not quite carry out this resolution. For some time the abuse of England and the English found and left me stolid: I bore it some fifteen minutes stoically enough; but this hissing cockatrice was determined to sting, and he said such things at last – fastening not only upon our women, but upon our greatest names and best men; sullying the shield of Britannia, and dabbling the union jack in mud – that I *was* stung. With vicious relish he brought up the most spicy current continental historical falsehoods – than which nothing can be conceived more offensive. Zélie, and the whole class, became one grin of vindictive delight; for it is curious to discover how these clowns of Labassecour secretly hate England. At last, I struck a sharp stroke on my desk, opened my lips, and let loose this cry: –

'Vive l'Angleterre, l'Histoire et les Héros! A bas la France, la Fiction et les Faquins!'[181]

The class was struck of a heap. I suppose they thought me mad. The professor put up his handkerchief, and fiendishly smiled into its folds. Little monster of malice! He now thought he had got the victory, since he had made me angry. In a second he became good-humoured. With great blandness he resumed the subject of his flowers; talked poetically and symbolically of their sweetness, perfume, purity, etcetera; made Frenchified comparisons between the 'jeunes filles' and the sweet blossoms before him; paid Mademoiselle St. Pierre a very full-blown compliment on the superiority of her bouquet; and ended by announcing that the first really fine, mild, and balmy morning in spring, he intended to take the whole class out to breakfast in the country. 'Such of the class, at least,' he added, with emphasis, 'as he could count amongst the number of his friends.'

'Donc je n'y serai pas,' declared I, involuntarily.

'Soit!'[182] was his response, and, gathering his flowers in his arms, he flashed out of classe; while I, consigning my work, scissors, thimble, and the neglected little box, to my desk, swept up-stairs. I don't know whether *he* felt hot and angry, but I am free to confess that *I* did.

Yet with a strange evanescent anger, I had not sat an hour on the edge of my bed, picturing and repicturing his look, manner, words, ere I smiled at the whole scene. A little pang of regret I underwent that the box had not been offered. I had meant to gratify him. Fate would not have it so.

In the course of the afternoon, remembering that desks in classe were by no means inviolate repositories, and thinking that it was as well to secure the box, on account of the initials in the lid, P. C. D. E., for Paul Carl (or Carlos) David Emanuel – such was his full name – these foreigners must always have a string of baptismals – I descended to the school-room.

It slept in holiday repose. The day-pupils were all gone home, the boarders were out walking, the teachers, except the surveillante of the week, were in town, visiting or shopping; the suite of divisions was vacant; so was the grande salle, with its huge solemn globe hanging in the midst, its pair of many-branched chandeliers, and its horizontal grand piano closed, silent, enjoying its mid-week Sabbath. I rather wondered to find the first classe door ajar; this room being usually locked when empty, and being then inaccessible to any save Madame Beck and myself, who possessed a duplicate key. I wondered still more, on approaching, to hear a vague movement as of life – a step, a chair stirred, a sound like the opening of a desk.

'It is only Madame Beck doing inspection duty,' was the conclusion following a moment's reflection. The partially-opened door gave opportunity for assurance on this point. I looked. Behold! not the inspecting garb of Madame Beck – the shawl and the clean cap – but the coat, and the close-shorn, dark head of a man. This person occupied my chair; his olive hand held my desk open, his nose was lost to view amongst my papers. His back was towards me, but there could not be a moment's question about identity. Already was the attire of ceremony discarded: the cherished and ink-stained paletôt was resumed; the perverse bonnet-grec lay on the floor, as if just dropped from the hand, culpably busy.

Now I knew, and had long known, that that hand of M. Emanuel's was on intimate terms with my desk; that it raised and lowered the lid, ransacked and arranged the contents, almost as familiarly as my own. The fact was not dubious, nor did he wish it to be so: he left signs of each visit palpable and unmistakeable; hitherto, however, I had never caught him in the act: watch as I would, I could not detect the hours and moments of his coming. I saw the brownie's work, in exercises left overnight full of faults, and found next morning carefully corrected: I profited by his capricious goodwill in loans full welcome and refreshing. Between a sallow dictionary and worn-out grammar would magically grow a fresh interesting new work, or a classic, mellow and sweet in its ripe age. Out of my work-basket would laughingly peep a romance, under it would lurk the pamphlet, the magazine, whence last evening's reading had been extracted. Impossible to doubt the source whence these treasures flowed: had there been no other indication, one condemning and traitor peculiarity common to them all, settled the question – *they smelt of cigars*. This was very shocking, of course: *I* thought so at first, and used to open the window with some bustle, to air my desk, and with fastidious finger and thumb, to hold the peccant brochures forth to the purifying breeze. I was cured of that formality suddenly. Monsieur caught me at it one day, understood the inference, instantly relieved my hand of its burden, and, in another moment, would have thrust the same into the glowing stove. It chanced to be a book on the perusal of which I was bent; so for once I proved as decided and quicker than himself, recaptured the spoil, and – having saved this volume – never hazarded a second. With all this, I had never yet been able to arrest in his visits the freakish, friendly, cigar-loving phantom.

But now at last I had him: there he was – the very brownie himself; and there, curling from his lips, was the pale blue breath of his Indian darling: he was smoking into my desk: it might well betray him. Provoked at this particular, and yet pleased to surprise him – pleased, that is, with the mixed feeling of the housewife who discovers at last her strange elfin ally busy in the dairy at the untimely churn – I softly stole forward, stood behind him, bent with precaution over his shoulder.

My heart smote me to see that – after this morning's hostility, after my seeming remissness, after the puncture experienced by his feelings, and the ruffling undergone by his temper – he, all willing to forget and forgive, had brought me a couple of handsome volumes, of which the title and authorship were guarantees for interest. Now, as he sat bending above the desk, he was stirring up its contents; but with gentle and careful hand: disarranging indeed, but not harming. My heart smote me: as I bent over him, as he sat unconscious, doing me what good he could, and I daresay not feeling towards me unkindly, my morning's anger quite melted: I did not dislike Professor Emanuel.

I think he heard me breathe. He turned suddenly: his temperament was nervous, yet he never started, and seldom changed colour; there was something hardy about him.

'I thought you were gone into town with the other teachers,' said he, taking a grim gripe of his self-possession, which half escaped him – 'It is as well you are not. Do you think I care for being caught? Not I. I often visit your desk.'

'Monsieur, I know it.'

'You find a brochure or a tome now and then; but you don't read them, because they have passed under this?' – touching his cigar.

'They have, and are no better for the process, but I read them.'

'Without pleasure?'

'Monsieur must not be contradicted.'

'Do you like them, or any of them? – are they acceptable?'

'Monsieur has seen me reading them a hundred times, and knows I have not so many recreations as to undervalue those he provides.'

'I mean well; and, if you see that I mean well, and derive some little amusement from my efforts, why can we not be friends?'

'A fatalist would say – because we cannot.'

'This morning,' he continued, 'I awoke in a bright mood, and came into classe happy; you spoiled my day.'

'No, Monsieur, only an hour or two of it, and that unintentionally.'

'Unintentionally! No. It was my fête-day; everybody wished me happiness but you. The little children of the third division gave each her knot of violets, lisped each her congratulation: you – nothing. Not a bud, leaf, whisper – not a glance. Was this unintentional?'

'I meant no harm.'

'Then you really did not know our custom? You were unprepared? You would willingly have laid out a few centimes on a flower to give me pleasure, had you been aware that it was expected? Say so, and all is forgotten, and the pain soothed.'

'I *did* know that it was expected: I *was* prepared; yet I laid out no centimes on flowers.'

'It is well – you do right to be honest. I should almost have hated you, had you flattered and lied. Better declare at once – "Paul Carl Emanuel – je te déteste, mon garçon!" – than smile an interest, look an affection, and be false and cold at heart. False and cold, I don't think you are; but you have made a great mistake in life, that I believe: I think your judgment is warped – that you are indifferent where you ought to be grateful – and perhaps devoted and infatuated, where you ought to be cool as your name. Don't suppose that I wish you to have a passion for me, Mademoiselle; Dieu vous en garde! What do you start for? Because I said passion? Well, I say it again. There is such a word, and there is such a thing – though not within these walls, thank Heaven! You are no child that one should not speak of what exists; but I only uttered the word – the thing, I assure you, is alien to my whole life and views. It died in the past – in the present it lies buried – its grave is deep-dug, well-heaped, and many winters old: in the future there will be a resurrection, as I believe to my soul's consolation; but all will then be changed – form and feeling: the mortal will have put on immortality – it will rise, not for earth, but heaven. All I say to *you*, Miss Lucy Snowe, is – that you ought to treat Professor Paul Emanuel decently.'

I could not, and did not, contradict such a sentiment.

'Tell me,' he pursued, 'when it is *your* fête-day, and I will not grudge a few centimes for a small offering.'

'You will be like me, monsieur: this cost more than a few centimes, and I did not grudge its price.'

And taking from the open desk the little box, I put it into his hand.

'It lay ready in my lap this morning,' I continued; 'and if Monsieur had been rather more patient, and Mademoiselle St. Pierre less interfering – perhaps I should say, too, if *I* had been calmer and wiser – I should have given it then.'

He looked at the box: I saw its clear warm tint and bright azure circlet pleased his eye. I told him to open it.

'My initials!' said he, indicating the letters in the lid. 'Who told you I was called Carl David?'

'A little bird, monsieur.'

'Does it fly from me to you? Then one can tie a message under its wing when needful?'

He took out the chain – a trifle indeed as to value, but glossy with silk and sparkling with beads. He liked that too – admired it artlessly, like a child.

'For me?'

'Yes, for you.'

'This is the thing you were working at last night?'

'The same.'

'You finished it this morning?'

'I did.'

'You commenced it with the intention that it should be mine?'

'Undoubtedly.'

'And offered on my fête-day?'

'Yes.'

'This purpose continued as you wove it?'

Again I assented.

'Then it is not necessary that I should cut out any portion – saying, this part is not mine; it was plaited under the idea and for the adornment of another?'

'By no means. It is neither necessary, nor would it be just.'

'This object is *all* mine?'

'That object is yours entirely.'

Straightway Monsieur opened his paletôt, arranged the guard splendidly across his chest, displaying as much and suppressing as little as he could: for he had no notion of concealing what he admired and thought decorative. As to the box, he pronounced it a superb bonbonnière – he was fond of bon-bons, by the way – and as he always liked to share with others what pleased himself, he would give his 'dragées' as freely as he lent his books. Amongst the kind brownie's gifts left in my desk, I forgot to enumerate many a paper of chocolate comfits. His tastes in these matters were southern, and what we think infantine. His simple lunch consisted frequently of a 'brioche,' which as often as not, he shared with some child of the third division.

'A présent c'est un fait accompli,' said he, re-adjusting his paletôt; and we had no more words on the subject. After looking over the two volumes he had brought, and cutting away some pages with his penknife (he generally pruned before lending his books, especially if they were novels, and sometimes I was a little provoked at the severity of his censorship, the retrenchments interrupting the narrative), he rose, politely touched his bonnet-grec, and bade me a civil good day.

'We are friends now,' thought I, 'till the next time we quarrel.'

We *might* have quarrelled again that very same evening, but, wonderful to relate! failed, for once, to make the most of our opportunity.

Contrary to all expectation, M. Paul arrived at the study-hour. Having seen so much of him in the morning, we did not look for his presence at night. No sooner were we seated at lessons, however, than he appeared. I own I was glad to see him, so glad that I could not help greeting his arrival with a smile; and when he made his way to the same seat about which so serious a misunderstanding had formerly arisen, I took good care not to make too much room for him; he watched with a jealous, side-long look, to see whether I shrank away, but I did not, though the bench was a little crowded. I was losing the early impulse to recoil from M. Paul. Habituated to the paletôt and bonnet-grec, the neighbourhood of these garments seemed no longer uncomfortable or very formidable. I did not now sit restrained, 'asphyxiée' (as he used to say) at his side; I stirred when I wished to stir, coughed when it was necessary, even yawned when I was tired – did, in short, what I pleased, blindly reliant upon his indulgence. Nor did my temerity, this evening at least, meet the punishment it perhaps merited; he was both indulgent and good-natured; not a cross glance shot from his eyes, not a hasty word left his lips. Till the very close of the evening, he did not indeed address me at all, yet I felt, somehow, that he was full of friendliness. Silence is of different kinds, and breathes different meanings; no words could inspire a pleasanter content than did M. Paul's wordless presence. When the tray came in, and the bustle of supper commenced, he just said, as he retired, that he wished me a good night and sweet dreams; and a good night and sweet dreams I had.

CHAPTER 30

M. Paul

YET THE READER is advised not to be in any hurry with his kindly conclusions, or to suppose, with an over-hasty charity, that from that day M. Paul became a changed character – easy to live with, and no longer apt to flash danger and discomfort round him.

No; he was naturally a little man of unreasonable moods. When over-wrought, which he often was, he became acutely irritable; and, besides, his veins were dark with a livid belladonna tincture, the essence of jealousy. I do not mean merely the tender jealousy of the heart, but that sterner, narrower sentiment whose seat is in the head.

I used to think, as I sat looking at M. Paul, while he was knitting his brow or protruding his lip over some exercise of mine, which had not as many faults as he wished (for he liked me to commit faults: a knot of blunders was sweet to him as a cluster of nuts), that he had points of resemblance to Napoleon Bonaparte. I think so still.

In a shameless disregard of magnanimity, he resembled the great Emperor. M. Paul would have quarrelled with twenty learned women, would have unblushingly carried on a system of petty bickering and recrimination with a whole capital of coteries, never troubling himself about loss or lack of dignity. He would have exiled fifty Madame de Staels, if they had annoyed, offended, outrivalled, or opposed him.

I well remember a hot episode of his with a certain Madame Panache – a lady temporarily employed by Madame Beck to give lessons in history. She was clever – that is, she knew a good deal; and, besides, thoroughly possessed the art of making the most of what she knew; of words and confidence she held unlimited command. Her personal appearance was far from destitute of advantages; I believe many people would have pronounced her 'a fine woman;' and yet there were points in her robust and ample attractions, as well as in her bustling and demonstrative presence, which, it appeared, the nice and capricious tastes of M. Paul could not away with. The sound of her voice, echoing through the carré, would put him into a strange taking; her long, free step – almost stride – along the corridor, would often make him snatch up his papers and decamp on the instant.

With malicious intent he bethought himself, one day, to intrude on her class; as quick as lightning he gathered her method of instruction; it differed from a pet plan of his own. With little ceremony, and less courtesy, he pointed out what he termed her errors. Whether he expected submission and attention, I know not; he met an acrid opposition, accompanied by a round reprimand for his certainly unjustifiable interference.

Instead of withdrawing with dignity, as he might still have done, he threw down the gauntlet of defiance. Madame Panache, bellicose as a Penthesilea,[183] picked it up in a minute. She snapped her fingers in the intermeddler's face; she rushed upon him with a storm of words. M. Emanuel was eloquent; but Madame Panache was voluble. A system of fierce antagonism ensued. Instead of laughing in his sleeve at his fair foe, with all her sore amour propre and loud self-assertion, M. Paul detested her with intense seriousness; he honoured her with his earnest fury; he pursued her vindictively and implacably, refusing to rest peaceably in his bed, to derive due benefit from his meals, or even serenely to relish his cigar, till she was fairly rooted out of the establishment. The professor conquered, but I cannot say that the laurels of this victory shadowed gracefully his temples. Once I ventured to hint as much. To my great surprise he allowed that I might be right, but averred that when brought into contact with either men or women of the coarse, self-complacent quality, whereof Madame Panache was a specimen, he had no control over his own passions; an unspeakable and active aversion impelled him to a war of extermination.

Three months afterwards, hearing that his vanquished foe had met with reverses, and was likely to be really distressed for want of employment, he forgot his hatred, and, alike active in good and evil, he moved heaven and earth till he found her a place. Upon her coming to make up former differences, and thank him for his recent kindness, the old voice – a little loud – the old manner – a little forward – so acted upon him that in ten minutes he started up and bowed her, or rather himself, out of the room, in a transport of nervous irritation.

To pursue a somewhat audacious parallel, in a love of power, in an eager grasp after supremacy, M. Emanuel was like Bonaparte. He was a man not always to be submitted to. Sometimes it was needful to resist; it was right to stand still, to look up into his eyes and tell him that his requirements went beyond reason – that his absolutism verged on tyranny.

The dawnings, the first developments of peculiar talent appearing within his range, and under his rule, curiously excited, even disturbed him. He watched its struggle into life with a scowl; he held back his hand – perhaps said, 'Come on if you have strength,' but would not aid the birth.

When the pang and peril of the first conflict were over, when the breath of life was drawn, when he saw the lungs expand and contract, when he felt the heart beat and discovered life in the eye, he did not yet offer to foster.

'Prove yourself true ere I cherish you,' was his ordinance; and how difficult he made that proof! What thorns and briars, what flints, he strewed in the path of feet not inured to rough travel! He watched tearlessly – ordeals that he exacted should be passed through – fearlessly. He followed footprints that, as they approached the bourne, were sometimes marked in blood – followed them grimly, holding the austerest police-watch over the pain-pressed pilgrim. And when at last he allowed a rest, before slumber might close the eyelids, he opened those same lids wide, with pitiless finger and thumb, and gazed deep through the pupil and the irids into the brain, into the heart, to search if Vanity, or Pride, or Falsehood, in any of its subtlest forms, was discoverable in the furthest recess of existence. If, at last, he let the neophyte sleep, it was but a moment; he woke him suddenly up to apply new tests; he sent him on irksome errands when he was staggering with weariness; he tried the temper, the sense, and the health; and it was only when every severest test had been applied and endured, when the most corrosive aquafortis had been used, and failed to tarnish the ore, that he admitted it genuine and, still in clouded silence, stamped it with his deep brand of approval.

I speak not ignorant of these evils.

Till the date at which the last chapter closes, M. Paul had not been my professor – he had not given me lessons, but about that time, accidentally hearing me one day acknowledge an ignorance of some branch of education (I think it was arithmetic) which would have disgraced a charity-schoolboy, as he very truly remarked, he took me in hand, examined me first, found me, I need not say, abundantly deficient, gave me some books and appointed me some tasks.

He did this at first with pleasure, indeed with unconcealed

exultation, condescending to say that he believed I was 'bonne et pas trop faible' (i.e. well enough disposed, and not wholly destitute of parts) but, owing he supposed to adverse circumstances, 'as yet in a state of wretchedly imperfect mental development.'

The beginning of all efforts has indeed with me been marked by a preternatural imbecility. I never could, even in forming a common acquaintance, assert or prove a claim to average quickness. A depressing and difficult passage has prefaced every new page I have turned in life.

So long as this passage lasted, M. Paul was very kind, very good, very forbearing; he saw the sharp pain inflicted, and felt the weighty humiliation imposed by my own sense of incapacity; and words can hardly do justice to his tenderness and helpfulness. His own eyes would moisten, when tears of shame and effort clouded mine; burdened as he was with work, he would steal half his brief space of recreation to give to me.

But, strange grief! when that heavy and overcast dawn began at last to yield to day; when my faculties began to struggle themselves free, and my time of energy and fulfilment came; when I voluntarily doubled, trebled, quadrupled the tasks he set, to please him as I thought, his kindness became sternness; the light changed in his eyes from a beam to a spark; he fretted, he opposed, he curbed me imperiously; the more I did, the harder I worked, the less he seemed content. Sarcasms of which the severity amazed and puzzled me, harassed my ears; there flowed out the bitterest innuendoes against the 'pride of intellect.' I was vaguely threatened with, I know not what doom, if I ever trespassed the limits proper to my sex, and conceived a contraband appetite for unfeminine knowledge. Alas! I had no such appetite. What I loved, it joyed me by any effort to content; but the noble hunger for science in the abstract – the godlike thirst after discovery – these feelings were known to me but by briefest flashes.

Yet, when M. Paul sneered at me, I wanted to possess them more fully; his injustice stirred in me ambitious wishes – it imparted a strong stimulus – it gave wings to aspiration.

In the beginning, before I had penetrated to motives, that uncomprehended sneer of his made my heart ache, but by-and-by it only warmed the blood in my veins, and sent added action to my pulses. Whatever my powers – feminine or the contrary – God had given them, and I felt resolute to be ashamed of no faculty of His bestowal.

The combat was very sharp for a time. I seemed to have lost M.

Paul's affection; he treated me strangely. In his most unjust moments he would insinuate that I had deceived him when I appeared, what he called 'faible' – that is, incompetent; he said I had feigned a false incapacity. Again, he would turn suddenly round and accuse me of the most far-fetched imitations and impossible plagiarisms, asserting that I had extracted the pith out of books I had not so much as heard of – and over the perusal of which I should infallibly have fallen down in a sleep as deep as that of Eutychus.[184]

Once, upon his preferring such an accusation, I turned upon him – I rose against him. Gathering an armful of his books out of my desk, I filled my apron and poured them in a heap upon his estrade, at his feet.

'Take them away, M. Paul,' I said, 'and teach me no more. I never asked to be made learned, and you compel me to feel very profoundly that learning is not happiness.'

And returning to my desk, I laid my head on my arms, nor would I speak to him for two days afterwards. He pained and chagrined me. His affection had been very sweet and dear – a pleasure new and incomparable: now that this seemed withdrawn, I cared not for his lessons.

The books, however, were not taken away; they were all restored with careful hand to their places, and he came as usual to teach me. He made his peace somehow – too readily, perhaps; I ought to have stood out longer, but when he looked kind and good, and held out his hand with amity, memory refused to reproduce with due force his oppressive moments. And then, reconcilement is always sweet!

On a certain morning a message came from my godmother, inviting me to attend some notable lecture to be delivered in the same public rooms before described. Dr John had brought the message himself, and delivered it verbally to Rosine, who had not scrupled to follow the steps of M. Emanuel, then passing to the first classe, and, in his presence, stand 'carrément' before my desk, hand in apron-pocket, and rehearse the same, saucily and aloud, concluding with the words –

'Qu'il est vraiment beau, mademoiselle, ce jeune docteur! Quels yeux – quel regard! Tenez! J'en ai le coeur tout ému!'[185]

When she was gone, my professor demanded of me why I suffered 'cette fille effrontée, cette creature sans pudeur,'[186] to address me in such terms.

I had no pacifying answer to give. The terms were precisely such as Rosine – a young lady in whose skull the organs of reverence and reserve were not largely developed – was in the constant habit of using. Besides, what she said about the young doctor was true enough. Graham *was* handsome; he *had* fine eyes and a thrilling glance. An observation to that effect actually formed itself into sound on my lips.

'Elle ne dit que la vérité,' I said.

'Ah! vous trouvez?'

'Mais, sans doute.'[187]

The lesson to which we had that day to submit was such as to make us very glad when it terminated. At its close, the released pupils rushed out, half-trembling, half-exultant. I, too, was going. A mandate to remain arrested me. I muttered that I wanted some fresh air sadly – the stove was in a glow, the classe over-heated. An inexorable voice merely recommended silence; and this salamander – for whom no room ever seemed too hot – sitting down between my desk and the stove – a situation in which he ought to have felt broiled, but did not – proceeded to confront me with – a Greek quotation!

In M. Emanuel's soul rankled a chronic suspicion that I knew both Greek and Latin. As monkeys are said to have the power of speech if they would but use it, and are reported to conceal this faculty in fear of its being turned to their detriment, so to me was ascribed a fund of knowledge which I was supposed criminally and craftily to conceal. The privileges of a 'classical education,' it was insinuated, had been mine; on flowers of Hymettus I had revelled; a golden store, hived in memory, now silently sustained my efforts, and privily nurtured my wits.

A hundred expedients did M. Paul employ to surprise my secret – to wheedle, to threaten, to startle it out of me. Sometimes he placed Greek and Latin books in my way, and then watched me, as Joan of Arc's jailors tempted her with the warrior's accoutrements, and lay in wait for the issue. Again he quoted I know not what authors and passages, and while rolling out their sweet and sounding lines (the classic tones fell very musically from his lips – for he had a good voice – remarkable for compass, modulation, and matchless expression), he would fix on me a vigilant, piercing, and often malicious eye. It was evident he sometimes expected great demonstrations; they never occurred, however; not comprehending, of course I could neither be charmed nor annoyed.

Baffled – almost angry – he still clung to his fixed idea; my susceptibilities were pronounced marble – my face a mask. It appeared as if he could not be brought to accept the homely truth, and take me for what I was: men, and women too, must have delusion of some sort; if not made ready to their hand, they will invent exaggeration for themselves.

At moments I *did* wish that his suspicions had been better founded. There were times when I would have given my right hand to possess the treasures he ascribed to me. He deserved condign punishment for his testy crotchets. I could have gloried in bringing home to him his worst apprehensions astoundingly realized. I could have exulted to burst on his vision, confront and confound his 'lunettes,' one blaze of acquirements. Oh! why did nobody undertake to make me clever while I was young enough to learn, that I might, by one grand, sudden, inhuman revelation – one cold, cruel, overwhelming triumph – have for ever crushed the mocking spirit out of Paul Carl David Emanuel!

Alas! no such feat was in my power. To-day, as usual, his quotations fell ineffectual: he soon shifted his ground.

'Women of intellect' was his next theme: here he was at home. A 'woman of intellect,' it appeared, was a sort of 'lusus naturae,' a luckless accident, a thing for which there was neither place nor use in creation, wanted neither as wife nor worker. Beauty anticipated her in the first office. He believed in his soul that lovely, placid, and passive feminine mediocrity was the only pillow on which manly thought and sense could find rest for its aching temples; and as to work, male mind alone could work to any good practical result – hein?

This 'hein?' was a note of interrogation intended to draw from me contradiction or objection. However, I only said –

'Cela ne me regarde pas: je ne m'en soucie pas;'[188] and presently added – 'May I go, monsieur? They have rung the bell for the second déjeuner.' (*i.e.*, luncheon).

'What of that? You are not hungry?'

'Indeed I was,' I said; 'I had had nothing since breakfast, at seven, and should have nothing till dinner, at five, if I missed this bell.'

'Well, he was in the same plight, but I might share with him.'

And he broke in two the 'brioche,' intended for his own refreshment, and gave me half. Truly his bark was worse than his bite; but the really formidable attack was yet to come. While eating his cake, I could not forbear expressing my secret wish that I really knew all of which he accused me.

'Did I sincerely feel myself to be an ignoramus?' he asked, in a softened tone.

If I had replied meekly by an unqualified affirmative, I believe he would have stretched out his hand, and we should have been friends on the spot, but I answered:

'Not exactly. I am ignorant, monsieur, in the knowledge you ascribe to me, but I *sometimes*, not *always*, feel a knowledge of my own.'

'What did I mean?' he inquired, sharply.

Unable to answer this question in a breath, I evaded it by change of subject. He had now finished his half of the brioche: feeling sure that on so trifling a fragment he could not have satisfied his appetite, as indeed I had not appeased mine, and inhaling the fragrance of baked apples afar from the refectory, I ventured to inquire whether he did not also perceive that agreeable odour. He confessed that he did. I said if he would let me out by the garden-door, and permit me just to run across the court, I would fetch him a plateful; and added that I believed they were excellent, as Goton had a very good method of baking, or rather stewing fruit, putting in a little spice, sugar, and a glass or two of vin blanc – might I go?

'Petite gourmande!' said he, smiling. 'I have not forgotten how pleased you were with the pâté à la crême I once gave you, and you know very well, at this moment, that to fetch the apples for me will be the same as getting them for yourself. Go, then, but come back quickly.'

And at last he liberated me on parole. My own plan was to go and return with speed and good faith, to put the plate in at the door, and then to vanish incontinent, leaving all consequences for future settlement.

That intolerably keen instinct of his seemed to have anticipated my scheme; he met me at the threshold, hurried me into the room, and fixed me in a minute in my former seat. Taking the plate of fruit from my hand, he divided the portion intended only for himself, and ordered me to eat my share. I complied with no good grace, and vexed, I suppose, by my reluctance, he opened a masked and dangerous battery. All he had yet said, I could count as mere sound and fury, signifying nothing; not so of the present attack.

It consisted in an unreasonable proposition with which he had before afflicted me: namely, that on the next public examination-day I should engage – foreigner as I was – to take my place on the first form of first-class pupils, and with them improvise a composition in French, on any subject any spectator might dictate, without benefit of grammar or lexicon.

I knew what the result of such an experiment would be. I, to whom nature had denied the impromptu faculty; who, in public, was by nature a cypher; whose time of mental activity, even when alone, was not under the meridian sun; who needed the fresh silence of morning, or the recluse peace of evening, to win from the Creative Impulse one evidence of his presence, one proof of his force; I, with whom that Impulse was the most intractable, the most capricious, the most maddening of masters (him before me always excepted) – a deity, which sometimes, under circumstances apparently propitious, would not speak when questioned, would not hear when appealed to, would not, when sought, be found; but would stand, all cold, all indurated, all granite, a dark Baal with carven lips and blank eye-balls, and breast like the stone face of a tomb; and again, suddenly, at some turn, some sound, some long-trembling sob of the wind, at some rushing past of an unseen stream of electricity, the irrational demon would wake unsolicited, would stir strangely alive, would rush from its pedestal like a perturbed Dagon,[189] calling to its votary for a sacrifice, whatever the hour – to its victim for some blood or some breath, whatever the circumstance or scene – rousing its priest, treacherously promising vaticination, perhaps filling its temple with a strange hum of oracles, but sure to give half the significance to fateful winds, and grudging to the desperate listener even a miserable remnant – yielding it sordidly, as though each word had been a drop of the deathless ichor of its own dark veins. And this tyrant I was to compel into bondage, and make it improvise a theme, on a school estrade, between a Mathilde and a Coralie, under the eye of a Madame Beck, for the pleasure and to the inspiration of a bourgeois of Labassecour!

Upon this argument M. Paul and I did battle more than once – strong battle, with confused noise of demand and rejection, exaction and repulse.

On this particular day I was soundly rated. 'The obstinacy of my whole sex,' it seems, was concentrated in me; I had an 'orgueil de diable.' I feared to fail, forsooth! What did it matter whether I failed or not? Who was I that I should not fail like my betters? It would do me good to fail. He wanted to see me worsted (I knew he did), and one minute he paused to take breath.

'Would I speak now and be tractable?'

'Never would I be tractable in this matter. Law itself should not compel me. I would pay a fine, or undergo an imprisonment, rather than write for a show and to order, perched up on a platform.'

'Could softer motives influence me? Would I yield for friendship's sake?'

'Not a whit, not a hair-breadth. No form of friendship under the sun had a right to exact such a concession. No true friendship would harass me thus.'

He supposed then (with a sneer – M. Paul could sneer supremely, curling his lip, opening his nostrils, contracting his eyelids) – he supposed there was but one form of appeal to which I would listen, and of that form it was not for him to make use.

'Under certain persuasions, from certain quarters, je vous vois d'ici,' said he, 'eagerly subscribing to the sacrifice, passionately arming for the effort.'

'Making a simpleton, a warning, and an example of myself, before a hundred and fifty of the "papas" and "mamans" of Villette.'

And here, losing patience, I broke out afresh with a cry that I wanted to be liberated, to get out to the air – I was almost in a fever.

'Chut!' said the inexorable, 'this was a mere pretext to run away: *he* was not hot, with the stove close at his back; how could I suffer, thoroughly screened by his person?'

'I did not understand his constitution. I knew nothing of the natural history of salamanders. For my own part, I was a phlegmatic islander, and sitting in an oven did not agree with me; at least, might I step to the well, and get a glass of water – the sweet apples had made me thirsty?'

'If that was all, he would do my errand.'

He went to fetch the water. Of course, with a door only on the latch behind me, I lost not my opportunity. Ere his return, his half-worried prey had escaped.

CHAPTER 31

The Dryad[190]

THE SPRING WAS ADVANCING, and the weather had turned suddenly warm. This change of temperature brought with it for me, as probably for many others, temporary decrease of strength. Slight exertion at this time left me overcome with fatigue – sleepless nights entailed languid days.

One Sunday afternoon, having walked the distance of half a league to the Protestant church, I came back weary and exhausted; and taking refuge in my solitary sanctuary, the first classe, I was glad to sit down, and to make of my desk a pillow for my arms and head.

Awhile I listened to the lullaby of bees humming in the berceau, and watched, through the glass door, and the tender, lightly-strewn spring foliage, Madame Beck and a gay party of friends, whom she had entertained that day at dinner after morning-mass, walking in the centre-alley under orchard boughs dressed at this season in blossom, and wearing a colouring as pure and warm as mountain-snow at sun-rise.

My principal attraction towards this group of guests lay, I remember, in one figure – that of a handsome young girl whom I had seen before as a visitor at Madame Beck's, and of whom I had been vaguely told that she was a 'filleule,' or god-daughter, of M. Emanuel's, and that between her mother, or aunt, or some other female relation of hers, and the professor – had existed of old a special friendship. M. Paul was not of the holiday band to-day, but I had seen this young girl with him ere now, and as far as distant observation could enable me to judge, she seemed to enjoy with him the frank ease of a ward with an indulgent guardian. I had seen her run up to him, put her arm through his and hang upon him. Once, when she did so, a curious sensation had struck through me – a disagreeable anticipatory sensation – one of the family of presentiments, I suppose – but I refused to analyze or dwell upon it. While watching this girl, Mademoiselle Sauveur by name, and following the gleam of her bright silk robe (she was always richly dressed, for she was said to be wealthy) through the flowers and the glancing leaves of tender emerald, my eyes became dazzled – they closed; my lassitude, the warmth of the day, the hum of bees and birds, all lulled me, and at last I slept.

Two hours stole over me. Ere I woke, the sun had declined out of sight behind the towering houses, the garden and the room were gray, bees had gone homeward, and the flowers were closing; the party of guests, too, had vanished; each alley was void.

On waking, I felt much at ease – not chill, as I ought to have been after sitting so still for at least two hours; my cheek and arms were not benumbed by pressure against the hard desk. No wonder. Instead of the bare wood on which I had laid them, I found a thick shawl, carefully folded, substituted for support, and another shawl (both taken from the corridor where such things hung) wrapped warmly round me.

Who had done this? Who was my friend? Which of the teachers? Which of the pupils? None, except St. Pierre, was inimical to me; but which of them had the art, the thought, the habit, of benefiting thus tenderly? Which of them had a step so quiet, a hand so gentle, but I should have heard or felt her, if she had approached or touched me in a day-sleep?

As to Ginevra Fanshawe, that bright young creature was not gentle at all, and would certainly have pulled me out of my chair, if she had meddled in the matter. I said at last: 'It is Madame Beck's doing; she has come in, seen me asleep, and thought I might take cold. She considers me a useful machine, answering well the purpose for which it was hired; so would not have me needlessly injured. And now,' methought, 'I'll take a walk; the evening is fresh, and not very chill.'

So I opened the glass door and stepped into the berceau.

I went to my own alley: had it been dark, or even dusk, I should hardly have ventured there, for I had not yet forgotten the curious illusion of vision (if illusion it were) experienced in that place some months ago. But a ray of the setting sun burnished still the gray crown of Jean Baptiste; nor had all the birds of the garden yet vanished into their nests amongst the tufted shrubs and thick wall-ivy. I paced up and down, thinking almost the same thoughts I had pondered that night when I buried my glass jar – how I should make some advance in life, take another step towards an independent position; for this train of reflection, though not lately pursued, had never by me been wholly abandoned; and whenever a certain eye was averted from me, and a certain countenance grew dark with unkindness and injustice, into that track of speculation did I at once strike; so that, little by little, I had laid half a plan.

'Living costs little,' said I to myself, 'in this economical town of Villette, where people are more sensible than I understand they are in dear old England – infinitely less worried about appearance, and less emulous of display – where nobody is in the least ashamed to be quite as homely and saving as he finds convenient. House-rent, in a prudently chosen situation, need not be high. When I shall have saved one thousand francs, I will take a tenement with one large room, and two or three smaller ones, furnish the first with a few benches and desks, a black tableau, an estrade for myself; upon it a chair and table, with a sponge and some white chalks; begin with taking day-pupils, and so work my way upwards. Madame Beck's commencement was – as I have often heard her say – from no higher starting-point, and where is she now? All these premises and this garden are hers, bought with her money; she has a competency already secured for old age, and a flourishing establishment under her direction, which will furnish a career for her children.

Courage, Lucy Snowe! With self-denial and economy now, and steady exertion by-and-by, an object in life need not fail you. Venture not to complain that such an object is too selfish, too limited, and lacks interest; be content to labour for independence until you have proved, by winning that prize, your right to look higher. But afterwards, is there nothing more for me in life – no true home – nothing to be dearer to me than myself, and by its paramount preciousness, to draw from me better things than I care to culture for myself only? Nothing, at whose feet I can willingly lay down the whole burden of human egotism, and gloriously take up the nobler charge of labouring and living for others?' I suppose, Lucy Snowe, the orb of your life is not to be so rounded; for you the crescent-phase must suffice. Very good. I see a huge mass of my fellow-creatures in no better circumstances. I see that a great many men, and more women, hold their span of life on conditions of denial and privation. I find no reason why I should be of the few favoured. I believe in some blending of hope and sunshine sweetening the worst lots. I believe that this life is not all; neither the beginning nor the end. I believe while I tremble; I trust while I weep.

So this subject is done with. It is right to look our life-accounts bravely in the face now and then, and settle them honestly. And he is a poor self-swindler who lies to himself while he reckons the items, and sets down under the head happiness that which is misery. Call anguish – anguish, and despair – despair; write both down in strong characters with a resolute pen: you will the better pay your debt to Doom. Falsify; insert 'privilege' where you should have written 'pain;' and see if your mighty creditor will allow the fraud to pass, or accept the coin with which you would cheat him. Offer to the strongest – if the darkest angel of God's host – water, when he has asked blood – will he take it? Not a whole pale sea for one red drop. I settled another account.

Pausing before Methusaleh – the giant and patriarch of the garden – and leaning my brow against his knotty trunk, my foot rested on the stone sealing the small sepulchre at his root; and I recalled the passage of feeling therein buried. I recalled Dr John; my warm affection for him; my faith in his excellence; my delight in his grace. What was become of that curious one-sided friendship which was half marble and half life; only on one hand truth, and on the other perhaps a jest?

Was this feeling dead? I do not know, but it was buried. Sometimes I thought the tomb unquiet, and dreamed strangely of disturbed earth, and of hair, still golden and living, obtruded through coffin-chinks.

Had I been too hasty? I used to ask myself; and this question would occur with a cruel sharpness after some brief chance interview with Dr John. He had still such kind looks, such a warm hand; his voice still kept so pleasant a tone for my name; I never liked 'Lucy' so well as when he uttered it. But I learned in time that this benignity, this cordiality, this music, belonged in no shape to me: it was a part of himself; it was the honey of his temper; it was the balm of his mellow mood; he imparted it, as the ripe fruit rewards with sweetness the rifling bee; he diffused it about him, as sweet plants shed their perfume. Does the nectarine love either the bee or bird it feeds? Is the sweet-briar enamoured of the air?

'Good-night, Dr John; you are good, you are beautiful; but you are not mine. Good-night, and God bless you!'

Thus I closed my musings. 'Good-night' left my lips in sound; I heard the two words spoken, and then I heard an echo – quite close.

'Good-night, mademoiselle; or, rather, good evening – the sun is scarce set; I hope you slept well?'

I started, but was only discomposed a moment; I knew the voice and speaker.

'Slept, monsieur! When? where?'

'You may well inquire when – where. It seems you turn day into night, and choose a desk for a pillow; rather hard lodging – ?'

'It was softened for me, monsieur, while I slept. That unseen, gift-bringing thing which haunts my desk, remembered me. No matter how I fell asleep; I awoke pillowed and covered.'

'Did the shawls keep you warm?'

'Very warm. Do you ask thanks for them?'

'No. You looked pale in your slumbers; are you home-sick?'

'To be home-sick, one must have a home; which I have not.'

'Then you have more need of a careful friend. I scarcely know any one, Miss Lucy, who needs a friend more absolutely than you; your very faults imperatively require it. You want so much checking, regulating, and keeping down.'

This idea of 'keeping down' never left M. Paul's head; the most habitual subjugation would, in my case, have failed to relieve him of it. No matter; what did it signify? I listened to him, and did not trouble myself to be too submissive; his occupation would have been gone, had I left him nothing to 'keep down.'

'You need watching, and watching over,' he pursued; 'and it is well for you that I see this, and do my best to discharge both duties. I watch you and others pretty closely, pretty constantly, nearer and oftener than you or they think. Do you see that window with a light in it?'

He pointed to a lattice in one of the college boarding-houses.

'That,' said he, 'is a room I have hired, nominally for a study – virtually for a post of observation. There I sit and read for hours together: it is my way – my taste. My book is this garden; its contents are human nature – female human nature. I know you all by heart. Ah! I know you well – St. Pierre the Parisienne – cette maîtresse-femme, my cousin Beck herself.'

'It is not right, monsieur.'

'Comment – it is not right? By whose creed? Does some dogma of Calvin or Luther condemn it? What is that to me? I am no Protestant. My rich father (for, though I have known poverty, and once starved for a year in a garret in Rome – starved wretchedly, often on a meal a day, and sometimes not that – yet I was born to wealth) – my rich father was a good Catholic; and he gave me a priest and a Jesuit for a tutor. I retain his lessons; and to what discoveries, grand Dieu! have they not aided me!'

'Discoveries made by stealth seem to me dishonourable discoveries.'

'Puritaine! I doubt it not. Yet see how my Jesuit's system works. You know the St. Pierre?'

'Partially.'

He laughed. 'You say right – "*partially*;" whereas, *I* know her *thoroughly*; there is the difference. She played before me the amiable; offered me patte de velours; caressed, flattered, fawned on me. Now, I am accessible to a woman's flattery – accessible against my reason. Though never pretty, she was – when I first knew her – young, or knew how to look young. Like all her countrywomen, she had the art of dressing – she had a certain, cool, easy, social assurance, which spared me the pain of embarrassment – '

'Monsieur, that must have been unnecessary. I never saw you embarrassed in my life.'

'Mademoiselle, you know little of me; I can be embarrassed as a petite pensionnaire; there is a fund of modesty and diffidence in my nature – '

'Monsieur, I never saw it.'

'Mademoiselle, it is there. You ought to have seen it.'

'Monsieur, I have observed you in public – on platforms, in tribunes, before titles and crowned heads – and you were as easy as you are in the third division.'

'Mademoiselle, neither titles nor crowned heads excite my modesty; and publicity is very much my element. I like it well, and breathe in it quite freely; but – but – in short, here is the sentiment brought into action, at this very moment; however, I disdain to be worsted by it. If, mademoiselle, I were a marrying man (which I am not; and you may spare yourself the trouble of any sneer you may be contemplating at the thought), and found it necessary to ask a lady whether she could look upon me in the light of a future husband, then would it be proved that I am as I say – modest.'

I quite believed him now; and, in believing, I honoured him with a sincerity of esteem which made my heart ache.

'As to the St. Pierre,' he went on, recovering himself, for his voice had altered a little, 'she once intended to be Madame Emanuel; and I don't know whither I might have been led, but for yonder little lattice with the light. Ah, magic lattice! what miracles of discovery hast thou wrought! Yes,' he pursued, 'I have seen her rancours, her vanities, her levities – not only here, but elsewhere: I have witnessed what bucklers me against all her arts: I am safe from poor Zélie.'

'And my pupils,' he presently recommenced, 'those blondes jeunes filles – so mild and meek – I have seen the most reserved – romp like boys, the demurest – snatch grapes from the walls, shake pears from the trees. When the English teacher came, I saw her, marked her early preference for this alley, noted her taste for seclusion, watched her well, long before she and I came to speaking terms; do you recollect my once coming silently and offering you a little knot of white violets when we were strangers?'

'I recollect it. I dried the violets, kept them, and have them still.'

'It pleased me when you took them peacefully and promptly, without prudery – that sentiment which I ever dread to excite, and which, when it is revealed in eye or gesture, I vindictively detest. To return. Not only did I watch you, but often – especially at eventide – another guardian angel was noiselessly hovering near: night after night my cousin Beck has stolen down yonder steps, and glidingly pursued your movements when you did not see her.'

'But, Monsieur, you could not from the distance of that window see what passed in this garden at night?'

'By moonlight I possibly might with a glass – I use a glass – but the garden itself is open to me. In the shed, at the bottom, there is a door leading into a court, which communicates with the college; of that door I possess the key, and thus come and go at pleasure. This afternoon I came through it, and found you asleep in class; again this evening, I have availed myself of the same entrance.'

I could not help saying, 'If you were a wicked, designing man, how terrible would all this be!'

His attention seemed incapable of being arrested by this view of the subject: he lit his cigar, and while he puffed it, leaning against a tree, and looking at me in a cool, amused way he had when his humour was tranquil, I thought proper to go on sermonizing him: he often lectured me by the hour together – I did not see why I should not speak my mind for once. So I told him my impressions concerning his Jesuit-system.

'The knowledge it brings you is bought too dear, monsieur; this coming and going by stealth degrades your own dignity.'

'My dignity!' he cried, laughing; 'when did you ever see me trouble my head about my dignity? It is you, Miss Lucy, who are "digne." How often, in your high insular presence, have I taken a pleasure in trampling upon, what you are pleased to call, my dignity; tearing it, scattering it to the winds, in those mad transports you witness with such hauteur, and which I know you think very like the ravings of a third-rate London actor.'

'Monsieur, I tell you every glance you cast from that lattice is a wrong done to the best part of your own nature. To study the human heart thus, is to banquet secretly and sacrilegiously on Eve's apples. I wish you were a Protestant.'

Indifferent to the wish, he smoked on. After a space of smiling yet thoughtful silence, he said, rather suddenly –

'I have seen other things.'

'What other things?'

Taking the weed from his lips, he threw the remnant amongst the shrubs, where, for a moment, it lay glowing in the gloom.

'Look at it,' said he: 'is not that spark like an eye watching you and me?'

He took a turn down the walk; presently returning, he went on:

'I have seen, Miss Lucy, things to me unaccountable, that have made me watch all night for a solution, and I have not yet found it.'

His tone was peculiar; my veins thrilled; he saw me shiver.

'Are you afraid? Whether is it of my words or of that red jealous eye just winking itself out?'

'I am cold; the night grows dark and late, and the air is changed; it is time to go in.'

'It is little past eight, but you shall go in soon. Answer me only this question.'

Yet he paused ere he put it. The garden was truly growing dark; dusk had come on with clouds, and drops of rain began to patter through the trees. I hoped he would feel this, but, for the moment, he seemed too much absorbed to be sensible of the change.

'Mademoiselle, do you Protestants believe in the supernatural?'

'There is a difference of theory and belief on this point amongst Protestants, as amongst other sects,' I answered. 'Why, monsieur, do you ask such a question?'

'Why do you shrink and speak so faintly? Are you superstitious?'

'I am constitutionally nervous. I dislike the discussion of such subjects. I dislike it the more because –'

'You believe?'

'No: but it has happened to me to experience impressions –'

'Since you came here?'

'Yes: not many months ago.'

'Here? – in this house?'

'Yes.'

'Bon! I am glad of it. I knew it somehow before you told me. I was conscious of rapport between you and myself. You are patient, and I am choleric; you are quiet and pale, and I am tanned and fiery; you are a strict Protestant, and I am a sort of lay Jesuit: but we are alike – there is affinity. Do you see it, mademoiselle, when you look in the glass? Do you observe that your forehead is shaped like mine – that your eyes are cut like mine? Do you hear that you have some of my tones of voice? Do you know that you have many of my looks? I perceive all this, and believe that you were born under my star. Yes, you were born under my star! Tremble! for where that is the case with mortals, the threads of their destinies are difficult to disentangle; knottings and catchings occur – sudden breaks leave damage in the web. But these "impressions," as you say, with English caution. I, too, have had my "impressions."'

'Monsieur, tell me them.'

'I desire no better, and intend no less. You know the legend of this house and garden?'

'I know it. Yes. They say that hundreds of years ago a nun was buried here alive at the foot of this very tree, beneath the ground which now bears us.'

'And that in former days a nun's ghost used to come and go here.'

'Monsieur, what if it comes and goes here still?'

'Something comes and goes here: there is a shape frequenting this house by night, different to any forms that show themselves by day. I have indisputably seen a something, more than once; and to me its conventual weeds were a strange sight, saying more than they can do to any other living being. A nun!'

'Monsieur, I, too, have seen it.'

'I anticipated that. Whether this nun be flesh and blood, or something that remains when blood is dried and flesh wasted, her business is as much with you as with me, probably. Well, I mean to make it out: it has baffled me so far, but I mean to follow up the mystery. I mean – '

Instead of telling what he meant, he raised his head suddenly; I made the same movement in the same instant; we both looked to one point – the high tree shadowing the great berceau, and resting some of its boughs on the roof of the first classe. There had been a strange and inexplicable sound from that quarter, as if the arms of that tree had swayed of their own motion, and its weight of foliage had rushed and crushed against the massive trunk. Yes; there scarce stirred a breeze, and that heavy tree was convulsed, whilst the feathery shrubs stood still. For some minutes amongst the wood and leafage a rending and heaving went on. Dark as it was, it seemed to me that something more solid than either night-shadow, or branch-shadow, blackened out of the boles. At last the struggle ceased. What birth succeeded this travail? What Dryad was born of these throes? We watched fixedly. A sudden bell rang in the house – the prayer-bell. Instantly into our alley there came, out of the bureau, an apparition, all black and white. With a sort of angry rush – close, close past our faces – swept swiftly the very NUN herself! Never had I seen her so clearly. She looked tall of stature, and fierce of gesture. As she went, the wind rose sobbing; the rain poured wild and cold; the whole night seemed to feel her.

CHAPTER 32

The First Letter

WHERE, IT BECOMES TIME TO INQUIRE, was Paulina Mary? How fared my intercourse with the sumptuous Hôtel Crécy? That intercourse had, for an interval, been suspended by absence; M. and Miss de Bassompierre had been travelling, dividing some weeks between the provinces and the capital of France. Chance apprised me of their return very shortly after it took place.

I was walking one mild afternoon on a quiet boulevard, wandering slowly on, enjoying the benign April sun, and some thoughts not unpleasing, when I saw before me a group of riders, stopping as if they had just encountered, and exchanging greetings in the midst of the broad, smooth, linden-bordered path; on one side a middle-aged gentleman and young lady, on the other – a young and handsome man. Very graceful was the lady's mien, choice her appointments, delicate and stately her whole aspect. Still, as I looked, I felt they were known to me, and, drawing a little nearer, I fully recognized them all; the Count Home de Bassompierre, his daughter, and Dr Graham Bretton.

How animated was Graham's face! How true, how warm, yet how retiring the joy it expressed! This was the state of things, this the combination of circumstances, at once to attract and enchain, to subdue and excite Dr John. The pearl he admired was in itself of great price and truest purity, but he was not the man who, in appreciating the gem, could forget its setting. Had he seen Paulina with the same youth, beauty, and grace, but on foot, alone, unguarded, and in simple attire, a dependent worker, a demi-grisette, he would have thought her a pretty little creature, and would have loved with his eye her movements and her mien, but it required other than this to conquer him as he was now vanquished, to bring him safe under dominion as now, without loss, and even with gain to his manly honour – one saw that he was reduced; there was about Dr John all the man of the world; to satisfy himself did not suffice; society must approve – the world must admire what he did, or he counted his measures false and futile. In his victrix he required all that was here visible – the imprint of high cultivation, the consecration of a careful and authoritative protection, the adjuncts that Fashion decrees, Wealth purchases, and Taste adjusts; for these conditions his spirit stipulated ere it surrendered: they were here to the utmost fulfilled; and now, proud, impassioned, yet fearing, he did homage to Paulina as his sovereign. As for her, the smile of feeling, rather than of conscious power, slept soft in her eyes.

They parted. He passed me at speed, hardly feeling the earth he skimmed, and seeing nothing on either hand. He looked very handsome; mettle and purpose were roused in him fully.

'Papa, there is Lucy!' cried a musical, friendly voice, 'Lucy, dear Lucy – *do* come here!'

I hastened to her. She threw back her veil, and stooped from her saddle to kiss me.

'I was coming to see you to-morrow,' said she; 'but now, to-morrow you will come and see me.'

She named the hour, and I promised compliance.

The morrow's evening found me with her – she and I shut into her own room. I had not seen her since that occasion when her claims were brought into comparison with those of Ginevra Fanshawe, and had so signally prevailed; she had much to tell me of her travels in the interval. A most animated, rapid speaker was she in such *tête-à-tête*, a most lively describer; yet with her artless diction and clear, soft voice, she never seemed to speak too fast or say too much. My own attention I think would not soon have flagged, but by-and-by, she herself seemed to need some change of subject; she hastened to wind up her narrative briefly. Yet why she terminated with so concise an abridgment did not immediately appear; silence followed – a restless silence, not without symptoms of abstraction. Then, turning to me, in a diffident, half-appealing voice, –

'Lucy –'

'Well, I am at your side.'

'Is my cousin Ginevra still at Madame Beck's?'

'Your cousin is still there; you must be longing to see her.'

'No – not much.'

'You want to invite her to spend another evening?'

'No. . . I suppose she still talks about being married?'

'Not to any one you care for.'

'But of course she still thinks of Dr Bretton? She cannot have changed her mind on that point, because it was so fixed two months ago?'

'Why, you know, it does not matter. You saw the terms on which they stood.'

'There was a little misunderstanding that evening, certainly; does she seem unhappy?'

'Not she. To change the subject. Have you heard or seen nothing of, or from Graham during your absence?'

'Papa had letters from him once or twice, about business I think. He undertook the management of some affair which required attention, while we were away. Dr Bretton seems to respect papa, and to have pleasure in obliging him.'

'Yes: you met him yesterday on the boulevard; you would be able to judge from his aspect that his friends need not be painfully anxious about his health?'

'Papa seems to have thought with you. I could not help smiling. He is not particularly observant, you know, because he is often thinking of other things than what pass before his eyes; but he said, as Dr Bretton rode away, "Really it does a man good to see the spirit and energy of that boy." He called Dr Bretton a boy; I believe he almost thinks him so, just as he thinks me a little girl; he was not speaking to me, but dropped that remark to himself. Lucy . . .'

Again fell the appealing accent, and at the same instant she left her chair, and came and sat on the stool at my feet.

I liked her. It is not a declaration I have often made concerning my acquaintance, in the course of this book; the reader will bear with it for once. Intimate intercourse, close inspection, disclosed in Paulina only what was delicate, intelligent, and sincere; therefore my regard for her lay deep. An admiration more superficial might have been more demonstrative; mine, however, was quiet.

'What have you to ask of Lucy?' said I; 'be brave, and speak out.'

But there was no courage in her eye; as it met mine, it fell; and there was no coolness on her cheek – not a transient surface-blush, but a gathering inward excitement raised its tint and its temperature.

'Lucy, I *do* wish to know your thoughts of Dr Bretton. Do, *do* give me your real opinion of his character – his disposition.'

'His character stands high, and deservedly high.'

'And his disposition? Tell me about his disposition,' she urged; 'you know him well.'

'I know him pretty well.'

'You know his home-side. You have seen him with his mother; speak of him as a son.'

'He is a fine-hearted son; his mother's comfort and hope, her pride and pleasure.'

She held my hand between hers, and at each favourable word gave it a little caressing stroke.

'In what other way is he good, dear Lucy?'

'Dr Bretton is benevolent – humanely disposed towards all his race. Dr Bretton would have benignity for the lowest savage, or the worst criminal.'

'I heard some gentlemen, some of papa's friends, who were talking about him, say the same. They say many of the poor patients at the hospitals, who tremble before some pitiless and selfish surgeons, welcome him.'

'They are right; I have witnessed as much. He once took me over a hospital; I saw how he was received: your father's friends are right.'

The softest gratitude animated her eye as she lifted it a moment. She had yet more to say, but seemed hesitating about time and place. Dusk was beginning to reign; her parlour fire already glowed with twilight ruddiness; but I thought she wished the room dimmer, the hour later.

'How quiet and secluded we feel here!' I remarked, to reassure her.

'Do we? Yes; it is a still evening, and I shall not be called down to tea; papa is dining out.'

Still holding my hand, she played with the fingers unconsciously, dressed them, now in her own rings, and now circled them with a twine of her beautiful hair; she patted the palm against her hot cheek, and at last, having cleared a voice that was naturally liquid as a lark's, she said: –

'You must think it rather strange that I should talk so much about Dr Bretton, ask so many questions, take such an interest, but – '

'Not at all strange; perfectly natural; you like him.'

'And if I did,' said she, with slight quickness, 'is that a reason why I should talk? I suppose you think me weak, like my cousin Ginevra?'

'If I thought you one whit like Madame Ginevra, I would not sit here waiting for your communications. I would get up, walk at my ease about the room, and anticipate all you had to say by a round lecture. Go on.'

'I mean to go on,' retorted she; 'what else do you suppose I mean to do?' And she looked and spoke – the little Polly of Bretton – petulant, sensitive. 'If,' said she emphatically, 'if I liked Dr John till I was fit to die for liking him, that alone could not license me to be otherwise than dumb – dumb as the grave – dumb as you, Lucy

Snowe – you know it – and you know you would despise me if I failed in self-control, and whined about some ricketty liking that was all on my side.'

'It is true I little respect women or girls who are loquacious either in boasting the triumphs, or bemoaning the mortifications, of feeling. But as to *you*, Paulina, speak, for I earnestly wish to hear you. Tell me all it will give you pleasure or relief to tell; I ask no more.'

'Do you care for me, Lucy?'

'Yes, I do, Paulina.'

'And I love you. I had an odd content in being with you even when I was a little, troublesome, disobedient girl; it was charming to me then to lavish on you my naughtinesses and whims. Now you are acceptable to me, and I like to talk with and trust you. So listen, Lucy.'

And she settled herself, resting against my arm – resting gently, not with honest Mistress Fanshawe's fatiguing and selfish weight.

'A few minutes since you asked whether we had not heard from Graham during our absence, and I said there were two letters for papa on business; this was true, but I did not tell you all.'

'You evaded?'

'I shuffled and equivocated, you know. However, I am going to speak the truth now; it is getting darker; one can talk at one's ease. Papa often lets me open the letter-bag and give him out the contents. One morning, about three weeks ago, you don't know how surprised I was to find, amongst a dozen letters for M. de Bassompierre, a note addressed to Miss de Bassompierre. I spied it at once, amidst all the rest; the handwriting was not strange; it attracted me directly. I was going to say, "Papa, here is another letter from Dr Bretton;" but the "Miss" struck me mute. I actually never received a letter from a gentleman before. Ought I to have shown it to papa, and let him open it and read it first? I could not for my life, Lucy. I know so well papa's ideas about me: he forgets my age; he thinks I am a mere school-girl; he is not aware that other people see I am grown up as tall as I shall be; so, with a curious mixture of feelings, some of them self-reproachful, and some so fluttering and strong, I cannot describe them, I gave papa his twelve letters – his herd of possessions – and kept back my one, my ewe-lamb. It lay in my lap during breakfast, looking up at me with an inexplicable meaning, making me feel myself a thing double-existent – a child to that dear papa, but no more a child to myself. After breakfast I carried my letter up-stairs, and having secured myself by turning the key in the door, I began to study the outside of my treasure: it was some minutes before I could get over the direction and penetrate the seal; one does not take a strong place of this kind by instant storm – one sits down awhile before it, as beleaguers say. Graham's hand is like himself, Lucy, and so is his seal – all clear, firm, and rounded – no slovenly splash of wax – a full, solid, steady drop – a distinct impress: no pointed turns harshly pricking the optic nerve, but a clean, mellow, pleasant manuscript, that soothes you as you read. It is like his face – just like the chiselling of his features: do you know his autograph?'

'I have seen it: go on.'

'The seal was too beautiful to be broken, so I cut it round with my scissors. On the point of reading the letter at last, I once more drew back voluntarily; it was too soon yet to drink that draught – the sparkle in the cup was so beautiful – I would watch it yet a minute. Then I remembered all at once that I had not said my prayers that morning. Having heard papa go down to breakfast a little earlier than usual, I had been afraid of keeping him waiting, and had hastened to join him as soon as dressed, thinking no harm to put off prayers till afterwards. Some people would say I ought to have served God first and then man; but I don't think Heaven could be jealous of anything I might do for papa. I believe I am superstitious. A voice seemed now to say that another feeling than filial affection was in question – to urge me to pray before I dared to read what I so longed to read – to deny myself yet a moment, and remember first a great duty. I have had these impulses ever since I can remember. I put the letter down and said my prayers, adding, at the end, a strong entreaty that whatever happened, I might not be tempted or led to cause papa any sorrow, and might never, in caring for others, neglect him. The very thought of such a possibility so pierced my heart that it made me cry. But still, Lucy, I felt that in time papa would have to be taught the truth, managed, and induced to hear reason.

'I read the letter. Lucy, life is said to be all disappointment. *I* was not disappointed. Ere I read, and while I read, my heart did more than throb – it trembled fast – every quiver seemed like the pant of an animal athirst, laid down at a well and drinking; and the well proved quite full, gloriously clear; it rose up munificently of its own impulse; I saw the sun through its gush, and not a mote, Lucy, no moss, no insect, no atom in the thrice-refined golden gurgle.

'Life,' she went on, 'is said to be full of pain to some. I have read biographies where the wayfarer seemed to journey on from suffering to suffering; where Hope flew before him fast, never alighting so near, or lingering so long, as to give his hand a chance of one realizing grasp. I have read of those who sowed in tears, and whose harvest, so far from being reaped in joy, perished by untimely blight, or was borne off by sudden whirlwind; and, alas! some of these met the winter with empty garners, and died of utter want in the darkest and coldest of the year.'

'Was it their fault, Paulina, that they of whom you speak thus died?'

'Not always their fault. Some of them were good, endeavouring people. I am not endeavouring, nor actively good, yet God has caused me to grow in sun, due moisture, and safe protection, sheltered, fostered, taught, by my dear father; and now – now – another comes. Graham loves me.'

For some minutes we both paused on this climax.

'Does your father know?' I inquired, in a low voice.

'Graham spoke with deep respect of papa, but implied that he dared not approach that quarter as yet; he must first prove his worth: he added that he must have some light respecting myself and my own feelings ere he ventured to risk a step in the matter elsewhere.'

'How did you reply?'

'I replied briefly, but I did not repulse him. Yet I almost trembled for fear of making the answer too cordial: Graham's tastes are so fastidious. I wrote it three times – chastening and subduing the phrases at every rescript; at last, having confected it till it seemed to me to resemble a morsel of ice flavoured with ever so slight a zest of fruit or sugar, I ventured to seal and despatch it.'

'Excellent, Paulina! Your instinct is fine; you understand Dr Bretton.'

'But how must I manage about papa? There I am still in pain.'

'Do not manage at all. Wait now. Only maintain no further correspondence till your father knows all, and gives his sanction.'

'Will he ever give it?'

'Time will show. Wait.'

'Dr Bretton wrote one other letter, deeply grateful for my calm, brief note; but I anticipated your advice, by saying, that while my sentiments continued the same, I could not without my father's knowledge write again.'

'You acted as you ought to have done; so Dr Bretton will feel: it will increase his pride in you, his love for you, if either be capable of increase. Paulina, that gentle hoar-frost of yours, surrounding so much pure, fine flame, is a priceless privilege of nature.'

'You see I feel Graham's disposition,' said she. 'I feel that no delicacy can be too exquisite for his treatment.'

'It is perfectly proved that you comprehend him, and then – whatever Dr Bretton's disposition, were he one who expected to be more nearly met – you would still act truthfully, openly, tenderly, with your father.'

'Lucy, I trust I shall thus act always. Oh, it will be pain to wake papa from his dream, and tell him I am no more a little girl!'

'Be in no hurry to do so, Paulina. Leave the revelation to Time and your kind Fate. I also have noticed the gentleness of her cares for you: doubt not she will benignantly order the circumstances, and fitly appoint the hour. Yes; I have thought over your life just as you have yourself thought it over; I have made comparisons like those to which you adverted. We know not the future, but the past has been propitious.

'As a child I feared for you; nothing that has life was ever more susceptible than your nature in infancy: under harshness, or neglect, neither your outward nor your inward self would have ripened to what they now are. Much pain, much fear, much struggle would have troubled the very lines of your features, broken their regularity, would have harassed your nerves into the fever of habitual irritation: you would have lost in health and cheerfulness, in grace and sweetness. Providence has protected and cultured you, not only for your own sake, but I believe for Graham's. His star, too, was fortunate: to develope fully the best of his nature, a companion like you was needed; there you are, ready. You must be united. I knew it the first day I saw you together at La Terrasse. In all that mutually concerns you and Graham there seems to me promise, plan, harmony. I do not think the sunny youth of either will prove the forerunner of stormy age. I think it is deemed good that you two should live in peace and be happy – not as angels, but as few are happy amongst mortals. Some lives *are* thus blessed: it is God's will: it is the attesting trace and lingering evidence of Eden. Other lives run from the first another course. Other travellers encounter weather fitful and gusty, wild and variable – breast adverse winds, are belated and overtaken by the early closing winter night. Neither can this happen without the sanction of God; and I know that, amidst His boundless works, is somewhere stored the secret of this last fate's justice: I know that His treasures contain the proof as the promise of its mercy.'

CHAPTER 33

M. Paul Keeps His Promise

ON THE FIRST OF MAY, we had all – *i.e.* the twenty boarders and the four teachers – notice to rise at five o'clock of the morning, to be dressed and ready by six, to put ourselves under the command of M. le Professeur Emanuel, who was to head our march forth from Villette, for it was on this day he proposed to fulfil his promise of taking us to breakfast in the country. I, indeed, as the reader may perhaps remember, had not had the honour of an invitation when this excursion was first projected – rather the contrary; but on my now making allusion to this fact, and wishing to know how it was to be, my ear received a pull, of which I did not venture to challenge the repetition by raising further difficulties.

'Je vous conseille de vous faire prier,'[191] said M. Emanuel, imperially menacing the other ear. One Napoleonic compliment, however, was enough, so I made up my mind to be of the party.

The morning broke calm as summer, with singing of birds in the garden, and a light dew-mist that promised heat. We all said it would be warm, and we all felt pleasure in folding away heavy garments, and in assuming the attire suiting a sunny season. The clean fresh print dress, and the light straw bonnet, each made and trimmed as the French workwoman alone can make and trim, so as to unite the utterly unpretending with the perfectly becoming, was the rule of costume. Nobody flaunted in faded silk; nobody wore a second-hand best article.

At six the bell rang merrily, and we poured down the staircase, through the carré, along the corridor, into the vestibule. There stood our Professor, wearing, not his savage-looking paletôt and severe bonnet-grec, but a young-looking belted blouse and cheerful straw hat. He had for us all the kindest good-morrow, and most of us for him had a thanksgiving smile. We were marshalled in order and soon started.

The streets were yet quiet, and the boulevards were fresh and peaceful as fields. I believe we were very happy as we walked along. This chief of ours had the secret of giving a certain impetus to happiness when he would; just as, in an opposite mood, he could give a thrill to fear.

He did not lead nor follow us, but walked along the line, giving a word to every one, talking much to his favourites, and not wholly neglecting even those he disliked. It was rather my wish, for a reason I had, to keep slightly aloof from notice, and being paired with Ginevra Fanshawe, bearing on my arm the dear pressure of that angel's not unsubstantial limb – (she continued in excellent case, and I can assure the reader it was no trifling business to bear the burden of her loveliness; many a time in the course of that warm day I wished to goodness there had been less of the charming commodity) – however, having her, as I said, I tried to make her useful by interposing her always between myself and M. Paul, shifting my place, according as I heard him coming up to the right hand or the left. My private motive for this manoeuvre might be traced to the circumstance of the new print dress I wore, being pink in colour – a fact which, under our present convoy, made me feel something as I have felt, when, clad in a shawl with a red border, necessitated to traverse a meadow where pastured a bull.

For awhile, the shifting system, together with some modifications in the arrangement of a black silk scarf, answered my purpose; but, by-and-by, he found out, that whether he came to this side or to that, Miss Fanshawe was still his neighbour. The course of acquaintance between Ginevra and him had never run so smooth that his temper did not undergo a certain crisping process whenever he heard her English accent: nothing in their dispositions fitted; they jarred if they came in contact; he held her empty and affected; she deemed him bearish, meddling, repellent.

At last, when he had changed his place for about the sixth time, finding still the same untoward result to the experiment – he thrust his head forward, settled his eyes on mine, and demanded with impatience –

'Qu'est-ce que c'est? Vous me jouez des tours?'[192]

The words were hardly out of his mouth, however, ere, with his customary quickness, he seized the root of this proceeding: in vain I shook out the long fringe, and spread forth the broad end of my scarf. 'A – h – h! c'est la robe rose!'[193] broke from his lips, affecting me very much like the sudden and irate low of some lord of the meadow.

'It is only cotton,' I alleged, hurriedly; 'and cheaper, and washes better than any other colour.'

'Et Mademoiselle Lucie est coquette comme dix Parisiennes,' he answered. 'A-t-on jamais vu une Anglaise pareille? Regardez plutot son chapeau, et ses gants, et ses brodequins!'[194] These articles of dress were just like what my companions wore; certainly not one whit smarter – perhaps rather plainer than most – but monsieur had now got hold of his text, and I began to chafe under the expected sermon. It went off, however, as mildly as the menace of a storm sometimes passes on a summer day. I got but one flash of sheet lightning in the shape of a single bantering smile from his eyes; and then he said: –

'Courage! – à vrai dire je ne suis pas fâché, peut-être même suis-je content qu'on s'est fait si belle pour ma petite fête.'

'Mais ma robe n'est pas belle, monsieur – elle n'est que propre.'

'J'aime la propreté,'[195] said he. In short, he was not to be dissatisfied; the sun of good humour was to triumph on this auspicious morning; it consumed scudding clouds ere they sullied its disk.

And now we were in the country, amongst what they called 'les bois et les petits sentiers.' These woods and lanes a month later, would offer but a dusty and doubtful seclusion: now, however, in their May greenness and morning repose, they looked very pleasant.

We reached a certain well, planted round, in the taste of Labassecour, with an orderly circle of lime-trees: here a halt was called; on the green swell of ground surrounding this well, we were ordered to be seated, monsieur taking his place in our midst, and suffering us to gather in a knot round him. Those who liked him more than they feared, came close, and these were chiefly little ones; those who feared more than they liked, kept somewhat aloof; those in whom much affection had given, even to what remained of fear, a pleasurable zest, observed the greatest distance.

He began to tell us a story. Well could he narrate: in such a diction as children love, and learned men emulate; a diction simple in its strength, and strong in its simplicity. There were beautiful touches in that little tale; sweet glimpses of feeling and hues of description that, while I listened, sunk into my mind, and since have never faded. He tinted a twilight scene – I hold it in memory still – such a picture I have never looked on from artists' pencil.

I have said that, for myself, I had no impromptu faculty; and perhaps that very deficiency made me marvel the more at one who possessed it in perfection. M. Emanuel was not a man to write books; but I have heard him lavish, with careless, unconscious prodigality, such mental wealth as books seldom boast; his mind was indeed my library, and whenever it was opened to me, I entered bliss. Intellectually imperfect as I was, I could read little; there were few bound and printed volumes that did not weary me – whose perusal did not fag and blind – but his tomes of thought were collyrium[196] to the spirit's eyes; over their contents, inward sight grew clear and strong. I used to think what a delight it would be for one who loved him better than he loved himself, to gather and store up those handfuls of gold-dust, so recklessly flung to heaven's reckless winds.

His story done, he approached the little knoll where I and Ginevra sat apart. In his usual mode of demanding an opinion (he had not reticence to wait till it was voluntarily offered) he asked: –

'Were you interested?'

According to my wonted undemonstrative fashion, I simply answered –

'Yes.'

'Was it good?'

'Very good.'

'Yet I could not write that down,' said he.

'Why not, monsieur?'

'I hate the mechanical labour; I hate to stoop and sit still. I could dictate it, though, with pleasure to an amanuensis who suited me. Would Mademoiselle Lucy write for me if I asked her?'

'Monsieur would be too quick; he would urge me, and be angry, if my pen did not keep pace with his lips.'

'Try some day; let us see the monster I can make of myself under the circumstances. But just now, there is no question of dictation; I mean to make you useful in another office. Do you see yonder farm-house?'

'Surrounded with trees? Yes.'

'There we are to breakfast; and while the good fermière makes the café au lait in a caldron, you and five others, whom I shall select, will spread with butter half a hundred rolls.'

Having formed his troop into line once more, he marched us straight on the farm, which, on seeing our force, surrendered without capitulation.

Clean knives and plates, and fresh butter being provided, half a dozen of us, chosen by our professor, set to work under his directions, to prepare for breakfast a huge basket of rolls, with which the baker had been ordered to provision the farm, in anticipation of our coming. Coffee and chocolate were already made hot; cream and new-laid eggs were added to the treat, and M. Emanuel, always generous, would have given a large order for 'jambon' and 'confitures' in addition, but that some of us, who presumed perhaps upon our influence, insisted that it would be a most reckless waste of victual. He railed at us for our pains, terming us 'des ménagères avares;' but we let him talk, and managed the economy of the repast our own way.

With what a pleasant countenance he stood on the farm-kitchen hearth looking on! He was a man whom it made happy to see others happy; he liked to have movement, animation, abundance and enjoyment round him. We asked where he would sit. He told us, we knew well he was our slave, and we his tyrants, and that he dared not so much as choose a chair without our leave; so we set him the farmer's great chair at the head of the long table, and put him into it.

Well might we like him, with all his passions and hurricanes, when he could be so benignant and docile at times, as he was just now. Indeed, at the worst, it was only his nerves that were irritable, not his temper that was radically bad; soothe, comprehend, comfort him, and he was a lamb; he would not harm a fly. Only to the very stupid, perverse, or unsympathizing, was he in the slightest degree dangerous.

Mindful always of his religion, he made the youngest of the party say a little prayer before we begun breakfast, crossing himself as devoutly as a woman. I had never seen him pray before, or make that pious sign; he did it so simply, with such child-like faith, I could not help smiling pleasurably as I watched; his eyes met my smile; he just stretched out his kind hand, saying,

'Donnez-moi la main! I see we worship the same God, in the same spirit, though by different rites.'

Most of M. Emanuel's brother professors were emancipated free-thinkers, infidels, atheists; and many of them men whose lives would not bear scrutiny: he was more like a knight of old, religious in his way, and of spotless fame. Innocent childhood, beautiful youth were safe at his side. He had vivid passions, keen feelings, but his pure honour and his artless piety were the strong charm that kept the lions couchant.

That breakfast was a merry meal, and the merriment was not mere vacant clatter: M. Paul originated, led, controlled and heightened it; his social, lively temper played unfettered and unclouded; surrounded only by women and children there was nothing to cross and thwart him; he had his own way, and a pleasant way it was.

The meal over, the party were free to run and play in the meadows; a few stayed to help the farmer's wife to put away her earthenware. M. Paul called me from among these to come out and sit near him under a tree – whence he could view the troop gambolling over a wide pasture – and read to him whilst he took his cigar. He sat on a rustic bench, and I at the tree-root. While I read (a pocket-classic – a Corneille[197] – I did not like it, but he did, finding therein beauties I never could be brought to perceive), he listened with a sweetness of calm the more impressive from the impetuosity of his general nature; the deepest happiness filled his blue eye and smoothed his broad forehead. I too was happy – happy with the bright day, happier with his presence, happiest with his kindness.

He asked, by-and-by, if I would not rather run to my companions than sit there? I said, no; I felt content to be where he was. He asked whether, if I were his sister, I should always be content to stay with a brother such as he. I said, I believed I should; and I felt it. Again, he inquired whether, if he were to leave Villette, and go far away, I should be sorry; and I dropped Corneille, and made no reply.

'Petite soeur,' said he; 'how long could you remember me if we were separated?'

'That, monsieur, I can never tell, because I do not know how long it will be before I shall cease to remember everything earthly.'

'If I were to go beyond seas for two – three – five years, should you welcome me on my return?'

'Monsieur, how could I live in the interval?'

'Pourtant j'ai été pour vous bien dur, bien exigeant.'[198]

I hid my face with the book, for it was covered with tears. I asked him why he talked so; and he said he would talk so no more, and cheered me again with the kindest encouragement. Still, the gentleness with which he treated me during the rest of the day, went somehow to my heart. It was too tender. It was mournful. I would rather he had been abrupt, whimsical, and irate as was his wont.

When hot noon arrived – for the day turned out as we had anticipated; glowing as June – our shepherd collected his sheep from the pasture, and proceeded to lead us all softly home. But we had a whole league to walk – thus far from Villette was the farm where we had breakfasted; the children, especially, were tired with their play; the spirits of most flagged at the prospect of this mid-day walk over chaussées flinty, glaring and dusty. This state of things had been foreseen and provided for. Just beyond the boundary of the farm we met two spacious vehicles coming to fetch us – such conveyances as are hired out purposely for the accommodation of school-parties; here, with good management, room was found for all, and in another hour M. Paul made safe consignment of his charge at the Rue Fossette. It had been a pleasant day: it would have been perfect, but for the breathing of melancholy which had dimmed its sunshine a moment.

That tarnish was renewed the same evening.

Just about sunset, I saw M. Emanuel come out of the front-door, accompanied by Madame Beck. They paced the centre-alley for nearly an hour, talking earnestly: he – looking grave, yet restless; she – wearing an amazed, expostulatory, dissuasive air.

I wondered what was under discussion; and when Madame Beck re-entered the house as it darkened, leaving her kinsman Paul yet lingering in the garden, I said to myself –

'He called me "petite soeur" this morning. If he were really my brother, how I should like to go to him just now, and ask what it is that presses on his mind. See how he leans against that tree, with his arms crossed and his brow bent. He wants consolation, I know: Madame does not console; she only remonstrates. What now – ?'

Starting from quiescence to action, M. Paul came striding erect and quick down the garden. The carré doors were yet open: I thought he was probably going to water the orange-trees in the tubs, after his occasional custom; on reaching the court, however, he took an abrupt turn and made for the berceau and the first classe glass-door. There, in that first classe I was, thence I had been watching him; but there I could not find courage to await his approach. He had turned so suddenly, he strode so fast, he looked so strange; the coward within me grew pale, shrunk and – not waiting to listen to reason, and hearing the shrubs crush and the gravel crunch to his advance – she was gone on the wings of panic.

Nor did I pause till I had taken sanctuary in the oratory, now empty. Listening there with beating pulses, and an unaccountable, undefined apprehension, I heard him pass through all the schoolrooms, clashing the doors impatiently as he went; I heard him invade the refectory which the 'lecture pieuse' was now holding under hallowed constraint; I heard him pronounce these words –

'Où est Mademoiselle Lucie?'[199]

And just as, summoning my courage, I was preparing to go down and do what, after all, I most wished to do in the world – viz., meet him – the wiry voice of St. Pierre replied glibly and falsely, 'Elle est au lit.'[200] And he passed, with the stamp of vexation, into the corridor. There Madame Beck met, captured, chid, convoyed to the street-door, and finally dismissed him.

As that street-door closed, a sudden amazement at my own perverse proceeding struck like a blow upon me. I felt from the first it was me he wanted – me he was seeking – and had not I wanted him too? What, then, had carried me away? What had rapt me beyond his reach? He had something to tell: he was going to tell me that something: my ear strained its nerve to hear it, and I had made the confidence impossible. Yearning to listen and console, while I thought audience and solace beyond hope's reach – no sooner did opportunity suddenly and fully arrive, than I evaded it, as I would have evaded the levelled shaft of mortality.

Well, my insane inconsistency had its reward. Instead of the comfort, the certain satisfaction, I might have won – could I but have put choking panic down, and stood firm two minutes – here was dead blank, dark doubt, and drear suspense.

I took my wages to my pillow, and passed the night counting them.

CHAPTER 34

Malevola

MADAME BECK called me on Thursday afternoon, and asked whether I had any occupation to hinder me from going into town and executing some little commissions for her at the shops.

Being disengaged, and placing myself at her service, I was presently furnished with a list of the wools, silks, embroidering thread, etcetera, wanted in the pupils' work, and having equipped myself in a manner suiting the threatening aspect of a clouded and sultry day, I was just drawing the spring-bolt of the street-door, in act to issue forth, when Madame's voice again summoned me to the salle à manger.

'Pardon, Meess Lucie!' cried she, in the seeming haste of an impromptu thought, 'I have just recollected one more errand for you, if your good nature will not deem itself overburdened?'

Of course I 'confounded myself' in asseverations to the contrary; and Madame, running into the little salon, brought thence a pretty basket, filled with fine hothouse fruit, rosy, perfect, and tempting, reposing amongst the dark green, wax-like leaves, and pale yellow stars of, I know not what, exotic plant.

'There,' she said, 'it is not heavy, and will not shame your neat toilette, as if it were a household, servant-like detail. Do me the favour to leave this little basket at the house of Madame Walravens, with my felicitations on her fête. She lives down in the old town, Numéro 3, Rue des Mages. I fear you will find the walk rather long, but you have the whole afternoon before you, and do not hurry; if you are not back in time for dinner, I will order a portion to be saved, or Goton, with whom you are a favourite, will have pleasure in tossing up some trifle, for your especial benefit. You shall not be forgotten, ma bonne meess. And oh! please!' (calling me back once more) 'be sure to insist on seeing Madame Walravens herself, and giving the basket into her own hands, in order that there may be no mistake, for she is rather a punctilious personage. Adieu! Au revoir!'

And at last I got away. The shop-commissions took some time to execute, that choosing and matching of silks and wools being always a tedious business, but at last I got through my list. The patterns for the slippers, the bell-ropes, the cabas were selected – the slides and tassels for the purses chosen – the whole 'tripotage,' in short, was off my mind; nothing but the fruit and the felicitations remained to be attended to.

I rather liked the prospect of a long walk, deep into the old and grim Basse-Ville; and I liked it no worse because the evening sky, over the city, was settling into a mass of black-blue metal, heated at the rim, and inflaming slowly to a heavy red.

I fear a high wind, because storm demands that exertion of strength and use of action I always yield with pain; but the sullen down-fall, the thick snow-descent, or dark rush of rain, asks only resignation – the quiet abandonment of garments and person to be drenched. In return, it sweeps a great capital clean before you; it makes you a quiet path through broad, grand streets; it petrifies a living city, as if by eastern enchantment; it transforms a Villette into a Tadmor. Let, then, the rains fall, and the floods descend – only I must first get rid of this basket of fruit.

An unknown clock from an unknown tower (Jean Baptiste's voice was now too distant to be audible) was tolling the third quarter past five, when I reached that street and house whereof Madame Beck had given me the address. It was no street at all; it seemed rather to be part of a square; it was quiet, grass grew between the broad gray flags, the houses were large and looked very old – behind them rose the appearance of trees, indicating gardens at the back. Antiquity brooded above this region, business was banished thence. Rich men had once possessed this quarter, and once grandeur had made her seat here. That church whose dark, half-ruinous turrets overlooked the square, was the venerable and formerly opulent shrine of the Magi. But wealth and greatness had long since stretched their gilded pinions and fled hence, leaving these their ancient nests, perhaps to house Penury for a time, or perhaps to stand cold and empty, mouldering untenanted in the course of winters.

As I crossed this deserted 'place,' on whose pavement drops almost as large as a five-franc piece were now slowly darkening, I saw, in its whole expanse, no symptom or evidence of life, except what was given in the figure of an infirm old priest, who went past, bending and propped on a staff – the type of eld and decay.

He had issued from the very house to which I was directed; and when I paused before the door just closed after him, and rang the bell, he turned to look at me. Nor did he soon avert his gaze; perhaps he thought me, with my basket of summer fruit, and my lack of the dignity age confers, an incongruous figure in such a scene. I know, had a young ruddy-faced bonne opened the door to admit me, I should have thought such a one little in harmony with her dwelling; but when I found myself confronted by a very old woman, wearing a very antique peasant costume, a cap alike hideous and costly, with long flaps of native lace, a petticoat and jacket of cloth, and sabots more like little boats than shoes, it seemed all right, and soothingly in character.

The expression of her face was not quite so soothing as the cut of her costume; anything more cantankerous I have seldom seen; she would scarcely reply to my inquiry after Madame Walravens; I believe she would have snatched the basket of fruit from my hand, had not the old priest, hobbling up, checked her, and himself lent an ear to the message with which I was charged.

His apparent deafness rendered it a little difficult to make him fully understand that I must see Madame Walravens, and consign the fruit into her own hands. At last, however, he comprehended the fact that such were my orders, and that duty enjoined their literal fulfilment. Addressing the aged bonne, not in French, but in the aboriginal tongue of Labassecour, he persuaded her, at last, to let me cross the inhospitable threshold, and himself escorting me up-stairs, I was ushered into a sort of salon, and there left.

The room was large, and had a fine old ceiling, and almost church-like windows of coloured glass; but it was desolate, and in the shadow of the coming storm, looked strangely lowering. Within – opened a smaller room; there, however, the blind of the single casement was closed; through the deep gloom few details of furniture were apparent. These few I amused myself by puzzling to make out; and, in particular, I was attracted by the outline of a picture on the wall.

By-and-by the picture seemed to give way: to my bewilderment, it shook, it sunk, it rolled back into nothing; its vanishing left an opening – arched, leading into an arched passage, with a mystic winding stair; both passage and stair were of cold stone, uncarpeted and unpainted. Down this donjon stair descended a tap, tap, like a stick; soon, there fell on the steps a shadow, and last of all, I was aware of a substance.

Yet, was it actual substance, this appearance approaching me? this obstruction, partially darkening the arch?

It drew near, and I saw it well. I began to comprehend where I was. Well might this old square be named quarter of the Magi – well might the three towers, overlooking it, own for godfathers three mystic sages of a dead and dark art. Hoar enchantment here prevailed; a spell had opened for me elf-land – that cell-like room, that vanishing picture, that arch and passage, and stair of stone, were all parts of a fairy tale. Distincter even than these scenic details stood the chief figure – Cunegonde,[201] the sorceress! Malevola, the evil fairy. How was she?

She might be three feet high, but she had no shape; her skinny hands rested upon each other, and pressed the gold knob of a wand-like ivory staff. Her face was large, set, not upon her shoulders, but before her breast; she seemed to have no neck; I should have said there were a hundred years in her features, and more perhaps in her eyes – her malign, unfriendly eyes, with thick gray brows above, and livid lids all round. How severely they viewed me, with a sort of dull displeasure!

This being wore a gown of brocade, dyed bright blue, full-tinted as the gentianella flower, and covered with satin foliage in a large pattern; over the gown a costly shawl, gorgeously bordered, and so large for her, that its many-coloured fringe swept the floor. But her chief points were her jewels: she had long, clear ear-rings, blazing with a lustre which could not be borrowed or false; she had rings on her skeleton hands, with thick gold hoops, and stones – purple, green, and blood-red. Hunchbacked, dwarfish, and doting, she was adorned like a barbarian queen.

'Que me voulez-vous?' said she hoarsely, with the voice rather of male than of female old age; and, indeed, a silver beard bristled her chin.

I delivered my basket and my message.

'Is that all?' she demanded.

'It is all,' said I.

'Truly, it was well worth while,' she answered. 'Return to Madame Beck, and tell her I can buy fruit when I want it, et quant à ses félicitations, je m'en moque!' And this courteous dame turned her back.

Just as she turned, a peal of thunder broke, and a flash of lightning blazed broad over salon and boudoir. The tale of magic seemed to proceed with due accompaniment of the elements. The wanderer, decoyed into the enchanted castle, heard rising, outside, the spell-wakened tempest.

What, in all this, was I to think of Madame Beck? She owned strange acquaintance; she offered messages and gifts at an unique shrine, and inauspicious seemed the bearing of the uncouth thing she worshipped. There went that sullen Sidonia, tottering and trembling like palsy incarnate, tapping her ivory staff on the mosaic parquet, and muttering venomously as she vanished.

Down washed the rain, deep lowered the welkin; the clouds, ruddy a while ago, had now, through all their blackness, turned deadly pale, as if in terror. Notwithstanding my late boast about not fearing a shower, I hardly liked to go out under this water-spout. Then, the gleams of lightning were very fierce, the thunder crashed very near; this storm had gathered immediately above Villette; it seemed to have burst at the zenith; it rushed down prone; the forked, slant bolts pierced athwart vertical torrents; red zig-zags interlaced a descent blanched as white metal: and all broke from a sky heavily black in its swollen abundance.

Leaving Madame Walravens' inhospitable salon, I betook myself to her cold staircase; there was a seat on the landing – there I waited. Somebody came gliding along the gallery just above; it was the old priest.

'Indeed Mademoiselle shall not sit there,' said he. 'It would displease our benefactor if he knew a stranger was so treated in this house.'

And he begged me so earnestly to return to the salon, that, without discourtesy, I could not but comply. The smaller room was better furnished and more habitable than the larger; thither he introduced me. Partially withdrawing the blind, he disclosed what seemed more like an oratory than a boudoir, a very solemn little chamber, looking as if it were a place rather dedicated to relics and remembrance, than designed for present use and comfort.

The good father sat down, as if to keep me company; but instead of conversing, he took out a book, fastened on the page his eyes, and employed his lips in whispering – what sounded like a prayer or litany. A yellow electric light from the sky gilded his bald head; his figure remained in shade – deep and purple; he sat still as sculpture; he seemed to forget me for his prayers; he only looked up when a fiercer bolt, or a harsher, closer rattle told of nearing danger; even then, it was not in fear, but in seeming awe, he raised his eyes. I too was awe-struck; being, however, under no pressure of slavish terror, my thoughts and observations were free.

To speak truth, I was beginning to fancy that the old priest resembled that Père Silas, before whom I had kneeled in the church of the Béguinage. The idea was vague, for I had seen my confessor only in dusk and in profile, yet still I seemed to trace a likeness: I thought also I recognized the voice. While I watched him, he betrayed, by one lifted look, that he felt my scrutiny; I turned to note the room; that too had its half-mystic interest.

Beside a cross of curiously carved old ivory, yellow with time, and sloped above a dark-red *prie-dieu*, furnished duly with rich missal and ebon rosary – hung the picture whose dim outline had drawn my eyes before – the picture which moved, fell away with the wall and let in phantoms. Imperfectly seen, I had taken it for a Madonna; revealed by clearer light, it proved to be a woman's portrait in a nun's dress. The face, though not beautiful, was pleasing; pale, young, and shaded with the dejection of grief or ill health. I say again it was not beautiful; it was not even intellectual; its very amiability was the amiability of a weak frame, inactive passions, acquiescent habits; yet I looked long at that picture, and could not choose but look.

The old priest, who at first had seemed to me so deaf and infirm, must yet have retained his faculties in tolerable preservation; absorbed in his book as he appeared, without once lifting his head, or, as far as I knew, turning his eyes, he perceived the point towards which my attention was drawn, and, in a slow, distinct voice, dropped concerning it, these four observations.

'She was much beloved.

'She gave herself to God.

'She died young.

'She is still remembered, still wept.'

'By that aged lady, Madame Walravens?' I inquired, fancying that I had discovered in the incurable grief of bereavement, a key to that same aged lady's desperate ill-humour.

The father shook his head with half a smile.

'No, no;' said he, 'a grand-dame's affection for her children's children may be great, and her sorrow for their loss, lively; but it is only the affianced lover, to whom Fate, Faith, and Death, have trebly denied the bliss of union, who mourns what he has lost, as Justine Marie is still mourned.'

I thought the father rather wished to be questioned, and therefore I inquired who had lost and who still mourned 'Justine Marie.' I got, in reply, quite a little romantic narrative, told not unimpressively, with the accompaniment of the now subsiding storm. I am bound to say it might have been made much more truly impressive, if there had been less French, Rousseau-like sentimentalizing and wire-drawing; and rather more healthful carelessness of effect. But the worthy father was obviously a Frenchman born and bred (I became more and more persuaded of his resemblance to my confessor) – he was a true son of Rome; when he did lift his eyes, he looked at me out of their corners, with more and sharper subtlety than, one would have thought, could survive the wear and tear of seventy years. Yet, I believe, he was a good old man.

The hero of his tale was some former pupil of his, whom he now called his benefactor, and who, it appears, had loved this pale Justine Marie, the daughter of rich parents, at a time when his own worldly prospects were such as to justify his aspiring to a well-dowered hand. The pupil's father – once a rich banker – had failed, died, and left behind him only debts and destitution. The son was then forbidden to think of Marie – especially that old witch of a grand-dame I had seen, Madame Walravens, opposed the match with all the violence of a temper which deformity made sometimes demoniac. The mild Marie had neither the treachery to be false, nor the force to be quite staunch to her lover; she gave up her first suitor, but, refusing to accept a second with a heavier purse, withdrew to a convent, and there died in her noviciate.

Lasting anguish, it seems, had taken possession of the faithful heart which worshipped her, and the truth of that love and grief had been shown in a manner which touched even me, as I listened.

Some years after Justine Marie's death, ruin had come on her house too; her father, by nominal calling a jeweller, but who also dealt a good deal on the Bourse, had been concerned in some financial transactions which entailed exposure and ruinous fines. He died of grief for the loss, and shame for the infamy. His old hunchbacked mother and his bereaved wife were left pennyless, and might have died too, of want; but their lost daughter's once despised, yet most true-hearted suitor, hearing of the condition of these ladies, came with singular devotedness to the rescue. He took on their insolent pride the revenge of the purest charity – housing, caring for, befriending them, so as no son could have done it more tenderly and efficiently. The mother – on the whole a good woman – died blessing him; the strange, godless, loveless, misanthrope grandmother lived still, entirely supported by this self-sacrificing man. She, who had been the bane of his life, blighting his hope, and awarding him, for love and domestic happiness, long mourning and cheerless solitude, he treated with the respect a good son might offer a kind mother. He had brought her to this house, 'and,' continued the priest, while genuine tears rose to his eyes, 'here, too, he shelters me, his old tutor, and Agnes, a superannuated servant of his father's family. To our sustenance, and to other charities, I know he devotes three parts of his income, keeping only the fourth to provide himself with bread and the most modest accommodations. By this arrangement he has rendered it impossible to himself ever to marry: he has given himself to God and to his angel-bride as much as if he were a priest, like me.'

The father had wiped away his tears before he uttered these last words, and in pronouncing them, he for one instant raised his eyes to mine. I caught that glance, despite its veiled character; the momentary gleam shot a meaning which struck me.

These Romanists are strange beings. Such a one among them – whom you know no more than the last Inca of Peru, or the first Emperor of China – knows you and all your concerns; and has his reasons for saying to you so and so, when you simply thought the communication sprang impromptu from the instant's impulse: his plan in bringing it about that you shall come on such a day, to such a place, under such and such circumstances, when the whole arrangement seems to your crude apprehension the ordinance of chance, or the sequel of exigency. Madame Beck's suddenly recollected message and present, my artless embassy to the Place of the Magi, the old priest, accidentally descending the steps and crossing the square, his interposition on my behalf with the bonne who would have sent me away, his reappearance on the staircase, my introduction to this room, the portrait, the narrative so affably volunteered – all these little incidents, taken as they fell out, seemed each independent of its successor; a handful of loose beads; but threaded through by that quick-shot and crafty glance of a Jesuit-eye, they dropped pendant in a long string, like that rosary on the prie-dieu. Where lay the link of junction, where the little clasp of this monastic necklace? I saw or felt union, but could not yet find the spot, or detect the means of connection.

Perhaps the musing-fit into which I had by this time fallen, appeared somewhat suspicious in its abstraction; he gently interrupted:

'Mademoiselle,' said he, 'I trust you have not far to go through these inundated streets?'

'More than half a league.'

'You live – ?'

'In the Rue Fossette.'

'Not' (with animation), 'not at the pensionnat of Madame Beck?'

'The same.'

'Donc' (clapping his hands), 'donc, vous devez connaître mon noble élève, mon Paul?'[202]

'Monsieur Paul Emanuel, Professor of Literature?'

'He, and none other.'

A brief silence fell. The spring of junction seemed suddenly to have become palpable; I felt it yield to pressure.

'Was it of M. Paul you have been speaking?' I presently inquired. 'Was he your pupil and the benefactor of Madame Walravens?'

'Yes, and of Agnes, the old servant; and moreover' (with a certain emphasis), 'he was and *is* the lover, true, constant and eternal, of that saint in Heaven – Justine Marie.'

'And who, father, are *you*?' I continued; and though I accentuated the question, its utterance was well-nigh superfluous; I was ere this quite prepared for the answer which actually came.

'I, daughter, am Père Silas; that unworthy son of Holy Church whom you once honoured with a noble and touching confidence, showing me the core of a heart, and the inner shrine of a mind whereof, in solemn truth, I coveted the direction, in behalf of the only true faith. Nor have I for a day lost sight of you, nor for an hour failed to take in you a rooted interest. Passed under the discipline of Rome, moulded by her high training, inoculated with her salutary doctrines, inspired by the zeal she alone gives – I realize what then might be your spiritual rank, your practical value; and I envy Heresy her prey.'

This struck me as a special state of things – I half-realized myself in that condition also; passed under discipline, moulded, trained, inoculated, and so on. 'Not so,' thought I, but I restrained deprecation and sat quietly enough.

'I suppose M. Paul does not live here?' I resumed, pursuing a theme which I thought more to the purpose than any wild renegade dreams.

'No; he only comes occasionally to worship his beloved saint, to make his confession to me, and to pay his respects to her he calls his mother. His own lodging consists but of two rooms; he has no servant, and yet he will not suffer Madame Walravens to dispose of those splendid jewels with which you see her adorned, and in which she takes a puerile pride as the ornaments of her youth, and the last relics of her son, the jeweller's wealth.'

'How often,' murmured I to myself, 'has this man, this M. Emanuel, seemed to me to lack magnanimity in trifles, yet how great he is in great things!'

I own I did not reckon amongst the proofs of his greatness, either the act of confession, or the saint-worship.

'How long is it since that lady died?' I inquired, looking at Justine Marie.

'Twenty years. She was somewhat older than M. Emanuel; he was then very young, for he is not now much beyond forty.'

'Does he yet weep her?'

'His heart will weep her always: the essence of Emanuel's nature is – constancy.'

This was said with marked emphasis.

And now the sun broke out pallid and waterish; the rain yet fell, but there was no more tempest; that hot firmament had cloven and poured out its lightnings. A longer delay would scarce leave daylight for my return, so I rose, thanked the father for his hospitality and his tale, was benignantly answered by a 'pax vobiscum,' which I made kindly welcome, because it seemed uttered with a true benevolence; but I liked less the mystic phrase accompanying it:

'Daughter, you *shall* be what you *shall* be!' an oracle that made me shrug my shoulders as soon as I had got outside the door. Few of us know what we are to come to certainly, but for all that had happened yet, I had good hopes of living and dying a sober-minded protestant: there was a hollowness within, and a flourish around 'Holy Church' which tempted me but moderately. I went on my way pondering many things. Whatever Romanism may be, there are good Romanists: this man, Emanuel, seemed of the best; touched with superstition, influenced by priestcraft, yet wondrous for fond faith, for pious devotion, for sacrifice of self, for charity unbounded. It remained to see how Rome, by her agents, handled such qualities; whether she cherished them for their own sake and for God's, or put them out to usury and made booty of the interest.

By the time I reached home, it was sundown. Goton had kindly saved me a portion of dinner, which indeed I needed. She called me into the little cabinet to partake of it, and there Madame Beck soon made her appearance, bringing me a glass of wine.

'Well,' began she, chuckling, 'and what sort of a reception did Madame Walravens give you? Elle est drôle, n'est ce pas?'

I told her what had passed, delivering verbatim the courteous message with which I had been charged.

'Oh la singulière petite bossue!' laughed she: 'Et figurez-vous qu'elle me déteste, parcequ'elle me croit amoureuse de mon cousin Paul; ce petit dévot qui n'ose pas bouger, à moins que son confesseur ne lui donne la permission!²⁰³ Au reste' (she went on), 'if he wanted to marry ever so much – soit moi, soit une autre – he could not do it; he has too large a family already on his hands; Mère Walravens, Père Silas, Dame Agnes, and a whole troop of nameless paupers. There never was a man like him for laying on himself burdens greater than he can bear, voluntarily incurring needless responsibilities. Besides, he harbours a romantic idea about some pale-faced Marie Justine – personnage assez niaise à ce que je pense[204]' (such was Madame's irreverent remark), 'who has been an angel in Heaven, or elsewhere, this score of years, and to whom he means to go, free from all earthly ties, pure comme un lis,[205] à ce qu'il dit. Oh, you would laugh could you but know half M. Emanuel's crotchets and eccentricities! But I hinder you from taking refreshment, ma bonne meess, which you must need; eat your supper, drink your wine, oubliez les anges, les bossues, et surtout, les Professeurs – et bon soir!'[206]

CHAPTER 35

Fraternity

'OUBLIEZ LES PROFESSEURS.' So said Madame Beck. Madame Beck was a wise woman, but she should not have uttered those words. To do so was a mistake. That night she should have left me calm – not excited, indifferent – not interested, isolated in my own estimation and that of others – not connected, even in idea, with this second person whom I was to forget.

Forget him? Ah! they took a sage plan to make me forget him – the wiseheads! They showed me how good he was; they made of my dear little man a stainless little hero. And then they had prated about his manner of loving. What means had I, before this day, of being certain whether he could love at all or not?

I had known him jealous, suspicious; I had seen about him certain tendernesses, fitfulnesses – a softness which came like a warm air, and a ruth which passed like early dew, dried in the heat of his irritabilities: *this* was all I had seen. And they, Père Silas and Modeste Maria Beck (that these two wrought in concert I could not doubt) opened up the adytum of his heart – shewed me one grand love, the child of this southern nature's youth, born so strong and perfect, that it had laughed at Death himself, despised his mean rape of matter, clung to immortal spirit, and, in victory and faith, had watched beside a tomb twenty years.

This had been done – not idly: this was not a mere hollow indulgence of sentiment; he had proven his fidelity by the consecration of his best energies to an unselfish purpose, and attested it by limitless personal sacrifices: for those once dear to her he prized – he had laid down vengeance, and taken up a cross.

Now, as for Justine Marie, I knew what she was as well as if I had seen her. I knew she was well enough; there were girls like her in Madame Beck's school – phlegmatics – pale, slow, inert, but kind-natured, neutral of evil, undistinguished for good.

If she wore angel's wings, I knew whose poet-fancy conferred them. If her forehead shone luminous with the reflex of a halo, I knew in the fire of whose irids that circlet of holy flame had generation.

Was I, then, to be frightened by Justine Marie? Was the picture of a pale dead nun to rise, an eternal barrier? And what of the charities which absorbed his worldly goods? What of his heart, sworn to virginity?

Madame Beck – Père Silas – you should not have suggested these questions. They were at once the deepest puzzle, the strongest obstruction, and the keenest stimulus, I had ever felt. For a week of nights and days I fell asleep – I dreamt, and I woke upon these two questions. In the whole world there was no answer to them, except where one dark little man stood, sat, walked, lectured, under the head-piece of a bandit bonnet-grec, and within the girth of a sorry paletôt, much be-inked, and no little adust.

After that visit to the Rue des Mages, I *did* want to see him again. I felt as if – knowing what I now knew – his countenance would offer a page more lucid, more interesting than ever; I felt a longing to trace in it the imprint of that primitive devotedness, the signs of that half-knightly, half-saintly chivalry which the priest's narrative imputed to his nature. He had become my Christian hero: under that character I wanted to view him.

Nor was opportunity slow to favour: my new impressions underwent her test the next day. Yes: I was granted an interview with my 'Christian hero' – an interview not very heroic, or sentimental, or biblical, but lively enough in its way.

About three o'clock of the afternoon, the peace of the first classe – safely established, as it seemed, under the serene sway of Madame Beck, who, in *propria persona*, was giving one of her orderly and useful lessons – this peace, I say, suffered a sudden fracture by the wild inburst of a paletôt.

Nobody at the moment was quieter than myself. Eased of responsibility by Madame Beck's presence, soothed by her uniform tones, pleased and edified with her clear exposition of the subject in hand (for she taught well), I sat bent over my desk, drawing – that is, copying an elaborate line engraving, tediously working up my copy to the finish of the original, for that was my practical notion of art; and, strange to say, I took extreme pleasure in the labour, and could even produce curiously finical Chinese facsimiles of steel or mezzotint plates – things about as valuable as so many achievements in worsted-work, but I thought pretty well of them in those days.

What was the matter? My drawing, my pencils, my precious copy, gathered into one crushed-up handful, perished from before my sight; I myself appeared to be shaken or emptied out of my chair, as a solitary and withered nutmeg might be emptied out of a spice-box by an excited cook. That chair, and my desk, seized by the wild paletôt, one under each sleeve, were borne afar; in a second, I followed the furniture: in two minutes they and I were fixed in the centre of the grande salle – a vast adjoining room, seldom used save for dancing and choral singing-lessons – fixed with an emphasis which seemed to prohibit the remotest hope of our ever being permitted to stir thence again.

Having partially collected my scared wits, I found myself in the presence of two men – gentlemen, I suppose I should say – one dark, the other light – one having a stiff, half-military air, and wearing a braided surtout; the other partaking, in garb and bearing, more of the careless aspect of the student or artist class: both flourishing in full magnificence of moustaches, whiskers, and imperial. M. Emanuel stood a little apart from these; his countenance and eyes expressed strong choler; he held forth his hand with his tribune gesture.

'Mademoiselle,' said he, 'your business is to prove to these gentlemen that I am no liar. You will answer, to the best of your ability, such questions as they shall put. You will also write on such theme as they shall select. In their eyes, it appears I hold the position of an unprincipled impostor. I write essays; and, with deliberate forgery, sign to them my pupils' names, and boast of them as their work. You will disprove this charge.'

Grand Ciel! Here was the show-trial, so long evaded, come on me like a thunder-clap. These two fine, braided, moustachioed, sneering personages, were none other than dandy professors of the college – Messieurs Boissec and Rochemorte – a pair of cold-blooded fops and pedants, sceptics, and scoffers. It seems that M. Paul had been rashly exhibiting something I had written – something he had never once praised, or even mentioned, in my hearing, and which I deemed forgotten. The essay was not remarkable at all; it only *seemed* remarkable, compared with the average productions of foreign school-girls; in an English establishment it would have passed scarce noticed. Messrs. Boissec and Rochemorte had thought proper to question its genuineness, and insinuate a cheat; I was now to bear my testimony to the truth, and to be put to the torture of their examination.

A memorable scene ensued.

They began with classics. A dead blank. They went on to French history. I hardly knew Mérovée from Pharamond. They tried me in various 'ologies, and still only got a shake of the head, and an unchanging 'Je n'en sais rien.'[207]

After an expressive pause, they proceeded to matters of general information, broaching one or two subjects which I knew pretty well, and on which I had often reflected. M. Emanuel, who had hitherto stood looking on, dark as the winter-solstice, brightened up somewhat; he thought I should now show myself at least no fool.

He learned his error. Though answers to the questions surged up fast, my mind filling like a rising well, ideas were there, but not words. I either *could* not, or *would* not speak – I am not sure which: partly, I think my nerves had got wrong, and partly my humour was crossed.

I heard one of my examiners – he of the braided surtout – whisper to his co-professor: 'Est-elle donc idiote?'

'Yes,' I thought, 'an idiot she is, and always will be, for such as you.'

But I suffered – suffered cruelly; I saw the damps gather on M. Paul's brow, and his eye spoke a passionate yet sad reproach. He would not believe in my total lack of popular cleverness; he thought I *could* be prompt if I *would*.

At last, to relieve him, the professors, and myself, I stammered out:

'Gentlemen, you had better let me go; you will get no good of me; as you say, I am an idiot.'

I wish I could have spoken with calm and dignity, or I wish my sense had sufficed to make me hold my tongue; that traitor tongue tripped, faltered. Beholding the judges cast on M. Emanuel a hard look of triumph, and hearing the distressed tremor of my own voice, out I burst in a fit of choking tears. The emotion was far more of anger than grief; had I been a man and strong, I could have challenged that pair on the spot – but it *was* emotion, and I would rather have been scourged, than betrayed it.

The incapables! Could they not see at once the crude hand of a novice in that composition they called a forgery? The subject was classical. When M. Paul dictated the trait on which the essay was to turn, I heard it for the first time; the matter was new to me, and I had no material for its treatment. But I got books, read up the facts, laboriously constructed a skeleton out of the dry bones of the real, and then clothed them, and tried to breathe into them life, and in this last aim I had pleasure. With me it was a difficult and anxious time till my facts were found, selected, and properly pointed; nor could I rest from research and effort till I was satisfied of correct anatomy; the strength of my inward repugnance to the idea of flaw or falsity sometimes enabled me to shun egregious blunders; but the knowledge was not there in my head, ready and mellow; it had not been sown in Spring, grown in Summer, harvested in Autumn, and garnered through Winter; whatever I wanted I must go out and gather fresh; glean of wild herbs my lap full, and shred them green into the pot. Messieurs Boissec and Rochemorte did not perceive this. They mistook my work for the work of a ripe scholar.

They would not yet let me go: I must sit down and write before them. As I dipped my pen in the ink with a shaking hand, and surveyed the white paper with eyes half-blinded and overflowing, one of my judges began mincingly to apologize for the pain he caused.

'Nous agissons dans l'intêret de la verité. Nous ne voulons pas vous blesser,'[208] said he.

Scorn gave me nerve. I only answered, –

'Dictate, Monsieur.'

Rochemorte named this theme: 'Human Justice.'

Human Justice! What was I to make of it? Blank, cold abstraction, unsuggestive to me of one inspiring idea; and there stood M. Emanuel, sad as Saul, and stern as Joab, and there triumphed his accusers.

At these two I looked. I was gathering my courage to tell them that I would neither write nor speak another word for their satisfaction, that their theme did not suit, nor their presence inspire me, and that, notwithstanding, whoever threw the shadow of a doubt on M. Emanuel's honour, outraged that truth of which they had announced themselves the champions: I *meant* to utter all this, I say, when, suddenly, a light darted on memory.

Those two faces looking out of the forest of long hair, moustache, and whisker – those two cold yet bold, trustless yet presumptuous visages – were the same faces, the very same that, projected in full gas-light from behind the pillars of a portico, had half frightened me to death on the night of my desolate arrival in Villette. These, I felt morally certain, were the very heroes who had driven a friendless foreigner beyond her reckoning and her strength, chased her breathless over a whole quarter of the town.

'Pious mentors!' thought I. 'Pure guides for youth! If "Human Justice" were what she ought to be, you two would scarce hold your present post, or enjoy your present credit.'

An idea once seized, I fell to work. 'Human Justice' rushed before me in novel guise, a red, random beldame with arms akimbo. I saw her in her house, the den of confusion: servants called to her for orders or help which she did not give; beggars stood at her door waiting and starving unnoticed; a swarm of children, sick and quarrelsome, crawled round her feet and yelled in her ears appeals for notice, sympathy, cure, redress. The honest woman cared for none of these things. She had a warm seat of her own by the fire, she had her own solace in a short black pipe, and a bottle of Mrs Sweeny's soothing syrup; she smoked and she sipped and she enjoyed her paradise, and whenever a cry of the suffering souls about her pierced her ears too keenly – my jolly dame seized the poker or the hearth-brush: if the offender was weak, wronged, and sickly, she effectually settled him; if he was strong, lively, and violent, she only menaced, then plunged her hand in her deep pouch, and flung a liberal shower of sugar-plums.

Such was the sketch of 'Human Justice,' scratched hurriedly on paper, and placed at the service of Messrs. Boissec and Rochemorte. M. Emanuel read it over my shoulder. Waiting no comment, I curtsied to the trio, and withdrew.

After school that day, M. Paul and I again met. Of course the meeting did not at first run smooth; there was a crow to pluck with him: that forced examination could not be immediately digested. A crabbed dialogue terminated in my being called, 'une petite moqueuse et sans-coeur,'[209] and in Monsieur's temporary departure.

Not wishing him to go quite away, only desiring he should feel that such a transport as he had that day given way to, could not be indulged with perfect impunity, I was not sorry to see him, soon after, gardening in the berceau. He approached the glass door; I drew near also. We spoke of some flowers growing round it. By-and-by Monsieur laid down his spade; by-and-by he recommenced conversation, passed to other subjects, and at last touched a point of interest.

Conscious that his proceeding of that day was specially open to a charge of extravagance, M. Paul half apologized; he half regretted too the fitfulness of his moods at all times, yet he hinted that some allowance ought to be made for him. 'But,' said he, 'I can hardly expect it at your hands, Miss Lucy; you know neither me, nor my position, nor my history.'

His history. I took up the word at once; I pursued the idea.

'No, monsieur,' I rejoined. 'Of course, as you say, I know neither your history, nor your position, nor your sacrifices, nor any of your sorrows, or trials, or affections, or fidelities. Oh, no! I know nothing about you; you are for me altogether a stranger.'

'Hein?' he murmured, arching his brows in surprise.

'You know, monsieur, I only see you in classe – stern, dogmatic, hasty, imperious. I only hear of you in town as active and wilful, quick to originate, hasty to lead, but slow to persuade, and hard to bend. A man like you, without ties, can have no attachments; without dependents, no duties. All we, with whom you come in contact, are machines, which you thrust here and there, inconsiderate of their feelings. You seek your recreations in public, by the light of the evening chandelier: this school and yonder college are your workshops, where you fabricate the ware called pupils. I don't so much as know where you live; it is natural to take it for granted that you have no home, and need none.'

'I am judged,' said he. 'Your opinion of me is just what I thought it was. For you – I am neither a man nor a Christian. You see me void of affection and religion, unattached by friend or family, unpiloted by principle or faith. It is well, mademoiselle; such is our reward in this life.'

'You are a philosopher, monsieur; a cynic philosopher' (and I looked at his paletôt, of which he straightway brushed the dim sleeve with his hand), 'despising the foibles of humanity – above its luxuries – independent of its comforts.'

'Et vous, mademoiselle; vous êtes proprette et douillette, et affreusement insensible, par-dessus le marché.'[210]

'But, in short, monsieur, now I think of it, you *must* live somewhere? Do tell me where; and what establishment of servants do you keep?'

With a fearful projection of the under lip, implying an impetus of scorn the most decided, he broke out –

'Je vis dans un trou! I inhabit a den, miss – a cavern, where you would not put your dainty nose. Once, with base shame of speaking the whole truth, I talked about my "study" in that college: know now that this "study" is my whole abode; my chamber is there and my drawing-room. As for my "establishment of servants" (mimicking my voice) 'they number ten: les voilà!'

And he grimly spread, close under my eyes, his ten fingers.

'I black my boots,' pursued he, savagely. 'I brush my paletôt – '

'No, monsieur, it is too plain; you never do that,' was my parenthesis.

'Je fais mon lit et mon ménage;[211] I seek my dinner in a restaurant; my supper takes care of itself; I pass days laborious and loveless; nights long and lonely; I am ferocious, and bearded, and monkish; and nothing now living in this world loves me, except some old hearts worn like my own, and some few beings, impoverished, suffering, poor in purse and in spirit, whom the kingdoms of this world own not, but to whom a will and testament not to be disputed, has bequeathed the kingdom of heaven.'

'Ah, monsieur; but I know!'

'What do you know? many things, I verily believe; yet not me, Lucy!'

'I know that you have a pleasant old house in a pleasant old square of the Basse-Ville – why don't you go and live there?'

'Hein?' muttered he again.

'I liked it much, monsieur; with the steps ascending to the door, the gray flags in front, the nodding trees behind – real trees, not shrubs – trees dark, high, and of old growth. And the boudoir-oratoire – you should make that room your study; it is so quiet and solemn.'

He eyed me closely; he half-smiled, half-coloured. 'Where did you pick up all that? Who told you?' he asked.

'Nobody told me. Did I dream it, monsieur, do you think?'

'Can I enter into your visions? Can I guess a woman's waking thoughts, much less her sleeping fantasies?'

'If I dreamt it, I saw in my dream human beings as well as a house. I saw a priest, old, bent, and gray, and a domestic – old, too, and picturesque; and a lady, splendid but strange; her head would scarce reach to my elbow – her magnificence might ransom a duke. She wore a gown bright as lapis-lazuli – a shawl worth a thousand francs: she was decked with ornaments so brilliant, I never saw any with such a beautiful sparkle; but her figure looked as if it had been broken in two and bent double; she seemed also to have outlived the common years of humanity, and to have attained those which are only labour and sorrow. She was become morose – almost malevolent; yet *somebody*, it appears, cared for her in her infirmities – somebody forgave her trespasses, hoping to have his trespasses forgiven. They lived together, these three people – the mistress, the chaplain, the servant – all old, all feeble, all sheltered under one kind wing.'

He covered with his hand the upper part of his face, but did not conceal his mouth, where I saw hovering an expression I liked.

'I see you have entered into my secrets,' said he, 'but how was it done?'

So I told him how – the commission on which I had been sent, the storm which had detained me, the abruptness of the lady, the kindness of the priest. 'As I sat waiting for the rain to cease, Père Silas whiled away the time with a story,' I said.

'A story! What story? Père Silas is no romancist.'

'Shall I tell monsieur the tale?'

'Yes: begin at the beginning. Let me hear some of Miss Lucy's French – her best or her worst – I don't much care which: let us have a good poignée of barbarisms, and a bounteous dose of the insular accent.'

'Monsieur is not going to be gratified by a tale of ambitious proportions, and the spectacle of the narrator sticking fast in the midst. But I will tell him the title – "The Priest's Pupil."'

'Bah!' said he, the swarthy flush again dyeing his dark cheek. 'The good old father could not have chosen a worse subject: it is his weak point. But what of "The Priest's Pupil"?'

'Oh! many things.'

'You may as well at once define *what* things. I mean to know.'

'There was the pupil's youth, the pupil's manhood – his avarice, his ingratitude, his implacability, his inconstancy. Such a bad pupil, monsieur! – so thankless, cold-hearted, unchivalrous, unforgiving!'

'Et puis?' said he, taking a cigar.

'Et puis,' I pursued, 'he underwent calamities which one did not pity – bore them in a spirit one did not admire – endured wrongs for which one felt no sympathy; finally, took the unchristian revenge of heaping coals of fire on his adversary's head.'

'You have not told me all,' said he.

'Nearly all, I think: I have indicated the heads of Père Silas's chapters.'

'You have forgotten one – that which touched on the pupil's lack of affection – on his hard, cold, monkish heart.'

'True; I remember now. Père Silas *did* say that his vocation was almost that of a priest – that his life was considered consecrated.'

'By what bonds or duties?'

'By the ties of the past and the charities of the present.'

'You have, then, the whole situation?'

'I have now told monsieur all that was told me.' Some meditative minutes passed.

'Now, Mademoiselle Lucy, look at me, and with that truth which I believe you never knowingly violate, answer me one question. Raise your eyes; rest them on mine; have no hesitation; fear not to trust me – I am a man to be trusted.'

I raised my eyes.

'Knowing me thoroughly now – all my antecedents, all my responsibilities – having long known my faults, can you and I still be friends?'

'If monsieur wants a friend in me, I shall be glad to have a friend in him.'

'But a close friend I mean – intimate and real – kindred in all but blood? Will Miss Lucy be the sister of a very poor, fettered, burdened, encumbered man?'

I could not answer him in words, yet I suppose I *did* answer him; he took my hand, which found comfort in the shelter of his. *His* friendship was not a doubtful, wavering benefit – a cold, distant hope – a sentiment so brittle as not to bear the weight of a finger: I at once felt (or *thought* I felt) its support like that of some rock.

'When I talk of friendship, I mean *true* friendship,' he repeated emphatically; and I could hardly believe that words so earnest had blessed my ear; I hardly could credit the reality of that kind, anxious look he gave. If he *really* wished for my confidence and regard, and *really* would give me his – why, it seemed to me that life could offer nothing more or better. In that case, I was become strong and rich: in a moment I was made substantially happy. To ascertain the fact, to fix and seal it, I asked –

'Is monsieur quite serious? Does he really think he needs me, and can take an interest in me as a sister?'

'Surely, surely,' said he; 'a lonely man like me, who has no sister, must be but too glad to find in some woman's heart a sister's pure affection.'

'And dare I rely on monsieur's regard? Dare I speak to him when I am so inclined?'

'My little sister must make her own experiments,' said he; 'I will give no promises. She must tease and try her wayward brother till she has drilled him into what she wishes. After all, he is no inductile material in some hands.'

While he spoke, the tone of his voice, the light of his now affectionate eye, gave me such a pleasure as, certainly, I had never felt. I envied no girl her lover, no bride her bridegroom, no wife her husband; I was content with this my voluntary, self-offering friend. If he would but prove reliable, and he *looked* reliable, what, beyond his friendship, could I ever covet? But, if all melted like a dream, as once before had happened – ?

'Qu'est-ce donc? What is it?' said he, as this thought threw its weight on my heart, its shadow on my countenance. I told him; and after a moment's pause, and a thoughtful smile, he showed me how an equal fear – lest I should weary of him, a man of moods so difficult and fitful – had haunted his mind for more than one day, or one month.

On hearing this, a quiet courage cheered me. I ventured a word of re-assurance. That word was not only tolerated; its repetition was courted. I grew quite happy – strangely happy – in making him secure, content, tranquil. Yesterday, I could not have believed that earth held, or life afforded, moments like the few I was now passing. Countless times it had been my lot to watch apprehended sorrow close darkly in; but to see unhoped-for happiness take form, find place, and grow more real as the seconds sped, was indeed a new experience.

'Lucy,' said M. Paul, speaking low and still holding my hand, 'did you see a picture in the boudoir of the old house?'

'I did; a picture painted on a panel.'

'The portrait of a nun?'

'Yes.'

'You heard her history?'

'Yes.'

'You remember what we saw that night in the berceau?'

'I shall never forget it.'

'You did not connect the two ideas; that would be folly?'

'I thought of the apparition when I saw the portrait,' said I; which was true enough.

'You did not, nor will you fancy,' pursued he, 'that a saint in Heaven perturbs herself with rivalries of earth? Protestants are rarely superstitious; these morbid fancies will not beset you?'

'I know not what to think of this matter; but I believe a perfectly natural solution of this seeming mystery will one day be arrived at.'

'Doubtless, doubtless. Besides, no good living woman – much less a pure, happy spirit – would trouble amity like ours – n'est-il pas vrai?'

Ere I could answer, Fifine Beck burst in, rosy and abrupt, calling out that I was wanted. Her mother was going into town to call on some English family, who had applied for a prospectus: my services were needed as interpreter. The interruption was not unseasonable: sufficient for the day is always the evil; for this hour, its good sufficed. Yet I should have liked to ask M. Paul whether the 'morbid fancies,' against which he warned me, wrought in his own brain.

CHAPTER 36

The Apple of Discord

Besides Fifine Beck's mother, another power had a word to say to M. Paul and me, before that covenant of friendship could be ratified. We were under the surveillance of a sleepless eye: Rome watched jealously her son through that mystic lattice at which I had knelt once, and to which M. Emanuel drew nigh month by month – the sliding panel of the confessional.

'Why were you so glad to be friends with M. Paul?' asks the reader. 'Had he not long been a friend to you? Had he not given proof on proof of a certain partiality in his feelings?'

Yes, he had; but still I liked to hear him say so earnestly – that he was my close, true friend; I liked his modest doubts, his tender deference – that trust which longed to rest, and was grateful when taught how. He had called me 'sister.' It was well. Yes; he might call me what he pleased, so long as he confided in me. I was willing to be his sister, on condition that he did not invite me to fill that relation to some future wife of his; and tacitly vowed as he was to celibacy, of this dilemma there seemed little danger.

Through most of the succeeding night, I pondered that evening's interview. I wanted much the morning to break, and then listened for the bell to ring; and, after rising and dressing, I deemed prayers and breakfast slow, and all the hours lingering, till that arrived at last which brought the lesson of literature. My wish was to get a more thorough comprehension of this fraternal alliance: to note with how much of the brother he would demean himself when we met again; to prove how much of the sister was in my own feelings; to discover whether I could summon a sister's courage, and he a brother's frankness.

He came. Life is so constructed, that the event does not, cannot, will not, match the expectation. That whole day he never accosted me. His lesson was given rather more quietly than usual, more mildly, and also more gravely. He was fatherly to his pupils, but he was not brotherly to me. Ere he left the classe, I expected a smile, if not a word; I got neither: to my portion fell one nod – hurried, shy.

This distance, I argued, is accidental – it is involuntary; patience, and it will vanish. It vanished not; it continued for days; it increased. I suppressed my surprise, and swallowed whatever other feelings began to surge.

Well might I ask when he offered fraternity – 'Dare I rely on you?' Well might he, doubtless knowing himself, withhold all pledge. True, he had bid me make my own experiments – tease and try him. Vain injunction! Privilege nominal and unavailable! Some women might use it! Nothing in my powers or instinct placed me amongst this brave band. Left alone, I was passive; repulsed, I withdrew; forgotten – my lips would not utter, nor my eyes dart a reminder. It seemed there had been an error somewhere in my calculations, and I waited for time to disclose it.

But the day came when, as usual, he was to give me a lesson. One evening in seven he had long generously bestowed on me, devoting it to the examination of what had been done in various studies during the past week, and to the preparation of work for the week in prospect. On these occasions my school-room was anywhere, wherever the pupils and the other teachers happened to be, or in their close vicinage, very often in the large second division, where it was easy to choose a quiet nook when the crowding day-pupils were absent, and the few boarders gathered in a knot about the surveillante's estrade.

On the customary evening, hearing the customary hour strike, I collected my books and papers, my pen and ink, and sought the large division.

In classe there was no one, and it lay all in cool deep shadow; but through the open double doors was seen the carré, filled with pupils and with light; over hall and figures blushed the westering sun. It blushed so ruddily and vividly, that the hues of the walls and the variegated tints of the dresses seemed all fused in one warm glow. The girls were seated, working or studying; in the midst of their circle stood M. Emanuel, speaking good-humouredly to a teacher. His dark paletôt, his jetty hair, were tinged with many a reflex of crimson; his Spanish face, when he turned it momentarily, answered the sun's animated kiss with an animated smile. I took my place at a desk.

The orange-trees, and several plants, full and bright with bloom, basked also in the sun's laughing bounty; they had partaken it the whole day, and now asked water. M. Emanuel had a taste for gardening; he liked to tend and foster plants. I used to think that working amongst shrubs with a spade or a watering-pot soothed his nerves; it was a recreation to which he often had recourse; and now he looked to the orange-trees, the geraniums, the gorgeous cactuses, and revived them all with the refreshment their drought needed. His lips meantime sustained his precious cigar, that (for him) first necessary and prime luxury of life; its blue wreaths curled prettily enough amongst the flowers, and in the evening light. He spoke no more to the pupils, nor to the mistresses, but gave many an endearing word to a small spanieless (if one may coin a word), that nominally belonged to the house, but virtually owned him as master, being fonder of him than of any inmate. A delicate, silky, loving, and loveable little doggie she was, trotting at his side, looking with expressive, attached eyes into his face; and whenever he dropped his bonnet-grec or his handkerchief, which he occasionally did in play, crouching beside it with the air of a miniature lion guarding a kingdom's flag.

There were many plants, and as the amateur gardener fetched all the water from the well in the court, with his own active hands, his work spun out to some length. The great school-clock ticked on. Another hour struck. The carré and the youthful group lost the illusion of sunset. Day was drooping. My lesson, I perceived, must to-night be very short; but the orange-trees, the cacti, the camelias were all served now. Was it my turn?

Alas! in the garden were more plants to be looked after, – favourite rose-bushes, certain choice flowers; little Sylvie's glad bark and whine followed the receding paletôt down the alleys. I put up some of my books; I should not want them all; I sat and thought, and waited, involuntarily deprecating the creeping invasion of twilight.

Sylvie, gaily frisking, emerged into view once more, heralding the returning paletôt; the watering-pot was deposited beside the well; it had fulfilled its office; how glad I was! Monsieur washed his hands in a little stone bowl. There was no longer time for a lesson now; ere long the prayer-bell must ring; but still we should meet; he would speak; a chance would be offered of reading in his eyes the riddle of his shyness. His ablutions over, he stood, slowly re-arranging his cuffs, looking at the horn of a young moon, set pale in the opal sky, and glimmering faint on the oriel of Jean Baptiste. Sylvie watched the mood contemplative; its stillness irked her; she whined and jumped to break it. He looked down.

'Petite exigeante!' said he; 'you must not be forgotten one moment, it seems.'

He stooped, lifted her in his arms, sauntered across the court, within a yard of the line of windows near one of which I sat: he sauntered lingeringly, fondling the spaniel in his bosom, calling her tender names in a tender voice. On the front-door steps he turned; once again he looked at the moon, at the gray cathedral, over the remoter spires and house-roofs fading into a blue sea of night-mist; he tasted the sweet breath of dusk, and noted the folded bloom of the garden; he suddenly looked round; a keen beam out of his eye rased the white façade of the classes, swept the long line of croisées. I think he bowed; if he did, I had no time to return the courtesy. In a moment he was gone; the moonlit threshold lay pale and shadowless before the closed front-door.

Gathering in my arms all that was spread on the desk before me, I carried back the unused heap to its place in the third classe. The prayer-bell rang; I obeyed its summons.

The morrow would not restore him to the Rue Fossette, that day being devoted entirely to his college. I got through my teaching; I got over the intermediate hours; I saw evening approaching, and armed myself for its heavy ennuis. Whether it was worse to stay with my co-inmates, or to sit alone, I had not considered; I naturally took up the latter alternative; if there was a hope of comfort for any moment, the heart or head of no human being in this house could yield it; only under the lid of my desk could it harbour, nestling between the leaves of some book, gilding a pencil-point, the nib of a pen, or tinging the black fluid in that ink-glass. With a heavy heart I opened my desk-lid; with a weary hand I turned up its contents.

One by one, well-accustomed books, volumes sewn in familiar covers, were taken out and put back hopeless; they had no charm; they could not comfort. Is this something new, this pamphlet in lilac? I have not seen it before, and I re-arranged my desk this very day – this very afternoon; the tract must have been introduced within the last hour, while we were at dinner.

I opened it. What was it? What would it say to me?

It was neither tale nor poem, neither essay nor history; it neither sung, nor related, nor discussed. It was a theological work; it preached and it persuaded.

I lent to it my ear very willingly, for, small as it was, it possessed its own spell, and bound my attention at once. It preached Romanism; it persuaded to conversion. The voice of that sly little book was a honied voice; its accents were all unction and balm. Here roared no utterance of Rome's thunders, no blasting of the breath of her displeasure. The Protestant was to turn Papist, not so much in fear of the heretic's hell, as on account of the comfort, the indulgence, the tenderness Holy Church offered: far be it from her to threaten or to coerce; her wish was to guide and win. *She* persecute? Oh dear no! not on any account!

This meek volume was not addressed to the hardened and worldly; it was not even strong meat for the strong: it was milk for babes; the mild effluence of a mother's love towards her tenderest and her youngest; intended wholly and solely for those whose head is to be reached through the heart. Its appeal was not to intellect; it sought to win the affectionate through their affections, the sympathizing through their sympathies: St. Vincent de Paul,[212] gathering his orphans about him, never spoke more sweetly.

I remember one capital inducement to apostacy was held out in the fact that a Catholic who had lost dear friends by death could enjoy the unspeakable solace of praying them out of purgatory. The writer did not touch on the firmer peace of those whose belief dispenses with purgatory altogether; but I thought of this, and, on the whole, preferred the latter doctrine as the most consolatory.

The little book amused, and did not painfully displease me. It was a canting, sentimental, shallow little book, yet something about it cheered my gloom and made me smile; I was amused with the gambols of this unlicked wolf-cub muffled in the fleece, and mimicking the bleat of a guileless lamb. Portions of it reminded me of certain Wesleyan Methodist tracts I had once read when a child; they were flavoured with about the same seasoning of excitation to fanaticism. He that had written it was no bad man, and while perpetually betraying the trained cunning – the cloven hoof of his system – I should pause before accusing himself of insincerity. His judgment, however, wanted surgical props; it was ricketty.

I smiled then over this dose of maternal tenderness, coming from the ruddy old lady of the Seven Hills;[213] smiled, too, at my own disinclination, not to say disability, to meet these melting favours. Glancing at the title-page, I found the name of 'Père Silas.' A fly-leaf bore in small, but clear and well-known pencil characters: 'From P. C. D. E. to L– y.' And when I saw this I laughed; but not in my former spirit. I was revived.

A mortal bewilderment cleared suddenly from my head and vision; the solution of the Sphynx-riddle was won; the conjunction of those two names, Père Silas and Paul Emanuel, gave the key to all. The penitent had been with his director; permitted to withhold nothing; suffered to keep no corner of his heart sacred to God and to himself; the whole narrative of our late interview had been drawn from him; he had avowed the covenant of fraternity, and spoken of his adopted sister. How could such covenant, such adoption, be sanctioned by the Church? Fraternal communion with a heretic! I seemed to hear Père Silas annulling the unholy pact; warning his penitent of its perils; entreating, enjoining reserve, nay, by the authority of his office, and in the name, and by the memory of all M. Emanuel held most dear and sacred, commanding the enforcement of that new system whose frost had pierced to the marrow of my bones.

These may not seem pleasant hypotheses; yet, by comparison, they were welcome. The vision of a ghostly troubler hovering in the background, was as nothing, matched with the fear of spontaneous change arising in M. Paul himself.

At this distance of time, I cannot be sure how far the above conjectures were self-suggested: or in what measure they owed their origin and confirmation to another quarter. Help was not wanting.

This evening there was no bright sunset; west and east were one cloud; no summer night-mist, blue, yet rose-tinged, softened the distance; a clammy fog from the marshes crept gray round Villette. To-night the watering-pot might rest in its niche by the well; a small rain had been drizzling all the afternoon, and still it fell fast and quietly. This was no weather for rambling in the wet alleys, under the dripping trees; and I started to hear Sylvie's sudden bark in the garden – her bark of welcome. Surely she was not accompanied; and yet this glad, quick bark was never uttered, save in homage to one presence.

Through the glass-door and the arching berceau, I commanded the deep vista of the allée défendue: thither rushed Sylvie, glistening through its gloom like a white guelder-rose. She ran to and fro, whining, springing, harassing little birds amongst the bushes. I watched five minutes; no fulfilment followed the omen. I returned to my books: Sylvie's sharp bark suddenly ceased. Again I looked up. She was standing not many yards distant, wagging her white, feathery tail as fast as the muscle would work, and intently watching the operations of a spade, plied fast by an indefatigable hand. There was M. Emanuel, bent over the soil, digging in the wet mould amongst the rain-laden and streaming shrubs, working as hard as if his day's pittance were yet to earn by the literal sweat of his brow.

In this sign I read a ruffled mood. He would dig thus in frozen snow on the coldest winter day, when urged inwardly by painful emotion, whether of nervous excitation, or sad thoughts, or self-reproach. He would dig, by the hour, with knit brow and set teeth, nor once lift his head, or open his lips.

THE APPLE OF DISCORD

Sylvie watched till she was tired. Again scampering devious, bounding here, rushing there, snuffing and sniffing everywhere, she at last discovered me in classe. Instantly she flew barking at the panes, as if to urge me forth to share her pleasure or her master's toil; she had seen me occasionally walking in that alley with M. Paul; and I doubt not, considered it my duty to join him now, wet as it was.

She made such a bustle that M. Paul at last looked up, and of course perceived why, and at whom she barked. He whistled to call her off; she only barked the louder. She seemed quite bent upon having the glass-door opened. Tired, I suppose, with her importunity, he threw down his spade, approached, and pushed the door ajar. Sylvie burst in all impetuous, sprang to my lap, and with her paws at my neck, and her little nose and tongue somewhat overpoweringly busy about my face, mouth, and eyes, flourished her bushy tail over the desk, and scattered books and papers far and wide.

M. Emanuel advanced to still the clamour and repair the disarrangement. Having gathered up the books, he captured Sylvie, and stowed her away under his paletôt, where she nestled as quiet as a mouse, her head just peeping forth. She was very tiny, and had the prettiest little innocent face, the silkiest long ears, the finest dark eyes in the world. I never saw her, but I thought of Paulina de Bassompierre: forgive the association, reader, it *would* occur.

M. Paul petted and patted her; the endearments she received were not to be wondered at; she invited affection by her beauty and her vivacious life.

While caressing the spaniel, his eye roved over the papers and books just replaced; it settled on the religious tract. His lips moved; he half-checked the impulse to speak. What! had he promised never to address me more? If so, his better nature pronounced the vow 'more honoured in the breach than in the observance,' for with a second effort, he spoke: –

'You have not yet read the brochure, I presume? It is not sufficiently inviting?'

I replied that I had read it.

He waited, as if wishing me to give an opinion upon it unasked. Unasked, however, I was in no mood to do or say anything. If any concessions were to be made – if any advances were demanded – that was the affair of the very docile pupil of Père Silas, not mine. His eye settled upon me gently; there was mildness at the moment in its blue ray – there was solicitude – a shade of pathos; there were meanings composite and contrasted – reproach melting into remorse. At the moment, probably, he would have been glad to see something emotional in me. I could not show it. In another minute, however, I should have betrayed confusion, had I not bethought myself to take some quill-pens from my desk, and begin soberly to mend them.

I knew that action would give a turn to his mood. He never liked to see me mend pens; my knife was always dull-edged – my hand, too, was unskilful; I hacked and chipped. On this occasion I cut my own finger – half on purpose. I wanted to restore him to his natural state, to set him at his ease, to get him to chide.

'Maladroite!' he cried at last, 'she will make mincemeat of her hands.'

He put Sylvie down, making her lie quiet beside his bonnet-grec, and, depriving me of the pens and penknife, he proceeded to slice, nib, and point with the accuracy and celerity of a machine.

'Did I like the little book?' he now inquired.

Suppressing a yawn, I said I hardly knew.

'Had it moved me?'

'I thought it had made me a little sleepy.'

(After a pause) 'Allons donc! It was of no use taking that tone with him. Bad as I was – and he should be sorry to have to name all my faults at a breath – God and nature had given me "trop de sensibilité et de sympathie"[214] not to be profoundly affected by an appeal so touching.'

'Indeed!' I responded, rousing myself quickly, 'I was not affected at all – not a whit.'

And in proof, I drew from my pocket a perfectly dry handkerchief, still clean and in its folds.

Hereupon I was made the object of a string of strictures rather piquant than polite. I listened with zest. After those two days of unnatural silence, it was better than music to hear M. Paul haranguing again just in his old fashion. I listened, and meantime solaced myself and Sylvie with the contents of a bonbonnière, which M. Emanuel's gifts kept well supplied with chocolate comfits. It pleased him to see even a small matter from his hand duly appreciated. He looked at me and the spaniel while we shared the spoil; he put up his penknife. Touching my hand with the bundle of new-cut quills, he said: –

'Dites-donc, petite soeur – speak frankly – what have you thought of me during the last two days?'

But of this question I would take no manner of notice; its purport made my eyes fill. I caressed Sylvie assiduously. M. Paul, leaning over the desk, bent towards us: –

'I called myself your brother,' he said; 'I hardly know what I am – brother – friend – I cannot tell. I know I think of you – I feel I wish you well – but I must check myself; you are to be feared. My best friends point out danger, and whisper caution.'

'You do right to listen to your friends. By all means be cautious.'

'It is your religion – your strange, self-reliant, invulnerable creed, whose influence seems to clothe you in, I know not what unblessed panoply. You are good – Père Silas calls you good, and loves you – but your terrible, proud, earnest Protestantism, there is the danger. It expresses itself by your eye at times; and again, it gives you certain tones and certain gestures that make my flesh creep. You are not demonstrative, and yet, just now – when you handled that tract – my God! I thought Lucifer smiled.'

'Certainly I don't respect that tract – what then?'

'Not respect that tract? But it is the pure essence of faith, love, charity! I thought it would touch you: in its gentleness, I trusted that it could not fail. I laid it in your desk with a prayer. I must indeed be a sinner: Heaven will not hear the petitions that come warmest from my heart. You scorn my little offering. Oh, cela me fait mal!'

'Monsieur, I don't scorn it – at least, not as your gift. Monsieur, sit down; listen to me. I am not a heathen, I am not hard-hearted, I am not unchristian, I am not dangerous, as they tell you; I would not trouble your faith; you believe in God and Christ and the Bible, and so do I.'

'But *do* you believe in the Bible? Do you receive Revelation? What limits are there to the wild, careless daring of your country and sect? Père Silas dropped dark hints.'

By dint of persuasion, I made him half-define these hints; they amounted to crafty Jesuit-slanders. That night M. Paul and I talked seriously and closely. He pleaded, he argued. *I* could not argue – a fortunate incapacity; it needed but triumphant, logical opposition to effect all the director wished to be effected; but I could talk in my own way – the way M. Paul was used to – and of which he could follow the meanderings and fill the hiatus, and pardon the strange stammerings, strange to him no longer. At ease with him, I could defend my creed and faith in my own fashion; in some degree I could lull his prejudices. He was not satisfied when he went away, hardly was he appeased; but he was made thoroughly to feel that Protestants were not necessarily the irreverent Pagans his director had insinuated; he was made to comprehend something of their mode of honouring the Light, the Life, the Word; he was enabled

partly to perceive that, while their veneration for things venerable
was not quite like that cultivated in his Church, it had its own,
perhaps, deeper power – its own more solemn awe.

I found that Père Silas (himself, I must repeat, not a bad man,
though the advocate of a bad cause) had darkly stigmatized
Protestants in general, and myself by inference, with strange names,
had ascribed to us strange 'isms;' Monsieur Emanuel revealed all this
in his frank fashion, which knew not secretiveness, looking at me as
he spoke with a kind, earnest fear, almost trembling lest there should
be truth in the charges. Père Silas, it seems, had closely watched me,
had ascertained that I went by turns, and indiscriminately, to the
three Protestant Chapels of Villette – the French, German, and
English – *id est*, the Presbyterian, Lutheran, Episcopalian. Such
liberality argued in the Father's eyes profound indifference – who
tolerates all, he reasoned, can be attached to none. Now, it happened
that I had often secretly wondered at the minute and unimportant
character of the differences between these three sects – at the unity
and identity of their vital doctrines: I saw nothing to hinder them
from being one day fused into one grand Holy Alliance, and I
respected them all, though I thought that in each there were faults of
form, incumbrances, and trivialities. Just what I thought, that did I
tell M. Emanuel, and explained to him that my own last appeal, the
guide to which I looked, and the teacher which I owned, must always
be the Bible itself, rather than any sect, of whatever name or nation.

He left me soothed, yet full of solicitude, breathing a wish, as
strong as a prayer, that if I were wrong, Heaven would lead me
right. I heard, poured forth on the threshold, some fervid
murmurings to 'Marie, Reine du Ciel,' some deep aspiration that *his*
hope might yet be *mine*.

Strange! I had no such feverish wish to turn him from the faith of his
fathers. I thought Romanism wrong, a great mixed image of gold and
clay; but it seemed to me that *this* Romanist held the purer elements of
his creed with an innocency of heart which God must love.

The preceding conversation passed between eight and nine
o'clock of the evening, in a school-room of the quiet Rue Fossette,
opening on a sequestered garden. Probably about the same, or a
somewhat later hour of the succeeding evening, its echoes, collected
by holy obedience, were breathed verbatim in an attent ear, at the
panel of a confessional, in the hoary church of the Magi. It ensued
that Père Silas paid a visit to Madame Beck, and stirred by I know
not what mixture of motives, persuaded her to let him undertake for
a time the heretic Englishwoman's spiritual direction.

Hereupon I was put through a course of reading – that is, I just glanced at the books lent me; they were too little in my way to be thoroughly read, marked, learned, or inwardly digested. And besides, I had a book up-stairs, under my pillow, whereof certain chapters satisfied my needs in the article of spiritual lore, furnishing such precept and example as, to my heart's core, I was convinced could not be improved on.

Then Père Silas showed me the fair side of Rome, her good works, and bade me judge the tree by its fruits.

In answer, I felt and I avowed that these works were *not* the fruits of Rome; they were but her abundant blossoming, but the fair promise she showed the world. That bloom, when set, savoured not of charity; the apple full-formed was ignorance, abasement, and bigotry. Out of men's afflictions and affections were forged the rivets of their servitude. Poverty was fed and clothed, and sheltered, to bind it by obligation to 'the Church;' orphanage was reared and educated that it might grow up in the fold of 'the Church;' sickness was tended that it might die after the formula and in the ordinance of 'the Church;' and men were over-wrought, and women most murderously sacrificed, and all laid down a world God made pleasant for his creatures' good, and took up a cross, monstrous in its galling weight, that they might serve Rome, prove her sanctity, confirm her power, and spread the reign of her tyrant 'Church.'

For man's good was little done; for God's glory less. A thousand ways were opened with pain, with blood-sweats, with lavishing of life; mountains were cloven through their breasts, and rocks were split to their base; and all for what? That a Priesthood might march straight on and straight upward to an all-dominating eminence, whence they might at last stretch the sceptre of their Moloch 'Church.'

It will not be. God is not with Rome, and, were human sorrows still for the Son of God, would he not mourn over her cruelties and ambitions, as once he mourned over the crimes and woes of doomed Jerusalem!

Oh, lovers of power! Oh, mitred aspirants for this world's kingdoms! an hour will come, even to you, when it will be well for your hearts – pausing faint at each broken beat – that there is a Mercy beyond human compassions, a Love stronger than this strong death which even you must face, and before it, fall; a Charity more potent than any sin, even yours; a Pity which redeems worlds – nay, absolves Priests.

My third temptation was held out in the pomp of Rome, the glory of her kingdom. I was taken to the churches on solemn occasions – days of fête and state; I was shown the Papal ritual and ceremonial. I looked at it.

Many people – men and women – no doubt far my superiors in a thousand ways, have felt this display impressive, have declared that though their Reason protested, their Imagination was subjugated. I cannot say the same. Neither full procession, nor high mass, nor swarming tapers, nor swinging censers, nor ecclesiastical millinery, nor celestial jewellery, touched my imagination a whit. What I saw struck me as tawdry, not grand; as grossly material, not poetically spiritual.

This I did not tell Père Silas; he was old, he looked venerable, through every abortive experiment, under every repeated disappointment, he remained personally kind to me, and I felt tender of hurting his feelings. But on the evening of a certain day when, from the balcony of a great house, I had been made to witness a huge mingled procession of the church and the army – priests with relics, and soldiers with weapons, an obese and aged archbishop, habited in cambric and lace, looking strangely like a gray daw in bird-of-paradise plumage, and a band of young girls fantastically robed and garlanded – *then* I spoke my mind to M. Paul.

'I did not like it,' I told him, 'I did not respect such ceremonies; I wished to see no more.'

And having relieved my conscience by this declaration, I was able to go on, and, speaking more currently and clearly than my wont, to show him that I had a mind to keep to my reformed creed; that the more I saw of Popery the closer I clung to Protestantism; doubtless there were errors in every Church, but I now perceived by contrast how severely pure was my own, compared with her whose painted and meretricious face had been unveiled for my admiration. I told him how we kept fewer forms between us and God; retaining, indeed, no more than, perhaps, the nature of mankind in the mass rendered necessary for due observance. I told him I could not look on flowers and tinsel, on wax-lights and embroidery, at such times and under such circumstances as should be devoted to lifting the secret vision to Him whose home is Infinity, and his being – Eternity. That when I thought of sin and sorrow, of earthly corruption, mortal depravity, weighty temporal woe – I could not care for chanting priests or murmuring officials; that when the pains of existence and the terrors of dissolution pressed before me – when the mighty hope and measureless doubt of the future arose in view – *then*, even the scientific strain, or the prayer in a language learned and dead, harassed with hindrance a heart which only longed to cry –

'God be merciful to me, a sinner!'

When I had so spoken, so declared my faith, and so widely severed myself from him I addressed – then, at last, came a tone accordant, an echo responsive, one sweet chord of harmony in two conflicting spirits.

'Whatever say priests or controversialists,' murmured M. Emanuel, 'God is good, and loves all the sincere. Believe, then, what you can; believe it as you can; one prayer, at least, we have in common; I also cry – "O Dieu, sois appaisé envers moi qui suis pécheur!"'

He leaned on the back of my chair. After some thought he again spoke:

'How seem in the eyes of that God who made all firmaments, from whose nostrils issued whatever of life is here, or in the stars shining yonder – how seem the differences of man? But as Time is not for God, nor Space, so neither is Measure, nor Comparison. We abase ourselves in our littleness, and we do right; yet it may be that the constancy of one heart, the truth and faith of one mind according to the light He has appointed, import as much to Him as the just motion of satellites about their planets, of planets about their suns, of suns around that mighty unseen centre incomprehensible, irrealizable, with strange mental effort only divined.

'God guide us all! God bless you, Lucy!'

CHAPTER 37

Sunshine

IT WAS VERY WELL FOR PAULINA to decline further correspondence with Graham till her father had sanctioned the intercourse, but Dr Bretton could not live within a league of the Hôtel Crécy, and not contrive to visit there often. Both lovers meant at first, I believe, to be distant; they kept their intention so far as demonstrative courtship went, but in feeling they soon drew very near.

All that was best in Graham sought Paulina; whatever in him was noble, awoke, and grew in her presence. With his past admiration of Miss Fanshawe, I suppose his intellect had little to do, but his whole intellect, and his highest tastes, came in question now. These, like all his faculties, were active, eager for nutriment, and alive to gratification when it came.

I cannot say that Paulina designedly led him to talk of books, or formally proposed to herself for a moment the task of winning him to reflection, or planned the improvement of his mind, or so much as fancied his mind could in any one respect be improved. She thought him very perfect; it was Graham himself, who, at first by the merest chance, mentioned some book he had been reading, and when in her response, sounded a welcome harmony of sympathies, something pleasant to his soul, he talked on, more and better perhaps than he had ever talked before on such subjects. She listened with delight, and answered with animation. In each successive answer, Graham heard a music waxing finer and finer to his sense; in each he found a suggestive, persuasive, magic accent that opened a scarce known treasure-house within, showed him unsuspected power in his own mind, and what was better, latent goodness in his heart. Each liked the way in which the other talked; the voice, the diction, the expression pleased; each keenly relished the flavour of the other's wit; they met each other's meaning with strange quickness, their thoughts often matched like carefully-chosen pearls. Graham had a wealth of mirth by nature; Paulina possessed no such inherent flow of animal spirits – unstimulated, she inclined to be thoughtful and pensive – but now she seemed merry as a lark; in her lover's genial presence, she glanced like some soft glad light. How beautiful she grew in her happiness, I can hardly express, but I wondered to see her. As to that gentle ice of hers – that reserve on which she had depended; where was it now? Ah! Graham would not long bear it; he brought with him a generous influence that soon thawed the timid, self-imposed restriction.

Now were the old Bretton days talked over; perhaps brokenly at first, with a sort of smiling diffidence, then with opening candour and still growing confidence. Graham had made for himself a better opportunity than that he had wished me to give; he had earned independence of the collateral help that disobliging Lucy had refused; all his reminiscences of 'little Polly' found their proper expression in his own pleasant tones, by his own kind and handsome lips – how much better than if suggested by me.

More than once when we were alone, Paulina would tell me how wonderful and curious it was to discover the richness and accuracy of his memory in this matter. How, while he was looking at her, recollections would seem to be suddenly quickened in his mind. He reminded her that she had once gathered his head in her arms, caressed his leonine graces, and cried out, 'Graham, I *do* like you!' He told her how she would set a foot-stool beside him, and climb by its aid to his knee. At this day he said he could recall the sensation of her little hands smoothing his cheek, or burying themselves in his thick mane. He remembered the touch of her small forefinger, placed half tremblingly, half curiously, in the cleft in his chin, the lisp, the look with which she would name it 'a pretty dimple,' then seek his eyes and question why they pierced so, telling him he had a 'nice, strange face; far nicer, far stranger, than either his mama or Lucy Snowe.'

'Child as I was,' remarked Paulina, 'I wonder how I dared be so venturous. To me he seems now all sacred, his locks are inaccessible, and, Lucy, I feel a sort of fear when I look at his firm, marble chin, at his straight Greek features. Women are called beautiful, Lucy; he is not like a woman, therefore I suppose he is not beautiful, but what is he then? Do other people see him with my eyes? Do *you* admire him?'

'I'll tell you what I do, Paulina,' was once my answer to her many questions. '*I never see him*. I looked at him twice or thrice about a year ago, before he recognized me, and then I shut my eyes; and if he were to cross their balls twelve times between each day's sunset and sunrise, except from memory, I should hardly know what shape had gone by.'

'Lucy, what do you mean?' said she, under her breath.

'I mean that I value vision, and dread being struck stone blind.' It was best to answer her strongly at once, and to silence for ever the tender, passionate confidences which left her lips, sweet honey, and sometimes dropped in my ear – molten lead. To me, she commented no more on her lover's beauty.

Yet speak of him she would; sometimes shyly in quiet, brief phrases; sometimes with a tenderness of cadence, and music of voice exquisite in itself, but which chafed me at times miserably; and then, I know, I gave her stern looks and words; but cloudless happiness had dazzled her native clear sight, and she only thought Lucy – fitful.

'Spartan girl! Proud Lucy!' she would say, smiling at me. 'Graham says you are the most peculiar, capricious little woman he knows; but yet you are excellent; we both think so.'

'You both think you know not what,' said I. 'Have the goodness to make me as little the subject of your mutual talk and thoughts as possible. I have my sort of life apart from yours.'

'But ours, Lucy, is a beautiful life, or it will be; and you shall share it.'

'I shall share no man's or woman's life in this world, as you understand sharing. I think I have one friend of my own, but am not sure; and till I *am* sure, I live solitary.'

'But solitude is sadness.'

'Yes; it is sadness. Life, however, has worse than that. Deeper than melancholy, lies heartbreak.'

'Lucy, I wonder if anybody will ever comprehend you altogether.'

There is, in lovers, a certain infatuation of egotism; they will have a witness of their happiness, cost that witness what it may. Paulina had forbidden letters, yet Dr Bretton wrote; she had resolved against correspondence, yet she answered, were it only to chide. She showed me these letters; with something of the spoiled child's wilfulness, and of the heiress's imperiousness, she *made* me read them. As I read Graham's, I scarce wondered at her exaction, and understood her pride: they were fine letters – manly and fond – modest and gallant. Hers must have appeared to him beautiful. They had not been written to show her talents; still less, I think, to express her love. On the contrary, it appeared that she had proposed to herself the task of hiding that feeling, and bridling her lover's ardour. But how could such letters serve such a purpose? Graham was become dear as her life; he drew her like a powerful magnet. For her there was influence unspeakable in all he uttered, wrote, thought, or looked. With this unconfessed confession, her letters glowed; it kindled them, from greeting to adieu.

'I wish papa knew; I *do* wish papa knew!' began now to be her anxious murmur. 'I wish, and yet I fear. I can hardly keep Graham back from telling him. There is nothing I long for more than to have this affair settled – to speak out candidly; and yet I dread the crisis. I know, I am certain, papa will be angry at the first; I fear he will dislike me almost; it will seem to him an untoward business; it will be a surprise, a shock; I can hardly foresee its whole effect on him.'

The fact was – her father, long calm, was beginning to be a little stirred: long blind on one point, an importunate light was beginning to trespass on his eye.

To *her*, he said nothing; but when she was not looking at, or perhaps thinking of him, I saw him gaze and meditate on her.

One evening – Paulina was in her dressing-room, writing, I believe, to Graham; she had left me in the library, reading – M. de Bassompierre came in; he sat down: I was about to withdraw; he requested me to remain – gently, yet in a manner which showed he wished compliance. He had taken his seat near the window, at a distance from me; he opened a desk; he took from it what looked like a memorandum-book; of this book he studied a certain entry for several minutes.

'Miss Snowe,' said he, laying it down, 'do you know my little girl's age?'

'About eighteen, is it not, sir?'

'It seems so. This old pocket-book tells me she was born on the 5th of May, in the year 18 – , eighteen years ago. It is strange; I had lost the just reckoning of her age. I thought of her as twelve – fourteen – an indefinite date; but she seemed a child.'

'She is about eighteen,' I repeated. 'She is grown up; she will be no taller.'

'My little jewel!' said M. de Bassompierre, in a tone which penetrated like some of his daughter's accents.

He sat very thoughtful.

'Sir, don't grieve,' I said; for I knew his feelings, utterly unspoken as they were.

'She is the only pearl I have,' he said; 'and now others will find out that she is pure and of price; they will covet her.'

I made no answer. Graham Bretton had dined with us that day; he had shone both in converse and looks: I know not what pride of bloom embellished his aspect and mellowed his intercourse. Under the stimulus of a high hope, something had unfolded in his whole manner which compelled attention. I think he had purposed on that day to indicate the origin of his endeavours, and the aim of his ambition. M. de Bassompierre had found himself forced, in a manner, to descry the direction and catch the character of his homage. Slow in remarking, he was logical in reasoning; having once seized the thread, it had guided him through a long labyrinth.

'Where is she?' he asked.

'She is up-stairs.'

'What is she doing?'

'She is writing.'

'She writes, does she? Does she receive letters?'

'None but such as she can show me. And – sir – she – *they* have long wanted to consult you.'

'Pshaw! They don't think of me – an old father! I am in the way.'

'Ah, M. de Bassompierre – not so – that can't be! But Paulina must speak for herself; and Dr Bretton, too, must be his own advocate.'

'It is a little late. Matters are advanced, it seems.'

'Sir, till you approve, nothing is done – only they love each other.'

'Only!' he echoed.

Invested by fate with the part of confidante and mediator, I was obliged to go on: –

'Hundreds of times has Dr Bretton been on the point of appealing to you, sir; but, with all his high courage, he fears you mortally.'

'He may well – he may well fear me. He has touched the best thing I have. Had he but let her alone, she would have remained a child for years yet. So. Are they engaged?'

'They could not become engaged without your permission.'

'It is well for you, Miss Snowe, to talk and think with that propriety which always characterizes you; but this matter is a grief to me; my little girl was all I had; I have no more daughters and no son; Bretton might as well have looked elsewhere; there are scores of rich and pretty women who would not, I daresay, dislike him; he has looks, and conduct, and connection. Would nothing serve him but my Polly?'

'If he had never seen your "Polly," others might and would have pleased him – your niece, Miss Fanshawe, for instance.'

'Ah! I would have given him Ginevra with all my heart; but Polly! – I can't let him have her. No – I can't. He is not her equal,' he affirmed, rather gruffly. 'In what particular is he her match? They talk of fortune! I am not an avaricious or interested man, but the world thinks of these things – and Polly will be rich.'

'Yes, that is known,' said I: 'all Villette knows her as an heiress.'

'Do they talk of my little girl in that light?'

'They do, sir.'

He fell into deep thought. I ventured to say: –

'Would you, sir, think any one Paulina's match? Would you prefer any other to Dr Bretton? Do you think higher rank or more wealth would make much difference in your feelings towards a future son-in-law?'

'You touch me there,' said he.

'Look at the aristocracy of Villette – you would not like them, sir?'

'I should not – never a duc, baron, or vicomte of the lot.'

'I am told many of these persons think about her, sir,' I went on, gaining courage on finding that I met attention rather than repulse. 'Other suitors will come, therefore, if Dr Bretton is refused. Wherever you go, I suppose, aspirants will not be wanting. Independent of heiress-ship, it appears to me that Paulina charms most of those who see her.'

'Does she? How? My little girl is not thought a beauty.'

'Sir, Miss de Bassompierre is very beautiful.'

'Nonsense! – begging your pardon, Miss Snowe, but I think you are too partial. I like Polly: I like all her ways and all her looks – but then I am her father; and even I never thought about beauty. She is amusing, fairy-like, interesting to me; – you must be mistaken in supposing her handsome?'

'She attracts, sir: she would attract without the advantages of your wealth and position.'

'My wealth and position! Are these any bait to Graham? If I thought so – '

'Dr Bretton knows these points perfectly, as you may be sure, M. de Bassompierre, and values them as any gentleman would – as *you* would yourself, under the same circumstances – but they are not his baits. He loves your daughter very much; he feels her finest qualities, and they influence him worthily.'

'What! has my little pet "fine qualities?" '

'Ah, sir! did you observe her that evening when so many men of eminence and learning dined here?'

'I certainly was rather struck and surprised with her manner that day; its womanliness made me smile.'

'And did you see those accomplished Frenchmen gather round her in the drawing-room?'

'I did; but I thought it was by way of relaxation – as one might amuse one's self with a pretty infant.'

'Sir, she demeaned herself with distinction; and I heard the French gentlemen say she was "pétrie d'esprit et de graces." Dr Bretton thought the same.'

'She is a good, dear child, that is certain; and I *do* believe she has some character. When I think of it, I was once ill; Polly nursed me; they thought I should die; she, I recollect, grew at once stronger and tenderer as I grew worse in health. And as I recovered, what a sunbeam she was in my sick-room! Yes; she played about my chair as noiseless and as cheerful as light. And now she is sought in marriage! I don't want to part with her,' said he, and he groaned.

'You have known Dr and Mrs Bretton so long,' I suggested, 'it would be less like separation to give her to him than to another.'

He reflected rather gloomily.

'True. I have long known Louisa Bretton,' he murmured. 'She and I are indeed old, old friends: a sweet, kind girl she was when she was young. You talk of beauty, Miss Snowe! *she* was handsome, if you will – tall, straight, and blooming – not the mere child or elf my Polly seems to me: at eighteen, Louisa had a carriage and stature fit for a princess. She is a comely and a good woman now. The lad is like her; I have always thought so, and favoured and wished him well. Now he repays me by this robbery! My little treasure used to love her old father dearly and truly. It is all over now, doubtless – I am an incumbrance.'

The door opened – his 'little treasure' came in. She was dressed, so to speak, in evening beauty; that animation which sometimes comes with the close of day, warmed her eye and cheek; a tinge of summer crimson heightened her complexion; her curls fell full and long on her lily neck; her white dress suited the heat of June. Thinking me alone, she had brought in her hand the letter just written – brought it folded but unsealed. I was to read it. When she saw her father, her tripping step faltered a little, paused a moment – the colour in her cheek flowed rosy over her whole face.

'Polly,' said M. de Bassompierre, in a low voice, with a grave smile, 'do you blush at seeing papa? That is something new.'

'I don't blush – I never *do* blush,' affirmed she, while another eddy from the heart sent up its scarlet. 'But I thought you were in the dining-room, and I wanted Lucy.'

'You thought I was with John Graham Bretton, I suppose? But he has just been called out: he will be back soon, Polly. He can post your letter for you; it will save Matthieu a "course," as he calls it.'

'I don't post letters,' said she, rather pettishly.

'What do you do with them, then? – come here and tell me.'

Both her mind and gesture seemed to hesitate a second – to say 'Shall I come?' – but she approached.

'How long is it since you became a letter-writer, Polly? It only seems yesterday when you were at your pot-hooks, labouring away absolutely with both hands at the pen.'

'Papa, they are not letters to send to the post in your letter-bag; they are only notes, which I give now and then into the person's hand, just to satisfy.'

'The person! That means Miss Snowe, I suppose?'

'No, papa – not Lucy.'

'Who then? Perhaps Mrs Bretton?'

'No, papa – not Mrs Bretton.'

'Who then, my little daughter? Tell papa the truth.'

'Oh, papa!' she cried with earnestness, 'I will – I *will* tell you the truth – all the truth; I am glad to tell you – glad, though I tremble.'

She *did* tremble: growing excitement, kindling feeling, and also gathering courage, shook her.

'I hate to hide my actions from you, papa. I fear you and love you above everything but God. Read the letter; look at the address.'

She laid it on his knee. He took it up and read it through; his hand shaking, his eyes glistening meantime.

He re-folded it, and viewed the writer with a strange, tender, mournful amaze.

'Can *she* write so – the little thing that stood at my knee but yesterday? Can she feel so?'

'Papa, is it wrong? Does it pain you?'

'There is nothing wrong in it, my innocent little Mary; but it pains me.'

'But, papa, listen! You shall not be pained by me. I would give up everything – almost' (correcting herself): 'I would die rather than make you unhappy; that would be too wicked!'

She shuddered.

'Does the letter not please you? Must it not go? Must it be torn? It shall, for your sake, if you order it.'

'I order nothing.'

'Order something, papa; express your wish; only don't hurt, don't grieve Graham. I cannot, *cannot* bear that. I love you, papa; but I love Graham too, because – because – it is impossible to help it.'

'This splendid Graham is a young scamp, Polly – that is my present notion of him: it will surprise you to hear that, for my part, I do not love him one whit. Ah! years ago I saw something in that lad's eye I never quite fathomed – something his mother had not – a

depth which warned a man not to wade into that stream too far;
now, suddenly, I find myself taken over the crown of the head.'

'Papa, you don't – you have not fallen in; you are safe on the
bank; you can do as you please; your power is despotic; you can
shut me up in a convent, and break Graham's heart to-morrow, if
you choose to be so cruel. Now autocrat, now czar, will you do
this?'

'Off with him to Siberia, red whiskers and all; I say, I don't like
him, Polly, and I wonder that you should.'

'Papa,' said she, 'do you know you are very naughty? I never saw
you look so disagreeable, so unjust, so almost vindictive before.
There is an expression in your face which does not belong to you.'

'Off with him!' pursued Mr Home, who certainly did look sorely
crossed and annoyed – even a little bitter; 'but, I suppose, if he
went, Polly would pack a bundle and run after him; her heart is
fairly won – won, and weaned from her old father.'

'Papa, I say it is naughty, it is decidedly wrong, to talk in that
way. I am *not* weaned from you, and no human being and no mortal
influence *can* wean me.'

'Be married, Polly! Espouse the red whiskers. Cease to be a
daughter; go and be a wife!'

'Red whiskers! I wonder what you mean, papa. You should take
care of prejudice. You sometimes say to me that all the Scotch, your
countrymen, are the victims of prejudice. It is proved now, I think,
when no distinction is to be made between red and deep nut-
brown.'

'Leave the prejudiced old Scotchman; go away.'

She stood looking at him a minute. She wanted to show firmness,
superiority to taunts; knowing her father's character, guessing his
few foibles, she had expected the sort of scene which was now
transpiring; it did not take her by surprise, and she desired to let it
pass with dignity, reliant upon reaction. Her dignity stood her in no
stead. Suddenly her soul melted in her eyes; she fell on his neck: –

'I won't leave you, papa; I'll never leave you. I won't pain you; I'll
never pain you!' was her cry.

'My lamb! my treasure!' murmured the loving though rugged
sire. He said no more for the moment; indeed, those two words
were hoarse.

The room was now darkening; I heard a movement, a step
without. Thinking it might be a servant coming with candles, I
gently opened, to prevent intrusion. In the ante-room stood no
servant; a tall gentleman was placing his hat on the table, drawing

off his gloves slowly – lingering, waiting, it seemed to me. He called me neither by sign nor word; yet his eye said: –

'Lucy, come here.' And I went.

Over his face a smile flowed, while he looked down on me: no temper, save his own, would have expressed by a smile the sort of agitation which now fevered him.

'Mr de Bassompierre is there – is he not?' he inquired, pointing to the library.

'Yes.'

'He noticed me at dinner? He understood me?'

'Yes, Graham.'

'I am brought up for judgment, then, and so is *she*?'

'Mr Home' (we now and always continued to term him Mr Home at times) 'is talking to his daughter.'

'Ha! These are sharp moments, Lucy!'

He was quite stirred up; his young hand trembled; a vital (I was going to write *mortal*, but such words ill apply to one all living like him) – a vital suspense now held, now hurried, his breath: in all this trouble his smile never faded.

'Is he *very* angry, Lucy?'

'*She* is very faithful, Graham.'

'What will be done unto me?'

'Graham, your star must be fortunate.'

'Must it? Kind prophet! So cheered, I should be a faint heart indeed to quail. I think I find all women faithful, Lucy. I ought to love them, and I do. My mother is good; *she* is divine; and *you* are true as steel. Are you not?'

'Yes, Graham.'

'Then give me thy hand, my little god-sister; it is a friendly little hand to me, and always has been. And now for the great venture. God be with the right! Lucy, say, Amen!'

He turned, and waited till I said 'Amen!' – which I did to please him: the old charm, in doing as he bid me, came back. I wished him success; and successful I knew he would be. He was born victor, as some are born vanquished.

'Follow me!' he said; and I followed him into Mr Home's presence.

'Sir,' he asked, 'what is my sentence?'

The father looked at him; the daughter kept her face hid.

'Well, Bretton,' said Mr Home, 'you have given me the usual reward of hospitality. I entertained you; you have taken my best. I was always glad to see you; you were glad to see the one precious thing I had. You spoke me fair; and, meantime, I will not say you *robbed* me, but I am bereaved, and what I have lost, *you*, it seems, have won.'

'Sir, I cannot repent.'

'Repent! Not you! You triumph, no doubt: John Graham, you descended partly from a Highlander and a chief, and there is a trace of the Celt in all you look, speak, and think. You have his cunning and his charm. The red – (well, then, Polly, the *fair)* hair, the tongue of guile, and brain of wile, are all come down by inheritance.'

'Sir, I *feel* honest enough,' said Graham; and a genuine English blush covered his face with its warm witness of sincerity. 'And yet,' he added, 'I won't deny that in some respects you accuse me justly. In your presence I have always had a thought which I dared not show you. I did truly regard you as the possessor of the most valuable thing the world owns for me. I wished for it; I tried for it. Sir, I ask for it now.'

'John, you ask much.'

'Very much, sir. It must come from your generosity, as a gift; from your justice, as a reward. I can never earn it.'

'Ay! Listen to the Highland tongue!' said Mr Home. 'Look up, Polly! Answer this "braw wooer;" send him away!'

She looked up. She shyly glanced at her eager, handsome suitor. She gazed tenderly on her furrowed sire.

'Papa, I love you both,' said she; 'I can take care of you both. I need not send Graham away – he can live here; he will be no inconvenience,' she alleged with that simplicity of phraseology which at times was wont to make both her father and Graham smile. They smiled now.

'He will be a prodigious inconvenience to me,' still persisted Mr Home. 'I don't want him, Polly; he is too tall; he is in my way. Tell him to march.'

'You will get used to him, papa. He seemed exceedingly tall to me at first – like a tower when I looked up at him; but, on the whole, I would rather not have him otherwise.'

'I object to him altogether, Polly; I can do without a son-in-law. I should never have requested the best man in the land to stand to me in that relation. Dismiss this gentleman.'

'But he has known you so long, papa, and suits you so well.'

'Suits *me*, forsooth! Yes; he has pretended to make my opinions and tastes his own. He has humoured me for good reasons. I think, Polly, you and I will bid him good-bye.'

'Till to-morrow only. Shake hands with Graham, papa.'

'No: I think not: I am not friends with him. Don't think to coax me between you.'

'Indeed, indeed, you *are* friends. Graham, stretch out your right hand. Papa, put out yours. Now, let them touch. Papa, don't be stiff; close your fingers; be pliant – there! But that is not a clasp – it is a grasp! Papa, you gripe like a vice. You crush Graham's hand to the bone; you hurt him!'

He must have hurt him; for he wore a massive ring, set round with brilliants, of which the sharp facets cut into Graham's flesh and drew blood: but pain only made Dr John laugh, as anxiety had made him smile.

'Come with me into my study,' at last said Mr Home to the doctor. They went. Their interview was not long, but I suppose it was conclusive. The suitor had to undergo an interrogatory and a scrutiny on many things. Whether Dr Bretton was at times guileful in look and language or not, there was a sound foundation below. His answers, I understood afterwards, evinced both wisdom and integrity. He had managed his affairs well. He had struggled through entanglements; his fortunes were in the way of retrieval; he proved himself in a position to marry.

Once more the father and lover appeared in the library. M. de Bassompierre shut the door; he pointed to his daughter.

'Take her,' he said. 'Take her, John Bretton; and may God deal with you as you deal with her!'

Not long after, perhaps a fortnight, I saw three persons, Count de Bassompierre, his daughter, and Dr Graham Bretton, sitting on one seat, under a low-spreading and umbrageous tree, in the grounds of the palace at Bois l'Etang. They had come thither to enjoy a summer evening: outside the magnificent gates their carriage waited to take them home; the green sweeps of turf spread round them quiet and dim; the palace rose at a distance, white as a crag on Pentelicus;[215] the evening star shone above it; a forest of flowering shrubs embalmed the climate of this spot; the hour was still and sweet; the scene, but for this group, was solitary

Paulina sat between the two gentlemen; while they conversed, her little hands were busy at some work; I thought at first she was binding a nosegay. No; with the tiny pair of scissors, glittering in her lap, she had severed spoils from each manly head beside her, and was now occupied in plaiting together the gray lock and the golden wave. The plait woven – no silk-thread being at hand to bind it – a tress of her own hair was made to serve that purpose; she tied it like a knot, prisoned it in a locket, and laid it on her heart.

'Now,' said she, 'there is an amulet made, which has virtue to keep you two always friends. You can never quarrel so long as I wear this.'

An amulet was indeed made, a spell framed which rendered enmity impossible. She was become a bond to both, an influence over each, a mutual concord. From them she drew her happiness, and what she borrowed, she, with interest, gave back.

Is there, indeed, such happiness on earth? I asked, as I watched the father, the daughter, the future husband, now united – all blessed and blessing.

Yes; it is so. Without any colouring of romance, or any exaggeration of fancy, it is so. Some real lives do – for some certain days or years – actually anticipate the happiness of Heaven; and, I believe, if such perfect happiness is once felt by good people (to the wicked it never comes), its sweet effect is never wholly lost. Whatever trials follow, whatever pains of sickness or shades of death, the glory precedent still shines through, cheering the keen anguish, and tinging the deep cloud.

I will go farther. I *do* believe there are some human beings so born, so reared, so guided from a soft cradle to a calm and late grave, that no excessive suffering penetrates their lot, and no tempestuous blackness overcasts their journey. And often, these are not pampered, selfish beings, but natures elect, harmonious and benign; men and women mild with charity, kind agents of God's kind attributes.

Let me not delay the happy truth. Graham Bretton and Paulina de Bassompierre were married, and such an agent did Dr Bretton prove. He did not with time degenerate; his faults decayed, his virtues ripened; he rose in intellectual refinement, he won in moral profit: all dregs filtered away, the clear wine settled bright and tranquil. Bright, too, was the destiny of his sweet wife. She kept her husband's love, she aided in his progress – of his happiness she was the corner stone.

This pair was blessed indeed, for years brought them, with great prosperity, great goodness; they imparted with open hand, yet wisely. Doubtless they knew crosses, disappointments, difficulties; but these were well borne. More than once, too, they had to look on Him whose face flesh scarce can see and live: they had to pay their tribute to the King of Terrors. In the fulness of years, M. de Bassompierre was taken; in ripe old age departed Louisa Bretton.

Once even there rose a cry in their halls, of Rachel weeping for her children;[216] but others sprang healthy and blooming to replace the lost: Dr Bretton saw himself live again in a son who inherited his looks and his disposition; he had stately daughters, too, like himself; these children he reared with a suave, yet a firm hand; they grew up according to inheritance and nurture.

In short, I do but speak the truth when I say that these two lives of Graham and Paulina were blessed, like that of Jacob's favoured son, with 'blessings of Heaven above, blessings of the deep that lies under.' It was so, for God saw that it was good.

CHAPTER 38

Cloud

BUT IT IS NOT SO FOR ALL. What then? His will be done, as done it surely will be, whether we humble ourselves to resignation or not. The impulse of creation forwards it; the strength of powers, seen and unseen, has its fulfilment in charge. Proof of a life to come must be given. In fire and in blood, if needful, must that proof be written. In fire and in blood do we trace the record throughout nature. In fire and in blood does it cross our own experience. Sufferer, faint not through terror of this burning evidence. Tired wayfarer, gird up thy loins, look upward, march onward. Pilgrims and brother mourners, join in friendly company. Dark through the wilderness of this world stretches the way for most of us: equal and steady be our tread; be our cross our banner. For staff we have His promise, whose 'word is tried, whose way perfect:' for present hope His providence, 'who gives the shield of salvation, whose gentleness makes great;' for final home His bosom, who 'dwells in the height of Heaven;' for crowning prize a glory, exceeding and eternal. Let us so run that we may obtain; let us endure hardness as good soldiers; let us finish our course, and keep the faith, reliant in the issue to come off more than conquerors: 'Art thou not from everlasting mine Holy One? WE SHALL NOT DIE!'

On a Thursday morning we were all assembled in classe, waiting for the lesson of literature. The hour was come; we expected the master.

The pupils of the first classe sat very still; the cleanly-written compositions prepared since the last lesson lay ready before them, neatly tied with ribbon, waiting to be gathered by the hand of the professor as he made his rapid round of the desks. The month was July, the morning fine, the glass-door stood ajar, through it played a fresh breeze, and plants, growing at the lintel, waved, bent, looked in, seeming to whisper tidings.

M. Emanuel was not always quite punctual; we scarcely wondered at his being a little late, but we wondered when the door at last

opened and, instead of him with his swiftness and his fire, there
came quietly upon us, the cautious Madame Beck.

She approached M. Paul's desk; she stood before it; she drew
round her the light shawl covering her shoulders; beginning to
speak in low, yet firm tones, and with a fixed gaze, she said –

'This morning there will be no lesson of literature.'

The second paragraph of her address followed, after about two
minutes' pause.

'It is probable the lessons will be suspended for a week. I shall
require at least that space of time to find an efficient substitute for
M. Emanuel. Meanwhile, it shall be our study to fill the blanks
usefully.

'Your professor, ladies,' she went on, 'intends, if possible, duly to
take leave of you. At the present moment he has not leisure for that
ceremony. He is preparing for a long voyage. A very sudden and
urgent summons of duty calls him to a great distance. He has
decided to leave Europe for an indefinite time. Perhaps he may tell
you more himself. Ladies, instead of the usual lesson with M.
Emanuel, you will, this morning, read English with Mademoiselle
Lucy.'

She bent her head courteously, drew closer the folds of her shawl,
and passed from the classe.

A great silence fell: then a murmur went round the room: I
believe some pupils wept.

Some time elapsed. The noise, the whispering, the occasional
sobbing increased. I became conscious of a relaxation of discipline, a
sort of growing disorder, as if my girls felt that vigilance was
withdrawn, and that surveillance had virtually left the classe. Habit
and the sense of duty enabled me to rally quickly, to rise in my usual
way, to speak in my usual tone, to enjoin, and finally to establish
quiet. I made the English reading long and close. I kept them at it
the whole morning. I remember feeling a sentiment of impatience
towards the pupils who sobbed. Indeed, their emotion was not of
much value; it was only an hysteric agitation. I told them so
unsparingly. I half ridiculed them. I was severe. The truth was, I
could not do with their tears, or that gasping sound; I could not
bear it. A rather weak-minded, low-spirited pupil kept it up when
the others had done; relentless necessity obliged and assisted me so
to accost her, that she dared not carry on the demonstration, that
she was forced to conquer the convulsion.

That girl would have had a right to hate me, except that, when
school was over and her companions departing, I ordered her to

stay, and when they were gone, I did what I had never done to one among them before – pressed her to my heart and kissed her cheek. But, this impulse yielded to, I speedily put her out of the classe, for, upon that poignant strain, she wept more bitterly than ever.

I filled with occupation every minute of that day, and should have liked to sit up all night if I might have kept a candle burning; the night, however, proved a bad time, and left bad effects, preparing me ill for the next day's ordeal of insufferable gossip. Of course this news fell under general discussion. Some little reserve had accompanied the first surprise: that soon wore off; every mouth opened; every tongue wagged; teachers, pupils, the very servants, mouthed the name of 'Emanuel.' He, whose connection with the school was contemporary with its commencement, thus suddenly to withdraw! All felt it strange.

They talked so much, so long, so often, that, out of the very multitude of their words and rumours, grew at last some intelligence. About the third day I heard it said that he was to sail in a week; then – that he was bound for the West Indies. I looked at Madame Beck's face, and into her eyes, for disproof or confirmation of this report; I perused her all over for information, but no part of her disclosed more than what was unperturbed and commonplace.

'This secession was an immense loss to her,' she alleged. 'She did not know how she should fill up the vacancy. She was so used to her kinsman, he had become her right hand; what should she do without him? She had opposed the step, but M. Paul had convinced her it was his duty.'

She said all this in public, in classe, at the dinner-table, speaking audibly to Zélie St. Pierre.

'Why was it his duty?' I could have asked her that. I had impulses to take hold of her suddenly, as she calmly passed me in classe, to stretch out my hand and grasp her fast, and say, 'Stop. Let us hear the conclusion of the whole matter. *Why* is it his duty to go into banishment?' But Madame always addressed some other teacher, and never looked at me, never seemed conscious I could have a care in the question.

The week wore on. Nothing more was said about M. Emanuel coming to bid us good-bye; none seemed anxious for his coming; none questioned whether or not he would come; none betrayed torment lest he should depart silent and unseen; incessantly did they talk, and never, in all their talk, touched on this vital point. As to Madame, she of course could see him, and say to him as much as she pleased. What should *she* care whether or not he appeared in the school-room?

The week consumed. We were told that he was going on such a day, that his destination was 'Basseterre in Guadaloupe:' the business which called him abroad related to a friend's interests, not his own: I thought as much.

'Basseterre in Guadaloupe.' I had little sleep about this time, but whenever I *did* slumber, it followed infallibly that I was quickly roused with a start, while the words 'Basseterre,' 'Guadaloupe,' seemed pronounced over my pillow, or ran athwart the darkness around and before me, in zig-zag characters of red or violet light.

For what I felt there was no help, and how could I help feeling? M. Emanuel had been very kind to me of late days; he had been growing hourly better and kinder. It was now a month since we had settled the theological difference, and in all that time there had been no quarrel. Nor had our peace been the cold daughter of divorce; we had not lived aloof; he had come oftener, he had talked with me more than before; he had spent hours with me, with temper soothed, with eye content, with manner home-like and mild. Kind subjects of conversation had grown between us; he had inquired into my plans of life, and I had communicated them; the school-project pleased him; he made me repeat it more than once, though he called it an Alnaschar dream.[217] The jar was over; the mutual understanding was settling and fixing; feelings of union and hope made themselves profoundly felt in the heart; affection and deep esteem and dawning trust had each fastened its bond.

What quiet lessons I had about this time! No more taunts on my 'intellect,' no more menaces of grating public shows! How sweetly, for the jealous gibe, and the more jealous, half-passionate eulogy, were substituted a mute, indulgent help, a fond guidance, and a tender forbearance which forgave but never praised. There were times when he would sit for many minutes and not speak at all; and when dusk or duty brought separation, he would leave with words like these: 'Il est doux, le repos! Il est précieux, le calme bonheur!'

One evening, not ten short days since, he joined me whilst walking in my alley. He took my hand. I looked up in his face; I thought he meant to arrest my attention.

'Bonne petite amie!' said he, softly; 'douce consolatrice!'[218] But through his touch, and with his words, a new feeling and a strange thought found a course. Could it be that he was becoming more than friend or brother? Did his look speak a kindness beyond fraternity or amity?

His eloquent look had more to say, his hand drew me forward, his interpreting lips stirred. No. Not now. Here into the twilight alley broke an interruption: it came dual and ominous: we faced two bodeful forms – a woman's and a priest's – Madame Beck and Père Silas.

The aspect of the latter I shall never forget. On the first impulse, it expressed a Jean-Jacques sensibility, stirred by the signs of affection just surprised; then, immediately, darkened over it the jaundice of ecclesiastical jealousy. He spoke to *me* with unction. He looked on his pupil with sternness. As to Madame Beck, she, of course, saw nothing – nothing; though her kinsman retained in her presence the hand of the heretic foreigner, not suffering withdrawal, but clasping it close and fast.

Following these incidents, that sudden announcement of departure had struck me at first as incredible. Indeed, it was only frequent repetition, and the credence of the hundred and fifty minds round me, which forced on me its full acceptance. As to that week of suspense, with its blank yet burning days, which brought from him no word of explanation – I remember, but I cannot describe its passage.

The last day broke. Now would he visit us. Now he would come and speak his farewell, or he would vanish mute, and be seen by us nevermore.

This alternative seemed to be present in the mind of not a living creature in that school. All rose at the usual hour; all breakfasted as usual; all, without reference to, or apparent thought of their late professor, betook themselves with wonted phlegm to their ordinary duties.

So oblivious was the house, so tame, so trained its proceedings, so inexpectant its aspect – I scarce knew how to breathe in an atmosphere thus stagnant, thus smothering. Would no one lend me a voice? Had no one a wish, no one a word, no one a prayer to which I could say – Amen?

I had seen them unanimous in demand for the merest trifle – a treat, a holiday, a lesson's remission; they could not, they *would* not now band to besiege Madame Beck, and insist on a last interview with a Master who had certainly been loved, at least by some – loved as *they* could love – but, oh! what is the love of the multitude?

I knew where he lived: I knew where he was to be heard of, or communicated with; the distance was scarce a stone's-throw; had it been in the next room – unsummoned, I could make no use of my knowledge. To follow, to seek out, to remind, to recall – for these things I had no faculty.

M. Emanuel might have passed within reach of my arm: had he passed silent and unnoticing – silent and stirless, should I have suffered him to go by.

Morning wasted. Afternoon came, and I thought all was over. My heart trembled in its place. My blood was troubled in its current. I was quite sick, and hardly knew how to keep at my post or do my work. Yet the little world round me plodded on indifferent; all seemed jocund, free of care, or fear, or thought: the very pupils who, seven days since, had wept hysterically at a startling piece of news, appeared quite to have forgotten the news, its import, and their emotion.

A little before five o'clock, the hour of dismissal, Madame Beck sent for me to her chamber, to read over and translate some English letter she had received, and to write for her the answer. Before settling to this work, I observed that she softly closed the two doors of her chamber; she even shut and fastened the casement, though it was a hot day, and free circulation of air was usually regarded by her as indispensable. Why this precaution? A keen suspicion, an almost fierce distrust, suggested such question. Did she want to exclude sound? what sound?

I listened as I had never listened before; I listened like the evening and winter-wolf, snuffing the snow, scenting prey, and hearing far off the traveller's tramp. Yet I could both listen and write. About the middle of the letter I heard – what checked my pen – a tread in the vestibule. No door-bell had rung; Rosine – acting doubtless by orders – had anticipated such reveillée. Madame saw me halt. She coughed, made a bustle, spoke louder. The tread had passed on to the classes.

'Proceed,' said Madame; but my hand was fettered, my ear enchained, my thoughts were carried off captive.

The classes formed another building; the hall parted them from the dwelling-house: despite distance and partition, I heard the sudden stir of numbers, a whole division rising at once.

'They are putting away work,' said Madame.

It was indeed the hour to put away work, but why that sudden hush – that instant quell of the tumult?

'Wait, madame – I will see what it is.'

And I put down my pen and left her. Left her? No: she would not be left: powerless to detain me, she rose and followed, close as my shadow. I turned on the last step of the stairs: –

'Are you coming too?' I asked.

'Yes,' said she; meeting my glance with a peculiar aspect – a look, clouded, yet resolute. We proceeded then, not together, but she walked in my steps.

He was come. Entering the first classe, I saw him. There, once more appeared the form most familiar. I doubt not they had tried to keep him away, but he was come.

The girls stood in a semi-circle; he was passing round, giving his farewells, pressing each hand, touching with his lips each cheek. This last ceremony, foreign custom permitted at such a parting – so solemn, to last so long.

I felt it hard that Madame Beck should dog me thus; following and watching me close, my neck and shoulder shrunk in fever under her breath; I became terribly goaded.

He was approaching; the semi-circle was almost travelled round; he came to the last pupil; he turned. But Madame was before me; she had stepped out suddenly; she seemed to magnify her proportions and amplify her drapery; she eclipsed me; I was hid. She knew my weakness and deficiency; she could calculate the degree of moral paralysis – the total default of self-assertion – with which, in a crisis, I could be struck. She hastened to her kinsman, she broke upon him volubly, she mastered his attention, she hurried him to the door – the glass-door opening on the garden. I think he looked round; could I but have caught his eye, courage, I think, would have rushed in to aid feeling, and there would have been a charge, and, perhaps a rescue; but already the room was all confusion, the semi-circle broken into groups, my figure was lost among thirty more conspicuous. Madame had her will; yes, she got him away, and he had not seen me; he thought me absent. Five o'clock struck, the loud dismissal bell rung, the school separated, the room emptied.

There seems, to my memory, an entire darkness and distraction in some certain minutes I then passed alone – a grief inexpressible over a loss unendurable. *What* should I do; oh! *what* should I do; when all my life's hope was thus torn by the roots out of my riven, outraged heart?

What I *should* have done, I know not, when a little child – the least child in the school – broke with its simplicity and its unconsciousness into the raging yet silent centre of that inward conflict.

'Mademoiselle,' lisped the treble voice, 'I am to give you that. M. Paul said I was to seek you all over the house, from the grenier to the cellar, and when I found you, to give you that.'

And the child delivered a note; the little dove dropped on my knee its olive-leaf plucked off. I found neither address nor name, only these words: –

'It was not my intention to take leave of you when I said good-bye to the rest, but I hoped to see you in classe. I was disappointed. The interview is deferred. Be ready for me. Ere I sail, I must see you at leisure, and speak with you at length. Be ready; my moments are numbered, and, just now, monopolized; besides I have a private business on hand which I will not share with any, nor communicate – even to you – PAUL.'

'Be ready?' Then it must be this evening; was he not to go on the morrow? Yes; of that point I was certain. I had seen the date of his vessel's departure advertised. Oh! *I* would be ready, but could that longed-for meeting really be achieved? the time was so short, the schemers seemed so watchful, so active, so hostile; the way of access appeared strait as a gully, deep as a chasm – Apollyon straddled across it, breathing flames. Could my Greatheart[219] overcome? Could my guide reach me?

Who might tell? Yet I began to take some courage, some comfort; it seemed to me that I felt a pulse of his heart beating yet true to the whole throb of mine.

I waited my champion. Apollyon came trailing his Hell behind him. I think if Eternity held torment, its form would not be fiery rack, nor its nature, despair. I think that on a certain day amongst those days which never dawned, and will not set, an angel entered Hades – stood, shone, smiled, delivered a prophecy of conditional pardon, kindled a doubtful hope of bliss to come, not now, but at a day and hour unlooked for, revealed in his own glory and grandeur the height and compass of his promise; spoke thus – then towering, became a star, and vanished into his own Heaven. His legacy was suspense – a worse boon than despair.

All that evening I waited, trusting in the dove-sent olive-leaf, yet in the midst of my trust, terribly fearing. My fear pressed heavy. Cold and peculiar, I knew it for the partner of a rarely-belied presentiment. The first hours seemed long and slow; in spirit I clung to the flying skirts of the last. They passed like drift cloud – like the rack scudding before a storm.

They passed. All the long, hot summer day burned away like a Yule-log; the crimson of its close perished; I was left bent among the cool blue shades, over the pale and ashen gleams of its night.

Prayers were over; it was bed-time; my co-inmates were all retired. I still remained in the gloomy first-classe, forgetting, or at least disregarding, rules I had never forgotten or disregarded before.

How long I paced that classe I cannot tell; I must have been afoot many hours; mechanically had I moved aside benches and desks, and had made for myself a path down its length. There I walked, and there, when certain that the whole household were abed, and quite out of hearing – there, I at last wept. Reliant on Night, confiding in Solitude, I kept my tears sealed, my sobs chained, no longer; they heaved my heart; they tore their way. In this house, what grief could be sacred?

Soon after eleven o'clock – a very late hour for the Rue Fossette – the door unclosed, quietly but not stealthily; a lamp's flame invaded the moonlight; Madame Beck entered, with the same composed air, as if coming on an ordinary occasion, at an ordinary season. Instead of at once addressing me, she went to her desk, took her keys, and seemed to seek something; she loitered over this feigned search long, too long. She was calm, too calm; my mood scarce endured the pretence; driven beyond common range, two hours since I had left behind me wonted respects and fears. Led by a touch, and ruled by a word, under usual circumstances, no yoke could now be borne – no curb obeyed.

'It is more than time for retirement,' said Madame; 'the rule of the house has already been transgressed too long.'

Madame met no answer: I did not check my walk; when she came in my way, I put her out of it.

'Let me persuade you to calm, meess; let me lead you to your chamber,' said she, trying to speak softly.

'No!' I said; 'neither you nor another shall persuade or lead me.'

'Your bed shall be warmed. Goton is sitting up still. She shall make you comfortable: she shall give you a sedative.'

'Madame,' I broke out, 'you are a sensualist. Under all your serenity, your peace, and your decorum, you are an undenied sensualist. Make your own bed warm and soft; take sedatives, and meats and drinks spiced and sweet, as much as you will. If you have any sorrow or disappointment – and, perhaps, you have – nay, I *know* you have – seek your own palliatives, in your own chosen resources. Leave me, however. *Leave me*, I say!'

'I must send another to watch you, meess; I must send Goton.'

'I forbid it. Let me alone. Keep your hand off me, and my life, and my troubles. Oh, Madame! in *your* hand there is both chill and poison. You envenom and you paralyze.'

'What have I done, meess? You must not marry Paul. He cannot marry.'

'Dog in the manger!' I said; for I knew she secretly wanted him, and had always wanted him. She called him 'insupportable;' she railed at him for a 'dévot;' she did not love, but she wanted to marry, that she might bind him to her interest. Deep into some of Madame's secrets I had entered – I know not how; by an intuition or an inspiration which came to me – I know not whence. In the course of living with her, too, I had slowly learned, that, unless with an inferior, she must ever be a rival. She was *my* rival, heart and soul, though secretly, under the smoothest bearing, and utterly unknown to all save her and myself.

Two minutes I stood over Madame, feeling that the whole woman was in my power, because in some moods, such as the present – in some stimulated states of perception, like that of this instant – her habitual disguise, her mask and her domino, were to me a mere network reticulated with holes; and I saw underneath a being heartless, self-indulgent, and ignoble. She quietly retreated from me; meek and self-possessed, though very uneasy, she said, 'If I would not be persuaded to take rest, she must reluctantly leave me.' Which she did incontinent, perhaps even more glad to get away, than I was to see her vanish.

This was the sole flash-eliciting, truth-extorting, rencontre which ever occurred between me and Madame Beck; this short night-scene was never repeated. It did not one whit change her manner to me. I do not know that she revenged it. I do not know that she hated me the worse for my fell candour. I think she bucklered herself with the secret philosophy of her strong mind, and resolved to forget what it irked her to remember. I know that to the end of our mutual lives there occurred no repetition of, no allusion to, that fiery passage.

That night passed: all nights – even the starless night before dissolution – must wear away. About six o'clock, the hour which called up the household, I went out to the court, and washed my face in its cold, fresh, well-water. Entering by the carré, a piece of mirror-glass, set in an oaken cabinet, repeated my image. It said I was changed; my cheeks and lips were sodden-white, my eyes were glassy, and my eye-lids swollen and purple.

On rejoining my companions, I knew they all looked at me – my heart seemed discovered to them; I believed myself self-betrayed. Hideously certain did it seem that the very youngest of the school must guess why and for whom I despaired.

Isabelle, the child whom I had once nursed in sickness, approached me. Would she, too, mock me?

'Que vous êtes pâle! Vous êtes donc bien malade, mademoiselle!'[220] said she, putting her finger in her mouth, and staring with a wistful stupidity which at the moment seemed to me more beautiful than the keenest intelligence.

Isabelle did not long stand alone in the recommendation of

ignorance; before the day was over, I gathered cause of gratitude towards the whole blind household. The multitude have something else to do than to read hearts and interpret dark sayings. Who wills, may keep his own counsel – be his own secret's sovereign. In the course of that day, proof met me on proof, not only that the cause of my present sorrow was unguessed, but that my whole inner life for the last six months, was still mine only. It was not known – it had not been noted – that I held in peculiar value one life among all lives. Gossip had passed me by; curiosity had looked me over: both subtle influences, hovering always round, had never become centred upon me. A given organization may live in a full fever-hospital, and escape typhus. M. Emanuel had come and gone; I had been taught and sought; in season and out of season he had called me, and I had obeyed him: 'M. Paul' – such had been the perpetual bulletin; and nobody commented, far less condemned. Nobody hinted, nobody jested. Madame Beck read the riddle; none else resolved it. What I now suffered was called illness – a headache: I accepted the baptism.

But what bodily illness was ever like this pain? This certainty that he was gone without a farewell – this cruel conviction that fate and pursuing furies – a woman's envy and a priest's bigotry – would suffer me to see him no more? What wonder that the second evening found me like the first – untamed, tortured, again pacing a solitary room in an unalterable passion of silent desolation?

Madame Beck did not herself summon me to bed that night – she did not come near me; she sent Ginevra Fanshawe – a more efficient agent for the purpose she could not have employed. Ginevra's first words – 'Is your headache very bad to-night?' (for Ginevra, like the rest, thought I had a headache – an intolerable headache which made me frightfully white in the face, and insanely restless in the foot) – her first words, I say, inspired the impulse to flee anywhere, so that it were only out of reach. And soon, what followed – plaints about her own headaches – completed the business.

I went up-stairs. Presently I was in my bed – my miserable bed – haunted with quick scorpions. I had not been laid down five minutes, when another emissary arrived: Goton came, bringing me something to drink. I was consumed with thirst – I drank eagerly; the beverage was sweet, but I tasted a drug.

'Madame says it will make you sleep, chou-chou,' said Goton, as she received back the emptied cup.

Ah! the sedative had been administered. In fact, they had given me a strong opiate. I was to be held quiet for one night.

The household came to bed, the night-light was lit, the

dormitory hushed. Sleep soon reigned: over those pillows, sleep won an easy supremacy; contented sovereign over heads and hearts which did not ache – he passed by the unquiet.

The drug wrought. I know not whether Madame had over-charged or under-charged the dose; its result was not that she intended. Instead of stupor, came excitement. I became alive to new thought – to reverie peculiar in colouring. A gathering call ran among the faculties, their bugles sang, their trumpets rang an untimely summons. Imagination was roused from her rest, and she came forth impetuous and venturous. With scorn she looked on Matter, her mate –

'Rise!' she said. 'Sluggard! this night I will have *my* will; nor shalt thou prevail.'

'Look forth and view the night!' was her cry; and when I lifted the heavy blind from the casement close at hand – with her own royal gesture, she showed me a moon supreme, in an element deep and splendid.

To my gasping senses she made the glimmering gloom, the narrow limits, the oppressive heat of the dormitory, intolerable. She lured me to leave this den and follow her forth into dew, coolness, and glory.

She brought upon me a strange vision of Villette at midnight. Especially she showed the park, the summer-park, with its long alleys all silent, lone and safe; among these lay a huge stone basin – that basin I knew, and beside which I had often stood – deep-set in the tree-shadows, brimming with cool water, clear, with a green, leafy, rushy bed. What of all this? The park-gates were shut up, locked, sentinelled; the place could not be entered.

Could it not? A point worth considering; and while revolving it, I mechanically dressed. Utterly incapable of sleeping or lying still – excited from head to foot – what could I do better than dress?

The gates were locked, soldiers set before them; was there, then, no admission to the park?

The other day, in walking past, I had seen, without then attending to the circumstance, a gap in the paling – one stake broken down: I now saw this gap again in recollection – saw it very plainly – the narrow, irregular aperture visible between the stems of the lindens, planted orderly as a colonnade. A man could not have made his way through that aperture, nor could a stout woman, perhaps not Madame Beck; but I thought I might: I fancied I should like to try, and once within, at this hour the whole park would be mine – the moonlight, midnight park!

How soundly the dormitory slept! What deep slumbers! What quiet breathing! How very still the whole large house! What was the time? I felt restless to know. There stood a clock in the classe below; what hindered me from venturing down to consult it? By such a moon, its large white face and jet black figures must be vividly distinct.

As for hindrance to this step, there offered not so much as a creaking hinge or a clicking latch. On these hot July nights, close air could not be tolerated, and the chamber-door stood wide open. Will the dormitory-planks sustain my tread untraitorous? Yes. I know wherever a board is loose, and will avoid it. The oak staircase creaks somewhat as I descend, but not much: – I am in the carré.

The great classe-doors are close shut; they are bolted. On the other hand, the entrance to the corridor stands open. The classes seem to my thought, great dreary jails, buried far back beyond thoroughfares, and for me, filled with spectral and intolerable memories, laid miserable amongst their straw and their manacles. The corridor offers a cheerful vista, leading to the high vestibule which opens direct upon the street.

Hush! – the clock strikes. Ghostly deep as is the stillness of this convent, it is only eleven. While my ear follows to silence the hum of the last stroke, I catch faintly from the built-out capital, a sound like bells or like a band – a sound where sweetness, where victory, where mourning blend. Oh, to approach this music nearer, to listen to it alone by the rushy basin! Let me go – oh, let me go! What hinders, what does not aid freedom?

There, in the corridor, hangs my garden-costume, my large hat, my shawl. There is no lock on the huge, heavy, porte-cochère; there is no key to seek; it fastens with a sort of spring-bolt, not to be opened from the outside, but which, from within, may be noiselessly withdrawn. Can I manage it? It yields to my hand, yields with propitious facility. I wonder as that great portal seems almost spontaneously to unclose; I wonder as I cross the threshold and step on the paved street, wonder at the strange ease with which this prison has been forced. It seems as if I had been pioneered invisibly, as if some dissolving force had gone before me; for myself, I have scarce made an effort.

Quiet Rue Fossette! I find on this pavement that wanderer-wooing summer night of which I mused; I see its moon over me; I feel its dew in the air. But here I cannot stay; I am still too near old haunts; so close under the dungeon, I can hear the prisoners moan. This solemn peace is not what I seek, it is not what I can bear; to me the face of that sky bears the aspect of a world's death. The park also will be calm – I know, a mortal serenity prevails everywhere – yet let me seek the park.

I took a route well-known, and went up towards the palatial and royal Haute-Ville; thence the music I had heard, certainly floated; it was hushed now, but it might re-waken. I went on; neither band nor bell-music came to meet me; another sound replaced it, a sound like a strong tide, a great flow, deepening as I proceeded. Light broke, movement gathered, chimes pealed – to what was I coming? Entering on the level of a Grande Place, I found myself, with the suddenness of magic, plunged amidst a gay, living, joyous crowd.

Villette is one blaze, one broad illumination; the whole world seems abroad; moonlight and heaven are banished: the town, by her own flambeaux, beholds her own splendour – gay dresses, grand equipages, fine horses and gallant riders throng the bright streets. I see even scores of masks. It is a strange scene, stranger than dreams. But where is the park? – I ought to be near it. In the midst of this glare the park must be shadowy and calm – *there*, at least, are neither torches, lamps, nor crowd?

I was asking this question, when an open carriage passed me filled with known faces. Through the deep throng it could pass but slowly; the spirited horses fretted in their curbed ardour. I saw the occupants of that carriage well; me they could not see, or, at least, not know, folded close in my large shawl, screened with my straw hat (in that motley crowd no dress was noticeably strange). I saw the Count de Bassompierre; I saw my godmother, handsomely apparelled, comely and cheerful; I saw, too, Paulina Mary, compassed with the triple halo of her beauty, her youth, and her happiness. In looking on her countenance of joy, and eyes of festal light, one scarce remembered to note the gala elegance of what she wore; I know only that the drapery floating about her was all white and light and bridal: seated opposite to her I saw Graham Bretton; it was in looking up at him her aspect had caught its lustre – the light repeated in *her* eyes beamed first out of his.

It gave me strange pleasure to follow these friends viewlessly, and I *did* follow them, as I thought, to the park. I watched them alight (carriages were inadmissible) amidst new and unanticipated splendours. Lo! the iron gateway, between the stone columns, was spanned by a flaming arch built of massed stars; and, following them cautiously beneath that arch, where were they, and where was I?

In a land of enchantment, a garden most gorgeous, a plain sprinkled with coloured meteors, a forest with sparks of purple and ruby and golden fire gemming the foliage; a region, not of trees and shadow, but of strangest architectural wealth – of altar and of temple, of pyramid, obelisk, and sphynx; incredible to say, the wonders and the symbols of Egypt teemed throughout the park of Villette.

No matter that in five minutes the secret was mine – the key of the mystery picked up, and its illusion unveiled – no matter that I quickly recognized the material of these solemn fragments – the timber, the paint, and the pasteboard – these inevitable discoveries failed to quite destroy the charm, or undermine the marvel of that night. No matter that I now seized the explanation of the whole great fête – a fête of which the conventual Rue Fossette had not tasted, though it had opened at dawn that morning, and was still in full vigour near midnight.

In past days there had been, said history, an awful crisis in the fate of Labassecour, involving I know not what peril to the rights and liberties of her gallant citizens. Rumours of wars, there had been, if not wars themselves; a kind of struggling in the streets – a bustle – a running to and fro, some rearing of barricades, some burgher-rioting, some calling out of troops, much interchange of brick-bats, and even a little of shot. Tradition held that patriots had fallen: in the old Basse-Ville was shown an enclosure, solemnly built in and set apart, holding, it was said, the sacred bones of martyrs. Be this as it may, a certain day in the year was still kept as a festival in honour of the said patriots and martyrs of somewhat apocryphal memory – the morning being given to a solemn Te Deum in St. Jean Baptiste, the evening devoted to spectacles, decorations, and illuminations, such as these I now saw.

While looking up at the image of a white ibis, fixed on a column – while fathoming the deep, torch-lit perspective of an avenue, at the close of which was couched a sphynx – I lost sight of the party which, from the middle of the great square, I had followed – or, rather, they vanished like a group of apparitions. On this whole scene was impressed a dream-like character; every shape was wavering, every movement floating, every voice echo-like – half-mocking, half-uncertain. Paulina and her friends being gone, I scarce could avouch that I had really seen them; nor did I miss them as guides through the chaos, far less regret them as protectors amidst the night.

That festal night would have been safe for a very child. Half the peasantry had come in from the outlying environs of Villette, and the decent burghers were all abroad and around, dressed in their best. My straw-hat passed amidst cap and jacket, short petticoat, and long calico mantle, without, perhaps, attracting a glance; I only took the precaution to bind down the broad leaf gipsy-wise, with a supplementary ribbon; and then I felt safe as if masked.

Safe I passed down the avenues – safe I mixed with the crowd where it was deepest. To be still was not in my power, nor quietly to observe. I took a revel of the scene; I drank the elastic night-air – the swell of sound, the dubious light, now flashing, now fading. As to Happiness or Hope, they and I had shaken hands, but just now – I scorned Despair.

My vague aim, as I went, was to find the stone basin, with its clear depth and green lining: of that coolness and verdure I thought, with the passionate thirst of unconscious fever. Amidst the glare, and hurry, and throng, and noise, I still secretly and chiefly longed to come on that circular mirror of crystal, and surprise the moon glassing therein her pearly front.

I knew my route, yet it seemed as if I was hindered from pursuing it direct: now a sight, and now a sound, called me aside, luring me down this alley and down that. Already I saw the thick-planted trees which framed this tremulous and rippled glass, when, choiring out of a glade to the right, broke such a sound as I thought might be heard if Heaven were to open – such a sound, perhaps, as *was* heard above the plain of Bethlehem, on the night of glad tidings.

The song, the sweet music, rose afar, but rushing swiftly on fast-strengthening pinions – there swept through these shades so full a storm of harmonies that, had no tree been near against which to lean, I think I must have dropped. Voices were there, it seemed to me, unnumbered; instruments varied and countless – bugle, horn, and trumpet I knew. The effect was as a sea breaking into song with all its waves.

The swaying tide swept this way, and then it fell back, and I followed its retreat. It led me towards a Byzantine building – a sort of kiosk near the park's centre. Round about stood crowded thousands, gathered to a grand concert in the open air. What I had heard was, I think, a wild Jager chorus; the night, the space, the scene, and my own mood, had but enhanced the sounds and their impression.

Here were assembled ladies, looking by this light most beautiful; some of their dresses were gauzy, and some had the sheen of satin; the flowers and the blond trembled, and the veils waved about their decorated bonnets, as that host-like chorus, with its greatly-gathering sound, sundered the air above them. Most of these ladies occupied the little light park-chairs, and behind and beside them stood guardian gentlemen. The outer ranks of the crowd were made up of citizens, plebeians and police.

In this outer rank I took my place. I rather liked to find myself the silent, unknown, consequently unaccosted neighbour of the short petticoat and the sabot; and only the distant gazer at the silk robe, the velvet mantle, and the plumed chapeau. Amidst so much life and joy, too, it suited me to be alone – quite alone. Having neither wish nor power to force my way through a mass so close-packed, my station was on the farthest confines, where, indeed, I might hear, but could see little.

'Mademoiselle is not well placed,' said a voice at my elbow. Who dared accost *me*, a being in a mood so little social? I turned, rather to repel than to reply. I saw a man – a burgher – an entire stranger, as I deemed him for one moment, but the next, recognized in him a certain tradesman – a bookseller, whose shop furnished the Rue Fossette with its books and stationery; a man notorious in our pensionnat for the excessive brittleness of his temper, and frequent snappishness of his manner, even to us, his principal customers; but whom, for my solitary self, I had ever been disposed to like, and had always found civil, sometimes kind; once, in aiding me about some troublesome little exchange of foreign money, he had done me a service. He was an intelligent man; under his asperity, he was a good-hearted man; the thought had sometimes crossed me, that a part of his nature bore affinity to a part of M. Emanuel's, (whom he knew well, and whom I had often seen sitting on Miret's counter, turning over the current month's publications); and it was in this affinity I read the explanation of that conciliatory feeling with which I instinctively regarded him.

Strange to say, this man knew me under my straw-hat and closely-folded shawl; and, though I deprecated the effort, he insisted on making a way for me through the crowd, and finding me a better situation. He carried his disinterested civility further, and, from some quarter, procured me a chair. Once and again, I have found that the most cross-grained are by no means the worst of mankind; nor the humblest in station, the least polished in feeling. This man, in his courtesy, seemed to find nothing strange in my being here alone; only a reason for extending to me, as far as he could, a retiring, yet efficient attention. Having secured me a place and a seat, he withdrew without asking a question, without obtruding a remark, without adding a superfluous word. No wonder that Professor Emanuel liked to take his cigar and his lounge, and to read his feuilleton in M. Miret's shop; the two must have suited.

I had not been seated five minutes, ere I became aware that chance and my worthy burgher friend had brought me once more within view of a familiar and domestic group. Right before me sat the Brettons and De Bassompierres. Within reach of my hand – had I chosen to extend it – sat a figure like a fairy-queen, whose array, lilies and their leaves seemed to have suggested; whatever was not spotless white, being forest-green. My god-mother, too, sat so near, that, had I leaned forward, my breath might have stirred the ribbon of her bonnet. They were too near; having been just recognized by a comparative stranger, I felt uneasy at this close vicinage of intimate acquaintance.

It made me quite start when Mrs Bretton, turning to Mr Home, and speaking out of a kind impulse of memory, said, –

'I wonder what my steady little Lucy would say to all this if she were here? I wish we had brought her, she would have enjoyed it much.'

'So she would, so she would, in her grave sensible fashion; it is a pity but we had asked her,' rejoined the kind gentleman; and added, 'I like to see her so quietly pleased; so little moved, yet so content.'

Dear were they both to me, dear are they to this day in their remembered benevolence. Little knew they the rack of pain which had driven Lucy almost into fever, and brought her out, guideless and reckless, urged and drugged to the brink of frenzy. I had half a mind to bend over the elders' shoulders, and answer their goodness with the thanks of my eyes. M. de Bassompierre did not well know *me*, but I knew *him*, and honoured and admired his nature, with all its plain sincerity, its warm affection, and unconscious enthusiasm. Possibly I might have spoken, but just then Graham turned, he turned with one of his stately firm movements, so different from those of a sharp-tempered undersized man; there was behind him a throng, a hundred ranks deep; there were thousands to meet his eye and divide its scrutiny – why then did he concentrate all on me – oppressing me with the whole force of that full, blue, steadfast orb? Why, if he *would* look, did not one glance satisfy him? why did he turn on his chair, rest his elbow on its back, and study me leisurely? He could not see my face, I held it down; surely, he *could* not recognize me; I stooped, I turned, I *would* not be known. He rose, by some means he contrived to approach, in two minutes he would have had my secret; my identity would have been grasped between his never tyrannous, but always powerful hands. There was but one way to evade or to check him. I implied, by a sort of supplicatory gesture, that it was my prayer to be let alone; after that, had he persisted, he would perhaps have seen the spectacle of Lucy incensed: not all that was grand, or good, or kind in him (and Lucy felt the full amount) should have kept her quite tame, or absolutely inoffensive and shadowlike. He looked, but he desisted. He shook his handsome head, but he was mute. He resumed his seat, nor did he again turn or disturb me by a glance, except indeed for one single instant, when a look, rather solicitous than curious, stole my way – speaking what somehow stilled my heart like 'the south-wind quieting the earth.' Graham's thoughts of me were not entirely those of a frozen indifference, after all. I believe in that goodly mansion, his heart, he kept one little place under the skylights where Lucy might have entertainment, if she chose to call. It was not so handsome as the chambers where he lodged his male friends; it was not like the hall where he accommodated his philanthropy, or the library where he treasured his science, still less did it resemble the pavilion where his marriage feast was splendidly spread; yet, gradually, by long and equal kindness, he proved to me that he kept one little closet, over the door of which was written 'Lucy's Room.' I kept a place for him, too – a place of which I never took the measure, either by rule or compass: I think it was like the tent of Peri-Banou.[221] All my life long I carried it folded in the hollow of my hand – yet, released from that hold and constriction, I know not but its innate capacity for expanse might have magnified it into a tabernacle for a host.

Forbearing as he was to-night, I could not stay in this proximity; this dangerous place and seat must be given up; I watched my opportunity, rose, and stole away. He might think, he might even believe that Lucy was contained within that shawl, and sheltered under that hat; he could never be certain, for he did not see my face.

Surely the spirit of restlessness was by this time appeased? Had I not had enough of adventure? Did I not begin to flag, quail, and wish for safety under a roof? Not so. I still loathed my bed in the school-dormitory more than words can express; I clung to whatever could distract thought. Somehow I felt, too, that the night's drama was but begun, that the prologue was scarce spoken: throughout this woody and turfy theatre reigned a shadow of mystery; actors and incidents unlooked-for, waited behind the scenes: I thought so: foreboding told me as much.

Straying at random, obeying the push of every chance elbow, I was brought to a quarter where trees planted in clusters, or towering singly, broke up somewhat the dense packing of the crowd, and gave it a more scattered character. These confines were far from the music, and somewhat aloof even from the lamps, but there was sound enough to soothe, and with that full, high moon, lamps were scarce needed. Here had chiefly settled family-groups, burgher-parents; some of them, late as was the hour, actually surrounded by their children, with whom it had not been thought advisable to venture into the closer throng.

Three fine tall trees growing close, almost twined stem within stem, lifted a thick canopy of shade above a green knoll, crowned with a seat – a seat which might have held several, yet it seemed abandoned to one, the remaining members of the fortunate party in possession of this site standing dutifully round; yet, amongst this reverent circle was a lady, holding by the hand a little girl.

When I caught sight of this little girl, she was twisting herself round on her heel, swinging from her conductress's hand, flinging herself from side to side with wanton and fantastic gyrations. These perverse movements arrested my attention, they struck me as of a character fearfully familiar. On close inspection, no less so appeared the child's equipment; the lilac silk pelisse, the small swansdown boa, the white bonnet – the whole holiday toilette, in short, was the gala garb of a cherub but too-well known, of that tadpole, Désirée Beck – and Désirée Beck it was – she, or an imp in her likeness.

I might have taken this discovery as a thunderclap, but such hyperbole would have been premature; discovery was destined to rise more than one degree, ere it reached its climax.

On whose hand could the amiable Désirée swing thus selfishly, whose glove could she tear thus recklessly, whose arm thus strain with impunity, or on the borders of whose dress thus turn and trample insolently, if not the hand, glove, arm, and robe of her lady-mother? And there, in an Indian shawl and a pale-green crape bonnet – there, fresh, portly, blithe, and pleasant – there stood Madame Beck.

Curious! I had certainly deemed Madame in her bed, and Désirée in her crib, at this blessed minute, sleeping, both of them, the sleep of the just, within the sacred walls, amidst the profound seclusion of the Rue Fossette. Most certainly also they did not picture 'Meess Lucie' otherwise engaged; and here we all three were taking our 'ébats' in the fête-blazing park at midnight!

The fact was, Madame was only acting according to her quite justifiable wont. I remembered now I had heard it said among the teachers – though without at the time particularly noticing the gossip – that often, when we thought Madame in her chamber, sleeping, she was gone, full-dressed, to take her pleasure at operas, or plays, or balls. Madame had no sort of taste for a monastic life, and took care – largely, though discreetly – to season her existence with a relish of the world.

Half a dozen gentlemen of her friends stood about her. Amongst these, I was not slow to recognize two or three. There was her brother, M. Victor Kint; there was another person, moustached and with long hair – a calm, taciturn man, but whose traits bore a stamp and a semblance I could not mark unmoved. Amidst reserve and phlegm, amidst contrasts of character and of countenance, something there still was which recalled a face – mobile, fervent, feeling – a face changeable, now clouded, and now alight – a face from my world taken away, for my eyes lost, but where my best spring-hours of life had alternated in shadow and in glow – that face, where I had often seen movements, so near the signs of genius – that why there did not shine fully out, the undoubted fire, the thing, the spirit, and the secret itself – I could never tell. Yes – this Josef Emanuel – this man of peace – reminded me of his ardent brother.

Besides Messieurs Victor and Josef, I knew another of this party. This third person stood behind and in the shade, his attitude too was stooping, yet his dress and bald white head made him the most conspicuous figure of the group. He was an ecclesiastic: he was Père Silas. Do not fancy, reader, that there was any inconsistency in the priest's presence at this fête. This was not considered a show of Vanity Fair, but a commemoration of patriotic sacrifice. The Church patronized it, even with ostentation. There were troops of priests in the park that night.

Père Silas stooped over the seat with its single occupant, the rustic bench and that which sat upon it: a strange mass it was – bearing no shape, yet magnificent. You saw, indeed, the outline of a face and features, but these were so cadaverous and so strangely placed, you could almost have fancied a head severed from its trunk, and flung at random on a pile of rich merchandise. The distant lamp-rays glanced on clear pendants, on broad rings; neither the chasteness of moonlight, nor the distance of the torches, could quite subdue the gorgeous dyes of the drapery. Hail, Madame Walravens! I think you looked more witch-like than ever. And presently the good lady proved that she was indeed no corpse or ghost, but a harsh and hardy old woman; for, upon some aggravation in the clamorous petition of Désirée Beck to her mother, to go to the kiosk and take sweetmeats, the hunchback suddenly fetched her a resounding rap with her gold-knobbed cane.

There, then, were Madame Walravens, Madame Beck, Père Silas – the whole conjuration, the secret junta. The sight of them thus assembled did me good. I cannot say that I felt weak before them, or abashed, or dismayed. They outnumbered me, and I was worsted and under their feet; but, as yet, I was not dead.

CHAPTER 39

Old and New Acquaintance

Fascinated as by a basilisk with three heads, I could not leave this clique; the ground near them seemed to hold my feet. The canopy of entwined trees held out shadow, the night whispered a pledge of protection, and an officious lamp flashed just one beam to show me an obscure, safe seat, and then vanished. Let me now briefly tell the reader all that, during the past dark fortnight, I have been silently gathering from Rumour, respecting the origin and the object of M. Emanuel's departure. The tale is short, and not new: its alpha is Mammon, and its omega, Interest.

If Madame Walravens was hideous as a Hindoo idol, she seemed also to possess, in the estimation of these her votaries, an idol's consequence. The fact was, she had been rich – very rich; and though for the present, without the command of money, she was likely one day to be rich again. At Basseterre, in Guadaloupe, she possessed a large estate, received in dowry on her marriage sixty years ago, sequestered since her husband's failure; but now, it was supposed, cleared of claim, and, if duly looked after by a competent agent of integrity, considered capable of being made, in a few years, largely productive.

Père Silas took an interest in this prospective improvement for the sake of religion and the church, whereof Magloire Walravens was a devout daughter. Madame Beck, distantly related to the hunchback, and knowing her to be without family of her own, had long brooded over contingencies with a mother's calculating forethought, and, harshly treated as she was by Madame Walravens, never ceased to court her for interest's sake. Madame Beck and the priest were thus, for money reasons, equally and sincerely interested in the nursing of the West-Indian estate.

But the distance was great, and the climate hazardous. The competent and upright agent wanted, must be a devoted man. Just such a man had Madame Walravens retained for twenty years in her service, blighting his life, and then living on him, like an old fungus; such a man had Père Silas trained, taught, and bound to him by the ties of gratitude, habit, and belief. Such a man Madame Beck knew, and could in some measure influence. 'My pupil,' said Père Silas, 'if he remains in Europe, runs risk of apostasy, for he has become entangled with a heretic.' Madame Beck made also her private comment, and preferred in her own heart her secret reason for desiring expatriation. The thing she could not obtain, she desired not another to win; rather would she destroy it. As to Madame Walravens, she wanted her money and her land, and knew Paul, if he liked, could make the best and faithfullest steward: so the three self-seekers banded and beset the one unselfish. They reasoned, they appealed, they implored; on his mercy they cast themselves, into his hands they confidingly thrust their interests. They asked but two or three years of devotion – after that, he should live for himself: one of the number, perhaps, wished that in the mean time he might die.

No living being ever humbly laid his advantage at M. Emanuel's feet, or confidingly put it into his hands, that he spurned the trust, or repulsed the repository. What might be his private pain or inward reluctance to leave Europe – what his calculations for his own future – none asked, or knew, or reported. All this was a blank to me. His conferences with his confessor I might guess; the part duty and religion were made to play in the persuasions used, I might conjecture. He was gone, and had made no sign. There my knowledge closed.

With my head bent, and my forehead resting on my hands, I sat amidst grouped tree-stems and branching brushwood. Whatever talk passed amongst my neighbours, I might hear, if I would; I was near enough; but, for some time, there was scarce motive to attend. They gossiped about the dresses, the music, the illuminations, the fine night. I listened to hear them say, 'It is calm weather for *his* voyage; the "Antigua" (his ship) 'will sail prosperously.' No such remark fell: neither the 'Antigua,' nor her course, nor her passenger, were named.

Perhaps the light chat scarcely interested old Madame Walravens more than it did me; she appeared restless, turning her head now to this side, now that, looking through the trees, and among the crowd, as if expectant of an arrival and impatient of a delay. 'Où sont-ils? Pourquoi ne viennent-ils?'[222] I heard her mutter more than once; and at last, as if determined to have an answer to her questions – which hitherto none seemed to mind, she spoke aloud this phrase – a phrase brief enough, simple enough, but it sent a shock through me –

'Messieurs et mesdames,' said she, 'où donc est Justine Marie?'

'Justine Marie!' What name was this? Justine Marie – the dead nun – where was she? Why in her grave, Madame Walravens – what can you want with her? You shall go to her, but she shall not come to you.

Thus *I* should have answered, had the response lain with me, but nobody seemed to be of my mind; nobody seemed surprised, startled, or at a loss. The quietest common-place answer met the strange, the dead-disturbing, the Witch-of-Endor[223] query of the hunchback.

'Justine Marie,' said one, 'is coming; she is in the kiosk; she will be here presently.'

Out of this question and reply sprang a change in the chat – chat it still remained – easy, desultory, familiar gossip. Hint, allusion, comment, went round the circle, but all so broken, so dependent on references to persons not named, or circumstances not defined, that, listen intently as I would – and I *did* listen *now* with a fated interest – I could make out no more than that some scheme was on foot, in which this ghostly Justine Marie – dead or alive – was concerned. This family-junta seemed grasping at her somehow, for some reason; there seemed question of a marriage, of a fortune, for whom I could not quite make out – perhaps for Victor Kint, perhaps for Josef Emanuel – both were bachelors. Once I thought the hints and jests rained upon a young fair-haired foreigner of the party, whom they called Heinrich Mühler. Amidst all the badinage, Madame Walravens still obtruded, from time to time, hoarse, cross-grained speeches; her impatience being diverted only by an implacable surveillance of Désirée, who could not stir but the old woman menaced her with her staff.

'Là voilà!' suddenly cried one of the gentlemen, 'voilà Justine Marie qui arrive!'

This moment was for me peculiar. I called up to memory the pictured nun on the panel; present to my mind was the sad love-story; I saw in thought the vision of the garret, the apparition of the alley, the strange birth of the berceau: I underwent a presentiment of discovery, a strong conviction of coming disclosure. Ah! when imagination once runs riot where do we stop? What winter tree so bare and branchless – what way-side, hedge-munching animal so humble, that Fancy, a passing cloud, and a struggling moonbeam, will not clothe it in spirituality, and make of it a phantom?

With solemn force pressed on my heart the expectation of mystery breaking up: hitherto I had seen this spectre only through a glass darkly; now was I to behold it face to face. I leaned forward: I looked.

'She comes!' cried Josef Emanuel.

The circle moved as if opening to admit a new and welcome member. At this instant a torch chanced to be carried past; its blaze aided the pale moon in doing justice to the crisis, in lighting to perfection the dénouement pressing on. Surely those near me must have felt some little of the anxiety I felt, in degree so unmeted. Of that group, the coolest must have 'held his breath for a time!' As for me, my life stood still.

It is over. The moment and the nun are come. The crisis and the revelation are passed by.

The flambeau glares still within a yard, held up in a parkkeeper's hand; its long eager tongue of flame almost licks the figure of the Expected – there – where she stands full in my sight. What is she like? What does she wear? How does she look? Who is she?

There are many masks in the Park to-night, and as the hour wears late, so strange a feeling of revelry and mystery begins to spread abroad, that scarce would you discredit me, reader, were I to say that she is like the nun of the attic, that she wears black skirts and white head-clothes, that she looks the resurrection of the flesh, and that she is a risen ghost.

All falsities – all figments! We will not deal in this gear. Let us be honest, and cut, as heretofore, from the homely web of truth.

Homely, though, is an ill-chosen word. What I see is not precisely homely. A girl of Villette stands there – a girl fresh from her pensionnat. She is very comely, with the beauty indigenous to this country; she looks well-nourished, fair, and fat of flesh. Her cheeks are round, her eyes good; her hair is abundant. She is handsomely dressed. She is not alone; her escort consists of three persons – two being elderly; these she addresses as 'Mon Oncle' and 'Ma Tante.' She laughs, she chats: good-humoured, buxom, and blooming, she looks, at all points, the bourgeoise belle.

So much for 'Justine Marie;' so much for ghosts and mystery: not that this last was solved – this girl certainly is not my nun; what I saw in the garret and garden must have been taller by a span.

We have looked at the city belle; we have cursorily glanced at the respectable old uncle and aunt. Have we a stray glance to give to the third member of this company? Can we spare him a moment's notice? We ought to distinguish him so far, reader; he has claims on us; we do not now meet him for the first time. I clasped my hands very hard, and I drew my breath very deep; I held in the cry, I devoured the ejaculation, I forbade the start, I spoke and I stirred no more than a stone; but I knew what I looked on; through the dimness left in my eyes by many nights' weeping, I knew him. They said he was to sail by the 'Antigua.' Madame Beck said so. She lied, or she had uttered what was once truth, and failed to contradict it, when it became false. The 'Antigua' was gone, and there stood Paul Emanuel .

Was I glad? A huge load left me. Was it a fact to warrant joy? I know not. Ask first what were the circumstances attendant on this respite? How far did this delay concern *me*? Were there not those whom it might touch more nearly?

After all, who may this young girl, this Justine Marie be? Not a stranger, reader; she is known to me by sight; she visits at the Rue Fossette; she is often of Madame Beck's Sunday parties. She is a relation of both the Becks and Walravens; she derives her baptismal name from the sainted nun who would have been her aunt had she lived; her patronymic is Sauveur; she is an heiress and an orphan, and M. Emanuel is her guardian; some say her godfather. The family junta wish this heiress to be married to one of their band – which is it? Vital question – which is it?

I felt very glad now, that the drug administered in the sweet draught had filled me with a possession which made bed and chamber intolerable. I always, through my whole life, liked to penetrate to the real truth; I like seeking the goddess in her temple, and handling the veil, and daring the dread glance. O Titaness amongst deities! The covered outline of thine aspect sickens often through its uncertainty, but define to us one trait, show us one lineament, clear in awful sincerity; we may gasp in untold terror, but with that gasp we drink in a breath of thy divinity; our heart shakes, and its currents sway like rivers lifted by earthquake, but we have swallowed strength. To see and know the worst is to take from Fear her main advantage.

The Walravens' party, augmented in numbers, now became very gay. The gentlemen fetched refreshments from the kiosk, all sat down on the turf under the trees; they drank healths and sentiments; they laughed, they jested. M. Emanuel underwent some raillery, half good-humoured, half, I thought, malicious, especially on Madame Beck's part. I soon gathered that his voyage had been temporarily deferred of his own will, without the concurrence, even against the advice of his friends; he had let the 'Antigua' go, and had taken his berth in the 'Paul et Virginie,' appointed to sail a fortnight later. It was his reason for this resolve which they teased him to assign, and which he would only vaguely indicate as 'the settlement of a little piece of business which he had set his heart upon.' What *was* this business? Nobody knew. Yes, there was one who seemed partly, at least, in his confidence; a meaning look passed between him and Justine Marie. 'La petite va m'aider – n'est-ce pas?' said he. The answer was prompt enough, God knows!

'Mais oui, je vous aiderai de tout mon coeur. Vous ferez de moi tout ce que vous voudrez, mon parrain.'[224]

And this dear 'parrain' took her hand and lifted it to his grateful lips. Upon which demonstration, I saw the light-complexioned young Teuton, Heinrich Mühler, grow restless, as if he did not like it. He even grumbled a few words, whereat M. Emanuel actually laughed in his face, and with the ruthless triumph of the assured conqueror, he drew his ward nearer to him.

M. Emanuel was indeed very joyous that night. He seemed not one whit subdued by the change of scene and action impending. He was the true life of the party; a little despotic perhaps, determined to be chief in mirth, as well as in labour, yet from moment to moment proving indisputably his right of leadership. His was the wittiest word, the pleasantest anecdote, the frankest laugh. Restlessly active, after his manner, he multiplied himself to wait on all; but oh! I saw which was his favourite. I saw at whose feet he lay on the turf, I saw whom he folded carefully from the night air, whom he tended, watched, and cherished as the apple of his eye.

Still, hint and raillery flew thick, and still I gathered that while M. Paul should be absent, working for others, these others, not quite ungrateful, would guard for him the treasure he left in Europe. Let him bring them an Indian fortune; they would give him in return a young bride and a rich inheritance. As for the saintly consecration, the vow of constancy, that was forgotten: the blooming and charming Present prevailed over the Past; and at length his nun was indeed buried.

Thus it must be. The revelation was indeed come. Presentiment had not been mistaken in her impulse; there is a kind of presentiment which never *is* mistaken; it was I who had for a moment miscalculated; not seeing the true bearing of the oracle, I had thought she muttered of vision when, in truth, her prediction touched reality.

I might have paused longer upon what I saw; I might have deliberated ere I drew inferences. Some perhaps would have held the premises doubtful, the proofs insufficient; some slow sceptics would have incredulously examined, ere they conclusively accepted the project of a marriage between a poor and unselfish man of forty, and his wealthy ward of eighteen; but far from me such shifts and palliatives, far from me such temporary evasion of the actual, such coward fleeing from the dread, the swift-footed, the all-overtaking Fact, such feeble suspense of submission to her the sole sovereign, such paltering and faltering resistance to the Power whose errand is to march conquering and to conquer, such traitor defection from the TRUTH.

No. I hastened to accept the whole plan. I extended my grasp and took it all in. I gathered it to me with a sort of rage of haste, and folded it round me, as the soldier struck on the field folds his colours about his breast. I invoked Conviction to nail upon me the certainty, abhorred while embraced, to fix it with the strongest spikes her strongest strokes could drive; and when the iron had entered well my soul, I stood up, as I thought renovated.

In my infatuation, I said, 'Truth, you are a good mistress to your faithful servants! While a Lie pressed me, how I suffered! Even when the Falsehood was still sweet, still flattering to the fancy, and warm to the feelings, it wasted me with hourly torment. The persuasion that affection was won could not be divorced from the dread that, by another turn of the wheel, it might be lost. Truth stripped away Falsehood, and Flattery, and Expectancy, and here I stand – free!'

Nothing remained now but to take my freedom to my chamber, to carry it with me to my bed and see what I could make of it. The play was not yet indeed quite played out, I might have waited and watched longer that love scene under the trees, that sylvan courtship. Had there been nothing of love in the demonstration, my Fancy in this hour was so generous, so creative, she could have modelled for it the most salient lineaments, and given it the deepest life and highest colour of passion. But I *would* not look; I had fixed my resolve, but I would not violate my nature. And then – something tore me so cruelly under my shawl, something so dug into my side, a vulture so strong in beak and talon, I must be alone to grapple with it. I think I never felt jealousy till now. This was not like enduring the endearments of Dr John and Paulina, against which while I sealed my eyes and my ears, while I withdrew thence my thoughts, my sense of harmony still acknowledged in it a charm. This was an outrage. The love born of beauty was not mine; I had nothing in common with it: I could not dare to meddle with it, but another love, venturing diffidently into life after long acquaintance, furnace-tried by pain, stamped by constancy, consolidated by affection's pure and durable alloy, submitted by intellect to intellect's own tests, and finally wrought up, by his own process, to his own unflawed completeness, this Love that laughed at Passion, his fast frenzies and his hot and hurried extinction, in *this* Love I had a vested interest; and whatever tended either to its culture or its destruction, I could not view impassibly.

I turned from the group of trees and the 'merrie companie' in its shade. Midnight was long past; the concert was over, the crowds were thinning. I followed the ebb. Leaving the radiant park and well-lit Haute-Ville (still well-lit, for this it seems was to be a 'nuit blanche' in Villette), I sought the dim lower quarter.

Dim I should not say, for the beauty of moonlight – forgotten in the park – here once more flowed in upon perception. High she rode, and calm and stainlessly she shone. The music and the mirth of the fête, the fire and bright hues of those lamps had out-done and out-shone her for an hour, but now, again, her glory and her silence triumphed. The rival lamps were dying: she held her course like a white fate. Drum, trumpet, bugle, had uttered their clangour and were forgotten: with pencil-ray she wrote on heaven and on earth records for archives everlasting. She and those stars seemed to me at once the types and witnesses of truth all regnant. The night-sky lit her reign: like its slow-wheeling progress, advanced her victory – that onward movement which has been, and is, and will be from eternity to eternity.

These oil-twinkling streets are very still: I like them for their lowliness and peace. Homeward-bound burghers pass me now and then, but these companies are pedestrian, make little noise, and are soon gone. So well do I love Villette under her present aspect, not willingly would I re-enter under a roof, but that I am bent on pursuing my strange adventure to a successful close, and quietly regaining my bed in the great dormitory, before Madame Beck comes home.

Only one street lies between me and the Rue Fossette; as I enter it, for the first time, the sound of a carriage tears up the deep peace of this quarter. It comes this way – comes very fast. How loud sounds its rattle on the paved path! The street is narrow and I keep carefully to the causeway. The carriage thunders past, but what do I see, or fancy I see, as it rushes by? Surely something white fluttered from that window – surely a hand waved a handkerchief. Was that signal meant for me? Am I known? Who could recognize me? That is not M. de Bassompierre's carriage, nor Mrs Bretton's; and besides, neither the Hôtel Crécy nor the chateau of La Terrasse lies in that direction. Well, I have no time for conjecture: I must hurry home.

Gaining the Rue Fossette, reaching the Pensionnat, all there was still; no fiacre had yet arrived with Madame and Désirée. I had left the great door ajar; should I find it thus? Perhaps the wind or some other accident may have thrown it to with sufficient force to start the spring-bolt? In that case, hopeless became admission; my adventure must issue in catastrophe. I lightly pushed the heavy leaf: would it yield?

Yes. As soundless, as unresisting, as if some propitious genius had waited on a sesame-charm, in the vestibule within. Entering with bated breath, quietly making all fast, shoelessly mounting the staircase, I sought the dormitory, and reached my couch.

Aye! I reached it, and once more drew a free inspiration. The next moment, I almost shrieked – almost, but not quite, thank Heaven!

Throughout the dormitory, throughout the house, there reigned at this hour the stillness of death. All slept, and in such hush, it seemed that none dreamed. Stretched on the nineteen beds lay nineteen forms, at full-length and motionless. On mine – the twentieth couch – nothing *ought* to have lain: I had left it void, and void should have found it. What, then, do I see between the half-drawn curtains? What dark, usurping shape, supine, long, and strange? Is it a robber who has made his way through the open street-door, and lies there in wait? It looks very black, I think it looks – not human. Can it be a wandering dog that has come in from the street and crept and nestled hither? Will it spring, will it leap out if I approach? Approach I must. Courage! One step! –

My head reeled, for by the faint night-lamp, I saw stretched on my bed the old phantom – the NUN.

A cry at this moment might have ruined me. Be the spectacle what it might, I could afford neither consternation, scream, nor swoon. Besides, I was not overcome. Tempered by late incidents, my nerves disdained hysteria. Warm from illuminations, and music, and thronging thousands, thoroughly lashed up by a new scourge, I defied spectra. In a moment, without exclamation, I had rushed on the haunted couch; nothing leaped out, or sprung, or stirred; all the movement was mine, so was all the life, the reality, the substance, the force; as my instinct felt. I tore her up – the incubus! I held her on high – the goblin! I shook her loose – the mystery! And down she fell – down all round me – down in shreds and fragments – and I trode upon her.

Here again – behold the branchless tree, the unstabled
Rosinante;[225] the film of cloud, the flicker of moonshine. The long
nun proved a long bolster dressed in a long black stole, and artfully
invested with a white veil. The garments in very truth – strange as it
may seem – were genuine nun's garments, and by some hand they
had been disposed with a view to illusion. Whence came these
vestments? Who contrived this artifice? These questions still
remained. To the head-bandage was pinned a slip of paper: it bore
in pencil these mocking words: –

'The nun of the attic bequeaths to Lucy Snowe her wardrobe.
She will be seen in the Rue Fossette no more.'

And what and who was she that had haunted me? She, I had
actually seen three times? Not a woman of my acquaintance had the
stature of that ghost. She was not of female height. Not to any man
I knew could the machination, for a moment, be attributed.

Still mystified beyond expression, but as thoroughly, as suddenly,
relieved from all sense of the spectral and unearthly; scorning also
to wear out my brain with the fret of a trivial though insoluble
riddle – I just bundled together stole, veil, and bandages, thrust
them beneath my pillow, lay down, listened till I heard the wheels
of Madame's home-returning fiacre, then turned, and worn out by
many nights' vigils, conquered, too, perhaps, by the now reacting
narcotic, I deeply slept.

CHAPTER 40

The Happy Pair

THE DAY SUCCEEDING this remarkable Midsummer night, proved no common day. I do not mean that it brought signs in heaven above, or portents on the earth beneath; nor do I allude to meteorological phenomena, to storm, flood, or whirlwind. On the contrary: the sun rose jocund, with a July face. Morning decked her beauty with rubies, and so filled her lap with roses, that they fell from her in showers, making her path blush: the Hours woke fresh as nymphs, and emptying on the early hills their dew-vials, they stepped out dismantled of vapour: shadowless, azure, and glorious, they led the sun's steeds on a burning and unclouded course.

In short, it was as fine a day as the finest summer could boast: but I doubt whether I was not the sole inhabitant of the Rue Fossette, who cared or remembered to note this pleasant fact. Another thought busied all other heads; a thought, indeed, which had its share in my meditations; but this master consideration, not possessing for me so entire a novelty, so overwhelming a suddenness, especially so dense a mystery, as it offered to the majority of my co-speculators thereon, left me somewhat more open than the rest, to any collateral observation or impression.

Still, while walking in the garden, feeling the sunshine, and marking the blooming and growing plants, I pondered the same subject the whole house discussed.

What subject?

Merely this. When matins came to be said, there was a place vacant in the first rank of boarders. When breakfast was served, there remained a coffee-cup unclaimed. When the house-maid made the beds, she found in one, a bolster laid lengthwise, clad in a cap and nightgown; and when Ginevra Fanshawe's music-mistress came early, as usual, to give the morning lesson, that accomplished and promising young person, her pupil, failed utterly to be forthcoming.

High and low was Miss Fanshawe sought; through length and breadth was the house ransacked; vainly; not a trace, not an indication, not so much as a scrap of a billet rewarded the search;

the nymph was vanished, engulfed in the past night, like a shooting star swallowed up by darkness.

Deep was the dismay of surveillante teachers, deeper the horror of the defaulting directress. Never had I seen Madame Beck so pale or so appalled. Here was a blow struck at her tender part, her weak side; here was damage done to her interest. How, too, had the untoward event happened? By what outlet had the fugitive taken wing? Not a casement was found unfastened, not a pane of glass broken; all the doors were bolted secure. Never to this day has Madame Beck obtained satisfaction on this point, nor indeed has anybody else concerned, save and excepting one, Lucy Snowe, who could not forget how, to facilitate a certain enterprise, a certain great door had been drawn softly to its lintel, closed, indeed, but neither bolted nor secure. The thundering carriage-and-pair encountered were now likewise recalled, as well as that puzzling signal, the waved handkerchief.

From these premises, and one or two others, inaccessible to any but myself, I could draw but one inference. It was a case of elopement. Morally certain on this head, and seeing Madame Beck's profound embarrassment, I at last communicated my conviction. Having alluded to M. de Hamal's suit, I found, as I expected, that Madame Beck was perfectly au fait to that affair. She had long since discussed it with Mrs Cholmondeley, and laid her own responsibility, in the business, on that lady's shoulders. To Mrs Cholmondeley and M. de Bassompierre she now had recourse.

We found that the Hôtel Crécy was already alive to what had happened. Ginevra had written to her cousin Paulina, vaguely signifying hymeneal intentions; communications had been received from the family of de Hamal; M. de Bassompierre was on the track of the fugitives. He overtook them too late.

In the course of the week, the post brought me a note. I may as well transcribe it; it contains explanation on more than one point: –

'DEAR OLD TIM' (short for Timon), – 'I am off you see – gone like a shot. Alfred and I intended to be married in this way almost from the first; we never meant to be spliced in the humdrum way of other people; Alfred has too much spirit for that, and so have I – Dieu merci! Do you know, Alfred, who used to call you "the dragon," has seen so much of you during the last few months, that he begins to feel quite friendly towards you. He hopes you won't miss him now that he is gone; he begs to apologize for any little trouble he may have given you. He is afraid he rather inconvenienced you once when he came upon you in the grenier, just as you were reading a letter seemingly of the most special interest; but he could not resist the temptation to give you a start, you appeared so wonderfully taken up with your correspondent. En revanche, he says you once frightened him by rushing in for a dress or a shawl, or some other chiffon, at the moment when he had struck a light, and was going to take a quiet whiff of his cigar, while waiting for me.

'Do you begin to comprehend by this time that M. le Comte de Hamal was the nun of the attic, and that he came to see your humble servant? I will tell you how he managed it. You know he has the entrée of the Athénée, where two or three of his nephews, the sons of his eldest sister, Madame de Melcy, are students. You know the court of the Athénée is on the other side of the high wall bounding your walk, the allée défendue. Alfred can climb as well as he can dance or fence; his amusement was to make the escalade of our pensionnat by mounting, first the wall; then – by the aid of that high tree overspreading the grand berceau, and resting some of its boughs on the roof of the lower buildings of our premises – he managed to scale the first classe and the grande salle. One night, by the way, he fell out of this tree, tore down some of the branches, nearly broke his own neck, and after all, in running away, got a terrible fright, and was nearly caught by two people, Madame Beck and M. Emanuel, he thinks, walking in the alley. From the grande salle the ascent is not difficult to the highest block of building, finishing in the great garret. The skylight, you know, is day and night left half-open for air; by the skylight he entered. Nearly a year ago, I chanced to tell him our legend of the nun, that suggested his romantic idea of the spectral disguise, which I think you must allow he has very cleverly carried out.

'But for the nun's black gown and white veil, he would have been caught again and again both by you and that tiger-Jesuit, M. Paul. He thinks you both capital ghost-seers, and very brave. What I wonder at is, rather your secretiveness than your courage. How could you endure the visitations of that long spectre, time after time, without crying out, telling everybody, and rousing the whole house and neighbourhood?

'Oh, and how did you like the nun as a bed-fellow? I dressed her up – didn't I do it well? Did you shriek when you saw her? *I* should have gone mad; but then you have such nerves! – real iron and bend leather! I believe you feel nothing. You haven't the same sensitiveness that a person of my constitution has. You seem to me insensible both to pain and fear and grief. You are a real old Diogenes.

'Well, dear grandmother! and are you not mightily angry at my moonlight flitting and run-away match? I assure you it is excellent fun, and I did it partly to spite that minx, Paulina, and that bear, Dr John – to show them that, with all their airs, I could get married as well as they. M. de Bassompierre was at first in a strange fume with Alfred; he threatened a prosecution for "détournement de mineur," and I know not what; he was so abominably in earnest, that I found myself forced to do a little bit of the melodramatic – go down on my knees, sob, cry, drench three pocket-handkerchiefs. Of course, "mon oncle" soon gave in; indeed, where was the use of making a fuss? I am married, and that's all about it. He still says our marriage is not legal, because I am not of age, forsooth! As if that made any difference! I am just as much married as if I were a hundred. However, we are to be married again, and I am to have a trousseau, and Mrs Cholmondeley is going to superintend it; and there are some hopes that M. de Bassompierre will give me a decent portion, which will be very convenient, as dear Alfred has nothing but his nobility, native and hereditary, and his pay. I only wish uncle would do things unconditionally, in a generous, gentleman-like fashion; he is so disagreeable as to make the dowry depend on Alfred's giving his written promise that he will never touch cards or dice from the day it is paid down. They accuse my angel of a tendency to play: I don't know anything about that, but I *do* know he is a dear, adorable creature.

'I cannot sufficiently extol the genius with which De Hamal managed our flight. How clever in him to select the night of the fête, when Madame (for he knows her habits), as he said, would infallibly be absent at the concert in the park. I suppose *you* must have gone with her. I watched you rise and leave the dormitory about eleven o'clock. How you returned alone, and on foot, I cannot conjecture. That surely was *you* we met in the narrow old Rue St. Jean? Did you see me wave my handkerchief from the carriage window?

'Adieu! Rejoice in my good luck: congratulate me on my supreme happiness, and believe me, dear cynic and misanthrope, yours, in the best of health and spirits,

GINEVRA LAURA DE HAMAL, née FANSHAWE.

'P.S. – Remember, I am a countess now. Papa, mama, and the girls at home, will be delighted to hear that. "My daughter, the Countess! My sister, the Countess." Bravo! Sounds rather better than Mrs John Bretton, hein?'

In winding up Mistress Fanshawe's memoirs, the reader will no doubt expect to hear that she came finally to bitter expiation of her youthful levities. Of course, a large share of suffering lies in reserve for her future.

A few words will embody my farther knowledge respecting her.

I saw her towards the close of her honeymoon. She called on Madame Beck, and sent for me into the salon. She rushed into my arms laughing. She looked very blooming and beautiful: her curls were longer, her cheeks rosier than ever: her white bonnet and her Flanders veil, her orange flowers and her bride's dress, became her mightily.

'I have got my portion!' she cried at once; (Ginevra ever stuck to the substantial; I always thought there was a good trading element in her composition, much as she scorned the 'bourgeoisie;') 'and uncle de Bassompierre is quite reconciled. I don't mind his calling Alfred a "nincompoop" – that's only his coarse Scotch breeding; and I believe Paulina envies me, and Dr John is wild with jealousy – fit to blow his brains out – and I'm so happy! I really think I've hardly anything left to wish for – unless it be a carriage and a hotel, and – oh! I must introduce you to "mon mari". Alfred, come here!'

And Alfred appeared from the inner salon, where he was talking to Madame Beck, receiving the blended felicitations and reprimands of that lady. I was presented under my various names: the Dragon, Diogenes, and Timon. The young Colonel was very polite. He made me a prettily-turned, neatly-worded apology, about the ghost-visits, &c., concluding with saying that 'the best excuse for all his iniquities stood there!' pointing to his bride.

And then the bride sent him back to Madame Beck, and she took me to herself, and proceeded literally to suffocate me with her unrestrained spirits, her girlish, giddy, wild nonsense. She showed her ring exultingly; she called herself Madame la Comtesse de Hamal, and asked how it sounded, a score of times. I said very little. I gave her only the crust of my nature. No matter: she expected of me nothing better – she knew me too well to look for compliments – my dry gibes pleased her well enough, and the more impassible and prosaic my mien, the more merrily she laughed.

Soon after his marriage, M. de Hamal was persuaded to leave the army as the surest way of weaning him from certain unprofitable associates and habits; a post of attaché was procured for him, and he and his young wife went abroad. I thought she would forget me now, but she did not. For many years, she kept up a capricious, fitful sort of correspondence. During the first year or two, it was only of herself and Alfred she wrote; then, Alfred faded in the background; herself and a certain new-comer prevailed; one Alfred Fanshawe de Bassompierre de Hamal began to reign in his father's stead. There were great boastings about this personage, extravagant amplifications upon miracles of precocity, mixed with vehement objurgations against the phlegmatic incredulity with which I received them. I didn't know 'what it was to be a mother:' 'unfeeling thing that I was, the sensibilities of the maternal heart were Greek and Hebrew to me,' and so on. In due course of nature this young gentleman took his degrees in teething, measles, hooping-cough: that was a terrible time for me – the mama's letters became a perfect shout of affliction – never woman was so put upon by calamity: never human being stood in such need of sympathy. I was frightened at first, and wrote back pathetically; but I soon found out there was more cry than wool in the business, and relapsed into my natural cruel insensibility. As to the youthful sufferer, he weathered each storm like a hero. Five times was that youth 'in articulo mortis,'[226] and five times did he miraculously revive.

In the course of years there arose ominous murmurings against Alfred the First; M. de Bassompierre had to be appealed to, debts had to be paid, some of them of that dismal and dingy order called 'debts of honour;' ignoble plaints and difficulties became frequent. Under every cloud, no matter what its nature, Ginevra, as of old, called out lustily for sympathy and aid. She had no notion of meeting any distress single-handed. In some shape, from some quarter or other, she was pretty sure to obtain her will, and so she got on – fighting the battle of life by proxy, and, on the whole, suffering as little as any human being I have ever known.

CHAPTER 41

Faubourg Clotilde

MUST I, ERE I CLOSE, render some account of that Freedom and Renovation which I won on the fête-night? Must I tell how I and the two stalwart companions I brought home from the illuminated park bore the test of intimate acquaintance?

I tried them the very next day. They had boasted their strength loudly when they reclaimed me from love and its bondage, but upon my demanding deeds, not words, some evidence of better comfort, some experience of a relieved life – Freedom excused himself, as for the present, impoverished and disabled to assist; and Renovation never spoke; he had died in the night suddenly.

I had nothing left for it then but to trust secretly that conjecture might have hurried me too fast and too far, to sustain the oppressive hour by reminders of the distorting and discolouring magic of jealousy. After a short and vain struggle, I found myself brought back captive to the old rack of suspense, tied down and strained anew.

Shall I yet see him before he goes? Will he bear me in mind? Does he purpose to come? Will this day – will the next hour bring him? or must I again assay that corroding pain of long attent – that rude agony of rupture at the close, that mute, mortal wrench, which, in at once uprooting hope and doubt, shakes life; while the hand that does the violence cannot be caressed to pity, because absence interposes her barrier!

It was the Feast of the Assumption; no school was held. The boarders and teachers, after attending mass in the morning, were gone on a long walk into the country to take their goûter, or afternoon meal at some farm-house. I did not go with them, for now but two days remained ere the 'Paul et Virginie' must sail, and I was clinging to my last chance, as the living waif of a wreck clings to his last raft or cable.

There was some joiners' work to do in the first classe, some bench or desk to repair; holidays were often turned to account for the performance of these operations, which could not be executed when the rooms were filled with pupils. As I sat solitary, purposing to adjourn to the garden and leave the coast clear, but too listless to fulfil my own intent, I heard the workman coming.

Foreign artizans and servants do everything by couples: I believe it would take two Labassecourien carpenters to drive a nail. While tying on my bonnet, which had hitherto hung by its ribbons from my idle hand, I vaguely and momentarily wondered to hear the step of but one 'ouvrier.' I noted, too – as captives in dungeons find sometimes dreary leisure to note the merest trifles – that this man wore shoes, and not sabots: I concluded that it must be the master-carpenter, coming to inspect, before he sent his journeymen. I threw round me my scarf. He advanced; he opened the door; my back was towards it; I felt a little thrill – a curious sensation, too quick and transient to be analyzed. I turned, I stood in the supposed master-artizan's presence: looking towards the door-way, I saw it filled with a figure, and my eyes printed upon my brain the picture of M. Paul.

Hundreds of the prayers with which we weary Heaven, bring to the suppliant no fulfilment. Once haply in life, one golden gift falls prone in the lap – one boon full and bright, perfect from Fruition's mint.

M. Emanuel wore the dress in which he probably purposed to travel – a surtout, guarded with velvet; I thought him prepared for instant departure, and yet I had understood that two days were yet to run before the ship sailed. He looked well, and cheerful. He looked kind and benign: he came in with eagerness; he was close to me in one second; he was all amity. It might be his bridegroom-mood which thus brightened him. Whatever the cause, I could not meet his sunshine with cloud. If this were my last moment with him, I would not waste it in forced, unnatural distance. I loved him well – too well not to smite out of my path even Jealousy herself, when she would have obstructed a kind farewell. A cordial word from his lips, or a gentle look from his eyes, would do me good, for all the span of life that remained to me; it would be comfort in the last strait of loneliness; I would take it – I would taste the elixir, and pride should not spill the cup.

The interview would be short, of course: he would say to me just what he had said to each of the assembled pupils; he would take and hold my hand two minutes; he would touch my cheek with his lips for the first, last, only time – and then – no more. Then, indeed, the final parting, then the wide separation, the great gulf I could not pass to go to him – across which, haply, he would not glance, to remember me.

He took my hand in one of his, with the other he put back my bonnet; he looked into my face, his luminous smile went out, his lips expressed something almost like the wordless language of a mother who finds a child greatly and unexpectedly changed, broken with illness, or worn-out by want. A check supervened.

'Paul, Paul!' said a woman's hurried voice behind, 'Paul, come into the salon; I have yet a great many things to say to you – conversation for the whole day – and so has Victor; and Josef is here. Come, Paul, come to your friends.'

Madame Beck, brought to the spot by vigilance or an inscrutable instinct, pressed so near, she almost thrust herself between me and M. Emanuel. 'Come, Paul!' she reiterated, her eye grazing me with its hard ray like a steel stylet. She pushed against her kinsman. I thought he receded; I thought he would go. Pierced deeper than I could endure, made now to feel what defied suppression, I cried –

'My heart will break!'

What I felt seemed literal heart-break; but the seal of another fountain yielded under the strain: one breath from M. Paul, the whisper, 'Trust me!' lifted a load, opened an outlet. With many a deep sob, with thrilling, with icy shiver, with strong trembling, and yet with relief – I wept.

'Leave her to me; it is a crisis; I will give her a cordial, and it will pass,' said the calm Madame Beck.

To be left to her and her cordial, seemed to me something like being left to the poisoner and her bowl. When M. Paul answered deeply, harshly, and briefly –

'Laissez-moi!'[227] in the grim sound I felt a music strange, strong, but life-giving.

'Laissez-moi!' he repeated, his nostrils opening, and his facial muscles all quivering as he spoke.

'But this will never do,' said Madame, with sternness. More sternly rejoined her kinsman –

'Sortez d'ici!'[228]

'I will send for Père Silas; on the spot I will send for him,' she threatened pertinaciously.

'Femme!' cried the professor, not now in his deep tones, but in his highest and most excited key, 'Femme! sortez à l'instant!'

He was roused, and I loved him in his wrath with a passion beyond what I had yet felt.

'What you do is wrong,' pursued Madame; 'it is an act characteristic of men of your unreliable, imaginative temperament; a step impulsive, injudicious, inconsistent – a proceeding vexatious, and not estimable in the view of persons of steadier and more resolute character.'

'You know not what I have of steady and resolute in me,' said he, 'but you shall see; the event shall teach you. Modeste,' he continued less fiercely, 'be gentle, be pitying, be a woman; look at this poor face, and relent. You know I am your friend, and the friend of your friends; in spite of your taunts, you well and deeply know I may be trusted. Of sacrificing myself I made no difficulty, but my heart is pained by what I see; it *must* have and give solace. *Leave me*!'

This time, in the '*leave me*,' there was an intonation so bitter and so imperative, I wondered that even Madame Beck herself could for one moment delay obedience; but she stood firm; she gazed upon him dauntless; she met his eye, forbidding and fixed as stone. She was opening her lips to retort; I saw over all M. Paul's face a quick-rising light and fire: I can hardly tell how he managed the movement; it did not seem violent; it kept the form of courtesy; he gave his hand; it scarce touched her, I thought; she ran, she whirled from the room; she was gone and the door shut in one second.

This flash of passion was all over very soon. He smiled as he told me to wipe my eyes; he waited quietly till I was calm, dropping from time to time a stilling, solacing word. Ere long I sat beside him once more myself – re-assured – not desperate, nor yet desolate; not friendless, not hopeless, not sick of life, and seeking death.

'It made you very sad then to lose your friend?' said he.

'It kills me to be forgotten, monsieur,' I said. 'All these weary days I have not heard from you one word, and I was crushed with the possibility, growing to certainty, that you would depart without saying farewell!'

'Must I tell you what I told Modeste Beck – that you do not know me? Must I show and teach you my character? You *will* have proof that I can be a firm friend? Without clear proof this hand will not lie still in mine, it will not trust my shoulder as a safe stay? Good. The proof is ready. I come to justify myself.'

'Say anything, teach anything, prove anything, monsieur: I can listen now.'

'Then, in the first place, you must go out with me a good distance into the town. I came on purpose to fetch you.'

Without questioning his meaning, or sounding his plan, or offering the semblance of an objection, I re-tied my bonnet: I was ready.

The route he took was by the boulevards: he several times made me sit down on the seats stationed under the lime-trees; he did not ask if I was tired, but looked, and drew his own conclusions.

'All these weary days,' said he, repeating my words, with a gentle, kindly mimicry of my voice and foreign accent, not new from his lips, and of which the playful banter never wounded, not even when coupled as it often was, with the assertion, that however I might *write* his language, I *spoke* and always should speak it imperfectly and hesitatingly. ' "All these weary days," I have not for one hour forgotten you. Faithful women err in this, that they think themselves the sole faithful of God's creatures. On a very fervent and living truth to myself, I, too, till lately scarce dared count, from any quarter; but – look at me.'

I lifted my happy eyes: they *were* happy now, or they would have been no interpreters of my heart.

'Well,' said he, after some seconds' scrutiny, 'there is no denying that signature: Constancy wrote it; her pen is of iron. Was the record painful?'

'Severely painful,' I said, with truth. 'Withdraw her hand, monsieur; I can bear its inscribing force no more.'

'Elle est toute pâle,' said he, speaking to himself; 'cette figure là me fait mal.'[229]

'Ah! I am not pleasant to look at – ?'

I could not help saying this; the words came unbidden: I never remember the time when I had not a haunting dread of what might be the degree of my outward deficiency; this dread pressed me at the moment with special force.

A great softness passed upon his countenance; his violet eyes grew suffused and glistening under their deep Spanish lashes: he started up; 'Let us walk on.'

'Do I displease your eyes *much*?' I took courage to urge: the point had its vital import for me.

He stopped, and gave me a short, strong answer – an answer which silenced, subdued, yet profoundly satisfied. Ever after that, I knew what I was for *him*; and what I might be for the rest of the world, I ceased painfully to care. Was it weak to lay so much stress on an opinion about appearance? I fear it might be – I fear it was; but in that case I must avow no light share of weakness. I must own a great fear of displeasing – a strong wish moderately to please M. Paul.

Whither we rambled, I scarce knew. Our walk was long, yet seemed short; the path was pleasant, the day lovely. M. Emanuel talked of his voyage – he thought of staying away three years. On his return from Guadaloupe, he looked forward to release from liabilities and a clear course; and what did I purpose doing in the interval of his absence? he asked. I had talked once, he reminded me, of trying to be independent and keeping a little school of my own: had I dropped the idea?

'Indeed, I had not: I was doing my best to save what would enable me to put it in practice.'

'He did not like leaving me in the Rue Fossette; he feared I should miss him there too much – I should feel desolate – I should grow sad – ?'

This was certain; but I promised to do my best to endure.

'Still,' said he, speaking low, 'there is another objection to your present residence. I should wish to write to you sometimes: it would not be well to have any uncertainty about the safe transmission of letters; and in the Rue Fossette – in short, our Catholic discipline in certain matters – though justifiable and expedient – might possibly, under peculiar circumstances, become liable to misapplication – perhaps abuse.'

'But if you write,' said I, 'I *must* have your letters; and I *will* have them: ten directors, twenty directresses, shall not keep them from me. I am a Protestant: I will not bear that kind of discipline: monsieur, I *will not.*'

'Doucement – doucement,' rejoined he; 'we will contrive a plan; we have our resources: soyez tranquille.'

So speaking, he paused.

We were now returning from the long walk. We had reached the middle of a clean Faubourg, where the houses were small, but looked pleasant. It was before the white door-step of a very neat abode that M. Paul had halted.

'I call here,' said he.

He did not knock, but taking from his pocket a key, he opened and entered at once. Ushering me in, he shut the door behind us. No servant appeared. The vestibule was small, like the house, but freshly and tastefully painted; its vista closed in a French window with vines trained about the panes, tendrils and green leaves kissing the glass. Silence reigned in this dwelling.

Opening an inner door, M. Paul disclosed a parlour, or salon – very tiny, but I thought, very pretty. Its delicate walls were tinged like a blush; its floor was waxed; a square of brilliant carpet covered its centre; its small round table shone like the mirror over its hearth; there was a little couch, a little chiffonnière – the half-open, crimson-silk door of which, showed porcelain on the shelves; there was a French clock, a lamp; there were ornaments in biscuit china; the recess of the single ample window was filled with a green stand, bearing three green flower-pots, each filled with a fine plant glowing in bloom; in one corner appeared a guéridon with a marble top, and upon it a work-box, and a glass filled with violets in water. The lattice of this room was open; the outer air breathing through, gave freshness, the sweet violets lent fragrance.

'Pretty, pretty place!' said I. M. Paul smiled to see me so pleased.

'Must we sit down here and wait?' I asked in a whisper, half-awed by the deep-pervading hush.

'We will first peep into one or two other nooks of this nut-shell,' he replied.

'Dare you take the freedom of going all over the house?' I inquired.

'Yes, I dare,' said he, quietly.

He led the way. I was shown a little kitchen with a little stove and oven, with few but bright brasses, two chairs and a table. A small cupboard held a diminutive but commodious set of earthenware.

'There is a coffee service of china in the salon,' said M. Paul, as I looked at the six green and white dinner-plates; the four dishes, the cups and jugs to match.

Conducted up the narrow but clean staircase, I was permitted a glimpse of two pretty cabinets of sleeping-rooms; finally, I was once more led below, and we halted with a certain ceremony before a larger door than had yet been opened.

Producing a second key, M. Emanuel adjusted it to the lock of this door. He opened, put me in before him.

'Voici!' he cried.

I found myself in a good-sized apartment, scrupulously clean, though bare, compared with those I had hitherto seen. The well-scoured boards were carpetless; it contained two rows of green benches and desks, with an alley down the centre, terminating in an estrade, a teacher's chair and table; behind them a tableau. On the walls hung two maps; in the windows flowered a few hardy plants; in short, here was a miniature classe – complete, neat, pleasant.

'It is a school then?' said I. 'Who keeps it? I never heard of an establishment in this faubourg.'

'Will you have the goodness to accept of a few prospectuses for distribution in behalf of a friend of mine?' asked he, taking from his surtout-pocket some quires of these documents, and putting them into my hand. I looked, I read – printed in fair characters: –

'Externat de demoiselles.[230] Numéro 7, Faubourg Clotilde. Directrice, Mademoiselle Lucy Snowe.'

And what did I say to M. Paul Emanuel?

Certain junctures of our lives must always be difficult of recall to memory. Certain points, crises, certain feelings, joys, griefs, and amazements, when reviewed, must strike us as things wildered and whirling, dim as a wheel fast spun.

I can no more remember the thoughts or the words of the ten minutes succeeding this disclosure, than I can retrace the experience of my earliest year of life: and yet the first thing distinct to me is the consciousness that I was speaking very fast, repeating over and over again:

'Did you do this, M. Paul? Is this your house? Did you furnish it? Did you get these papers printed? Do you mean me? Am I the directress? Is there another Lucy Snowe? Tell me: say something.'

But he would not speak. His pleased silence, his laughing down-look, his attitude, are visible to me now.

'How is it? I must know all – *all*,' I cried.

The packet of papers fell on the floor. He had extended his hand, and I had fastened thereon, oblivious of all else.

'Ah! you said I had forgotten you all these weary days,' said he. 'Poor old Emanuel! These are the thanks he gets for trudging about three mortal weeks – from house-painter to upholsterer, from cabinet-maker to charwoman – Lucy and Lucy's cot, the sole thoughts in his head!'

I hardly knew what to do. I first caressed the soft velvet on his cuff, and then I stroked the hand it surrounded. It was his foresight, his goodness, his silent, strong, effective goodness, that overpowered me by their proved reality. It was the assurance of his sleepless interest which broke on me like a light from heaven; it was his (I will dare to say it) his fond, tender look, which now shook me indescribably. In the midst of all, I forced myself to look at the practical.

'The trouble!' I cried, 'and the cost! Had you money, M. Paul?'

'Plenty of money!' said he heartily. 'The disposal of my large teaching-connection put me in possession of a handsome sum: with part of it I determined to give myself the richest treat that I *have* known or *shall* know. I like this. I have reckoned on this hour day and night lately. I would not come near you, because I would not forestall it. Reserve is neither my virtue nor my vice. If I had put myself into your power, and you had begun with your questions of look and lip – Where have you been, M. Paul? What have you been doing? What is your mystery? – my solitary first and last secret would presently have unravelled itself in your lap. Now,' he pursued, 'you shall live here and have a school; you shall employ yourself while I am away; you shall think of me sometimes; you shall mind your health and happiness for my sake, and when I come back – '

Here he left a blank.

I promised to do all he told me. I promised to work hard and willingly. 'I will be your faithful steward,' I said; 'I trust at your coming the account will be ready. Monsieur, monsieur, you are *too* good!'

In such inadequate language my feelings struggled for expression: they could not get it; speech, brittle and unmalleable, and cold as ice, dissolved or shivered in the effort. He watched me still: he gently raised his hand to stroke my hair; it touched my lips in passing; I pressed it close, I paid it tribute. He was my king; royal for me had been that hand's bounty; to offer homage was both a joy and a duty.

The afternoon hours were over, and the stiller time of evening shaded the quiet faubourg. M. Paul claimed my hospitality; occupied and afoot since morning, he needed refreshment; he said I should offer him chocolate in my pretty gold and white china service. He went out and ordered what was needful from the restaurant; he placed the small guéridon and two chairs in the balcony outside the French window under the screening vines. With what shy joy I accepted my part as hostess, arranged the salver, served the benefactor-guest.

This balcony was in the rear of the house, the gardens of the faubourg were round us, fields extended beyond. The air was still, mild, and fresh. Above the poplars, the laurels, the cypresses, and the roses, looked up a moon so lovely and so halcyon, the heart trembled under her smile; a star shone subject beside her, with the unemulous ray of pure love. In a large garden near us, a jet rose from a well, and a pale statue leaned over the play of waters.

M. Paul talked to me. His voice was so modulated that it mixed harmonious with the silver whisper, the gush, the musical sigh, in which light breeze, fountain, and foliage intoned their lulling vesper.

Happy hour – stay one moment! droop those plumes, rest those wings; incline to mine that brow of Heaven! White Angel! let thy light linger; leave its reflection on succeeding clouds; bequeath its cheer to that time which needs a ray in retrospect!

Our meal was simple: the chocolate, the rolls, the plate of fresh summer fruit, cherries and strawberries bedded in green leaves, formed the whole; but it was what we both liked better than a feast, and I took a delight inexpressible in tending M. Paul. I asked him whether his friends, Père Silas and Madame Beck knew what he had done – whether they had seen my house?

'Mon amie,' said he, 'none knows what I have done save you and myself: the pleasure is consecrated to us two, unshared and unprofaned. To speak truth, there has been to me in this matter a refinement of enjoyment I would not make vulgar by communication. Besides' (smiling), 'I wanted to prove to Miss Lucy that I *could* keep a secret. How often has she taunted me with lack of dignified reserve and needful caution! How many times has she saucily insinuated that all my affairs are the secret of Polichinelle!'[231]

This was true enough: I had not spared him on this point, nor perhaps on any other that was assailable. Magnificent minded, grand-hearted, dear, faulty little man! You deserved candour, and from me always had it.

Continuing my queries, I asked to whom the house belonged, who was my landlord, the amount of my rent. He instantly gave me these particulars in writing; he had foreseen and prepared all things.

The house was not M. Paul's – that I guessed; he was hardly the man to become a proprietor; I more than suspected in him a lamentable absence of the saving faculty; he could get, but not keep; he needed a treasurer. The tenement, then, belonged to a citizen in the Basse-Ville – a man of substance, M. Paul said; he startled me by adding: 'a friend of yours, Miss Lucy, a person who has a most respectful regard for you.' And, to my pleasant surprise, I found the landlord was none other than M. Miret, the short-tempered and kind-hearted bookseller, who had so kindly found me a seat that eventful night in the Park. It seems M. Miret was in his station, rich, as well as much respected, and possessed several houses in this faubourg; the rent was moderate, scarce half of what it would have been, for a house of equal size, nearer the centre of Villette.

'And then,' observed M. Paul, 'should fortune not favour you, though I think she will, I have the satisfaction to think you are in good hands; M. Miret will not be extortionate: the first year's rent you already have in your savings; afterwards Miss Lucy must trust God, and herself. But now, what will you do for pupils?'

'I must distribute my prospectuses.'

'Right! By way of losing no time, I gave one to M. Miret yesterday. Should you object to beginning with three petites bourgeoises – the Demoiselles Miret? They are at your service.'

'Monsieur, you forget nothing; you are wonderful. Object? It would become me indeed to object! I suppose I hardly expect at the outset to number aristocrats in my little day-school; I care not if they never come. I shall be proud to receive M. Miret's daughters.'

'Besides these,' pursued he, 'another pupil offers, who will come daily to take lessons in English; and, as she is rich, she will pay handsomely. I mean my god-daughter and ward, Justine Marie Sauveur.'

What is in a name? – what in three words? Till this moment I had listened with living joy – I had answered with gleeful quickness; a name froze me; three words struck me mute. The effect could not be hidden, and indeed I scarce tried to hide it.

'What now?' said M. Paul.

'Nothing.'

'Nothing! Your countenance changes; your colour and your very eyes fade. Nothing! You must be ill; you have some suffering; tell me what?'

I had nothing to tell.

He drew his chair nearer. He did not grow vexed, though I continued silent and icy. He tried to win a word; he entreated with perseverance, he waited with patience.

'Justine Marie is a good girl,' said he; 'docile and amiable; not quick – but you will like her.'

'I think not. I think she must not come here.' Such was my speech.

'Do you wish to puzzle me? Do you know her? But, in truth, there *is* something. Again you are pale as that statue. Rely on Paul Carlos: tell him the grief.'

His chair touched mine; his hand, quietly advanced, turned me towards him. 'Do you know Marie Justine?' said he again.

The name re-pronounced by his lips overcame me unaccountably. It did not prostrate – no, it stirred me up, running with haste and heat through my veins – recalling an hour of quick pain, many days and nights of heart-sickness. Near me as he now sat, strongly and closely as he had long twined his life in mine – far as had progressed, and near as was achieved our minds' and affections' assimilation – the very suggestion of interference, of heart-separation, could be heard only with a fermenting excitement, an impetuous throe, a disdainful resolve, an ire, a resistance of which no human eye or cheek could hide the flame, nor any truth-accustomed human tongue curb the cry.

'I want to tell you something,' I said; 'I want to tell you all.'

'Speak, Lucy; come near; speak. Who prizes you if I do not? Who is your friend, if not Emanuel? Speak!'

I spoke. All leaped from my lips. I lacked not words now; fast I narrated; fluent I told my tale; it streamed on my tongue. I went back to the night in the park; I mentioned the medicated draught – why it was given – its goading effect – how it had torn rest from under my head, shaken me from my couch, carried me abroad with the lure of a vivid yet solemn fancy – a summer-night solitude on turf, under trees, near a deep, cool lakelet. I told the scene realized; the crowd, the masques, the music, the lamps, the splendours, the guns booming afar, the bells sounding on high. All I had encountered I detailed, all I had recognized, heard, and seen; how I had beheld and watched himself; how I listened, how much heard, what conjectured; the whole history, in brief, summoned to his confidence, rushed thither truthful, literal, ardent, bitter.

Still as I narrated, instead of checking, he incited me to proceed; he spurred me by the gesture, the smile, the half-word. Before I had half done, he held both my hands, he consulted my eyes with a most piercing glance: there was something in his face which tended neither to calm nor to put me down; he forgot his own doctrine, he forsook his own system of repression when I most challenged its exercise. I think I deserved strong reproof; but when have we our deserts? I merited severity; he looked indulgence. To my very self I seemed imperious and unreasonable; for I forbade Justine Marie my door and roof; he smiled, betraying delight. Warm, jealous, and haughty, I knew not till now that my nature had such a mood; he gathered me near his heart. I was full of faults; he took them and me all home. For the moment of utmost mutiny, he reserved the one deep spell of peace. These words caressed my ear: –

'Lucy, take my love. One day share my life. Be my dearest, first on earth.'

We walked back to the Rue Fossette by moonlight – such moonlight as fell on Eden – shining through the shades of the Great Garden, and haply gilding a path glorious, for a step divine – a Presence nameless. Once in their lives some men and women go back to these first fresh days of our great Sire and Mother – taste that grand morning's dew – bathe in its sunrise.

In the course of the walk I was told how Justine Marie Sauveur had always been regarded with the affection proper to a daughter – how, with M. Paul's consent, she had been affianced for months to one Heinrich Mühler, a wealthy young German merchant, and was to be married in the course of a year. Some of M. Emanuel's relations and connections would, indeed, it seems, have liked him to marry her, with a view to securing her fortune in the family; but to himself the scheme was repugnant, and the idea totally inadmissible.

We reached Madame Beck's door. Jean Baptiste's clock tolled nine. At this hour, in this house, eighteen months since, had this man at my side, bent before me, looked into my face and eyes, and arbitered my destiny. This very evening he had again stooped, gazed and decreed. How different the look – how far otherwise the fate!

He deemed me born under his star: he seemed to have spread over me its beam like a banner. Once – unknown, and unloved, I held him harsh and strange; the low stature, the wiry make, the angles, the darkness, the manner, displeased me. Now, penetrated with his influence, and living by his affection, having his worth by intellect, and his goodness by heart – I preferred him before all humanity.

We parted: he gave me his pledge, and then his farewell. We parted: the next day – he sailed.

CHAPTER 42

Finis

MAN CANNOT prophesy. Love is no oracle. Fear sometimes imagines a vain thing. Those years of absence! How had I sickened over their anticipation! The woe they must bring seemed certain as death. I knew the nature of their course: I never had doubt how it would harrow as it went. The Juggernaut[232] on his car towered there a grim load. Seeing him draw nigh, burying his broad wheels in the oppressed soil – I, the prostrate votary – felt beforehand the annihilating craunch.

Strange to say – strange, yet true, and owning many parallels in life's experience – that anticipatory craunch proved all – yes – nearly *all* the torture. The great Juggernaut, in his great chariot, drew on lofty, loud, and sullen. He passed quietly, like a shadow sweeping the sky at noon. Nothing but a chilling dimness was seen or felt. I looked up. Chariot and demon charioteer were gone by; the votary still lived.

M. Emanuel was away three years. Reader, they were the three happiest years of my life. Do you scout the paradox? Listen.

I commenced my school; I worked – I worked hard. I deemed myself the steward of his property, and determined, God willing, to render a good account. Pupils came – burghers at first – a higher class ere long. About the middle of the second year an unexpected chance threw into my hands an additional hundred pounds: one day I received from England a letter containing that sum. It came from Mr Marchmont, the cousin and heir of my dear and dead mistress. He was just recovering from a dangerous illness; the money was a peace-offering to his conscience, reproaching him in the matter of, I know not what, papers or memoranda found after his kinswoman's death – naming or recommending Lucy Snowe. Mrs Barrett had given him my address. How far his conscience had been sinned against, I never inquired. I asked no questions, but took the cash and made it useful.

With this hundred pounds I ventured to take the house adjoining mine. I would not leave that which M. Paul had chosen, in which he had left, and where he expected again to find me. My externat became a pensionnat; that also prospered.

The secret of my success did not lie so much in myself, in any endowment, any power of mine, as in a new state of circumstances, a wonderfully changed life, a relieved heart. The spring which moved my energies lay far away beyond seas, in an Indian isle. At parting, I had been left a legacy; such a thought for the present, such a hope for the future, such a motive for a persevering, a laborious, an enterprising, a patient and a brave course – I *could* not flag. Few things shook me now; few things had importance to vex, intimidate, or depress me: most things pleased – mere trifles had a charm.

Do not think that this genial flame sustained itself, or lived wholly on a bequeathed hope or a parting promise. A generous provider supplied bounteous fuel. I was spared all chill, all stint; I was not suffered to fear penury; I was not tried with suspense. By every vessel he wrote; he wrote as he gave and as he loved, in full-handed, full-hearted plenitude. He wrote because he liked to write; he did not abridge, because he cared not to abridge. He sat down, he took pen and paper, because he loved Lucy and had much to say to her; because he was faithful and thoughtful, because he was tender and true. There was no sham and no cheat, and no hollow unreal in him. Apology never dropped her slippery oil on his lips – never proffered, by his pen, her coward feints and paltry nullities: he would give neither a stone, nor an excuse – neither a scorpion, nor a disappointment; his letters were real food that nourished, living water that refreshed.

And was I grateful? God knows! I believe that scarce a living being so remembered, so sustained, dealt with in kind so constant, honourable and noble, could be otherwise than grateful to the death.

Adherent to his own religion (in him was not the stuff of which is made the facile apostate), he freely left me my pure faith. He did not teaze nor tempt. He said: –

'Remain a Protestant. My little English Puritan, I love Protestantism in you. I own its severe charm. There is something in its ritual I cannot receive myself, but it is the sole creed for "Lucy."'

All Rome could not put into him bigotry, nor the Propaganda itself make him a real Jesuit. He was born honest, and not false – artless, and not cunning – a freeman, and not a slave. His tenderness had rendered him ductile in a priest's hands, his affection, his devotedness, his sincere pious enthusiasm blinded his kind eyes sometimes, made him abandon justice to himself to do the work of craft, and serve the ends of selfishness; but these are faults so rare to find, so costly to their owner to indulge, we scarce know whether they will not one day be reckoned amongst the jewels.

And now the three years are past: M. Emanuel's return is fixed. It is Autumn; he is to be with me ere the mists of November come. My school flourishes, my house is ready: I have made him a little library, filled its shelves with the books he left in my care: I have cultivated out of love for him (I was naturally no florist) the plants he preferred, and some of them are yet in bloom. I thought I loved him when he went away; I love him now in another degree; he is more my own.

The sun passes the equinox; the days shorten, the leaves grow sere; but – he is coming.

Frosts appear at night; November has sent his fogs in advance; the wind takes its autumn moan; but – he is coming.

The skies hang full and dark – a rack sails from the west; the clouds cast themselves into strange forms – arches and broad radiations; there rise resplendent mornings – glorious, royal, purple as monarch in his state; the heavens are one flame; so wild are they, they rival battle at its thickest – so bloody, they shame Victory in her pride. I know some signs of the sky; I have noted them ever since childhood. God, watch that sail! Oh! guard it!

The wind shifts to the west. Peace, peace, Banshee – 'keening' at every window! It will rise – it will swell – it shrieks out long: wander as I may through the house this night, I cannot lull the blast. The advancing hours make it strong: by midnight, all sleepless watchers hear and fear a wild south-west storm.

That storm roared frenzied for seven days. It did not cease till the Atlantic was strewn with wrecks: it did not lull till the deeps had gorged their full of sustenance. Not till the destroying angel of tempest had achieved his perfect work, would he fold the wings whose waft was thunder – the tremor of whose plumes was storm.

Peace, be still! Oh! a thousand weepers, praying in agony on waiting shores, listened for that voice, but it was not uttered – not uttered till, when the hush came, some could not feel it: till, when the sun returned, his light was night to some!

Here pause: pause at once. There is enough said. Trouble no quiet, kind heart; leave sunny imaginations hope. Let it be theirs to conceive the delight of joy born again fresh out of great terror, the rapture of rescue from peril, the wondrous reprieve from dread, the fruition of return. Let them picture union and a happy succeeding life.

Madame Beck prospered all the days of her life; so did Père Silas; Madame Walravens fulfilled her ninetieth year before she died. Farewell.

NOTES

DCM: Pierre Grimal: *Penguin Dictionary of Classical Mythology*, edited by Stephen Kershaw, translated by A. R. Maxwell-Hyslop (Penguin, Harmondsworth 1991)

SOED: *Shorter Oxford English Dictionary*

1   (p. 2) central characters in Bunyan's *The Pilgrim's Progress*, to which the subsequent quotation also refers

2   (p. 11) modesty covering of lace or muslin at the neck of a dress

3   (p. 17) Psalms 22:1; Matthew 27:46; Mark 15:34

4   (p. 23) See Genesis 37:1 Samuel 3; Daniel 6. The subsequent quotation is adapted from Genesis 37:35.

5   (p. 24) eastern female slave or concubine (SOED)

6   (p. 25) Mount Chimborazo, in the Andes

7   (p. 32) a spirit that wails under the windows of a house when one of the inmates is about to die, according to Scottish and Irish folklore (SOED)

8   (p. 43) Sea-Mud

9   (p. 43) In Greek mythology Charon was the boatman who ferried the souls of the dead across the River Styx to Hades. (DCM)

10 (p. 46) a mailboat which also carried both goods and passengers

11 (p. 46) indecorous

12 (p. 47) pretty young girls

13 (p. 47) thing (thingumajig)

14 (p. 48) mistresses, masters, pupils in a school

15 (p. 48) to the devil

16 (p. 00) Luckily I know how to get things going.

17 (p. 49) from Richard Lovelace's 'To Althea, from Prison' (1649)

18   (p. 52) Englishwoman
19   (p. 52) public stage-coach
20   (p. 53) roadway
21   (p. 54) What are you doing there? That's my trunk.
22   (p. 56) main gate
23   (p. 56) girls' boarding school
24   (p. 57) England
25   (p. 57) There's no one like English women for these sorts of adventure; how fearless they are!
26   (p. 57) That's for evening prayers.
27   (p. 62) in English or in Irish
28   (p. 63) goddess of the dawn (DCM)
29   (p. 63) governess
30   (p. 64) tyrannical king of Crete (DCM)
31   (p. 64) female form of Ignatius (Loyola, founder of the Jesuits)
32   (p. 65) shoes of silence, slippers
33   (p. 66) for the poor
34   (p. 66) arbour
35   (p. 67) waffles
36   (p. 67) white wine
37   (p. 67) brown bread
38   (p. 69) Don't tell it to my enemies; see 2 Samuel 1:20
39   (p. 69) Tell me now, do you really feel too weak?
40   (p. 69) forward
41   (p. 69) These are Labassecourians, open, frank, blunt, and somewhat rebellious.
42   (p. 70) It's true.
43   (p. 70) young lady
44   (p. 70) nursemaid
45   (p. 72) maintaining an air of innocence
46   (p. 72) That's good. That will do.
47   (p. 73) I have lied several times.
48   (p. 74) Lord, this is hard. I don't want to do it any more. It bores me too much.
49   (p. 75) Because when you're dead, you'll go straight to the fires of Hell.
     Do you believe that?
     Certainly I believe it; everyone knows it; and besides the priest told me. To ensure your salvation up above, it would be better to burn you alive down here.
50   (p. 77) So-so . . . That will do.
51   (p. 77) according to what they say

52 (p. 77) good-looking, but more a handsome man than an attractive one

53 (p. 78) sky-blue sash

54 (p. 79) set of jewellery

55 (p. 79) Greek philosopher renowned for his austere style of living (SOED)

56 (p. 80) A visitor for Mademoiselle Fanshawe!

57 (p. 80) Listen, my dear grumbler.

58 (p. 81) callow youth

59 (p. 81) But not at all ! I am his queen, but he is not my king.

60 (p. 82) The thinkers, men who are deep and passionate, are not to my taste . . . Let me have good-looking fops and attractive rogues! Long live joys and pleasures! Down with deep passions and strict virtues! I love my good-looking colonel. I will never love his rival. I'll never be the wife of a bourgeois, not me!

61 (p. 83) their future

62 (p. 83) Take care, my child.

63 (p. 83) What a poisonous pest that Désirée is!

64 (p. 84) Désirée needs a particularly watchful eye.

65 (p. 84) This child has a broken bone.

66 (p. 84) Someone get hold of a cab immediately.

67 (p. 85) sugared water

68 (p. 85) That will be better.

69 (p. 85) Thank you, Madame: very good, excellent! . . . You showed a much-needed coolness, worth a thousand outbursts of misplaced feeling.

70 (p. 88) Daniel 3:1

71 (p. 90) An ordinary woman's bluntness and frankness

72 (p. 91) Poor Dr John . . . this dear young man! the best creature in the world!

73 (p. 91) women's laced boots

74 (p. 93) song such as those sung by Venetian gondoliers (SOED)

75 (p. 93) working girl, sometimes used to suggest a flirtatious one

76 (p. 95) a character defeated by Christian in Bunyan's *The Pilgrim's Progress*

77 (p. 98) Look here, how clean she is, this young Miss Lucy. So you like this alleyway?

78 (p. 99) Sisera had subjugated the Israelites for twenty years when Jael killed him as he slept, by driving a tent-pin into his temple; see Judges 4.

79　(p. 101) a real British prude according to what you say – a kind of monster, sharp and rough like an old grenadier corporal, and bad-tempered as a nun

80　(p. 102) What a tale! . . . Nobody's been there.

81　(p. 104) What a lovely night! . . . How fine it is! how fresh the air is! . . . Good-night, my good friend, sleep well!

82　(p. 106) Conrad, as spiritual guide, urged Elizabeth into a life of self-deprivation and self-denial.

83　(p. 106) characters in Sir Walter Scott's *Old Mortality* (1816)

84　(p. 109) hat of a soft green colour

85　(p. 110) The brat hasn't got anything wrong with her, has she? Not much.

86　(p. 111) Ah, really? So there's nothing behind it – no mystery, no flirtation, for example?
No more than is in my hand.
What a pity! And I was just beginning to get a few ideas about it.
Really! well that was at your own expense.

87　(p. 116) I know very well that she has no principles, perhaps even no morals, but her bearing in class is always proper and even dignified; that's all that's needed. Neither the parents nor the pupils look much further than that, and so, consequently, neither do I.

88　(p. 117) Oh, very well then – two or three spoons and as many forks, in silver.

89　(p. 118) Are you no more than dolls? Haven't you any passions, the rest of you? Don't you feel anything? Is your flesh made of snow, your blood of ice? What I want is that this should be alight, with its own life, and soul!

90　(p. 120) As for St Pierre, she's got the air of an old flirt playing the innocent.

91　(p. 121) That's it! I know her: it's the Englishwoman. Too bad. Completely English, and thus completely prudish as she may be – she will do what I want, or I'll know the reason why.

92　(p. 124) I heard it all. It's good enough. Now do it again . . . Again! And don't make faces! Suppress your nerves!

93　(p. 125) 'Sir . . .
'Well, what is it, miss?
I'm hungry.
What do you mean, you're hungry! What about the cold buffet? . . . Ah, that's true.

94　(p. 127) Have courage, my friend. Keep cool, have a little self-possession, M. Lucien, and everything will be all right.

95 (p. 129) It may be better than your model, but it's not right.

96 (p. 131) Be quiet! You won't get past me unless it's over my dead body, and the only woman you'll dance with is the garden nun.

97 (p. 141) So you are going to be enthroned like a queen, tomorrow you'll be on a throne beside me? Undoubtedly you are relishing in advance the delights of authority. I believe I discern in you some sort of radiance, you ambitious little creature!

98 (p. 142) I took warning from that.

99 (p. 143) The poor thing!

100 (p. 146) Psalm 88:15

101 (p. 148) Father, I am a Protestant.

102 (p. 149) Francois Fénelon, renowned for his success in winning converts to Catholicism

103 (p. 155) character in *The Arabian Nights*

104 (p. 155) Roman household gods (DCM)

105 (p. 173) In Shakespeare's *A Midsummer Night's Dream*, Titania, Queen of the Fairies, is magically made to fall in love with Bottom the weaver, who has been transformed into an ass.

106 (p. 182) a magnificent room

107 (p. 182) very worthy, agreeable and respectable

108 (p. 182) madam his mother, the dignified lady of the manor

109 (p. 187) What are you doing here!
But, sir, I'm enjoying myself.
Enjoying yourself! with what, may I ask? But first, do me the honour of getting up: take my arm, and let us move to the other side.

110 (p. 188) Be quiet, and sit down there – there!
But, sir.
But, miss, sit down, and don't move – do you understand? not until someone comes to find you, or till I give you permission. What a dreary corner! and what ugly pictures!

111 (p. 188) The life of a woman: the categories are Young Girl, Wife, Young Mother, Widow; all four are ironically described as Angels.

112 (p. 190) Truly! You're not worth much.

113 (p. 190) That's not important. A superb woman – of imperial bearing, Junoesque, but not someone I'd want for a wife, or daughter, or sister. Thus you must not cast one look more in her direction.

114   (p. 191) in classical mythology, a grove of golden apples given to Hera when she married Zeus (DCM)

115   (p. 196) Shetland pony (SOED)

116   (p. 196) statue made by the Greek sculptor Phidias, fifth century BC

117   (p. 196) Roman equivalent of the Greek goddess Hera. Protector of women, and especially married women, she embodied femaleness. (DCM)

118   (p. 200) a novel by Oliver Goldsmith (1766)

119   (p. 210) a Cretan hero renowned for his wisdom and justice (DCM)

120   (p. 216) Moses saw the Promised Land from Mount Nebo; see Deuteronomy 34: 1–4.

121   (p. 216) Miss, you are sad.
Sir, I have good cause to be.
You are sick at heart and in spirit.

122   (p. 218) Timon of Athens, a famed misanthrope, eponymous hero of Shakespeare's play (SOED)

123   (p. 220) angel who shies away from company

124   (p. 220) British bear

125   (p. 223) Cyclops in Greek mythology were one-eyed giants (DCM)

126   (p. 223) Isaac, who asked Esau to hunt for some meat to eat before he died; see Genesis 27

127   (p. 226) You're only young once.

128   (p. 226) I understand, I understand: I know what it means to be just a friend.

129   (p. 226) I see clearly that you are contemptuous of me and my belongings.

130   (p. 227) But of course, darling, you can have two if you want.

131   (p. 233) imaginary flower which never fades (SOED)

132   (p. 236) The Syrian Naaman acknowledged God but also worshipped the Syrian deity Rimmon.

133   (p. 238) the brightest of the stars

134   (p. 240) A queen renowned for her beauty. The French actress Rachel, whose acting Charlotte Brontë saw in London in 1851, is generally thought to be the model for the fictional Vashti here.

135   (p. 241) character in Sir Walter Scott's *The Talisman* (1825)

136   (p. 241) Flemish painter (1577–1640) whose female figures were characteristically fleshy

137 (p. 241) a valley near Jerusalem associated with human sacrifice (SOED)

138 (p. 242) Pythia was the priestess of Apollo at Delphi, who delivered the oracles in a state of divine frenzy. (SOED)

139 (p. 250) from a story in *The Arabian Nights*, signifying imaginary food and drink

140 (p. 251) god of healing and medicine

141 (p. 254) Turkish dignitaries

142 (p. 255) They were unable to help king Nebuchadnezzar to solve the riddle of his dream; see Daniel 2.

143 (p. 261) from Robert Burns's song 'Auld Lang Syne'

144 (p. 267) from Hamlet's soliloquy, 1, 2, 129

145 (p. 273) Yes, yes, my good friend, I give you permission with all my heart. Your work in my house has always been admirable, full of zeal and good judgement: you have every right to enjoy yourself. So go out as much as you like. As for your choice of acquaintances, I am happy with it; it is wise, worthy and commendable.

146 (p. 274) There's something really remarkable in the English character ... I would not know how to say 'how', but in the end the English have certain ideas peculiar to them, about friendship, love everything. But at least there is no need to keep an eye on them.

147 (p. 276) in Hebrew a name meaning 'no glory'

148 (p. 281) Scots dialect for lad

149 (p. 282) devoutness ... composure

150 (p. 283) swear word ... holy

151 (p. 284) The Maiden's Lament

152 (p. 290) speaker's platform

153 (p. 291) What did you think?

154 (p. 297) Little she-cat, with your soft, sweet manner! you seem sad, subdued, dreamy, but you're not; it is I who tell you this: Wild creature! with a flame in your soul, and your eyes flashing!

155 (p. 297) Yes, I do have a flame in my soul, and I must have it!

156 (p. 299) This great fop of an Englishman.

157 (p. 299) Good! Now we can see daylight! So say, my friend. Mr Paul, I forgive you.

158 (p. 300) John Knox, who founded Scottish Presbyterianism, was outspokenly critical of the conduct of the Catholic Mary, Queen of Scots.

159 (p. 303) What's going to happen to me? Monsieur is going to kill me, I'm sure; because he's in such a temper!

160 (p. 304) From this moment on, entry to the classroom is forbidden. The first person to open that door, or to pass that division, will be hanged – be it Madame Beck herself!

161 (p. 305) I want the impossible, something incredible.

162 (p. 306) There now, I'm bereaved of my glasses.

163 (p. 307) a strong woman – a terrible Englishwoman – a little break-all

164 (p. 308) Napoleon

165 (p. 309) So you don't want me for your neighbour, you think you're a caste above me; you treat me like a pariah. So be it! I'll sort things out. Stand up, girls!

166 (p. 309) Is this far enough away?
Monsieur is the judge.
You know very well that's not true. It's you who have created this huge gulf: I haven't raised a finger.

167 (p. 309) the false idol of these pagan idiots, the English

168 (p. 310) intractable character

169 (p. 311) ardour

170 (p. 311) going off like gunpowder!

171 (p. 311) getting carried away . . . warmth

172 (p. 00) doll's colours, a nose more or less nicely formed (M. Paul is referring to Dr John.)

173 (p. 311) embroidered collars

174 (p. 312) further decoration

175 (p. 312) baubles

176 (p. 312) society fashions

177 (p. 312) homespun . . . grey as dust

178 (p. 312) Keep the ribbon!

179 (p. 315) bright orange

180 (p. 318) Is that everything?

181 (p. 320) Long live England, History and Heroes! Down with France, Fiction and Scoundrels!

182 (p. 320) In that case I won't be there.
Fine!

183 (p. 327) a queen of the Amazons and a renowned warrior (DCM)

184 (p. 330) He fell into a deep sleep while listening to Paul preach; see Acts 20:9.

185 (p. 330) How handsome he is, miss, this young doctor! What eyes – what a look! My heart is really moved by him!

186 (p. 330) That brazen girl, that shameless creature.
187 (p. 331) She's only saying what's true.
           Ah! Do you think so?
           Absolutely.
188 (p. 332) That doesn't concern me; I don't care about it
189 (p. 334) pagan deities
190 (p. 336) wood-nymph
191 (p. 353) I advise you to invite yourself.
192 (p. 354) What's going on? Are you playing tricks on me?
193 (p. 354) It's the pink dress!
194 (p. 355) And Miss Lucy is as smart as ten Parisian women . . .
           Have you ever seen an Englishwoman like her? Look at her
           hat, her gloves, her boots!
195 (p. 355) Don't worry! To tell the truth I am not annoyed,
           even perhaps pleased that someone has made herself look so
           pretty for my outing.
           But my dress is not pretty, sir – it is only neat.
           I like neatness.
196 (p. 356) an eyewash (SOED)
197 (p. 358) a play by the French seventeenth-century dramatist
           Pierre Corneille
198 (p. 358) Yet I have been very hard on you, very demanding.
199 (p. 359) Where is Miss Lucy?
200 (p. 359) She is in bed.
201 (p. 364) character in Voltaire's *Candide* (1759) who transfixes
           the hero with her beauty but after a passage of time becomes
           ugly and withered
202 (p. 368) Ah, well then, you must know my good pupil, my Paul?
203 (p. 370) She is odd, isn't she? The strange little hunchback!
           And just think, she hates me, because she thinks I'm in love
           with my cousin Paul; that devout little man who dare not
           move unless he's got permission from his confessor!
204 (p. 371) someone rather foolish to my thinking
205 (p. 371) as pure as a lily
206 (p. 371) Forget angels, hunchbacks, and above all, Professors
           – and so good-night!
207 (p. 374) I know nothing about that.
208 (p. 376) We are acting in the interest of truth. We have no
           wish to hurt you.
209 (p. 377) a little heartless mocker
210 (p. 378) And you, miss, you are neat and sweet, and terribly
           tough-skinned for all that.

211 (p. 378) I make my own bed and do my housework.

212 (p. 387) French priest who started a charitable foundation

213 (p. 387) Rome (i.e. Catholicism)

214 (p. 390) too much sensitivity and feeling

215 (p. 407) a mountain near Athens, famous for its marble quarries

216 (p. 409) a reference to Herod's massacre of baby boys. It suggests that Paulina and Dr John suffer the death of a child. See Matthew 2.

217 (p. 413) An unreal hope; drawn from a story in *The Arabian Nights*.

218 (p. 413) Rest is sweet! It is a precious thing, calm contentment! . . . Good little friend! sweet consoler!

219 (p. 417) references to *The Pilgrim's Progress*; see note 76, above

220 (p. 419) How pale you are! You must be really ill, miss

221 (p. 428) one which can shrink or expand at will; from a story in *The Arabian Nights*

222 (p. 432) Where are they? Why don't they come?

223 (p. 433) She raised the spirit of Samuel at Saul's bidding; see 1 Samuel 28.

224 (p. 436) The little one will help me, yes? . . .
     But of course, I will help you with all my heart. You can do what you like with me, godfather.

225 (p. 440) Don Quixote's horse, in the novel by Cervantes

226 (p. 446) at death's door

227 (p. 449) Leave me!

228 (p. 449) Get out of here!

229 (p. 451) She is very pale . . . that face makes me ill.

230 (p. 453) girls' day school.

231 (p. 456) a reference to Punch, who announces secrets in a loud stage whisper

232 (p. 460) Hindu god, mounted annually on a cart; bystanders were sometimes caught beneath the wheels. It is usually a reference to an unavoidable fate.

"One of the few kings of American fiction."—*New York Times*

Chasing Destiny

"[A] strong, sexy heroine." —*Kirkus Reviews*

"Sultry prose . . . lively." —*Publishers Weekly*

Genevieve

"[A] sizzling, sexy, downright gritty love story." —*Library Journal*

"Explicit . . . red-hot . . . sex-drenched . . . [and] instantly en-grossing." —*Publishers Weekly*

Drive Me Crazy

"Smart, gritty, and gripping . . . another winner." —*Publishers Weekly*

"May be his best novel to date . . . a page-turner." —*Booklist*

Naughty or Nice

"There are three kinds of physical love in these pages: hot, red-hot, and nuclear." —*Publishers Weekly*

"A very funny and engrossing novel . . . laugh-out-loud humor." —*Booklist*

continued . . .

Also by Eric Jerome Dickey

Waking with Enemies
Chasing Destiny
Genevieve
Drive Me Crazy
Naughty or Nice
The Other Woman
Thieves' Paradise
Between Lovers
Liar's Game
Cheaters
Milk in My Coffee
Friends and Lovers
Sister, Sister

Anthologies

Voices from the Other Side: Dark Dreams II
Got to Be Real
Mothers and Sons
River Crossings: Voices of the Diaspora
Griots Beneath the Baobob
Black Silk: A Collection of African American Erotica
Gumbo: A Celebration of African American Writing

Cappuccino (movie)—original story

Comic Books

Storm (Six-issue miniseries, Marvel Entertainment)

ERIC JEROME DICKEY

Sleeping with Strangers

NAL NEW AMERICAN LIBRARY

New American Library]
Published by New American Library, a division of
Penguin Group (USA) Inc., 375 Hudson Street,
New York, New York 10014, USA
Penguin Group (Canada), 90 Eglinton Avenue East, Suite 700, Toronto,
Ontario M4P 2Y3, Canada (a division of Pearson Penguin Canada Inc.)
Penguin Books Ltd., 80 Strand, London WC2R 0RL, England
Penguin Ireland, 25 St. Stephen's Green, Dublin 2,
Ireland (a division of Penguin Books Ltd)
Penguin Group (Australia), 707 Collins Street, Melbourne, Victoria 3008,
Australia (a division of Pearson Australia Group Pty. Ltd.)
Penguin Books India Pvt. Ltd., 11 Community Centre, Panchsheel Park,
New Delhi–110 017, India
Penguin Group (NZ), 67 Apollo Drive, Rosedale, Auckland 0632,
New Zealand (a division of Pearson New Zealand Ltd.)
Penguin Books, Rosebank Office Park, 181 Jan Smuts Avenue,
Parktown North 2193, South Africa
Penguin China, B7 Jaiming Center, 27 East Third Ring Road North,
Chaoyang District, Beijing 100020, China

Penguin Books Ltd., Registered Offices:
80 Strand, London WC2R 0RL, England

Published by New American Library, a division of Penguin Group (USA) Inc. Previously
published in a Dutton edition.

First New American Library Printing, April 2008
10   9   8   7   6   5   4   3   2

 REGISTERED TRADEMARK — MARCA REGISTRADA

New American Library trade paperback ISBN: 978-0-451-22233-6

LIBRARY OF CONGRESS CATALOGING-IN-PUBLICATION DATA:
Dickey, Jerome.
Sleeping with strangers / Eric Jerome Dickey.
p. cm.
ISBN: 978-0-525-94999-2
1. African American men—Fiction. 2. Assassins—Fiction. 3. Suspense fiction.
4. Love stories. I. Title.
PS3554.I319 S58 2007
813'.54—dc22   2007008330

Set in Janson Text
Designed by Spring Hoteling

Printed in the United States of America

for Dominique

One

way of the transgressor

"What's your goddamn name?"

I stared at the huge man who wore the preacher's collar. He'd been crippled by paid-for violence, dragged downstairs, and tossed onto the marble floor. His arrogant face and body bruised by the brass knuckles that were at my side. He was a big man, much bigger than I. He looked like John Coffey, from *The Green Mile*, in a $3,000 suit and gators.

"Who are you? Why are you doing this? What's your goddamn name?"

I yawned, exhausted from traveling. I told him, "I don't have a name."

"What do you mean, you don't have a name?"

I had rented a hotel room near Oakland University. Oakland University was in Rochester, Michigan. Not Oakland, California. This Oakland wasn't black. The winters in Michigan were not to be played with. I had on a serious coat, one big enough to shelter my weapons.

From the hotel, I had traveled a few miles away, was creating terror at midnight in the Bloomfield Villas subdivision. On Oak Avenue in Birmingham, Michigan. A sweet $2 million home.

Four-sided brick. Four bedrooms. Three full baths. A half bath on the main floor.

We were in the basement. A finished basement that was laid to the bone. Marble. Golden fixtures. Game room. Full gym. Bar. Bathroom. Jacuzzi. Kid's playroom. Wine room.

I had disabled his alarm system in less than ten seconds. People bought million-dollar homes and never had the phone company move the D-Mark box inside their cribs. If they didn't have backup power, all it took was a pair of dime-store wire cutters to slice the phone lines and shut down the alarm system. I already knew what kind of system had been installed before I crept around back and cut a single wire. I had information on the floor plans for the house, had studied its layout before I compromised his mansion. I had sat in the dark, just another shadow, waiting for the reverend to come home. Church had run longer than I had expected.

He shouted, *"What political organization are you representing?"*

"It's freezing down here. I hate the cold."

"In God's name *who are you?*"

"Is this marble floor heated? Has to be. Marble gets damn cold."

"Who. Are. You?"

His voice echoed, but no one could hear him scream.

Pictures of the reverend and his family were on the walls. Photos of people who could be his parents and in-laws, political figures and church members, were in every nook and cranny. High-end art from Europe, sculptures from many parts of Africa, Ralph Lauren paint on every wall, the place was decorated to the bone. On the back wall was the largest high-def television I had ever seen. Had to be one hundred inches wide. Had to have been imported straight from Japan. Picture so clear it seemed like I should be able to get up and walk right into the screen.

It was so clear I should've been able to leave this world and leap into a better life.

There were gold-trimmed stairs. He had spent the congregation's money well.

I tugged at my leather gloves, said, "I'm watching the news. Do you mind?"

My cellular was in my hand. I took a picture of the injured man, sent it to the person who was responsible for this job. The phone on this end was a clone, stolen and untraceable, just like the one on the other end, both to be disposed of when the evening came to its premeditated conclusion. I looked out the window again, stared at the freezing tundra. The weather was in the low twenties, was going to hit zero before long. My breath fogged in front of me.

Reverend raised his pain-filled voice and asked, "How much are they paying you?"

I looked at him.

"I'll pay you one hundred thousand to reverse this shit and . . . and . . ."

"Do unto others."

He growled, "An eye for an eye."

"In the name of the Lord."

"I'm offering you one hundred thousand dollars."

Religion had vacated his tone, replaced by vulgarity and desperation.

I said, "Let me think about it."

I went back to watching *Local 4 News*.

There were accidents on Stephenson Highway, Thirteen Mile Road, and on the connector ramp to the Lodge Freeway. Weather was getting so bad that all of the public schools were being closed. New Haven Marquette Elementary, Monnier Elementary, many more.

I said, "I didn't know there was a Beverly Hills, Birmingham, and Berkley in Michigan."

After talking about layoffs at the Big 3 automotive businesses that dominated the Detroit economy, they talked about more layoffs at Lear and Johnson Controls.

I shook my head. "Economy is fucked up here. Didn't know it was that bad."

Then they reported on a rap war. Two rappers had gone at it Tupac and Biggie style. One called himself Sledgehammer. The other called himself the Big Bad Wolf. They both made cuts dissing each other. And fighting each other. Fights between their crews had just broken out at a radio station up in New York. A few people were shot, more than a few had been hurt.

The reverend struggled to breathe. "Are you . . . planning . . . to kill me?"

"Will you please shut up?"

He shouted, *"If this is a robbery, get to robbing and get the hell out of my home."*

"What part of shut up don't you understand?"

"I have a family." He was crying. "A beautiful wife. A daughter. A little boy."

I forgot about the news and looked at him. His right eye was swollen, the size of a baseball. His left eye wasn't too much smaller.

"There isn't any money here at the house, I swear, but let me ring my wife. She will pay whatever you ask, without question, without reporting the incident. Let me talk to my children. I want you to hear their voices. Hear the love. You have a heart, don't you? You have children?"

He spat on the floor. Blood and saliva. Marked the floor with his DNA.

I looked at my watch.

Reverend sounded like he was in the pulpit, fire and brimstone in his voice, as if he were in charge. "I have two. Two wonderful children. Both attend Christian schools."

Confirmation was due five minutes ago.

Palms sweating. Listening for sirens. That had left me more than nervous.

"Greater Life Academy. A *Christian* school. Children must attend schools that are not afraid to acknowledge Jesus and give praise to the Lord. Do you believe in the Lord? My daughter is six. My son is four. Straight-A students."

"Hallelujah, Reverend. Now shut the fuck up."

He closed his eyes, prayed.

Back to the news. The mayor's recent State of the City address was being talked about, debated, said the mayor was forthright when he said Detroit was in serious trouble, refused to let Motown die on his watch, pundits saying the city was already dead and needed to be funeralized.

"Reverend . . . is that you and a group of protestors standing behind the mayor?"

"Is that what this is about?"

"With the religious power you have, you could get a political stronghold on Detroit."

"Is that what this is about? My announcement that I was considering running for mayor?"

"Wow. Look at that close-up of you as the mayor is speaking. Man, you look pissed off."

"Because we disagree with all the mayor has done. Under his rule, Detroit has been run into the ground. I'd rather live in Ninth Ward of New Orleans than watch my Detroit fall apart."

"Ninth Ward. Cutthroat City. Where you were born."

"I was born . . . in the Mighty 9. Came to Detroit when I was a boy."

"Now you're going up against the mayor of Motown."

"Did he send you to do this?"

"You sure publicly disagreeing with the sitting mayor was the right thing to do?"

"That overrated, pimp-suit-wearing son of a . . . does he have something to do with this?"

"He sort of reminds me of Suge Knight. Whatever happened to Suge?"

"Is the mayor behind this? Is this about the church protesting and demanding the mayor to step down so we can once again make Detroit the great city it once was? Watch us. We will put the motor back in the Motor City. We will be mo' better than when we were Motown."

"Running for mayor. Didn't know you were that famous."

"I am a man of God. I have been a pillar of the community for three decades."

"Big church?"

"Twenty thousand members and growing. My message is broadcast around the world."

"I don't know you."

"They know me from Seattle to South Africa. So you may want to reconsider."

"Hot damn. You're famous. International. Maybe I should get your autograph."

"Please, let me go."

There were enough pictures of him and politicians to display his lust for power. His photos told me he was a man who had to be in control. Now he had no control.

His joy was in controlling the sheep of this city.

One sheep had stepped away from his flock, refused to bow down to his power.

My eyes wandered the room again. The reverend had a lot. Seeing his wordly possessions reminded me that I'd been robbed of all I owned. Robbed by Thelma. I thought about Thelma. Thought about the last time I saw her. I thought about all she had taken from me. I should've put a bullet in her heart and killed my anger.

My eyes went to the pictures of the reverend's family. Images of his children and his wife all over the place. So much love in the picture between him and his wife. That forever love.

Sometimes I wanted that. What I saw in those pictures, I wanted that shit for myself.

I said, "I caught feelings for this woman a long time ago."

The reverend grunted. "What you say?"

"Was talking, telling you about this girl. Met her at a pool hall in California. I was about an hour outside of Los Angeles, in North Hollywood. The old man they called Big Slim ran this hot spot. A bona fide thieves' paradise. A simple girl, she was. At least she was back then. Beautiful, exotic girl dressed in Salvation Army clothes. But the part of her I found so beautiful, nobody could see. She didn't see it herself. I saw beyond her daddy issues, the issues she had with her mother, saw beyond the sibling rivalry she had, saw beyond all of that shit in her life."

"What's your problem, son?" Reverend coughed, spat up blood. "Speak your mind."

"Arizona."

"It happened in Arizona."

"No. That's her name. Arizona."

"Speak your mind, son."

"Sure you want to hear this?"

He grunted, struggled to breathe. "Speak your mind."

"She was seeing somebody else. Flimflam man. A high roller. But I put my bid in. She laughed in my face, told me that if I wanted to be with her, I needed a million dollars in the bank."

He released more pain.

I whispered, "A million dollars."

"So that is what motivates you. Your love for a woman."

"My hate for one woman fuels my anger while my love for another fuels my purpose."

"Hate is cancer of the soul. Tell me about the one you hate."

"I don't want to talk about that whore."

"A man should not speak of a woman with such venom."

"No, Reverend. *Whore* is accurate. She's a woman of the night. She's a whore."

"Like Mary Magdalene."

"The one I like, I've been trying to get a million dollars in the bank ever since I met her."

"The one you hate is a whore."

"Yeah."

"The one you love, she hung out in a den of thieves and wrongdoers."

"She's a thief." I nodded. "Runs scams. An artful dodger. Bona fide flimflam woman."

"A thief and a whore. Criminals and the unrighteous. Transgressors. Like you."

"I don't scam or steal. I've been stolen from. But I never steal. Never been a righteous man, not like you. Guess you could say criminals always end up being drawn together."

His pain was getting the best of him. Sweat dripping from his skin like rain.

Then my cellular phone vibrated. It was a text message. I flipped the phone open and finally saw a three-word message. *Funds transferred, proceed.* Followed by a smiley face.

I told him, "Time for us to raise up out of here."

"Where are you taking me?"

"Cold as hell outside."

"Can I please get my coat?"

"Afraid not."

"I need to take my Bible. A man of God must always travel with His word near his heart."

"Sure." I took a deep breath, both tired and irritated. "Get your Bible."

He loosened his collar and limped his gigantic frame across the room, went to the wall filled with leatherbound books, and with his injured hands struggled to pull out a worn Bible.

It was a beautiful red Bible with golden letters across the front.

He said, "This was my first Bible. My *first*. It was Father's *first* Bible. He was a minister. He owned it before me. And this Bible, it is to be my son's first Bible. *Hallelujah*, glory to *Gawd*."

He held his Bible to his chest like it was his salvation. Or his bulletproof vest.

Again, in a shaky voice, he said, "Who are you?"

"I don't have a name."

"You have to have a name."

"Why?"

"So people know who to be afraid of." He laughed a pained laugh. "How are people going to know who to be afraid of? You can't be afraid of someone who doesn't have a name."

"I don't need a name."

"What if Jesus didn't have a name? What if Satan didn't have a name? Good or evil, everyone must have a name. We name what we praise, we name what we fear."

The Bible he held, though his hands were wounded; at least two fingers were broken.

He said, "The wrong you're doing . . . stop doing evil while you can. Stop because one day somebody will come for you. One day what you do to other people, that will be done to you."

His righteous words slowed me down, sent a chill through my frame.

I said, "Hopefully you and my employer can work this out for the best."

"Two hundred thousand. I'll get you two hundred thousand in thirty minutes."

"Both of you care about the future of Detroit."

"The mayor. It's that self-righteous, arrogant motherfucka. I knew it."

"Let's go."

"I'll get you three hundred thousand to kill that son of a bitch."

"You have that kinda cash on hand?"

"Not here. At my church. In the safe. No one has access to the safe."

"No one?"

"There is only one person I trust."

"Don't tell me God has the combo to your safe?"

"I mean here on earth. Only one person on earth I trust."

"Who?"

"Do we have a deal?"

I almost smiled. Three hundred thousand would put me much closer to my goal.

I shook my head. "Sorry. I never double-cross my clients."

He asked, "And you're going to kill me?"

"Yes."

"Why?"

"Because some people deserve to die."

A rush of fear and desperation bloomed in the reverend's face. He began praying. With those damaged fingers he fumbled with the Bible. Struggled to open the damn thing.

The pain in his hands was too great. But he never stopped praying.

He dropped the Bible and it popped open. God's words had been hollowed out and replaced with a snub-nose .38. That four-inch barrel leapt out, hit the marble floor hard, slid ten inches in my favor. His swollen eyes met mine, panic came out of his body on the winds of the loudest scream I'd ever heard. I raced for his .38 like I was racing to stop my own death.

He tackled me like he was a Pro Bowler, lifted me up quick and fast, ran with me, knocked over North African sculptures; the sheep became a raging bull as he slammed me into the one-hundred-inch television against the wall. I swung at his head, connected a few times, but it did no damage, not enough to take him down. He slammed me into the wall again and again.

I gritted my teeth, grunted with each blow. One final slam and I screamed.

Pain consumed me like fire and I went limp, almost blacked out.

He was winded, out of shape, and had to let me go.

I went down fast and hard. So did he.

He collapsed and lay there praying and breathing hard. I lay there rolling in pain.

Reverend made it to his feet first, staggered away from me, limped toward the .38.

"Satan will not defeat me. Not in my home. Not in the Lord's house."

He picked the gun up, frantic, grunting, his swollen fingers getting the best of him.

"Son of a bitch. The mayor . . . I'll kill every motherfucking devil he sends my way."

He wasn't the reverend anymore. He was a pissed-off gangster born in New Orleans.

He grunted and with his aching fingers raised the .38, pointed it at my head.

I was staring at the long barrel of death.

Time slowed down.

By sunrise, the reverend would be a hero. Attacked in his home by an assassin. Then killing the assassin. God was on his side. He'd be a statewide hero by noon. His congregation would be with him on the evening news. CNN would call. Larry King would want to chat with him. *USA Today* would cover this, a picture of the reverend on the cover, followed by a photo of the reverend and his family on page two. He would become the next mayor of Detroit.

All from my death.

There were three explosions.

The first bullet whizzed by my head and hit the wall.

The second bullet would've been in my left eye, had I still been there.

I scampered across the frozen marble, rolled, and yelled out my own fear, came up one knee, crouched, now a smaller target. Sweat in my eyes, pain in my lower back, I had come up facing my enemy, my hand reaching underneath my coat, pulling my .22 from its holster.

I was trapped against the wall, broken television behind me, death in front of me.

It was a .38 against a .22.

The third explosion came from my gun.

I had aimed at his chest, but my pain lowered my gun and my shot was way off, the bullet hitting his right leg. He screamed, staggered, went down on one knee.

He wasn't running. They always ran. He was coming after me. Minister by trade, soldier at heart. He'd become the wounded animal going after his hunter.

His next shot hit the marble floor near my feet. The next hit the shattered television behind me.

If I hadn't beaten him down, if his hands weren't broken, I'd be dead right now.

There were two more explosions. Both came from the .22 I was holding.

One tore into his left arm, that brand-new pain slowing him down.

The second ripped opened a tiny hole in the front of the reverend's head.

There was another explosion, one last echo. The final sound from the battle. His gun fired at the ground, the bullet ricocheting off the marble and shattering glass.

The gun fell from his swollen hand; the reverend slumped into his death. He lay there like a big rag doll, his body in a pool of blood, part of his brain decorating the wall behind him.

I swallowed. Trembled. Looked down at the gun in my hand.

For a moment I was seven years old. There was no joy in killing, not for me. The nauseous feeling that came after I did a job told me there was no joy at all.

I used the camera phone, took a photo, sent that image to the other side of the country.

I was still trembling.

First I was as cold as a Siberian wasteland. Cold and detached, like a whore with her john. It was as if I were watching someone else do horrible things. Then I realized I was drenched, face damp. Sweat glands were pumping hard. Chest rising and falling.

My cellular rang.

Sweat in my eye, I pulled myself together and answered, "Talk to me."

"Is he . . . the reverend . . . did you . . ."

I panted. "You get the picture I sent you?"

"Yes."

I got my breath and firmed my tone. "Then don't ask stupid questions."

Another chill hit me. Like Death was in the room collecting souls, passing through me, its icy fingers grabbing at my insides, knowing it wasn't my time, but warning me nevertheless.

I asked, "Where are you?"

"My suite. Mayflower Hotel. Downtown Seattle."

"Why are you in Seattle?"

"I'm . . . I'm . . . uh . . . T. D. Jakes conference."

"Pull yourself together. You're at a conference. Doing what?"

"Hosting events for the preachers' wives, giving seminars on family values."

"Lots of people have seen you."

"Thousands. Was onstage at the convention center all day."

"Washington State Convention and Trade Center."

Her voice trembled. "Yes."

"Good. You have your alibi."

"My husband . . . the reverend . . . he's due here tomorrow."

"He won't make it."

"So it's . . . it's really . . . it's done."

"Where are your kids?"

"Sleeping. Different part of the suite."

"You're alone."

"I've sequestered myself from the others in anticipation of this moment."

"You sound drunk."

"Had to . . . Yes, I've had a few drinks."

"Sober up. Go take care of your kids. This time tomorrow they'll know they don't have a daddy. Get yourself some rest. And you'll have to face the media and plan a funeral."

"Detroit can bury that cheating bastard in a cardboard box for all I care."

"Either way, you have to tell your kids their daddy is gone."

"He was fucking the babysitter. Cliché, but true. The babysitter was a live-in. That black bitch was living under my roof. I went to Puerto Rico to visit my family. She took me to the airport. Was all up in my face smiling. I was gone for two weeks. Had taken the kids with me, but had forgotten to turn off the hidden camera. It recorded two weeks of . . . of . . . them fornicating."

She sobbed smooth and easy, made anguish sound beautiful. Soft music was playing in the background. Yolanda Adams. Hadn't heard her spiritual ambiance until that moment.

"In my own house. They did it in my house. Disrespected me right under my nose."

I held the phone, staring at their wonderful photos. He was dressed in an expensive suit, like he was the Donald Trump of Christianity. She was his stunning wife. Power and Beauty.

Then I looked down at that hollowed Bible, looked at the reverend's smoking gun.

Anger rose up inside me.

I said, "He said there is three hundred thousand in the safe at church."

She paused. "What else did he tell you?"

"That you have the combination."

"I see."

"There's probably more undeclared tithe money sitting around."

"Okay. So there is a little money in the safe. Big deal."

"I want twenty percent of the three hundred thousand."

"What? Twenty percent of . . . you've already been paid."

"The loaded gun tucked inside the red Bible, you failed to get me that information."

She didn't say anything. Her breathing betrayed her true knowledge.

I said, "Think of it as a sixty-thousand-dollar penalty. Or think of it as sixty thousand reasons for me to not catch a red-eye to Seattle. Think what you want. Just wire it to me."

"If I refuse to wire it to you?"

I paused, then whispered, "Marriott."

That one word halted her.

I said, "You're not staying at the Mayflower. You're at the Marriott Waterfront."

That deflated her arrogance.

I said, "Who do you think sent that basket of fruit to the presidential suite?"

She made a sound that radiated her fear.

"Send my money. Or I will find you, Mrs. Reverend."

I closed the phone, stepped over the reverend, went inside a small room hidden off to the side, one that housed the central vacuum system. It also housed systems for DSL, the phone lines, the DVR, the system for the home surveillance. I took the brains of the system, took the recording of me walking up to this property, and got ready to head out into the freezing night air.

Again I trembled, battled another wave of nausea, then pulled it together.

If I had listened closer, I might've heard the sound of a terrified vixen making calls, then the sound of $60,000 being transferred to a numbered account in a faraway land.

I opened all the windows. The frigid air would throw off his time of death.

At the basement door, breath fogging out of my mouth, I wrapped my scarf around my neck, pulled my beanie down over my head, and prepared to ride through an area that reminded me of South Park and the Dilworth District; big-money areas in North Carolina that had plantation homes situated at least a quarter mile from the streets. North Carolina. Where I was born.

I looked back.

Over the years I'd learned that the most common reason for murder for hire was in relation to the dissolution of an intimate relationship. Especially when a lot of money was involved. If he had three hundred thousand in a safe, I'd love to see his bank account.

Now Mrs. Reverend would be doing the breaststroke in a pool filled with Benjamins.

The red Bible rested at her deceased husband's side. My eyes went to the cover.

In golden letters, a name stared up me.

Through my pain I whispered, "Gideon."

I killed the lights, limped across the garden, each uneven step crunching frozen grass.

The reverend was right. Every man needed a name.

People needed to know who to praise.

Or who to fear.

Gideon.

My name would be Gideon.

Strangers

Two

the damned don't cry

She wore black.

The hue of grief and mourning.

The color of a new death.

Tears ran from behind her dark shades. She'd taken them off right after she got into her seat, while the rest of the plane was trying to get settled. She sobbed as the plane took off, the expression on her face revealing her anxiety. College Park and the Dirty South faded behind us. Tissue to her face, she shook her head like it was too late to change her mind, wiped away so many tears. More appeared. The redness of her eyes was as strong as the heat of the sun.

The woman dressed in Prada and Rolex was drying one tear at a time.

The black dress she wore. Reminded me of Audrey Hepburn. *Breakfast at Tiffany's.* She didn't remind me of Audrey Hepburn. Just the dress. It had class.

I'd seen her crying at the gate, looking like she was about to have a breakdown, then we boarded the British Airways aircraft with the rest of the world travelers. I hoped she wouldn't bounce her leg and cry the entire eight hours we would be on this flight, hoped she wouldn't sob and blow her nose all the way to London. She put her shades back on, hiding from the world.

I had my own problems. I'd made a bad move in Tampa and almost lost my life. Hadn't been that careless since the reverend in Detroit. That Detroit contract had been years ago.

My face ached. Would ache for a while. I had taken a BC Powder, the only thing that ever seemed to work for my pains. The swell above my left eye didn't hurt as much, but my bottom lip still throbbed. My wounds were less than a week old.

She wept. The woman dressed in death cried like she was at her mother's funeral.

She felt my energy, might have caught me peeping at her, and shifted away from me.

Thick book resting in her lap, she ran her hands through her big Afro, hair with old-school flair and contemporary highlights, hair with two personalities, two moods, and glanced at me. No words, just a quick, almost embarrassed glimpse as she raised her dark shades and dabbed her bloodshot eyes. She took a deep breath, shook her head, took off her high-priced sunglasses, eased them into the seat pocket, made her leg bounce, and fastened her seat belt. She straightened out her clothes, continued manufacturing more tears than she could wipe away.

My face. My hand. Both hurt bad. I opened and closed my fingers, felt pain in my hand.

I was glad to be leaving the U.S. Needed to get far away from what I'd done.

I grunted with my suffering, ached, and the woman dressed in mourning cried.

As soon as I began to drift and land in a peaceful place, my agony grabbed me, woke me up with a start. My hands became swollen fists, my teeth clenched, until I realized where I was.

She was looking at me, her mouth wide-open, almost terrified.

The unknown woman smelled nice, her aisle seat one empty

seat away from my window seat, and she was dressed in a black dress that hit right below her knees, her black heels now off, seat reclined, overhead light on. Her toes were pretty. Sexy. She reached into her purse and took out two miniature bottles of pinot, a small plastic cup, filled her cup, and began sipping.

Bouncing her leg. Sobbing. Shaking her head. Drinking.

She wiped her eyes again and again, got her crying under control, and picked up her book. I saw the cover. *Skin in Darkness*, a collection of erotic novellas by Maxim Jakubowski.

I broke the silence, asked, "Good book?"

She shrugged. "Better than reading wretched legal documents."

"What do you do?"

"I was an attorney." She hesitated. "Used to work in law. Not anymore."

I repeated, "Not anymore?"

More tears fell from her eyes, and she turned away.

Our conversation ended.

I had all the information I wanted.

I thought she was British, had assumed that because of her proper demeanor, but she was American. She said *attorney*, not *barrister*. She was born outside of the U.S. Her accent told me that. But her accent wasn't primary, didn't subdue the few words she had given me. She was born somewhere else and moved to the States. She was married. She was rich.

Didn't take much information to create a package.

She blew her nose. Dried her eyes. Went back to her book, her body angled away from mine. That shapely leg was bouncing, drawing my attention to her flesh. Forcing me to notice.

Had been a while since I'd been inside a woman. Had been too long.

She was beautiful. Intelligent voice with a hint of accent, just enough to make her words ring as exotic. Like Arizona. But not like Arizona. The lady next to me cried. Arizona would never shed a tear. Had known Arizona for a criminal's lifetime and never saw her shed a single tear, not even when she had been slapped in the face by the man she was with when I met her, not when she was betrayed by the man she was seeing, not even when she was betrayed by her own family. We had that in common. The part about being betrayed by people we cared about.

I put on my headphones, popped in a DVD.

The crying woman never said a word. She wore a silver cross, one that hung to the swell of her breasts. Her wedding ring was the size of a weapon, large enough to kill any man or slay any conversation of a particular kind. She wiped her eyes, went to the bathroom, came back, her red-rimmed eyes taking her right back to her erotica, her black dress clinging to her like unseen hands made of high-end fabric.

Drink service came by. I went for the hard stuff. Whiskey. The good stuff. I took my liquor straight up, no chaser. She ordered two more bottles of white wine, sipped on her first glass as soon as it was handed to her, wiping away her tears and falling back into a world that Maxim had fabricated, that strange woman not wanting to be disturbed until her liquor was gone.

She shifted, moved her leg in an easy, stimulated way. I cleared my throat, my peripheral catching her peeping around, checking to see if anyone was watching her in her literary voyeurism. I was right there with her. As she read, with every page, she was being read.

I wondered if she was wet. If the folds of her secrets were moist.

A while later a sensual noise rose in her throat. A sinful and naughty sound. Again she shifted. Another noise. More shifting. She licked her lips. Then, another sex-inspired noise.

She returned to the real world, looked around, took her headset off, closed her book, disturbed, no doubt stimulated by what she had read, or by the cups of wine, maybe both.

She finished her second glass of wine, asked, "What movie are you watching?"

"Sci-fi." I hit the pause button. *"Battlestar Galactica."*

She swallowed, a deep frown set in her face. "My husband . . . his favorite show."

I didn't know if her abrupt disdain was because of her husband or sci-fi. My bet was the husband. Even the people who disliked sci-fi never rendered a stare of contempt for the genre.

Still frowning, she went back to her book, returned to sex and fantasy, her silver cross taking refuge in the sweet mystery of her bosom, her wedding ring glittering in the faint overhead light.

She began working on her third glass of wine. Not as many tears right now. Even in the middle of sorrow she was esculent, in the sensual sense of the word. Nice brown skin. Her voice had been strong, professional, accented with a mild erotic tone. She was streamlined, everything in its place, as if she had gone shopping for T&A and other accessories, shopped all over the world until she'd found the perfect match for everything, then draped it all in the color of death.

I looked at my hands and expected to see streaks of crimson, but there was no blood, just swollen hands. For a moment I saw the dead bodies scattered in the parking lot. My flesh turned hot. Had to focus to keep from feeling nauseous. Stomach hadn't felt weak in years.

My subconscious was playing itself out, fucking with me.

Mild turbulence shook me away from that memory. As soon as the turbulence eased up, that nauseous feeling ceased. The FASTEN SEAT BELTS sign went off, and one of the flight attendants came down the aisle, looking at passengers, then stopped at my row.

No way would they send a flight attendant to look for me on a plane.

But then again, there wouldn't be a way for me to get off a plane.

The flight attendant held the seats to stay balanced.

He said, "We have a bit of a situation."

I tensed. But I smiled too.

The woman in black put her book down, dried her eyes, tensed as well. No smile.

Flustered, the flight attendant stood over me, his British accent so thick and cockney that I had a hard time understanding what he was trying to explain to me and the woman in black.

"The flight is full and unfortunately we have to do a tad bit of rearranging."

I stared at the attendant, anger and dread in my injured expression.

He asked, "Is that middle seat taken?"

The woman in black looked at the vacant seat, we glanced at each other, the first moment we connected, if there was a connection, and we bonded like soldiers in a war, like strangers who had a common enemy, and that enemy wore a blue uniform, white shirt, red tie.

I said, "Harvey is sitting there."

"Harvey?"

"My rabbit. Don't tell me you can't see Harvey."

The woman in black didn't miss a beat, said, "I see him. Hard to miss a six-foot rabbit."

The flight attendant was confused, then made a face that said he wasn't amused.

"So that seat is available." The flight attendant shrugged as if our tribulations were no one's but our own. "Tell your rabbit we have a full flight. We have to make a few adjustments."

The male flight attendant hand-signaled. Halfway down the aisle, a female flight attendant acknowledged the gesture; then she waved toward the front of the plane.

The woman in black cursed. Called the flight attendant a *bloody blood clot*.

She was from the islands. Married. Crying. I wondered if she was crying, reading erotica, and on her way to attend a funeral, or if she had just buried someone she loved.

A moment later another woman was being ushered down the narrow aisle, her supersized and overstuffed backpack and coat being held in front of her.

"Oh, God." The woman in black groaned. "Not her."

The young woman heading our way. Her easy brown complexion the same hue as sugar in the raw. Dressed in tight jeans. T-shirt cut to expose her stomach, a stomach that had done hundreds of sit-ups. The swell of her breasts made it hard for any man to maintain eye contact. Her T-shirt read MAKE POVERTY HISTORY. But the jeans sent another type of message.

The girl snapped at the flight attendant, "I don't see why I have to change seats."

She was black American.

The way those dungarees fit her small waist and rocked her thick thighs was obscene. Tight, low-rise pants that were well below her belly button. Built for both speed and comfort.

The flight attendant remained proper. "Please, ma'am. The other couple, they have a baby and they were supposed to have those seats assigned to them. They need the seats designated for babies. It's policy."

"Show me that policy in writing."

"We apologize for the inconvenience."

"Well, you're going to be apologizing to the NAACP as soon as I land. Wait, is there a NAACP in England? Has to be a NAACP office in Brixton. That's where the black people at."

"You can check, ma'am, upon your arrival. Somehow I doubt if there is one of those."

"Well, could you stick me in first class as compensation?"

"Afraid not, ma'am."

"At least hook a sister up with a free drink or something."

The flight attendant walked away, left in a hurry, left the angry girl and her pissed-off attitude standing in the aisle. She cursed and flipped the bird. Her headset was around her neck, her iPod on her hip, her music loud, spilling into the aisle, Prince singing about Lolita.

The angry girl looked at us. "Sorry, but they put me on the back of the bus. No wonder their asses are being investigated for price-fixing. Need to investigate them for seat-fixing too. And they need Jesus. They sent an employee home because she wore a crucifix. Heathens."

The woman in black raised her head, did that with reluctance, got up with a sigh.

The angry girl looked the woman in black in her face, smiled, said, "Hey, it's you again."

The woman in black dabbed her eyes with a napkin, created a smile. "Surprise."

"Sorry about this. But they moved three of us because of a baby. You're stuck with me, I guess. Better me than the three-hundred-pound woman wearing floral spandex. They sent her wobbling the other way. Bet those people are mad as hell right about now. All because of a damn baby."

They shuffled around a bit, tried to get by each other.

"Can you believe what they did to me? First they *asked* me to move. I said no. Actually, I told his ass *hell* no. That's why I booked online and checked the box for a *window seat*. So I could put my head against the window and sleep. So I wouldn't have to move to let people out every time they want to get up. Then they kick me to the back of the plane like it's the back of the damn bus. This is a long flight and people will want to get up. I bought a ticket from Orbitz and I checked the box for a *window seat* and I had a damn *window seat* and now I'm being forced to get stuck in a *middle* seat? Why didn't they ask some of those *white* people to move? Why me?"

The woman in black sighed. Shifted.

The angry girl went on, "Then that anorexic-looking, pale-ass bitch got all the flight attendants, all of them in my face, trying to encourage me to move back here. Had everybody watching the black girl, trying to see what I was going to do. I wanted to knock that bitch the fuck out."

The woman in black sighed again.

The angry girl asked the woman in black, "How are you feeling now?"

"Better. Can't believe I'm on a plane to London."

"You're still crying?"

"Off and on."

The woman in black hurried by our new seatmate and headed toward the long line of people waiting to get into the claustrophobic-size bathroom. Our reluctant seatmate opened and slammed the overhead bins; each time she tiptoed, her tight jeans slipped down below decency. She marched up and down the aisle, complaining, hunting for some place to put her backpack and coat. She stuffed her coat in a bin about ten rows up, struggled to get her backpack in a bin in the same area, not enough room, went down five rows, found another bin, same result, gave up, and dragged her gear back to the seat, bent over, and squeezed her backpack in the little space we had, that move making her low-rise jeans fall even lower, low enough to see she was wearing a blue thong, a lacy number that contradicted the rest of her urban gear, and struggled to stuff her backpack underneath her seat, gave up, let it rest at her feet, her legs on either side of her luggage. Her left leg would be touching mine for the entire flight. She tried to shift, but there was nowhere to shift, no room left, would be even less when the woman in black came back.

"*Hate* damn middle seats. Can you believe that shit?"

The girl sucked her teeth, shook her head, enraged.

"This *sucks*. This really *sucks*. Can't wait to find the NAACP."

She saw me looking at her, saw me shifting, watching her struggle.

She gave up a stiff smile, her headset still dangling, music loud, Prince still wailing.

She asked, "Mrs. Jones hanging in there or what?"

"What?"

"The lady who is sitting next to you. Mrs. Jones. She was going through it at the airport."

"Mrs. Jones . . . a friend of yours?"

"Nah. Met her when we were in line getting tickets. Had a problem with mine and had to go to the counter. Had an e-ticket but they couldn't find my damn info. Nothing but drama."

"What's up with her?"

"Heartbroken. Running away from home."

"She's too old to run away from home."

"I'm just repeating what she told me. Heartbroken and running away from home."

"That explains all the crying."

She took a deep breath. "She told me she hopped on a damn plane and decided she was going to London. She's *never* been to England. She just passed by LAX, went inside, broke out her American Express, and bought a ticket. Being traumatized will make you do that. Just snap, break out a platinum card, slap down your passport, hop on a plane, and go as far away from your problems as you can afford to go. Or being in love. Being in love will make you spend your last dime. Will make you borrow money against your future. Love is an investment, you know?"

"I heard it could be traumatic."

"Watch what you say. I'm in love, which is different than being traumatized. Or crazy. I decided this morning to just get up and go see my boyfriend. Well, I didn't just decide. We were talking and he told me he wished I were there, in London. He's an actor. I'm an actor too."

"Are you?"

"Or an actress. Some call us actors, some say actress. I don't care as long as they spell my name right on my check. But things are slow, not working right now. My agent sucks. I do massages on the side. No happy endings. People always ask. Men. And women too. Would you believe women ask other women for happy endings? I guess all the touching, you know, the dark room with candles, the soft music, I guess, you know, people are bound to get aroused."

"I guess. Touching does create arousal."

"My boyfriend is in London. He's starring in a play. *Rent.* You heard of *Rent*?"

I shook my head.

"You haven't heard of *Rent*?" She beamed. "It's a play and a movie."

"What's it about? People struggling . . . to pay their rent?"

"Nah. It's like . . . like . . . like *Brokeback Mountain* and *Queer as Folk* meets *The L Word* with the crackhead from *Jungle Fever* and it's set in the eighties. I have it on DVD if you want to—"

"I'll pass on that one."

"Sure? It's really good. It's about love and loving unconditionally."

"I'll pass. I'm sure. But if you have something with Clint Eastwood or Wesley Snipes . . ."

"My boyfriend, he's so good. From Boston. Never thought I'd fall in love with a black man from Boston. Hell, didn't know there were any black men in Boston. Besides Bobby Brown. Maybe that's why he left. Got tired of being the only black man in Boston. Just kidding. Lots of black people in Boston. My honey is straight gangsta. Public-housing baby. From Mattapan, aka *Murderpan*. Aka *Ratattattattapan*. You know Boston? I looked it up. Used to be Jewish area, but when black people showed up, white flight like a mofo. He grew up around Blue Hill Avenue. Blue Hill Ave., like the movie. My boo is six-four. Two hundred plus. Bona fide soldier."

I shifted, hoped she was done.

She said, "My boo plays the part of the landlord. A *straight* part. He's not a homophobe, but he wouldn't audition to play a gay role to save his life, not at this point in his career. He said you didn't see Denzel and Sidney Poitier or James Earl Jones playing no fag, and I'm not talking about a cigarette. No, sir. They played straight men all the way down the line. He wants to be famous and not get typecast, like, like, you know, like other famous actors. Wesley Snipes almost made it, but he played a transvestite and *BAM*, career went downhill from there. Wonder if he's going to pay the IRS that twelve million or be on the run like he was in that movie with Tommy Lee Jones."

I put my things to the side, let my tray table up, told her to let me out.

I had to get out of that corner. Was starting to feel claustrophobic like an American soldier during Vietnam, held captive in a small cage, being tortured by the enemy in Vietcong.

As soon as I was free, she put her headset on, bobbed to Prince.

The lady in black was hanging out in the back of the airbus, near the bathroom.

I headed that way.

Still anxious.

Still looking for trouble.

Still swimming in Lake Panic.

Something told me I was being watched.

I looked behind me.

He was wearing a dark gray suit.

Had bandages on his face.

And he was coming toward me.

Three

the man with the broken nose

A man in a dark gray suit was coming down the aisle.

Dressed like he was a high-end preacher. Yellow book in hand, like it was his Bible. He was halfway down the airbus before he stopped walking. Came to an abrupt stop.

Midfifties I'd guess. Seasoned.

Pretty unremarkable except for the huge Band-Aids over his broken nose. The Band-Aids were bloodied, large enough to obscure the top part of his face. He'd suffered a good blow.

We paused.

He regarded my injuries. I did the same with his.

Yellow book in hand, he turned around and went back toward business class.

I turned around, heading deeper into the poverty section of the plane.

My mind photographed what I had seen. Injured man in suit. I doubted if those were Fortune 500 injuries. Light-skinned man. Could've been black or white. Bald. Gray suit and red shirt. The shirt was the $200 kind and the suit had to cost ten times that.

I looked back again.

Book in hand, he made his way back through the curtains that separated the classes.

In the end, it wasn't his injury that made me notice him, I'd seen many injuries on people. It was his clothes and his deep-set eyes. His eyes had maintained an unblinking cold stare.

He could've been the air marshal.

For a moment I saw the dead bodies scattered in the parking lot. My flesh turned hot. Maybe they knew about Tampa. Maybe my fake passport had been compromised and they knew. Maybe they'd be waiting for me at the other end of this journey.

Mrs. Jones was in front of me, staring at me. Standing up, she was stunning, the way her black dress hung over her breasts and the swell of her modest ass was like two shots of Viagra.

That was the effect she was starting to have on me.

The lady in black wiped her eyes, smiled at me. "I'm impressed."

"How so?"

"You lasted a whole five minutes with Chatty Cathy."

"I was ten seconds from asking for a parachute."

"You were going to jump?"

"Was about to throw her out."

"And you'd waste a parachute?"

"Good point."

She laughed.

I said, "So you're Mrs. Jones."

She smiled. "What else she tell you?"

I smiled. "Nothing. Was she supposed to tell me something?"

Her smile faded. She let go of her illusion. "Sorry for crying. Trying to stop, I really am."

"What's wrong?"

"Guess I'm just mentally and emotionally tired of being mentally and emotionally tired."

"When you're done crying, you'll be good as new."

She smiled again, this one real.

We stood back there, moving around that tight space, a line of people going in and out of the toilets. I realized why she was there. She was avoiding going back to her seat. Me too.

She asked, "Can you . . . uh . . . can you recommend any hotels in London?"

"Which part? In the city, outside the city? What area did you have in mind?"

"Anywhere. First timer. Never been to London."

"Maybe Central London. Try Bloomsbury. Nice hotels in that area. Try Myhotel."

"You own a hotel?"

"No, it's called Myhotel. Nice place. Sushi bar. Great lounge."

"Sounds . . . sounds . . ."

"Sexy?"

"Well, I wasn't going to say that."

"It's trendy and hip and sexy."

She shifted. "Is that where you're staying? At the trendy and hip and sexy hotel?"

"Depends."

"Depends on what?"

Point-blank I asked, "Your husband's not meeting you across the pond?"

"No." She hesitated. That simple question changed the temperature. "No, he's not."

"So you're alone?"

She looked down at her wedding ring, took in a slow breath. I had been too obvious.

But the man part of me had to go there. Always had to try, even if it was in vain.

Hunters. We were all hunters.

I asked, "Your marriage . . . your husband . . . everything okay?"

"All I can say is . . . we make promises we know we can't keep. Promises that start with *always* and end with *forever.* We take on the impossible and fail miserably. Or stick it out and pretend that there was some great reward for enduring a life lived in depression and torture."

Again, we paused.

I said, "A cynic."

"You noticed."

"Of course."

She motioned toward the Chatty Cathy who had invaded our space.

Mrs. Jones said, "I used to be just like her."

"Talkative?"

"No. Idealistic. Happy. Ignorance is truly bliss."

She wiped her eyes with the back of her hands. Crying again.

I asked, "Would you like to do dinner?"

"Dinner? On the plane?"

"In London."

"You're asking me out to dinner?"

"Yes."

We stared a bit. Her eyes went down. Maybe she was appraising my crotch. Or admiring her wedding ring. Maybe she was just looking at the floor. Wasn't sure.

I said, "You're a beautiful woman."

"Makeup running. Eyes swollen. I don't feel beautiful."

"Well, you are."

She bit her top lip, disturbed, thinking.

I said, "What's on your mind?"

"This."

"What about this?"

"This . . . this . . . you're flirting with me. I haven't been flirted with in . . . forever."

"Then your husband should be charged with neglect."

"Or should I charge you with criminal trespass?"

"Can't jail a man for thinking about doing something."

Mild turbulence. More staring between us. I held her gaze

the way her dress held her slender frame, with both respect and disrespect, tight and loose all at once.

Her brown eyes narrowed.

She waved her wedding ring. "Testing the waters?"

"I'm a good swimmer."

We stood there, saying nothing as people went in and out of the bathroom.

She touched her wild hair and walked away. She looked back. We stared at each other for a moment, maybe five long seconds. Then she went inside one of the vacant bathrooms.

I headed down the aisle, passed my seat, kept going until I got to the blue curtain, stopped like I was at the rim of a foreign country, flight attendants guarding that area like border patrol. I looked for the man with the broken nose. That $6,000-a-seat section had reclining chairs, half facing forward, half facing backward, the seats in sets of two, side-by-side recliners with red partitions in between. Two rows up. I saw his dark gray suit pants, his shoes.

He was in a rear-facing seat, one row in. I crept across the border.

The yellow book was in his lap. He held it like it was his Bible. Two empty whiskey bottles were on his tray. He was horizontal. Might've been sleeping. His monitor was on a movie. The thick covers they gave the privileged were pulled up to his injured nose.

On the way back I looked at other passengers. No one was interested in me.

There was an overweight woman in floral spandex squeezed between two people. There was a crying baby in the section of the plane the happy actress had come from. So the happy actress wasn't a setup, so far as I could tell. The woman in black seemed legit too. Nobody could cry that long without being in emotional strife. There were no dots to connect. There was no conspiracy, none that I could find. And there weren't any vindictive rappers on the plane.

I looked at my swollen hands. There was a mild tremble.

I grabbed a few newspapers, headed back to my third-world section of this flying world.

The front page of the *New York Times* had an article on THE DAY HIP-HOP DIED. Three days ago rapper Big Bad Wolf, aka Big Bad, had been slaughtered in a dark alley down in Tampa.

The paper said the scene was gruesome, looked like a gang war had broken out.

That was how it was supposed to look. Like the battlefield at the end of a war.

I was almost done with this business.

In a few hours, outside of the three properties I owned, I'd have a million dollars in cash tucked away. I remembered being homeless, on the run, living on the streets of Montreal.

I tossed the *New York Times* into an empty seat, kept the British papers in hand.

On the way back, with guilt swirling inside me, everybody looked suspicious.

At this rate, by the time the plane landed, the small children would be suspects.

But no one was after me.

Not on a plane.

An airplane was the safest place to be.

It would be a different story when I was on the ground.

When I was close to my seat, I saw something else.

Something that made me clench my teeth.

I had been robbed.

Four

between tears and laughter

The happy actress had jacked me for my window seat.

My newspapers had been moved to the middle. Her stuffed backpack was crammed at her feet, the tray table down. Not only had she stolen my seat, she had her elbows spread out and she'd gotten too comfortable; most of the space and the shared armrest was now hers.

Without complaining I took the middle seat.

The girl slid her headset off. "I wasn't finished talking about my boo."

"There's more?"

"We've been together for three years now. We met doing this play in L.A. A musical, actually. He was the lead. He was so good. I was the understudy for the female lead. She got sick. So I got to kiss him every night. I mean we kissed for real. Well, nobody told me I wasn't supposed to tongue-kiss him. But I did. He was holding my butt and everything. You know, got into the part. We got a standing ovation. Actors have to get into the role, you know?"

She laughed.

Down the way, food service for the second-class fliers had

begun. Flight attendants were coming down both aisles of the airbus, feeding the two rows on both sides, doing the same for the five seats in the middle, throwing us food in cardboard boxes the way zookeepers feed monkeys.

She went on, "We started kicking it after that. The first year was re-mark-able. We were shacking. Well, he was staying at my apartment in West Hollywood, splitting the rent. He's been on the road with *Rent* for two years, so we haven't had a chance to be together too much, only when he came home on break. But we send e-mails and text-message and don't really talk because he's always either distracted or in theater mode, always jibber-jabbering and going on and on about the play and the people in his cast when I want to talk about us or have some sexy conversation. Don't think we've had any real sexy conversation in at least two months. At least. Maybe three. Hard being the patient girl-friend, you know? Not one of my stronger points. Because, I mean actors and actresses, we need attention, need to be in the spotlight, you know?"

"In other words you're self-centered and narcissistic, you know?"

"That was mean."

"You talk a lot, you know?"

"I'm wound up." She laughed. "And I'm tired. I ramble when I'm exhausted."

She put her headphones back on. She searched, found a magazine in her seat. *Pride*. London's version of *Ebony*, a red-haired Toni Braxton gracing the cover. I glimpsed the cover and saw it had articles on great sex saving Samuel Jackson's marriage; lesbian love; black men and oral sex being the last taboo. She went straight to the article on black men and oral sex.

When I thought she was comfortable, she took off her headset.

She tapped my leg and said, "One more thing, then I'll let you get back to your movie. Mrs. Jones, she's married but she said she was about to get divorced, that her marriage was *irre-*

trievably broken. *Irretrievably.* That's why she's crying like somebody cut off her foot."

"Okay. Her marriage is *irretrievably* broken. Your point?"

"Check it out; she's not the one who wants the divorce, if you get my drift."

"So she's scorned and rejected."

"Did she tell you that she hopped on a plane with no goddamn luggage? She told me she was going to London, no luggage, no clothes, no nothing. All she has is what she has on. Would you believe that? Not even a clean pair of drawers. Crazy, huh?"

"I wouldn't call that crazy."

"C'mon, man. What woman in her right mind leaves without shoes? Without drawers?"

"A rich woman who doesn't want to be found."

"Hmmm. Hadn't thought about it from that angle."

"You done trying to play Nancy Drew?"

"I'm done." She yawned. "She's all screwed up and here I am going to hook up with my boyfriend, about to have the time of my life in London, and she's . . . I feel sorry for her. God, hope she doesn't start bawling again. Can you imagine being on the plane for hours sitting next to somebody going to work your nerves from the U.S. to the U.K.?"

"I think I can."

"That was mean."

"I thought you were done talking."

"Winding down." She yawned again. "What's your name?"

I stared at her, stunned and irritated by her rambling.

I said, "Gideon."

"Gideon. The hero of Israel who saved his people from the Midianites."

"Somebody knows the Bible."

"Top to bottom. Book of Judges."

"Yeah."

"I'm Lola. In case you were wondering. Lola McVeigh."

"Nice to meet you, Lola McVeigh."

"Lola McVeigh but I use the stage name Lola Mack. Sexy and cool, huh? Lola, like Lola Falana. Mack like the movie *The Mack*. And like that Mark Morrison song 'Return of the Mack.'"

I rubbed my temples, really did wish a door would blow off and suck Lola out of the plane.

Lola shifted, hummed a bit, put on a huge smile. "Can't wait to see my boyfriend."

"Lola. Please. Give it a rest."

She said, "You're sexy, got this rugged way about you that's hot, you know that?"

"Uh . . . Lola . . ."

"Not hitting on you. Just saying. I got a man. My man is so damn fine it's ridiculous. Was just pointing out you got this mad aphrodisiac thing working, but you probably know that."

"You finished?"

"Nnnnope. Even with your face beat up like that, you look good. Man, either you got it bad, or somebody got it worse. Serious, what happened to your face? All red and swollen around the eyes. Hands scratched up. Looks like somebody just kicked your ass or vice versa."

"Fell down."

"Did you fall down on somebody else's wife?"

I opened my eyes, actually laughed. "What did you say you did for a living?"

"Actress. Singer. Masseuse with no happy endings. Oh, 'happy endings' are orgasms."

"I know what a happy ending is."

She laughed. "I know this guy at the Ritz who does that for his clients, men or women."

"Men or women?"

"He services both. Men and women ask me to give them a happy ending all the time."

I asked, "Women want happy endings from women?"

"Devil talk has your ears burning now, huh? I'll be quiet now."

"No, tell me about this women and happy ending thing."

"See, talk about sex and a man is all ears."

"Go to sleep, Lola."

The woman in black returned, tipsy, two bottles of wine in her hands, moving at a slow pace. She eased into her seat, found her seat belt, adjusted it, found her sex-filled novel again.

In the softest, kindest voice I'd ever heard, Lola asked her, "Sure you're gonna be okay?"

The woman in black nodded, went to her wine and her book, shutting us out.

Lola said, "This is Gideon. Gideon, like the Bible."

Mrs. Jones said, "Gideon."

"Gideon, this is Mrs. Jones. Like the love song 'Me and Mrs. Jones' or the movie called *Devil in Miss Jones*, only this isn't that Mrs. Jones, not the one in the song or the woman in the nasty movie. You met Gideon, Mrs. Jones?"

Mrs. Jones said, "We chatted. He recommended a hotel in Bloomsbury."

"Which hotel?"

"Myhotel."

"You own a friggin' hotel? You rolling like that?"

"No, that's the name of it. Myhotel. Right, Gideon?"

I nodded.

Lola frowned. "That's a *stupid* name for a hotel."

Food service finally made it back to us.

We all let out our tray tables, ate the bland food without talking. When we were done, Lola took our trash, stacked it all up on her tray. She let her seat back, popped in her earphones, cranked up Prince, and fell into that purple world.

Mrs. Jones picked up the *Pride* magazine, went straight to the article about great sex saving Samuel L. Jackson's marriage. I asked Mrs. Jones to let me out. Needed to stretch my legs. I wandered the aisle, went to the back, did some stretches, then made a bathroom run.

When I came back, Mrs. Jones had moved to the middle seat, *Pride* magazine in her lap. The armrest between her and Lola was up. Lola was giving Mrs. Jones a shoulder massage. Mrs. Jones's eyes were tight, face looking ethereal.

Lola said, "Turn a little bit so I can work on your neck."

Soft moans from Mrs. Jones. *"Oh God, Lola, oh God, oh God."*

"No wonder you can't stop crying. All these knots and rocks in your shoulders and back."

"Lola, Lola, oh God, Lola." Mrs. Jones shivered and sighed and moaned. *"Oh, God."*

"If I had my table and oils, I could really hook you up."

I let the armrest between the aisle and middle seat up, Mrs. Jones's warm leg rubbing up against mine. First she twitched. Then her leg started to shake. Lola asked her if she was okay. Mrs. Jones bit her bottom lip and let out soft moans, held on to the armrest like somebody was licking figure eights on her fleshy folds. Her hand ended up on my hand, felt her quivering from deep inside, felt her riding the waves of pleasure. Lola was humming, singing low, sounding like an angel, doing that without thought as she finished her work. Mrs. Jones let my hand go, stopped moving. Lola whispered her name. No answer. The woman in black was sleeping. Light snores, like she hadn't slept in years.

I was aroused. Very aroused.

Lola looked over at me, winked, then whispered, "Told you I was the bomb."

"Never doubted you."

"Soon as I get to London, I'm going to give my boyfriend one. With a very happy ending."

A while later Lola put her headset back on.

I looked at my hands again. I could've been dead.

I'd stop at a million dollars.

The flight attendants came back down the aisle, collecting trays and trash.

Mrs. Jones shifted, leaned up against me, still in a deep sleep.

Mrs. Jones. The heartbroken runaway. Her marriage *irretrievably* broken.

Lola wiggled, still in my stolen seat, her head against the window, snoring a little.

Lola McVeigh. Stage name Lola Mack. The hopeless romantic.

And me, the man with the gentle smile that hid so much anger.

Thelma. The source of my anger.

Hadn't thought about her for a few hours.

Anger rose so high it choked me. Couldn't get her out of my mind.

It had been years.

I'd be in England soon. Close to Amsterdam once again.

Thelma.

Some people deserved to die. Thelma was at the top of that list.

Amsterdam. Window 120. All of a sudden those images flashed in my mind.

I handed the trays and trash to the flight attendant without waking Mrs. Jones or Lola, opened another BC Powder, washed it down with the last of my hard liquor, then let my seat back. I had hoped the caffeine in the BC Powder would keep me awake. But I leaned against Mrs. Jones's softness, her bushy hair like a pillow, her warmth and easy breathing soothing me.

Her energy soothed me the same way Lola's touch had soothed her.

I slipped into a dreamless slumber. But my sleep never stayed dreamless for long. Just like every flight had some turbulence. Tampa remained on my mind, found its way through the darkness and into my dreams. So did my last trip to the Netherlands.

Memories of Amsterdam rose up and created a thick shadow that darkened all thoughts of Tampa. Holland was personal, a promise I needed to keep before I finished this career.

I had eliminated many, but there was one person I had to destroy to find my own peace.

Five

you can't escape forever

Four summers ago.

Amsterdam Centraal was hot and humid, packed with tourists, most loaded down with huge backpacks. Signs were everywhere warning neophytes to beware of pickpockets. Summertime. The season of tourists, when the thieves came out of hibernation.

I had flown into Schiphol Airport, then caught the train into Amsterdam Centraal. Wearing worn jeans and a tank top, backpack and sandals on, I put on my shades and followed the crowd, took a number and waited my turn, then exchanged dollars for euros at the train station, tried to use some of the Dutch I remembered, told the old, stout attendant *bedankt* for her help, not sure if that was the right word, but she smiled and in stiff English told me that I was welcome in return.

We smiled after butchering each other's language.

She looked at me with endearing eyes, no idea of what was going on inside me.

I'd come here on business. Business from me always put grief in the hearts of others.

My whole life had been one big business trip. I'd never played. Never had fun.

Business was wearing me down.

She said, "American, no?"

I nodded. "Yes. American."

"If you taxi, use the TCA taxi. The others will give you a higher rate, overcharge you."

"*Bedankt.*"

"Make sure you stop at the Sex Museum. It is by McDonald's. Look for McDonald's. The museum has the biggest penis. Maybe three hundred centimeters tall."

"A nine-foot-tall penis?"

"And maybe one hundred eighty centimeters around."

"Did Shaq donate his organ?"

She didn't understand my American NBA humor. "Take picture. Then go take picture of the marble penis fountain at Casa Rosso. The penis gushes all day and night."

"*Bedankt.*"

"And McDonald's has a urinal shaped like a woman's mouth with big red lips. It was in the newspaper. Crazy people angry, so it might not be there for long. Photograph as well."

"*Bedankt.*"

"The *Opstapper*. The weather is very nice so ride the *Opstapper* to sightsee everything."

"*Bedankt.*"

"But the best way to see Amsterdam is from the canals. Look for St. Nicholas Boat Club."

I became patient, let the old woman finish telling me where to find the best shopping and where to buy Mark Raven art, let her tell all she wanted to tell me before I left her window.

I headed out into the heart of Amsterdam, a liberal city that had more weed-selling coffeehouses than Seattle had Starbucks. A place that sold international pussy the way IHOP sold Rooty Tootys. Air was so damn clear here, skies so damn blue, more beautiful than the godly blue that hovered over North Carolina. The area around the train station was buzzing with languages I couldn't comprehend. Coffee in hand, I was almost run down by an old woman on her bicycle. She was yapping on her cellular phone as she sped by. Others were pedaling and smoking. One was pedaling and putting on makeup. I looked to my left, saw the Amstel Brewery, a Heineken sign on top of that brick structure, the Museum of Sex straight ahead.

In the land of wooden shoes and bicycles, my target was less than a mile away.

For a few moments I stood on the sidewalk, part of me wanting to turn around.

But I mumbled, "Some people deserve to die."

Anger checkmated reason.

I bypassed the cabs, headed by the bicycle parking lot, a lot that was at least three levels high, passing at least a thousand parked bicycles along the way. Most of the population was on bicycles. Maybe that's why, relative to the overeaters in America, everybody looked so goddamn slim and sexy. Even the ugly had sex appeal, bad teeth and all. There was something different about the European women. There was something about America, maybe that racial divide that existed from coast to coast, that beast that created fear based on ignorance, maybe that made American people unlikable. Between racism and classism, not many people liked anybody.

Maybe it was that every other building here was a coffee shop and every coffee shop sold weed, that and the open sex market, that made the Dutch people more congenial. Getting high kept you mellow. Sex killed stress. America had laws and taboos about both. Amsterdam didn't have the racial divide, no hyphenated citizens. There were no black-Dutch, at least on job applications there wasn't a box to check. Race belonged to America, for the most part.

But hate belonged to the world.

Hate ruled the world.

Hate ruled my heart.

Hate was making me a rich man.

I moved deeper into the dark and seedy part of the city, if only in reputation and not in appearance, and stopped at Lunchroom 52, a coffee shop that faced the Oude Kerk, a Gothic, old church that cast its shadows over all the windows in this red-light district. As if God were looking down on, maybe looking over, all the whores, taking care of all the children of Mary Magdalene.

Most of the glass windows that housed the whores were in sets of threes, un-air-conditioned rooms smaller than a jail cell, fans blowing on high, recirculating odors that had permeated sheets and walls, the edges of their worn mattresses no more than two feet from the alley, the room barely big enough to house a sink and a bed with come-stained sheets. She'd been easy to find because all the windows had numbers the way homes had addresses. She worked out of window 120. A sign in the window said that all major credit cards were accepted.

I didn't bring any weapons, no way to transport deadly hardware on a plane. From canal to canal, warning signs were posted, letting everybody know that it was illegal to possess any kind of weapon. The second part of that warning was that, in a country where the world's oldest profession was legal, where people could buy hash or marijuana at any coffee shop, hard drugs weren't allowed. The warning ended with a notice that there was a regular police patrol.

I was more concerned with the warning about the weapons.

No weapon was needed. I knew at least twenty-two ways to kill with my bare hands.

I contributed to the local economy and bought three packs of weed. Purple haze. The pure stuff. The pre-rolled dope was cut with tobacco. I rolled a joint. Smoked it as I sipped a Heineken. Even when it was legal, it felt like the police should rush in and handcuff everybody in the place. But all over, in every seat facing the canals, people were firing up their medicinal cigarettes like they were Kool Menthol, that secondhand smoke giving the city a contact high.

I studied the roads and canals, mapped my exit. Her information was already memorized, already knew in which section of Raamverhuur I would be able to find her working her window. I knew she was renting a one-bedroom flat near Wijde Kerksteeg and Warmoesstraat. I knew she was renting because even though selling pussy was legal, it was hard for a whore to own a home, the lenders didn't want to gamble and lend the whores money.

The business was legit, but the whores weren't trusted.

Never trust a whore.

I took her pictures out of my pocket. I had several, all with different-colored hair.

She was a beautiful woman.

I checked window 120 again, her red light still dark, the red velvet curtains closed. As I walked the narrow alleys, some whores had their doors open, sat on the edges of their beds smoking, fans on high, faces made up and damp with sweat, looking like mannequins in a Victoria's Secret window who would come to life for a price. Some were on cellular phones, a few jumped out in bondage gear, whips in hand, playfully swatting the asses of young men as they walked by. One grabbed a man and tried to entice him and his wallet into her tiny room. Other working women were tapping on their windows and smiling that insincere whore's smile.

Nothing they did shocked or amused me.

The lack of sleep and heat was getting to me. Amsterdam rarely had hot days. That day heat was rising as if the devil was passing through town. I walked around looking at the whores, looked at all the girls in all of the windows. Unimpressed until a girl working in a window near Brouwersgracht and Palmstraat caught my eye. She was working window 693. I paused and stared. At first I thought she was someone I knew, someone I wanted to be with. The girl in window 693 was exotic and dark. Her beauty was disturbing. Scared me that she reminded me of someone I desired.

I stared at her awhile.

I fell into a trance.

I stood in front of her window.

Filipino music played from the boom box sitting at her feet.

She wore six-inch clear-heeled shoes. Red lingerie. Arched eyebrows. Long black hair.

Same type of outfit that was in a thousand red-lit windows within a square mile.

She eased off her barstool, adjusted her tits, came to her window.

As crowds passed and evaluated her, she stared at me.

Her eyes were glazed over.

She opened her door.

I didn't move.

She extended her hand.

Almost touched me.

I backed away from her, left taking steps backward, and watched her as long as I could.

I only went a few feet, then I turned and looked at her again.

My breathing had become ragged and uneven.

I turned around, went to go back to her.

Just that quick another man was at her window, being led inside.

I shook it off.

Shook away that desire.

Desire for a woman who she reminded me of.

I regained my focus.

Reminded myself why I was here.

I was here for the woman who worked window 120.

She wasn't in the window.

I had her home address.

So I walked the canals toward where my target lived. To the apartment she rented.

Too many people were out. I didn't go to her door. Stood a block away.

I waited.

Thirty minutes passed.

Then an hour.

She came out wearing a long dress. Her hair in long, blond

braids. Had seen her hair in many colors, but had never seen her mane braided before. She was bringing a bicycle down the stairs. I walked toward her. Tourist season. People were all over the *rue*. Too many eyes to take her right now. If I had known she was home, I could've broken in and had this over with.

I could do this right now and be gone, could blend with the crowd.

I walked toward her, my steps quick.

I was almost close enough to grab her braids when she started pedaling. Her legs were strong and she took to the bicycle lane fast, made her horn *ching-ching* and mixed in with the cars and bicyclists and pedestrians that shared the same narrow roads without complaint.

There wasn't any need to run after her. I knew where she was going.

She was going to work her window.

I had time.

I went back toward Brouwersgracht and Palmstraat, went back to window 693. The exotic girl was there, her curtain open, her red light on. I stood in front of the window.

I stared at the doppelgänger of someone I desired. Her doppelgänger stared at me. Her disturbing beauty anchored me.

I put my hand on her window, my palm resting right above the VISA AMERICAN EXPRESS MASTERCARD ACCEPTED sign. She took everything but food stamps.

I could have her. By cash or credit, I could buy an illusion. I could finance fantasy.

She slid off her barstool; put her hand up to mine, the scratchy glass separating us.

I nodded.

She opened the door to her world.

Thirty minutes later I was back near window 120.

Another thirty minutes passed before those red velvet curtains opened.

I froze where I was. Waited for her to appear. And within a minute, she did.

There she stood in white lingerie. Her face was made up. Her blond braids had been covered with a dark wig. A wig with a Cleopatra cut that hung down over her shoulders. Presentation of her wares in full effect. I stood off to the side. Men slowed at her window, most in groups, some alone, all of them in awe. Group after group paused and stared at her as she stood in that window, gave her more attention than the other whores received.

People hired me to exact death for different reasons, but most contracts, if not all, had one thing in common: freedom. The death of one person always freed another from some prison.

I wanted to get out of my prison. I wanted my own freedom.

My target pulled up a barstool, sat, waited for work to come her way. Men and women stared at her, but she made eye contact with no one, her eyes on the ground most of the time.

It seemed dehumanizing, sitting on display while people passed by on the cobblestones, sitting for hours, almost naked, with people staring like they were watching animals at the zoo.

I approached her from the side, was standing against the wall in front of her window, listening to the Bob Marley tunes coming from the beat box on the floor of her tiny space, looking inside her world, seeing a small bed and a sink that housed a few toiletries, looked at her as droves of people passed between us, had been frowning at her for five minutes before she looked up.

I said, "*Suces moi*, Thelma?"

She heard her birth name and almost fell off her barstool.

Her hand went up to her mouth, then her eye, before she crossed her arms over her breasts. I walked to her window, a few inches of glass separating, my reflection lying on top of her face, our bodies lining up, most of our features lining up in a surreal way.

She asked, "How did you find me?"

"I found you."

She shivered. "What do you want from me?"

"Some people deserve to die."

Terror took over her eyes. Her jittery body language showed her fear.

I tried her door. Despite the heat, most of the girls had their windows open. Window 120 was locked. Inside this peaceful country that bred pickpockets, she'd been living in fear.

Teeth clenched, I whispered, *"Open the goddamn door."*

The curtains closed. Her red light darkened.

I tapped on her window. I said, "Open the door. *Pute.*"

She heard me. I know she heard me.

Three men showed up a few minutes later. I had expected at least one more.

They walked up on me, gangster intentions in their eyes.

I turned around and walked away. Took to the narrow alleys, kept my pace normal, headed down a strip that was empty, no surveillance cameras overhead.

They were on my heels the entire stroll.

I was nervous. Nervousness was a mainstay I'd learned to live with.

I turned fast, the biggest of the three had his arm cocked, his fist aimed at me, and I took a blow to my jaw, staggered into the brick wall. That blow had hurt me. Sobered me. I worked through the pain, traded blows in a filthy alley, bobbed and weaved his destruction, put my right knee in his gut, and when he bent, came up and landed a fist in the big man's throat.

He was good at giving but horrible at receiving pain.

One blow landed and he stumbled from me, was about to fold. My fear was on him unleashing a barrage of elbows that left his face a bloody mess. He went down gagging.

Then there were the two more, both looking surprised, scared, and angry.

I was all on the next one, had put a simple foot in his nuts, made him fold in agony, a blow that hurt my ankle as well. While the second one went down, the third one swung at me, missed, and I went after him, my ankle aching, and I tackled him, grappled with him, wrestled him to the ground, and slammed my fist into his face as many times as my hand could stand.

I delivered one final enraged blow that cracked his ribs.

I looked up at the one I had downed with a groin shot.

He was slowed by agony and frozen in fear.

I pounced and attacked him, left him in the same state as his coworkers.

Without thought, I picked up a brick. Raised it high, brought it down on the big man's hands, bones cracking with each blow. Then I did the same to his two friends.

Sweating, favoring my left ankle, I limped away, bruised and battered, damn near thirty broken fingers and more than a few broken ribs writhing in pain in the filthy alley behind me.

I was kind to them that day. I had smashed their hands. Smashed hands couldn't grab guns and shoot, couldn't pull out knives; smashed hands couldn't hit you with a sucker punch. I'd learned that early in my career. Take out the hands first. Take out their legs to keep them from running for help. They crawled away from me, made it to their feet, and stumbled down the canal, never looking back. I could've beat them senseless. But I walked away. Their hands were so mangled that they'd have to pop a Viagra and use their dicks to dial for an ambulance.

I limped back to window 120. The red light was off. The curtains open. The bed empty.

She was gone.

Insane and fuming, I rushed back toward her apartment, moved as fast as I could, limped down the canals, stopping when the pain in my ankle felt too great. I was going to break into her apartment, but didn't have to. Her door was ajar. She had run back, gathered her things, and left minutes before I had arrived. The place she had rented was tiny, outside of the paint she'd left on the wall, door to door, closet to closet, it was mostly empty, a few things left on the floor in haste.

The bicycle had been dropped and left in the kitchen.

I supposed she had taken too much to leave on a bicycle.

I imagined she was running with fear in her heart and suitcases in her hands.

I took that bicycle with me when I left.

Injured, I rode toward the train station.

Didn't find her at the station.

I rode from Amsterdam Centraal to the Anne Frank Museum, then back to Rembrandt Square. Sweating and searching every canal, looked in so many coffee shops I had a contact high, looked in every red-lit window until my eyes owned the same devilish hue.

Then I was too tired, was in too much pain to keep going.

I checked into Hotel de Gerstekorrel, a short walk from McDonald's and the Sex Museum. From my bed it was a two-minute stroll down the canal back to window 120.

I tended to my wounds and iced my ankle and, after very little sleep, checked out of the hotel the next morning, rode the canals again, began searching for the runaway at sunrise, riding while the party people were staggering back to their rented rooms, while the unshowered whores were bicycling home, was on the cobblestone roads before the street was crowded with bicycles.

I rode until the sun started to set again.

During peak business hours I checked window 120. A new Dutch girl was there. I asked for the woman who was there the day before. She said that that woman was gone, then offered me her services. I passed. I walked the canals, looked in every window, just in case she had changed. She could've moved two blocks away, could've leased a new window in one of the other two red-light areas in the city, could've started selling her worn hole out of someone's home.

Wherever she had gone, she was still a whore.

Whoring was all she knew.

Like killing was I all knew.

"Gideon?" Lola's soft voice. "Let your seat back up and put your seat belt on."

"We're here?"

"Can't wait to run through customs and get to my boo."

The plane was descending into London. The plane went down as my anxiety rose up.

I looked over at Mrs. Jones. She was reading the *New York Times*.

The picture of the Big Bad Wolf was staring at me as I came back to this world.

The Big Bad Wolf was everywhere.

I didn't know if Mrs. Jones had opened that paper to taunt me.

Didn't know if she was one of them.

The plane taxied into the airport.

"I am so pumped up." Lola yawned. "This time tomorrow, me and my boo will be riding the London Eye and drinking champagne while we're *way, way, way* up in the sky. By next week I'll be chilling and watching *EastEnders*, *Kumars at No. 42*, *Big Brother*, living on *Love Island* with my boo, riding the red buses, tubes, and trains, being knackered and happy."

We landed. The ding came that told us we could get up.

Mrs. Jones was still quiet.

Lola was still hyped.

I said, "So, your boyfriend is in *Rent*."

"You have to come to the play. Both of you. You have to see my boo rock it."

"And you said you want to play the Mimi part."

"Hello? You hearing me? I want to get in *Rent* and play Mimi so fucking bad."

"Who is Mimi?"

"She's the stripper strung out on drugs. Awesome part. Her solo is off the chains."

"Then you'd get to be on tour with your boyfriend."

I helped Lola with her backpack, grabbed mine.

Lola said, "You know? When I get in *Rent*, it's going to be on and popping. We're going to be rocking and shacking up and doing the damn thing U.K. style. Shit, we're going to be like Ruby Dee and Ossie Davis. Just watch. You're gonna look up and see me onstage playing the hell out of Mimi, spotlight on this ass, people applauding, the whole friggin' nine."

I thought about how the flight attendant had brought Lola back here.

How they had strategically sat her next to me.

Didn't know if Lola Mack had been sent back here to keep an eye on me.

Lola went on, "Can't believe you haven't seen *Rent*. Mrs. Jones, did you see the play?"

Mrs. Jones shook her head, still no eye contact.

Lola asked, "The movie?"

Mrs. Jones offered the same distant and unkind response. She focused on moving with the crowd. There was some sort of holdup. We had landed but we weren't getting off the plane.

As if they were waiting on law enforcement.

I kept Lola talking, kept making everything look normal.

I asked, "Which is better, the play or the movie?"

"I like the play better. Theater person, you know? They used most of the original actors from the play in the movie, but ten years or more had gone by since it was on Broadway . . . or off-Broadway . . . wherever it was . . . and the actors . . . well, they looked old as shit. For that play, they were just too old, you know? I mean, like, Hollywood old, not real people old."

I answered Lola, "Is that right?"

We finally started moving.

I said, "So the actors in the movie were too old for your taste."

"The play was written for people in their later teens and twenties. Not pushing forty. Who wants to watch some over-the-hill, old-ass actors almost in their forties acting like they were fags and addicts in their late teens and early twenties? Oh, you know in London, a *fag* is a cigarette, so don't get offended if someone asks you for a fag or says they haven't had a fag all day, or say they can't stop because they've been fagging since they were a teenager."

"Thanks for the info on fags."

"Snap. My bad. You're not gay, are you? I mean, I don't want to offend you if you are."

"Not gay. Not offended."

Then we were leaving the plane. Making turn after turn, customs being at least a mile away from where we landed. Lots of walking. Lots of jet-lagged people on moving sidewalks.

Lola said, "I have gay friends, I mean real friends, not associates. A woman is supposed to have gay friends, you know? We all need men who dress well and won't try to screw us in our lives. And gay men are the best dancers. Gay clubs are the best clubs. Anyway, I live my life guided by love. I treat people the way I like to be treated. Serious. I don't hate anybody. Not the kind of person born to be a hater. What they do and how they do it ain't any of my business."

"That's the way people should live."

Mrs. Jones was behind me. Still silent. That newspaper still in her hands.

Big Bad Wolf's face refused to stop taunting me.

Then we were corralled at customs, standing in the long line for non-U.K. citizens.

Moving up one by one.

The agents were checking passports and asking questions, then stamping passports.

Police were all around.

As were the drug- and bomb-sniffing dogs.

I flipped open my bogus passport. Reminded myself what my name was this time.

Hoped this passport hadn't been flagged.

My nerves had me shifting and sweating.

Lola smiled at me. "You okay?"

"Jet lag."

"Me too."

I said to Lola, "You were saying about the play?"

"Oh, yeah. The play, those old-ass actors, even the chick that played Mimi . . . Rosario Dawson . . . she's *so* beautiful . . . but too damn old to play nineteen, you know? Why couldn't they hire age-appropriate, out-of-work überactors? It's better to act up than act down, you know? They needed to hire somebody who could act and sing and dance and pass for nineteen."

"In other words, instead of Rosario Dawson, they should've given you the part."

Lola laughed. "Yeah, I'm hating."

I said, "You're stuck on yourself, you know that?"

"Duh. I'm an actress."

"Right, right. Part of that narcissistic lot."

"Stop being mean to me."

Mrs. Jones was in front of me.

Lola was behind me.

Mrs. Jones was directed to an agent.

She handed him her blue passport.

She said a few things to the agent.

Then she glanced back at me.

From the newspaper she held, Big Bad Wolf's face was staring at me.

Mrs. Jones was let through without too many questions.

I thought she would walk on, keep going, and head into London.

But she stopped and waited.

No tears in her eyes.

No expression on her face. As if the tears had been a sham.

I'd grown up around treacherous women. Had worked with cons and killers all my life.

Mrs. Jones waited.

I felt trapped.

I was directed to the same customs agent. While Mrs. Jones stood there, the picture on the front page of her newspaper glaring at me, I took easy steps toward the agent.

Throat tight, palms damp, I handed him my passport.

The agent stared at me. Stared hard. Treachery lived in his blue eyes.

Mrs. Jones and her wretched newspaper remained in front of me.

One of the customs agents looked at Mrs. Jones. He nodded at her. She nodded in return. A coconspirator to this treachery.

She touched her wild mane in a telling way, like she was signaling the authorities.

The customs agent in front of me swiped my passport.

Something went wrong.

He swiped my passport again.

He read the screen and stared at me with a stiff poker face.

Stared at my injuries.

He looked me over again. Stared at the passport, stared at me.

Not too far away more policemen appeared.

Sledgehammer.

I thought about Sledgehammer.

Going to meet him had been a big fucking mistake.

Six

big bad wolf

Sledgehammer aka Sledge.

Überrapper of the year.

He hated being called Hammer. Said he was better than that old-school rapper. Did a record and spent a million on a hardcore video with him screaming about how he hated being called Hammer. A sledgehammer was what John Henry used, not a small, pathetic hammer.

I had a package on him before we met. That meeting was just a few days ago.

His birth name was Ronald Chin. Asian with a black man's disposition. He'd grown up in Harlem on Eighth Avenue and changed his name. Now his legal name was Sledgehammer Jackson.

Married for six years. Two kids from that marriage. One kid out of wedlock. Child support current. Taxes paid. Had bought his parents a brand-new house. Gave to charities. Went to church off and on, but based on his tax write-off, he sent his tithes on time.

People claimed that he paid Karrine Steffans a grip to not mention him in her book.

Others claimed he was mentioned by the name Papa.

Had to know who I was dealing with. If he had a record.

If he had police ties. Or Mafia ties. Or gang affiliation.

If he was in debt.

Had to see how liquid the man was, know what he could afford.

Lot of rappers bragged about money and cars but still had to put their bling on layaway.

The rap game had been profitable for Sledge.

More than twenty times as profitable as my occupation of choice had been for me.

What he rapped about doing was what I did without rapping about it.

Sledge had done a series of concerts that week at HiFi Buys Amphitheatre in Lakewood, down off 166 in the heart of the hood, then had an after-party downtown at Club Vision, the club on Peachtree that would soon be closed down, destroyed, condos rising where party central once stood. The day after the last show he'd rode out to Cascade Heights and closed down J. R. Crickets, a hot-wing joint that doubled as a sports bar. That building was the dividing line between the megachurches that sat across from million-dollar homes and the start of low-income housing and crackhead row. When I pulled up, I saw that J. R. Crickets was on full blast. Looked like a dozen televisions were on the walls, most on sports channels, the eight or nine booths were packed, so were the bar tables and the seats lining the bar. The women outnumbered the men ten to one. The best peaches Georgia had to offer. Women with small waists and big butts, not many had more than C cups, hair to perfection, were all over the place.

At least eight men were there who could stunt-double for Michael Vick. Three of the eight came up when I walked to the door. They came up fast, like three moving walls.

The first bodyguard: "'Sup, dawg?"

Big guy, huge shoulders. Reminded me of Michael Jai White. Had seen Michael Jai White on a flight to ATL the night before. Coach. AirTran. Him with a woman. Me solo.

I said, "Gideon. Here to talk to Sledge."

"Need to pat you down."

"Men don't touch me. Unless we're fighting."

"Then you ain't coming up in here."

"Tell your boss Gideon came through. And I won't be re-turning his call."

I walked away.

Behind me I heard one of them barking into the two-way.

I was passing Wachovia Bank when one of the bodyguards ran and caught up with me.

He said, "Didn't know that was you. *That* Gideon."

"What Gideon is that?"

"Uh . . . look . . . Sledge is waiting on you. You don't come back, I lose my job."

I went back. Now the bodyguards looked scared. All of them moved out of my way.

The music was blasting so loud the windows were shaking. *Killing 'em with a Sledgehammer.* That was his hit, his trademark song. The room was crowded. People were dancing in the aisles, hot wings and beers in hand. Music thumping, I passed under banners for Atlanta Hawks, Miami, Alabama, the bar-and-grill showing love for so many Southern teams.

I passed by the Michael Jai White look-alike.

He regarded me with his eyes; I offered him the same greet-ings and salutation.

I'd killed bigger and stronger men many times over.

I went inside without being searched. But three Michael Vicks followed me inside, led me beyond banners for Morehouse, Spelman, and Florida State, then two more added to that posse and walked me by the Pac-Man machine and booths, led me out on the covered patio facing Cascade Road. Coors banners swinging overhead, two hundred people were in the main part, an area that was made to hold about one hundred, but only thirty were on the patio. Twenty of the thirty were women. They were in the VIP section, drinking Patrón and playing dominoes.

When I walked out, Sledgehammer frowned up at me, that nervous look in his eyes.

Two of his boys pulled their jackets back, showed me they were strapped.

They did that to impress the girls.

I said, "You're expecting me."

Sledgehammer stood up. He was all of five foot six. All muscle, but that five foot six became five-eight with the added vertical help from his thick Air Jordans. His thick build and his photos made him look like he was six foot nine. His attitude added a few inches to his deficit.

He growled, "Yeah. I'm expecting you."

Sledge was an Asian rapper but he had a deep voice and sounded blacker than Isaac Hayes. He didn't look as Asian as the stereotypes because he wore his hair in stylish cornrows, he dressed hip-hop and swaggered like a felon. The only thing that was Asian about him was his eyes and size, but as soon as he started talking, you forgot about that. He sounded like Florence and Normandie, 125th Street in Harlem, East Oakland, he sounded like everything black.

Sledgehammer came over to me, extended his hand. A hand that was as soft as a newborn's backside. His palm was damp. His hand was shaking. At first I thought he was afraid of me. But his fear was larger than that of the moment. The number of bodyguards he had posted up spoke of his true fear. He was terrified. Had been scared stiff for a while. The number and size of the bodyguards around me told me that his paranoia was off the meter.

All of this security was because Sledge was afraid of the Big Bad Wolf.

I asked, "What name you want me to call you?"

"Sledge is cool. Or Sledgehammer. Never call me Hammer."

I nodded. Looked at all the eyes grimacing at me. A patio full of men who carried hardware for decoration, as accessories to the bling-bling gold fronts they wore, men who had never shot anyone and would run as soon as the first piece of hot lead whizzed through the air.

I nodded. "Let's get to business."

I followed Sledge past the scent of lemon pepper hot wings, past the sweet aroma of barbecue hot wings, past the Heineken and Budweiser ads, past the lemon and four-layer-chocolate and caramel cakes, followed him past the women up front doing ka-raoke like they were *Dreamgirls* wannabes.

Two of the guards went out the back door first. After they had checked out the parking lot, they signaled and I followed Sledge outside. I'd never seen this much paranoia in my life. Never been around this much fear. His stretch SUV limo was parked at the back door, facing the exit. All the windows were tinted midnight black. I'd bet the glass and side paneling were bulletproof.

Once we got inside his pimped-out ride, his guards stood by the stretch SUV, backs to us.

I sat at one end, near the door. He sat at the other. Godfather at the head of the table.

Sledge said, "You don't talk much, do you?"

"Get to the business."

"Yeah. Guess I better." He lost his hip-hop smile and shook off some of his nervousness. "Actually this beef between me and that motherfucker started four years ago, when our group split, had to leave them haters and do my own thing, made my CDs, did a few movies, but they never let it go, kept slandering me, and this craziness came to a head two months ago."

"Another bona fide war between the rappers."

"Call it what you want. We were at an award show and shit got crazy backstage. Then we ran into them again when I was about to do some shit at a radio station in New York."

I coughed, waited for him to get to the point.

"*New York Times* covered the melee between our bodyguards in Manhattan. Shit was crazy. Would you believe that motherfucker came at me like that? You didn't hear the CD that motherfucker dropped? YouTube, MySpace, shit all over the Internet and shit."

I sat still, not moving.

"Motherfucker jocked the beats from Ice Cube's 'No Vaseline.' Back in the day, after he left NWA, Ice Cube had slammed Eazy-E, Dr. Dre, had slammed his whole crew."

I stared at him, still silent.

"Me and Big Bad Wolf were in the same group too. I started that group. Motherfucker. I started the group that gave his punk ass a name. Shit, I gave him that name. Big Bad Wolf. I was reading that book back then and told the motherfucker he should call himself that shit."

Again, not a word from me as irritation rose up to my chest.

"Motherfucker coming at me like I'm some bitch."

I checked my watch.

"Yeah, we started out with the same crew. Motherfucker got mad when the spotlight hit me, and when I started blowing up, that hating bitch turned on me, dissed me the way Kool Moe Dee had slammed LL Cool J. Coming at me the same way everybody coming at 50 Cent."

"Sledge, either open the door or move the conversation forward to its conclusion."

He pulled it together, ran his jittery hand over his braids, took a few deep breaths, let his inner terror escape on a thin stream of air, nodded, then said, "Want you to listen to this shit."

He popped in a CD. It was a recorded interview.

On air, during a live discussion, Big Bad had gone too far and called my client's wife a whore, called his four-year-old child ugly, referred to him as a *gook*, a lo mein eater, then thumped his chest and said that he'd love to do an R. Kelly on Sledge's little girl.

He said, "That itself is a good enough reason to bust a cap in a fool's cranium."

On CD, Big Bad went on, said he wanted to skeet-skeet on the face of the Sledge's seed, kept saying he wanted to come and piss on the child's face. It was revolting and disgusting.

Threatening to abuse a kid. That got to me. But I didn't let it show.

He said, "Shit got my wife scared, man. Got my children scared."

"You scared?"

He trembled. "What you hearing, that bullshit went out live on the number one hip-hop station in the world. Millions heard that shit. You hear me? That shit went to millions. Millions."

In the song, Big Bad called Sledge a *faggot-ass chink*. Said he was going to come after Sledge's kids and *slant-eyed, whore wife*. Then, as the Mary J. wannabe sang, Big Bad threw down a hard-core rhyme claiming that him and his homies had run a train on my client's wife, said they were all hitting it hard, *fucking that slant-eyed ho' from the flo' to the do', fucked her so hard her eyes weren't slanted no mo'*, claimed they had fucked my client's wife, *gave the bitch what she needed, fucked the bitch until her pussy bleeded*, while my client was onstage performing at a show at the Fox Theater in Oakland.

I wanted to ask him if that part was true, but decided against it.

Live on radio, after the song ended, the DJ interviewed Big Bad and he laughed it up and boasted that he had fucked my client's wife in her ass while one of his homies ejaculated all over the woman's face. Big Bad laughed along with the NYC DJ on the top-rated morning show, which broadcast on the Web at the same time, and dared my client to call the station. Dared Sledge-hammer Jackson to meet him in the parking lot. Like he was the Big Bad Wolf. Actually, he was the Big Bad Wolf.

"And bring me some goddamn Chinese food, ya punk-ass wigger chink."

The broadcast ended with the Big Bad Wolf of rap going freestyle, then shouting out his trademark rap, *I'll huff and puff and blow down your weak lyrics.* . . .

The CD was shut off abruptly.

Forehead crinkled with anger, Sledge said, "Fifty large."

"He rolls at least six deep. With a team of felons. This would be a special case."

"One hundred."

I said, "Add twenty-five to that and we can talk."

Stress-sweating and trembling, he added fifty to that. Then offered me an extra twenty-five for anyone else I had to kill to get to his enemy.

He said, "An extra twenty large if you can make it happen in the next fourteen days."

"Make it an extra fifty and we might have a deal."

"If it's done in the next two weeks, I'll make it an extra seventy-five."

I nodded. Anger and fear had him throwing a lot of money on the table.

Something bloomed inside me. Greed.

My overseas account would be right at a million dollars when all was said and done.

Arizona was on my mind.

Desire had followed greed.

Whenever Arizona came to mind, irrational feelings rose up inside me.

Didn't care about Sledge or Big Bad.

Just wanted a million in my account before I saw her again.

I said, "So you want this done in New York."

"Not in New York. I live in and love New York. New York has had enough problems."

"Where?"

"Make it go down in that motherfucker's hometown. Put blood on the streets of Tampa."

"How do I get him to Tampa?"

"He's in Tampa all next week. I got the word that mother-fucker there recording his next CD and shit. I know where he hangs out. Strip club. He always goes to the same strip club."

I asked Sledge where he would be when it all went down, just in case.

He said, "For the next fourteen days I'll be out of the country. Taking my family with me."

I nodded.

"I want to send my own message. To him and every mother-fucker like him. Motherfuckers like him been fucking with me since I grew up on Eighth Ave. Tired of this shit."

His bodyguards tapped on the window. Seconds later Sledge let the window down. His boys were checking to make sure he was all right. While we wrapped up our business, another one of the bodyguards came out back, one of the finest girls Atlanta had to offer at his side.

Sledge let the window down. I moved where I couldn't be seen.

He snapped, "What?"

The girl leaned her breasts toward the window. She said, "You forgot about me already?"

"Who you?"

"Last night at Body Tap. I danced for you for about an hour."

She turned around, showed him her ass and tits, made her body shake, smiling.

Sledge said, "Oh, yeah."

She slapped her backside. "Sure you remember me now?"

"The business major at Spelman, right?"

She smiled.

Sledge said, "Hold tight until I get out of this meeting."

The window rolled up on her enthusiasm.

I said, "When my deposit is verified, we'll take it to the next level."

We shook hands. His hand was still dank and trembling.

I asked, "What's the matter?"

"This is crazy. I'm actually going through with this shit. But he started it, you know? He used to be my homie. We came down here, hooked up with Dupri, went to New York, met Jay-Z . . . damn shame it came down to this. But it is what it is. He brought this on himself."

I got out. And the heavy-bottomed girl smiled at Sledge and crawled inside.

I headed out front, walked a block east, passed by Wachovia Bank, and went into the parking lot that housed Big Daddy's Soul Food and other businesses. I put on my helmet and gloves, got on my motorcycle, and headed up Cascade, breezed by John A. White Golf Course and sped toward Langhorn, then made a left and got on I-20 heading east, back toward Stone Mountain.

My phone buzzed in my pocket.

The deposit had been transferred.

The deal had been sealed.

I'd been homeless.

Abused.

A fugitive.

Now I was damn near a millionaire.

I should've been happy.

For the first time ever, I wished the money hadn't come.

London

Seven

strangers in a strange land

Gatwick Airport sparkled with European flair.

Marble and glass, everything contemporary from the rooter to the tooter.

With my fake passport, I had made it through customs, no alarms sounding.

When I took my jet-lagged stroll by the last of the police officers, I took a deep breath.

Lola was excited, eyes wide. "This is an airport? This joint looks like both the Grove and the Beverly Center in Los Angeles. Look at all these places to shop. They have so many stores in here . . . off the chains . . . this is like walking down Rodeo Drive."

Mrs. Jones was quiet and unimpressed, the opposite of Lola.

Lola went on, "Caffè Nero. They have a friggin' Burberry store up in here. Chez Gerard, whatever that is. HMV. Lacoste. Nike. Nine West. Starbucks. WHSmith. This is awesome."

Local time was eight thirty in the morning, my body still on eastern time, my every cell crying for a warm bed and few more hours of sleep. We'd been on the ground just long enough to battle our way through customs and make our way over to the

North Terminal; Mrs. Jones walked at my right side, her expensive heels clinking. My backpack was hanging from my right shoulder and I was pulling an overpacked suitcase that had bad wheels, Lola's cheap luggage. Lola had her backpack on and was pulling her second suitcase, that one having better wheels. Since she had so much to carry, I'd waited for her at baggage claim. Kept her talking, kept her laughing. Kept my eyes on the police.

"Aww, man." Lola cursed at her phone. "Cellular doesn't work here."

I shook my head. "Not unless you have tri-band."

"Damn Verizon. I have to find a Verizon store and handle this."

"No Verizon here. If you had T-Mobile, you could upgrade, make the phone international."

"They have Starbucks every ten feet but they don't have one Verizon store?"

"You need a phone with a SIM card."

"What's a SIM card?"

"SIM card. Subscriber Identity Module. Gets you international service. About the size of a postage stamp. Stores all kind of info. Like saved telephone numbers. Text messages."

Lola cursed. "How am I going to survive without a phone?"

"You can get a SIM card for about five bucks U.S. over in Chinatown."

"Yeah, but I need a freakin' T-Mobile phone. You okay with that bag, Gideon?"

I asked, "Did you have to pack your entire life in these bags, Lola?"

"I'm a girl, Gideon. I never know what kinda mood I'm going to be in, so I have to bring clothes to match my mood. Assholes made me pay extra. Said my bags were too heavy."

"How much did your bags weigh?"

"One was like ninety pounds. The other one weighed a little over a hundred."

"How long are you staying with your boyfriend?"

"The rest of my life. I'm going to be his Mimi, without the drug habit."

Mrs. Jones fell back behind us. I glanced and saw her break her cellular in half, then she dropped the remains in a trash can. She caught up with us, then once again she fell behind.

She had freed herself of her electronic leash.

Lola asked, "Gideon, think I could borrow a few dollars?"

"Pounds. Or quid. Same thing."

"Okay, pounds," Lola said. "Can I borrow a few pounds, quids, whatever they use?"

"For what?"

"Check it. Kinda broke. Spent all of my money on the plane ticket. Was gonna ask my boyfriend to come get me. No signal, no cellular. I don't have enough to make a phone call."

"How much you need?"

"How many pounds or quid do you get for a dollar anyway?"

I motioned to a huge screen right above a money exchange station.

EXCHANGE RATES	
US/CAD	1.1244
US/AUD	1.3237
US/ZAR	6.1190
US/Euro	0.7971
US/SF	1.2521
US/BP	0.5534
US/Yen	114.24
US/Rub	27.26
US/Yuan	8.0099
US/Rupee	45.01
US/Mexican	11.11

She said, "Eighty cents for a dollar? The euro is kicking the dollar's butt."

"Not eighty cents. That means eight-tenths of a euro for a buck. London is still on the pound system. Look at BP. British pound."

"Are you serious? Does that mean . . . I'm confused. Fifty-five cents for a damn dollar?"

"Means fifty-five percent of a pound for a dollar. Less than that once they take their commission."

"That's *robbery*. We need to be in Mexico. You can buy Mexican for like five dollars."

"How much British money you need?"

"Well, I'll need enough to get to Embankment. My boo is chilling down in that area. The theater is on St. Martin's Lane. He said his hotel was a two-minute walk from the theater."

"You have the address?"

"Got it right here."

"No problem. I'll get you to your man."

"Cool. My boo will have my back after that. I can get some money from him and kick you down what I owe you. Just holla at me down there and I'll bring you what I owe you."

"Don't worry about it."

"You sure?"

"I'll get you a day pass for all the zones. Just in case."

"And can you throw in enough for me to buy some condoms?"

"Condoms?"

"In case he doesn't have any. Lose your momentum, spoil the mood."

"How many condoms will you need, Lola?"

"A dozen should get me through the weekend. At least until Sunday."

"Today is Friday. And you want a dozen?"

"You're right. I should get more."

Tired and irritable, we ate upstairs at Brasserie Bar.

Lola had three scrambled eggs and smoked salmon. I had veggie sausages, grilled tomatoes, and fried eggs. Mrs. Jones sat across from me, away from Lola, without talking. Mrs. Jones hadn't said much to Lola since we'd left the plane and made it through customs.

She hadn't said anything to Lola since that massage.

At the table next to us were four Africans, all speaking French. Beyond them were Europeans speaking a language I couldn't make out, not at first. One of the Europeans, a young Slavic blonde wearing a T-shirt with a picture of Folasade Coker, a Nigerian writer, across the front, had put her backpack on the floor near mine. It was a generic blue backpack, identical to mine.

The blonde smiled at me, then told her male friend, *"Is dit het echte leven?"*

He responded, *"Is dit enkel fantasie?"*

I looked down at their backpack.

Lola said, "These accents."

I asked, "What do you mean?"

"All kinds of African. German. Russian. Don't hear a lot of that gibberish in L.A. And I haven't seen a Mexican for hours. Not one Mexican in sight. This is straight-up weird. I mean, if there are no Mexicans, who keeps the city clean? Who cuts the grass? Who babysits?"

One of the Europeans next to us said, *"Open uw ogen."*

I turned to them, smiled, and said, *"Kijk tot de hemelen en zie."*

They laughed. The blonde looked at me again. She nodded.

Lola said, "What language is that?"

"Dutch."

"You speak Dutch?"

"Not really." I winked at her. "You were saying this feels like an alternate universe, huh?"

"People, especially the black people over here, they sound so smart. Speak all these languages. Their accents are the bomb. Even the stupid people sound like they have Ph.D.s."

Mrs. Jones drank her latte from Caffè Nero without acknowledging Lola, but her red eyes came to mine. She was in London, free to go, but she was still here with me.

Lola headed to the bathroom, left me and Mrs. Jones sitting at the table.

I asked the woman dressed in the color of sorrow if she was okay.

She asked me, "Why do you like *Battlestar*?"

"It's filled with Greek mythology and Christianity and atheism and zodiac references. . . . Caprica . . . that's their home planet . . . Caprica . . . as in Capricorn."

"The number twelve comes up a lot."

"As in twelve disciples and twelve signs of the zodiac and twelve colonies."

"The number twelve keeps coming up, implying earth was part of something larger."

"So you like the show."

"I despise it. Only way I used to spend time with my husband on Friday nights."

"Guess you won't be asking to borrow my DVDs."

She hesitated, looked a little embarrassed. "Seen enough. Felt like I was forced to. Had to pay attention just so we would have something to talk about. Just so we could . . . communicate. Just to get some conversation out of him. But I . . . I guess I don't have to watch that nonsense anymore."

We let that settle between us. That tension returned.

Her eyes were on her sparkling wedding ring. She spoke without moving her gaze.

"My husband . . . he doesn't touch me."

"I find that hard to believe."

"He hasn't touched me for years."

"As beautiful as you are? I'd never stop touching you."

I put my hand on hers. Her eyes came to mine.

She asked, "Are you testing the waters?"

I smiled. "Only if you're inviting me for a swim."

The Dutch-speaking Europeans finished their breakfast, grabbed their backpacks, and left. Again the blond girl looked at me. She was nervous. I saw it in her eyes.

She said, "*Scaramouche.*"

I nodded, said, "*Bismillah.*"

They left, talking first in Dutch, then changing to French. My focus went back to Mrs. Jones. I was looking in her eyes, holding her hand. She was holding my hand too.

She said, "You're a liar, Gideon."

"What have I lied about, Mrs. Jones?"

"No luggage."

"You don't have any luggage either."

"Are you on the run?"

"I have a backpack."

"A small backpack. And you didn't bring a coat."

"Neither did you."

"My trip wasn't planned."

I winked at her. "Maybe we have more in common than we realize."

"Your voice . . . your tone . . ."

"What about it?"

She said, "You're intelligent. Very. I'd guess you're an attorney or a thief of some sort."

"Is there a difference?"

"Not that it matters." She smiled. "I love the way your hand feels on mine. Love touching you."

"Are you flirting with me, Mrs. Jones?"

We sat there looking at each other, in provocative silence, until Lola came back.

The man with the broken nose passed by. Gray suit and red shirt looking wrinkled. He was on his cellular. He took a seat at a table near us and took out a London Underground map.

He was preoccupied, didn't notice us.

A second cellular phone rang.

He put down the first mobile and answered the second one, his face all business.

He juggled phone calls. Then hung up both and took out that yellow book again.

He had come through customs and wasn't carrying anything, not even a backpack. All he had was that yellow book.

I said, "Looks like he had a rough night."

"His eyes are black as hell." Lola rubbed her nose, as if seeing his made her conscious of her own. "Thought that was from plastic surgery or something."

"He's traveling light."

Lola said, "Not as light as Mrs. Jones. Not like you have much luggage yourself."

I regarded Mrs. Jones. Inside that moment, I was once again suspicious of her too.

She said, "Maybe he left an unhappy life. Maybe he had been cheated on, cuckold. Maybe his kid, or kids, became his worst nightmare. Maybe he had to leave or go insane."

Lola and I looked at Mrs. Jones.

Mrs. Jones said, "Maybe he's trying to start over without baggage."

I said, "What about his face?"

"We're all wounded in some way. Maybe he came here to heal."

Her mind was on something else, something more promising, something more urgent.

After the man looked at the menu, he sat back, rubbed his eyes, and opened that yellow book. He took out a pair of reading glasses, struggled to get them over his bandaged nose, gave up, and held the book close to his eyes. He bothered me. I kept him in my periphery. He never glanced my way, just read his book and checked his watch. He ordered breakfast and ate like he was in a rush, or starving, not at the easy pace of the Europeans. He ate like an American, and most Americans ate like they were convicts, fast and in a hurry, like men and women in prison.

We left before he did, left him eating and reading his book, the pages and words right up to his eyes. I looked back as we took the escalator, looked again as we left the airport.

He never spied my way.

We rode the Gatwick Express nonstop toward London's Victoria Station.

It was going to be a thirty-minute ride.

Thirty minutes before I was alone with Mrs. Jones.

Thirty more minutes of Lola.

We sat in the red seats, two facing forward, two facing backward. Lola crashed across from me. Mrs. Jones sat next to me, again not talking to Lola, avoiding any contact with the animated woman, but every now and then gazing at Lola, a quick glance before looking away.

Mrs. Jones kept her eyes on the graffiti and countryside we were passing.

Lola bounced around, humming and smiling her ass off, then said, "This is crazy."

I asked, "What?"

"Gas is cheap as hell. We just passed a gas station and gas was a dollar a gallon."

"Wrong money. That was in pounds. One pound is about two dollars."

"My bad. Then two dollars a gallon. Still damn good."

"They measure in liters, not gallons. Four liters equal one gallon."

"That shit's too much like algebra for me. How much is gas over here, Brainiac?"

"Petrol is about eight dollars a gallon."

"*Get the fuck out.* No wonder they're in these itsy-bitsy-ass clown cars."

Lola closed her eyes and, at last, did the same with her mouth.

Then Mrs. Jones's eyes returned to mine. She licked her lips, sighed, shifted around, spoke to me in restless silence.

Her eyes went to my backpack. Then her eyes met mine head-on.

She remained expressionless, then turned her head away.

Again she wiped her eyes. Tears came and went.

I asked her, "How are you feeling?"

She set free one soft word. "Scared."

Victoria Station.

British accents dominated the international chatter; announcements from a woman who sounded like Miss Moneypenny reminded everyone to *Mind the gap* and to please tap in and tap out their Oyster cards. British culture met us head-on as we followed the WAY OUT signs from the trains up to the streets, blended in with the pace and pandemonium that was equal to being at Union Station in D.C. during rush hour. It was damn cold. Everyone had on gloves, scarves, hats, and coats. On the escalator we followed the rules and stood to the right so the impatient people could hurry by on the left. Lola was behind me, Mrs. Jones in front. Lola called to Mrs. Jones, offered to let Mrs. Jones use her Old Navy coat, said she had an extra one in her bag, but Mrs. Jones refused her offer without looking back, only gave Lola the somewhat detectable shake of her head. Still not a single word for Lola.

Something was wrong. Something bigger than the two women at my side.

Instinct told me to look back. Instinct told me to always look back. Instinct had me on edge, being on edge created paranoia. Paranoia was my alarm clock.

The man with the broken nose was back there, map of the tubes unfolded in his hands.

This time I put my luggage down and followed my paranoia.

I asked, "You okay? Need help?"

He looked up from his map. "Weren't you on my flight from Atlanta?"

"Yeah. Saw you on the plane too."

"You're American?"

"Yeah."

"Good. Maybe you can help me. I'm trying to figure out how to get to Tower Hill. The directions my friend gave me didn't make sense. I asked inside, but the accents are killing me."

His accent was soft and Southern. Genial. Like Billy Bob Thornton in a good mood.

I looked at his map.

He looked toward Mrs. Jones and Lola.

He said, "Beautiful women you're with."

"Yeah, they are."

"Saw the woman in the black dress crying at the airport."

"She's doing much better."

I saw the yellow book he was holding. *Divorce for Dummies*.

He was nobody.

Just another nobody.

"That's good to hear. Now, how do I find Tower Hill?"

I told him to go back inside, find out what zone he was going to, buy a travel card, down to the tubes, follow the yellow line on the map, and take the Circle Line to Tower Hill. It was morning rush hour in London, so he'd get there faster and cheaper if he took the tube.

He checked his watch and rushed back inside the station.

Then I watched him until he vanished. I looked around.

No police.

No trouble.

I let all my anxiety mix in with the voices from the city.

Mrs. Jones looked at me.

I smiled at the woman whose marriage was irretrievably broken.

Eight

body heat

We hustled by the nine-to-five crew.

We found the long line for the hackney carriages, what they called the black cabs. Ugly, bulky cabs that looked like they were from the seventeenth century. I gave Lola enough British currency to get to the theater district, then, even though we were all pretty much heading in the same direction, offered my cab to Mrs. Jones. Desire danced. She hesitated, didn't answer, just stood in the cold, still silent. Mrs. Jones was ready to get away from Lola. Lola was ready to get away from us so she could get to the man of her dreams. And I wanted Mrs. Jones to myself.

I told her, "I can show you my hotel room. Then you can decide."

There was a moment of indecision, a few breaths of contemplation.

Mrs. Jones climbed inside my cab. She sat facing forward, legs closed.

I pulled down a seat, sat across from her, facing backward, looking at her as we traveled.

I put my hand on her knee. My eyes searched hers for either rejection or approval.

There was no approval, but there was no rejection either.

Only tears. The tears returned.

I asked, "What that wedding ring set you back?"

"Guess."

My fingers traced her kneecaps, moved up her thigh, back to her knees. Her eyes were on my fingers, watching me, her breathing tight, almost asthmatic.

I said, "Ten, maybe fifteen."

"Try twenty."

"I hope taxes and a big rebate were included."

"I was talking years. It set me back twenty years of my life."

My fingers moved between her thighs, back to her knees, kept feeling her heat.

She looked at my hand, then slowly raised her watery eyes to mine.

She said, "My husband . . . he doesn't touch me."

"Is that right?"

"He has been with other women. He fell in love with someone else."

"Sorry to hear."

"So I've . . . I've . . . I've had to turn to other men."

"Desire is a beast that must be fed."

My hand moved up her leg, stopped right above her thigh. For a moment I was in North Carolina, not far from Pope and Fort Bragg military bases, at a strip club on Bragg Boulevard. Then I was in Tampa, on Martin Luther King Boulevard, on the front row of the midnight show at Crazy Horse, putting my money in the garters of naked women.

This was not a dancer at Déjà Vu. Not a whore in Brazil. This was a real woman.

"Do you think that's wrong, my turning to other men . . . to be made to feel like . . . a woman? . . . I mean . . . every woman needs to be made to feel like a woman . . . to feel special."

"When you're honest with yourself, oftentimes you betray someone else."

"This is true."

"Everyone needs to be touched. We all need contact, you know?"

She yielded a weak shrug. "I mean, is it really cheating when it comes to that?"

I repeated, "When you're honest with yourself, you betray someone else."

She wiped her eyes. "I broke my vows to God and the church."

"We're all sinners, Mrs. Jones. All of us."

"I wanted to be righteous."

"Even the righteous man is just a sinner living in between sins."

"I allowed other men to touch me, men who wanted to own me because I was unattainable. Men who knew my forever love was somewhere else, for someone else, they wanted me in the ways I wanted my husband to want me."

"It's a human thing, Mrs. Jones. To need to be touched is a human thing."

"It was just two men. Over ten years. Only two men."

"We all need to be touched."

"Three if you count . . . well, one experience was oral, wasn't really sex, you know?"

My hand moved up her leg, stopped short of her vagina, but I felt the heat. The heat from a woman could make a man's instincts go cold while his vision went bad. At the wrong time, the heat from a woman made it hard for a man to see beyond the end of his dick.

This was all I could see right now. This was all I wanted to see.

I whispered, "And you need to be touched."

"Desperately."

She closed her eyes. Bit her bottom lip.

I whispered, "You're vulnerable right now."

"I am. So very. So very. Vulnerable."

"I'd be taking advantage of you."

"Perhaps I'd be taking advantage of you. Using tears to get what I need."

There was a raging furnace between her legs. My finger grazed her panties. She jerked, tightened her thighs around my hand. Then she caught her breath and relaxed.

I asked, "Are you?"

"Am I what?"

"Using your tears?"

"Would it matter? The end result will be the same."

"You want me to touch you."

"At this moment, what I need supersedes what I want."

Her words remained the hymn of love gone bad. What had been sweet to the tongue now had a bitter taste. She was juggling love and hate, not knowing which one to drop.

She said, "On the train. The way it creaked and moaned. Like sex. The way it moved side to side. Like lovers. Like new lovers engaged in give-and-take. The train moved like sex."

"I didn't notice."

"I noticed. God, I noticed. It was . . . stimulating. I was imagining you. Us."

I moved to her side of the cab, put both arms around her, held her, pulled her breasts close to my chest, one hand moving across her body, her curves very nice.

She sighed, trembled.

She brought her hands up my back, gradually held on to me.

I whispered, my lips on her ear, told her how beautiful she was.

She said, "You don't have to say that."

"You are."

Again she cried, this time her tears came with a smile.

The taxi stopped. The area bustling. Signs said the British Museum wasn't far away. We were in Bloomsbury. Parked in front of Myhotel. Redness dominated Mrs. Jones's eyes. I doubt if mine looked any better. The skies made it seem as if it were an hour before sunrise.

Mrs. Jones shifted, more nervous than before, said, "My watch says two in the morning."

"It's ten. Set your watch to Greenwich Mean Time; get acclimated to the time change."

I paid the driver and we got out of the taxi on Bayley Street, the narrow avenue in front of Myhotel, stood on the double yellow lines that marked the no-parking zone, the equivalent of America's red curbs. Sky gray, cold, rain starting to fall. Since she wore no coat and I didn't have one to offer, Mrs. Jones shivered; her nipples were standing tall.

I asked, "Sure you want to come up to my room?"

Without hesitating she answered, "Carpe diem."

"What was that?"

"Carpe diem." She looked out at Bayley Street, evaluated Bedford Square. "It means the enjoyment of the pleasures of the moment without concern for the future."

"Would you like to engage in pleasure without concern for the future?"

Her breath caught inside her throat. She closed her eyes and nodded once.

Again, in the softest voice, she whispered, "I don't want to be alone."

We went inside a warm five-star hotel that owned a fabulous sushi bar.

Mrs. Jones took a seat right inside the glass doors, remained in a small seating area, fidgeting and facing the streets while I checked in. Her eyes and thoughts remained in the direction of all the red-and-white St. George's Cross flags hanging from the windows of almost every flat. She saw me watching her, pushed her prim and proper lips up into a loose smile.

She asked, "How much does a condo cost in this area?"

"At least a million pounds."

"How many square feet?"

"Doubt if those flats are much larger than this room."

"Remarkable."

"Read it was a good investment. With housing costs rising something like thirty percent, those flats will be worth a lot more in a few months."

I turned my back and checked in. That took a few minutes. She waited in silence, back straight, legs crossed, right foot barely bouncing, proper and sophisticated.

Room key in hand, I headed for the elevator.

She followed, her wild hair down, eyes avoiding the hotel staff, not saying a word.

On the elevator I put my hand to her face.

We were alone. In a lift easing up. Easing up like I wanted to ease inside her. My warm hand on warmer flesh. Mrs. Jones let out a spiraling moan. Her tongue grazed my palm. Drove me insane. I held her close, put my hand between her legs. Felt her global warming.

The woman dressed in black moaned. The woman dressed in mourning shuddered.

She closed her eyes tight as the vertical carriage took us closer to a brand-new sin.

I wanted to rip that dress off her, wanted to fuck her right there, fuck her between floors.

Already I was caught up.

Caught up and unaware of the evil that was happening over four thousand miles away.

At that moment, at Turtle Beach, a resort in Trinidad, a family was yawning and piling inside a rental van for a family outing. A young Asian man walked with a hip swagger, along with his beautiful African-American wife, his three interracial kids. His parents. His in-laws. At least ten people altogether. One big family vacation. They were making a forty-five-minute drive from Port-of-Spain to Maracas Bay. Yesterday he had partied at Chacacabana, the day before at Macqueripe. Today was another day for tanning and parasailing while the children enjoyed their grandparents and played in the warm waters. Maybe even a day for taking a trip to Tobago.

The Asian man looked at the front page of the *Trinidad Guardian*. It showed that the Big Bad Wolf had died in Tampa. As planned. The Asian man had thrown barbecues, spent money on exotic dancers and Cristal, been celebrating the death of his enemy like he'd won the lottery.

Now it was family time.

His beautiful wife finished loading their beautiful children inside the van, leaned over, and kissed him. She was happy too. She had been humiliated and ridiculed across the country.

Now it was over.

The Big Bad Wolf was dead. His enemy had been destroyed. Now they were free.

The Asian man turned the key to start the van.

The van exploded.

On a peaceful morning in the islands, fire and screams filled the tropical air.

That Asian man was born with the name Ronald Chin.

Had changed his name to Sledgehammer Jackson.

The world knew him as Sledge.

His death was filled with fire and brimstone. On a piece of land surrounded by water.

I wouldn't hear about that revenge until later.

I wouldn't know I was a wanted man for a few hours.

Being hunted was the last thing on my mind.

Right now I was the hunter.

Hunting for carnal joy.

Underneath gray clouds, my mind was on a different prey.

Right now my mind was on the pursuit of a brand-new pleasure.

My mind was on fucking Mrs. Jones.

Nine

wag

The man with the broken nose found Tower Hill.

Trains had been delayed due to service. He had been lost most of the morning.

He was still lost in Savage Gardens; one of the landmarks he had been given, a hotel called Novotel, was down the street. He couldn't find 1 Pepys Street. He walked the block, passed by Fenchurch Street Station, The English Club, Cheshire Cheese, Ladbrokes betting shop.

He made a frustrated sound, double-checked his instructions, then went back to Tower Hill tube station and started over. He was in EC3. EC3 was the postal code. And that postal code was posted on the corner of almost every building. Once again he passed the first landmark, looked up, and saw the blue heritage plaque on the wall of the flat where the Reverend P. T. B. "Tubby" Clayton had lived. Again he passed the Wine Library. And St. Olave's Church.

He didn't want to ask for directions. Not this close to his destination.

He didn't need to be remembered.

Again he circled the block, passed by all the pubs and betting shops. Then he found the apartment building. It had been right in front of him, its address etched in glass and impossible to read. The building was on a narrow street barely wide enough for a taxi to negotiate, faced Novotel, was directly across from the hotel's main entrance.

He took a deep breath and almost smiled. He had found where the famous barrister lived.

He was running late. Very late. He hated to waste time. Time was unrecoverable.

As he walked to the glass door, he saw the beautiful barrister rushing off the lift, tension in her face. Without looking up she hurried across the marble floor in the pristine lobby.

She looked just like her photograph. Actually better. Not many did.

The woman was part of the elite group known as WAGs. Wives and Girlfriends of footballers. Stunning woman. Long yellow hair. Could pass for a Spice Girl. He had made it to her flat just in time to catch her leaving, dark sweats on, iPod on, heading out for her morning jog.

She came out of her flat, jogged right past him, never looked at him.

He hated the way he was invisible to women. Especially to beautiful women.

He turned around and watched her hair bouncing as she passed by buildings where historical figures had resided, crossed the narrow street, darting toward Trinity Square, arrogant enough to ignore Smart cars and mopeds. As if she owned the road. Her form was bad. Her back wasn't straight. She moved her arms too much. Ran flat-footed. Six miles. The package said she always ran six miles. His intel said that took her an hour. And she still had cellulite.

With better form she could knock a minute off each mile in no time.

He couldn't help her with the cellulite.

He had an hour. Plenty of time to read some more of his book. *Divorce for Dummies*.

The WAG always ran toward Embankment. Part of him wished he could've gone running with her. He touched his nose, yawned as he walked up to her flat, took keys out of his pocket.

One was a sensor key. He waved it in front of the sensor pad. The glass doors opened.

He took the elevator to the fourth floor. Went to her flat, stopped in front of her door.

He had almost put the key in the lock, then decided to ring the doorbell.

No one answered. Her new boyfriend stayed with her every other week.

The boyfriend she had started up with a few months after her marriage.

The man with the broken nose rang again. No one answered.

He used the key, and with a simple turn the dead bolt was undone.

He walked into a well-lit flat, closed the door, engaged the dead bolt.

It was quiet.

Birds-of-paradise were on a glass table, along with a mushy card from her lover.

Red leather furniture. Granite counters and marble floors. Stainless-steel appliances.

From the window in her living room he had a view of Novotel.

He wondered how much a suite cost in that swank hotel.

He went and looked in both bedrooms. Her king-size bed was unmade. The second bedroom had been converted into an office. He wondered how much a tiny place like this cost. Compared to what real estate cost in Texas, the property prices were outrageous in London.

He was hungry. The rabbit food on the flight hadn't done a thing for him. He hated the food at the airport. He had stopped at Tesco, a grocery-store-type place, to get a muffin. But the English had all of their muffins and rolls in open containers. He watched people pick over the food before they chose the one they wanted. Hands that had touched unsanitary tube rails and doorknobs, hands that touched their penises and vaginas and wiped their asses and masturbated and picked noses, those filthy hands were picking over fresh muffins and rolls, not taking the first muffin or roll they contaminated, leaving the tainted one on the pile, that infected one rolling over on the fresh ones. Unsanitary. He thought that shit was plain old disgusting.

He looked inside the WAG's refrigerator. Saw a lot of ready-made food from Marks & Spencer, crisps on the counter, *fruit and fibre* cereal, and a few figs, nothing of interest.

He looked at the package of crisps. Had no idea what those were. Saw a picture of potato chips on the package. He realized the English called their potato chips *crisps*.

He went to the bathroom, put his book on divorce down, looked at his nose.

Broken. He got a little angry. Someone had gotten the best of him.

It had happened four days ago. Jacksonville, Florida. At the Modis Building. A $10,000 job, half his usual fee. He'd done the job, then gone back to his room at the Omni, iced up his nose, and waited for a bootleg doctor to show up and fix his face. He sat there in pain watching Angela Spears deliver the noon news. He fell into a trance, watching the news anchor on WTLV. Beautiful woman. Just like his wife. Or soon-to-be ex-wife. She had a smile that made a man want to relocate to Jacksonville. Angela Spears did, not his soon-to-be ex-wife.

He wanted to touch himself, his hand drifting, but they switched to a man doing weather.

He took some pain medication, sat on the bed, and read about Jacksonville.

He wanted to get out of Texas. Away from those memories.

He thought about Jacksonville, thought long and hard. Read that crime was up in that area, but crime was up all over the world. Might even marry a J'ville woman. Like Angela Spears.

He wondered if she was married. He had to get marriage out of his head. He had heard someone say not to let money ruin his marriage. That got a small laugh out of him.

He mumbled, "Shit. It's the other way around. Don't let marriage ruin your money."

He cared about his money. What was left of it. But he loved being married.

He read that J'ville was one of the most recession-proof cities in the country. No local or state income tax. Office space was cheaper than in L.A., New York, and most spots in between. Five colleges, so he could talk his daughter into going to college down there. She was only ten, but he was thinking ahead. Maybe his son, Skeeter, would like it down there.

Maybe he'd go back to school himself. Finally work on that Ph.D. His two brothers and three sisters all had Ph.D.s. He only had a master's. He was the dumb one.

He'd spent his youth being married. Then widowed. Then married again.

He wanted another wife. A new one. A beautiful one. Like his first wife.

Maybe have four more kids. He wanted a big family. He loved kids.

Even if he didn't luck up on a beautiful newscaster, the area was crawling with military, so there were plenty of hardworking women in uniform in search of civilian men. Hiking and biking, could do both of his favorite sports. Had to be plenty of marathons in the area. The same for triathlons. He could train year-round, like in Texas. Hard not to love a place that had 113 miles of pristine beaches. And had a professional football team. As far as he was concerned, Jacksonville had more perks than the first-class lounge in heaven. Spanish influence was everywhere. Spectacular archways and stained-glass windows.

He could start over in Jacksonville.

Maybe he'd meet a Spanish woman this time.

He'd think about that some more after he left London.

After he was done with the WAG.

His nose ached. He had a high threshold for pain, but still it ached.

He took bandages out, was starting to change them when the front door opened.

An hour hadn't passed. Only ten minutes had gone by.

Barely enough time for her to run a mile.

Her profile said that she *always* ran six, showered, then went to her office.

Sounded like she dropped her keys at the door, dropped them hard. She moved with an urgency, came running down the short hallway toward the bathroom, moving and moaning like she was in agony.

She bolted into the bathroom, iPod still on, her running pants already halfway down.

She had cut her run short because she had to pee.

Everything couldn't be factored in. Nothing ever went according to plan.

Not until then did she look up.

Then they were eye to eye.

The WAG stopped pissing, jumped up from the toilet.

Her iPod blasted a song by the Pussycat Dolls as she opened her mouth to scream.

The man with the broken nose charged and hit her in the nose. Right-handed punch. Like when he worked out on the bag. His punch had great form. She went down hard, just like that. Unconscious, just like that. Nose crushed, just like his. Bladder emptying itself.

If it were in a movie, it would've been funny, like *Scary Movie.*

He said, "Sorry about that, ma'am. Not polite for a man to hit a woman. Just business."

He tied her hands and feet. Pussycat Dolls singing for a man to loosen up their buttons.

Then he stood behind her, covered her head with a plastic bag.

Suffocation left no blood. Minimal amount of noise.

As the WAG twitched, he was thinking how the U.K. weather sucked. Thinking that he couldn't wait to get back to Gatwick and catch the next plane back to the States.

Long day. But he'd be back in time to pick the kids up from school tomorrow.

He looked down at the WAG. Pretty woman. As if there were ugly WAGs.

Nice breasts. Sweet hips. A childbearer. She could've had some beautiful children.

He took out his cellular. Took a photo of the WAG. Sent the image to his client.

Damn shame, he thought. *Damn shame.*

He undressed her. Dropped her smelly clothes in the compact washer.

He started a load of laundry. Then mopped up the piss in the bathroom.

He left the floor spotless. He was anal. Liked things clean and in their place.

Then he took out the map of London, wanted to see how far he'd be from a different tube.

The type was too small, but he tried to comprehend the tubes. London confused him. Always had. Frustrated, feeling vulnerable, he sighed when he had to put his reading glasses back on. Glasses he'd bought at Hartsfield International for $10.

He'd left his prescription reading glasses at home.

He reminded himself to go ahead and make that appointment for LASIK surgery.

IRS wanted money. Attorneys wanted money. Kids wanted money. Church wanted tithes. He didn't have an extra three thousand for LASIK, but he had to do what he had to do.

Mortgage had to be paid. The gardener had to be paid. He needed the money.

He dressed nice, but being broke and looking broke were two different things.

That's why he had left working at the university and gone back to picking up contracts.

For the money. The tax-free kind of money you got under the table.

He had come back because he needed the cash.

His ex would get the kids, the house, half the pension.

All he'd walk away with would be the memories.

And he wished he could let his soon-to-be ex take those bittersweet memories too.

The first few years had been good. New was always good. New was always exciting.

Having kids changed her for the worse. She was a horrible mother.

Being a parent had been the best thing that ever happened to him.

He was a great father. He did what he had to do to make sure his kids had what they needed. He just needed a woman in the house. A man was supposed to take a wife.

He picked up his self-help book. He'd find a new wife, he hoped, before long.

He dragged the WAG's naked body down the hallway, Jacksonville on his mind.

Then he passed by a black dress, saw it hanging in her bedroom, the clothes the WAG had no doubt planned on wearing this morning, saw that blackness, and his thoughts shifted.

To the beautiful woman he'd seen on the plane. The one who had been crying.

He would've stayed another day just to have a ten-minute conversation with her.

Divorce for Dummies in his pocket, dragging a dead WAG across the tile floor, he wondered where the woman in black was right now. He wished he had asked her her name.

He wished he had given her a handkerchief to dry her tears.

Ten

woman on the run

Myhotel. Third floor.

Hotel rooms in Europe were diminutive, but my suite was decent, big enough for a king-size bed, a desk, and a small contemporary sofa that was against the wall between the two windows. The sofa was one step away from the bed. The windows were two steps away from the bed, double windows starting three feet above the floor and extending to the ten-foot ceiling. The dark curtains were thick enough to make a red dress for Scarlett O'Hara; both of those curtains pulled back, still open, the gray skies and London's Victorian architecture peeping, a thousand windows facing this room, two thousand eyes acting as spies in the house of love.

Above the desk, a Sony flat-screen television was anchored to the wall, it now being on a music station, Corinne Bailey Rae singing, her voice wonderful any time of the day.

Mrs. Jones sat on the bed. Crossing, uncrossing her legs. Hands smoothing out the already perfect bedspread. Her eyes going to the dresser, to the CD player, to the television, looking at everything but me. I went to her, put my fingers in her thick hair. The texture of her mane was strong, had a wonderful scent, fresh, maybe jojoba oil. Her eyes came to mine.

She asked, "How do we do . . . how do we negotiate this?"

"The times you committed adultery, how did you do it?"

"Those men . . . we weren't total strangers . . . not like this."

"Where did you meet them?"

"One . . . we were in law school together."

"The other."

"At Starbucks. Used to see him . . . we talked a lot . . . became friends before . . . it happened. It wasn't my intent. But it happened. To my regret. He was intense . . . so needy . . . bought a house near mine . . . cars . . ." She took a breath and shook away that memory. "Let me be quiet."

I whispered, "How would you like to do this?"

"Don't know." Her voice thinned. "I don't know how to do this."

"Yes, you do."

"Should I get . . . should I undress now . . . what?"

"Do you want to get undressed now?"

"Damn you, Gideon."

I stood over her, my groin at her eye level.

She opened, closed her hands.

Her lips barely parted as she whispered, "I am so wet, so marinated right now."

She leaned into my body, took a lungful of air, then shifted toward me, turned her face to the side, rested her face on my groin, took a deep breath, and released a soft growl.

The beast inside her was waking up.

She breathed on me, the warmth of her gasps moving through the material of my sweats, her heat giving me an abrupt hardness as she rubbed her face on that sudden erection, did it with passion, exhaled on that rigidity, took shallow inhales and curt exhales as she moved her lips side to side, as she leaned forward and moved her mouth deeper into my groin, over and over the sweetest moans escaping her full lips.

I whispered, "Take your panties off."

Her hand pulled up her dress, did that in increments, exposed flesh up to her thigh, and that hand went underneath all of that blackness and mystery, tugged as she shifted to her left side, then tugged as she shifted to her right side, her ass shifting as she uncovered her secrets, her face still on my crotch, her warm breath on what was hard, creating an unexpected fire.

In her hand, her panties were black, dangling from the ends of her fingers.

Mrs. Jones dropped that soft blackness to the floor.

I looked down at the silver cross resting in the swell of her breasts.

She gazed up at me, swallowed, her chest rising and falling at an anxious rate.

Tears sat in her eyes.

I leaned into her, undid her bra, dropped it on her panties.

Mrs. Jones lay back, her eyes closed.

I put my hands at her knees, pushed her legs apart.

Then.

She moved my hand away and closed her legs. Not a hard move, very gentle, and I complied. I moved away from her, took a step backward, gave her the right to choose.

She sat up, eyes now wide, wiping unhappiness from her eyes, shaking her head.

Mrs. Jones stood up, adjusted her dress, found her underwear, stuffed her unmentionables inside her purse, moved across the room, leaving without announcement.

Hands clenched, teeth tight, still shaking her head, her wild hair moving as if it were a tree in a breeze; she stopped at the door, struggled with herself, then gazed at me.

I went to her, kissed her chin, raised her head. My lips went to her cheek, to her salty tears. Then her tongue eased out, greeted me, awkward and desperate all at once. She dropped her purse and devoured me. Greedy sounds came from her, sounds so primal they almost scared me.

I whispered, "Slow down."

"Okay, okay."

But she didn't slow down. Then we were tugging at each other's clothes, kissing, unable to get undressed fast enough, fighting to get undressed, both of us giving up, my hands squeezing her breasts, her hands squeezing my ass, my mouth sucking her neck, her nails digging into my skin, breathing and panting hard.

The phone rang. She jumped. It disrupted her pace, caused her to pull away.

She asked, "You need to get that?"

"It's the Hanso Foundation. They'll call back."

She came back to me, came back in a hurry.

My hand went between her legs, first raising her dress again, then two fingers finding what was wet, moving inside what was hot. Mrs. Jones was on the bed. Mrs. Jones was whimpering, moaning. Mrs. Jones wasn't crying anymore. Pleasure dominated sadness.

We moved around, touching each other, shifting positions until I got behind her. I entered her. Not all at once. Moved deeper with invitation. It was a subtle invasion of the kingdom that belonged to another man. A land, based on what she had told me, he no longer wanted to rule.

"Where are you from, Gideon? How old are you? Were you in the army or any other branch of the military? Have you done time? Tell me something about you . . . anything . . ."

"This is all you need to know, Mrs. Jones."

"No fair."

Mrs. Jones was on her left side, her right leg in the air, her limbs loose and lithe, fluid and ambitious, as I moved in and out of her, her body lean and more flexible than it had appeared, her pretty face craned back for a kiss. She sucked my tongue like she hadn't been fed sensuality in a long time, maybe was used to sex without the kissing. Mrs. Jones still had her expensive black dress on, parts of that top-shelf material pulled up, parts of it pulled down, most of if bunched up around her midsection; she still had on her high-heeled shoes; my sweats were dangling from my right leg; everything we had carried to the room had been dropped between the bed and the front door.

Mrs. Jones frowned when she cried but smiled when she was getting fucked. She shed her aristocratic demeanor and made wonderful sounds, never said a coherent word.

The bed rocked. The wind blew. The heater hummed. The moans grew. In the few minutes we'd been here, the room had moved from ten below freezing to ten degrees above hell.

The clothes got in the way and we struggled to get that dress up over her head, it getting caught up on her wild hair, that moment causing her to release a nervous laugh. Mrs. Jones was so damn beautiful when she laughed. She was a girl at heart; her laugh told me that.

She kicked off her expensive shoes, put her legs up high, and I sucked her pretty toes. Wildness invaded her; convulsions had her grabbing the sheets. I sucked her toes and slid a finger inside her. Then I sucked her toes and slid two fingers inside, first deep, then rubbing that part of her that felt like a magical button. That had her pulling the sheets to her, her back arching.

My tongue moved from her toes to her knees; she responded to that with twitches and shudders, then to the back of her knee, down her thigh, and settled between her legs. My tongue made circles, I sucked on her clit, licked figure eights, gave her the sweetest torture. Her head moved side to side, jerked and moaned like the devil inside her was fighting for freedom.

I turned her over, put her ass up high, her beautiful face in the white pillow, and from behind I rubbed my energy up against her dampness. Moved it back and forth until she reached for me, until she stroked me, until she put my energy inside her. She moved against me hard, then I slapped her backside, spanked the right side, then the left cheek, did that over and over, made her cringe and stop. I moved slow, kept control of my own pleasure, didn't want my energy to spill too soon, moved from lovemaking to a straight-up mean fuck, tried to see what speed she liked, what she loved, tried to have fun and find out if she wanted the smooth or rough.

When I pinched her nipples, she closed her eyes, she moaned that she was coming.

I watched her. Felt her. Enjoyed her orgasm as much as she did.

I sat up, my back against the headboard. She straddled me. Wiggled until I slipped back inside. Moved with me. This dance between strangers working so well. She held on to me, her cross swaying as she moved up, then her cross sticking to her damp skin as she came down on me hard. My thrusts were hard, almost brutal and unkind, but she came down on me with equal or greater force each time, clenching her teeth, growling, challenging me, telling me to give her all I had, grunting for me to bring it on and give her the best I could for as long as I could.

Mrs. Jones was insatiable, couldn't tell if I was fucking her or if she was fucking me.

I turned her over, flipped her around again, had to change positions, break that devastating rhythm before I shot my load. She frowned back at what was going in and out of her, stared at it with moans and detachment, moved like an exhibitionist but had the gaze of a woman who was a voyeur at heart. She moved like the freak in her had died and she needed me to give it major resuscitation. Sharp noises. Short words that made no sense. Mild shrieks. Tight-eyed groans.

On her back, head tossed back, her skull deep inside the pillow, she panted and jerked as I moved my tongue up and down that narrow slit.

Then with me on my back she held my balls and licked the sides of my handle, then took me in her mouth. I smiled and played with her hair, moved my hips up, went deeper inside her face. She worked magic.

She told me she wanted me back inside her.

Sharp breathing came from both of us. Her hands pulled at

her hair, making what was untamed even wilder. I understood her bohemian mane now. It didn't match the high-street clothes she wore, wasn't intended to complement the professional part of her personality. That hair matched this part of her, the part she kept hidden, the part she let shine behind closed doors.

Missionary. Her legs around my back. Moving slowly. Going deep. Stopped when it felt too good. Kissed her lips, sucked her tongue, and delayed the inevitable.

She stared at me, but her eyes were out of focus, seeing something else.

Or somebody else.

I asked, "What was that look?"

She smiled, came back to the here and now, found her focus, found me.

I asked her again.

She whispered, "Lola Mack."

It was my turn to smile.

Her eyes closed, her voice less than a whisper now. "She made me come."

"On the plane."

She groaned. "Had a goddamn orgasm at thirty-six thousand feet in the air."

I moved slow, felt her body start to quiver again, that right leg shaking, mild convulsions.

I said, "I'm inside you and you're thinking about Lola Mack."

"Yes."

"Imagining Lola Mack?"

"I'm not going to answer that."

I fucked her harder, fucked her and growled, "Are you imagining her?"

She surrendered. "Yes."

"Did you like that? When she made you come, did you like that?"

"God, you're . . . you're . . . your . . . it's getting so hard."

"Did you like that?"

"Imagining me and Lola . . . imagining us . . . that turns you on, doesn't it?"

"Did you like that?"

"Would that turn you on?"

"Answer me, dammit."

"Fuck you."

"Answer me."

"So damn hard. You are so damn hard."

"Did you like that?"

"God, you are fucking—"

"Answer . . ."

"—the shit out of me."

"Answer . . . answer . . . me . . . answer me."

I slowed down, caught my breath. She did the same. Her eyes opened wide, not blinking, as if she were gone to some ethereal place far away.

She whispered, "She made me come . . . when she massaged me . . . she . . . I came like a river . . . was too embarrassed to get up and . . . or make her stop . . . so I pretended to be asleep."

I asked, "On the plane . . . you come good?"

"Not as good as . . . as . . . as I'm about to come now."

She was shaking, holding me. Her nonstop whimpers were so sensual, so arousing.

I was grunting, mixing my sex sounds with her orgasmic squeals.

Pleasure was about to rush out of me. I pulled out, told Mrs. Jones that I was about to come. She lay back, waiting, panting like she was in heat, licking her lips, her eyes on my penis, watching, wanting to see, wanting to see, wanting to see. It was taking me too long to come. She took my penis and stroked me. Stroked me and took me over that ridge. I grunted as my seeds left me, as they spilled and decorated her stomach, as they created a river between her breasts.

Now she had a pearl necklace to go with her diamond ring.

She ran her fingers through the river of lifeless life, closed her eyes and played with those unborn children, children with nowhere to swim, children who would not hunt for an egg at breakfast time. Mrs. Jones licked her lips, hesitated, that urge rose in her face, that urge she couldn't suppress any longer, the urge she had to give in to. She sucked her fingers.

She hummed and licked her fingers like she was finishing a bucket of KFC.

Eleven

deadly is the female

Mrs. Jones had become an exotic vampire.

I smiled; what she was doing was so damn erotic. She grinned at me in return, now feeling safe with what she was doing in front of me. When she was done, she closed her eyes.

I said, "Lola Mack made you come."

She shook her head in disbelief, gave me a shallow chuckle, her eyes getting tighter.

"I couldn't look at Lola when we got off the plane. Hated her happy ass. Tried to avoid her after customs. Thought she would get her damn luggage and run to her boyfriend's hotel."

I chuckled. "She looked happy when she got in that taxi."

"That's how a woman smiles when she's horny and knows it's about to get handled."

"You have the same smile now."

She licked her fingers. "I know."

I lay down on her, that river becoming our glue, and we kissed. We moved from deep kisses to softer kisses as we cooled down, like two athletes at the end of a workout. She moved away from me, got her own pillow, put her back to me. I put my arm around her. She shifted and I took that as a hint, so I moved my arm away. Reached for the remote, hit the ON button.

I changed channels and stopped at TV6. Every few minutes they played that irritating opening for the *Simpsons*, this one using real people instead of animations.

She whispered, "Horrible. That's just plain horrible."

"That a woman made you come?"

"No, that *Simpsons* intro thing. The cartoon is much better. That's horrible."

A moment passed.

I changed the channel, found Prime Minister Tony Blair in the middle of a loan scandal.

I looked at Mrs. Jones. She stopped staring at my backpack, looked at me.

Mrs. Jones said, "Blair sucks."

I agreed. "He's just another Bush."

"Blair has a better vocabulary."

"Bush has better teeth."

"Tell me about your backpack."

I pretended she didn't faze me, surfed BBC1.

Pictures of Big Bad with birth and death dates lit up my room. Clips of his videos and interviews played in the background. The news had put together a package. In big Vegas-style lights BIG BAD. White Adidas to the bone. Shaking, doing the *Boom Boom Click* dance moves that came out of the Dirty South. Doing the walk-it-out. Pool Palace. Lean-wit-it-rock-wit-it. Rag Top. Everybody in the video dressed like they were his clones.

He said, "I'm *bling-tabulous*, baby. *Bling-tabulous*."

The reporter said that this gang killing had left a trail of destruction rivaled only by the Japanese beetle. A thousand police lights and coroner vans were behind that strip club.

The news called it a gang war.

Fans were showing up with flowers and candles and testimonies.

They had his wife and kids on the news too. She was crying, so were the kids.

Two days ago the members of his former group were interviewed.

Sans Sledge.

Yesterday Sledge's publicist had issued a heartfelt comment.

They said Sledge was too shocked and broken up by the loss of an old friend to speak.

I changed the channel, moved on to BBC2, ITV, Channel 4, and Channel 5. One station was showing *Friends. Will & Grace* and *Just Shoot Me* were warming up, next at bat. Another channel had news, said that there was a thirty-minute delay on some trains in some areas. That was followed by a special report giving props to the area that had the worst teeth in the U.K.

I changed the channel again. Leeds University students were demanding the resignation of Dr. Frank Ellis for supporting the right-wing "bell-curve" theory, which said black students were genetically inferior. Not exactly the kind of shit I wanted to hear about right now.

I thought Mrs. Jones was going to sleep, but she kept shifting positions, bothered.

I asked her what was wrong. She said her entire life was on her mind.

She said, "Thinking about . . . I had an interesting childhood."

I muted the television, turned and faced Mrs. Jones.

She whispered, "My first sexual experience . . . was unexpected. Like this."

"This reminds you of that."

"Was with a girl." She chuckled. "Never told anybody that. Not even my husband."

"What happened? How did that come about?"

"It started off . . . we called ourselves practicing . . . for the day we were with a boy. We practiced . . . kissing our hands . . . then each other . . . first lips closed . . . then French . . . then

touching . . . what to expect boys to touch . . . and it . . . it became something else for a while."

"Did it?"

"After school we'd . . . be together. Do things. Things we
thought boys would do."

"Like?"

"It was innocent. Tried to teach each other how to kiss.
Learned about our bodies."

"How did it end?"

"Our parents found out . . . it got ugly."

"So you're bi?"

"Not at all. Was just something I did when I was a young
girl, experimental, that's all. With that one girl. No one else.
Something that happened . . . decades ago. A lifetime ago."

Silence from me while she shifted a lot.

She said, "Can't believe I told you that. My husband doesn't . . .
didn't know that."

"Really?"

"There is . . . was a lot he doesn't . . . didn't know about me."

It was too quiet. I turned on the radio. I searched for Miles, or
Wes, or Trane, stopped surfing at Choice FM. Beverley Knight's
remake of an old Al Green song was going off as Corinne Bailey
Rae took the floor with her original music and told the U.K. to
put their records on.

I closed my eyes. The bed moved when Mrs. Jones got up.
My hands ached. So did my face. Pins and needles were under
my skin. All of those sensations were reminders. Days had passed
and my insides still rattled with nervousness, like they did before
a job. It was so vivid.

Wondered how many Hail Marys a man like me would have
to say to see glory.

Corinne Bailey Rae went off and Amy Winehouse came on.
"Moody's Mood for Love."

I opened my eyes; Mrs. Jones was preoccupied, trying to
clean her black dress.

I walked to the window, pulled the thick, red curtains back. London was gray and overcast, the same mood Mrs. Jones had been in before we crossed that line, and she was drifting back toward the land of melancholy. She wasn't crying. That was good.

My thoughts stayed back in Tampa.

Mrs. Jones remained in her own world as well.

She said, "My dress is ruined."

"Come stains?"

"Jism blots all over. This dress cost four hundred dollars. Now it's ruined."

"Now it's a Lewinsky."

"It's fucked-up, that's what it is."

She got back in the bed.

Never should have brought her anxiety and problems up to my room.

I went back to the bed. Mrs. Jones had pulled the cover up over her petite butt.

"Lola made you come."

"Damn that talkative bitch."

I said, "Doubt if she's talking right now."

"She's probably fucking the shit out of her boyfriend."

We laughed hard, me because in that moment, I heard the ghetto rise up and walk out on the tongue of a sophisticated woman. The timbre of hard times and ruthlessness in her tone.

For a moment I imagined Mrs. Jones being my woman.

I asked, "What if your husband went away?"

"He's already left me."

"No . . . what if . . . if . . . what if he ceased to exist?"

"Died?"

I let that idea sit for a moment, then asked, "Would that make you happy?"

Silence charged into the room, followed by the muffled return of Mrs. Jones's tears.

She hurried into the bathroom, closed the door hard. I heard sobbing, water running, then the shower. She came back out wearing a towel, covering all she had shared with me.

I thought about Thelma.

Mrs. Jones said, "When he was a teenager, my husband used to rob banks."

"Your husband was a bad boy."

"He ran with gangs. And his older brother. Yeah. He robbed banks."

"You don't say. And here I am using an ATM to get my money."

"Your sense of humor is awful."

"Have to work on my timing, that's all."

"My husband. He doesn't know I know he was a stickup man."

"How did you find out?"

"His mother told me. Before we married, his mother told me."

"And you still married him."

She went into a trance.

"Gideon."

"Yes, Mrs. Jones."

She looked unnerved.

I asked, "Do I scare you?"

"You made me wet. On the plane, in the galley, when you were flirting, you made me wet."

"Did I?"

"You made me wet, then Lola put her hands on me. She fanned the flames you created."

Mrs. Jones pulled her dress on, tried to smooth away the wrinkles, and picked at the jism stains, sat at the end of the bed, not blinking, eyes glued to the wall.

She wiped away her tears, whispered, "How much would something like that cost?"

"You talking about a new dress?"

"No. The other thing. To make someone . . . cease to exist. What's the going rate?"

"What would it be worth to you?"

Then the whispers ended and she was blinking again, crying harder.

Her voice turned ragged. "Are you fucking with me, Gideon?"

I remained calm. "I'm not fucking—"

"Are you testing me—"

"—with you."

"Then what are you doing?"

"I'm just asking a question."

"To see what kind of person I am?"

She went on breathing hard for a while, tugging at her hair, shaking her head.

She said, "I come from a long line of bad people. I'm not proud of it, but that's who I am."

I looked at her, waited for her to say more or shut down. Either way didn't matter.

She said, "My father . . . he made money in Jamaica. He did illegal things."

"Drugs."

"I'm not saying."

"Jamaica is between where they manufacture the drugs and the people who buy drugs."

She nodded. "Lots of kidnappings. Lots of murders."

"And Kingston has a murder rate that ranks number one, I do believe."

"So you've been to Kingston?"

"Saw a lot of beautiful things, met some beautiful women, but what's up with the brothers walking the streets with their dicks hanging out of their pants? Is that a fashion statement?"

She almost smiled.

"I'm serious. Why do they walk around with their dicks hanging out?"

"Because they can."

"Is that against the law?"

"I didn't study Jamaican law." Her smile vanished. "My father, he took us to America."

"From Jamaica."

"He came to my room. I was a child. I was six, maybe five. But I remember his fear. He came and picked me up. In the middle of the night. Picked me up fast. He had me in his arms when he ran to get my mother. She was sleeping. Rushed us to an airfield. We left everything behind. Left abruptly, in our pajamas, my mother in her housecoat and house shoes, and I never knew why, but I did know why. The suitcase filled with money told me some of the why."

"That's wild."

"I'm telling you things I never told my husband. Things I've never talked about."

We exchanged expressions.

I asked, "Did you change your names once you got here . . . I mean there, to the U.S.?"

She smiled a life-weary smile that was a mask for her swift embarrassment.

"We changed names, changed everything." She whispered to herself for a moment. "Maybe I inherited my father's old ways. Maybe anger and revenge live in my blood."

"Meaning what exactly?"

"Meaning I'd better get away from you before I make someone cease to exist."

I shrugged. "We were just being hypothetical."

She whispered, "Contemplation is prelude to commission."

"Is it?"

"Like we contemplated fucking."

"Then we were fucking."

"Now we're two people contemplating murder."

Silence moved between us, wedged us further apart, put us back in our corners.

She whispered, " 'For what I am working out I do not know. For what I wish, this I do not practice, but what I hate is what I do . . . but now the one working it out is no longer I, but sin that resides in me. For I know that in me, that is, in my flesh, there dwells nothing good. For ability to wish is present with me, but ability to work what is fine is not present. For the good that I wish I do not do, but the bad that I do not wish is what I practice . . .'"

I said, "And she quotes the Bible."

She went on, her voice a perplexed whisper, the good and bad inside her fighting like rabid pit bulls, her face showing her inner struggle, revealing her angst. "I find, then, this law in my case: That when I wish to do what is right, what is bad is present with me . . ."

Somebody tapped on my door. We both jumped, only in different ways, for different reasons. Mine was the mild panic of a man worried about the law. Mrs. Jones jumped like a married woman who realized she was in the bedroom with another man, his come still on her breath, his seeds drying on her skin.

I asked who it was.

"Housekeeping. You would . . . do you like your room to be serviced, yes?"

We heard workers giggling in the hallway. Their accents thick enough to cut with a blade, maybe Polish or Romanian, could've been some other Eastern Bloc tongue.

I told them to go away, nothing was needed right now. They sounded like grown women but giggled like naughty teenagers. They apologized in chorus. That giggle meant they had heard us moaning. Their accents faded into the room across the hallway.

Mrs. Jones said, "My name was Henrietta Kellogg. That was my birth name."

"You changed it."

"My parents changed it. I woke up in America with a new identity."

"So you know how to leave an old life behind."

"Where I was from, money fixed all problems. Everybody had a price. Everyone from the police to the neighbor. You paid them off, made your problems go away. You made people go away. And if they didn't have a price . . . if they didn't have a price . . ."

"They slept under the dirt."

"My father . . . he tried to kill someone for me . . . he tried . . . his old ways came back."

"Why did he try to kill someone for you?"

"Because I asked him to." She paused. "Because I *told* . . . *begged* him to."

She wiped her eyes with the back of her hand.

I nodded.

She said, "It didn't happen. He tried. It went wrong. It went bad for all of us."

"Your husband? Your father tried to kill your husband for you?"

"Someone else. I don't want to talk about that. Not ever. I want to forget it all."

I listened.

"So, yesterday, I did just like I did when I was a child." She took a breath. "I ran away. Got on a plane. Left my name. Clothes. Everything I owned. I ran away from my life."

"Sounds traumatic."

"We shed the skins of who we used to be."

"Can't imagine what you went through. What you're going through."

"I'm going through . . . my life. Once again uprooted from friends. From my culture. From my world. Only when I was a little girl, I had my doll to comfort me. No doll, not this time."

She stared out the window for a moment. Looked like she was counting raindrops.

She whispered, "I can be someone different every day. I can become a new woman every day until I like the woman I become, then I can become her for a while, if not forever."

She finished dressing.

Mrs. Jones said, "Too bad I didn't know you last year."

"Is that right?"

She walked toward the door.

She asked, "Have you slept with a lot of married women?"

"Only the ones who have given up on their husbands."

"Then you have slept with a lot of married women."

I didn't answer.

"I saw you exchange backpacks. Your bag is heavier."

"What does that tell you?"

"You're a criminal."

"And you're an attorney."

"Not any longer."

"What are you now?"

"I don't know."

Mrs. Jones didn't look back at me, just left the room.

Twelve

this gun for hire

Mrs. Jones had bedded a contract killer and walked away.

I went back to the window.

The skies were darker, the rain coming down with the same silky cadence, a tempo that was steady but not urgent. Down on the cobblestone walkway it was about four degrees Celsius, which translated to about forty Fahrenheit. To my right, an Asian man wearing a bright yellow raincoat was out on the corner holding up a big sign that advertised his Chinese buffet was the best in the area, marching back and forth in the rain as Europeans and Africans hustled up and down Tottenham Court Road, umbrellas held high, most dressed in dark colors, casual and cosmopolitan, this metropolitan section of the world that housed Protestants, Catholics, and followers of Islam, looking like a mixture of Seattle, Rittenhouse Square in Philly, all of that with blended architecture, the historic and outdated along with the contemporary and chic.

I waited. It was cold out there, freezing by L.A. standards. Too bitter for the thin dress Mrs. Jones had on. All the other women who had on skirts wore black leggings, some with funky patterns, but Mrs. Jones's legs were bare. No way would she take to the cold dressed the way she was. Without a coat. Expected to hear a tap at the door, any second I would hear her taps.

The phone rang again.

I took my time, answered on the third ring. Expected to hear Mrs. Jones's jet-lagged and disheartened tone. Wanted it to be her. The voice on the other end was fresh. My work calling.

My instructions were curt. "Walk Tottenham Court Road until you see Freddie Mercury."

"You're in London?"

"Freddie Mercury will be on the left."

"Why can't I just walk until I see Tupac and Biggie?"

Then I was talking to a dial tone.

Time to go to work.

My attention went to the blue backpack. The one the Dutch woman at Gatwick had traded for mine. I unzipped the bag. Old Navy sweats and underwear were packed on top, white socks there as well. Under the clothing was a computer, a TX-series Sony Vaio that weighed no more than two pounds. The three-prong power cable was made for the U.S. They had been kind enough to throw in a dual-wattage international converter set.

What had the most weight was a white box. I opened it. Inside was a sweet piece of hardware, a nine with its silencer packed off to the side. A SIG-Sauer was in the bag too, as I had requested. After the incident with the reverend I started using a bigger gun with a bigger bullet.

Other tools were in the backpack. Ice pick. Piano wire. Custom gloves.

I touched the guns and once again I was seven years old. Saw that big, ugly man beating my mother. A big man they called Mr. Midnight. He was choking her. Screaming at her and killing her. Had her by the neck, her body raised up sky-high, my mother naked and kicking wildly as she suffocated, her feet banging against the wall as he rag-dolled her around the room, my mother's feet knocking over lamps as she clawed at his hands.

Like Mrs. Jones and her family had fled Jamaica, me and my mother fled Charlotte. My mother took the cash out of that dead man's wallet and packed our clothes. He was my first kill. Not for profit, the ones that came later were put in a different category, at least they were in my mind.

While we sat in the back of a Greyhound bus, she held me in her arms, that smoking Smith & Wesson in her big purse, and told me who my father was.

Before that day, I never knew I had a father.

My mother told me that my father was an army man. He bragged that he used to jump out of planes, took sniper training, made Delta Force. While they drank and got high, while he paid my mother to do the kind of things a man paid a woman in her profession to do, he ran his strong hands through her long hair and held her close, treated her like a lady, a cigarette in his hand and liquor on his breath, and told her his secrets, told that young woman that the government still needed mercenaries. He was being sent to Latin America, somewhere in Honduras and Nicaragua, so he could deal with arms traders.

He met my mother on his sojourn to South America. He needed to relieve some stress, made a stop at a brothel in Montego Bay, where all the tender-legged women lined up for inspection, and picked the prettiest woman in the whorehouse, sweet girl from Charlotte, North Carolina. Nine months after that I was born in the city named after King George III's wife, the queen being a woman from Germany, Mecklenburg, hence the name of the county of my birth.

My father was strong, used to fight bulls bare-handed, beat them every time.

That was some of what my mother told me; I've added to the truth she gave me.

Like James Frey, in my own omniscient voice, I have embellished my own history.

As far as I know, my entire history, including what my mother said, could be a lie.

I hurried back to the window, hoping I hadn't missed Mrs. Jones.

She was leaving the hotel, moving into the streets, not looking in the right direction for traffic. She was in the middle of the road when a Smart car whipped around the corner; the driver slammed on his brakes and slid fast. Mrs. Jones was almost run down. In America, traffic came from the left. In London, a world that was reversed, traffic assaulted pedestrians from the right. Mrs. Jones had looked the wrong way, her mind now realizing this world drove on the opposite side of the street. Barely in London for three hours and she was almost killed, almost run down like Natalie Portman in the opening of the movie *Closer*. Mrs. Jones stood in the middle of the street, shaken, the driver blowing his horn as he struggled to maneuver around Mrs. Jones.

Mrs. Jones looked up at the window. She saw me. Stared. Then, without expression, turned her head away. I no longer existed in her world.

Forty-degree wind made her dark dress sway. Purse on her arm, she lowered her head, took quick steps to beat the traffic and negotiate Tottenham Court Road at the Odeon. Again she stood in the rain, pondered both directions like she was trying to ponder the rest of her life.

Then she looked down. At every intersection were markings on the pavement, big and bold, white lettering, telling pedestrians which way to scan for traffic: LOOK RIGHT. LOOK LEFT. I wonder how many Americans and Parisians were run down before they came up with that idea.

Mrs. Jones went left toward the high-tech district, passed by the red phone booths, phone booths that had business cards from every whore in the area posted inside.

The night I killed that evil man, my mother remained calm. Unbelievably calm. He'd almost murdered her and she never fell apart. She was calm to the point of being cold. She put a sheet over his body while we ate, packed, wiped our prints away from everything in that rented space, then left before the sun made friends with Mecklenburg County. My mother didn't shed a single tear. Neither did I. I read my comic books and became the echo of her emotions.

I asked my mother, "Where we going?"

"Quebec. On the island of Montreal."

I asked, "We have friends on that island?"

"My only friend died a long time ago."

"You have any friends?"

"Only one I ever had died. She was killed by one of her johns."

My mother was smoking, sweating.

I asked, "How am I supposed to make friends if we keep moving?"

"We'll stop moving one day. But right now we have to leave before the police come."

Once again I'd have to become someone else.

I asked, "Why we have to go this time?"

"Because they will take you away from me. They will lock me up and put you in the system. I grew up in the system. The system is no place for a child to be. There is no love."

I looked down at my hand. I moved my trigger finger back and forth. Felt the weight of that .22 in my hand, even though I wasn't holding that weapon. Smelled the cordite on my skin.

I asked my mother, "Did I do a bad thing?"

"Some people deserve to die." She shook her head. "Your daddy told me. Bad people need to die. It makes the world a better place."

I told myself that by killing that man and saving my mother, I was a superhero, that I had made the world a better place. I was still making the world a better place for someone.

Below me, on Bayley Street, over on Tottenham Court, nothing but crowds and strangers.

Mrs. Jones had vanished underneath a dark sky that was a doppelgänger for her mood.

Disappeared like her wicked family did on a terrifying night in Jamaica.

I smelled my fingers, the sweetness of her vagina still living on my tongue.

Thirteen

the woman in white

His broken nose ached.

He was sitting at a bistro table, Starbucks Coffee at Tower Bridge Piazza.

The area around Shad Thames and Horsleydown Lane looked like the old country.

He was only a few yards away from where he had dropped the WAG.

He had done as he was ordered. The WAG's estranged husband wanted her dropped on the spot he had proposed to her. He had paid a lot of money to make sure that happened.

People were mumbling about a body that had been found in the Thames this morning.

People thought it was suicide. London was a dark and dreary, depressing place that had plenty of self-killings. But the man with the broken nose knew the truth.

Glasses on, he was reading *Divorce for Dummies*, drinking a tall house coffee. No cream. Sugar. With his cellular up to his ear. Frustration was crawling up and down his spine.

Jaw tight, he told his soon-to-be ex-wife, "I'm in London. Left a message on your cellular."

"I'm leaving you. I'm moving on with my life."

"Let's not go through this again. I can't handle this right now."

"And I'm taking our daughter. I'm taking Melanie. Skeeter can stay with you. Boys should be with their fathers. You can teach him things I can't. No child support. Agreed?"

"I'm tired of the threats. Let's get this divorce over with, can we? This is worse than that crap Alec Baldwin and Kim Basinger are going through. You need to calm the fuck down."

"Don't tell me to calm the eff down. Don't you dare tell me to calm the eff down."

"You're killing me over here, you know that? It's what, still the middle of the night in Texas and you're blowing up my phone. Why do you do this to me? Why harass me?"

"I'm leaving you."

"Don't talk about it. Be about it."

"I'm leaving you."

"And I want you to leave. I was served. I signed. What else do you want?"

"But I'm not taking Skeeter. I can't deal with Skeeter. I can't handle Skeeter."

Pressure at both temples. He wondered if Paul McCartney was this stressed.

He snapped, "Don't do this to me, not right now."

"Two weeks you've been gone. When are you coming back?"

He took a breath. "Trying to get back to Katy sometime tomorrow."

"I can't handle Skeeter. Come get him. He should be with his father."

His cellular rang. Not the one in his hand, the one in his pocket.

The hotline.

He told his soon-to-be ex-wife to hold on.

She asked, "Hold on? I'm falling apart. Why should I have to hold on?"

"Business call coming in. Need to take it."

She hung up on him.

He almost called her back. But there was no need trying to put toothpaste back in the tube. That was both futile and messy. He flipped one phone closed. Flipped the other one open.

He answered, "Talk to me, Sam."

"Got another job for you."

He grunted out his frustration. "Where?"

"London."

"Need to leave. London's going to be on fire in the next few hours."

"Top dollar on the next one."

"Top dollar? What's top dollar?"

He listened. What he heard caused him to put his book to the side.

He said, "That's a lot of money."

"Can get you half in the next day or so."

"What's the job?"

"Cleanup. High-profile."

High-profile. People liked to clean up after big jobs, jobs that drew too much attention. The contractors liked to assassinate the contract killers to prevent them from testifying or even spreading rumors about who hired them. Rotten business. Profitable, but rotten to the core.

Everybody was expendable in the name of self-preservation.

The man with the broken nose asked, "From what job?"

"Can't say."

"Well, is it a European cleanup?"

"Something back in North America."

"North America runs from Mexico to the North Pole."

He sipped his coffee. Cleanups were the most dangerous. Killer against killer.

But wives cost money. Kids cost money. Coffee cost money.

He asked, "Who is the package on? Who is the hit on, Sam? Man or woman?"

"Don't know. Not like there is a Hit Man's Registration Act to keep you guys in line."

"Save the jokes. Get me a package."

"Will do."

"If I'm staying, I'll need some perks. And I need some additional hardware."

"Place your order. I can get almost anything."

"Had my eye on a Desert Eagle .50. Titanium finish."

"Israeli gun. Big bullets. Loud bang."

He said, "Hadn't planned on staying. Need money. Not to be held against my fee."

"Use the American Express that came with the passport and tickets."

"Need suits. And you know what kind of suits I wear."

"Then buy the kind of suits you wear."

"Need a place to hole up."

"Get a hotel. Use the AmEx. Get some rest."

"I don't want to be in London no more than another day. Get me that package."

He hung up that cellular.

Then flipped open the other one. Started putting in the 713 area code to his soon-to-be ex-wife's cellular. Made it to the last number and paused. He hated her. He really did.

He wished he had thrown her into the Thames.

Now he was stuck in London.

He had planned on returning to Gatwick. An hour trip. Go through customs. Another hour. Wait for three or four hours to board a flight at British Air. Take a nine-hour flight back to Atlanta. Again through customs. Then wait for another plane. After that a two-hour flight to Houston. Drive the forty-five minutes to Katy. Get Mexican food for dinner.

Then listen to his soon-to-be-ex bitch about how much she hated her life.

Listen to her brag about her new boyfriend. How he takes her out.

He hung up the phone.

He didn't want to rush home to that. He'd take a nap, buy a couple of suits, maybe head out to the Brick Lane Market and take a glimpse at the Bengali culture. He'd picked up a travel guide. *London in 24 Hours*. Had circled a few things that looked interesting. A restaurant on Portobello Road looked nice. Brochure said it was across the street from a famous tattoo shop that had been seen in the opening of a Julia Roberts movie, one she had done with some wimpy British guy. Might find his way over to the Ten Bells pub. Maybe just relax for a few hours and do like the brochure recommended, become a tourist and take in some of Dickensian London.

He picked up a newspaper. Morning edition. Front page announced that Europe had 55 million hard drinkers, a third of them women who had started drinking by the age of thirteen. No wonder they had some of the unfriendliest faces on the planet. Hard to smile with a hangover. Next page was about a man who had been served divorce papers, and minutes later he poured gasoline around the house, lit a match, and damn near blew up the neighborhood.

He understood that man.

Women. When they didn't have a man, unhappy. When they had a man, unhappy. Not married, unhappy. Married, unhappy. No kids, unhappy. Had kids, unhappy. Go figure.

He was done with women. With dating. With marriage. For a long while.

Then.

A woman walked in dressed in all white. That color out of season, at least it was out of season by Texas standards. No white after Labor Day was the rule in the South. In the blacks and grays, she stood out. But she would've stood out anyway. She was bald, for the most part.

Stunning woman. High cheekbones, round face, full lips.

Dark skin. Small breasts. Small waist that led to a healthy, round backside.

He looked at her, her bald head and angelic colors hard to ignore on a gloomy day.

Especially since she had to be at least six foot three in her heels. She was so damn vertical, tall enough to walk up to a man of average height and stick her breast directly in his mouth. She smiled at him, her features too astonishing to be obstructed by hair.

His voice vanished.

But he nodded at her. Then he looked away. Then he wished he hadn't looked away.

A moment later she was standing near his table, looking around the room, coffee in hand.

All the seats in Starbucks were filled. Except the one in front of him.

She smiled. "Is this seat taken?"

He stood up like a gentleman, motioned at the seat.

She got comfortable in her chair, took off her coat, put her purse in her lap.

He asked, "What are you drinking?"

"Caramel Macchiato. I'm addicted. Have to have one as soon as I wake up. Then I have to have a blueberry green-tea Frappuccino before I go to bed. Starbucks gets my money."

He motioned at his coffee. "Same here. One in the morning. One at night. Addicted."

Then she asked, "What are you drinking?"

"Coffee in the morning. Black with sugar. Triple grande mocha with nonfat later on."

She checked her watch. "Was crazy getting here. You see all the police and news stations on the bridge?"

"What's going on? Filming a movie or something?"

"You didn't hear about the woman who jumped off the bridge?"

"This bridge?"

"You're joking. You're sitting here and didn't know what was going on out there?"

"Just got to London. Literally. Walked in jet-lagged and got a cup of coffee."

She sipped. "Here on holiday or business? I'm guessing business."

"The suit gave it away, huh?"

"That and being near the financial district. How long you here?"

"Looks like I'll be here a couple of days."

"What brings you here? What business?"

He remembered all the real estate businesses that had lined Shad Thames. He said, "Looking at real estate investments. Had a meeting with agents at Rive, another at Cluttons."

"You like the area?"

"Yeah. It's calm. Kind of secluded. Peaceful. Queen's Walk looks like a good place to take a jog. Was looking at the terrace houses. And apartments. For investment."

"I love it over here. Bakeries. Wine merchants. Indian restaurants. Everything."

She looked at him, her eyes focused on his broken nose. He waited for her to ask.

He was ready to lie. Amazed him how he kept track of all of his lies.

She said, "You're American."

He nodded. "American. You?"

"I'm Motswana."

"What country is that?"

"Botswana. Miss Universe was from Lobatse, Botswana."

"Didn't know that."

"When Mpule Kwelagobe won Miss Universe, it was ecstatic at home, never before have we won such a coveted prize. She really represented us. Look her up on Wikipedia."

"I'll make sure I do that." He smiled. "So you're Motswana from Botswana."

"Sure am."

"Is that where they are razing the villages, killing men, women, and children?"

"I think you're thinking of Darfur. I'm not from there. It's tragic and horrible there."

"Not good with African geography. Sorry. Where's your homeland?"

"Southern Africa."

"Never would've guessed you were African. I mean, South African."

"Hell no." She laughed, but she had some attitude. "Not *South* African. Botswanans really hate being referred to as South Africans just because people don't understand the difference between South Africa and Botswana, or that they don't know none other than South Africa."

"So it's Southern Africa."

"Not South Africa."

"Educate me. I like to get things like that right. I don't know much about Africans. But I can relate, in some ways. People over here think all Americans are the same and we're not."

"The way you call me African. It's funny."

"What's funny about that?"

"I wasn't African until I left Africa."

"Sorry? What were you in Africa?"

"At home I am Motswana. I leave home and they call me *African*. They talk about Africa like it's a borough. Africa is a *continent*. So, that irritates me to no end. No matter where you are from—Ethiopia, South Africa, Niger—we lose our identity and become African. Like when you leave America, they call you American. I'm sure in America they call you something else."

"Texan. Live in Texas. So I get called a lot of names. Not many flattering."

She laughed a little. "I've heard of Texas. Is that near California or New York?"

"Neither. Middle of America, as far south as you can go before hitting Mexico."

"My American geography . . . sorry. All I know for sure is New York and California."

"Texas is in the south. Right above Mexico. Texas is the second-largest state."

"What's the largest?"

"Alaska. About twice the size of Texas. Alaska is north and west, next to Canada."

"How big is Texas?"

"Takes two days to drive across Texas."

"Two days? To drive across one state?"

"Two days."

"Good Lord. I could be in ten countries in two days."

"Well, when Texas was founded, they had a provision that it could be broken up into ten smaller states, but I guess they never got around to it. Yep. Two days to drive across Texas."

"I'd go crazy if I were in a car that long."

They laughed.

He said, "I don't know anything about Botswana."

She told him that she had gone to Our Lady of the Desert Primary School from ages six to twelve, then to Mater Spei College until she was seventeen. After that, Botswana Institute of Administration & Commerce, then to Birmingham College of Food.

He said, "Birmingham, Alabama?"

"Birmingham, England. It's north of here."

"Food college?"

"I wanted to be a chef. Wanted to have my own restaurant. And I will one day."

"So you can cook?"

"Of course. Now I work and go to Bournville College on the weekends."

She told him she was on the way to work. He offered to walk

her out. He followed her across the rugged roadway, streets made of uneven brick, maybe to give that cobblestone feel. They took to the stairs, went up, came out almost at the spot he had dropped the WAG.

It was amazing.

Above, all across the bridge were police cars and ambulances. News reporters as well.

People were looking over the railing like it was a tourist attraction. Yards away people lined up to visit the Tower, where hundreds were executed. Murder was entertainment. He wondered if he had earned a spot on that tour. Wondered if soon people would come from all over the world to see this spot, if they would have cameras and pose in front of Death's handiwork the same way other tourists lined up to visit the horrors of the London Dungeon. Almost twenty pounds to watch re-created gruesome events, scenes of gory torture, murders, atrocities, group rates available. He could only hope his work would one day be included.

She said, "Did you hear what they said when we were walking by?"

"What did they say?"

"That they think the woman was dead before she was in the water."

"Thought you said she jumped."

"I did. People jump from the bridges all the time. A man jumped from London Bridge last week. They never found his body. Now they are saying she was killed and thrown into the river."

"That's horrible. What is this world coming to?"

"Crazy things happen here. Did you know on the tubes, people jump in front of the trains all the time? Especially on New Year's Eve. So many people kill themselves that way."

Dark skies and chilly winds, they walked toward the tube, commotion behind them.

He looked down at the muddy waters. An old fear rose up inside him.

Old horrors never died.

He remembered when he was a child. His father had thrown him into a lake. To teach him how to swim. He remembered that terror. Drowning. Remembered thinking he was going to die. He held his breath. Suffocating. Remembered thinking that was a horrible way to die.

He remembered waking up, coughing the water out of his lungs.

He remembered how he cried.

He remembered how his brothers and sisters laughed.

He remembered how once he caught his breath, his old man threw him right back in.

He hated water. He hated rivers. He hated lakes. He hated swimming pools.

She asked, "Where are you going? Business meeting?"

"No business for a while. Looking for a hotel in this area."

She pointed. "Over there. Novotel. That hotel is nice. It has a very nice gym."

Then an awkward moment. How to say good-bye. He didn't want to say good-bye.

He asked, "Where do you work?"

"East London."

"Anyway, can I . . . uh . . . call you or . . . something?"

"Depends."

"On what?"

"Where am I from?"

"Batswana."

"*Bots*wana. Not *Bats*wana."

"Botswana."

"I should give you a lashing."

"So I messed up a vowel."

She laughed. "What do they call me at home?"

"Motswana."

"What part of Africa am I from?"

"Southern Africa, not South Africa."

"Impressive."

"Do I get a gold star on my paper?"

"You have to stay after school and write *Botswana* on the board a thousand times."

"Bummer."

She handed him one of her cards. The Bank of New York. One Canada Square.

He saw that she had already had the business card in the palm of her hand.

Her name was Tebogo Otsile. Assistant treasurer. Corporate trust.

She said, "Tebogo. But they call me Tebby."

"My name is Bruno. And people call me Bruno."

He smiled. She smiled.

She said, "Call anytime. Or e-mail. If not, it was still nice meeting you, Bruno."

"I'll call you, Tebby. Just tell me when is a good time."

"Anytime, Bruno. Call if you need something, call if you just want to call."

"Maybe we could meet at Starbucks and chat."

"That would be lovely."

"You could tell me more about Botswana."

"And you can tell me more about America. I plan to move there one day."

"Do you?"

"Yes. I want to become an American. I want to have my own restaurant. I'm desperate to leave London and move to America. I'd go to the airport and leave right now if I could."

There was a pause between them.

She said, "I love your American accent."

Then she waved good-bye and headed into the Tower Hill tube station.

The last thing he saw as she vanished was her smile.

And that angelic whiteness in a sea of dark and dreary colors.

His cellular rang again. Not the personal one. The hotline.

He answered, "Talk to me."

All the shyness in his voice now replaced by brutal harshness.

"Located a Desert Eagle. Titanium finish. Found it in Banglatown."

"That was quick."

"Everybody knows everybody in this area. Made a few calls. Called a guy I know out at the military base and he put me in contact with a supplier I know in Brixton. Found what you need in the East End. Sure you want a Desert Eagle? Weighs five pounds. Supplier is getting it, adding a markup to stay in the loop. So pricewise you're looking at about seventeen hundred pounds."

"How do I get it from your contact?"

"Already arranged pickup."

"How will I know the contact?"

"My contact will recognize you."

He touched his nose. "What about the cleanup job?"

"Will have information on that job later today. No later than tomorrow."

"If you don't have it tomorrow, I'm on a plane."

"Understood."

He was told where to pick up the Desert Eagle.

He hung up, then looked at the white-and-gray business card in his callused hand.

Tebby never asked about his broken nose. But he had never mentioned her bald head.

His other phone rang. The friends and family line.

He answered, "Hello. This is Edward Johnson."

"And this is Melanie Marie Johnson."

"Melanie." He laughed. "Hey, baby. How's daddy's little princess?"

"Mommy told me you were in London."

"Yeah. You mad? I'm going to have to stay a few days."

"No, it's cool. I want all the Harry Potter books."

"You already have all the Harry Potter books."

"Not from London. I want them with the London publisher's cover and the price tag in pounds. I want it authentic. In hardback if you can find them. Please, Daddy, please?"

"Okay. I'll try and find them."

"I want to make all of my friends jealous."

"That's not a guarantee. I'll do my best."

"And magnets. Buy me Harry Potter magnets. I'll pay you back out of my allowance."

"You always say that."

"And take a picture of the *Cutty Sark*. Kisses. Love you, Daddy."

"Love you too."

They hung up.

Damn shame how a ten-year-old kid had him doing flips for her.

He smiled. If only buying Harry Potter books could fix all of his problems.

So little joy in the world. He'd make sure his ten-year-old got as much joy as possible.

He checked into Novotel. He had wanted something more discreet. But the woman he had met. Tebby. Maybe she lived in the area. She was at that Starbucks, after all. Maybe she'd meet him at Starbucks again. Or in the area for dinner and drinks. He checked in, got his room key, but didn't go up to his suite; instead he came right back out for the tube.

He wanted to have on clean clothes when he saw her again.

Maybe a nice European suit with one-and-a-quarter-inch cuffs.

No way he could wear the same clothes and see her again.

A Motswana woman from Botswana. That in itself was intriguing.

His phone rang again. The hotline.

He answered, "Talk to me."

"The contract is on a guy who uses the handle Gideon. He calls himself Gideon."

"That's it? Just Gideon?"

"That's it."

"Was expecting something more menacing."

"Well, Bruno isn't exactly gruesome."

"It's Italian. It's Mafia. I like the *Godfather* movies. Bruno is a kick-ass name."

"Well, this guy calls himself Gideon."

"What else you got for me?"

"Got more information coming in later."

"Don't keep yanking my chain."

"I assure you that a package is being sent to me as we speak."

"Could you be a little more vague, Sam?"

"My apologies to you, Bruno. They are dragging on the other end."

"Well, tell them to be professional. Respect my fucking time."

"But I should have the info soon."

"When is soon? Thanksgiving? Christmas?"

"Within the hour. In the meantime, my cranky friend, get some sleep."

He rubbed his jet-lagged eyes. "Call me when you get the package."

He hung up.

Harry Potter books.

He had to find Harry Potter books.

If his princess wanted Harry Potter himself, he'd kidnap the boy, take the bastard to her.

He was anxious to take this contract, kill the target, then go back home, eat some authentic Mexican food.

As far as he was concerned, Gideon was already a dead man.

And that was nothing but business. He was in the business of killing.

Fourteen

like oil on my skin

I was inside Benjy's deli.

The dead entertainer I was supposed to look for was standing across the street.

I was on the edge of the theater district, six lanes of insane traffic separating me from the Dominion Theatre. On top of the Dominion a larger-than-life-but-smaller-than-legend-size golden statue of Freddie Mercury was on the roof. The Queen Musical, *We Will Rock You*.

I was waiting between Chinatown and Bloomsbury, underneath the shadows of Centre Point Tower. Next door was a grungy-looking theatre-club that advertised Betty-somebody and some punk-rock-looking group whose name was the acronym GAY. I sipped on a green tea, reading Metro.Co.UK, an article about poor areas having the fewest free ATMs. The poor getting scammed, being once again penalized for being poor.

I looked up, didn't see her, checked my watch, went back to the paper.

Channel 4 was planning to screen Britain's first marathon masturbation event, called Wankathon. They were giving prizes to people who could have the most orgasms and masturbate the longest. Faking an orgasm could get you disqualified, and the record for the longest masturbation session was eight and a half hours. The Brits were special people.

Saw nothing about Tampa. Had to let that go. Was getting obsessed.

I looked at my watch and yawned. Sleep was trying to invade my body.

The people next to me were speaking French with a distinctive accent and vocabulary. "Secret Lovers" was on the sound system, Atlantic Starr sounding twice as popular here as they did on the other side of the pond. No matter if I was at a club over in Brixton or walking through one of the shops in Oxford Circus, I always heard more American music than I did British.

Above me, a small television was on. Still on the story about the dead WAG.

I looked across the street at the tube exit. A Filipina with skin the hue of sunrise over Ipanema was over in the crowd by Freddie Mercury, coming up from the tube.

She put her cellular up to her face.

My cellular rang.

I answered, "I'm inside Benjy's."

She hung up.

Black jeans. White sweater. Long black coat. Umbrella up high.

First she crossed in front of Centre Point; that left her one more intersection to negotiate before she made it to me. She passed by a man with a sign advertising Internet access at the cost of one British pound per hour. She passed by two police officers. They don't carry guns, just handcuffs. Hard to be afraid of a gunless cop. A cop with no gun was a security guard.

London was filled with thieves. On the tubes and in stores were continuous announcements to watch out for pickpockets, who preyed on the inattentive. Cafés had signs posted telling patrons to beware of thieves they called slashers, nimble-fingered crooks who would cut open your bags and catch the goods as they fell out. Plenty of nimble fingers in the U.K. lot who worked in groups and had mastered the art of distraction and blocking.

The woman coming my way would put all of London's criminals to shame.

Her name was Arizona. People in my dark world knew her as Queen Scamz.

I fell in lust with her the moment I laid eyes on her, as most straight men did. That was in North Hollywood, when she was a young girl who had nothing but ambition in her eyes. Back then she was in love with Scamz, the man who slapped her silly, the man who had made her his number one, then, in the blink of an eye, replaced her with her own sister. Back then Arizona was a flight attendant, using her job pre-9/11 to be a mule for some of Scamz's illegal ventures, and her sister was working as a teller at a Wells Fargo in Hollywood. Arizona had brought her in on a job. Once her sister met Scamz, she had ambitions of her own, and her desires paid no mind to upstaging and dethroning Arizona.

We had that in common. Both of us had been betrayed by people we cared about.

Arizona crossed the street. Two men were about ten yards behind her, had been behind her since she exited the tube. Both of those men wore thick coats on top of black hoodies.

Arizona came in the door, umbrella at her side, bags under her eyes, lips tight.

I watched the men who were keeping up with her.

They kept going toward Leicester Square, now looking at other women.

I rubbed my temples, released my paranoia, let it float up toward the ozone.

Arizona made her way to where I was sitting, said, "You're early."

"Early is on time. On time is late."

She nodded. "And late is unacceptable."

I stood to hug her, but she extended her hand.

I said, "So it's like that."

She nodded once, her hand still extended, firm in her decision.

I extended my hand for a curt handshake, all business.

Last time I saw her we did things that would make porn stars take notes.

She opened the *Evening Standard* newspaper in her hand. Once again the Big Bad Wolf stared at me. It was international. Nothing to be proud of. It had followed me across the pond.

I said, "Already saw it."

She said, "This place is too small, too crowded. Let's walk and talk."

We fought the crowd, passed by Borders. Soho Original Books. Blackwell's. Lovejoys. Murder One. Henry Pordes. One look down any street and it was obvious that the British were literary. Bookshops were every ten feet, if not less, each one filled with book-hungry customers.

She asked, "WAG job?"

"Wasn't me. Sounded like a crime of passion. That was a hit?"

"Heard somebody was looking for somebody to take that contract."

"And you didn't refer me?"

"Needed you for horse-and-grass country. Need you to handle Lakenheath."

Brazilian. Indian. Chinese. International food was everywhere, just like hiking down Broadway in New York, or being on South Beach, minus the palm trees and sunshine. There were enough Burger Kings and McDonald's and Pizza Huts to make every foreigner feel at home. But it was the other shops I always noticed. In my world Starbucks ruled; here Starbucks was outnumbered by both bookshops and alternative coffee spots like Caffè Nero.

I said, "Why you pick me for this job?"

"Got fucked over on a Katrina scam."

"You know what I mean. I know him."

"He's afraid of you."

"And I'd be a fool to go after him."

"Asshole owes me a lot of money. No one else I can send to make my point. Everyone else is afraid of him. He knows you. Respects you. He'll be cool with you. He'll listen to you."

"How much he get you for?"

"The amount is irrelevant. But it's a lot. I taught him how to work FEMA like FEMA was nothing more than a pigeon drop. He made a quick grip. Refused to pay my percentage."

"Double cross on a Katrina scam? Scamming a scammer?"

"You know? Motherfuckers still don't think I'm for real. Some of them misogynistic pricks still refuse to take a woman seriously, Gideon. Looks like I have to send out another message."

"Hard business for women. Maybe you should get out and slow down. Have babies."

"I'm not the type for being barefoot and pregnant."

"Too bad. You have pretty feet."

"I was going to call Switchblade Molly in on this one, but she's too messy."

"She did some good work for your boy Scamz back in the day."

"She did. But that was ten years ago. When she was younger. She earned her moniker one hundred times over."

"I'll ride up to Lakenheath Village and take care of it."

We hurried by theaters, coffeehouses, bars, and Internet cafés, put her umbrella up high, dodged puddles, and headed toward one of the busiest spots in London. She told me there was a nice Starbucks across from the Odeon, this location being the home of the U.K. movie premieres, the U.K. version of Holly-wood's Grauman's Chinese Theatre. The area had been cleaned up. The small patch in the center of the square used to be a haven for junkies. Now it was safe to wander through the grass without tripping over piles of old, used needles, and still-damp condoms.

She asked, "You been back to New Orleans since Katrina?"

"Nope. Just saw it on the news. How bad was it up close?"

"Ninth Ward looks like a bomb was dropped on it. Houses stacked on top of houses. Cars on top of cars. Insurance companies don't want to pay. That's the scam right there. They blame the flooding on the levee, not Katrina. Don't get me started on that crap. Material cost has shot through the roof. And gas prices are crazy. And they are still pulling dead bodies out of the buildings. Hell, most of the evacuees are running scams. Half of them weren't doing anything before Katrina, then they were getting two grand a month from FEMA, so they came up big-time."

"FEMA. Bet you tapped into that and made a mint."

"FEMA stands for Fuck Everybody with Melanin in America."

"Of course."

"And, yeah, I hit FEMA harder than Katrina hit New Orleans."

We passed by several spots to buy theater tickets. Saw a big poster for *One Flew over the Cuckoo's Nest*, Christian Slater starring in that one. *Stomp* had huge posters too.

I spied the TKTS booth, the only freestanding building in the square, but didn't see any ads for *Rent*. So many productions were posted. Impossible to notice everything.

I held Arizona's umbrella up over our heads as we entered the square and passed by all the tourist traps and souvenir shops, made our way across the cobblestone walkway leading to the center of the square and went inside Starbucks. Arizona ordered a latte. I went to the counter, ordered a house coffee, then found out that they didn't honor the U.S.'s Starbucks gift cards in this country. The man behind the counter apologized, and I paid in pounds and pence.

I told the server, "Lots of coffee drinkers. Thought Brits liked teas."

"There are no real Brits left in the London area. Immigrants have taken over. And immigrants bring their own tastes with them. I'm a Brit by birth and I only drink tea."

I thanked him and moved on.

This Starbucks was large, most of the seating being in the back of the space. By the time I had put four sugars in my tall cup of joe, Arizona had a table in the back of the room, away from everyone, but still surrounded with enough noise to keep other people out of our conversation.

She said, "Did you see the statue of Shakespeare out front?"

"Shakespeare was a master plagiarist. He stole Francis Bacon's work."

"Before we have that debate, let's get to the business I have for you."

Arizona opened her bag, took out a folder, a profile on my target.

She said, "Inside is a travel card good for all week."

"Why didn't you get me an Oyster card? I could've done a top up."

"Don't use an Oyster. It's an electronic card, just like the Octopus card in Hong Kong. Those cards leave electronic bread crumbs. So every time you touch in or touch out, Big Brother knows where you are. Use an Oyster and Scotland Yard knows your travel habits. They know where you get on the tube, where you get off the tube. They know where you get on the buses."

"You have an Oyster card."

"Mine was bought with a hot credit card. Under a fake name. A man's name. And I switch Oyster cards throughout the day."

"So you have extras."

"I'm prepared."

She dug into her bag, took out another Oyster card, threw it to me.

I said, "You think like a man."

"I'm too smart to be a man. That's why I'm a woman."

"Did you go to terrorist training school or something?"

"I'm too smart to be a terrorist too."

I yawned. "All the CCTV cameras. London is starting to feel like one big-ass prison."

"Put up some barbed wire and it would be. Surveillance cameras are both underground and on the platforms. Cameras are on the buses. Bobbies walking the street like guards."

"Are you a terrorist?"

"Just letting you know. If you're traveling, if you're trying to not be seen, trying not to be found, pay cash for a travel card, ride the tube, blend with the crowd, and vanish in the system."

Then she handed me a passport, this one deep red. It had the same photo as my blue one, the one made in the U.S. For the next few hours I would be a British citizen named Clive.

I asked, "This clean?"

"From a newborn. That's the best way to do identity theft. Not from the dead, but from a newborn. Takes years, since a newborn or a kid won't apply for credit anytime soon."

She tapped the information.

She said, "Handle Lakenheath as soon as you can."

Her fingers lingered on the information. I reached for her hand. She jerked it away.

I asked, "Why the attitude?"

"As soon as it's done, the rest of the money will be transferred to your account."

We sat there, Arizona finishing off the last of her coffee.

The moment reminded me of sitting at the kitchen table and watching my mother drink Folgers coffee in the morning. We used to leave our rattrap in the heart of the neglected

Dalton Village, abandon West Charlotte, and ride through the sweet, much-loved areas like Myers Park, ride by those homes in South Charlotte screaming and pointing like I was on a ride at Six Flags Over Georgia. Looked at big homes the way people admired art at the Louvre. Loved them in the wintertime. Didn't really snow in Charlotte, but the ice storms would come and make all the bare trees look like they were silver master-pieces. So much beauty inside that danger.

When I gazed at Arizona, I saw the opposite, so much danger inside beauty.

Arizona spoke in a soft, almost vulnerable tone. "I started watching *Battlestar Galactica*."

"No shit?"

"Because of you, I watched that show because of you."

"You say that like it's a bad thing."

"Liked the Cylons. Love when slaves rise up and defeat the master. Racism. Battles amongst the classes. Sexism. Fear. So much hate wrapped around one television show."

"Like . . . life. Hate has put a lot of money in my pockets."

She said, "I have a theory on why people don't respect black Americans."

"I'm listening."

"Because black Americans never rose up and defeated their master. They were enslaved by the master and had to be freed by the master. There was no victory."

"The Cylons will be respected."

"No, the Cylons will be *feared*. That's *better* than being respected."

Her intense stare, it didn't wane.

Without transition she asked, "Who's the woman who went to the hotel with you?"

I took a breath. "A square. Met her on the plane."

"Don't mess with squares. What do you know about her?"

"She was looking for a room, checked out the hotel."

"Is that right? Where is she now?"

"Well, Arizona, I offered you first right of refusal."

"Keep it professional, Gideon."

"So New York and Chapel Hill didn't happen?"

"No idea what you're talking about."

"You're breaking my heart."

"When did you get a heart?"

"Why are you being so damn nasty to me?"

"Doesn't matter. I'm a bang-and-go kind of gal anyway. At least that's how you see me."

"Yeah, you're breaking my heart."

"Better yours than mine. Actually mine has already been shattered."

"Can't break what has already been broken."

"Abso-fucking-lutely."

"Hold up. How did you know someone came to the hotel with me?"

"Maybe I came to see you. Maybe I thought about Chapel Hill and New York and wanted to see you again. Maybe I was going to surprise you and get beans and eggs and toast for breakfast. Maybe I was outside your hotel room. Maybe I heard you fucking your concubine."

If water fell on her skin, it would sizzle away.

She dug inside her bag, took out three CDs. Miles, Wes, and Coltrane.

She put them on the table, slid those legends toward me, her anger controlled.

I had given her those CDs as a gift. Now she was rejecting the memory.

I said, "Keep 'em."

Arizona shook her head. I saw the tempest in her expression, the frost in her eyes.

That femme fatale owned beauty and more danger than an ice storm in North Carolina.

Then I saw another kind of danger.

I said, "Sit down."

"Fuck you."

I gave her a broad smile. "No, sit down."

"I'm not your whore. I don't work for you."

I added a light laugh. "We're being watched."

She hesitated. "Don't play with me."

"We're being trailed."

Fifteen

chinatown

That had Arizona's attention.

I told her that the men who had followed her from the tube were in the room. Their hoodies had been pulled back. I got a clear view of our present danger. One was bald, the other sported locks. They had slipped inside and posted up in the section of Starbucks between us and the front door. There was only one way in and one way out. They weren't that close. The coffeeshop was large, could be divided into three sections, us being in the back third. Neither had a coffee or a newspaper. They were waiting for something, and I knew it wasn't the tube.

I told Arizona all of that with smiles and laughter.

Arizona sat back down, did that real ladylike, crossed her legs, played with her hair.

Then she chuckled and smiled like everything was okay.

I did the same, kept the game going.

She asked, "You sure they're following me? They could be following you."

"They were behind you when you showed up at Freddie Mercury."

"Who are they?"

"Thought they might be part of the Tampa crew."

"Thought you handled them."

"Rappers are like roaches."

"Cockroaches."

"Can't kill 'em all."

"Not even with a nuclear explosion."

Between us, we'd offended so many people that death or justice could come at any time with any face. I'd been that death for many people, enough to earn me damn near a million.

Arizona tensed. Then she smiled again. "Okay, I'll leave first. See if they follow me."

"Which way?"

"Pass by Häagen-Dazs Café, get to Charing Cross, make a left, first narrow street turn left again, that'll take you off the main drag and into Chinatown. Head toward car park on the right."

I nodded. "Left out of Starbucks and two more lefts to car park."

"Gideon. If it's the police on my ass, let it go, okay? Let them take me and let it go."

That hurt my heart. "Just make it around the block as soon as you can."

"You know the rules. If it's the police and they're after you, I'll have to do the same."

"I know."

Arizona took a small package out of her bag.

She said, "Forgot to put this jewelry with your special order."

She slid that package across the table toward me.

Arizona picked up Miles, Trane, and Wes, held them in her hand, put on a sweet smile, blew me a kiss good-bye, got up, and walked away. I picked up a left-behind copy of *The Daily Telegraph*, pretended I was reading about the twelve who bankrolled Tony Blair into a loan crisis, then spied toward the front of Starbucks again, toward the two men who had raised my senses.

I wanted them to be after me, not Arizona. I'd lead them in the opposite direction.

But the second she walked out of Starbucks, they were hot on her trail.

As soon as they hit the front door, I was on my feet, grabbed what Arizona had left behind, opened it as I moved with quickness, walking fast enough to keep them in sight.

Brass knuckles. Arizona had given me brass knuckles.

Arizona was making her way through the sea of people crowding Leicester Square.

They were focused on her, gradually getting closer, keeping her in sight.

I was right behind them, separated by a decent crowd of tourists and locals.

I expected one—if not both—to look back. They never did.

They weren't pros. Not even close. But that didn't make them any less of a threat.

They got closer to Arizona.

I sped up, got closer to them.

The neon signs and Eastern structures of Chinatown rose up.

Two lefts and a right later, I ran into a wall of Chinese food.

The stench of egg fried rice and lo mein took me back to Tampa, turned my stomach.

Arizona moved through all the Asians on the plaza, strolled like she was about to pass by the car park and head toward the section of Soho dedicated to the queer and gothic, but she made an abrupt right turn, her casual walk changing into a fierce run.

That sudden change in direction and sprint surprised her stalkers.

The men broke into a trot trying to catch her.

Arizona was fast, moved like greased lightning.

She'd been chased before. She'd been chased and never been caught.

I broke into a sprint, cold and damp air in my face, trying to keep up with them.

They raced inside the covered lot, looked left and right, heard something, footsteps running, and they ran up the curved exit. When they made it to the next floor, they were winded. Confused. They looked between cars, then looked behind them, saw me standing there. Watching. Relaxed. Hands in my pockets, I faced my new dilemma eye to eye.

I said, "Amazing how she vanishes. Like smoke. Poof. She's gone."

A few automobiles and a motorcycle exited the car park with us staring.

We were up a level, away from the eyes of the public.

I took a step forward, my foot landing in a puddle, splashing water.

The one with dreadlocks was five foot eleven, the shorter of the two. His silent friend was taller, larger, owned the mean face. Obviously the enforcer.

I asked, "Who sent you?"

"Who the fuck are you?" Dreadlocks was the spokesman.

Hands in pockets, eyes on my new friends, I inhaled deeply, let it out slowly.

They came closer. Closer. I went numb. Detached myself from the moment.

Then they were close enough to hurt me.

The smaller one stayed back at least three steps.

The big one came at me ready to do damage. He came after me like I had gone after others. I held my position. Nervous. Scared. Excited. Sweating. Numb. I was all of that.

I knew twenty-two ways to kill a man with my bare hands. But only one way to die.

In an accented voice Dreadlocks asked, "Where is Queen Scamz?"

A car was zooming down the ramp. The car was half the size of a Mini Cooper, even smaller than the popular Smart car. It was one of the short and slender LUV cars big enough for two anorexic midgets. That car was quiet and moved like a bullet.

The car hit Dreadlocks dead on, flipped him, and knocked his ass to the side. His dreads whipped around his face as he grunted and slammed into one of the concrete pillars, went down headfirst, landed in a way that told me he wouldn't be getting up anytime soon, if at all.

Arizona put on her brakes, got out of that fuel-efficient weapon on four wheels.

The big one that had come up on me with fists doubled, that crash had stolen his attention. Now he was suffering blow after blow, bending, grunting, bleeding, going down hard and fast. Ten hard and fast blows from my right hand to his face and ribs left his face broken beyond belief. I had slipped on the brass knuckles Arizona had slid me. He'd wake up in a London hospital, pissing blood, a tube in his nose, and a shit bag strapped to his hip.

Then I was surprised. The other one, after being run down, moaned and got up.

Head bloodied, dreadlocks swaying, he staggered toward the exit. His right arm looked broken. He was whimpering and limping like a monster out of a late-night creature feature. Moved like he was in "Thriller." Arizona's arms pumped and her heels clacked on the pavement as she ran after him.

He tried to speed up, but only made it to a slow, stumbling, pain-filled trot.

Arizona stopped running, walked after him, looking around, weapon in hand.

He must've been delirious, in shock, because he headed up the ramp.

Arizona didn't run, just walked after the crippled man.

I was a few feet behind her, made sure the one on the ground stayed on the ground.

They vanished around a curve.

When I caught up with the pandemonium, Arizona wasn't walking anymore.

She was focused, aiming, had her arm pulled back. Knife in hand. She slung her blade.

A painful sound echoed from around the corner.

Then Arizona was walking again, her steps a lot quicker.

Dreadlocks was on the ground trying to pull a five-inch blade out of the back of his thigh.

I told Arizona, "Your aim is pretty good."

"Was aiming at his neck."

"Your aim sucks."

"Fuck you."

"Thought I taught you better."

"Well, I'm not as good as you. But I'm good enough, dammit."

While Arizona stood over Dreadlocks and put pressure on the blade, I put my shoe stiff against the back of his neck, my weight pushing his face deep into the cold pavement. Fear rose up from the trembling man. Piss drained from between his legs and mixed with his river of blood.

Arizona frowned at me. "Do you mind?"

"Sorry."

I backed away, became her wingman.

This was her show. I kept a lookout and let her have it her way.

Arizona's voice filled with anger as she demanded, "Who hired you?"

He refused to answer.

She brought the blade out again.

For a moment I thought she was about to cut his throat.

He battled with the hurting.

She pressed on the knife. "See what I mean? Motherfuckers think I'm a joke."

Arizona brought the blade down into his arm; that improved his hearing and memory.

"Lakenheath. Call came from Lakenheath. Military guy. That's all I know."

He tried to scream, but the blade had been moved to his neck; that muted his agony.

Arizona fumed, "How much you get paid?"

"Twenty-five hundred euros."

Either way Arizona was insulted at such a low offering.

She asked, "Where you from?"

"Haarlem."

"You don't sound like you're from New York."

I interrupted, "His accent is Dutch. He's talking about Haarlem in the Netherlands."

Arizona snapped at me, "Do you mind?"

I raised my hand in apology.

She took her fury back to Dreadlocks.

"Holland? You came from Holland?"

He nodded again. "On the train. We came on the train."

"To kill me?"

He didn't answer. She pressed on that knife. Drew more blood.

He confessed, "Hurt you. Break your arms. Your knees. Cut off all of your hair. Rape you. But we weren't going to rape you. Honest."

"Just cut off my hair and break my knees and crush all my bones."

"That's all."

Her eyes told me she was about to become a murderer.

Then she backed away.

She asked, "Are we done? Or do I need to take this to the next level?"

Again he managed a nod, then he shook his head.

I looked at Arizona.

She shook her head. "Fucking amateurs."

Arizona knew what this was about.

Arizona took her blade, the blade that had her fingerprints all over the handle, and wiped the blood on the man's coat, dropped the weapon inside her bag, and walked around the curve toward the edges of Chinatown, headed back the same way we had come with a generous pace.

I called out to her, asked, "What about your car?"

"Not mine. Hot-wired it."

"That was quick."

"Used to be quicker. Leave it where it is."

A few seconds passed, enough time for Arizona to get to the first level.

I headed toward the big guy I had taken down.

He was fucked up, crawling across the pavement, trying to run away from his pain.

I walked by him.

I dropped the brass knuckles inside my pocket.

Looked back at the wrecked LUV and the men on the ground.

I buttoned my coat, adjusted my scarf, and walked away.

At the bottom of the ramp, hundreds of Asians were moving through the area, a few were looking at the mouth of the car park. They looked at it all from a distance. Maybe they had heard the whole thing. I expected them to either point fingers or run away from me. But they stood, smoked hand-rolled cigarettes, and watched in silence. Like we were a show on HBO.

Arizona was standing to my left, the way we had come.

Head down, shoulders hunched, I headed that way.

When I got to her, she pushed the CDs back into my hands.

Two men lay bleeding on frozen concrete and we were back to that heated argument.

I said, "These were for you."

"Take them back to your hotel and give them to your concubine."

She moved on, shoulders hunched, her head down as well.

Arizona lit up a Djarum, walked away blowing smoke, leaving the scent of cloves behind.

I followed her. She'd become a female version of James Dean.

She sped up.

Now she was running from me, heading across St. Martin's Lane into Covent Garden, her cellular phone in hand. She was outside the tube station before she slowed down.

My cellular rang. I answered.

Arizona snapped, "Stop following me."

"I'm trying to make sure you're okay."

"If I need you, I will call you."

I pressed on, "When I finish here, I want to get away from all of this. I want to take you with me."

"Gideon, I'm not your girlfriend. Not trying to be. Never will be."

In a few words she stripped my heart down to nothing.

I hung up.

My phone rang. It was Arizona.

She said, "Look, on the business tip, I have another job for you."

"Outside of the work here in London?"

"Holland. Looks like I need to send a message to someone in Holland."

"The Holland boys said they were working for Lakenheath."

"Don't believe everything you hear."

"What do you know that I don't know?"

"Just handle Lakenheath. Holland will be there. Go do what you do best."

That put fire in my gut.

"Now on personal level, stop following me, Gideon. Please stop, okay?"

She stopped and faced me, stood waiting for me to leave her alone.

She said, "No expectations, no disappointments."

She hung up. I did the same.

Dark clouds clung to heaven's floor, rain fell, I turned around, went the other way.

Way down, at least a block away, I thought I saw bandages on the nose of a bald man in a dark suit. The man from the airplane. He was turning around, hurrying away from me.

Like he had been following me. Following us. Now he had been seen.

I jogged to the corner and looked into the crowd. Didn't see him. Saw lots of men in suits. But none were bald. Too many narrow streets feeding into narrow streets to check them all. Maybe paranoia and tiredness were teaming up with my guilt and making me see things. I rubbed my eyes and looked back. Hurried back toward where I had left Arizona. She was gone. Didn't know if she had kept going through Covent Garden toward the Embankment or had hurried down into the tube station.

I called Arizona's cellular. Her calls were being diverted.

I left her a message. "I think those guys had a wingman. Be careful. Hit me back."

Rain fell soft and easy. I crossed into Leicester Square, heard the wail of ambulances roaring toward Chinatown, saw policemen on BMW motorcycles zooming the same way.

I kept going, made a right at TGIF, moved by theaters and pubs, zigzagged toward the red-light district, always looking back, or checking windows to see if I was being trailed. The way the city was laid out, all the narrow streets that fed into even narrower streets, with the number of tube stations and places to vanish in an instant, no wonder Jack the Ripper was never caught.

I stopped at the edges of the red-light district, an area that, in the middle of the day, looked respectable; vendors were out in the cold selling fruit, fish, odds and ends. People were inside Somerfield food-shopping. Others were at the various porn stores, shopping there too.

Men were slipping inside narrow doors that led to Russian and Asian pussy for sale.

I looked up, saw African whores, Spanish whores, red lights in almost every window.

I moved on toward Oxford Circus, Thelma on my mind.

I'd find her one day.

No matter where she'd run, I'd find her and finish what we'd started.

I stopped and bought warmer clothes.

Needed heavier jeans, thermals, a turtleneck, boots, and a short leather jacket that zipped. Had to dump what I had on, in case blood had splattered on me from the crime scene we'd just created. Thirty minutes later I came out in Soho looking brand-new from head to toe and in between, dumped my old clothes, then hit the main drag at Oxford Circus, an area as busy as Chicago's Magnificent Mile, blended with the crowd. I went down into the tube, waited on a Central Line train to take me to the Northern Line, would take that line one stop over to Goodge and get off there. I walked back to the room and grabbed my backpack.

Had to take the tube to the Liverpool station.

It was time to go visit a man on Arizona's behalf.

Like I had done for her when we connected in New York.

When that delinquent debt had to be settled.

Only this was somebody I knew.

We weren't the best of friends, but we were a long way from being enemies.

This was a merciless business.

A different kind of coldness came and hugged me.

The kind of iciness that came with my complex occupation.

It was time to bundle up and go to work.

My hands trembled again as I changed from the tube to the Stansted Express and headed toward horse-and-grass country. The place that in the summertime, with all the fertilizer in the air, they called horse-and-*smells-like-ass* country. My hands trembled the entire forty-six minutes I was on the train, trembled as the airport came in sight. They wouldn't stop trembling.

As I exited the train, that feeling of death moved through me, tried to cling to me, but I shook it off. In the middle of the terminal, people all around me, I stopped walking. A wave hit me. Coldness. Followed by numbness. Followed by an almost unbearable heat.

I looked down at the three CDs I still had in my hand.

Memories of New York clung to me. I thought about the fun we'd had in Chapel Hill.

I stuffed those CDs in my backpack and found my way to underground parking.

I walked until I found a row of motorcycles, stopped in front of a BMW 1200. Light blue, helmet attached to locking strap. Keys were in my backpack. I took out a black key and a red key. The black key opened the sidesaddles, where I found gloves. Two small bottles were there as well. One was a small bottle of Jack Daniel's. The other a special order. The same key also unlocked the helmet and started the engine. The bike was still warm. Hadn't been here too long.

Minutes after that, I was easing around the roundabout, getting a feel for the machine, then I was speeding down M11 north. Thoughts of Arizona, thoughts of Chapel Hill never left. As I changed from A11 to A14 and back to A11 again, as I zoomed down a two-lane highway by grass and horses and sheep, as I slowed for speed cameras as I entered Suffolk County, Miles, Wes, and Coltrane stayed on my mind.

Sixteen

contract killer

Docklands Light Railway.

Aboveground train. Heading toward Canary Wharf.

The man with the broken nose had been turned around all morning. He had taken the tube to Embankment. But he was supposed to be at Bank to catch the DLR. Embankment had sounded like Bank. When he realized he was at the wrong location, Embankment not Bank, he looked for Bank on the tube map again. That labyrinth of tubes was confusing. Didn't look like it was that far. Hoping to have better luck, he had taken to the streets, got lost again, ended up at Covent Garden, then hurried back inside the tube, took the Piccadilly to the Central Line, finally made it to Bank and the DLR.

Brits and their fucking accents. Felt like he was in a damn Harry Potter movie.

That reminded him. He had to find a bookstore. Had to buy books and magnets.

For a moment, when he was lost at Covent Garden, it felt like he was being followed.

But no one was there.

No one had boarded the train with him. No one on the platform shadowed him.

The ride was shoulder to shoulder.

People were forced to touch other people.

His personal space no longer existed.

He hated public transportation. One look and he could tell the tubes were a breeding ground for germs, people coughing and sneezing and blowing their noses all over, breathing the same germ-ridden air stop after stop, nasty hands touching the same seats and holding the same contaminated rails, everyone forced to be right up on each other in flu and cold season. Two hundred and seventy-five tube stations. Two hundred and seventy-five places to get contaminated. Maybe a million people crammed on the tube each day. If bin Laden dropped a virus at Victoria, London would be extinct in two days, the rest of the free world in less than a week.

He understood why people in Tokyo wore those Michael Jackson–style surgical masks.

The DLR was better. He had his own seat. A grubby seat, but he had his own space.

And he had a better view to see if he was being trailed.

The WAG had become the talk of London.

He had to make sure someone hadn't targeted him for cleanup.

That being-followed feeling he had had at Covent Garden had stayed with him.

Until now.

He let it go and took out his over-the-counter reading glasses, opened his self-help book.

He had his glasses on, adjusted over his bandaged nose, again reading pages in *Divorce for Dummies*. He didn't look up. His contact would know him. Hard for him to not be recognized, broken nose and all. Still, for some reason, even with that, he was invisible to most people.

No one ever noticed Clark Kent until he became Superman.

That always worked in his favor.

He put his book down and picked up a discarded *London Lite*. A sex-slave market was being operated out of Heathrow. Young Malaysian women were being tricked into coming to London, ending up working at brothels in Campden Hill Gardens, Notting Hill, and Hyde Park, a few feet from Tony Blair's swank Connaught Square property.

He shook his head. Would kill them all if they even glanced at his little girl.

The DLR stopped at West India Quay.

A small crowd rushed on the train. Men. Women pushing strollers. Boys with backpacks. Four teenage girls boarded last. One took a can of Red Bull out of her backpack. Another took out plastic cups. A third took out a bottle of Scotch and became the bartender.

They made drinks and moved to the front of the car. Like it was no big deal.

The fourth young girl was staring at him. He nodded. She stood up. Thin kid, five feet tall, if that. Black parachute pants with a thousand silver zippers. Black military shoes. Black hoodie with a white smiling face on the front. Red-and-black fingerless gloves, fingernails the color of midnight. Her hoodie was pulled down over her head, only parts of her face showing. Her eyes as red as week-old ketchup that had been left out in the sun. She had a copy of *The Voice* in one hand and a green backpack in the other. The backpack had some weight. A black iPod was on her narrow hip, headsets were on, hip-hop blasting. Sounded like British rap.

The girl looked him in the face, exchanged a slight nod, then sat next to him.

The girl said, "Sam I am."

Her tongue ring showed.

He nodded. "Green eggs and ham."

She looked Cherokee Indian. Her accent very London, like everyone's.

Her breath smelled like hard liquor, cigarettes, and beans.

He moved to the back of the train. No one was there.

She followed.

They sat at the same time.

She asked, "What's happened to the nose, mate?"

"Nothing I care to talk about."

"Looks like you got in a row and got your bloody ass kicked."

"You have my order?"

The girl nodded. "Need anything let me know. I have a connection at Scotland Yard that's pilfering a mad load of guns from the Operation Trident program. Guns they take from minorities. Right now I could supply Iraq. Revolvers, machine guns, MAC-10 if you want to do a spray-and-pray. Crack cocaine, cannabis, CS sprays. I can get anything you need."

"How old are you?"

"Fourteen. If you need some Charlie, I can get you a deal."

He nodded. Wondered what his daughter would be like in four years.

He said, "I need clean barrels for the Eagle."

"How many?"

"Half a dozen."

"Have drops in Colindale and High Barnet, then I'll get you what I can. François might have them. Tell Sam to tell me and I'll get you what you need. Remember. Handguns. MAC-10. Cocaine. Crack. Cannabis. I'm the one you need to go to. Ask Sam. He'll tell you."

The train slowed down. The next exit Mudchute.

"Or if you know somebody chav or stoosh, I can get you gold, Burberry, anything bling."

Cellular up to her ear, the girl exited at the next stop.

The girls who were drinking Red Bull and Scotch exited too. They handed her a cup of their mixed drink. They all walked away like nothing they were doing was a big deal.

He wondered what *chav* and *stoosh* meant.

The green backpack was left behind. So was a newspaper. He

looked at the front page. Article on the new trend sweeping across the nation, rich trailer trash going to third-world countries and buying black and brown babies like they were shopping at a pet store. The things rich trailer-trash people did when they were bored. The newspaper had no messages, no significance. It was tossed.

He pulled the backpack closer to him.

Then he pulled out one of his cellular phones. Dialed.

A man answered. "Talk to me."

"What kind of shit was that?"

"So you met Zankhana."

"What kind of name is that?"

"Hindu."

"Shouldn't she be in school playing tetherball?"

"Guess you haven't heard about the kids over here. They are the worst."

"This gunrunning teenage alcoholic know what she's doing?"

"Big shoot-outs in London over the last few weeks. Albanians' card club in Park Royal, three dead. Guy shot up a McDonald's in Brixton. Another man shot in the face at Harlesden."

"And London doesn't have a death penalty."

"Abolished in the United Kingdom under the 1965 Murder Act."

"So you're telling me that fourteen-year-old Zankhana supplied all the guns."

"Zankhana is a piece of work. All the gangsters know her. She supplied guns in both sides of a shoot-out in Colindale. Then supplied guns to the crews who went in for vindication."

"Fourteen years old."

"Will be lucky to see fifteen."

"What's her connection with the Trident thing at Scotland Yard?"

"Indirect connection. She works for somebody older. Druggie named François Bertin."

"Fucking Frenchman."

"You've got issues with the French?"

"Just the Frenchmen who spit out bullshit poetry."

The man with the broken nose thought about his soon-to-be ex-wife, took a breath.

He asked, "What else you have for me?"

"Still working on the second one. Contract is coming in from the States. The buyer has the funds but is having a problem moving the funds at this time. But the money is there."

"They're being watched."

"Not sure. But if they are, not our problem."

"Don't waste my time. I could be on a plane right now."

"Worst-case scenario. Would you be interested in bartering for a Benz?"

"You shitting me?"

"Client has a brand-new CLK63 AMG Cabriolet."

"Cabriolet. A convertible."

"AMG."

"An AMG?"

"V-eight engine."

"Get out."

"Lovely car. Would look good in Texas."

"What year?"

"This year's model."

"What's that cost on a piece of work like that?"

"Off the showroom floor?"

"What's this one worth?"

"Almost one hundred thousand."

"Uh-huh. And how would that get into my possession?"

"Client would report it stolen. I'd arrange for the new paper-work and IDs."

"Oh, yeah. Why don't you just send me to jail? Just get me the money."

"Bruno, the car is brand-new. Look it up on the Internet."

"They have brand-new prisons filled with dumb fucks too. Don't waste my time."

"Just thought I'd ask. Promised the client I'd put that out there."

"This contract." He took a breath, touched his nose. "You have the package?"

"The information on Gideon is coming."

"Don't bullshit me, Sam."

"I assure you it's coming."

"Don't fuck me around, Sam. You don't want to fuck me around."

He hung up. He exited the DLR at Cutty Sark for Maritime Greenwich. Needed to get souvenirs for his daughter. And there was this other thing on his mind. As he walked he took out the other phone. Dialed.

His call was transferred.

She said, "Good afternoon."

"Tebby. Bruno. The guy from Starbucks."

"I know who this is. How are you?"

"Is this too soon to call? Was trying to wait, but I wanted to call you."

"Did you?"

"Is this too soon? I mean, I can call you back if this is too soon."

He heard the smile in her voice. "Not at all. I wanted to chat with you as well."

Butterflies in his belly, he stood to the side talking to her.

He asked, "Are you available to get together later? Only here a couple of days and I—"

"I love the cinema."

"Cinema?"

"Movies. We call them the cinema here."

"Oh, movies. Nice. We could do that. I like the cinema too."

"Well, the Prince Charles Cinema has some nice movies. Or if you like theater and want to know more about South Africa, there is a wonderful play about South Africa at Stratford."

"Haven't been to a play in a while. What's it called?"

"Township Stories."

"Is that like *Lion King*?"

"Not at all. But it's a good crime thriller that shows the gritty reality of South African life. They say Zenzo Ngqobe is excellent. Think he plays a cold-blooded assassin in the play."

"A cold-blooded assassin." He smiled. "Let's go see that."

"That would be lovely."

"But I have to tell you one thing. More like two."

"Yes."

"I'm going through a divorce. It's not over, hasn't been finalized, but that's weeks away. And I have two kids back in the States. A son and a daughter. Just wanted you to know that."

"Bruno."

"Yes."

"I'm divorced. And I have two children. Their father does not send a dime to help them. Two boys. Back in Botswana."

There was a long pause.

Bruno said, "Really?"

"Really."

"Well, I'm on my second marriage. My first wife died. Breast cancer."

Another pause.

The silence on the other end of the line told him that he had said the wrong thing.

Had said too much too soon.

The past should be given in measured doses, not all at once.

Tebby said, "Should I meet you at the theater? Or would you prefer to not be seen with a divorced woman who has two children? Would you rather be with a woman with hair?"

He hadn't blown it. He smiled.

He asked, "What theater and what time?"

She laughed. He laughed too.

Tension dissipated.

She told him where to meet her, then said, "I will meet you there, Bruno."

"Okay. Would you like to go for dinner before the play?"

"After would be better. That way we don't have to rush before the theater."

"Okay. Dinner after the play."

"I love your voice, Bruno. Love the way you sound so . . . American."

"Love your accent too."

"Have to get some things sorted out here at work."

"Have a good day."

"Cheers, Bruno."

She hung up.

His smile refused to end.

While he walked by all the shops that led to the *Cutty Sark,* he felt free.

He didn't think about his divorce.

Or the IRS.

Or buying Harry Potter books.

Or his son.

He only thought about Tebby.

He was happy.

Seventeen

murder by contract

Back at his swank hotel room, the man with the broken nose took his coat off.

He put the souvenirs from the *Cutty Sark* on the dresser and took off his Italian shoes.

Then he put the backpack on the queen-size bed.

It felt like Christmas. Like he was opening a Christmas present.

He unzipped the backpack. Took out a box.

He took his time, opened the box with patience. And there it was.

Desert Eagle .50. Not a regular Eagle. This bird was dressed in titanium.

He had owned one years ago, but not with this finish.

Almost five pounds. Not many men could control an Eagle's recoil. Its thunder so loud indoor ranges prohibited them. The Eagle was all about the big hunt. It was made for a real man.

There was a tap on the hotel room door.

He put a pillow over the Eagle, left his bird within reach. Adjusted his pants. Looked through the peephole. It was the man from concierge. He was bringing up a small FedEx box.

The package had arrived. He took the package, gave a tip, closed the door.

He opened the box as he walked across the room.

Stacks of information and photographs.

And a book.

He pushed the book to the side. Stared at the photograph.

He put his glasses on and took a better look.

He muttered, "No way. No fucking way."

He took out his cellular phone. The hotline.

Sam answered, "Talk to me, Bruno."

"This is the Gideon son of a bitch?"

"That's Gideon."

"No fucking way. I was on the plane with this guy."

"What plane?"

"The plane I just took to London."

"You're kidding me."

"Same fucking guy."

"They say he did the job in Tampa last week. Big bloody mess. All over the news."

"Haven't been watching the news. So, this hit . . . this about the thing he did in Tampa?"

"Let's pretend I didn't say as much as I already did."

"So he's a psycho."

"Be careful. He's a smart one. He's sneaky and brutal. I'll get you photos from this thing that just went down in Tampa. If you get on the computer, I can send you a link to YouTube, they have it out there too. A two-minute clip. This Gideon guy took out eight or nine guys by himself."

"What weapon?"

"No gunshot wounds. No knife wounds."

"Military background?"

"Nobody knows. For all I know he was raised by the Shaolin monks."

"What's the James Patterson book for?"

"Show him the book."

"What, he in a book club or something?"

"Show him the book. Look at his eyes. It'll mess him up."

"Will he go ballistic?"

"Not in a public place. Do it and exit. That will fuck with his head. Get him off-balance."

"So this is a cleanup and it has to do with the Tampa job."

"Need anything else, call me."

They hung up.

He studied the package. Studied Gideon.

Saw Gideon's credentials.

A few pictures from a bloody crime scene in Tampa were in the package.

He was glad he didn't have a weak stomach.

This business had been profitable for Gideon.

Very profitable.

Another knock at the hotel door.

He looked out. Saw a short, old man in a nice suit. He opened the door.

The old man said, "Mr. Bruno Brubaker?"

He nodded.

"You need me, no?"

"Who are you?"

"Friend of Sam. I brought you suits to try."

He was a Russian Jewish man, his back mildly crooked, his suit impeccable. The old man entered pushing a tall rack filled with suits and shirts, each suit in its own suit bag, everything else new and in the box. On the rack was a bag filled with belts and ties. Another had shoes.

Bruno found two suits to his liking. Four shirts. Two belts. Two pairs of shoes.

Bruno handed the old man his American Express card.

The man sat at the small desk and closed out the transaction.

Each suit cost £1,000. Two thousand U.S. dollars.

The belts were £200. The shoes were £600 a pair. The old man charged him £100 for two shirts, gave him two for free.

He'd paid a fortune for his clothing. But he'd pay five times that much today.

There was a woman he wanted to impress. A woman who looked like a queen.

The Russian gathered the rest of his things. Handed Bruno a business card.

"In case you need anything else while in London."

He nodded. "I do need one more thing."

"Tell me what you need, my friend."

"Underwear. Boxers or briefs."

"Sorry, no boxers and briefs. No socks. Only what I have on. You want to buy?"

He shook his head. "Well, thanks anyway."

"With a good salesman, everything is for sale."

"Well, I don't know how they do it where you come from, but where I'm from, men don't wear other men's underwear. Sorry, but I'm not one to wear another man's underwear."

"Stores all over. Get to any high street."

"High street?"

"Any main street. Any big street."

"Okay. I'll find a high street."

"Cheers to you, my friend."

"Cheers."

The old man left, back bent, pushing his cart of wares toward the elevator.

Picture of his next job in one hand, gun in the other, the man with the broken nose went back to the window, looked out at the sideshow. He loved the weight of the Eagle in his hand.

He wouldn't need the gun tonight. His hunt would begin tomorrow.

Eighteen

path of the unrighteous

I burgled my way inside a single-story Tudor home.

I'd traveled north and engaged in criminal acts right outside Royal Air Force Lakenheath. Eyes burning, in need of rest, I sat and waited for my contract to come home.

American flags decorated the walls of the modest home. Not one thing in the place was expensive, nothing was beyond his military income. Nothing was out of character. Plaques praising the sergeant's marksmanship, leadership, and dedication, all sorts of commendations took up every inch of one wall in the living room. Pictures of his six children were on another wall. Not a single photo of either his first or second ex-wife. His oldest kid went to USC. The kid below that one was stationed at Lackland. His youngest was almost in middle school. Had pictures of him and his kids out at Thetford Forest working out on the Go Ape obstacle course. Pictures of him on the Breckland Pines Golf Course. From a glance everything looked ordinary.

Six kids, one of the six in college, four young enough for child support, all that and two ex-wives latching on to your pension, that was enough to keep a military man bankrupt.

Enough to make a man walk on the other side of the law to earn his bread and butter.

I looked in the two bedrooms, the second bedroom filled with golf clubs and weights, 350 pounds on the bench press. I looked in closets, made sure no one else was here hiding out. I was inside the home of a warrior. I expected somebody to jump out and strike like a rattlesnake, knife or a gun in hand. The modest home was empty.

I went to the kitchen, pulled out a chair.

Leg bouncing, I rubbed my face, slapped myself, sat and waited with the patience of Job.

My mind remained on Chapel Hill.

Chapel Hill had been a month ago.

Before Tampa.

I closed my weary eyes. Remembered what I needed to forget.

But North Carolina had good memories too.

I remembered that day.

The sun was going down when Arizona called my hotel room. I was on the bed, reading *The Daily Tar Heel*. My work hadn't made the news. That was good. The news talked about rape and Duke's lacrosse team, then about a West Charlotte prostitution exclusion zone, showed poor people getting arrested for buying sex. Maybe the lacrosse team should've been hanging out in that zone. Saw that Damego Lee was charged with stabbing his girlfriend to death. Other news was about an immigration rally being sponsored by the Carolina Hispanic Association.

Arizona got to the point, said one word. "Lobby."

"Okay, boss."

"Smart-ass."

"See you in a sec."

I dropped the paper on the bed, that article about the prostitution zone staring up at me.

The good people of North Carolina were being locked up for buying pussy.

Buying pussy.

Less than a minute later I was in the lobby.

Arizona was looking studious and collegiate, sporting a beat-up Carolina-blue backpack. Everybody in the area wore Carolina blue. From skies to clothes, that was the only color for miles. I offered to carry her backpack, but she shook her head.

I handed her a package.

She asked, "What's this?"

"Luwak coffee."

"Wow. For me?"

"For you."

"Thanks."

The gourmet coffee I handed her was rare and exotic, labor-intensive and time-consuming to produce, made with the help of the marsupial Luwak of Indonesia, and cost more than most hard drugs. With a schoolgirl smile, she stuffed her present inside her backpack.

In silence we headed down the one-way street, took Columbia Street toward Franklin. She lit a Djarum cigarette, but didn't smoke it. Lit it, took that initial puff to get the fire going, just inhaled its exotic, clovelike scent, then dropped the Djarum, used her foot to put out the fire.

We went to the Top of the Hill, a local restaurant and brewery, sat up on the third floor facing the Varsity Theater, sipping beers and looking out over Kerr Drug store, Starbucks, Subway, Wachovia Bank, and all the mom-and-pop shops lining Franklin. The outskirts of campus were like Mayberry. With the area that housed the brown- and black-skinned minorities being miles away, minorities that built these colleges and businesses being out of sight and out of mind, this area was a regular Pleasantville. The drugstore sold popcorn for fifty-nine cents. The movie theater had two screens. It was a Dockers, Old Navy, and backpack world. I had on dull-gray sweats. Dark shades. Baseball cap turned backward. Arizona was dressed in plain jeans and a Carolina blue hoodie, hair pulled back, a simple ponytail, white tennis shoes.

I was close to my birthplace. Felt comfortable under skies painted Carolina blue.

Arizona said, "You did a good job yesterday."

"Thanks."

"The bell tower? You dropped him from the bell tower?"

"Didn't drop him. Just encouraged him to fall."

She nodded in agreement. "The message has been sent out."

"Effective?"

"Misogynistic assholes who owe me are paying up. That put fear in their hearts."

"If they don't respect you . . ."

"Make them fear you. And truth be told, fear works better than respect."

A group of strangers passed by. One of them stopped, asked Arizona if she was a member of No Entry, a South Asian dance group.

One of the men asked, "Ain't you Chinese?"

"I'm Filipina. Not Chinese." She shook her head. *"Kantutin mo ang nanay mo."*

He asked, "What was that?"

"Puputulin ko titi mo."

Confused, as if in their eyes there was no difference, they went away.

I asked her, "What did you say?"

"Told that redneck asshole to go fuck his mother. And threatened to cut off his dick."

Back to her perfect English. No hint of a Filipina accent. When she switched gears, her Tagalog was authentic. But her English was clear, perfect, and neutral. Owned no race, creed, or color. Like mine. We'd both studied hard at becoming neutral. Neutral people were never remembered. Neutral people were invisible to the rest of the world.

Arizona sipped her brew. "You never exterminate the same way twice, do you?"

"Try not to repeat myself. Don't need a signature."

Last time I saw her she was in New York, room 3607 at the Parker Meridien, wearing a $2,000 suit and a watch that made a Rolex look like a dime-store gift, and shoes that were so sexy they made me get an erection. Now she looked like a grunged-out college student, Wal-Mart and Target to the bone. Always so different. She was a chameleon, always dressed so she would fit in, taught how to blend in and go unnoticed, schooled by the best of grifters.

I said, "You should come to Atlanta with me. I have some business to take care of."

"What kind of business?"

"Sledge. Decided to meet with him. On the strength of your referral."

"He laundered some money for me."

"I hate rappers."

"Me too. But I owed him a favor."

"Come with me."

"I'll pass. But thanks."

We drank. We relaxed.

I said, "Want to catch a movie?"

Arizona whispered, "We're not squares, Gideon."

"It's just a movie."

"Last time it was just a play."

"So you remember New York."

"I remember New York."

I said, "Come on. My treat."

We hit Starbucks, then caught *Basic Instinct 2*. Ten minutes into the movie we thought about walking out, laughed, and called that fiasco of a film *Basically It Stinks, Too*. Movie was so bad that only four people were in the theater. A huge, dark theater that didn't have the latest sound technology. Like I said before, only two movies played at that local spot. Mayberry. And those two movies only played twice a day. Very Mayberry. No discounts for students. No wonder all the bars along the strip were full. Inside the dark theater, the other people were on the right side, close to the front. Old Tar Heels with bad vision. We sat in the back, far left side.

Arizona's hand came to my lap, rubbed, then she brought her other hand over, undid my sweats, fished inside, took out my penis. She stroked me. She watched the movie and stroked me until I started to rise. Then she paused. Shifted. She leaned, put her face in my lap.

She did what naughty squares would do at a moment like this.

Arizona stroked me while she looked at the movie, not impressed with what was on the big screen. She put her head back in my lap, took me in her throat with small, slow thrusts.

She said, "This movie is horrible."

Sharon Stone continued getting sexed as Arizona opened her soda, sipped a little, took some ice inside her mouth, then leaned over, took me inside her jaws again. One of my hands gripped my seat, the other held the back of her head. She worked me good, worked until I came, then kept working me until I was almost hard again.

While I caught my breath, Arizona ate popcorn and sipped on the last of her soda.

Arizona smiled. "That's payback for what you did to me in New York."

"Is that right?"

"So that debt is paid in full."

We left the sorry movie and went back to the Top of the Hill. More beers. Loud and obnoxious college students were getting wasted. Sober X hangover patches were on every other arm, and condoms were in just as many pockets. Meaningless sex was on the horizon.

The Terry Wiley Band was playing the best soul, funk, and blues, a serious party band. I convinced Arizona to mix with the blue-blooded crowd and dance with me. She was the queen of the grifters, but at the end of the day she was still a woman who loved to feel the groove.

I whispered in her ear, "Let me eat you out."

She pushed me away from her. "All about control, Gideon. You know that."

"What are you afraid of?"

"I lost control once . . . with Scamz . . . can't afford to get caught up like that again."

"You haven't gotten over him."

"It ended abruptly. There was no closure. No real closure."

"Want to talk about it?"

She didn't answer.

The conversation disconnected for a moment. Her lips turned down almost as if she were experiencing some sort of a love-hate relationship deep inside her soul.

We left the party, took a slow stroll down Cameron Avenue, cut through campus between Phillips and Memorial Hall, her hand in mine, me holding her delicate fingers as we headed toward middle campus, taking in her softness as we headed toward north campus.

She stared at the buildings. "I never went to college. I never made it out of high school."

"And you're smarter than most."

"Got my Ph.D. in the streets."

"And richer than most."

"Made my money hustling. Like my mother did. And my mother's mother."

Temperature was dropping. Had made it up to the midsixties, now it was nose-diving toward the low forties. We strolled back toward my historic, five-star hotel. The good old Carolina Inn. Up and down Columbia Street there was enough foliage to make a forest, nothing but easygoing trees and that peaceful feeling surrounding all the bricked structures.

We went inside the lobby, chilled out in the chairs next to the concierge.

She said, "I have the same nightmare over and over."

"What nightmare is that?"

"Watching Scamz get shot in the chest. Keep hearing the shotgun blast. See the blood."

"Heard it was nasty."

"I was inside the pool hall. We had just left a club. Me. Scamz. My sister."

"Your sister."

"That backstabbing, jealous bitch."

"Tell me how you really feel."

"We'd all been out. We were waiting on him, standing right next to him. He got into an argument with this guy. Shotgun went off. Me and . . . my sister . . . we saw him die. I saw him take his last breath. That sound . . . life leaving him . . . hollow look in his eyes . . . I see it in my dreams."

"How does it make you feel?"

"Happy. Sad. Depends on the day."

She thanked me for the Luwak, gave me a one-arm hug, as if what had happened at the Varsity was just a way of thanking me for the exotic coffee from Indonesia. She was always about fair exchange, never robbed me. Arizona adjusted her backpack and went toward valet parking and got her car. A simple Saturn. Dents in the side. Nothing to write home about.

The doorman held the door open for me, gave me that Southern service that made this historic hotel so enviable. I went back inside, headed down the hallway, went to room 160.

I showered. Decided I'd drive around town, revisit my old childhood haunts in West Charlotte, maybe ride as far as Greenville, Asheville, or Spartanburg.

While I was drying off, there was an urgent banging at my door.

I eased into my bag, pulled out my friend, a Beretta Elite,

stood to the side of the peephole, kept my voice even, and called out, "Who is it?"

"Open up."

Weapon down at my side, I took a deep breath, relaxed, opened the door. Arizona was sitting on the carpet. Her back to the door. She looked back, saw the weapon in my hand, saw my naked body. She stood up. Still she was unnerved, had a stressed expression.

I said, "Thought you were gone."

She shifted from foot to foot.

Her backpack was gone. She had left it in her car.

That meant she was back for a moment. To tell me what was on her mind.

I saw it in her face. Bad news. Angst. I had done or said something to offend her.

She said, "There is something . . . me and you . . . it's rough . . . like Tracy and Hepburn."

"Just when I thought it was smoothing out and becoming more like Bogart and Bacall."

"This thing between us . . . it bothers me."

"Well, it really bothers me too."

She held her strained expression as if she were living in the middle of a moral dilemma.

She whispered, "What would you do with Arizona . . . if she came inside your room?"

She spoke of herself in the third person. With detachment. Inanimate object. A divided soul.

I played along. "My favorite scenario is giving you a candlelit bath, washing your hair, drying you off, Miles Davis playing in the background, having your legs apart, giving you some serious mouth passion, and putting you to bed . . . then watching you sleep."

"You have any Monk?"

"And I have Miles. *Kind of Blue*. Got Coltrane. *Equinox. My Favorite Things*."

"You're making me weak."

"I was trying to make you wet."

"You did that when we were at the Top of the Hill."

"I did? How?"

"The way you look at me. Same way you're looking at me now."

"My look bothers you?"

"Monk and Coltrane."

"I have Miles and Wes too."

"Yeah. You're making me weak."

"Good."

"Don't know if I'd be able to handle all of that."

"We can always start with Monk, ride the Trane a few Miles toward Wes."

She didn't move.

I said, "Come on in."

"So far as my personal life . . . I'm very discreet . . . require total discretion."

"Don't worry. I don't kiss and tell."

"It's bad for business."

"I understand."

I went back to the bed, put my Beretta back in my bag.

She stood at the door, staring at me. Right then she was no different from all the college girls we had passed by tonight. I saw how she could've been a square, saw the normal in her.

She made a frustrated sound. *"Malibog ako. Gusto kitang kantutin."*

"Translate that shit."

"This is a booty call, Gideon. Just a booty call."

"A booty call."

"You're a male whore. It can't ever be more than a booty call."

That stung. Not in a painful way. Just introduced a reality, a part of me that might be coded deep into my DNA. My father, a man on the move. My mother, a whore.

I said, "You're a thief."

"I'm not a low-level thief. I run scams. I'm a businesswoman. I am the queen of my industry."

"I stand corrected."

She said, "I don't romanticize my existence. Not any longer. My eyes are open. The world is like *Lord of the Flies*. All about survival of the fittest. Survival of those who aren't afraid to be cruel. I don't care if you're a clergy or the president of a Fortune 500 company, don't care if you're homeless or a trust-fund baby, being good, following the rules, that shit doesn't work."

"Cool. I won't bullshit you and you don't bullshit me."

"Please. You tell me you want to make love. Save that rhetoric for the squares. They love that shit. First off, you don't know how to make love. You know how to fuck. Which is ironic. The better a man fucks, the more a woman will be convinced that he is making love to her."

She reached under her hoodie, hand going to the small of her back, fumbled with a strap, and pulled out a Ruger Mark III. She put her cold steel on the nightstand.

She glanced at me, swallowed.

The weapons were gone. Her shield was down.

She said, "So let's stop talking and fuck."

I held her small head in my hand, moved to her slow and easy, eased my lips on hers, moved my tongue around her lips, then eased my tongue inside her mouth, slow-grooved her with my tongue, my kiss a long and easy song, pure jazz, like I was Trane, Wes, Monk, and Miles.

"Stop being all romantic, Gideon. Fuck me means *fuck* me."

Then I dropped the romantic notions and fucked her.

I yanked most of her clothes away, did the same with mine, entered her doggie style, had her bent over the dresser, her holding the dresser while I fucked her booty-call style.

Over and over she moaned, "*Gusto kong kantutin tulad ni-to . . . susmariosep.*"

I wasn't nice. I stopped being pretty. I fucked like I wanted to hurt her.

"*Isa pa . . .*"

I pulled her hair and fucked her the way a thief needed to be fucked.

"*Sigi pa . . . do that . . . gusto ko yan . . .*"

I tried to fuck the arrogance and pain and rejection out of her.

"*Sigi pa . . . do that . . . gusto ko yan . . . again . . . isa pa.*"

I tried to fuck her to me.

I tugged the rest of her wrinkled clothes off her, took her to the bed, eased her down, put my weight on her, made the bed sigh, eased back inside her, and kept the party going.

Arizona's moans told me she wanted more.

I said, "Keep talking to me in Tagalog."

"Why?"

"It turns me on."

She smiled a little. Said things I didn't understand, things that excited me.

I held her breasts and kissed her, pinched her nipples while our tongues danced.

Kept sucking her breasts.

Then my tongue craved to taste what was between her legs. I licked the edges . . . just around the edges . . . circles . . . tongue moving slow and easy like a Sunday drive down Route 66.

She stopped saying things in Tagalog. Nails in my back, she begged for me to stop eating her out and fuck her.

"You're trying to control me with your tongue."

"Come for me."

"No."

"Come for me."

"No . . . no . . . shit . . . oh . . . damn you."

"Coming?"

"Don't stop . . . don't stop."

I did stop.

Left her hanging at the edge of orgasm.

Left her twitching.

"Damn you . . . Gideon . . . damn you."

"Open your legs."

I got on top of her, broke her skin a little at a time.

She said, "You're driving me crazy."

"Then we're even."

I kissed her like I had wanted to kiss her for a decade. Sucked her neck like I was a madman in search of sanity. The touch of her breasts magnifying my madness.

I teased her and drove myself insane.

Then I backed away. Left her suffering.

She clawed at me, begged me to not back away.

She said, "Stop playing and fuck me."

I didn't fuck her, not right then.

I was in control.

I wasn't going to let her control me.

I'd never let a woman control me.

I turned her over, put her on her knees, her face in the pillow, pulled her ass back toward me, my hands on her waist, made sure she kept her ass up high.

She said, "Gideon, give it to me. Please."

I rubbed my length against her over and over, let her feel what I wanted to give.

"That feels good. Shit. That's making me come."

She looked so feminine. So vulnerable. So damn sexy.

Then I went inside her. Went deep. Held her waist.

And I stroked her.

Didn't want it to end. Even if that was all we had. Wanted to make it last.

I tried to grab the edges of forever and make it stretch beyond eternity.

She came.

And the way she moved, I couldn't hold on any longer.

I came.

I came and kept moving until the well was dry.

I moved away from her, panting.

She did the same, running her fingers through her mane.

"Damn you, Gideon."

"Yeah. Damn you too."

A few minutes later Arizona sat on the edge of the bed, unlit Djarum in hand.

Djarum. The brand of clove-smelling cigarettes her dead lover used to smoke.

He didn't matter to me. Never did.

I told her, "Love you. Mean it."

She dragged her fingers through her hair, sighed, didn't look back at me.

I said, "You hear what I said?"

She shifted until she was sitting in profile, frowned, put the Djarum down, shook her head. *"Tahimik ka na."*

"Something wrong?"

"Don't say that. No love talk. Please. Don't do that."

"Took me ten years to get you to make love to me."

"We've had sex twice. We flirted and things . . . we crossed that forbidden line in New York. We mixed business with sex. Don't make it sound like something it's not, okay? We had sex. And today . . . we both needed this and so we got this from each other. Maybe I needed this. That's all. Just sex. Keep it real. Don't get foolish. Love talk is for squares, Gideon."

"Why did you come back?"

"You caught me at a good time. I just needed to . . . I needed some sexual healing."

"Sexual healing."

"I'm horny."

"Queen Scamz gets horny?"

"Ain't I a woman?"

"Yeah." I chuckled. "You're a woman. Best of the best."

She leaned back, kissed me. Growled as she sucked my tongue.

She asked, "Are we done or can you go another round?"

"Still horny?"

"Very. Get like this when it's close to that time of the month."

"Not done. Was letting you catch your breath."

"Well, let's get this party started."

"Staying the night?"

She shook her head. "I can stay a little while longer."

"Make me feel special."

"Fuck me again, Gideon. Like you just fucked me. Pull my hair, fuck me like that again. Don't be so gentle. I like gentle, but I don't want gentle right now. Fuck me like that again."

Coltrane adding to the soundtrack created by her moans, I pulled her hair and fucked her from wall to floor, made her stand up and touch her toes while I fucked her senseless.

Then I took her to the bed, again missionary, tongue to tongue.

She came.

She came again.

"Give it to me . . . that's it, Gideon . . . give it to me . . . don't stop . . . that's it."

I kept going until I couldn't fight it anymore.

I came.

She laughed.

I laughed too.

We stayed like that awhile.

Nothing was said after that.

Sweat dried.

North Carolina winds blew against the windows.

The room went from being hot to cold.

Then we pulled the covers up over us.

She whispered something in Tagalog. Something soft, emotional, and sweet.

I didn't know what she said.

I didn't ask.

All I know was I put my arm around her, pulled her to me, kept her close to my heart.

In silence she held on to my penis.

I fell asleep.

But the next morning she was gone. Had left like she was my overnight whore.

Or had left like I was the whore.

I jerked awake. Jumped to my feet. Spun around. Disoriented.

I had fallen asleep. Had my head down on the kitchen table.

That was fucked up. Dozing off, even for two seconds, could've sent me to the Big Sleep. I stretched, bounced up and down, splashed water on my face.

Took me a moment to remember I was eighty miles from London.

A vintage military jeep was pulling up out front.

The engine shut off.

My breathing shortened. Heart rate increased tenfold.

My palms were wet as rain. I took a few deep breaths.

He was here.

Sergeant was home.

It was time for the dance to begin.

Nineteen

one false move

I took another hard breath and wondered which way this was going to go.

Peaceful. Or with a hellified row.

I wanted him to see me when he came in. Wasn't going to hide.

A key was put in the door. My heart crept up my chest and stopped in my throat.

The door opened.

He came inside. Dressed in military fatigues. Rough face. Looked like Sergeant Rock.

He paused when he saw me sitting at his table, *Stars and Stripes* newspaper in my hand.

He frowned at me for a moment. A long, hot moment.

He spoke right above a whisper. "Gideon."

"Sergeant."

He looked like a sixty-year-old Sergeant Rock and sounded like Johnny Cash.

I kept my hands where he could see them. "Sorry to sneak up on you like this."

"This a social call?"

"Arizona asked me to stop by."

He nodded, said, "The slant-eyed bitch raised the stakes and sent Gide-fucking-on."

"Guess you could say that."

"She tell what it was about?"

I nodded. "FEMA scam. That's all she said. Don't need the details."

"Why didn't the bitch bring her narrow ass up to horse-and-grass her damn self?"

"Probably the same reason you sent the guys from Holland to talk to her."

"Guess that didn't deter her." He almost smiled. "Of all people, she sent Gideon."

I nodded.

"Well, Gideon, so far as the boys from Holland, those weren't my men. Arizona has her own problems in Holland. She knows who sent those boys over here. Don't let her fool you."

"Does that matter?"

His frown deepened.

"I should've sent some military boys down. Never should've let her send Dutch boys."

"Who is the mysterious *her* that hired the Dutch boys?"

"Arizona knows. Oh, she knows. I should've handled that problem myself."

"You should've. But you didn't. And now I'm up here trying to smooth it out."

"The Dutch boys hurt her any?"

"Not at all."

"Too bad."

"Sorry to disappoint you."

"Too fucking bad that slant-eyed cunt didn't get any justice."

"The Dutch boys will be crippled for life. If that makes you feel any better."

"I don't need this in my home. Don't want this battle on my territory."

"I understand. Your being military and all. Could be hard to explain to the higher-ups."

"Is that right? How do you see this, Gideon? How do you see this playing out?"

"News of a military man's investment in a FEMA scam ever hit the paper . . . can't even imagine what that would do to the country. Or to a man's career. No matter how much paper he has stacked. Family shamed. All because of a little Filipina girl. Wouldn't look good at all."

"Your advice? So I don't end up falling on my sword, your advice?"

"Cut your losses. Pay your bills. Walk away clean. With money in the bank."

"Money in the bank."

"I'm not the one, but you know Arizona will send somebody."

"So I'd best make a call to my moneyman and rectify this little problem."

"That would be my suggestion."

"Is that a threat?"

"Only a suggestion."

His hands were trembling, shaking worse than mine.

I was scared. He was scared. That meant everything was normal.

He said, "Some entertainers were massacred. Back in the States. Saw it on CNN."

"Really?"

"Some rapper. Happened in Tampa. Heard it was a mess."

"Didn't hear about it."

"Last time you been to Tampa?"

"Never been to Tampa."

"When you get here?"

"Few hours ago."

"You been to visit a WAG since you got here? They just found one floating in the river."

"Wasn't me."

He took out a cigarette, popped it in his mouth, used his lighter to fire up the cancer.

He asked, "Do you mind?"

I shrugged. "Your house."

"I take it that if I don't make a call, we will have a problem."

"There is already a problem, you know that."

He said, "You know that Arizona bitch, you can't trust her. Didn't care for her when she was Scamz's bitch. Don't care for her now. Scamz was a fair man. She's stolen Scamz's name. That evil bitch, nobody can afford to work with her, not and make a profit. Everybody hates her. She'll double-cross you, do you know that? She'd double-cross her own mother to turn a profit."

I didn't say anything.

He inhaled, spoke when he exhaled. "Never should have gotten in bed with that cunt."

He looked at me, put the cigarette out, and dialed a number. He was put on hold; while he waited, he stood up, never took his grimace off me. I didn't move an inch.

He asked, "You fucking her?"

"Maybe I should be asking you that question."

"Don't let pussy come between men. Pussy starts wars and good men die."

"What about Iraq?"

"George W. Bush is a pussy."

"And Blair must be his twin."

"I'll remember that one. Twin pussies. The boys'll get a good laugh out of that one."

He said some things to whoever was on the phone, nodded, cursed, hung up the phone, then he sat down.

He wasn't happy. Not at all.

Sergeant said, "Be careful. Men get fooled by sex. All men do."

I nodded.

We waited.

I took my eyes off him for a second, long enough to open my backpack.

In the blink of an eye, he made an M&P .40 appear. Smith & Wesson's military gun.

Everything slowed down.

I asked, "You going to shoot me?"

"What's in the bag? Show me. Use one hand. Your left hand. Move slow."

I showed him that, except for the pint of Jack, the backpack was empty.

"Somebody called one of my friends this morning. Looking for a Desert Eagle."

"Wasn't me."

"Wasn't you?"

"Nah. I'm a nine guy. Beretta time to time. A SIG. Maybe a .22. Nothing that big."

"My friend didn't know who the guy was. Told him he would have to look elsewhere. You're here in London and somebody happens to call up looking for a large-caliber, gas-operated semi-automatic pistol manufactured in Israel. Hope you're smarter than that, Gideon. For your own sake. Piece like that is too easy to follow back to the source. Hope that wasn't you."

"You know I'm not a show-off."

"Whoever it is, watch it, bet they trace the gun to find him . . . arms dealer selling off a .50-caliber gun dressed in titanium. That's over-the-top. That's six-o'clock news if ever I heard it."

"Titanium?"

He nodded. "That bitch will be easy to find. A big-ass loud gun. Whoever he is has to be a loose cannon. A man who has to have the biggest dick that screams the loudest orgasm."

"No insecurities over here."

"Just looking out for you. I have always been partial to you, Gideon. As a friend."

I nodded back at him, keeping my hands where he could see them at all times.

"If that was you buying the Eagle, take my advice, throw it

in the river and walk away." He kept his eyes on mine. "Too easy to trace, too showy, too loud."

"Wasn't me."

He put his S&W on his lap. His piece smiled at me.

He said, "Pardon the lack of trust. Somebody calls up for an Eagle, then you show up . . ."

"I showed up after you sent a hurt squad after Arizona."

"Like I said, what a coincidence."

"You say we're friends and you still have that barrel aimed at my gut."

"If I didn't like you, you'd be on that floor with two in your chest and one in your head."

"Make sure we exchange Christmas cards this year. Since we're friends."

"You got a weapon on you?"

"Just a pint of Jack."

"Sure about that?"

"You can search me."

"Don't need to be that close to you. So I'll take your word on that."

"I'm just the messenger."

"So the slant-eyed bitch just wants to play it like this. Who does that cunt think she is?"

"Queen Scamz. She thinks she's Queen Scamz."

My phone vibrated.

He jumped for his gun again.

Then he relaxed. Wiped his forehead with the back of his free hand.

The money he owed Arizona had been transferred.

I said, "See how easy that was?"

"Tell the bitch to suck my dick. You can quote me on that. And tell her to lick my balls while she's at it. Quote my ass on that too. Jacking me for my goddamn retirement money."

My phone vibrated again.

The money Arizona owed me had been transferred as well.

He stood across the room from me.

Again he asked, "You ain't fucking her, are you?"

"Let's keep this business."

"You know you ain't the only one she fucking. Get you a regular girl if you have to have a steady one. A girl like Arizona will be the death of you. Regular girl might break your heart and take your money, might even take your house, but they leave you breathing in the end."

I remained across the room from him, kept my hands where he could see them.

He asked, "You fucking her? And that is a damn business question, if you must know."

I shook my head.

He said, "Two hundred. I'll give you two hundred to put a bullet in her head."

"Pounds?"

"U.S. dollars. She ain't worth half what I'm offering you, and you know that."

He was talking two hundred thousand.

In this business a nickel was five thousand and a dime was ten.

I said, "Thought you'd spent your retirement money."

He gave me a one-sided grin. "FEMA supplemented my never-rising income. You know the exchange rate is killing us over here. Can't afford to buy shit off base. Not a damn thing."

I sat down. He did the same, his gun at his side, finger on the trigger.

My hands were damp, throat dry, heart maintained a steady gallop.

I said, "Two hundred is a lot of money. You must have a nice wad stashed away."

"Don't worry about what I got." He nodded. "You want the contract or not?"

I said, "Let's take a drink and talk about that."

I took the bottle of whiskey out of my backpack. Jack Daniel's. The brand we drank.

I sat the bottle down.

I asked, "Coke?"

He went to the small refrigerator.

I asked, "How you like living over here in England?"

"Either cold as hell or hot as hell. Gets hot as hell and ain't no air conditioners in England. No dryers, so when it's cold as hell, you can't hang your clothes out to dry. In the summertime you have to hang clothes on the back porch to dry."

"I was here once in the summer. Never came up here and went on base."

"On base, black women have light-skinned babies with curly hair. White women have brown-skinned babies with curly hair. Black is fucking white and white is fucking black. This is about as kum-ba-yah as it gets. Just like it is down in London. Same all over Europe. America is the most advanced country and still refuses to acknowledge the natural course of evolution."

He put a liter of Coca-Cola down.

He said, "This is the *real* thing. From home. Not that NutraSweet shit from London."

I said, "Glasses or straight from the bottle like winos in an alley?"

He went back to the cabinet, never taking his eyes off me, gun barrel aimed at the floor.

He said, "London kills me with that eat-in/takeaway bullshit. They add a surcharge to your meal if you eat at McDonald's or Pizza Hut or anywhere. All those mayonnaise-eating bastards. They put mayo on everything. I got some mustard here if you want some. You won't be able to find mustard in London. Hot sauce either. Got a few bottles if you need some."

"Thanks."

He sat in front of me.

I poured him a shot of Jack.

He thanked me, then asked, "You drinking?"

"Probably shouldn't. I'm on a motorcycle. Streets are damp. Not a good idea."

"Have a word with Jack before what I'm holding has two or three words with you."

He stared at his glass. Smiling. Waiting. Trembling. His fear controlled.

I said, "You think I put a little something extra in Jack?"

"Talk to Jack, not to me. Better hurry up, 'cause my trigger finger is getting twitchy."

I eased the bottle up to my lips, took a hit.

A minute went by.

He said, "Sip a little more. For good measure."

I did. Another minute went by.

He relaxed, but he never moved his hand away from his military gun.

I said, "For two hundred, if you're serious, I'll celebrate and drink the whole bottle."

"So you'll take the contract on that slant-eyed bitch?"

"I'd kill that slant-eyed bitch and my favorite whore for two hundred."

"Your favorite whore." He chuckled. "How is Thelma?"

"Have no idea."

"You ain't seen her?"

"Saw her in Amsterdam a few years ago."

"That why you in London?"

"What do you mean?"

"Guess you didn't know. She's in London."

"London?"

"Thelma's been working in London for at least two years. I see her from time to time."

"Where in London is she working?"

"Down in W1. A few doors down from a store called Le Pig something or another."

"Didn't know that."

"She's on the Internet. She's got herself an ad on craigslist. org under erotic services. She had a nice ad out at eros.com in the classifieds. Think she's still out at halfprice.com too."

"Sounds like she's keeping busy."

"Sent some business her way a time or two. Military is prison and so is marriage. Few married guys up here like to get away from their families and go down to the city for a day trip."

"Thought Thelma had run to Brazil or was hiding out somewhere in South America."

"She got in trouble down there. Then, from what I hear, she was over in Berlin for a while. Since the wall came down and prostitution became legal, all the girls are going there."

"Yeah. Heard all the whores were running to Germany."

"They have damn near half a million sex workers. Half a million. Wall-to-wall pussy. And for the man on the move, they have drive-through sex stalls in Germany. I shit you not."

"So Thelma went to Germany."

"She was over there working twelve-hour shifts. The young girls are lucky to get five to ten guys a day. Thelma said there was too much competition. After that she was working in Den Haag, Spijk, and Apeldoorn for a while. Then she came to London. Smaller market."

"Had no idea."

"You ain't been in touch with her?"

I shook my head.

He shook his head. "Damn shame."

"It is what it is."

"Look her up. If you go visit her, tell her Sergeant said hello. When I make it back down to Central London, tell her I'll visit her. Would love to buy her a drink and talk old times."

For a moment I smelled that whore's perfume on his skin.

"Let's talk contract," I said. "Have to hit the road. Almost a hundred miles to London."

I extended the bottle to him for a toast. His glass clinked my bottle.

I said, "Half up front. Other half when it's done. I'll send visual confirmation."

"SOP." That meant Standard Operating Procedures. "Where's that cunt Arizona hiding?"

"She's in London. Not sure where she's hiding out. But she's in contact."

"Sending somebody after me." He sipped. "She has a lot of nerve, you know that?"

He drank his shot. He looked around at his modest life. Looked at all the flags and trophies and commendations. Looked at the sum of his military career in a single glance.

He said, "Six more months with Uncle fucking Sam and I'm out of this bitch."

"Where to?"

"Retirement. Gonna chill out and retreat to a small island. Someplace peaceful. And away from everything that's going on in the world. Sit back and watch countries destroy each other. Take on an exotic wife. Get the best wife with the sweetest pussy that my money can buy. Even if she doesn't love me, she'll love the lifestyle I can afford. Dick can still hold up an American flag and squirt, so I'ma have as many children as her body can handle. Maybe take on more than one wife. A man should be able to have as many women as he could afford."

"Only takes one to make a rich man broke. Only takes one to steal all of your money."

He rubbed his eyes. Blinked a few times.

I took a small hit of the Jack. Did the same as it burned my throat.

I said, "This is some good shit."

"Jack has a nice kick. Top-shelf?"

I sipped a little more. "Only the best."

He poured himself another shot. Tossed it back. "I'ma grow a beard like Jerry Garcia. Let my hair go long like John Lennon. Work out twice a day, run five miles every morning and swim naked in one of God's beautiful bodies of water every evening.

Read the Bible from cover to cover. Repent. Find Jesus and get to know the Lord like my mama knew Him."

I smiled at him. Watched him throw back another shot.

He said, "But I'll have to go down and visit Thelma before. On a weekend. No congestion fees on the weekend. Goddamn robbery. You know about the congestion fees?"

"I heard they were about to go up. Heard the congestion zones were getting wider."

"I mean, you know about the checkpoints and the cameras that record you as soon as you hit the zone? They are on you as soon as you hit the city. And it's a rip-off. Eighteen U.S. dollars a day to drive into Central London. Parking fees not included. That's more than my car note to drive there a week."

"I heard."

"But what I'm telling you, Gideon, it's bigger than the fees. It's Big Brother's never-blinking eye. Be careful. Cameras track all moving vehicles. As soon as you hit the congestion zone, they run your plates and hit you with a bill for congestion charges so fast it could make your head spin, so that means Big Brother knows your every move. I park at Epping, catch the train down. Takes all damn day, and if the Central is down, I'm fucked, but I ain't paying no . . . no . . ."

He rubbed his eyes again. Coughed and smiled.

He refilled. My bottle clinked his glass, another toast.

He said, "But before I get religious, I want a bullet in that slant-eyed cunt's head."

"We're talking about Arizona now."

"Damn right."

"However you want it done, it's done."

"Always running her hand through her goddamn hair. And cut her damn hair off. Make gook-looking bitch bald." He rubbed his eyes. They were out of focus. "But don't cut it until after she's apologized and transferred my damn money back to my . . . not until she's sent every last dime of my money back . . . back . . . back . . . my money . . . my . . . money . . . back . . ."

Then his smile turned upside down. Panic lines grew in his forehead.

His vision was blurring, his breathing shutting down at a rapid pace.

I said, "Thanks for telling me where Thelma was working. I'll pay her a visit."

"Son of a . . . you son of a . . ."

"Sorry. This is business. Just business. I hate it, but this is how it is."

Eyes wide, he looked at his glass, maybe saw the film inside, and frowned at me.

His gun went off. Shot where my stomach would've been if I hadn't moved. The gun came up over the table, followed me. The next bullet exploded where my chest had been two seconds before. The third shot hit where I was a half second before that.

By the fourth explosion, I was across the room. I was nervous. Scared. Alert.

No way a man could dodge bullets and not feel his own death dancing in the room.

Agony seized him. He dropped the Smith & Wesson and grabbed his throat.

Death was charging his way. I kicked the gun out of his reach.

Sergeant convulsed. Wet his pants. A river of fear ran from between his legs.

I didn't poison the Jack. That would've been expected. I'd laced his drinking glasses with the tasteless, odorless venom. No matter which glass he'd picked up, it was poisoned.

I'd sipped from the untainted bottle.

Face red, he tried to get up, but crashed to the floor face-first, eyes wide-open.

His legs kicked, twitched, finally stopped moving. His bowels released, stenched the air.

I couldn't let him live. Not after he said he'd kill Arizona.

He had sent men to cripple and rape her.

My heart thumped inside my chest. But I didn't have time to wait for it to slow.

I put on rubber gloves and picked up his glass. Grabbed the one I didn't use. Picked up the bottle of Jack too. I washed his glasses out. Washed them all to prevent collateral damage.

I dried the glasses, put them back in the cabinet, stood over the sink, waiting for that nauseous feeling to go away. I was sweating and numb. I was living in my own darkness.

Had to remain on task.

In a couple of hours the poison in his system wouldn't be detectable.

Natural causes. It would look like death by natural causes.

I wiped down the bottle of Jack, then put the bottle in his hand long enough for his fingerprints to take. I put the bottle on the table, let it turn over and spill. Jack rained to the floor. Wanted it to look like he had knocked it over. Wouldn't make sense to empty the bottle, no need to toss it. I left his weapon where he had dropped it.

Had to.

Bullet holes were everywhere.

I'd let the police explain the bullet holes.

Maybe they'd think he'd gotten drunk, gone mad, started shooting, had a heart attack.

I didn't give a shit.

Better him than Arizona laid up in a hospital, raped and beaten.

I couldn't allow that to happen.

Five minutes later I was on A11 doing seventy, horses at my side, sadness in my heart.

The sadness went away when the anger returned.

Thelma was here. Right up under my nose.

Twenty

erotic gherkin

Hours had gone by.

The grayness of London had changed to a mild black.

The coldness remained, most of that chill surrounding my heart.

Not many tall structures polluted London's skyline, so the contemporary Erotic Gherkin could be seen from almost everywhere. It was actually the Swiss Re Tower, but the locals loved calling it the Erotic Gherkin, maybe because it was smooth and looked like an exotic vibrator rising from the ground. Hard to believe that Foster got away with that architectural design.

If he had put two round buildings at the base, it would've been a dick pointing at the sky.

Arizona said, "Good job. What you did in Lakenheath, good job."

I didn't say anything. Didn't want to rejoice in my wrongdoing.

She said, "After what happened this morning in Chinatown, I started thinking."

"And those thoughts were?"

"Come work for me. Exclusively."

"Other shit is on my mind right now."

"I'm listening."

She had boarded the Stansted Express at the Seven Sisters platform. She smelled top-shelf. She had on an expensive business suit, long black coat, boots, hair pulled back in a bun.

I told her, "If I wanted to work for somebody, I'd get a nine-to-five."

She flipped me off.

I said, "You get my messages?"

"I get a lot of messages. Remind me of your messages."

"Guy from the plane. Red shirt. High-end suit. Broken nose. Saw him again."

"That guy. Where?"

"After Chinatown. You ran away and when I turned around, he was behind me."

"The wingman you left me a message about."

"You thought I was bullshitting?"

"What happened?"

"I went after him. Lost him. He vanished somewhere in Covent Garden."

"So he was behind me."

"He was behind us. He could've hid out in the market."

She bounced her leg.

I asked, "How many people are after you?"

"About half as many as should be after you."

I repeated, "When you ran away, I turned around and he wasn't too far behind me."

"We'd just straightened out the Dutch boys. Maybe Sergeant used him as backup."

I shook my head. "Doubt it. He was on the flight from the U.S. with me."

"Maybe it was Lakenheath. Maybe Sergeant tried to get to me before I got to him."

"Wasn't Sergeant."

"Why so sure he didn't put a hit out on me too?"

"Because he offered me a contract on you."

That broke her pace. She saw the seriousness in my eyes. "How much?"

I told her. She remained poker-faced, but her leg bounced a little faster.

She said, "The guy in the suit, black, white, European?"

"Could be all of the above or none of the above."

"Bald."

"Yeah."

"A hit man shaves his body to get rid of DNA."

"Wait. Sergeant said he had a partner. A woman."

Arizona didn't say anything. Her face told me she knew.

She said, "His partner, the bitch he was dealing with, she's in Holland."

"So she arranged the Dutch boys?"

"The bitch did. She sent them to rape . . . she sent them."

Arizona was nervous. Her discomfort was as subtle as the sweat on the tip of her nose.

She said, "I need you to go to Amsterdam."

"Get me a package."

Her cellular rang. She looked at the number and took the call.

She frowned a little, then frowned a lot, then looked at me.

When she hung up, she cursed and shook her head.

I asked, "What happened?"

"Sledgehammer was murdered a few hours ago."

That got my attention.

I asked her when that happened. She told me that it was this morning.

He'd been killed after I made it to London, around the time I was bedding Mrs. Jones.

I asked, "How?"

"My contact said Sledge's van exploded." That was her answer.

"Sledge and his family were having a family outing in Trinidad. At least ten members of his family were inside the van."

"His family? His wife and kids?"

"Wife. Kids. Parents. In-laws. Everyone was piled in the same van."

Fear was in her eyes. Or maybe that was just a reflection of what I felt at the moment.

She said, "Consider my offer. Work for me. It would benefit both of us."

"I get it. You need me. You need protection."

"I fear no one but God."

"You're afraid. If I hadn't been on it and saw the cats at Starbucks, you're worried about what would've happened. You're scared because right now you'd be laid up in London Hospital. Every bone in your body broken while the police asked questions and brought a rape kit."

She swallowed. Had never seen her this rattled before. She said, "Be my partner."

"Answer me. How many people are after you? Who else would come after you?"

"All business. Without the sex. I think I need a male partner so these ignorant fools will take me seriously. And you, Gideon, would be perfect. People hear your name and know they are about to take a shortcut to hell. Hey, what's that puzzled expression all about? I lose you?"

"So those days are behind us."

"Draw your own conclusions."

"You're killing me over here."

"We'd have to be professional. Anything else would be a disaster."

"And how would a man with my impeccable résumé fit into your fine organization?"

"You could travel with me. I have a lot of business going on. I'd school you, bring you up to speed on the various operations I have going on with this aspect of the business."

"While you're playing one-minute manager, would I get to wear high-end suits?"

"I love a man in a suit. You know I do. I can get you the best. Only the best."

"I'm not interested in being your replacement for Scamz."

"No one is Scamz, Gideon. Scamz is irreplaceable."

She reminded me of Lil' Kim, still obsessed with Notorious B.I.G. We stared at each other a moment, then she looked away. My contempt wouldn't let me turn my head away.

She said, "Your reputation is growing, becoming almost mythical. Come work for me."

I shook my head.

My throat tightened. After what the Dutch boys said they had been paid to do, I felt like I was betraying her. She'd get over it. Everyone betrayed in this business.

At Liverpool we dropped that conversation, left the train, and found our way to the tube.

As we breathed polluted air, the train rocked and pitched. One commuter stumbled. Others held on. There was enough noise to keep our conversation away from other ears.

I rubbed my hands together, touched Arizona's leg, said, "I'm close to a million dollars."

"Your point?"

"This girl I met at this pool hall in North Hollywood, back when she was half-naked and hustling, trying to feed her mother, hustling to take care of her sister, I had a thing for her, and I was bold enough to ask her to be mine. She told me if I had a million dollars she would be mine."

"I bet that young girl was broke and needy, probably had low self-esteem."

"Or would've done what it took to take care of her mother."

"Bet her mother is dead now. Bet her mother died with a needle in her arm."

"I heard she took care of her little sister too."

"That's what a big sister does when her mother is in the gutter smoking crack. Somebody has to grow up. Somebody has to become the adult. Somebody has to sacrifice."

Arizona turned away. People boarded the train and our conversation died.

I asked, "You have more work for me?"

"I do. And I need your help on the Amsterdam problem."

"And all of this madness and drama is connected to the same FEMA problem?"

"Need you to take the contract without question. Want that part of my life over."

"Without question."

"Yes. Without question."

"It sounds more personal than business."

"Sometimes there is no difference."

"Like I said, get me the package."

"It's forthcoming. Give me a day or two."

"Problem?"

She hesitated. "No problem. No problem at all."

"Guy from the plane. Let's assume you're being followed. How you want to handle it?"

"Need to make a few calls. See what I can find out about a contract man."

"His nose is broken."

"A contract man with a broken nose."

We rode, the tube rocking the crowd ever so gently. Next to us a group of professional Chinese women were talking; all of them had cockney accents. Black people were talking in French across from us. I'd been in America too long. Some things I'd never get used to.

A couple got on, carrying an infant. Arizona looked at them, almost smiled.

I moved over and sat next to Arizona.

I asked, "You ever think about having babies?"

"This isn't . . . I'm not living the have-a-baby lifestyle."

"You ever think about getting out of the business and being a full-time square?"

"Too late. I'm too caught up in the world I'm living in now. This is who I am."

I nodded.

She said, "I want children. Love. I want the things that make a woman feel beautiful."

"If the time was ever right, down the road, would you want that beautiful life with me?"

She sighed. My words aged her a hundred years, put stress lines in her forehead.

She said, "I care about you, Gideon."

"You say that like it's a bad thing."

"I want to *not* have these feelings for you or any man."

"What are you afraid of?"

"I will not let you come into my world and dismantle me."

"I told you I loved you. You rejected me. You're the one doing the dismantling."

"I will not allow you to break me into pieces. And it hurts me to say this . . ."

"Say it."

"Anong gusto mo sa buhay ko?"

"In English."

"You know we can't be together."

"Tell me why."

"Not like regular people. We're not regular people. We're damaged. Gideon, you and I have that in common. We are both damaged. Beyond repair."

She was a con artist. I killed people.

She asked, "The woman you met on the plane, what do you know about her?"

"Why?"

"Not trying to get personal. Trying to protect you. You're thinking with your dick and I'm trying to make sure your dick doesn't get you killed, the same way leaving the dick in charge has buried so many other men. With that said, what the fuck do you know about the woman?"

I took a hard breath and exhaled. "Nothing."

"Was she with the man with the broken nose?"

"Not at all. She sat next to me the whole flight."

"Same flight."

"Yeah."

"She made herself available to you as soon as your plane landed."

"Yeah."

"Eight hours after you met her."

"Yeah."

"And you fucked her."

"Yeah, I fucked her. You want the details?"

"You have to be careful."

"I am careful."

"When it comes to this business, soft legs and pussy is a great disguise."

"I am careful."

"Bullshit. Sleeping with strangers will have you waking with enemies."

"Which are you?"

Her lips turned down. "Unbelievable. You are unbelievable."

It was my turn to look frustrated, my turn to age one hundred years.

I thought about how Sergeant had offered me a ton of money to put Arizona to bed. For a moment, I imagined her gone, dead by my hand, the longing I owned dead as well.

She snapped, "How do you meet a bitch on the plane, end up fucking her as soon as you get here?"

"How do you fuck me, then say we didn't? How do you vanish for months at a time?" I threw my hands up. "Don't get mad at me for doing my own thing while you do yours."

"Let's not . . . let's remain professional."

"Fuck being professional. Let's be personal."

She leaned forward, looked in my eyes, remained calm. "Sure. Let's."

"I've worked hard, bent over backward because I wanted to be with you."

"Who asked you to?"

"Who asked me to?"

"That's what I said."

"I tell you I have close to a million stacked up and you blow me off."

"Because I can't be bought. I'm not a whore."

"What?"

"You asked me how much it would take for me to be with you, like I'm some sort of a whore. I'm not for sale. *I'm not a goddamn whore.* I'm not your mother. I'm not my sister. I don't go running to the highest bidder. I'm not my own mother. I am none of those people."

My laughter was gone. I gritted my teeth.

She said, "I'm not for sale."

"*You* said a million dollars. Those were *your* words, not *my* price."

"Of course. I said an amount that to me, at the time, years ago, was unreachable."

"So, in other words, you've always been unreachable to me."

"Maybe it's the other way around."

"What are you talking about?"

"Like a fool I came to you, came to surprise you, but you had that woman in your bed."

"If you were in my bed, would you be there when I woke up the next morning? Would you decide it didn't happen again, file it away with Chapel Hill and New York?"

She nodded. "This is why business and pleasure should not mix."

I nodded back. "You don't want me, so what difference does it make who I'm fucking?"

She reached into her bag, took out a package, tossed it, made it land next to me.

Luwak coffee. The present I had given her in North Carolina.

I said, "You're giving that back too?"

"Don't bring me coffee, talk to me for hours, walk around holding my hand, make me start to feel things I haven't felt in years, don't be nice to me, do the things in bed . . . the things you do . . . don't do all of that then take some whore to bed with you and act like it's no big fucking deal."

"You run hot and cold, push me away, tell me whatever we did didn't fucking happen—"

"Why in the hell do you think I came to London? *To see you.* I could've handled this business with you over the phone. Same goes for the business in North Carolina and New York."

"I tell you I have damn near a mill saved up and you—"

"Does it look like I need *anything* from any man? I'm not that destitute girl you met years ago. I have *hustled* my way through my pains and heartaches. A million dollars? Before long I'll have that ten times over. Your problem is that you're . . . you're . . . a whore. Just like your mother."

I dared her to say that shit again.

"Just like your mother. *Puta ka.*" She growled. "*Puta ka. Putang ina mo.*"

Then there were long, hate-filled stares.

The tube rocked. People around us. Nothing I could do. Arizona knew that.

I smiled. "Arizona, your mother was a cock-sucking, strung-out, broke-ass crackhead who fucked strangers and sucked un-washed dick to get high, and you're disrespecting me like that?"

"Son of a whore. That's all you are. The son of a whore."

"That's why Scamz used to smack your ass silly. Smacked you and fucked your sister because you didn't have what it took to keep a real man. And you still don't have what it takes."

She put her hand in her bag like she was about to pull out a weapon.

The female British voice announced we were approaching King's Cross. The train stopped. People rushed off as others hurried on, raced for vacant seats. Others stood, jockeyed for space, got between us with their backpacks and luggage, separated jealousy and anger.

I said, "How do you suck the Jesus out of my dick at a movie, get your nut, then leave like a goddamn whore? How do you do that? Learn that from your mother? Her mother?"

"Do I suck dick better than your mother?"

That shut me down. Flames rose in my eyes.

"Bitch." I gritted my teeth, my voice a deep growl. "I'll fuck your ass up."

Arizona said some things to me in Tagalog, and judging by her expression they were vile and horrible things. She struggled by people, exited the tube, rage pacing her stride. I left the Luwak coffee on the seat, bumped around people, made it off the train just as the doors shut, more people separating us, chased her toward the WAY OUT sign, ran up the stairs after her like a damn square. She hurried away. Arizona knew I was there, heard me calling her name.

Both of us were beyond upset.

I was losing control. Not cool, not cool at all.

This was too damn volatile. Needed to turn around. But I chased her.

I was dynamite chasing a woman made of nitroglycerin.

She headed toward the escalator, got on, and moved with the impatient people on the left side, kept up with the ones who walked and ran to the top. Her slender legs pumped as she moved by people standing to the right, as she held her coat and bag tight to her chest, worked her heels and sprinted by advertisements for both the yellow pages and the theater.

Halfway up she slowed her pace and scowled back at me, her

small mouth tight, her body rising up toward the surface. We traded scowls until, once again, she vanished.

Grimacing, I went back to the tube, decided to let Arizona handle her own problems.

I battled London's cold and dreary weather.

London was a scandalous woman and I knew her sex-and-music district well, took to the small alleys with the clubs, places that were scary from the outside and not much better inside.

She was here.

I could smell her.

I'm surprised I didn't sense she was here.

The stench of Chinese food and heinous memories had battered my senses.

A boy in his late teens asked me if I was looking for girls, told me he had three upstairs. That there was no charge to look. I asked what his working women looked like. He described them, said all the girls were Russian. I shook my head, moved on.

Another man handed me a business card and walked on. The advertiser was half-naked, a dark-skinned African woman, her hair had dark roots, turned pink as it left her scalp, becoming fire red, wild hair that shot out like a fireworks show on the Fourth of July. The card said she worked in Central London, on Edgware Road; her rates started at £80 for half an hour, for full and personal service she charged £140, outcalls started at £250 for one and a half hours.

It wasn't her.

I dropped that card and moved on.

I was close. If she was still here, this would be her postal code.

Some places left their doors open, signs welcoming American money. Around £60 for half an hour of sex. Girls were selling themselves all over Chinatown and at Shepherd's Market.

I'd find her.

If she was here, I'd find her.

London was another hedonistic place, not the best, but far from being the worst, just had to know which rocks to turn over, which alleys to walk to rent pleasure.

I knew where to go. Outside of being Pleasure Alley, Soho had a strip of places for cultured businessmen to stop and buy hard-core porn before going home to the family.

Soho was where the whores went to work undisturbed by the law.

No matter how long it took, I'd find her tonight.

The anger I'd received from Arizona, it would get used before I went to bed.

I needed my own vengeance.

My personal anger had dug its claws into my flesh and dragged me to Soho.

My rage was looking for a whore.

A whore I should've killed in Amsterdam.

Twenty-one

women are trouble

Phone call from his ten-year-old daughter as he waited for the tube at Tower Hill.

"But, Dad . . . Skeeter is eating *all* the cereal. My *favorite* cereal. The *last* box."

"Melanie. Baby. What time is it over there in Texas?"

"It's one o'clock. And he's eating all the cereal. He always eats all the cereal."

She went on and on. In full-blown drama mode. Like her mother.

He took the phone away from his ear.

He was standing midway on the platform, District Line, when a couple, a tall and muscular black man wearing a BOSTON cap, and a woman, short and light-skinned, maybe a Zadie Smith type, maybe an octoroon, he thought, stopped right by him. More like she stopped in front of him, her face tense with anger, and the tall black man followed her, his steps heavy, face laced with frustration. The guy wearing the BOSTON cap had on a leather coat, long and black. She wore an oversize black coat, about the size to fit the tall man she was with, and across the back of the jacket, in big red letters, was the word RENT. Her red scarf and red gloves matched the crimson marquee across her back.

She was upset. "You ran after her. Were gone an hour. Sneak off for a shag, did you?"

"No, I didn't sneak off and shag anybody."

Her accent was British. His accent wasn't.

"You prefer shagging her? If so, then go to her. Go to her now."

"Could you not do this bullshit right now?"

The man with the broken nose watched them. They were the loudest on the platform. Not screaming, but the only ones that could be heard, the British being a quiet lot.

"You pathetic wanker. Liar. You're still shagging her. If I hadn't come back from Birmingham with me parents, you would've been shagging her in our bed nonetheless."

She stormed away from him, her heels clacking across the concrete.

The tall guy waited a moment, took a few hard breaths, then he followed her.

They resumed their argument to the end of the platform.

The man with the broken nose stopped watching the show, put the phone to his ear.

His daughter was still ranting about her older brother eating all the cereal.

He asked his daughter, "Where is your mother?"

"I just told you Mom was in her room syncing her iPod."

"Syncing her iPod?"

"She's on iTunes downloading movies and videos and television shows and music."

"Tell your mother to stop syncing her iPod and make Skeeter stop eating your cereal."

"She yelled at me, told me to leave her alone, then she closed her door in my face."

"Geesh."

"Skeeter had cereal last night and this morning. I won't have any cereal for breakfast. What am I supposed to eat for breakfast, Daddy? He's eating the cereal."

He put the phone down again.

Glasses on, he checked his watch, saw it was seven, took his glasses off, tucked them away, looked up at the monitor, saw a tube was due in two minutes, then stood to the side of the crowded platform and looked over the tube map. The concierge had told him he could catch the District or the Circle. But he didn't trust the man's Romanian accent. He read the map. The Circle would take him to Liverpool, then the Central to Stratford. He was confused. He was at the District Line. He could run to the Central Line, but running would mess up his shower. Decided to take the District Line to Mile End, change to Central Line for one stop to Stratford Station. He hoped he was there in thirty minutes. He had to get to Stratford. To the Theatre Royal Stratford East.

The best seats cost £18 and he wanted to get the tickets before they were gone. This was his day off. No guns. No packages to take care of. No soon-to-be ex-wife.

No IRS. No lawyers.

He put the phone back up to his ear. Loved his kid, but wanted her off the phone.

He asked, "What do you want me to do about it? I'm in London, for Christ's sake."

"Daddy—did you hear what I said? I asked you about Harry Potter."

"Look, I'm on the tube platform and—"

"Harry Potter Harry Potter. Please please please get my Harry Potter books."

"Take the cereal from your brother."

"He'll slap me in my head if I take his cereal."

"Make him a ham-and-cheese sandwich. Cut the edges off. He'll like that."

"He'll throw the sandwich at me."

"I have to go."

"Last time he threw his cereal at me. The whole bowl. Milk was all on my hair."

"Look . . . you're going to have to be a big girl and handle the situ—"

"Daddy—I'm ten years old. He's fifteen. He's ten times bigger than I am big."

"Stop exaggerating."

"Daddy. Help me."

"Bang on your mother's door." He took a breath. "I have to go."

She hung up, screaming at her brother to stop eating up her favorite cereal.

He hopped on the tube. So many crazy people were on the tube. He'd never seen so many iPods and books in one place. Everybody wore earphones, crowded next to each other and disconnected from each other. The closer people were, the further they were apart. That's why he loved Katy. People were nice in Katy. People talked to each other in Katy. With all the books and iPods the tube looked like a cross between an electronic and a book convention.

The loud couple moved around looking for space, came his way, stopped next to him.

They were still arguing. It was obvious the woman wouldn't let the argument die.

The tall guy with the BOSTON cap asked the might-be-an-octoroon wearing the oversize RENT jacket, "Who did I help get the audition? Who has the part? You or Lola?"

"Did you tell Lola that? Did you tell Lola that you told them to not audition her? Does she know I'm Mimi? She's not Mimi. I am Mimi."

"Not now."

"*But did you tell her?* Did the words come from your mouth and go to her ears?"

"Please." He adjusted his BOSTON cap, infuriated. "Let's talk about this later."

"You left me looking like a fool and you chased her. Do you know how that makes me feel? You left me and you ran after her. You were gone almost an hour. You left me for her."

Boston didn't say anything.

The girl folded her arms, closed off body language.

She asked, "You still love her, don't you? You prefer her to me. Tell me. You pathetic lying wanker. Tell me. Do you prefer her? I bloody hate you. You know that? I bloody hate you."

Boston gritted his teeth, then grabbed the girl, grabbed her rough, five thousand pounds of anger in his eyes.

Looked like Boston was about to knock the bejesus out of the might-be-an-octoroon.

The man with the broken nose was about to say something, was about to get involved.

But the guy wearing the BOSTON cap pulled the might-be-an-octoroon to him and kissed her, tongue and all.

She fought it for a moment, twisted, struggled, slapped his shoulders, very theatrical, then went limp in his arms, again dramatic.

The man with the broken nose moved by them, went to the opposite end of the car, found peace and quiet, and an empty seat. On the seat was a newspaper. *The Mirror.* Special edition.

The front page was about the dead WAG.

He popped a square of cinnamon gum in his mouth, picked up the paper, fixed his $10 glasses over his injured nose, started reading about the heinous crime that had London in a choke hold. The papers said the crime was brutal. Done in public. With no reliable witnesses.

He looked down at the other end of the train.

That couple was still kissing.

Tebby smiled.

Still dressed in the colors of angels. Six feet tall, like a goddess. Standing out in a sea of darkness and gloom. He saw her when he stepped off the tube. She was waiting.

Tall and bald. Her long coat flowing like a cape. But the bald head.

She made being bald look chic and daring and beautiful.

He greeted her with a broad smile, asked, "How was your day?"

"Lovely because I thought of you all day."

He smiled. "I thought about you all day too."

She complimented him on his new suit, then extended her hand. He took her hand.

Her skin was soft. And warm. Very warm. And electric. Very electric. His throat dried and his voice tried to shrink.

Seeing her again was enough. Holding her hand was more than he had expected.

She took the lead and he followed her, maneuvered through the mostly black crowd toward Great Eastern Road. The tube station was huge. A DLR station was there as well. A freight yard not too far away. Across the street was a mall. She told him that the theater was on the other side of the plaza, but they could walk through the mall and come out right at the theater.

As he walked, one of his cellular phones rang.

The phone that chimed was the hotline.

Sam was calling.

Either with news on Gideon. Or a new contract.

But he didn't answer. Not while he was holding Tebby's hand.

Not while everything in his life was, for once, perfect.

Inside the small theater the actors were already onstage.

The stage set up to show different locations. The play hadn't started, but the actors were on stage interacting, ignoring the audience, already creating the atmosphere of South Africa. Men to the side drinking and gambling. A young man on a bed, resting between a younger girl's legs, a girl dressed in a school uniform. A mixed-race boy reading a book. Much more.

The actors moved with spirit, the set changed, the play began.

With a brutal rape.

He heard sobbing and looked at Tebby. Tears remained in her eyes. The play had moved beyond the initial rape and murder, eventually showed a schoolgirl fleeing her home after a lifetime of squabbling and abuse, only to find solace in the arms of a gangster, and Tebby was still crying. Not loud. Gentle tears. A serial killer was on the loose, the play was dramatic and brutal, but since the part with the schoolgirl fleeing, Tebby had quietly been sobbing.

The man with the broken nose reached over and took Tebby's hand.

The play ended as it began. With brutality and abuse.

The actors received a standing ovation.

Tebby looked at him as if she were saying this was her life, her world.

He put his finger up to her damp cheek. Then he kissed her cheek.

While the crowd applauded, Tebby moved closer, put her head on his shoulder.

He asked Tebby, "You need a moment?"

She nodded.

Inside his pocket, his cellular vibrated. The hotline was on fire.

Twenty-two

detour

Leicester Square was alive, crowded and lit up like it was Times Square.

The man with the broken nose hated the crowd, he hated crowds, preferred the easiness of Katy, Texas, over this craziness. Too many people. He had paused in front of the rows of people off the side of the three cinemas, artists sketching mediocre caricatures of tourists, hundreds of people filing into clubs and restaurants between the Leicester Square tube and the Piccadilly tube. They walked by Burger King, Starbucks, Häagen-Dazs, and steak houses.

He moved on with Tebby.

Tebby said, "You haven't said anything about the play."

"I didn't know what to say. Saw you were disturbed by the performance."

"I wanted a different ending."

"You didn't like the ending?"

She shrugged. "Yes. And no. It made sense. But I wanted something else."

He said, "Seemed appropriate to me. Made sense."

"The killer got away."

The man with the broken nose shrugged.

Tebby nodded. "Wanted a happy ending. We all want happy endings. Everybody does."

He thought about the scenes with the killing the most. How when dying, people clung to life to their last breath. Like they were suffocating. Like when he was a kid drowning in water.

He didn't ask Tebby why she'd cried during the scenes portraying rape and murder, more of the former than the latter. He just thought about his little girl. It was a brutal world.

Tebby led him by the Prince Charles Cinema in the heart of the square. Another Häagen-Dazs Café. Pizza Hut. Tokyo Diner. Cork & Bottle. All Bar One. New Diamond. Mr. Kong.

She asked, "See anything to your liking?"

He pointed at Bella Italia, an Italian restaurant between Baskin-Robbins and Club Metro.

The man with the broken nose took Tebby there. He was still holding Tebby's hand.

He said, "You haven't asked me about my nose."

"And you haven't asked me about my bald head."

"I figured if you wanted me to know about your bald head, you'd tell me."

"Same for your nose."

He wanted a table where he could keep his back to the wall, so he could watch whoever came into the room. Old habits that had kept him alive this long. Tebby told him she wanted to sit upstairs in the window, said that way they could see all of Leicester Square and people-watch as they ate dinner. Mild tension rose up inside him. The corner of his lips turned downward.

First date. In London. With a queen from Botswana.

He complied.

After they ordered, he said, "So you say you're from Francistown in Botswana."

Tebby said, "Francistown. That's where I was born."

"Haven't heard of a lot of the places in Africa you mentioned."

Tebby asked, "Do you read? If so, what books?"

"I read. I lean toward Dostoyevsky. Kafka. What about you?"

"African writers. Bessie Head. Zoë Wicomb. Nelson Mandela. Coetzee. People like that. Oh, I'm reading Constance Briscoe's book. *Ugly*. Heard her mum is suing her over things she said."

"Connie Briscoe?"

"Constance. She's a judge here. Wrote her story. Abused as a child by her mum."

"Is that right."

"Her mum beat her, starved her, abandoned her when she was thirteen."

"Sounds . . . depressing, if you don't mind me saying so."

"She was physically and mentally abused. Now she is a judge."

"Amazing. But still sounds depressing."

"We can do anything when we decide to win no matter what. You should read it."

He wanted to order drinks. Tebby recommended shandy. Beer flavored with lemonade. Her favorite drink. So he ordered shandy.

Tebby asked, "Where were you born in Texas?"

"Moved to Texas when I was a kid. Grew up in a little city called Roscoe. Was born in West Memphis, Arkansas."

"Never heard of that West Memphis place. Is that similar to L.A. or New York?"

"Neither. Sounds like the place you grew up, to tell the truth."

"I doubt if it's anything like where I grew up. We didn't have electricity."

"No electricity?"

"No one did. It was no big deal. We didn't know we were supposed to have electricity."

He wasn't good at small talk. Wished he hadn't said the *Ugly* book sounded depressing.

Not like his life had been the source of inspiration for many.

A moment later Tebby asked, "Your father only had one wife?"

"Yeah. Yours?"

"Six wives, my father had. Maybe seven."

"Six or seven wives?"

"Africans. Polygamy. It still exists. Men have many wives."

"Brothers and sisters? You have brothers and sisters?"

"Of course. Do I know them all? Of course not."

The food came and they began eating.

He said, "So, why are you bald? Since you put it out there a while ago."

"My best friend back home, my childhood friend, her name is Lorato Modiri."

"Okay."

"She has cancer. She lost all of her hair."

"Sorry to hear that. I really am."

"That is why I shaved my head. I had long hair. Long, beautiful hair. So did Lorato. The chemotherapy has taken all of her hair. So I shaved my head to show her my love. My support."

That warmed him.

He said, "You're amazing."

"So are you, Bruno."

When they were done eating, Tebby went to the toilet.

His phone buzzed. The hotline.

He took out his phone. Voice strong and confident, he answered, "Talk to me."

"Got another job."

"Pitch it to me."

"Gambling debt. Jamaican."

"The sponsor?"

"Jamaican that runs this betting shop in Croydon. Jamaican-on-Jamaican thing."

"Get me the package."

"Talk soon."

"Yeah. Talk soon."

He hung up.

Tebby was making her way back through the crowd.

He watched the way other men and women stared at her.

Tebby had her cellular phone up to her face.

He wondered who she had tipped away to call.

Her children.

An old lover who spoke French and spat out bullshit poetry.

A current lover that she would go visit as soon as she finished dinner.

He sighed. Killing was so much easier than dating.

He looked out the window. At the crowd. So many people in a small space.

Hip-hop boys were passing out flyers, trying to lure the pretty women into clubs.

A white man with a Bible was off to the side preaching the word to no one.

A hundred pubs and twice as many clubs were in the square. Thousands of people were passing by. He witnessed at least three hundred nationalities per minute.

Then he almost jumped to his feet.

Gideon.

He thought he saw Gideon coming down Bear Street, a street that angled in from Charing Cross and Trafalgar Square into the heart of the pandemonium. The man with the broken nose wasn't sure. *Im-fucking-possible.* His heart raced as he watched the man that looked like Gideon, spied him passing by the venues that sold half-price theater tickets. It was dark, it was crowded, thousands of people were down below, but he focused on that singular face as it came closer.

As if on cue, Gideon stopped right out front of Bella Italia, looked back toward Café Rimini and Vue, then moved by the long line of people trying to get inside Metro Club & Bar.

It was Gideon without a doubt. And he was alone.

He was in perfect position for a bullet to the head.

The man with the broken nose reached for his gun. But he didn't have a weapon.

His Desert Eagle was back in his hotel room.

He took out his cellular, started dialing Sam's number.

Had to know if the money was in place.

If the money was in place, he would handle that contract to-night.

"Bruno, are you ready?"

Phone in his hand, he looked up at this woman.

A tall woman. Dressed in white. Her smile as big as her ear-rings.

For a moment he had no idea who she was.

Then he remembered.

Tebby.

The woman was Tebby.

She said, "Ready to leave?"

He hesitated. "Ready."

He took her hand and rushed her out of the restaurant, headed in the direction Gideon had gone, looking for him in the crowd, then seeing Gideon again.

Tebby said, "Thank you for dinner."

"You're welcome."

He thought Gideon was heading toward the Piccadilly Circus tube, but Gideon turned down a side street that went toward Shaftesbury Avenue, moved through that crowd.

Holding Tebby's hand, the man with the broken nose paused, his heart still racing, palms damp, jaw tight, droves of people moving around him as he stared at his vanishing target.

He asked Tebby, "What's down there?"

"Wardour Street goes into Soho. Chinatown. Red-light district. Strip clubs."

"Is that right?"

"Harmony has a big store down there. Largest adult store in the area."

"Didn't know that."

"Want to go?"

"Actually, I'm tired, ready to turn in, so I'd better get you back to the tube."

"You're right. I need to get the tube south and find where to change."

"South? You're not going back to Tower Hill?"

"To Brixton. South London."

"Thought you lived somewhere up by Tower Hill."

"Oh, no. Can't afford that area. Was in the financial district looking for another job. I won't be able to afford to open my own restaurant with the job I have, not on this salary."

"Then let me . . . I'll walk you to the tube."

Charing Cross was in the opposite direction, at least ten minutes. Longer with Tebby's slow and easy pace. By the time he walked to Charing Cross, stuck her on a tube, and ran back to Soho, Gideon's trail would be cold. Gideon's trail was almost cold now.

He could do this now. Get home to his children.

He was anxious. "How long will it take you to get to Brixton?"

"Depends. If I leave now, I should be fine." She checked her watch. "If I miss the last tube, then I have to catch the bus. And if the tube stops before I get home, I still have to get off and take a bus or a taxi. Getting to Brixton could be tricky. And that could take a while."

He was determined. "No, let me put you in a taxi."

"That's not necessary."

"I insist. Let me put you in a taxi."

He held her hand as they walked.

Desire.

He felt her desire.

It was subtle, but it was there.

With him trying to end the evening, that desire became more pronounced.

More obvious.

She said, "If you wanted to go through Soho, look at some shops . . ."

"It's late."

"I know. Just don't want the night to end so abruptly."

A six-foot-tall, beautiful woman from Botswana had offered to stroll into the red-light district and browse a porn store with him. The gods could be so cruel.

Tebby asked, "Everything okay?"

"What you mean?"

"You're . . . different all of a sudden. Did I do or say something wrong?"

He said, "I'm . . . it was a long flight. Six-hour time change. No sleep. Had a long day."

"And I didn't bring clothes. If I went with you, I'd have to leave in a couple of hours to get back home in time to change for work. I'd be exhausted. So I guess I need to go home."

He flagged down a hackney, gave Tebby £60, more than enough to get her home. He hugged her good-bye. He was trying to rush, but he felt her trying to make it linger.

She said, "I'm glad I went to Starbucks today."

"Me too."

She leaned forward. He leaned to her. She gave him her tongue. A slow, soft kiss.

When it ended, he felt light-headed. She looked intoxicated.

He said, "Tomorrow?"

"Should I bring an extra bag with me? Or would that be inappropriate?"

That frankness caught him off guard.

He smiled. "Yes. Bring an extra bag."

"Then I will bring an extra bag. Clothes for work. Just in case."

"Talk soon?"

"Talk soon. Cheers."

As the taxi pulled away, he sprinted back toward the street he had seen Gideon take.

He peeped inside porn shops. Passed by strip shows advertising American-style pole dancing. Then came out in the heart of the red-light area. Saw men going in and out of doors.

Saw women up in the windows, red lights glowing as they smoked hand-rolled cigarettes.

He found Gideon. Spied him passing by two little boys who were in the streets playing soccer. He watched Gideon look inside the doorway that led to every working woman.

The man with the broken nose eased through the crowd.

Moving by the kids playing soccer, he watched Gideon, focused, searching.

He got closer. Twenty yards. Ten yards. Point-blank range. Without a gun.

The filthy soccer ball stole his attention, hit his leg. The little boys ran by him without apology.

Then Gideon disappeared inside the doorway of the house of whores.

The man with the broken nose slowed at the door.

The whore asked Gideon, "Blow job or full service?"

He saw the back of Gideon's head, the golden legs of the working woman who was up at the top of the stairs. The man with the broken nose moved on, lurked across the street from a queer porn shop, then found a better hiding spot in Tyler's Court, an alley that was about six feet wide and no more than thirty yards away from the door Gideon had entered.

He jogged down the alley, searched for something he could use as a killing device. Nothing. He couldn't find a bottle on the streets. Nothing to serve as a good shank.

He ran back to the end of the alley. Watched men walking in and out of doors.

The kids were still playing soccer, kicking a dirty ball up and down a street that smelled like shit. He stood in the shadows wondering if Gideon was armed, wondering if Gideon was in that flat on a contract, waited with his heart beating loud enough to mute all sounds, reminding himself that Gideon had massacred several men in Tampa, knowing Gideon had acted alone, that he had done what was impossible, had killed a small army without any weapons.

That meant Gideon was good at hand-to-hand combat.

This might not be the place. Or the time. Not for hand-to-hand.

A bullet in the head was always the best.

Hand-to-hand wasn't his ideal scenario.

He waited. People going up and down Berwick, some taking the alley, he waited.

He kept his eye on the whore's door, watching the boys chase the shitty soccer ball.

Gideon's package had been impressive. It seemed like Gideon had a reputation.

The man with the broken nose told himself he needed a larger reputation.

A larger reputation yielded more money.

He could kill Gideon and take his name. Take both his name and his fame.

Or just be known as the man who killed Gideon.

He waited, wishing he had time to get his Desert Eagle and come back.

He waited, thinking about Tebby.

Wondering, if he hadn't seen Gideon, how their night would've ended.

It didn't matter. He wouldn't call her again. It always started off nice. And ended badly.

When a man grew older, he grew wiser, learned to play the ending.

He'd learned from his own experiences.

He'd let the romantic evening with Tebby die with that first and last kiss.

His phone rang. The hotline.

Sam answered, "Talk to me."

"I found Gideon. And I'm getting ready to kill him."

He'd never see Tebby again.

He'd kill Gideon and catch the first flight back to Katy.

Twenty-three

valley of darkness

The green cardboard sign outside the first door I passed said
MODEL UPSTAIRS.

Hand-painted on the wall inside the next door was the same advertisement.

Berwick Street. Central London. Postal code W1.

Red lights were perched in almost every windowsill, red bulbs hanging inside dingy windows.

Openings to every door had at least one fading sign made from cheap cardboard, damp cardboard that had been cut by hand and warped by the elements, written on in block-style lettering that looked like it had come from someone who had a third-grade education at most.

A soccer ball rolled by my feet. Two young boys, neither any more than six, ran by me, chasing the ball. One had blond, curly hair. He had on yellow-and-green footballer's gear, Brazil's team, the number 10, and the name RONALDINHO across his back. The other boy had dark skin, maybe the darkest skin I'd ever seen, his footballer gear blue-and-white, the colors of Chelsea, the number 8 and the name LAMPARD across the rear of his jersey.

Five little girls stood to the side cheering them on. Miniature footballers and wannabe WAGs. Those preschool kids were out during the sexual hours, on their own. Not afraid of the night or the adults passing by in search of pleasure and drugs. They were at home in this world.

So was I.

Every door was open. They were waiting; women with working names like Michelle, Sarah, and Elena were in their windows waiting to show customers how friendly they could be for the right price. The doors that had cheap signs that said YOUNG ASIAN MODEL were ignored. Thelma wasn't Asian. Door after door, I searched London's red-light district, where the whores called themselves models. I doubted if any of these women would appear on Tyra Banks's show.

The sign was yellow. The handwriting familiar and as unique as her own fingerprints.

DIAMOND. SEDUCTIVE AND FULLY EXPERIENCED. ALL SERVICES. LOVES A&O.

Her cheap, wooden door was barely on the hinges of a small, indiscreet opening between British Sex Shop and Blue Boy Paradise DVD Shop, the latter having more than enough copies of blue movies with men being friendly with men in every square inch of its front window.

She was working on a narrow street lined with porn shops and peep shows.

I looked down the avenue. The blond kid was kicking the ball to his friend.

The children of whores were entertaining themselves in the midnight hour.

Nobody noticed me.

I could find my peace and sanity in five minutes. Maybe less.

A man rushed down the concrete stairs.

He hit the streets smiling, looking relaxed and anxious to get away before he was exposed. He made eye contact and surrendered the red-faced chuckle of a man who had just finished fucking, then hurried down Berwick, not looking back until he was down by Vinyl Junkies.

He looked back and gave me the thumbs-up.

That meant the pussy was good. Give it a shot. The ride was worth the ticket.

I turned into the opening, a piss odor assaulting my senses. Chipped concrete stairs led up to more chipped concrete stairs. Dull white walls and more foul odors greeted me. Paint was peeling away from the walls and ceiling. Exposed pipes and crooked stairs were an eyesore. Handrail was about to fall free. Light fixtures outdated, would bet the same for the electrical throughout the building. Another step inside and I saw the ceiling was sagging. A handyman could spend three years on this property doing modernization and improvements.

The stairway was steep. All I could see were her feet. And from her angle all she could see were my jeans and boots. I recognized her feet. My heartbeat sped up.

I stepped up until I could see most of her body, from waist down.

Then went up a few stairs until I could see her up to her neck.

It was her.

She was at the top of the dingy stairway, in the cramped space, sitting on a shiny barstool, a brand-new barstool that was in contradiction with everything else. She sat there, reggae playing in the background, legs crossed, like she was a queen sitting on her throne.

Bob Marley sang his redemption song. Everyone wanted redemption.

I wanted revenge.

She was on her cellular phone, finishing up a cigarette. She released a quick exhalation that stopped short of exuding boredom.

She asked me, "Blow job or full service?"

"Are you as good as the Russian and Asian girls?"

"First off, I'm better than the Russians. Or the Asians. I'm better than anything you'll find on Tisbury or Peter Street. And the Asians give you an awful blow job and the worst sex you ever had. They won't give you your money's worth. With me, you get a wicked time. And no up sale. My rate is all-inclusive. So, with that said, tell me what you need and I'll tell what it will cost."

"Is that right, Thelma?"

She stood up with quickness when I said her birth name, a name she hadn't probably heard or gone by in years. Her shiny barstool screeched across the rugged concrete landing.

I went up a few more stairs, until I could see her face, until she could see mine.

"What's the matter, Thelma?"

Disbelief widened her eyes.

I said, "Haven't seen you since Amsterdam. Not since you were in window 120."

She saw that it was really me and dropped her cigarette, fumbled for it, and dropped her mobile phone. Her mobile hit the stairs, came apart, the battery flying out. I picked up the phone, the battery, put it back together, took a couple of steps up, and tossed it back to her. She tried to catch it, but it fell again, this time near her feet. She left it where it was, not worried about re-connecting and finishing her phone call in the proper way. I took three more steps. Heard her deep breathing. If I didn't know any better, I'd think she was trembling. The red light over my head, darkness still shadowing most of my features.

Seconds slipped by with droves of witnesses hurrying down the cobbled road behind me.

She lit another cigarette. In a trembling voice she asked, "How did you find me?"

"I found you."

"You're angry. You're still angry."

I took another step up. "Very angry."

She backed away from me.

I asked, "You don't think I'd kill you, do you?"

"You're so damn angry." She touched her left eye, did the same to her lips and chin, made a terrified face, cringed like she still felt the pain. "You beat me up pretty bad."

"With cause."

"You went insane."

"You were gone when I came back."

"I was in the hospital pissing blood."

"You should've been in a mental institute."

"What I did was wrong. But I never struck you. Not once."

I was one step below her by then. Close enough to inhale her perfume. Smelled the scent of seven or eight colognes mixed into the sweat that had dried on her skin. The scent of many men lived on her flesh. Today had been a good day for her. I'd showed up after the rush.

She took my hand, pulled me closer, kissed both sides of my cheeks, then kissed me on my lips. Her lipstick was thick, red. I wiped it away. It stained my hands like blood.

She softened her voice, asked, "How've you been?"

"Was about to ask you the same, Thelma."

"Please, stop calling me Thelma."

"Your name is Thelma."

"You're my son. Please. Call me Mother."

Twenty-four

prelude to fury

Her cellular rang.

Her ring tone was hip-hop. Beyoncé. Thelma picked up her cellular phone, looked at the number, pressed a button to divert the call, then sat back down on her barstool.

I leaned against the wall, left her potential customers a clear shot of her wares.

She asked, "What name are you using now?"

"Gideon."

"The name you had when we were in Montreal, that was the name I liked best."

"I don't give a shit what you like."

She paused. "You found me. You actually found me."

"Ran into Sergeant."

"He told you."

"Right before he died."

Her face lit up. She shook her head. Grief covered her face. Her eyes watered.

She asked, "You?"

I nodded.

Her lip trembled. She swallowed. "No. Not Sergeant. Why?"

"Because some people deserve to die."

Her grief magnified. As did her fear of me.

Looked like she wanted to run. Then realized there was nowhere to run.

Then she jumped.

Someone was sneaking up behind me.

I remembered Amsterdam, how she had sent trouble to find me.

I jerked around, ready to attack whoever was creeping up behind me.

I wouldn't be as nice to them as I was to the thugs in Amsterdam.

A man in a suit was standing in the ragged doorway. His face unseen.

Thelma called down, "What can I do for you today?"

He crept up the stairs, took slow steps, walked halfway up before stopping.

He said, "Diamond?"

"Yes."

"You were referred to me."

"By whom?"

"Ahmad."

"Okay." She said that like she had no idea who Ahmad was. "What can I do for you?"

He wore a suit and worn dress shoes. Eyeglasses with small lenses. Hair black and cut short. Thick and with so much body hair he looked like he had the werewolf syndrome. His coat was open wide, his gut spilling over his belt.

He whispered, "How much for straight sex?"

"Twenty pounds."

"How much time?"

"Ten minutes."

"How much for a blow job?"

"Sex and blow job, thirty pounds. If you want multiple positions, forty."

"I would like to get the sex and blow job for thirty quid, please."

"Thirty pounds up front."

"How soon can I see you?"

"Catch me in about an hour."

"Have to get the tube home to the family. I don't have that much time to spare."

"Then come back in fifteen to thirty. You'll have enough time to make the last tube."

"You take Visa?"

"Cash. Until you become a regular. Then I'll accept credit."

"I'll go to the cash machine, be right back."

"A cash machine is right across the street at Somerfield."

"Somerfield is closed."

"Use the one inside Blue Boy. Tell them I sent you."

The man waved and hurried away, checking his watch.

It was hard to do, but I raised my head and looked in my mother's eyes.

We stared for a moment.

She said, "A son should never hurt his mother."

"And a mother should never do the hurtful . . . the damaging things you did to her son."

Again we stared. Two unfeeling, poker-faced stares.

She said, "You killed Sergeant."

I nodded.

Her grief magnified. "I was drunk. When that thing happened, I was drunk."

"And I was angry."

"You almost killed me."

"You did so many horrible things to me."

"I almost died that night."

"Almost."

"You're still angry."

"Very."

"You were so angry in Amsterdam. I'd never seen you look like that."

"This is what you created. I'm your Frankenstein monster."

She swallowed.

I had marched up to her door like I was the Cylons invading New Caprica. Had come to her filled with bile, hate poisoning my every thought. Hate was a virus. Revenge its only cure.

I said, "'You can't play God and wash your hands of the things you've created because sooner or later the day comes and you can't run from the things you've done anymore.'"

I had just quoted *Battlestar Galactica*; a speech Adama had given had hit close to home, stayed with me. That same quote reminded me of other whispers from a shallow grave.

Nothing was said for a moment.

Her eyes were blank, haunted. She mumbled, kept repeating, "Sergeant is dead."

She said that like there had been a deeper connection between them.

More than sex for hire. More than sharing drinks.

She said, "Ever since Amsterdam, almost every night, without fail, I've dreamed about you coming to murder me. I knew you'd come. I knew you'd find me. I knew you'd be angry."

"We'll get that taken care of before I leave London."

She shuddered.

"Diamond?" That British accent came from behind me. "Are you Diamond?"

A man in a leather jacket was down in the doorway. Tall. White. Dorky. Ugly as hell.

Her voice trembled. "Can I help you, handsome?"

"What you charge for back door?"

"Sixty quid. That includes blow job and multiple positions."

"Now a good time?"

"Why don't you come up here and wait."

The man passed by me, went up top, passed by my mother, went into her flat.

I smiled, my grin unadulterated anger.

She smiled in return, hers still laced with fear.

I terrified her. She had let that stranger up so she could feel safe. So I wouldn't do her harm right now. If I did, she'd have a witness to my rage. If I needed to, I could kill him easier than I could kill her, just as fast. In every war there was collateral damage. Somebody was always in the way of victory.

"Good to see you're still selling the hole I came out of."

She swallowed, almost came undone. "I have to go."

"One question before you go make that money."

"What, Son?"

"Don't call me Son."

"You are my son. I will call you my son."

I paused, then worked my way to one of the many questions that had been in my mind all of these years. "You stole from that man. Did you not steal from that man?"

"What man?"

"The man who tried to kill you. The man I killed for you. The first person I killed."

"Mr. Midnight."

"I think he caught you trying to steal from him."

"That's not what happened."

"His attack wasn't unprovoked."

"Shouldn't matter why he attacked me. You were supposed to save your mother."

"He tried to kill a thieving whore."

"Now you have become him."

"Bullshit. I became what you made me."

"My sweet little Frankenstein."

"I'll be back for you. Before I leave, I will be back."

"I know. I'll be here."

"One more question."

"Yes, Son?"

"Who was my father?"

"I told you. He was in the army. Special Forces."

"Where is he now?"

"Only saw him that one time."

"Then how do you know that man was my father?"

"Maybe I made sure he was your father."

"What does that mean?"

"I put his sperm inside me when he left. I took the condom and put his sperm inside me."

"Why?"

"Because I liked him. Because he was a real man. He was the kind of man I would've wanted to be my husband. Because I wanted part of him to stay with me."

"Why?"

"Because I wanted to have a baby. Because I was tired of being alone. After my best friend was killed, maybe I had a hard time dealing with life. I hated being alone in this world."

My anger had me blazing.

I said, "See you soon."

"How much time do I have?"

"Not much. Get your house in order."

"I'll be here. I'll be ready."

Then she backed away, eased inside her apartment, and closed the door.

Her perfume remained, mixed in with the toxic stench that was assaulting my senses.

I turned around, took the slimy concrete stairs to the cold and slimy rue, once again greeted by droves of strangers and neon signs advertising sex. I headed up the narrow road.

It was starting to rain again. Even if it stormed forty days and forty nights, it would never rain hard enough to wash away this scum.

Numb. I was numb. I slowed down between a cloth shop and

the Islamic Centre. I looked back, saw half-dressed women standing in dingy windows, cigarettes burning between their fingertips, lips painted, eyes done, boredom in their eyes, red lightbulbs over their heads.

"How much does she charge you for her services?"

Coming toward me, money in hand, it was the fat, hairy man I'd just seen in her doorway.

He adjusted his glasses, asked, "How much she charges you, mate?"

My eyes went to him. My hands turning into fists.

He asked, "I think thirty quid is a bit much for straight sex and a bloody blow job."

Darkness rose. I was about to lose my freedom and kill that man.

He repeated, "They all say she's good, but if you ask me, she looks a little worn around the edges. What you think? Was she worth it? Did she give you full service or only a blow job?"

"Away from me."

"What was that?"

I shoved him so hard he stumbled and fell down.

He rolled side to side, got up, cursed me. I went toward him, hands in fists. He ran away. I scowled at the stiff-lipped people who were staring at me.

I marched away, shoulders hunched.

Like Frankenstein.

From time to time my mother used to send women to my room. I'd wake up and some beautiful stranger would be stimulating me, doing whatever my mother had paid them to do. The last time . . . I was sixteen. Maybe seventeen. Had dropped out of school by then. I had fallen asleep. Nocturnal emission. Might've been masturbating in my sleep. Don't know what I was dreaming about. Or who. Halle Berry. Vivica Fox. Nia Long. Maybe all of those heavenly creatures at once. Woke up when I started having an orgasm. Looked down and expected to see the

Filipina woman I had grown accustomed to, or maybe the face of a stranger from Ethiopia, or Russia, hoped to see the eyes of an exotic woman smiling up at me, sucking my dick as her introduction. But I woke up with my drunken mother in my bedroom; the woman who had birthed me had taken me inside her mouth like I was a john from the streets.

I knew it had to be a mistake. She wouldn't do that on purpose.

Then she looked up at me. She looked in my eyes.

I wanted to push her away. But my orgasm had traveled beyond the point of no return; no matter how I wanted to, that overwhelming sensation had gone too far to turn it around.

I shuddered, cursed, held her head, pulled her hair. She made me come.

My drunken mother had assaulted me. Raped me with her mouth.

I yanked her up to her feet and hit her. The first blow was a backhand across her face.

She grabbed her bloodied mouth, tried to run. I caught her, threw her into the wall.

She tried to get out the door and I grabbed her leg, dragged her back inside.

Like Mr. Midnight had done, I grabbed her hard and quick, picked her up by her neck.

She scratched my hands, kicked her feet, gagged.

I was going to kill her and throw her dead body in the streets.

Was going to kill her quick and without mercy, kill like she had taught me to do.

I had already found out she'd been stealing from me, pimping me.

When she stopped moving, I yanked my hands from her throat.

I dropped her. I thought she was dead. Hoped she was dead.

And I left her just like that. I left her battered and bruised body in the middle of the floor.

That had fucked me up.

When I came back, she wasn't there. She never came back.

Left me there, a high school dropout; the only skill I had was the one she had taught.

Neon ADULT CINEMA and XXX signs lit up Berwick Street and Soho.

Soho. *So many Hos.* Maybe that's what *Soho* stood for.

I tried to move on, but I couldn't. I was stuck in my past. I looked back at Thelma's door. Saw another man standing in the piss- and smoke-smelling stairwell reading her cheap, handwritten cardboard sign, then saw that man lower his head and hurry up the filthy stairs.

I could've been done. Could've ended my misery. With the heel of my hand I could've hit her nose, shoved her bone back into her brain. It would've been quick for her. And over for me.

The soccer ball was kicked hard, bounced off one of the boys, rolled my way.

The kids were playing football as if they were in the middle of a park.

The damp and filthy soccer ball rolled by me. I caught up with it, stopped it with my foot, then looked back. Both of the young boys were waiting, jumping up and down.

I wondered if they understood what their mothers were doing in those disgusting rooms.

I kicked the ball back to them, the blond boy losing the race to the dark-skinned boy.

The blond boy looked at me, put his hands up and shrugged, then ran and chased his friend. I watched them battle for the ball awhile, overwhelmed by my own childhood memories.

Then they started chesting the ball, controlling the ball, passing it back and forth.

The blond kid was good, but the dark-skinned boy was a regular Pelé in the making.

I watched the boys play. Watched the innocent.

Thelma's red light was off. Like a black cab that had a paying customer.

I stared at my mother's window.

Tears in my eyes, I hurried away, headed down the uneven and damp streets that reeked of sin and shame, shoulders hunched like I was walking down the Boulevard of Broken Dreams.

I was leaving my revenge behind for one reason.

I was being followed.

I'd left her dilapidated flat and two minutes later I was being followed.

Like in Amsterdam. But only one person was following me this time.

I moved through the crowd, looking for his reflection in the storefronts.

I caught a glimpse.

Saw the man following me had on a suit. Saw the bandages on his nose.

Him again.

I was confused. Him being on the plane. My mother. Tried to put all of this together.

The pieces didn't fit. The dots wouldn't connect. But that didn't mean they didn't.

The stench of Chinese food assaulting me, I made a thousand turns.

He stayed behind me, kept a few people between us.

I didn't know if he was carrying. I only knew I was naked right now.

Then I ducked inside the tube station. Put hundreds of people between us.

Hundreds of witnesses. Which didn't mean much. A man got his throat cut while he rode the tube in Croydon. Got his throat slashed wide-open in a crowd. And nobody saw anything.

I got on the tube.

My wounded admirer did the same. Rushed on the same car, only at a different door.

I pretended I was reading a left-behind paper, saw him without looking at him.

He never looked directly at me, but at the same time he never took his eyes off me.

I tucked the paper under my arm, took out my cellular to phone Arizona, needed backup.

But there was no signal underground.

Death was riding this train, like it was the 309.

I was on my own.

I ended up leading my stalker to Knightsbridge.

I took to the crowded strip outside Harrods. Blended with thousands of shoppers.

He was still behind me. Had taken the heavily populated tubes along with me.

Big crowd. An ocean of people with bags in their hands going in every direction.

Lots of corners. I made a few turns and he lost me.

He lost me because now I was behind him. The rabbit had become the fox.

He gave up looking for me and I followed him back down into the tube.

He saw me in the crowd. He saw me without looking directly at me. I did the same without looking directly at him. My position let him see the mouse had become the cat.

I was near one door and he was at the door at the opposite end.

Then we killed the game and looked at each other.

I nodded. He did the same.

With those simple gestures, this had been confirmed.

We kept our eyes on each other.

He rode the Piccadilly Line down one exit and jumped off

at South Kensington, an area where a small flat went for over a million pounds, then rushed through the underground through-way. He started running. I did too. I chased him through an underground tunnel that extended the better part of a mile and came out at the base of Hyde Park, a few blocks shy of Prince Albert Hall. He ran uphill toward the high street, dashed through traffic and bolted into the park, sped past the huge golden tribute to Prince Albert, a tribute surrounded by lights and sculptures. Those bright lights kept me from losing him. He kept running, never slowing down. I was running behind him. I chased him through the darkness and light, ran another good mile across the park to the Bayswater Road and came out by the Corus Park Hotel. He went to his right, bolted across the streets and through traffic, headed by the Swan restaurant, another intersection, looked back, saw I was still there, then bolted inside the Lancaster Gate tube.

He had me by thirty seconds.

I chased him into the tube station, slapped my Oyster card on the sensor, and waited for the gate to open. People were at the elevator, but I heard his feet racing down winding stairs that went into the bowels of the earth. I went that way as fast as I could. I was halfway down the two-hundred-step descent when I heard a train stopping down below. I stumbled, got my balance, raced around a few people, and tried to catch him. I was catching up, had made it down the stairs and was racing through the final tunnel that led to the trains, but he had me by a good twenty seconds. Just enough time for him to jump on the Central Line before the doors closed.

He looked back at me.

Scowling as the train pulled away.

He didn't look fifty anymore. He looked like he could pass for thirty.

The next train was in two minutes. But he could've gotten off the Central Line tube anywhere from the next stop at

Marble Arch or where the train ended an hour away at Epping.

I was drenched, winded.

He hadn't broken a sweat.

I had chased him over three miles and he hadn't broken a sweat.

Twenty-five

out of control

Eight stops later he exited the Central Line at Bank, nose aching.

He exited the tube at one of the busiest stations in Central London, got off looking to see if Gideon was following him. The man with the broken nose was shaken. He was sweating. Running like that had aggravated his nasal fracture. Pain was rising and spreading across his face. Felt like blood was dripping from his nose. The bruising around his eyes felt magnified, his eyes again feeling swollen. He slowed down. He could run over twenty-six miles, wanted to do a one-hundred-mile run at some point, but with the hard time breathing, running in a suit and shoes and having to inhale through his mouth on a cold and damp night, he was momentarily spent.

He'd run away from Gideon expecting the man to give up chasing him in less than a quarter mile. No one chased for much longer than one lap. Gideon had kept up. That surprised and . . . frightened him. Gideon was a killer too, after all. Then he expected to hear a gunshot ring out. His contact told him that Gideon had picked up a SIG. And with that contract out, the man knew his days were numbered. Gideon had run like a monster that had been set on fire.

A monster he could've put to sleep. If only he had been prepared.

He didn't have his Eagle with him. He could've completed the transaction in that shit-smelling alley in Soho. But the money wasn't in place. The goddamn money wasn't in place.

If he did the job before he was paid, then he wouldn't get paid for the job.

Business. Just business.

He had decided to follow Gideon. See where he was hiding out. But that went wrong.

Now the enemy knew he was out there. The enemy was aware.

That changed everything.

He felt like he had been hunted. Nobody hunts the hunter.

He touched his face, didn't see blood, but it ached again, still felt he looked like some sort of sweaty, grotesque monster that had risen from the pits of hell. In a dark Italian suit.

Every man on the tube had on a dark suit. Every other man was running for the tube as if his life depended on it. But he was the only one with his face bandaged up.

That fucker in Jacksonville had hit him with something made of lead. He wanted to kill that fucker all over again.

He ran over to the Monument side of the tube. Took the District Line to Tower Hill. Came out and walked up the stairs, both his feet and muscles aching. His anger never-ending. One hundred and fifty meters later he was coming up on Novotel. Across the narrow street women were putting flowers on the curb and in the doorway at 1 Pepys. Mourners had been doing that all day. Like the dead WAG was their replacement for the late Princess Diana.

Touching his nose, he passed by the teary-eyed mourners. That fucking fracture. He knew he needed rhinoplasty. That was cool. He was going to start a new life. With a new nose.

He changed his bandages. Took aspirin. Wondered how much a good nose job cost.

Then he looked at the package again. Stared in amazement. Gideon was doing well for himself. Nothing like reading about someone else's success to magnify your own failures.

He'd do much better than that. He was confident. Once the soon-to-be-ex was gone.

He showered. He wasn't tired anymore. His feet no longer ached.

He owned too much rage to rest. Gnashing his teeth. His father would be disappointed.

Then he put on his custom-made holster. His suit coat.

He picked up the Desert Eagle. Made sure it was loaded.

He put the Desert Eagle inside the holster. The Eagle was in its nest.

He took the earplugs out of the package, dropped them in his pocket.

No need going deaf. No workers' comp in this line of work. No 401(k) either.

All cash-and-carry.

Prepared, he left Novotel, again passing by all the flowers and mourners.

His night wasn't over. The hunter still had to hunt.

Tonight somebody was going to die.

And he would die a good death.

Twenty-six

night of the hunter

I took the Central Line, looking for that broken-nosed bastard at every stop.

I'd see that motherfucker again. I knew that. Just had to see him before he saw me.

I saw men in suits.

Men in dark suits.

Men dressed like preachers.

"The wrong you're doing . . . stop doing evil while you can. Stop because one day somebody will come for you. One day what you do to other people, that will be done to you."

That voice from the past came and haunted me, whispers from a shallow grave.

It felt like a knife being stabbed inside my wounded spirits.

Those words didn't come from a television show.

It was the voice of the minister I had killed a long time ago.

I'd never forgotten what he'd said as he begged for his life.

That I would have my day.

That day had come.

Someone had come for me.

Seemed like every man on the train wore a dark suit.

Pallbearers dressed in the color of death.

Every man wore the hue of mourning.

European men. Nigerian men. Russians. Swedish. Old men. Young men.

A killer owned no particular type of face.

And not all killers were men. There were a lot of Black Widows in the world.

In some cases women were the best. They were the last to be suspected.

Ten minutes later I was hurrying by that golden image of Freddie Mercury, making that night-chilled jog past all the people who were partying hard in Soho, Chinatown, and Leicester Square. Rain started to fall as I made it to the Odeon in Bloomsbury, came down with a steady rhythm as I hunched my shoulders and rushed by the red phone booths that served as warm places for picture-perfect whores to post their cards and advertise their well-traveled wares.

No one was behind me.

What was in front of me would be a bigger surprise.

Myhotel was buzzing long after the midnight hour.

The bar that was off to the right side, called Mybar, was packed, all the tables were taken and the drinks were plenty from wall to wall, Europeans at tables, legs crossed, smoking hand-rolled cigarettes and listening to jazz, saw all of that before I sliced through the cold and made it across the damp street.

When I shook the chill off my bones, pulled open the glass doors, and stepped inside the lobby, I stopped moving. Stopped because I was surprised to see her, of all people, sitting on the leather sofa. I thought our last good-bye was the last time I'd ever see her face again. She shifted, coughed, turned, and I saw a frown so deep she was damn near unrecognizable. She was waiting in the small lobby, alone, arms folded.

Her face was painted with ten shades of anger.

I wanted to keep going, but I paused in front of her.

I'd been chased.

Now she was here.

As if it were all part of a bigger plan.

She looked up, her expression changed, moved from being murderous to unsure.

My expression owned no trust.

She wiped tears from her eyes and sighed, that expression now sheer embarrassment.

I squatted, put my hand on her chin, wanted to look in her face, look for trouble.

She whispered, "Surprise."

"What are you doing sitting out here in the cold, Lola Mack?"

"This is a nice hotel. That sushi bar is off the chains. Cool the way the sushi is on the conveyor-belt thing and rotates around the bar and you grab what you want, huh? I ain't ever seen anything like that before in my life. Food passes by and people grab what they want to eat."

"Lola. Focus. Look at me. Thought you were with your boy-friend?"

"I'm . . . I was . . ." Her stomach growled and she moved with the pain. She wiped the tears from her eyes, pulled her-self together, said, "Looking for Mrs. Jones. I'm looking for Mrs. Jones."

I licked my lips, tried to recall Mrs. Jones's flavor. It was gone. "Mrs. Jones isn't here."

"Damn. Where is she?"

"She didn't . . . she moved on. Got a room somewhere else, I guess. Have no idea."

"Didn't know what to do."

"What's going on?"

"Now I'm the one crying, huh? Damn shame. I'm crying like Mrs. Jones was crying."

"What happened?"

Her bottom lip trembled. She took a hard breath. "I didn't have anywhere to go."

Again I asked, "What happened with your boyfriend?"

"That jerk." That murderous look reappeared in her eyes. "Son of a bitch."

"What happened?"

"Son of a bitch said he missed me . . . said he loved me . . . wished I was here . . . and . . . I mean . . . I spent my last dime . . . got on a plane . . . gave up auditions . . . came over here . . . The lies . . . he's been lying to me for God knows how long . . . *Rent* closed down months ago . . . He's been here . . . because . . . because . . . he met somebody while he was touring . . . and . . . and he stayed here . . . He lied to me and stayed here . . . said he met somebody . . . Shit happens, he said . . . That's it . . . shit happens . . . and he shrugged . . . Told his ass he better talk to me . . . tell me something . . . Said he was working on the show and met somebody . . . and they'd been traveling together for months . . . they'd been doing it for months . . . now . . . He said he's in love . . . been shacking up with somebody . . . in love and shacking up. And I'm his damn girlfriend. I mean, how messed up is that? I know we haven't seen each other, but I didn't know it was like that. I mean, we've been having phone sex and text sex and . . . and I spent a lot of money at Victoria's Secret too . . . another reason my charge card is over the limit . . . this is so fucked up. I came here to be with him and—"

"Lola."

"I'm rambling."

"Yes. You are rambling."

"I got my butt played. This is so humiliating."

I looked at her two overpacked suitcases, at her stuffed backpack.

She carried too much shit to be in this business. We traveled light.

Again I thought about the man I had chased.

It bothered me that he had appeared as soon as I left my mother.

Made me wonder if my mother had sent him after me.

Confused and anxious, I looked around.

Nobody inside the lobby seemed to be concerned with me.

The left side housed the sushi bar. It was packed too.

No one over there was concerned with me either.

I asked Lola, "How long have you been sitting here in the cold?"

"Forever. Was too tired to leave. And the tubes shut down, so that means my travel card has expired. Got frustrated." Her voice cracked as tears fell. "Didn't have anywhere to go."

"So you're telling me you're stranded."

"Yeah. Broke and stranded and stuck with all this damn luggage."

"Where have you been since you got to London?"

She shrugged. "Walking around like a damn homeless fool from America."

"You walked around dragging two hundred pounds of luggage?"

"Call me Erykah Badu, because I'm a damn bag lady."

First I rubbed my temples.

Then I thought about Mrs. Jones, leaving this warm hotel, almost being run down in front of the hotel, standing in her anger and sorrow, cold rain falling on her hot skin, her hair wild as her dress fluttered, carrying no luggage but dragging all of her invisible anguish behind her.

Lola nodded. "I don't have any money. Told you, maxed out my charge card flying my butt over here. Stupid, huh? Love makes you do stupid shit. And I spent the few dollars . . . I mean pounds . . . spent every pence of that funny-looking money I borrowed from you. The travel card, it sure came in handy. Well, I rode the train . . . thinking . . . got off one train . . . got on another . . . did that for hours . . . like a damn homeless person . . . tried to figure out what I could do . . . don't know nobody."

"Slow down. Catch your breath. Breathe. Talk to me. When is your return flight?"

"Uh . . . bought a one-way ticket. All I could afford. I figured I'd crash with my boo . . . with that son of a bitch I thought was my boo . . . figured I would be with him and not need anything . . . we used to be like that . . . now I don't have a ticket back. I know, I know. Stupid is as stupid does."

She wiped her eyes a thousand times. That murderous glare came and went.

She said, "He said he's in love with somebody else. *In love*. Asked him how in the hell could he be in love with somebody else and he said some stupid shit, said love had its own laws."

Not knowing what to say, I said nothing. Part of my mind still back on Berwick.

She said, "First I get thrown on the back of the plane, now this shit. I *hate* London."

Drama had built a nest on my doorstep. I had enough going on. I didn't want Lola to be here, but I couldn't kick her out in the cold. I rubbed my eyes, my own tiredness swooping in on me.

Her eyes were on the sushi bar. Anguish was in her face as she watched people eat.

I asked, "Have you eaten?"

"I was in Pizza Hut and these tourists left some of their pizza and I grabbed it before it was tossed. And they left some soda too. Did you know Pizza Hut had apple soda? The apple soda was off the chain. Ever tried it? Apple soda. Pizza Hut carries it over here. Cool, huh?"

"You ate somebody's leftovers?"

Tears fell from her eyes. "I know. That's fucked up, huh?"

My eyes searched the darkness. I was an open target. Needed to get out of this lobby.

I went to the front desk, tried to get a room for Lola. Something away from me, on a different floor. They told me the hotel was booked solid. I looked out at the cold rain. Not the best kind of weather for Lola to go out and hunt for a hotel. Not this time of night. Not with all of her backpacks and luggage. And I didn't want to go back out into Bloomsbury, not since I'd had that footrace, not with somebody hot on my trail. I told myself that I was safe here. If he knew I was here, he wouldn't have needed to follow me. I went back to the front door. Looked out. Dark clouds. Freezing air. Rain.

Then I went back to Lola.

Didn't have a lot of options at this point.

I said, "Why don't you come up to my room and get comfortable."

"No, that's okay."

"You don't really have a choice."

She hesitated. "I don't want to be an inconvenience."

Her stomach growled.

I said, "Hungry, huh?"

"Little bit. Yeah. I'm starving right about now."

"Let's get your two tons of luggage situated and get you some real food."

"For real?"

"Let's kill the fatted calf and get you situated."

"I need a bath."

"Come on up."

"You sure?"

"Your stomach is growling so loud it sounds like two bears fighting."

"Had that slice of cold pizza around noon."

"Thirteen hours ago."

"I'm used to eating three squares. I'm getting missed-meal cramps."

"How does room service sound? You like sushi? Could have them bring up some sushi."

"Hell yeah, I *love* sushi. But I'll be happy with McDonald's."

I smiled at her. "You didn't come all the way to London to eat clown food, did you?"

"You sure about sushi? It costs a grip. And with the exchange rate, it'll be a *super*grip."

"If you want a bottle of wine, order that too."

"Sushi and a bottle of wine?"

"Take a long bath. Eat. Drink. Be a queen for a while."

"Thank you, thank you, *thank* you. I want to jump up and down and *scream*."

"Please don't."

Again she cried, a different kind of tears. "I can't pay you back, not right now."

"Don't worry about it."

"I mean . . . I will, I promise." She wiped her eyes. "I'm not a freeloader, I promise I'm not."

"Just don't talk me to death, okay?"

She laughed.

We dragged all of her luggage toward the lift. Then I felt uneasy. Lola had shown up here right after I'd been chased.

Maybe Lola getting placed next to me on the plane wasn't a coincidence.

Maybe when I hooked up with Mrs. Jones it threw off her plan.

Right now it was all about having my enemies closer.

While we waited for the lift, the receptionist called me back to the front desk.

She handed me a FedEx box. The sender's name was written in bold letters. **Scaramouche**. No return address. My eyes went toward the darkness out on Bayley Street, to a group of drunken people coming inside. She wasn't there. But she was there at the same time.

Arizona had delivered information for the other jobs. I went back to the bar, looked around, but didn't see her. She would only be seen when she wanted to be seen, I knew that.

There was no note to say it, but I understood. Arizona was saying she was sorry for acting like a square, for the things she said, we could still be associates, we could still do business. She had work for me. And there was money to be made.

Lola held the lift door open for me. I struggled, crammed all of her luggage inside the small vertical carriage.

She wiped her teary eyes. "You look like somebody just killed your favorite cat."

I wanted to say I'd accepted a contract and killed a friend.

And I'd found the source of my pain and anger on Berwick Street. That soon I'd go back to Berwick. Might go back to Soho in the middle of the night.

And I would leave Berwick Street with blood on my hands.

But I pushed my lips up into a strained smile and sighed. "I don't like cats."

She laughed like she really wanted to start crying again. "Me either."

FedEx underneath my arm, I got on the lift, two hundred pounds of luggage separating us.

She took her tears to one side of the small vertical carriage, I took to the other.

Lola was nervous.

"Gideon . . . found out a lot about London today. Being homeless gives you time to read. Lot of black people over here. Some areas are like Compton and Detroit and Oakland. Found out that most people thought black people were new to England. But black people have been here more than fifteen minutes. People think we just got over here like in the forties, came here to play jazz and run away from wars. But blacks have been here forever. Have fought in every war with Britain. Romans brought black warriors with them to Britain. And black people still don't own shit."

I said, "Three."

"Huh?"

"Push the button for three. I'm on the third floor."

"Oh. I'm sorry. Guess I was rambling."

"I guess."

"Sorry. I'll stop. At least I'll try to."

When the elevator door closed, Arizona's scent became stronger. I inhaled, the vague scent of cloves and expensive perfume, her body gone but her essence remaining in the dank air.

Cloves.

The scent of a love gone by.

Like her man Scamz used to smoke.

Like she now smoked.

Arizona had been here. She'd been inside this elevator.

I expected to see her waiting outside my door when the elevator opened.

I looked for my golden-skinned Cylon. Looked for the grifter who had chosen to employ fear to gain respect.

And, like a Cylon, I wanted to destroy my creator.

We were both Cylons.

The third-floor hallway still smelled of cloves.

I looked up and down the hallway. No one was there.

She'd been here moments ago.

I didn't trust Arizona.

Women and treachery. Deceit and murder had been a part of my life.

My eyes went to Lola.

I didn't know what her angle was. Didn't know what her game was.

She didn't say anything, just kept her eyes down while we dragged her luggage down the slender hallway.

I opened the door, let Lola inside my room. I left both of her bags at the foot of the bed. She shifted, took off her backpack, put that load down in front of the desk.

She took her coat off, looked around. "This is a nice room."

"Thanks."

"I mean this is a really nice room."

"Order some food."

"Thanks, Gideon. I really mean it."

I repeated myself, maybe sounded a little irritated, told her, "Order some food."

She wiped her eyes with the back of her hands, got on the phone, called room service.

Shrimp tempura roll. Spicy tuna roll. Rainbow roll. Tuna tataki. Spicy squid roll. Softshell crab roll. Island roll. Tobiko with quail egg. She ordered a bottle of shirakawago sansannigori, a bamboo leaf sake. The way she ordered, she had to be starving.

Still I kept thinking about having my enemies closer.

I watched Lola, no trust in my eyes, wondering what game she was playing.

I stared at her and kept hearing whispers from a shallow grave haunting me.

It was the voice that had once belonged to a reverend in Detroit.

"The wrong you're doing . . . stop doing evil while you can. Stop because one day somebody will come for you. One day what you do to other people, that will be done to you."

Twenty-seven

wetwork

He was still swimming in anger, the undertow pulling him under.

He'd find Gideon.

Tonight.

As soon as he was done with this little matter.

He'd been sidetracked.

Sam had called.

Another target had been located. The money was in place.

The man with the broken nose went for the bird in the hand.

He had taken his unbridled rage outside the city to north London, was in Bruce Grove. Again he was in a footrace. He had found his contract, the Jamaican with the gambling debt.

The Jamaican was fleeing. That was expected. His profile had said he was a runner.

The man with the broken nose chased the Jamaican the way Gideon had chased him.

He chased him through urban areas that looked like Houston's Fifth Ward, New Orleans's Fourth Ward, South Central, East Oakland, Harlem, and Blackhaven in Memphis combined.

He convinced himself that he had tested Gideon. Wanted to see how strong Gideon was.

Told himself that fear didn't make him run; it was only a test.

Fear was there. Fear was part of the business. Fear kept a man alert.

But fear wasn't why he had run.

He'd run three sub-six-minute miles. In a suit and shoes. Gideon had almost caught him. Not many men could run three sub-six miles fully dressed. Wearing street shoes.

His father would've chastised him, shouted at him. If he had still been around. His father had been the ultimate sprinter in his youth and then a marathon man in his later years.

He used to hear his father talk to his friends about doing big jobs in other states, the sound of death in his voice. All the men wore suits. They always wore suits. And they all carried big guns. When the men left, his father would loosen his tie, then come and play with him and his siblings.

His father would leave at night. Not come home for days at a time.

No one ever questioned what he did or asked where he was.

He ran because his father loved to run. He had admired his father.

Even though he never went to visit his old man after they came and took him away.

His brothers and sisters didn't go visit their old man either.

But his mother did. His mother went to see his father once a month.

Conjugal.

It had been that way for the last twenty years.

His old man didn't want to look at his kids through Plexiglas. Not then, not now. He said he didn't want them to see the man he'd become as he rotted in a four-by-five cement room.

His father had never run from anyone. Not even the police when they came to get him.

The house had been surrounded.

His old man finished his coffee.

Kissed his kids.

Kissed their mother.

Then undressed.

Went outside naked, smoking a Lucky Strike cigarette. "You sons of bitches looking for me?"

Guns aimed at him, he kept on smoking his cigarette.

His old man had balls.

But unlike his fearless father, the man with the broken nose regretted that he had run from Gideon. Gideon had chased him the way Pacino had chased De Niro in the movie *Heat*.

This time he was Pacino, not De Niro.

He chased the Jamaican by homeless who slept in the doorways of businesses.

Chasing the Jamaican wasn't a test. Unlike Gideon, this contract had been paid for.

And the Jamaican knew it was his night to die.

The man with the broken nose wondered how it felt when you had been dealt a hand made of aces and eights.

He chased his prey.

The Jamaican's back-length locks were flying like a cape as he sprinted by the row of eateries on the strip by Loks 4 Life, raced downhill by Chicken Express and Regency Car Park, stumbling through Bruce Grove, waving for the night buses to stop, but the buses didn't slow down. He ran toward Seven Sisters, toward his flat, ran toward his weapons and friends.

Just like the package said he would do.

He chased the Jamaican another mile. A fast mile. The Jamaican looked back.

The Jamaican was tired.

The man with the broken nose was right behind him.

He wanted the Jamaican terrified.

He wanted him to die a thousand deaths before he caught him.

So he slowed down.

Let the Jamaican run his best run.

They were running against the wind.

Running against the rain.

Another mile went by, this one not as fast as the one before.

No longer a challenge.

He was tired of chasing. The chasing had been fun, but he had things to do tonight.

Still running, he took the Eagle out of its nest.

A piece of hot lead tore through the Jamaican's right leg as he stumbled by the Seven Sisters tube. The Jamaican fell, got back up limping, left a trail of blood marking his final steps.

Not many people were out, not like in Soho and Oxford Circus in Central London. It was cold. The tubes had closed. And it was an area where muggings at gunpoint had shot up in numbers. And it was raining. Few residents heard the screaming Jamaican, few had seen him hobbling down the high road, blood running out of him like rainwater, praying for mercy and strength.

The man with the broken nose took easy steps and caught the Jamaican.

Like a blubbering five-year-old child, the Jamaican cried and begged for mercy.

The man with the broken nose looked down on his prey.

But he saw Gideon. All he could think about was Gideon.

A double-decker bus was speeding down the high road toward Bruce Grove.

He knew that what the bus driver and his passengers on the 279 saw would have them in need of therapy the rest of their lives. He threw the Jamaican headfirst into its path.

Nobody had seen his face.

They'd only seen the horror in the eyes of a bloody Jamaican.

He could do better than Gideon had done in Tampa.

He could do much better.

Desert Eagle in hand, the man with the broken nose jogged into the darkness.

He didn't jog far. He didn't hide. He took out his earplugs and slowed to a stroll.

Nobody would see anything.

Nobody would hear anything.

Everyone would be too afraid that trouble would come looking for them.

He headed down Holloway Road toward Holloway Station.

When he was near, he found a black cab.

He got in, headed back toward Central London.

Infuriated.

He'd find Gideon. He'd make Gideon run. Like the Jamaican.

His cellular rang. It was his family phone. He didn't answer.

His family had called minutes ago. When he was creeping up on the Jamaican. That ringing phone had alerted the Jamaican. That ringing had been the bell at the start of their race.

He touched his nose. It ached. Damn it ached.

He was dropped off on Charing Cross and Shaftesbury.

Leicester Square was to his left.

Bloomsbury was to his right.

Gideon wasn't far.

He felt it.

He looked to his left. Pondered Leicester Square.

Then changed his mind, looked toward his right. He took steps toward Bloomsbury.

He paused. Darker clouds were in that direction. The weather horrendous.

He headed straight, went down Shaftesbury toward Piccadilly Circus, passed Chinatown, then slowed and looked to his right, took his search back toward the red lights in Soho.

The whore.

Maybe the whore Gideon had visited was his favorite whore.

Maybe she knew things that would help him end this transaction.

Men always said secret things to whores.

He had had therapeutic conversations with a few working women over the years.

Men always revealed secrets to whores.

Streets were damp. A few puddles. The rain had stopped. But it was still cold.

His nose still ached.

He touched his bandages, walked through the piss-and-shit stench, again passing by the children, young boys and girls kicking a shit-smelling soccer ball down narrow Berwick Street. He went to the door that Gideon had entered. Looked up and saw pretty feet at the top of the stairs.

Her friendly voice came down and greeted him, "Full service or blow job?"

He took the stairs, the weight of the Desert Eagle hardly noticeable.

He stopped when he was face-to-face with Gideon's whore.

She'd talk.

He'd beat the whore and make her talk.

Twenty-eight

shadow of doubt

Close to an hour later.

Lola had unpacked a few things, was on the other side of the frosted bathroom door.

She was crying and running her bathwater.

Or crying and plotting. I wasn't sure what she was doing. I was waiting to find out.

I sat on the far side of the bed, on the edge, my eye on the bathroom door, my mind on the man I had chased. And Arizona. The FedEx box was in front of me. Still unopened.

My gun was on the floor, at my feet. Just in case.

The room smelled like jasmine, Lola's scent, the aroma of purity and deception.

Empty sushi plates were on a tray we'd left on the floor near the door. I had a small glass of sake on the nightstand, and Lola had taken the rest of the bottle into the bathroom with her.

The fish smell might permeate the room, so I got up long enough to leave the tray in the hallway. Then I called room service to come get the tray before the hall smelled like sushi. I stumbled over a suitcase. The room had become an obstacle course. Lola's luggage and backpack took up most of the space.

Almost two in the morning. Nine P.M. on the East Coast. Six on the West Coast.

The television was on the news. First the never-ending talk about the WAG.

I wasn't interested.

Then news about Sledgehammer's death in Trinidad came on.

It confirmed what Arizona had told me a few hours ago.

That bothered me.

It scared me.

Not much had scared me over the years.

But this had me opening and closing my hands.

I clenched my teeth.

That report was followed by news about the demise of the Big Bad Wolf of rap.

The blood that had been shed in Tampa unnerved me as well.

I turned the television off. Was only so much of that shit I could take.

I opened the FedEx box. Saw pictures of two people. One of an overweight man. A local. This contract came in from Texas. Had nothing to do with Arizona. The other contract was Amsterdam. Those images kept my eye. Several pictures of a beautiful young woman.

Her name was Sierra.

Sierra was Arizona's younger sister.

My mouth dropped open.

Arizona had sent me a package on her little sister.

The package said Sierra was living and working out of Holland.

The men who came to cripple and rape Arizona were from Holland.

I tried to remember what Sergeant had said.

It wasn't too hard to connect the dots.

Arizona's sister was in bed with Sergeant as well.

Both were in on the FEMA scam. Shit went bad. Arizona

wanted her cut. Sergeant refused. Sierra had supplied the brawn to damage Arizona and take her out of the business.

Sierra had sent men to do major damage to Arizona.

Un-fucking-believable.

Sierra was working in Holland.

I stared in her eyes like I was staring inside another ancient memory.

She looked like the girl I had visited. The girl from window 693.

I put her picture down.

This shit was too deep.

A new SIM card was inside the box. I put my SIM card inside my mobile, turned it on. One number already programmed into the memory. Programmed without a name. Arizona's contact number.

After the shit we just went through, she had the nerve to drop this shit off at my hotel.

I pulled up her number, had my finger over the SEND key.

Arizona knew this would fuck me up.

That's why she didn't tell me. She sent me a fucking package.

I put the mobile away. Sipped my sake. Took a deep breath.

Again I stared at the picture of Arizona's younger sister.

Sierra was the spitting image of her older sister, only slightly darker, her body a bit fuller.

Arizona wanted her younger sister dead.

Still found it hard to believe Sierra had supplied the men who came after Arizona.

I wanted to chastise them both. But that would make me hypocritical.

I wanted Thelma to be in the same state.

I whispered, "The pot calls the kettle black."

My mind shifted.

Went to a dark place.

Thought about Thelma.

Thought about my mother.

I rubbed my eyes, rubbed away all memories.

I went to the window and looked out, opened and closed my hand.

I heard Lola in the bathroom. Still singing.

I grimaced out toward Berwick Street. A son should never hit his mother.

But I had.

We had done all of the things a mother and son shouldn't do.

Felt like I was about to have a panic attack. I sat down again. Sipped more sake. Stress had me feeling like I was about to have a stroke.

Rubbed my eyes. Eyes were on fire. Was tired in more ways than one.

My dark thoughts stayed there with my mother.

Couldn't remember the number of times she was locked up.

In those days, when she was taken away, whether we were in Chicago, Memphis, or Stillwater, I'd sit at home, would stay in our apartment for days, until she was free, cooking for myself, not answering the phone, going to school, doing homework, being as normal as I could, hoping she would come back. There was always food there. Enough for me to get by for days. Once she was incarcerated for a month. I was fourteen years old then. A grown man.

She walked in the door a month later, came in as if she had been gone fifteen minutes.

Miniskirt. High-heel shoes. She was amazing. She had pictures of Dorothy Dandridge, Sophia Loren, Audrey Hepburn, Tina Turner, Marilyn Monroe, Lauren Bacall, Lana Turner, and Eartha Kitt Scotch-taped all over our small apartment. Even with the wigs, shoes, and clothes she had, she was none of those women, yet she was all of those women at once.

My mother said, "I have something I need you to take care of for me."

I looked at her. No hello. No talk about missing me. She was so expressionless.

My mother slid me a picture of a man. A knife was next to the picture.

She said, "This john beat one of my friends."

She dropped pictures on the table. Red-haired woman. Face bloodied. Eyes swollen. Teeth knocked out. She looked horrible. The hazards of her chosen occupation.

"She fought him good. Did her best. But she's a tiny little woman. He beat her bad. You can see how he busted her face up. Bastard dropped his wallet when he ran out of the motel."

I pushed the pictures back to her.

Pushed the pictures away like I was rejecting the lifestyle she offered.

She reached inside her purse, put a stack of wrinkled money on the table.

I counted the small bills. Five hundred dollars.

She said, "We have to eat. You have to eat. We have to pay rent."

I went back to my book, to the complicated equations I was trying to comprehend.

She whispered, "Please?"

I ignored her.

My mother put her arms around me, rubbed her hands up and down my body.

She grabbed between my legs, rubbed my groin. I didn't stop her. Hoped she would quit. That excited me. I pretended nothing she did fazed me. She ran fingers over me, touched me and rubbed me in places, held me in ways a mother should never handle her son.

"You're getting to be a big boy. A real big boy."

I jerked away from her.

She laughed. It was her real laugh. She'd changed. Become a sadistic soul at heart.

I was embarrassed. Her whore's touch had stirred me. The stimulation showed.

She asked, "When was the last time you had some pussy?"

"When was the last time you sold some?"

"I'm more worried about the next time. Last time pays no bills."

"Trying to study."

"Son, I met this young girl. Twenty. From Hollywood. Long black hair. I can get her to give you some pussy. She's a good friend. Showed her your picture. She thinks you're cute."

"Is she a whore?"

"All women are whores. Just some have the sense to get paid."

That had become the language of our household.

Years of living on the run had hardened us.

After that back-and-forth with my mother, I went to the kitchen, poured a glass of water, wanted to get away from her. I liked it when she was gone. Liked it when she was in jail.

Mother followed me. "Ever had your little man sucked?"

"Stop it. Will you stop it?"

"She'll suck your dick for you if I tell her to."

She made a peanut butter and jelly sandwich. Left the bread open on the counter. I went behind her, cleaned up her crumbs. Had to before the roaches came out to feast.

"She's from Antigua. Trifling husband walked out, left her with all the bills. Good thing God gave her a pussy for bartering, else she'd starve to death, her and her five-year-old son."

My mother tapped the table. Five hundred dollars and a man's information stared at me.

I said, "I can't. It makes me sick. I get sick. I want to throw up."

"When I first started, every time a john left, I would get nauseated. Pretend you're somebody else. I do that and it helps. Let it be somebody else, another part of you that's doing the stuff you don't like doing. When I'm at work entertaining those men, when they have their hands on me, it's not me they're touching. Not me at all."

I went back and looked at the money on the table.

She said, "We have to eat. We have bills. We need the money."

We headed for the car. I had the knife in my hand.

Later on I'd find out that the lady who hired me had given my mother $1,500. My mother had asked for two thousand, but that fifteen was all the woman could afford. People would pay her as much as five thousand and I'd never see more than five hundred.

Inside every whore there lived a pimp who was trying to get out.

My mind was on fire, each thought like gasoline being thrown on flames.

I wanted to be alone right now. Needed to be alone so I could think.

Needed to sip on sake and do some reevaluation.

I looked at the luggage in the room. Two hundred pounds of somebody else's problems.

Too late for that. Too late to be alone.

Lola's suitcases and backpack were in front of me.

One was open. One wasn't. One was turned upside down, harder to get to.

I crept to the one that was right side up and open, most of its contents already taken out. What was packed wasn't folded, just tossed in, like she had left home in a hurry.

Lola was not a neat freak, not at all. She had already turned my room into a pigpen.

With easy movement, I looked through her things, felt around for anything suspicious. Lola had been gone for hours. She could've picked up anything since she made it to London. I searched. She had more lingerie than any one woman should be allowed to own, enough sexy gear to let me know that she had planned to spend a lot of bedroom time with her boyfriend. Lots of shoes. Dresses. Jeans. Workout clothes. Two new vibrators, one black and the other pink, both about five inches long. I moved all of that stuff aside and found what I was looking for. First, inside her wallet, was a picture of her and her boyfriend. Then, next to the DVD, I found an old theatrical playbill from *Rent* stuffed inside her backpack. It was a program from when he was touring with the production back in the States. I was searching for information on the man who had shattered her heart. And I wanted to make sure she wasn't part of something larger.

Outside of having two vibrators and a clit stimulator, nothing looked suspicious.

No weapons. No multiple passports.

No reason to take her down and leave her rotting in a mews out in horse-and-grass.

I put everything back the way I found it.

The vibrators. Two of them. Those were her weapons. Unless she was planning to torture me West Hollywood style, what she was carrying was harmless.

Two colorful vibrators.

I chuckled.

I wondered if she took both of her vibrators at the same time.

I gathered up everything I had taken from the FedEx box, then went to the room safe. Each room had one hidden away from plain sight. I read the instructions and reprogrammed the safe with a new pass code, then tucked everything from the FedEx box inside, locked it away.

Lola was singing another song, something about going out tonight. Sounded like she was howling part of the song. She was all into the tune. That almost made me laugh.

Then I was glad Lola was here. It was awkward, but it was nice chilling with a square.

Sergeant had said men like us shouldn't become personal with the women in our business.

I'd never forget that.

I'd put myself in the middle of shit between Arizona and her sibling, a problem that involved Sergeant. Had to be bad if her sister had sent men to do things worse than death.

I regretted that contract on Sergeant. Wished I'd taken his offer before he sipped his Jack. Needed to put up two shots of Jack and drink one, then apologize and pour one on the ground. Sergeant was right. I should take his advice, retire to a tropical island, find a pretty woman, maybe have some babies, get out of this business before it killed me. It had killed him. Just like it had killed a lot of us. Scamz had been gunned down in a pool hall. Sledge had been blown up in a van. I couldn't count or remember the number of people who had been assassinated in between.

I'd been followed like it was the prelude to my demise.

I sipped more sake. Looked at the clock.

Almost two thirty. Barely dinnertime back in the States.

I lay across the sofa, television on, BBC news showing another terrorist bombing that had blown up red buses and part of the tube system. It was like the universe was sending me a message. Now I was nervous. Imagined getting blown into a thousand little pieces.

I closed my eyes.

Focused on my breathing.

Relaxed.

Let the sake take me into a peaceful darkness.

Then came the dream. I knew the dream would come again, like it did on the plane.

I was back in Tampa.

Bodies all around me.

The stench of Chinese food making me want to puke.

Twenty-nine

we who are about to die

Two days after meeting with Sledgehammer.

Portable GPS at my side. Destinations programmed into memory.

Not too far from Tampa International Airport, down in the stadium area, a block or so from the Yankees' spring-training camp, driving in the shadows of their International Plaza. Nervous, I followed the trail of tattoo, pawn, and brake shops that shot down Dale Mabry, saw Asian massage parlors, the type that had discreet business signs and darkened windows.

Had to check out the lay of the land, plan an emergency escape route, if needed.

I didn't have to import weapons. Weapons were everywhere. All I had to do was find a hardware store. And finding pepper spray or Mace was easy. Within an hour I had hit four stores and had everything I needed. I found my way back to Dale Mabry Highway, headed toward the stadium, spied the area, and parked in a lot next to Mons Venus, Tampa's most famous spot for pole swingers. This lot was where Big Bad and his crew always parked.

This was where they would die.

I was tempted to lounge inside Mons Venus. Twenty to thirty

for a lap dance and I could touch the women anywhere except on the cookie. Thirty bucks to get dry-humped by one of the most beautiful women in the world. Paying thirty for that with no upsale wasn't too bad.

I didn't go inside.

I waited.

One hour turned into two. Two turned into three. Three became four.

Just when I was about to call it a bust, a stretch SUV pulled up in the dark parking lot, music blasting, wheels spinning. The Big Bad Wolf had arrived. My heart sped up. Hands went clammy. I took a deep breath. Focused. I got out of my ride and headed toward the parking lot.

Their music was loud enough to muffle a nuclear explosion.

They were too busy getting high to notice a shadow coming their way. As they unloaded, one man in thick jeans, a short leather jacket, and boots, he saw me first. They were an army dressed in oversize gear. I eased part of the way out of the shadows.

The one that had seen me barked, "What the fuck you want?"

"An autograph. I'm a big fan."

Then another. "We ain't doing no motherfuckin' autographs."

Both sported bulletproof vests.

Big Bad Wolf got out of the SUV.

Big guy. Saggy jeans. Long blond hair in dreadlocks. Tattoos all over. His teeth reflected, even in the dark. His mouth was decorated with a half million worth of platinum with white gold–plated, diamond-encrusted crowns, the 18-karat kind.

I held up what was in my gloved left hand.

I said, "Chinese food. You said to bring you some Chinese food, right?"

He knew.

Right then, he knew that Death was here.

I had marked that spot. Where I stood, my weapon was on

the ground. I grabbed what I had hidden and ran at them. Three of them charged at me. They were bad as hell, until they saw what was in my hands. A sledgehammer. I was holding what people used to knock down buildings. It was too late for them to stop their charge. I swung hard, connected in the chest of one of the attackers, saw pain and surprise light up his eyes as he fell on his friend. The second one was hit between his eyes before he could get back to his feet.

Then a third one met the same fate, the sledgehammer taking him down.

The third one was dressed better, wore a suit.

This was what I had become. I was so far from being seven years old and riding down the streets of Charlotte admiring the big houses. So far from being the little boy who wanted to go to Six Flags. For money, this was all about collecting money, all about trying to be somebody.

Two more of Big Bad's crew got it bad. Those men were dead before they understood what was going on.

Faces smashed so bad it would take two seasons of *Nip/Tuck* to fix what was left. And even if it was put back the way it was ten minutes ago, their brains were swollen beyond repair.

Big Bad Wolf ran like he was Little Red Riding Hood.

I pulled a knife from its sheath at my waist, threw the knife hard and fast. Not my best throw, but it was good enough. It hit his calf hard and deep. He went down, his face sliding across the asphalt. He grabbed his wound, looked up, and saw me holding a sledgehammer high over my head. His lips moved; the music was so loud nothing could be heard.

He was terrified. He was sorry for the shit he had said. He didn't want to die.

Nobody wanted to die.

The sledgehammer came down hard.

His face was smashed in. Just like my client wanted. Killed him with a sledgehammer.

That feeling of nausea swept through me, slowed me down.

Left me vulnerable.

Then I was hit hard.

Two more of the terrified hood rats pulled it together, attacked me at the same time. They were late getting out of the SUV. They came after me. Assaulted me the same way their music was attacking my ears. The first one hit me like he was a professional boxer. He was fast, but he was high on chronic, still managed to hit me with too many hard blows to count. Don't know. Was numb after the first blow clipped my eye, was going down after the second blow hit my mouth. I was dazed. Another blow hit my face and I went down like Sonny Liston.

The weapon was far away from me.

Death was standing in the shadows, smiling, not picky about who he claimed.

His drunken homeboy kicked me until I grabbed his foot, grappled with him while his buddy threw blow after blow at my head and back. I didn't let go. I held on to that foot, made my way up his leg, yanked his oversize jeans until they fell and tangled at his feet, put my weight into him, made him stumble, got some room, and yanked his weight from up under him.

Death applauded.

Floundering, spinning, struggling to get his balance, he hit the ground quick and hard.

His hard-hitting buddy kicked me and I stumbled over him.

They were shouting, screaming. But the music in the SUV drowned out all of their calls.

I tackled the one who hit like a boxer, lifted him up the same way a minister in Detroit had done me on the night he died, on the icy night we fought to the death. I growled like an animal, lifted him up, and crashed him into the pavement, drove him into the concrete as hard as I could.

That hurt him. That shit hurt me too. Knocked the wind out of me as well.

Death was laughing.

Had to get up. Had to get the fuck out of here.

But the first one I had dropped pulled his pants back up, wobbled to his feet before I did.

The second one struggled, got help from his friend, made it to his feet before I did too.

I heard debris on the filthy asphalt crunching as they stumbled toward me.

Death hovered over me with its sardonic smile.

From the ground, I looked up at both of them. They were breathing hard. They were in pain. I was breathing hard.

Bloody mouth, eye swollen, fists hurting, neon lights, vision blurry, this was my death.

Saw both of them standing over me. Screaming at each other. The one I had tackled pointed at the SUV. His homeboy stumbled back inside the SUV and came back with a gun.

By then the one I had tackled was holding my sledgehammer.

Death started doing cartwheels and back flips.

I hadn't killed the one person I promised myself I would kill.

I hadn't killed Thelma.

The one I had tackled was panting, cursing me, struggling to raise the sledgehammer while his wounded buddy kept his gun trained on me. I was on my knees, trying to get up, head tilted toward my executioners.

The pepper spray on my belt. That's what I was going for.

I sprayed at the eyes of the one with the sledgehammer, then rolled to my left.

He screamed and swung the sledgehammer, hit the ground where I used to be.

I kept rolling.

He swung hard, like Thor swinging his mighty Mjolnir, the hammer that destroyed all it touched. But he was hurting bad and the sledgehammer was heavy. He didn't have the muscles or concentration to use it like I had. He was freaking out. He was terrified. Death was on the ground, those cold spirits rising though him. The one with the sledgehammer kept swinging. His friend ducked, but he ducked in the wrong direction. He ducked in the direction of the swinging sledgehammer. He was hit in the center of his forehead. Instant death.

The gun fell to the ground. I went after the gun.

Panic had the best of the last one. He kept swinging the sledgehammer and hit the SUV.

Winded, he stopped. First he screamed. Then he was crying. Like a child. He was breaking down.

Then the gun I had in my hand, I pulled the trigger, put hot lead in his belly.

He grabbed his wound, let the sledgehammer drop, stumbled, fell against the SUV.

Another bullet in his gut made him slump a little more, but he wrestled with gravity and refused to fall to the ground.

I limped across the pavement, picked the sledgehammer up. Now it weighed a ton. With the butt of the hammer I knocked him down, then stood over him. He begged. Winded, wounded, sweating, in pain once again, I grunted as I raised the sledgehammer high, like a kid at the circus pretending to be the strong man, closed my eyes, grunted again as I brought the hammer down hard into the center of his chest. His insides crunched with internal injuries.

With the exception of my heavy breathing and bad music, the alley became soundless.

My vision blurred. I staggered. Went down on one knee, then the nausea hit me again. I fought it, didn't lose my insides. Held my DNA inside. The trembles. I pushed it all back.

I blinked away my agony and saw that I was surrounded.

Dead, their bodies broken and twisted like rag dolls, sprawled on uneven asphalt.

The parking lot had become a graveyard waiting on tombstones.

Death grabbed the collars of the expired, dragged their broken bodies into the shadows.

As Death vanished into the night, the chill that had me changed to numbness.

My emotions were gone. I'd detached. Like my mother had taught me.

I staggered to the Chinese food, took it, and stood over Big Bad.

I poured lo mein all over his shattered face.

I looked over, saw one of them moving his leg. The one who was dressed like a businessman was still groaning. He was still breathing.

Nausea rose, gave me a new battle. If I threw up, my DNA would be all over the concrete. That queasiness and my pains stopped me from going to finish him off.

The man I'd been paid to kill was gone.

My job was over.

Seven out of eight were dead.

I couldn't kill anymore. Not that night.

Empty Chinese food container in one hand, gun tucked in my pants, sledgehammer in the other, I limped away, that stench in my nostrils, knowing I'd never eat Chinese food again.

There was a crash.

I jerked awake, reaching for the gun I had hidden on the floor.

Lola was in the room.

I saw her coming toward me. Her hair was in a ponytail. No makeup on her face.

She gave me that Hollywood smile.

"Lola?"

"Didn't mean to wake you."

"You okay?"

She grunted.

She had on blue sweatpants, gray sweatshirt. Old Navy sweats.

Lola was sneaking up on me. Something heavy was dragging at her side.

I thought it was her luggage.

I saw that her suitcases had been moved.

The second suitcase, the one that had been left upside down, it was wide open.

And was empty.

A suitcase that had weighed over one hundred pounds was empty.

I asked, "What are you doing?"

"Are you afraid?"

"Just sleepy."

"I think you're afraid."

"What do you mean? Afraid of what?"

Then I saw what she had at her side.

It was a sledgehammer.

She said, "The Big Bad Wolf."

Fear magnified.

"I think you're afraid of the Big Bad Wolf."

She grunted and raised the weapon high over her head.

Lola became a silhouette standing over me with a sledgehammer in her hands.

She growled, "Who's afraid of the Big Bad Wolf?"

Lola brought the sledgehammer down.

She brought the hammer down hard.

Thirty

beauty betrayed

The sledgehammer crashed into the sofa where my head had been.

The hammer was too heavy for her.

I had the gun, had it off pause and ready to go.

I didn't want to shoot her.

But I would.

Gun aimed at her, I made it to the television, grunted out my fear, pointed the gun at her.

She held the sledgehammer high again.

I snapped, *"Back the fuck down, Lola."*

Lola grimaced, raised the sledgehammer high, came running at me.

I pulled the trigger.

Pst. Pst. Pst. Pst.

Shot her over and over, the silencer making the bullets exit like a coarse whisper.

Blood stained her sweats as she stumbled backward.

Lola dropped the sledgehammer. It fell across the nightstand, destroyed a lamp.

The light from the lamp blinking on and off, fizzing out, Lola crumpled into her death.

I stood there, teeth tight, focused, gun trained on her.

That lamp kept fizzing in and out.

Shadow and light.

Shadow and light.

Chest rising and falling, I waited.

Caught my breath, looked at the damage she had caused.

Looked at what I had done.

I cursed a thousand times.

Then I eased the gun down, leaned against the dresser, neck sweating like rain.

Lola was dead.

Her body riddled with bullets.

Blood was everywhere.

That light refusing to die, fizzing in and out, from shadow to light.

The noise from that sledgehammer had to wake up everybody in the hotel.

Out toward Centre Point, I saw lights coming on in every flat in Bloomsbury.

If anyone was in their window, they could've seen what just went down.

Soon there would be sirens.

Soon the place would be surrounded.

Had to get the fuck out of here.

Had to wipe the room down and get the fuck out of here.

Lola Mack was dead.

I'd been set up. She'd been sent by my enemy.

Then.

Noise came from behind me.

The sound of the broken lamp crumpling, being pushed to the side.

Lola wasn't on the floor.

She was already on her feet.

That light still going from light to dark.

Bullet holes in her sweatshirt showed me that she had been wearing a bulletproof vest.

She had the sledgehammer back in her hands.

Again she took the sledgehammer, grunted, and raised it high.

She handled the weight from her weapon much better this time.

Her control was much better.

Because she handled it with **rage**.

Rage had given her a new level of strength and a new speed.

Again she came at me.

She came at me fast.

She came at me hard.

She came at me with that sledgehammer raised high.

Gun raised, I aimed at her again.

Head shot this time.

Fuck her face being so damn pretty.

It was time for a bona fide kill shot.

I pulled the trigger.

Click.

The gun was empty.

Lola was on me.

That sledgehammer was up high, at its peak, about to come down with deadly force.

It came down toward my head.

I threw my hands up in vain.

This was my death.

This was my Tampa.

I jumped awake.

Still on the sofa.

Heart beating inside my ears.

I fumbled through my panic, grabbed the gun from the floor.

Felt its weight in my hand.

No dream this time.

No goddamn dream this time.

Gun in hand, I panted, pointed left, pointed right.

Was suffocating. Room was so hot I was suffocating.

Lola wasn't there.

Nothing was there.

Nothing was in front of me but fear and shadows.

I stood up, gun still going left to right, then right to left.

No broken lamps.

No Lola.

No sledgehammer.

I looked in her suitcases again.

Saw nothing in either.

Just clothes.

And vibrators.

The second suitcase.

I went to it.

Eased it over.

Opened it.

A hundred pairs of shoes. And clothes. That's all. A lot of damn shoes and more clothes.

I closed her suitcase.

Turned it back over.

I swallowed. Pulled it together.

Then I sat back down on the sofa.

There was another crash.

I jumped, again the gun aimed at the bathroom door.

The noise had come from inside the bathroom.

I listened.

Lola had dropped something. She was still messing around in the bathroom.

Gun in my lap, I rubbed the nightmare out of my eyes, took a deep breath, shook off the anxiety the best I could, then looked at the clock. Almost two hours of nightmares had passed.

I had slipped.

Sweetness and humidity flowed from the bathroom, blended with the room's warm air.

Lola was humming. Singing some song with the words 525,600 in the lyrics.

I waited for her to step out of the bathroom wearing sweats, big socks, a baggy T-shirt, maybe her hair in a ponytail, have on the terry-cloth robe that the hotel supplied in each suite.

Like in my dream.

The gun remained ready to handle whatever problem that femme fatale brought.

Finger on trigger, just in case that nightmare was a storm warning.

Just in case this moment was a déjà vu.

The bathroom door opened, that bathroom light disrupting the room's darkness, and she stood at the sink brushing her hair, her body draped in a red satin number that ran out of material right below the curve of her backside. Her breasts gave a wonderful shape to that shiny material.

Nothing like my dream.

Just like that I was staring at her. Fucking mesmerized.

She picked up her glass, took in the last swallow, mumbled something that had *son of a bitch* in it at least ten times, then brushed her hair over and over. I tried to not watch her and failed miserably. Never expected her to look like that.

I put the gun back in its hiding place.

Stared at Lola.

Her hair was down, hanging beyond her shoulders, cascading down her back.

Had no idea her hair was that long.

Satin flowed over the curves of her tight frame.

Her nipples were pushing their way through that smooth material.

I swallowed.

She moved and one of her straps slipped, showed most of her right breast.

Foolish thoughts came and went.

Lola tiptoed out of the bathroom.

Her arms were toned, legs toned, stomach flat and tight. A Hollywood body. The kind that hit the gym two, maybe three times a day. The kind that lived on tofu and salads.

Lola glanced at me. Her eyes told me that she was surprised I was awake.

She went back to the bathroom, took the robe off the hook, eased it on.

Lola said, "I'll grab a pillow and sleep on the sofa. Cool?"

"Take the bed."

"I can't do that."

"Take the bed."

She was tipsy. Her words slurred. "I can't put you out of your bed."

"Take the bed."

"Thanks. Bathroom's all yours."

I grabbed a few things, managed to slide my gun inside a towel when she wasn't looking, and headed for the bathroom, closed the door, turned on the shower. Her smell was in here. She had finished the sake, the empty bottle left on the counter.

Maybe this wasn't a good idea, now for another reason.

Gun on the counter, I stood there for a minute.

Shaking that nightmare away.

"One day what you do to other people, that will be done to you."

I shoved that ghost out of my mind, showered, and pulled on a pair of sweats.

When I came back out, Lola was under the covers, the white robe off to the side, but not out of her reach. The furry cover that had been on top of the white comforter, some brown leopard-print thing that would make the people at PETA have a heart attack, was off to the side. I adjusted the temperature in the room, took it down a few centigrades, and crashed on the sofa.

The gun was slipped under a pillow on the sofa. Still within reach.

Minutes went by. Besides the mild sounds brought on by the winds, no noises came from outside the double-pane windows. London was quiescent. Or in bed with their lovers.

I sat up for a minute, readjusted the covers.

She whispered, "Gideon."

"Thought you were sleeping."

"Just, you know, being quiet."

"Why you being so quiet?"

"Because you told me to shut up."

"No, I didn't."

"You said for me to be quiet. Said don't talk you to death."

"Oh."

"So I've been . . . I'm being quiet."

"You okay?"

"No."

"What's wrong?"

"Gideon, it's a king-size bed. I feel bad with you on that hard sofa."

"I'm cool."

"We can share the bed."

"You sure?"

"It's a big bed. We're adults. We can put pillows between us or something."

I moved to the bed, got under the covers, but kept to the far side of the bed, stayed within arm's reach of my gun. I couldn't count the number of nights I'd slept that way, gun within reach.

Lola moved around a lot. Couldn't get comfortable. I was fidgety too.

Lola whispered, "Gideon."

"Yeah."

"Think I drank too much sake."

"You gonna throw up?"

"No."

"What's the problem?"

"Something else."

"What?"

"My mind is messed up. Son of a bitch is in bed with somebody else right now."

She wept a little.

Lola said, "That's all I keep thinking about."

"You want to talk about it?"

"I feel so alone right now. I feel so unhappy."

"Anything I can do?"

"Gideon?"

"Whassup?"

"I can't sleep. And I have all of this energy. Want a massage?"

"You don't have to."

"I really need to do something."

"You've been up for hours. Aren't you tired?"

"Exhausted, but not tired. Need to . . . use this anxiety . . . this energy."

"Okay."

Lola got up, moved to her things, opened her bag, took out lotions and oils, took out the things she had planned on surprising her lover with, took out tools from her trade.

Lola paused, thinking. "Look in my eyes, Gideon."

I did.

She whispered, "Breathe with me."

I did.

Lola put her hands on my face. I felt a surge. Her touch was electrical. Sent energy through my body. Fear abandoned me. We sat there gazing into each other's eyes, our breathing finally becoming synchronized, the palms of her hands caressing my face.

I touched her cheeks in return.

She shook her head, did that in a polite way, and moved my hand away.

I understood. She was serious about her work, even when she was tipsy.

She asked, "How did you hurt your face?"

"Fight."

"Figured that much."

Unnerved. I waited for her to pry, ask me more questions.

Lola whispered, "Relax."

I did my best.

She said, "You have a lot of tension and hostility in your body."

"You can tell by looking in my eyes?"

"You have a lot of yin fighting with yang."

"Doesn't everybody?"

"Not like you. Never seen so much light and so much darkness at the same time."

I thought I had scared her. She didn't pull away. We gazed, kept breathing together.

She whispered, "Lie down. Facedown."

"Okay."

"Take your clothes off first. If you're comfortable. Or I can massage you through your clothes if you want, but it would be a lot better if—you know. Only if you're comfortable."

I stripped down to my birthday suit.

I closed my eyes and Lola fell quiet, rested her hands on my upper body, then moved her healing to my lower back, warmed oils in her hands and worked on me, that relaxing massage flowing from my back to my legs, her touch easing down to my feet. Her hands never left my body, always maintained contact, took her time, her movements both rhythmic and sensitive, long, gliding strokes that led to deeper ones. She used her body weight more than arm strength for the deep strokes, and during gliding strokes, since she didn't have her professional table, she made do with the bed I was on, adjusted her technique and remained fluid.

I was floating away and groaning like Mrs. Jones had groaned on the flight to London.

Felt like it was a warm summer day and I was resting underneath Carolina blue skies.

I relaxed, released my paranoia, and enjoyed her touch on my skin.

She whispered, "Turn over."

My erection betrayed me. My penis betrayed me. Lola didn't say anything. Didn't react. Her touch didn't stop, just moved to my chest, arms, and hands, glided down to my legs.

Her hands brushed my hard-on, took a slow journey toward my legs. Her tender touch made me want to explode. After she finished my legs and feet, her hands teased across my skin, glided back up, and brushed my genitals again. Then her hands touched my inner thighs, her touch staying near my hard-on, near that erection, her hands moving toward that stiffness.

I opened my eyes. Looked at her as she stroked me.

She blushed.

I blushed too.

She whispered, "Somebody is as tense as I am."

"Yeah."

She hesitated, tendered her tone. "You have a girlfriend?"

"Nope. No girlfriend."

Her voice tendered. "I don't have a man."

"I guess we don't have anybody."

"Guess not." Lola paused, tendered her voice even more. "I can try erotic if you like."

"Thought this was erotic."

"I mean . . . you know . . . happy ending. If you want me to, I can try."

"Don't want to do anything that would make you uncomfortable."

"I'm very comfortable with you. Very."

"I'm putting you up . . . you don't have to . . ."

"I want to. I like you. I'm feeling you. And I want to. That okay?"

"Sure."

"Sure you don't have a girlfriend?"

"I'm sure."

"Don't want to disrespect anybody, you know."

"Nobody to disrespect."

With her warm hands, she cradled my genitals, held on to my erection, her touch sending a new surge, her eyes asking me if that was okay. I nodded. She massaged me right there, focused on my genitals, every now and then her fingers and hands making sweeps up and down my body, her touch moving that sensation all over me, balancing it out.

She did different massage strokes that felt so damn good, firm and consistent stroking, alternating between those strokes. Lola had my penis resting on my belly, had cupped my balls with one hand, the heel of the palm of the other hand gliding up and down the underside of the penis, doing that from root to tip. Then she brought one hand down, stroked my penis from top to the bottom, and when it hit the bottom, she released it. Insanity rose. Again she changed, took my penis in her hand and held it for a moment, held it with gentleness, and gave it a quick up-and-down stroke. She did that for a while, then changed to slow up-and-down strokes, then changed, gave two quick up-and-down strokes. Caressed. Then gave three quick strokes.

I was in Fiji. The sunrise was in a thousand colors. A happy ending was on the horizon.

But Lola slowed down when my moans got too deep, when I moved against her motions.

She whispered, "Relax."

I focused on my breathing, calmed down.

I gazed at her. She stopped stroking me, but didn't let my penis go.

Lola got on top of me, hovered over me, slight contact, took her straps away, let her breasts hang, then moved her breasts across my skin, tickled her breasts from my face down to my erection, kept my genitals ablaze with desire, came back up again, eased back down.

She sat on the bed next to me. Lola's leg touched mine and I almost came. Her skin was hot. She brushed her leg against mine and she released a soft moan. I moved closer to her. Her breathing halted, then she swallowed. I put my hand on her shoulder, my fingers moving across that red satin until I felt her flesh. She made another sound, this one getting caught in her throat. Our legs rubbed, skin moved back and forth across skin. Her hand came up, touched my bare chest. She moved closer to me. I brought my hand up, touched her breasts. God, have mercy. They were full, soft, nipples erect. I moved closer to her, pulled her toward me.

I needed her. Needed to let her help me forget about a lot of things.

My mouth went to her neck, eased to her right breast, licked, sucked, then licked and sucked, then my tongue went to her left breast, licked and sucked. Again she moaned. My tongue traced up to her lips. I kissed her. Her kiss was intense, sucked my tongue to the point of pain, then she eased up. She held on to me. Her nails dug into my skin.

My hand went down to her waist, underneath her satin.

She moaned good and long. Moaned like she needed this too.

Two fingers slid inside her while my thumb rested on her swollen clit. Her legs tensed, her breathing did the same. She held me tighter. I found the right rhythm, the right pressure, and Lola moved against my hand. I kissed her, used my trigger finger, gave her a slow clit massage; finger-fucked her until my hand became sweetened with her juices. Her nostrils flared and she pushed her hips into my hand, her moans deepening as her nails dug deeper into my skin. My mouth moved back to her breasts and I sucked and bit her nipples, finger-fucked her while her jaw clenched and she sank deeper and deeper into that well of pleasure. She jerked, made sounds that told me she was on fire. I sucked her breasts as she trembled.

She moaned like she was singing the sweetest song.

Lola turned her body.

I shifted, got on top of her, did a slow grind, kissed her for a while.

"Gideon?"

"Yeah."

"If you want to . . . you know . . . we can . . . you know."

"If I want to what, we can what?"

"Don't make me say it."

I kissed her again, sucked her tongue, did the same with her full lips.

I said, "Say it."

"You want me to say it?"

"Say it."

"Damn you. You know you ain't right."

"Say it."

"You excite me."

"Do I?"

"I'm wet right now. Looking at you, I'm wet. Touching you made me wet."

"Are you?"

"Touch me. Feel me."

I touched her again. I felt what was damp and on fire.

She kissed me.

Her voice became a sweet song. "I have a dozen condoms."

We kissed and moved against each other, my hardness rubbing her softness.

"Get the condom," I told her as we kissed. "Let me massage you for a while."

"Let's trade happy ending for happy ending."

My heart beat fast, this time for a different reason.

The heat I felt was a welcome heat.

I had a feeling that Lola was dangerous, but in a different way.

I put a finger back inside her.

She moaned. "Sake has me feeling right."

Lola moved against my hand.

This was the real deal.

Right then I knew I didn't need to worry about that gun anymore.

Not right now.

I kept my hand on what might have been her true weapon, on the heat between her legs.

Thirty-one

warm place to hide

Lola reached underneath her pillow.

With nervous breath and a smooth motion, I stopped her hand.

My smile masked my lingering suspicion. "What are you hiding?"

"Okay, now I'm really embarrassed."

I moved my hand away.

She pulled out a condom.

Lola surrendered a shy smile.

I helped her out of her red satin. I kissed her breasts, licked her skin, laid her back, moved her knees apart, and went down on her. Held her ass, put my tongue between her legs.

Hands on my head, Lola shifted her hips toward my face, released a slow, long moan.

Lola struggled to open the condom, gave up, handed it to me, and sat back with her hands in her hair, waited while I ripped open the package and struggled to roll it on. She scooted toward the head of the bed, knees together. I moved toward her and she got on her back, her legs easing apart, and I crawled between her warm thighs, found my position between the gates to a new paradise. I kissed her again. Her hand found its way back to my penis. She checked to make sure I was wrapped up tight, then she kissed me and guided me. I moved toward her, grazed the edges, made her moan.

Then I sank inside her.

Lord, have mercy.

She held her breath for a moment, her nostrils flared, her back arched, her legs tightened, and she let out a slow, saccharine-filled sigh. My moan was abrupt, guttural.

I was on top of her, looking down on her, her hair framing her beautiful face.

Lola was beautiful, not cute. Cute was temporary. Beautiful was timeless.

She closed her eyes, frowned while I stirred her. A sensual frown.

My hands went in her hair, pulled her face to mine. She gave me her tongue.

"You can pull my hair if you want to. It's real. No tracks."

"Breasts real?"

"All me, baby."

"All you?"

"All me."

"No weave?"

"Hair. Ass. Breasts. Fingernails. Everything on me is real."

Deep. I sank deep. Came out and sank deep again. Each kiss more intense than the last, each kiss twice as desperate, each moan louder, each stroke devastating, more fulfilling.

I pulled her hair while I kissed. Pulled her mane and stroked her good.

Her frown deepened, became the most beautiful ugly face I'd ever seen.

Her knees came up, she locked her legs around my back, held on to me as I pumped, as I searched for the rhythm she wanted. I moved her legs, had her on her side while I was on my knees, stroking her, making her gasp and throw her head back. Then, as the rain began to fall outside the window, as the winds kicked in, I was behind her, my hands cupping her breasts while I kissed and nibbled her damp skin, my own sweat dripping from my face, adding to hers.

Lola didn't talk while she fucked, just gave it as good as she got, moved like an ambitious woman who was still trying to learn how to get it right, and held me as we made our way around the bed, everything so fluid, changing positions more than a few times, ending up with her on top of me, rising and falling, eyes still tight, face cringing with pain and pleasure, then when she was about to come, she moved up and down, made skin slap skin so hard, did that like the devil inside her had been released, gasped and moaned a lot. The second time her legs wobbled, she made sounds like she was drowning. I was behind her, that prickly hot rush in my thighs, legs braced, buttocks tight, my world a wonderful blur, had Lola's face deep in the pillow, pounding and long-stroking my way toward my own nirvana. My jaw clenched with determination. Again, her nostrils flared. She made curt sounds like *mmm* and *ahhh* and came violently, collapsed on the bed and came gripping the sheets. I didn't stop. She had an exceptional way of rolling her hips, responded to what she was feeling, and moved in subtle ways I'd never seen a woman move before.

I gave her two happy endings, the second being more intense, more joyous than the first.

Then I was making the ugly face, straining, pumping hard, her hands pulling me into her, encouraging me to reach satisfaction. My happy ending came with power. God, it came hard.

Anxiety and frustration and fear poured out of me.

While I came I thought about her.

Thought about the first time in New York.

Thought about the last time in Chapel Hill.

I looked down, expected to see Arizona.

In those final moments, that was who I had imagined was beneath me.

Reality brought a different face into focus.

I rested on top of Lola, dizzy, catching my breath, the room now feeling too damn hot.

She panted like she was woozy as well, ran her nails over my skin. "Was that okay?"

I swallowed, my brain still buzzing. "Brilliant. It was great."

"I can do better . . . just . . . you know . . . jet lag . . . been up for over twenty-four hours . . . tired."

"How was it for you?"

"Better than sake. Good Lord, that was better than sake."

I rolled off her. She slid from under me at the same time, turned over on her back.

"Thanks, Gideon. Damn, I needed that."

"I could tell."

"If you . . . you know . . . want to . . . again . . . you can."

"What are you trying to say?"

"Well, I do have eleven condoms left."

"We'll have to do something about that."

Lola blushed, the combination of sex and sake tightening her light brown eyes.

We kicked the covers away from us, were silent for a moment, listening to the rain.

My mind was on Berwick Street. My headache and anger trying to come back.

I went to the wall and turned the heat off. Then I flushed the condom and used the bathroom. When I went back to the bed, Lola was on her back, staring at the ceiling, her postcoital bliss a different kind of frown. Looked like she was dealing with her own headache.

I got back in the bed, became irritated by silence, asked Lola if she was okay.

She rolled over toward me. Whispered, "Sure you want me to start talking?"

"I'll cut you off if you start rambling."

"That's mean."

"Talk. I'll take my chances."

"I've been saving myself and being loyal to that son of a bitch . . . he's over here shagging and shacking . . . has his bitch living with him . . . should've known . . . things had gotten strange between us anyway." She cleared her throat. Even now her voice was soft, pleasant, no hint of pain, but the angst was there, just well disguised. "I think I was used to not seeing him. Sex wasn't popping no more. He never did it twice. One nut, he was done. Hated that. Last time I saw him he was tossing my salad and I was looking up at the ceiling wondering when he started doing that. I mean, was I supposed to like that? I had to focus on the ceiling so I wouldn't poot in his mouth. That's what that made me feel like doing, pooting. I hoped that he didn't think I was going to toss his salad in appreciation of him tossing my salad. I don't even like salads."

"Lola."

"Rambling. Sorry."

"No, you're on my arm. Need to shift."

"Oh. My bad."

Lola sat up, took a deep breath, rose to her feet, and staggered toward the bathroom. She stopped at the bathroom door, ran her hand over her hair like she was still dizzy.

She said, "I had wanted to meet the cast from *Rent* while I was here. Thought that *maybe*, you know, *maybe* I could get an audition for Mimi's part, would consider coming on as a swing, as long as I got to stay here in London and work and spend some time with my . . . with that son of a bitch . . . make it work . . . and now, guess that ain't gonna happen."

Her breasts were so damn nice. Stood high and full, nipples dark and large.

"Son of a bitch. I ever see that son of a bitch again . . . and I'm the motherfucker who encouraged him to audition for *Rent*. I'm the one who bought him a plane ticket to fly to New York and audition. I helped him with his vocals. Too bad my family ain't over here. They would handle this. I should look in the phone book and see if I can find any McVeighs."

I watched how her small waist curved down into her strong backside, watched her firmness. She sat on the toilet, took a long-overdue piss. When she was done, she turned on the water and washed her hands, caught a glimpse of her first grabbing a towel, then saw her washing between her legs. She came back with towels, cleaned me, then tossed the towels.

Lola cuddled up next to me, her soft and firm leg moving against mine, her sake-scented breath on my skin, her hand on my chest. She held me like we had been lovers for a lifetime.

I held her breast. Squeezed it, touched the nipple.

In return she held my penis. That reminded me of Arizona. She had held my penis after sex. Maybe that was what women did. Lola stroked my penis for a while. Then she stopped. She shifted around a lot. Sighed a lot, shook her head a lot. Made her foot bounce a lot.

Lola said, "What am I going to do? I'm stuck over here without a dime to my name."

"I'll get you back to America."

"Will you? Just get me to any part of North America: New York, Miami, Boston. Wait . . . not Boston. Son of a bitch is from Boston. Anywhere else is cool. Alaska. Canada. I don't care. Just get me back over the damn Atlantic and I'll figure out something once I get there."

"Lola, relax. I'll fly you back home."

"I'll pay you back, I promise. I'm not a freeloader."

My hand moved over her body, and she touched my hand, eased it back down between her legs. My trigger finger found her spot, massaged her until she moaned and came again.

"God, you are so good with that finger."

"Like the way I massage?"

"Hell yeah. Want me to get another condom?"

"In the morning. Will that be okay?"

"Condoms on the dresser. Just tap me on my shoulder. Or flip me over."

"Really?"

"Actually, it's been seven months. I'm angry and tired and horny as shit. And since I'm a free agent, this is my coochie, so, hey, you want to get up in my loving, get up in my loving."

"Eleven condoms left."

"Hey, you gave me the money to buy 'em. Feel free to use 'em all."

"You game?"

"Right now I'm game like a motherfucker."

She held me the way I had held Arizona that first time we had been together.

We kissed again.

Whores didn't kiss. Whores didn't cuddle. Whores never stayed the night.

Lola wasn't a whore.

For a moment I felt uncomfortable, wanted her gone. Not gone, just wasn't used to women staying after the deed was done. Either they left or they were paid and vacated.

Squares hung around. Squares wanted to cuddle. Squares wanted breakfast.

Squares had a heart. Right now I needed to be with somebody who had a heart.

Even if that meant that in the end, squares became too emotional.

When it came to the heart, squares were deadly and dangerous in their own way.

I'd become too emotional with Arizona. I'd become dangerous to her.

Always a vicious fucking cycle. The one you wanted always wanted something else.

"Son of a bitch. After all I did for him. He lived with me, I cooked for him, did everything."

"Would you be sad if something bad happened to him?"

"*Hell no.*"

She had said that without hesitation, her angst-ridden voice laced with pure venom.

My anger rose up and I almost offered to ease her pain. Almost. Caught myself.

Guess I'd heard that angered and vindictive tone so many times.

Lola whispered, "Good night."

"You can sleep now?"

"I think so. For a while."

She stopped shifting, breathing slowed, sleep imprisoned her before ten minutes had passed. I looked at her for a few moments, gazed at the condoms, her electric touch still sending sensual currents through my body, and despite only being tired, my nature wanted to rise. Arizona never offered herself to me like this, not without reluctance. Lola. Damn. I wanted to lose myself inside her again, get inside her womb, try to find my own release and move toward peace.

I wondered if, to her, I was the whore. A slut. If I was my mother's child.

You're a whore like your mother.

My thoughts stayed on my mother. Saw her bright red lipstick. Felt her hands on me.

While the stranger in my bed slept, I moved the gun from its hiding place to the backpack, then I stood in the window. The rain came down hard on London's dark side, the wind howled like a beast in chains, screamed like it was warning people that this was the land of butchers and train robbers, where they used to have public hangings at Old Bailey, where Braveheart was tortured, where the KGB dumped bodies in the Thames, where women were executed within the confines of the Tower of London.

With all the lights off I was looking down, searching for Jack the Ripper, making sure no one was watching or waiting, the man with the broken nose no longer an immediate concern of mine, Arizona's anger and recent threat now being more urgent. Arizona had sent a package, but that didn't mean anything. In this world people sent you roses before they put you in the ground.

Like I had shared a drink with Sergeant before I sent him to an early grave.

I remained in the window, naked, the room dark, staring out toward Centre Point.

Arizona's insults had fucked me up beyond repair. Beyond forgiveness.

Then I smelled her on my skin. My mother. I inhaled the stench of my mother.

From time to time I caught her scent deep in my skin. That whore reek was there. The horrible smell of a woman who didn't bathe between johns, only rinsed between her legs, her own cheap perfume and salty sweat mixed with the stink of cologne and musty odor of many men.

Like your mother.

My mother, my enemy.

I looked toward Berwick Street, no more than ten minutes away.

Wondered if the woman who had birthed me was on her back or her knees.

Over the years, wherever we lived, I had watched the men come and go.

I felt her heat where I shouldn't feel her heat, her red lipstick stains where they shouldn't have been. Then, once again, I saw Thelma on the ground, beaten and laid out like a rag doll.

Anger rose up inside me, mixed with all the other bad feelings I was having.

Then Lola groaned, turned over.

She was probably the nicest girl I'd ever met.

I was the last kind of man she needed to be laid up with.

But I was afraid of her.

She'd looked in my eyes and recognized my inner struggle.

That struggle had me awake now.

I had to move on.

I'd leave London in the morning. Would leave now but Lola

was here. I'd have to wait until morning, get her packed, get her to Gatwick, put her on a plane, get Lola back home.

I'd part ways with Lola, put these memories behind me, move on with my life.

Leave the past behind.

I sat on the sofa. Watched Lola sleep. A square. For once I was in bed with a real nice girl. Lola shifted and I moved back to the bed, got under the covers, my skin next to hers. She moved closer to me, her breasts on my skin, her hand holding me close. Moments like this made the square that lived inside me want to try that love thing. But I wasn't a square. I'd killed too many people to ever be forgiven. And one day, just as I'd gone after so many, someone would come for me. This was my world. Yeah, I should've gotten Lola her own room. I knew that. If I had to walk from Bloomsbury to Mansion House, I should've checked every hotel until I found a vacancy.

Eyes trained like a sentry, staring out at the darkness and the rain, I fell asleep.

It was a deep, peaceful sleep, the kind that didn't torture me with bad dreams.

But as soon as peace covered me and warmed my body, Lola nudged me.

I jerked awake. Her sweet face was close to mine.

I said, "Want me to get a condom?"

In a shaky voice she whispered, "Somebody's at the door."

That woke me up. I sat up, heard nothing. I asked, "You sure?"

"They've been moving around out there for a while. At least five minutes. I looked out the peephole, didn't see anybody. But I can hear them out there."

I pulled the covers back, eased my feet down on the thin carpet.

Lola moved to the edge of the bed, her breasts a beautiful silhouette in the darkness.

Sledge had been blown up in Trinidad.

I had been followed by the man with the broken nose.

"The wrong you're doing . . . that will be done to you."

I stood up and listened. Heard movement outside my door.

She whispered, "You expecting company?"

I put my finger to my lips, shook my head, had to figure out how to handle this.

I whispered, "Go inside the bathroom. And close the door."

Now Lola owned fear.

Lola did what I asked, grabbed the white robe and hurried to the bathroom.

I rushed to the backpack, grabbed my loaded nine, silencer on, crept to the peephole.

It was Death's peak business hours.

And Death had a business that was open 24/7.

I spied out the peephole.

A new kind of fear gripped me, its sharp claws running deep.

It was worse than anything I imagined.

I'd fought in Chinatown. Been stalked. After that I'd killed in Lakenheath. Was stalked again in Soho. Was slaughtered in my dreams. And I hadn't been in London twenty-four hours.

The night wasn't over.

Trouble had found me.

And the bad part was this was only beginning.

I knew how to end trouble before it started.

I raised my gun to the peephole.

This motherfucker had balls.

Acknowledgments

Before we get started . . .

If you're holding *Sleeping with Strangers*, its sequel, *Waking with Enemies*, picks up where *SWS* leaves off, and moves on full speed ahead.

If you're holding *Waking with Enemies*, make sure you read *Sleeping with Strangers* first.

Well, this is the back of the book, so I guess it's kinda late to say that, huh?

Duh.

Oh well.

☺

I started playing *What if?* and working on *Sleeping with Strangers* and *Waking with Enemies* back in March 2006, tried to come up with a story line. Initially I wanted to create a dark narrative, maybe come up with an antihero who had his or her adventure play out while driving across the States, some sort of West-Coast-to-East-Coast voyage, his or her motivation (or motivations) yet to be determined, but I didn't come up with a decent way to keep that interesting for me.

No story came to mind. Not at that moment.

The well was dry.

Then I changed gears, decided to try and find a way to include most of the cities I hit on tour, London included, in one story. That meant I had to write and tour all at once. Had to take notes while people were keeping me busy. Trust me, that wasn't easy. Any writer will tell you, writing on tour, being creative while dealing with jet lag, no real sleep, and trying to be productive while sitting at the airport—it just ain't happening. But I gave it a shot. A lot of spots I went to on tour I was barely there a day, some places only a few hours, and didn't see much outside of an airport, one or two bookstores and a hotel that I couldn't tell you how to get to if my life depended on it. All I knew was that I needed a good character. An antihero who traveled a lot.

And I wanted it to be noir. And sexy. And a challenge. Didn't want to recycle plots.

Enter Gideon.

I was in my office writing one day and when I turned around, there he was.

Gun in one hand and a knife in the other, the guy scared me at first. Could tell he was troubled. Thought he had come for me. But he said he just wanted to be in the book. Said he had a lot of personal shit he needed to work through and maybe being in a book would help.

I said cool. Told him he had a part. He left. Then I upgraded my security system.

If you believe that, I have a freeway I want to sell you out in Los Angeles.

Gideon started off being a serial killer. I played the *What if?* game and wrote scenes with him, well, at work. Tijuana. Jacksonville. Detroit. Brazil. Some, if not all, of those original scenes made the final cut. Somewhere along the way, my man Gideon evolved into being a contract killer. When I'd flown to the U.K. (much love to Bill, Claire, and the rest of the staff at Turnaround Publishing) to promote *Genevieve*, I had moved on, started writing the scenes that included the supporting cast. Eventually the man with the broken nose showed up and asked me if I needed somebody like him to be in this one. I tried to say no, but he pulled the Eagle out of its nest and that convinced me. Truth be told, I liked the crazy bastard. Great character. Every novel needs a supporting cast, and since this tale involved killers and grifters, for the most part, it gave me a chance to reach back into the Dickey Universe, tap on a few doors, and ask Arizona, one of my favorite characters, if she wanted to be in this one. She asked me if she would get a hot sex scene. I said no. She slammed the door in my face. I knocked again. She wouldn't answer. Then I yelled that I would put her in a damn steamy scene. She said she wanted *two*. Damn women. Anyway, I told her I would promise her one, and I'd do my best on a second one. Then she demanded to be more than a grifter, wanted to carry weapons and kick some ass. I told her that grifters didn't carry. She didn't give a shit. I think she had seen one too many Angelina Jolie movies. Anyway, my agent called her fictional agent and we got it worked out. She lit up her Djarum, grabbed her boots, and came along for the ride. Despite being so demanding, she's good people. If you like those kind of people. The queen of the grifters. I have no idea why I like her, but I do. She's evolved since she first drove onto the pages of *Thieves' Paradise*, become a little more intense since *Drive Me Crazy*, now she's operating on an international level.

Anyway, once my plane landed in London, so did the rest of the story.

I have to thank my U.K. peeps for helping a brother out while he was over there locked up in hotels and flats, writing from sunup to sundown, taking a nap, then back in front of the laptop until sunup again. My U.K. peeps were great, showed me around London on buses and tubes, drove me around in clown cars that had steering wheels on the wrong side of the dashboard.

They were there for me whether it was sweltering, raining, or bloody cold.

Kayode Disu, thanks for collecting me at Gatwick, making sure I was okay, getting me to Paris and back in a day, and getting me and my luggage back to Gatwick every time I came over.

My homie Monique Pendleton out at www.myspace.com/soulful_women, I think you've read every version of Gideon, saw changes in plots and subplots, well over a thousand pages, that's my estimate, and I thank you for that. And thanks for making sure the book kept that Brit flavor.

Inca Nixon, my girl Sam from the Islands, Tosh from wherever, thanks for coming down from horse-and-grass to hang out and show me around. See y'all at TGIF in Piccadilly soon!

To my military peeps stationed at Lakenheath and Mildenhall, be safe and see you soon. Neo Gwafila-Bulayani, thanks for Botswana and looking over the details of Tebby.

My boys at Progressive Entertainment (www.myspace.com/UKFridays), thanks for the birthday celebration. I'll see you guys at the Motion Bar soon. Save me a spot!

To my U.K. publisher, Bill, Claire, and the entire staff at Turnaround, thanks for everything. The events were fantastic and I look forward to returning.

If you peeps find me a place to live, I'll become a U.K. citizen and rent an accent so fast . . . you have no idea. We just have to come up with something better than beans and toast.

☺

Everything I got right, I thank my friends.

Until I can find a scapegoat, I'll take the blame for all I got wrong.

Time to thank the rest of my crew. The ones on this side of the pond.

John Paine, thanks for the input and the notes. Writing is all about rewriting.

DeMarMc, thanks for reading this one over and over and over and . . .

Lon in IAH, once again, thanks for the information early on. It made a big difference.

Christine Pattyn, thanks for Motown! Hope to make it to your club one day!

Lolita Files! You're the best! Thanks for being you!

Hazel Verzola in Montreal, thanks for the Tagalog!

Thanks to my agent, Sara Camilli. How many books before I get to book number 100?

To my wonderful editor, Julie Doughty, much love. You rock!

Brian Tart, thanks for believing in this double-sized project. I hope it has wings and flies.

To Lisa Johnson, Beth Parker, and all the people in publicity, thanks for everything.

And a special thanks to you. You, the person holding this book.

You didn't think I'd skip you, did you?

O faithful reader, thanks for coming back.

And if you're a new reader, thanks for coming on board.

I hope you enjoy this journey across the pond.

And if you're across the pond, I hope you find this tale enjoyable.

In case I forgot anyone, which wasn't intentional, here's your chance to shine.

I wanna thank _____ for _____ because without your help I'd be _____ at a _____ with _____ and wishing I was _____ in _____. You're the best of the best!

Make sure you check out www.ericjeromedickey.com. Or stop by www.myspace.com/ericjeromedickey.

Holla!

EJD
12/18/06
Latitude 33.76N and Longitude -84.4W
5:34 A.M.

Read on for an excerpt from

Waking with Enemies

**the exciting sequel to *Sleeping with Strangers*,
by Eric Jerome Dickey**

Available now from Dutton.

Death kept moving back and forth outside my door.

But Death never showed its face.

On the other side of my pulled curtains, the skies were gray, winds were blowing hard enough to sway trees, and the rain was falling, a rain that, in this weather, felt like ice water.

London's weather was as devastating as my mood.

I was in Bloomsbury, that abhorrence from my past crimes and sins fueling me as I stood by the door, listening for sounds in the hallway, gun in my hand, loaded, angst on high.

I'd done a job in Tampa. Had killed more than a few men in the name of profit.

A gruesome hit that would stay with me the rest of my days.

That job had been a few days ago, and now that hit had turned upside down. A rapper named Sledge had paid me a king's fortune to kill his rival, another rapper known as the Big Bad Wolf. I had slaughtered Big Bad and his crew, barely made it away from that job with my life, and since then Sledge had been assassinated. And I had been followed to London by a bald man who sported a broken nose, a man who had been sent to kill me as an act of vengeance.

I eased closer to the door and listened.

So much violence and death had happened since I landed in the U.K.

My mind was racing as I tried to remember it all; gun in hand, I was trying to put the pieces together. Yesterday afternoon I'd been stalked from Covent Garden to Soho, then around midnight I had realized I was being trailed as I left Soho, had flipped the script on my stalker and chased him, realized he was the same man I'd seen on my flight from America to the U.K., his broken nose making him stand out, and I had confronted him, chased him through Kensington Gardens only to have him vanish at Lancaster Gate.

Only a few hours had passed since that footrace.

And now someone was lurking outside my hotel room.

Freezing rain was falling as dark clouds strangled and smothered the sunrise.

Gun in hand, I listened to see if the messenger was outside moving around.

Behind me, in my room, I heard terrified breathing.

I looked back, saw two huge suitcases on the floor.

I'd forgotten she was here.

A naked woman was terrified, inside my hotel room, hiding in the bathroom.

Her name was Lola Mack.

She was an actress-slash-masseuse I had met on the same flight to Gatwick.

Hers was a long story, one that started with happiness in the U.S. and ended up here with her being in excruciating pain, the kind of pain that came from her flying across the Atlantic only to get rejected by the man she was in love with, that rejection coming a few hours ago.

About five hours ago she had ended up in my room, about three hours ago she had ended up in my bed. Now she was hiding in the bathroom as I tried to deal with this situation.

Bad timing. Bad fucking timing.

Now her life might be on the line.

There was another sound.

Once again trouble was shifting around outside my door.

Every time I did a job, I made enemies. I had done well so I had many enemies.

My mental Rolodex was spinning, so many enemies in my mind.

Too many to remember.

That terrified breathing echoed in the bathroom.

Even now I wondered if the woman hiding in the bathroom was part of a conspiracy.

That beautiful woman might've been sent to keep me here.

She had been waiting for me.

Right here.

In the lobby.

And she had bedded me.

Without hesitation.

She claimed she was an actress. Grifters were actors. Contract killers were actors.

I'd spent years hiding my feelings from the rest of the world. So I was an actor too.

I played it again in my mind.

A man had followed me first from America, then trailed me in Covent Garden, did the same in Soho, that confrontation coming to an abrupt end at Lancaster Gate.

Right after that Lola was waiting for me in the lobby.

She had found my hotel.

Paranoia whispered in my ear and told me she was part of the setup.

I was about to go to the bathroom, put the gun in her face, demand answers.

I'd kill Lola Mack if I had to. I'd kill her like she had killed me in my nightmares.

As soon as I made a step, there was a loud sound outside my door.

I jumped, aimed the gun at the door.

I eased back to the peephole.

Then Lola flushed the goddamn toilet. Something crashed to the bathroom floor.

I was heading toward Lola when the handle on the hotel door shook.

They were out there testing the door.

I tensed, expected the door to get kicked open right after that.

Gun aimed, I crept back toward the door.

I spied out again.

My stalker moved right in front of my door.

A bold and daring, confident stance.

I saw a face. Brown skin with long, braided hair. Same hairstyle one of the Dutch boys who had attacked me and a grifter named Arizona had sported yesterday. We'd had a battle in the heart of Chinatown during the noon hour. My stalker looked right into the peephole, looked right in my eye, that tense face becoming clearer. A beret covered those braids, French-style.

Now my problem was unhidden, still staring into the peephole.

I swallowed.

Didn't know how to deal with this.